THIS IS NOT A TALE OF OUR OWN WORLD.

It is a world like ours in many ways, but one where dragons live in their own lands, wary of humans. One with Sorcerers, light and dark. One where Pipers can control things around them merely by playing a Song.

Yet tales of other worlds *can* reach us, sometimes. All it takes is a little magic, and the Pipers have always known something that – for us – is easy to forget:

There is magic in music.
Listen...

TO MY SON ELIAS,
WHO HEARD IT ALL FIRST

First published in the UK in 2018 by Usborne Publishing Ltd., Usborne House, 83-85 Saffron Hill, London EC1N 8RT, England. www.usborne.com

Cover and inside illustrations by George Ermos

Title typography by Leo Nickolls

A CIP catalogue record for this book is available from the British Library.

ISBN 9781474945677 04819/2 JFMAMJJASO D/18
Printed in the UK.

A DARKNESS OF DRAGONS

S.A. PATRICK

1
The Ice Beast

The screams of the children brought the villagers running.

The little ones often played among the tall pines at the southern edge of Patterfall. This high in the mountains, winter was always hard; the pines offered shelter from the icy winds that blew through the valley.

As the villagers ran towards the sound, the panicked children emerged from the trees and came rushing through the snow. The first to reach them was Frer, the eight-year-old son of the baker.

"It's come! It's come!" said the boy.

"Steady, child," said Greta, the village Elder. "Tell me what it is. A bear?"

He shook his head. "No, Elder. It's the Ice Beast!"

With that, he ran past them to safety.

"The child is just scared," the Elder told the other villagers, because the Ice Beast was a legend, nothing more. A legend as old as the village itself, about an extraordinary creature formed of snow and ice – a creature that absolutely *did not exist*.

There *were* extraordinary creatures in the world, of course. Some, like dragons, were at least as intelligent as humans; others, like basilisks and manticores, were terrifying monstrosities.

But there was nothing like that anywhere *near* Patterfall. Dragons lived on a different continent, far to the east; as for the terrifying monstrosities, they were thankfully rare, and limited to the remotest parts of the world.

Only those foolish enough to get lost on the valley roads in deep winter ever claimed to have seen the Ice Beast – people who were exhausted and frightened, seeing things that weren't really there.

Yet the villagers could see movement a short way inside the forest.

Something large. Something white.

"*No*," the Elder said aloud. "It can't be!"

But it was.

The Ice Beast was the height of a large man, and seemed to be made entirely of snow. Its legs and arms were as thick as tree trunks. The head was a featureless white ball, but every villager could imagine where the terrifying mouth was, fangs dripping, ready to sink into the flesh of anyone who got too near.

Its slow steps drew a heavy crunch from the snow underneath. From its head came a steady moaning.

And the villagers kept moving towards it.

"Go!" they called to the children as they passed them. "Run to your homes!"

There was one child left, though. One small boy, too frightened to move, standing directly in the creature's path – Hap Werner, only four years old.

"Little Hap," called the Elder. "You go home now! Go on with you!"

But Hap shook his head, rooted to the spot. The creature was getting closer to him.

With no time to waste, the Elder raised the shovel she was carrying. "I'll have you, Beast!" she cried, and ran towards the creature. The other villagers followed, wielding what weapons they had – hoes, pitchforks, brooms.

The Elder was first to reach it, and she swung her shovel hard, hitting the Ice Beast's head; the creature made a strange noise before falling to the snowy ground with a thud.

There it lay, motionless, as the villagers surrounded it, ready to hit it again if it moved even a fraction.

But where the shovel had hit its head, a few chunks

of ice and snow were now gone, revealing something underneath. The villagers stared at what they saw: a very cold, very red nose, and below that, a very human mouth.

"*Ow...*" the mouth groaned.

For a moment the villagers looked at each other in shock. Then they began to scrape away what they could of the ice and snow that clung to the stranger. With each chunk removed he was smaller, lighter, yet what they found underneath was a curious giant, the legs and arms unnaturally thick. Only when more ice was cleared did it make sense to them.

Clothes.

Layer upon layer of shirts and trousers: dozens, perhaps more. The stranger's neck was thick with a hundred scarves, the hands and head puffed out by gloves and hats. Torn strips of material were densely wrapped around the face, gaps left only for the mouth, nose and eyes.

Too heavy to carry, they dragged the unconscious stranger to the village, his legs and feet still ice-bound. In the village hall a fire was roaring, and they propped him up in a chair in front of the blazing logs, then began cutting and unravelling the layers with care. In one corner of the hall, the pile of discarded garments grew, while the unconscious stranger shrank, until all that was left was a thin figure slouched in a chair, with a long coat over his simple clothing.

It was a *boy*, his hair dark and scruffy.

"Look how young he is, he can't be more than thirteen!" said a villager. "How did he survive his journey?"

"A good question!" said the Elder. "To emerge from the forest where he did, he must have come through Andig's Pass. An icy hell this time of year."

"It's certain death for anyone crazy enough to go that way!" said the villager.

"And yet this boy made it through," said the Elder, thoughtful. "There must be more to him than meets the eye!" She reached inside the boy's coat and searched the deep pockets within. After a moment, she slowly pulled out her hand; with it came a wooden flute, the length of her forearm. Those watching gasped as they saw.

It was *not* a flute, of course. The small finger holes were far more numerous, the layout much more complex, than on any flute they had ever seen.

This was not a flute.

It was a *Pipe*.

The Elder lifted it up. "The Piper has come," she said in awe, and the people cheered. The doors of the village hall were flung open, and the news was passed on to those waiting outside. Everyone took up the call:

"The Piper has come! *The Piper has come!*"

2
The Stranger

When the boy finally opened his eyes, he found himself on a small bed, in a room he didn't recognize, wearing a simple nightshirt that he was certain didn't belong to him. He sat up and tried to recall how he'd got there, but nothing came. Nothing but a sense that there was something very important that he needed to remember…

"You're awake at last," came a voice. Startled, the boy turned and saw an old woman sitting in a chair in the shadows of the corner. She stood and brought the chair over to the bedside. "My name is Greta," she said. "I'm the Elder of Patterfall."

"Of where?" said the boy.

"Patterfall," said Greta, looking worried. "This village."

"I'm sorry," he said. "I don't remember much. About anything."

Greta nodded. "Perhaps that's to be expected. The stress of your journey here has robbed you of your memory."

"Will it come back?"

"I've seen this kind of thing before," said Greta. "You're not the first to have stumbled out of the forest close to death, although you're certainly the youngest. Your memory will return soon enough. Something will spark it back to life. Do you remember anything about your journey?"

He thought for a moment, but all that came was that terrible dark walk through the forest, one step after another with no end. His eyes widened. "I don't even remember my own name!"

"I think I can answer that one," said Greta. She stood and fetched a coat that was hanging on a hook on the far wall. "When we found you, you were snowbound from head to toe, and wearing layer upon layer of clothes. Underneath them all was this coat. Is it yours?"

The boy smiled when he saw it, feeling relief at remembering even such a small thing. "Yes," he said. "It is."

"Then here," said Greta. She turned back the collar of the coat, to reveal a name embroidered in neat stitches. "I suspect this is your name."

The boy read the name aloud: "Patch Brightwater."

It felt right, and with the name came another small piece of his memory. "My grandmother stitched it in my coat, so I'd not lose it."

Greta smiled. "It's very good to meet you, Patch Brightwater!" she said. "It's *more* than good. You see, I know why you came here." She reached into Patch's coat pocket and pulled out the Pipe. "You came to save us!"

Patch stared. "Me?" he said, and Greta nodded. "I'm a Piper?" He reached out slowly and took the Pipe in his hands. As he held it, more memories came back to him, precious fragments and images. Moments, he realized, from his training at Tiviscan. *Yes*, he thought, *Tiviscan Castle, the home of the Pipers' Council.* The place where those hoping to become Pipers go to learn the Piper's Art.

There was still so much missing, but as his fingers moved over the holes in the Pipe, he knew that the Songs were clear in his mind.

"I *am* a Piper," said Patch at last, and now the tears came, flowing down his cheeks and past his broad smile.

Greta gave him a kindly pat on his hand. "You're much younger than we expected, I admit..."

Patch was filled with a sudden worry – the same feeling he'd had when he'd woken, that there was something very important he still needed to remember.

"But no ordinary traveller could have made it through

that snow!" said Greta. "We summoned a Piper, and here you are!"

Another memory came to him then. "Wait... There was an emergency. I was in a hurry." He looked to Greta, and she nodded to encourage him. "I think...there was a trader. He had the only cart heading this way, him and his family." His eyes narrowed as he concentrated. "The road was blocked, the snow too deep. As we turned, the cart's axle snapped. The trader unhitched his horse, mounted it with his wife and child, and rode off."

"They left you?"

Patch sighed. "Who can blame them? I looked in the cart for food, and all I found was clothing – the trader's wares. At first I stayed in the shelter of the cart, and played a heating Song on my Pipe to keep me warm. But the cold became too great; my fingers grew numb and I had to stop. So I put on layer after layer of clothes, and waited for the weather to improve, but it just kept getting worse. Finally I started to walk. There's a simpler heating Song that can be whistled – lip-playing, we call it. I used that for a time, until my dry lips cracked in the chill and I was forced into silence. I kept walking, all through the night..." He thought of how *long* that terrible icy walk had seemed. *Endless.*

"And you reached us!" said Greta. "You mentioned an emergency, Patch, and that's exactly what our village has! One that will leave us all in poverty, and perhaps end our lives. As soon as we knew how dangerous things had become, we sent a messenger to Wassil, the nearest town. The messenger took the only horse strong enough to make it through the deep snow; his mission was to summon a Piper. You!"

"Tell me, Greta," said Patch. "Tell me what I've come here to do."

Greta paused, looking weighed down with worry. "In summer," she said, "the fertile valley gives us enough grain to last a year, for our cattle and our bellies and for seeding the next year's crops, with some left over that we can sell. Each winter, the roads become impassable. The village remains isolated until late spring. Our dogs and our cats deal with any vermin from the forest. But not this year. One by one, our dogs went lame, our cats grew fearful, and the food in our homes was plundered. At first we couldn't understand what was doing it. They were not seen, and they left no signs."

Patch's face grew pale. "What…what was it?"

"Rats," said Greta. "More than we've ever known. Bigger than we've ever known. Smarter than we've ever known. Anything we did, it wasn't enough. They ate no poison. They triggered no traps." Greta shook her head, visibly distressed. "Nothing we've done has stopped them. They are frightening, Patch. And now they're all in the grain storehouse in the centre of the village, but we dare not attack them. They like it there, protected from the cold, with enough food to last them a few weeks. But when that's done, they'll find all our hidden stores. They'll consume everything we have. And then—" She closed her eyes, unable to speak for a moment. "None of the villagers have been hurt by them, yet. Not one. But when the grain is gone that will surely change."

Patch stared at her in horror. "Change? What do you mean?"

"We are trapped in the village, but so are the rats. When they're hungry enough, they'll come for us! You can see why we're desperate."

"Rats..." he said, thinking. What had he been taught? "Infestations are a common thing for Pipers to deal with, be it rats, mice, cockroaches." He let his fingers move over the Pipe, and smiled as he realized they were already marking out the notes of the Song he needed. "It's strange," he said. "There's so much I don't remember, but my training comes back to me easily."

"We should have called for a Piper weeks ago," said Greta. "But some of the villagers were afraid to."

"Afraid?" said Patch. "They have nothing to fear from me!"

"They thought of what happened in Hamelyn."

Patch opened his mouth to answer, but then the memory of the Hamelyn Piper returned to him like a slap to the face.

It was the greatest shame of Pipers – ten years ago, the town of Hamelyn had been infested by rats. A Piper came, a Piper with nothing but evil in his heart; once he had got rid of the rodents he played another Song, and led the children of Hamelyn off into the night. And what had become of them? To this day, nobody knew. Even after the Hamelyn Piper had been caught and thrown into the deepest dungeon, he had never revealed the truth.

For centuries, Pipers had been trusted completely, their honour beyond question as they wandered the lands, seeking work – helping crops to grow, say, or finding the right place to dig a well. A price would be agreed, and the work would be done.

The events in Hamelyn almost destroyed that trust. Never again would a Piper be able to simply turn up and offer their services. Now, Pipers had to be officially summoned, so that people could be sure that the Pipers who came were qualified and trustworthy.

"They have no need to worry," said Patch. He pulled back the blanket that covered his lower half and swung his legs out of the bed. "There's no time to waste. My clothes?"

"The clothing you wore under your coat has been cleaned in readiness," said Greta. "But I think you need to eat and rest first, to regain your strength."

"Nonsense," he said. "Waiting just means the rats eat more of your precious grain!" The rats, Patch thought, couldn't be as bad as Greta had made out. They were scared, these villagers, and their fear had made everything seem so much worse that it really was. He would cure them of their rats, and cure them of their fear!

He tried to stand, but his legs gave way at once and he fell back onto the bed, breathless.

"You see?" said Greta. "You've been unconscious for two days. You must eat and drink, and rest some more. Only then will you have the strength to deal with those rats. Tomorrow!"

Patch knew she was right; he was only just getting his breath back, and the mention of food had made him realize how hungry he was. "Tomorrow it is," he said.

Patch ate his fill, and slept well. In the morning, after a bowl of stew for breakfast, he got dressed and spent some time exercising his fingers. Nothing more of his memory had come back yet, but he was confident about his Piping – and that was all that mattered.

Greta knocked on the door and entered. "Are you ready?" she asked.

"Almost," said Patch. "First, though, we need a plan – a way to kill the rats! Somewhere to drown them, say."

"Follow me," said Greta.

Beside the village was a river twenty feet across, a simple

wooden bridge spanning its fast-flowing water. They followed it a short way downstream until they came to a cliff edge. There, the river became a roaring waterfall.

"This is where our village gets its name."

"Patterfall?" said Patch. "I would have expected something more gentle."

"The village has been here for three hundred years," said Greta. "Back then, the river was little more than a stream. Things have changed."

"No kidding." He crept forwards to the precipice and looked over. The drop was at least a hundred feet, and the base of the waterfall was littered with jagged rocks. The falling water would dash the rats against the sharp stones, so a quick death was assured. "This will do it," he said.

When they got back, everyone had gathered around the oak tree that stood in the heart of the village. They cheered at the sight of the Piper.

Patch waved to them, and Greta led him to the front of the large grain storehouse where the rats had taken up residence.

The cheering fell away to silence as the people of the village waited for the Piper to begin.

Greta walked to the doors of the storehouse. She removed the chains that had been thrown across the doors, then placed a huge key into the lock and turned it. She looked to Patch, who nodded. Slowly, Greta pulled the doors open, returning quickly to Patch's side. All eyes watched as he studied his quarry.

Then Patch, his body completely rigid, fell backwards in a dead faint.

3

The Piper of Patterfall

Patch came to, the flagstones cold under his back. He opened his eyes and saw Greta's worried face.

"Take my hand!" she whispered, supporting him as he stood.

"Let's try that again," said Patch, but his breathing grew more and more rapid, and his grip on Greta became ever tighter.

He didn't want to look through the storehouse doors again, but he had no choice.

He looked.

Rats!

Sleeping among mounds of grain and bags of seed and sacks of corn, sleeping in groups of three and groups of ten and – Patch shivered – groups of far *more* than ten. Brown rats, white rats, speckled rats, long rats, short rats. One had a tail with curious markings, ringed with red hoops all down its length.

All were asleep, but nowhere, not anywhere he looked, could Patch see a rat that could be called "small", or "thin".

Some were too fat even to curl up for their sleep, looking like big furry marrows or hairy loaves of bread. The fattest of all was a great rat pumpkin that surely couldn't have moved even if it wanted to, its feet sticking straight out, high off the ground, its belly making a dent in the grain where it lay.

Not a sound came from them – except perhaps, if he'd been brave enough to step inside and listen with a careful ear, the noise of little ratty snores and burps.

Rats, content and asleep.

Huge rats.

A vast number of huge rats.

He turned to Greta and opened his mouth to speak. No words came.

"You thought I was exaggerating," she said.

Patch nodded. He took a very long breath, and let out a very long sigh.

"Is it too hard a task?" said Greta.

Patch saw hope drain from the Elder. *No*, he thought, *I won't give in*. These people needed him, and they had saved his life.

But he could hardly pretend this was a selfless act. *He* was trapped here, just as the villagers were. Yet the rats did seem oddly cosy; they were so peaceful that it was a bit of a stretch to imagine them bearing down on him with blood-drenched maws.

He shivered. His mind had already started to imagine it.

He turned and addressed Greta. "The Art of Piping," he started, but it came out squeaky. He cleared his throat and tried again. "The Art of Piping," he repeated, in the confident voice that came from reciting such a well-learned passage, "has many magics. The Song most often used for clearing pests of whatever kind is called the Dream. This magic fills the target's mind full of the wonderful things that they most desire, and makes them think those things can be found by following the music of the Pipe." He looked at the rats, his mouth suddenly dry. "There are…*more* than I expected, I admit, but you avoid thinking about the number, you see. Then it's just as if there were ten, or twenty, rather than—" He gestured towards the rodents, then reached into his coat and took out his Pipe.

The Dream, he thought, grateful that he could remember his training. His fingers were already moving against the Pipe, rehearsing the intricate patterns that would draw the rats to their doom.

He put the Pipe to his lips and began.

* * *

It started with a simple melody, six notes repeated with a little variation. Patch played this half a dozen times, then took his mouth from the pipe.

Yet the music continued. Greta's eyes were wide with astonishment. "It...it keeps *playing—*"

"Of course," said Patch. "Otherwise you couldn't add layers, and it's the layers of a Song that make it so powerful."

Now, Patch started another melody – overlapping the first, seeming to shift away from it, then towards it again. Beside him, Greta was smiling, *grinning*, at the sound.

With the second melody holding, Patch added another sequence, then another, and another. The real work was being done. There was a change in the overall sound, a change that spoke of things that *could be.*

The Dream. The Dream was forming.

Patch's fingers moved in what seemed like effortless complexity. Suddenly he frowned and stopped playing. His hands fell to his sides, the Song starting to fade. He looked at Greta, anxious.

"What's wrong?" she asked, but Patch's attention was stolen by the sound that started among the villagers. The sound of cheering and applause.

He looked from the villagers to Greta, confused. "Why are they clapping?"

"They've never heard anything like that," said Greta.

"It was... It was—" She shook her head, grasping for the word. "It was *beautiful.*"

"Maybe so," said Patch. "But it didn't *work.*" He nodded towards the storehouse. The rats hadn't even stirred. "I don't understand! They should be filled with the knowledge that their dreams, *all* their dreams, await them if they follow the sound!" He began to mutter to himself.

It was Greta who realized what was wrong. "Patch, look at those animals." They both looked. "Do you think they *could* find somewhere better? They are warm, and sleeping in a building full of food! Don't you think they're already in their dream?"

"Of course!" said Patch, putting a hand to his forehead. "Think, think!" he said to himself. He began to stride up and down, his Pipe clenched behind his back. "Wait!" he said at last. "There's another way. But it's a little bit –" he paused for a moment, before finishing – "a little bit *unusual.*"

"Unusual" wasn't the first word that had come to Patch's mind.

When Greta had pointed out the reason for the Dream's failure, he'd hunted around in his memory for an alternative. *Maybe I can't remember enough of my training after all*, he'd thought, and that was a *terrible* thought, because part of his mind had got really very *good* at imagining how the rats would go about feasting on him if he botched this whole thing.

But eventually one idea *had* come, a Song that was so clear and so strong, something he *knew* would work, because he somehow knew that he was particularly good at it. Unfortunately, there was one other thing that he knew about the Song.

He knew that using it was absolutely against the laws of Piping, and had been ever since the Hamelyn Piper had played it to such devastating effect.

In short, it was *illegal*, and "illegal" was the word that he'd almost said to Greta. "Unusual" seemed a lot less alarming, so he'd gone with that instead.

He tried to recall what "illegal" meant for a Piper, and images came to him, images of very serious-looking Pipers in black-and-purple robes. *Oh, yes*, he thought. *Them.*

The Custodian Elite, they were called. If a Piper was to break the laws of Piping, the Custodian Elite would be the ones who brought them to justice.

Still, this was an emergency, and surely even the Custodian Elite would understand.

"This one is called the Dance," he said, then he raised his Pipe and started to play.

4

The Dance

Layer upon layer, the Dance took shape in his Pipe. At the sound of it he felt a familiar joy grow in his heart.

Soon the Song had formed. At first, the sleeping rats seemed oblivious to it. Then one of them stirred – the strange rat with the red-ringed tail. With a yawn it stood and sniffed the air, and saw Patch. Its paws came up to its mouth in a way that was strangely human, as if it was shocked. It waved frantically, shaking its head and squeaking, almost as if it was trying to warn the others.

How peculiar, Patch thought.

The strange rat clamped its paws tightly over its ears, attempting to shut out the sound – as if that would make any difference! – but after a few seconds the animal's rear paws were tapping to the rhythm, its agitation vanishing as it started to whirl and swish from side to side, caught in the Dance. All thought of escape had gone, Patch knew. The only thing it would know, from now until the moment it hit the rocks at the bottom of the waterfall, was the joy of the music.

In the centre of the storehouse floor was a small clearing, and that was where the red-ringed rat made its way. One by one, the other rats woke and followed, hopping and marching in time to the Song that Patch played. A circle of rats formed in the clearing, all on their hind legs, their little paws grasping those of the rats either side of them. As the ring completed, another larger ring started to link up outside the first.

It's working, Patch thought, thrilled and relieved in equal measure. *It's working!*

It wasn't long before ten circles of rats danced round and round, more rodents joining them every second. The circles danced one way, then turned and danced the other. The faces of the rats were happy, and gleeful squeaks could be clearly heard over the music.

The centre of the floor was almost full, so the rest of the rats formed groups in the hollows and spaces where they found themselves. The fattest rats, unable to dance, waggled their paws and heads and feet with smiling eyes and loud cheering squeaks.

All the rats were caught in the Dance now.

It's time, he thought. *Time to take the Dance outside to the river, and the waterfall!*

He backed away from the storehouse. In each of the dancing groups, the rats paired up and began skipping to the exit, with the fattest being rolled out by some of the others.

Patch glanced towards the villagers; anxiety was written on their faces. They wouldn't have to worry for much longer. He turned towards the bridge that crossed the river. From there, he would guide the rats into the water and keep them entranced until they went over the precipice. Greta was already heading to the bridge – the sight of the rats streaming out of the storehouse was enough to make anyone want to get away as quickly as they could.

Patch couldn't hurry, though. As he played, he took slow steps and kept glancing behind him, making sure his pace was right.

Hundreds of rats – thousands! – were pouring out of the doors, following Patch in a line ten rats across, spinning and jigging their way along, twenty feet behind him.

Had he been walking at normal speed he would have reached the bridge within a minute. Matching the pace of the rats, it took five times longer to get there, his fingers racing over the Pipe.

He reached the middle of the bridge and sent the rats towards the water. Line by line, the rats waded in, and each line kept dancing as they swam, forming a little circle as the strong current carried them downstream. Entire circles of rats would turn one way then another, before diving under the water, their tails and feet sticking out and moving from side to side in perfect time, before they brought their heads back up and danced on.

When a third of them were in the river, Patch looked to the waterfall's edge; so did Greta, who was now standing beside him.

"It almost seems cruel," said Greta. "Look at them, with no idea what's coming!"

Patch shook his head and took his lips from the Pipe. "They'll dance all the way down to the sharp rocks below," he said. "The whole time, they'll be happy."

"And we'll be free," said Greta, suddenly overwhelmed. "The village is saved!" She stepped forward and embraced him, then quickly stepped back again with an apologetic nod.

Patch smiled. He was almost overwhelmed, both with emotion and fatigue. It was only excitement that was keeping him on his feet, he knew. It would be a while yet before he fully recovered from his icy journey to the village, and he was still close to exhaustion.

Greta waved to the cheering crowd. Patch waved at them too, but only briefly – the Song could start to unravel if he didn't maintain its melodies. He turned back to the rats, nearly half of them now in the water.

He'd glanced so briefly at the villagers, he couldn't be blamed for not noticing one *very* important detail…

The villagers' feet had started to tap.

Almost there, Patch thought.

The frontmost rats were floating downriver and close to the point of no return, where the water quickened before hurtling into the void. The rearmost were just entering the water now.

He looked at Greta, expecting to see triumph on her face, watching the rats get ever nearer to oblivion.

Instead, Greta was staring past him, back down towards the villagers. Patch turned to follow her gaze, and gasped:

The people of the village were dancing.

Dancing in a column that was speeding towards the river, their grinning faces lit up with absolute glee.

"Oh no!" said Patch, horrified.

"What's gone wrong?" said Greta.

"The Song spilled out beyond the rats," he said. "The villagers are caught in the Dance!"

He looked to the rats near the waterfall, then back to the people. He played his Pipe, trying to add in a separation, to keep the rodents on their way and send the people back.

He quickly realized that it wasn't working.

Next option, he thought: *wait until most of the rats have gone over the falls, and bring the Dance to an end.*

But the people were so much *faster* than the rats, and many would be in the water by then. *Too risky*, he thought. There were children among the dancers. The water could sweep them to their deaths, however short a time they were in the river. Besides, could everyone even *swim*?

He added counter-rhythms that should slow the Dance down. That way, most of the rats would simply drift to their fate.

It had no effect. Closer the villagers came. Closer to the river's edge.

Greta grabbed his shoulder. "Patch! You have to do something!"

If he merely stopped playing, the Song would take too long to fade. As the first line of people stepped into the icy water, Patch knew there was only one option left.

He took the Pipe from his lips and snapped it in half.

At once the Dance died.

The grins on the faces of the villagers dropped away. Those who found themselves standing in the ice-cold river looked at their sodden legs, baffled. Panicked squeals came from the rats, who were now scrabbling their way towards the riverbank, finding purchase at the river's edge. The villagers watched as the rats helped each other and emerged from the water, scurrying back towards the village.

Patch's heart sank. He had come so close to success, but would have to start again once he'd recovered enough strength to…

The villager nearest the bridge raised a trembling arm, pointing right at Patch.

"He tried to kill us!" the villager screamed.

"Uh, no, I—" said Patch.

"He almost drowned us all!" cried another.

Greta stepped forward. "Wait!" she shouted. "That's not what happened!"

But the accusations kept mounting. Soon it seemed as if the whole village wanted his blood.

"He's like the Hamelyn Piper!" they cried. "Twisted, evil! Lock him up and throw away the key!"

"Um, Greta?" whispered Patch. "Maybe I should, uh, run away…"

She shook her head. "If you run, they'll chase you down like a mad dog! Your only chance is to reason with them."

"He's got Greta under a spell!" a villager cried.

Greta's eyes narrowed with anger. "*I'm not under any spell!*" she shouted, and the villagers fell silent at once, looking at her like children caught misbehaving by a parent. "Now all of you just calm down and listen! Angry decisions are bad ones, don't I always say?"

Nods and grumbles came from the villagers. Some agreed with Greta, but it was clear that many didn't. For Patch it was torture. Wherever he looked he saw suspicion and hate-filled eyes. It proved too much for him. Thinking this was his only opportunity to get a head start, he made a terrible mistake.

He began to run.

Over the bridge he went. The villagers were taken by surprise, but soon most were giving chase.

"Don't hurt him!" yelled Greta.

Patch hadn't yet realized the madness of his action – indeed, as he ran and found the road leading out of the village, he was hopeful. It didn't look impassable by any means! Pure white snow, flanked by trees, running straight on into the distance. He could outrun the villagers! He could keep ahead of them, and…

Suddenly the snow was too deep to run through. Too deep to *walk* through. He lost his balance and stumbled, falling face-down into white. His limbs felt impossibly heavy as he looked back to the villagers.

"Send him over the waterfall," one of them yelled, fist in the air. "See how he likes it!" It got a hearty cheer from the others.

Perhaps Greta could talk them out of it. Perhaps not.

Patch was so tired he almost didn't care.

The villagers fell suddenly silent and halted, staring past him. Patch looked at the road ahead. In the distance, the tops of the trees were shaking. The movement came nearer; the air itself was twisting, spinning.

The deep snow in the road was being hurled out to either side, as a corkscrew of white approached.

"He's summoned the Devil!" screamed one villager, running away. Some followed, terrified, but most were transfixed by the sight.

He could hear it now – a harsh whirring, almost like the buzz of wasps. And under that sound was another: rhythm and melody blending together in a Song for the wind.

When the twisting air broke through the last of the snow, Patch wasn't surprised by what he saw. Two horses, on a road that was clear of snow behind them. The riders wore the black and purple garb of the Custodian Elite.

Exhausted, he let his head fall. He half-laughed, and half-sobbed. He was safe. The villagers couldn't harm him now.

He heard the horses stop, then the crunch of boots in snow as one of the riders approached. Patch lifted his head and strained to look up. The face looming over him was young; with a shock, Patch realized it was familiar.

"Patch?" said the young man. "Patch Brightwater?"

Patch squinted at the young man's face.

I know you, he thought. *How do I know you?*

Ever since he'd woken in Patterfall, he'd known there was something very important that he needed to remember; at long last, that very important thing came back to him, and with it came everything else, all his lost memories returning at once.

"Oh no," he said. His head dropped back down to the snow.

He wasn't a Piper, not really. He'd fled from Tiviscan in disgrace before completing his training.

And now he knew just how much trouble he was in.

5
A Rat of Distinction

Patch woke from a dream.

He'd been walking hand in hand with his mother, feeling the kind of total happiness that he'd not felt in a long time. He'd only been three years old when both his parents had died, leaving him to be raised by his grandparents. He'd been left with no memories of his father at all, and only that single precious memory of his mother: holding her hand, looking up to see her smiling at him.

He was in a small room with a bare flagstone floor; there was a little window and a thin mat for a bed. It was cold. A fleece and a blanket covered him, and without it he suspected he would freeze.

He could feel a weight around his ankle – it was a manacle. Wrapping his covers around his back, he followed the chain to an iron ring on the wall. Out of the window, he could see the grain storehouse, its doors locked tight once more. He was wearing the clothes he'd fallen unconscious in, but his coat had been removed. On the floor was a tin bowl with a few hunks of stale bread, and a cup of water.

Hearing a clatter of keys, Patch turned to the door, and when it swung open he saw the face of the Elite Piper who had brought his memory rushing back. Erner Whitlock was his name; two years his senior, at fifteen. One of the three best Pipers that Patch had trained with.

"Erner," said Patch, looking at the robes Erner wore – rich purple on thick black cotton. "The Custodian Elite! The clothes suit you. I knew you'd pass your final trials."

Erner nodded. "I wish you'd been there to see it," he said. "Three of us went through the trials, and all three succeeded!"

"Who were the other two?"

"Mort and Kara. Mort is apprenticed with the Marinus Pipers in the Eastern Seas, but Kara was like me – Custodian Elite. She's gone to Skamos."

Patch could picture them both. Mort was a tall, strong lad with a love of the sea; Marinus Pipers were keenly sought by merchant ships, and needed a knack for whipping up winds and fending off pirates, which the Eastern Seas had plenty of. Kara, meanwhile, had been Erner's match in every task they'd ever done. Skamos was an important place, the only human city left on the continent known as the Dragon Territories. Peace between humans and dragons had always been fragile, but problems at Skamos had almost tipped things into war more than once. The Custodian Elite there had a crucial role in stopping that happening.

"Pirates and dragons," said Patch. "Exactly what they wanted. It's good to hear."

Erner stepped forward and gave him a sudden, brief hug. "I've missed you, Patch. We all did."

For a moment, Patch couldn't speak. The thought of all he'd left behind in Tiviscan was too much. Six months ago, just like Mort and Kara, he had known exactly what lay in his future – for him, it would be a glorious career in the Custodian Elite, bringing justice and help to those most in need. Then he'd thrown it all away, leaving Tiviscan behind, struggling to make ends meet. And now...the future wasn't something he even wanted to think about. "So," he said at last, changing the subject, "*Apprentice* Whitlock then!"

"It still sounds strange to my ears," said Erner.

An apprenticeship lasted two years, after which the title changed from "Apprentice" to "Fortis", which was the first proper rank of the Elite. Patch thought of the other figure he'd seen in the snow: "Who are you apprenticed to? What rank are they?"

"A Virtus," said Erner.

"Impressive!" said Patch – "Virtus" was the highest rank of all, and it was rare for them to take on an apprentice. "Which Virtus is it?"

Erner smiled awkwardly, and Patch could tell he was almost embarrassed to say it. "Virtus Stone."

Patch stared. "Good God, Erner. *Rundel* Stone?"

"Himself," said Erner.

The name of Rundel Stone brought two strong emotions to Patch. First, a deep sense of pride that his friend had been taken on as apprentice by such a legendary man – Stone was one of the Eight, the group of heroes who had finally captured the Hamelyn Piper.

The second emotion was utter despair, that the very same man held Patch's fate in his hands. Pity, the story went, was not a word Rundel Stone knew.

"Virtus Stone is making preparations to deal with the village's rat problem," said Erner. "While he does that, I'm to question you about...recent events."

"Hang on," said Patch. "Elite Pipers, dealing with rats?"

"With this many rats, people think of Hamelyn," said Erner. "The pride of all Pipers is at stake! We came to Patterfall because we happened to be in Wassil when the call for help was received, and the Virtus immediately volunteered. We arrived just in time to stop you being lynched. According to the villagers you burst out of the forest half-dead and with amnesia. They assumed you were the Piper they'd sent for, and you assumed the same. What were you doing in the forest?"

"I, um, just happened to be travelling nearby," said Patch. "The merchant's cart I was getting a ride on broke, and I was abandoned. The merchant hadn't known how dangerous the region was at this time of year."

"The villagers told us what happened to them, when you tried to deal with the rats."

Patch hung his head. "I broke the law," he said. "I played the Dance, yes. But I didn't mean for the people to get caught up in it!"

Erner nodded, sorrow in his eyes. "There's something else, Patch," he said. "It's the reason Rundel Stone and I were in Wassil. There was a great mystery we'd come to solve."

"Um...go on." Patch didn't like where this was going.

"A few months ago, the Pipers' Council became aware of tales of travelling musicians whose music was said to be the best anyone had ever heard. Witnesses all said the same thing: people danced like they'd never danced before. It seemed that the musicians had a mysterious Piper among them, and that the Piper had been playing the most illegal Song of them all. The Song that you played for the rats, Patch. The *Dance*. Forbidden, since Hamelyn!"

"Er...gosh," said Patch. He *really* didn't like where this was going.

"The Council grew even more concerned, because every description of this mystery Piper was different. In one place, people had seen a tall, thin woman. In another, a short, wide man. One week, old. Another week, young. The Council was scared, Patch. Scared! A Piper who played the Dance even though it was forbidden! A Piper powerful enough to change physical appearance from one day to the next! Unheard of! A dark and evil Piper, the Council assumed. *Toying* with us. So they sent Rundel Stone to hunt this villain down. And myself, of course."

Patch coughed. When he'd fled from Tiviscan, earning money for food and lodging hadn't been easy. Piping was all he knew, but as a failed student fleeing in disgrace, working as a Piper was impossible. After a week on the road, hungry and tired, he'd met a travelling band of musicians who were barely scraping a living themselves. He'd offered to play the flute for them, but they already had a flute player.

That was when he'd had the idea.

He told them of a wonderful tune he knew, a sea shanty they'd never heard before, and convinced them to try it out. While the band performed, Patch stayed hidden and played the Dance in secret, making sure the audience had the time of their lives. Tips flowed, of course, and the grateful band gave him some of the money. They asked him for another tune, and so it went on.

That was how he had spent the seven months since he'd left Tiviscan: staying with a band for a few weeks, then parting company and setting off to find another band before anyone got suspicious.

He thought of all the bands he'd been with, and of the flute players in them – a tall, thin woman; a short, wide man. Old, and young.

Meanwhile, the Council had heard rumours of an evil Piper, and the varying descriptions they got were simply those of the different flute players.

I scared the Council, he thought, amazed.

He opened his mouth to confess, and stopped. There was a pained look in Erner's eyes.

"You already know it was me," said Patch.

Erner nodded. "Changing the bands you played with was clever," he said. "It made it difficult for us to track you down, but we got word from Wassil and headed there at once. It seems you'd left the town just before we arrived."

Patch sighed. "Someone had been asking too many questions. I figured it was time to scarper, and the merchant who gave me a ride was the only one leaving that day."

"Yet fate led all of us to Patterfall," said Erner. "Virtus Stone has examined your broken Pipe, and the history of its Songs was still there to hear. I can't tell you how shocked I was to discover that it was *you* we'd been chasing all along!" He shook his head, saddened. "Why, Patch? Why would you take such a risk? Playing the Dance to deal with the rats was one thing, but playing it to entertain *people*?"

"It was the only way I could earn money, Erner. Nobody was harmed, and I didn't think anyone would find out." The look of disapproval on Erner's face was almost unbearable. "So," said Patch, "you'll take me back to Tiviscan, then. To certain imprisonment."

Erner seemed utterly deflated. "The Dance is absolutely forbidden. Ten years is the penalty." He walked over to the small window and looked out, silent for a moment. "There's some room for hope, though. The Lords who preside on your case can reduce the sentence by half – the rash actions of a trainee Piper without a malicious bone in his body."

"Five years, then," said Patch. "If pity is taken." He wondered if it might have been better if he'd died in the snow.

After Erner left, Patch lay down on his thin mat and despaired. Exhausted, he fell into an uneasy sleep. A curious sound, somewhere between scratching and rubbing, dragged him slowly back from slumber. He became aware of a gentle weight on his chest.

He opened his eyes and saw a rat.

It was the rat with the red-ringed tail, and it was looking at him.

The part of his brain that had done such a good job of imagining the rats *attacking* him went into overdrive. With a sudden yelp he sat up and backed away as far as he could, flinging the rat off him. It landed and gave him a very obvious glare, then raised a paw out to its side.

"I'm sorry! I'm sorry!" said Patch, gathering his blanket around himself. "Don't kill me!"

The rat looked to the ceiling and let out a tiny sigh, then nodded in the same direction as its paw.

"You're...you're not here to kill me?" said Patch, looking around frantically to see if the other rats were about to pour out of every crevice and devour him.

The rat shook its head and impatiently jabbed its paw towards the wall, its glare intensifying.

Patch stared at the rodent. He followed the line of its paw. On the flat stone of the wall beside him, written in chalk, were the words *Help me.*

The rat picked up a small piece of chalk from the floor and scurried over to the wall, ignoring Patch's whimper.

Patch wondered if he was still asleep, or if madness had taken him. All he could do was stare at the animal as it wrote more letters on the wall. At last it squeaked at him, and he read aloud what the rat had written.

Help me. I am the young daughter of a rich nobleman. I have been cursed by a Sorcerer into the shape of a rat. You will be well rewarded!

Patch looked at the rat, and the rat nodded. "Right," said Patch, and hid under his blanket. He clearly wasn't asleep, so madness seemed the only possibility.

After a few seconds he could feel the rat on top of him. He peeked out; it had its paws clasped together, pleading. "No!" he said. "You're not real!" The animal kept looking at him, forlorn and pitiful. A tiny tear formed and fell down the side of its face.

Patch felt a horrible stab of guilt. "Okay, enough!" he said. "Stop crying! I'll help." The rat gave a little jump for joy. "But why me?"

As if in answer, there was a sudden cheer from outside. Both Patch and the rat looked to the small window. Patch stood, and as he did the rat scampered up onto his shoulder. Patch walked to the window and looked out; a crowd of villagers had assembled by the oak tree, watching Virtus Stone and Erner as they approached the storehouse.

Patch turned his head to the rat. "The other rats all just went back to the storehouse?" he said. The rat nodded and slapped a paw to its forehead. "Not the smartest, are they?" said Patch, and the rat shrugged. Then the penny dropped. "*Ah!* You need protection from the Pipers, and who better to provide it than another Piper?" The rat nodded. "You'll be safe here," he said, wondering what Rundel Stone would play to get rid of the rodents. Stone had studied Patch's broken Pipe, so he probably knew the

Dream wouldn't work. Which Song would he try?

Stone took out his Pipe, and Patch could see that it was very dark in colour. There was an old rumour that Rundel Stone's Pipe was made of obsidiac, one of the rarest magical substances in the world. It was a form of obsidian – black volcanic glass – only ever found in the Dragon Territories. Stone's Pipe couldn't actually be *made* of obsidiac, of course – no piece big enough had ever been found, and even if one had been, the material was impossible to carve. But it could certainly have been coated in an obsidiac glaze, if the obsidiac was finely ground and mixed with resin. Such a glaze had once been highly prized in Pipe-making, as the resulting Pipes were immensely powerful. However, obsidiac was considered holy by dragons; as a result, the Piper's Council had banned its use in new Pipes long ago, in an effort to keep peace.

The Virtus raised his Pipe and began.

Patch listened carefully to the first notes, trying to identify the Song. He frowned. "I'm not sure what that is," he said. "The safest thing would be to wrap you in my blanket, little rat. Then, however the Song tries to compel you, you'll be unable to move and—"

He stopped talking.

The Virtus had started a rhythmic section, complex and primal. It was ringing a bell in Patch's mind. A great big worrying bell, one with *panic* written all over it.

"Oh," said Patch. "Oh no."

He had placed the rhythm. He knew the Song.

It was called the Dispersal, and it was a Song of execution – a terrifying thing, one of the most difficult Songs to perform.

Yet here was the Virtus, using it against a vast pack of rats.

The effect of Dispersal was simple. Every part of the target, every tiny *fragment*, would be utterly destroyed, the target reduced to its components – a devastating, instant unravelling that left nothing behind. Those components were widely dispersed, spread so thinly that not even a speck of blood would remain. Only dust, scattered across a thousand miles.

Patch listened in horror. The Dispersal was a highly selective Song, and the Virtus was allowing it to spread out, knowing that only his target – the rats – would be affected, without risk to the villagers. *All* rats within the bounds of the village would be killed, and perhaps for some distance beyond.

Patch had no idea if any defence was possible.

"Uhhh..." he said. "Um..." The rat put its paws over its ears so it couldn't hear, as it had done with the Dance, but Patch shook his head and it put its paws down again. "A Song isn't just heard with the ears," he said. "Every single *part* of you hears it." The rat stared at him, terrified.

Patch looked around the small room and his eyes settled on the tin bowl the bread was in. "Worth a try," he muttered. He grabbed it, tipping the bread out. "Quickly," he said to the rat. "Under the bowl!" The rat ran to him, and he turned the bowl upside down on top of it. "Keep entirely inside," he said. "And whatever you do, whatever you hear, don't come out!"

He placed his hands on the bowl and thought about what he could do. To keep the rat safe, he needed to play a counter-Song, and create a bubble of protection that surrounded the animal. He had no Pipe and would have to play it by lip, which made it harder – especially since his lips were still cracked and sore – but the bubble wouldn't need to be big.

Time was running out. Virtus Stone's Song was building. Patch could hear the chatter of the nervous villagers, as they sensed the sheer force of the music.

Here goes, he thought. With one ear on the Song outside, he began. The counter-rhythm he whistled was almost identical to the core rhythm of the Dispersal, but with a few carefully chosen added beats. Next, he whistled a modified version of the Song's secondary melody. Without a Pipe, all he could do was switch from rhythm to melody and back again, faster and faster, his lips getting ever closer to the upturned bowl.

The protective bubble began to form just in time. He

could sense it surrounding the metal of the bowl, a bubble that would guide the flow of the Song safely away, and not let it penetrate.

He tensed, knowing the moment was close. The bowl started to vibrate as the counter-Song struggled to hold together. On the floor nearby, the piece of chalk began to shake, then it rose up onto one tip, spinning. Patch felt his hair stand on end, and the chain around his ankle grew oddly warm.

The Dispersal reached a sudden crescendo and the force of it hit him, almost knocking him over. He managed to keep his hands firmly on the bowl, but he despaired as he felt his counter-Song shatter. From outside came the anguished cries of terrified villagers.

Then silence.

Shaking, Patch took his hands away from the bowl, wary of lifting it. Who knew *what* he might find there. "Hello?" he said. "Little rat?" There was a pitiful squeak. "It's okay," he said. "You're safe. You can come out now." The rat peeked out, trembling, looking at him for more reassurance. "Really," said Patch.

Outside, the shocked silence of the villagers was broken by hesitant cheers. "They've gone!" cried a voice. "Look! The rats have all gone!" The cheers grew.

The rat emerged from under the bowl and looked at Patch, a question in its eyes. Its companions were all dead,

Patch realized – turned to dust and scattered across vast distances. "Yes," said Patch. "The other rats... They've all gone."

The rat slumped.

Patch waited a moment before he spoke again. "I have two questions," he said. "First, were any of the other rats human too?" The rat shook its head, which was a huge relief. "And second," he said, lifting the piece of chalk from the floor and offering it to the rat. "What's your name?"

The rat took the chalk and wrote two words on the wall. Patch looked at them and smiled. He held out his hand, taking the rat's paw and gently shaking it. "Good to meet you, Wren Cobble," he said. "I'm Patch Brightwater."

Wren dashed up Patch's arm to his shoulder, and gave his neck a grateful hug.

6

Journey to Tiviscan

"How old are you, Wren?" said Patch.

Wren ran down from his shoulder, and wrote *13* on the wall.

"Same as me!" he said. "And educated enough to read and write! A benefit of your wealthy family, I suppose. I was in training at Tiviscan Castle from the age of ten. It's a free education, for those with the gift of Piping. That education will come in handy now that I'll never be a real Piper—"

Wren frowned at him.

"Oh, I mean it," said Patch. "I've played an illegal Song. The Custodians will take me to Tiviscan, I'll be put on trial, and jailed for five years at the very least! As a criminal, I'll never be permitted to work as a Piper." He sighed; his gaze moved to Wren's chalk-written plea for help, and he read the last part aloud: "*You will be well rewarded!*" He turned to Wren. "I'm thankful that your parents are rich. Don't think me greedy, but when I'm released from the dungeons in five years, I'll need that reward." He gave her a weak smile, then bowed his head and closed his eyes. If he'd still been looking at her, he would have seen a curious expression cross Wren's face: a mixture of guilt and worry.

Patch opened his eyes again. "You'll have one heck of a story to tell your parents," he said. "When you get back home."

Wren shook her head and started to write again, Patch waiting patiently as she slowly drew out each letter: *Not until curse lifted.*

"I'm sure your parents—" started Patch, but Wren jabbed at the words she'd written and added an exclamation mark.

Not until curse lifted!

"Fair enough," said Patch. He could sympathize, really – his grandparents thought he was still training to become a Piper, and the idea of them finding out the truth made him feel ill. He would leave them to their happy ignorance for as long as he could. "We'll have to get help from the Custodian Elite, then. They're in the best position to know what can be done for you."

She shook her head firmly.

"Saving you from that Song is one thing, Wren," he said.

"But as a prisoner, I won't be able to do anything more to help you. You'll need the Custodians. Let me talk to them."

Wren shook her head again, and mimed a lumbering monster. Patch laughed, because he understood who she meant.

"He's *Rundel Stone*," he said. "One of the Eight who hunted down the Hamelyn Piper. There isn't a more respected Custodian in the world! He's no monster."

Wren put her hand to her chest before taking it away sharply, as if it was painful. The Cold Heart of Justice, she was saying – Stone's famous nickname.

Patch sighed. He could understand why Wren would be wary of putting herself at the man's mercy. There were plenty of stories about how Stone sometimes applied the law far too strictly, and as a rat, Wren had certainly been guilty of stealing food and scaring the villagers. "Yes, but who can blame him for his cold heart?" said Patch. "He vowed to find the children of Hamelyn and bring them home, safe and sound. Rundel Stone and the rest of the Eight did all they could: they caught the Hamelyn Piper, and brought him to Tiviscan to be imprisoned. But the children weren't found, and their fate is still unknown. Rundel Stone couldn't keep his vow. That's enough to leave anyone with a cold heart."

Wren was standing with her arms folded. She wasn't having it.

"Very well," said Patch. "We'll leave Stone out of it. I know his apprentice, Erner Whitlock. Honest and decent. You'll like him. When I get a chance to talk to him alone, I'll *have* to tell him about you, okay? There's no other choice."

After a long pause, Wren gave him a reluctant nod.

"Strange to think I'll actually *meet* Rundel Stone," said Patch. He recited the rhyme every child knew – the names of the Eight, the heroes assembled by the Piper's Council to capture the Hamelyn Piper. "Palafox, Corrigan, Kellenfas, Stone," he said. "Casimir, Hinkelman, Drevis and Throne. My grandmother has a way with stories, and she told me their adventures every night. A race against time, hunting across every nation of these lands and into the Islands of the Eastern Sea, until they finally caught the Hamelyn Piper and locked him away to rot in the dungeons of Tiviscan Castle." He paused, knowing that it was in those very dungeons that he would be spending the next five years – or maybe ten! "To be jailed by one of my heroes…"

Wren nodded, downhearted. She set down her chalk, climbed onto his shoulder again, and curled up.

Patch was glad of the company. "It's at least a week's journey to Tiviscan Castle from here by horse. Ever seen it?"

Wren shook her head.

"It's impressive," he said. "It sits on a cliff, and the dungeons extend deep into the rock. The deepest of the dungeons is called the Dark. No natural light reaches it." He sat on the floor, miserable. "The Hamelyn Piper is imprisoned in the Dark, of course. At the deepest point of the deepest dungeon. It's said that each night the prisoners in the dungeons can hear him scream – scream until he's hoarse and can cry out no more."

He fell silent and closed his eyes.

After a while, Wren ran down to the ground and picked up her chalk. She wrote, but Patch was lost to his misery. She squeaked to get his attention.

You're too young for prison, she'd written.

"I'm not," he said. "Children younger than me have been jailed there." The Tiviscan dungeons were mainly used for those who broke the laws of Piping, so almost all the prisoners were Pipers themselves. Even the youngest child, discovering their own Piping ability for the first time, could accidentally break the law and end up in a cell. Although, Patch knew, it would often be just for a day, to scare them and make sure they didn't do it again. He honestly didn't know the longest time someone his age had been imprisoned for. Perhaps he would be setting a new record.

He could see that Wren was trying to think of something else to write.

"Look, I know you're trying to cheer me up," he said. "And thank you. But the only things that are important are that you're okay, and I'm not alone."

Wren nodded. She set down her chalk and clapped her paws together to get rid of the chalk dust, coughing as a little cloud of it engulfed her.

"It'd be easier with a quill and paper," said Patch. An image of a tiny feather cut to a quill came into his mind, and he smiled. "Perhaps Erner will get you that. Although..." A thought had occurred to him. "Have you heard of Merisax hand speech?" Wren shook her head. "Merisax is a language used by mercenaries and pirates. My dream was to join the Custodian Elite, and they're required to be fluent, so I spent a lot of time learning it." Ah yes, his dream... Long since shattered. He sighed. "Anyway, with Merisax you only use your *hands* to talk. It allows for total silence in setting an ambush – you can hold a conversation without giving away your position. It's also useful in battle. Or in a loud tavern. Or any time you can't speak—" He gestured towards Wren and paused, waiting for the penny to drop. When it did, Wren's face lit up. "How about I run through some phrases, to give you a feel for it?"

She gave him a brisk nod and sat facing him, eager to begin.

"*Yes, No*," said Patch, thumbs up, then thumbs down. "*Hurry up. Slow down. Come over here. Go away.*" With each example, he gave Wren enough time to mimic the sign he was showing her. "*Keep going. You're an idiot. Pass the rum.*" Next he made a throat-slitting motion. "*Kill*," he said.

"Lots of variants of kill, actually. Lots. That's pirates and mercenaries for you, I suppose. *Kill quickly. Kill slowly. Kill everyone. Don't kill anyone.*" He thought for a second. "That last one's probably not used much. Let's see... *Don't do that here. I'm bleeding. You're bleeding. Please stop the bleeding. You're on fire. The ship is on fire. The ship is sinking. Oh no it's a shark. Maybe we should murder the captain.*"

Wren studiously copied each action, deep in concentration.

Patch continued. "*You smell terrible. Run away. If you do that again I'll kill you.* The eyes are important for that one," said Patch. "Otherwise it's a bit too much like *Pass the rum*. I expect that's caused a few fights in its time. Anyway, that should give you the flavour of it. What do you think?"

Yes, kill everyone, oh no it's a shark, signed Wren.

"Well," said Patch. "It's a start."

It was several hours before Erner Whitlock returned, and by then Wren had shown herself to be exceptionally quick at learning Merisax. Patch reckoned she would soon get to grips with it – something that had taken Patch months to achieve.

When the keys rattled in the door, Wren hid under Patch's blanket. Patch stood as Erner came inside.

"Your coat," said Erner, handing it to Patch. "We'll be setting off shortly."

Patch put the coat on, immediately glad of its familiar feel. He looked at Erner, and noticed that the Apprentice Piper was uneasy. "Are you okay?" he asked.

Erner smiled nervously. "I should be asking *you* that. Patch, I want you to know that I—" He stopped and shook his head. "I'm sorry, about how things are."

Patch put his hand on Erner's shoulder. "I know," he said. "It's the way it must be, though. How's your boss?"

"Virtus Stone is unusually quiet," said Erner. "He's even moodier than normal."

"I could have guessed he was in a bad mood when he chose the Dispersal to deal with the rats," said Patch. "A bit over the top, don't you think?"

Erner shrugged. "The Virtus is the best Piper I've ever seen, by far. To him, the Dispersal is *easy,* and it was certain to do the job." He paused, before lowering his voice. "To be honest, it *was* overkill. I think he's cross from all this traipsing across frozen terrain, chasing you."

"I hope he cheers up on the journey back," said Patch. It seemed like a good opportunity to mention Wren. "Actually, there's something I need to talk to you about—"

"Silence!" came a voice. Rundel Stone swept through the doorway, and Patch took a step back from Erner. Even given the circumstances, Patch felt awed to be in the presence of a legend. "We leave in five minutes. The weather conditions are deteriorating. I've purchased another horse from the villagers for our *burden*." He looked with disdain at Patch when he said it; instinctively Patch opened his mouth to object, but the glare from the Virtus stopped him. "No speaking!" said Stone. "Understand? Not now, not while we travel. *Never.* You are a criminal. A *disgrace* to Piping. Oh, I know all about you, Patch Brightwater. I make it my business to know. A promising young student, you wanted to join the Custodian Elite, but instead you embarrassed yourself and vanished with your tail between your legs. Then you chose to *misuse* the skills you'd managed to learn, to lead me on a merry chase while my time would have been far better spent elsewhere, dealing with problems that – unlike you – *actually matter*."

Patch opened and closed his mouth in silence, like a dying fish.

"Five minutes!" said Stone. He turned to Erner. "Come, Apprentice," he said, and left. Erner gave Patch a regretful look and went with his master, locking the door behind him.

Wren poked her head out from her hiding place.

"So much for meeting your heroes," said Patch. "We'll get to speak to Erner on his own, sooner or later." He held his coat open. "Handmade by my grandfather, this coat. Deerskin. His gift to me when I first went to Tiviscan. A little big back then, but now it's perfect. Cool in summer, warm in winter, with endless pockets. Come on then, hop inside."

Wren wasn't too sure.

"I will *not* squash you," said Patch. "I promise."

When Stone and Erner came back a few minutes later, Wren was snuggled up in his pocket. Patch was led outside. The Elite Pipers' horses stood waiting, a smaller horse beside them. Next to the horses stood Greta, the only person there to bid him farewell; the other villagers of Patterfall had stayed indoors.

"Good luck, Patch," said Greta. She looked at Stone. "Don't be harsh on the lad. He meant well."

Rundel Stone said nothing in reply.

As Stone had instructed, Patch stayed silent as they rode. It made him miserable. He had too much time to think – about his past, and about his future. Neither was a place he was keen to visit. With Stone's expert Piping to clear the snow, it only took a day of travel for them to get out of the valley and reach lower altitudes. Heading south, winter's icy grip weakened quickly. Wren was a little pocket of extra warmth near his heart.

Each night, they camped in the cover of woods and forests, using three of the traditional Piper's shelters that had been part of Patch's training – tiny oilskin tents that, when folded up, took hardly any space in their horses' packs, but when assembled gave just enough room for a single curled-up sleeper. The tents kept out the cold, but even better was how the privacy let Patch help Wren learn her Merisax signs at night, until the light from the fire dwindled.

Each morning, Erner hunted for prey soon after dawn, when rabbit and fowl were more vulnerable to one of the various luring Songs. While he was gone, Stone got to work lighting a fire. Only on the third morning did they swap roles. When Stone went to hunt, Patch realized the chance had come to talk to Erner.

"Morning, Erner," said Patch, emerging from his little tent.

Erner had just struck his firesteel to light the fire. "Morning, Patch," he replied.

"Um, Erner?" said Patch.

Erner looked up, the fire doing well. "Yes?" he said, at which point Wren emerged from Patch's pocket, scurried to his shoulder, and waved.

"A rat!" said Erner, startled. Wren signed something, and Erner's surprise turned to astonishment. "That's Merisax hand speech!" he said. He watched the rat intently as she repeated what she'd signed. He stared in shock. "You want me to *what*?" he said, appalled.

"She didn't mean that," said Patch. "She's learning." He turned to Wren and signed: both hands opening and closing in fists. "*This* is 'Help me', Wren," he said. "What you just signed… Well, it's very much *not*, and I don't want to *ever* see you do that again."

Wren grumbled.

"No, I *won't* tell you what it means." Patch turned back to Erner. "Erner, this is Wren. She's human, she was cursed by a Sorcerer, and she needs help. She lived among the rats in the village, and I suspect she was the reason those rats were so successful at avoiding traps and poison." He glanced at Wren, who was trying to look as innocent as possible, but given how bright she'd shown herself to be, Patch had no doubt about it.

Erner's eyes widened in horror. "Wait…there were *people* among the rats?"

"None of the other rats were human," said Patch. "Luckily. Wren came to me when the Dispersal was about to happen, and I protected her from it, but with me in prison she'll need someone else to—"

"You *protected* her?" said Erner. "From *that* Dispersal? I felt how powerful it was."

Patch waved away the compliment. "Trust me, it wasn't easy. Look, we'd rather not involve the Virtus and he'll be back any minute."

"Why don't you want to involve the Virtus?" asked Erner.

Wren signed something incredibly rude again, and Patch thought that this time she knew *exactly* what she was saying. He turned to Erner. "She thinks that Rundel Stone is so stubborn he'd probably arrest her for being, I don't know, a talking rat without a *licence*. Or something."

Erner laughed wholeheartedly, then suddenly stopped. "Ah. I see your point."

Patch nodded. "Exactly," he said.

7

Trial of a Piper

Erner agreed to keep Wren's presence a secret, and to begin investigating a cure for her curse the moment they reached Tiviscan.

As they continued their journey, Wren's grasp of Merisax came on in leaps and bounds, and teaching her provided Patch with a welcome distraction from what awaited him when they reached their destination.

At last, ten days after setting off from Patterfall, the three horses trudged through rain on the rising road; ahead, they could see the sheer cliff on which Tiviscan Castle sat, overlooking forest. To the rear of the Castle was Tiviscan town, a ramshackle spread of buildings that flowed from the Castle's gates towards grassy plains and hills.

The Castle rose high and seemed larger than was

possible, since at its base it continued *into* the rock of the cliff. It was hard to tell where the Castle ended. Some parts of it were ancient beyond measure, older even than Piping. Originally, it was a village carved into the rock itself – networks of tunnels, tombs and homes that lay within the cliff. As the Castle grew, it grew down as well as up.

The oldest and deepest of those tunnels formed the dungeons where Patch would soon find himself. He thought of them, and shivered.

They reached the Castle gates, passing under the massive double archways and through the courtyard market, which was busy despite the rain. They dismounted at the vast central Keep, and Virtus Stone led them through the iron-clad Keep gate, into a dim stone entrance hall.

There were two sets of steps ahead. One set was plain stone, leading downwards. The other led up, and was far grander: the steps were marble, and the walls beside it were carved with images from the history of Piping.

The first carving showed the earliest days when Pipers knew only the simplest Songs. They were more like monks or knights back then, and travelled the world bringing help where they could, for no reward but food and shelter. A simple life, based on a proud code of honour – an ideal which was reborn much later, when the Custodian Elite were founded.

The next few carvings showed the discovery of new

Songs and new skills, as the Piper's Art was refined over centuries.

A great and glorious history, Patch thought, was carved into those walls.

And then he saw a carving that depicted a battle: army facing army, but only one side had Pipers in their ranks. It took Patch a moment to realize which battle was being represented, and when he did he sighed with sorrow.

The Pipers in that battle had been paid to fight. The opposing army was being slaughtered.

The history of Piping was not always great or glorious, thought Patch.

Stone stopped walking and looked at him, raising an eyebrow. He followed Patch's eyeline to the carving. "Ah," he said. "The Battle of Dornley Flats. I see you disapprove."

"Of course I do," said Patch. "Before then, Pipers could only fight for causes that were *just*, not for money."

"Pipers didn't invent war, boy," said Stone. "The many nations of these lands have always quarrelled with each other. Sometimes those quarrels grow. Sometimes they become wars. If Pipers have skills that are useful to an army, shouldn't they be able to profit from them?"

Patch didn't answer.

"Besides," said Stone, "no ruler – no king, queen, baron or overlord – wants the Pipers' Council as an enemy, for without the Council's approval they could hire no decent

Pipers to help in their battles. They'd be forced to use *outcast* Pipers, poorly skilled, poorly trained! Their forces would be at a severe disadvantage. That fact keeps the Pipers' Council safe, and all Pipers too, something you'd be wise to remember."

"Maybe," said Patch. It might have been the truth, but it left a sour taste in his mouth.

"Up past those carvings lies the Chamber of the Council," said Stone. "That's where you would have graduated if you'd proved your worth. Think how different your life could have been! As it is, your trial tomorrow could be the last time you ascend those stairs." He shook his head with a sigh and raised his arm, pointing ominously to the other steps. "We go *that* way."

Stone led them down the spiralling steps, followed by Patch, with Erner at the rear. It got darker as they descended, and a horrible stench rose from below.

They came to a locked gate. Stone knocked, and a burly man opened it.

"Prisoner for trial –" said Stone – "by the name of Patch Brightwater." He turned to Erner. "Accompany him to the holding cell," he said. "I'll inform the Council of our success."

"Come on through," said the burly man. He closed the

gate once Patch and Erner were inside. "My name's Furnel, lad," he said to Patch. "This way."

Furnel led them to a dank corridor lit by oil lamps. Patch saw a row of small cells, with one door open. Furnel pointed to the door, and Patch went inside. There was just enough space to lie down, and a sickly light came through the bars in the door. On the cold floor was some straw, and a rough blanket that at first touch felt like it might give him splinters. The door was shut behind him and he could hear Furnel and Erner walking away.

Wren came out of his pocket and ran up to his shoulder. *Horrible place*, she signed, anxious.

Patch nodded. Five years, he thought. Five years in a cell that would probably be even worse than this. And that was if he was lucky enough to have his sentence reduced.

A few minutes later, Erner opened the door and handed him a bundle of clothes. "The jailor insisted you change into these," he said. "Prison clothing must be worn by the accused at a trial."

Patch took them. Rough cloth trousers, rough cloth shirt.

"You can keep your boots," said Erner.

"What about my coat?" said Patch.

Erner shook his head. "I'll look after it until your release."

Patch set Wren on the floor and changed, then handed

Erner his clothes and coat. "There's one other thing I want you to look after," he said. He turned to Wren, whose eyes widened.

What are you talking about? she signed.

"I'll take good care of her," said Erner. "You have my word."

No chance! signed Wren. *I'm staying with Patch! Someone has to lift his spirits!*

"You can't stay with me, Wren," said Patch. "The dungeons are no place for you." She folded her arms and avoided eye contact. "Please, Wren. Erner will find the help you need. I'll make it through. In five years, I'll be out. And you can bring me that reward!" When he said it like that, it almost sounded *possible.*

Wren looked to Patch, then to Erner, and back again. Her shoulders sagged, and her head dropped. She nodded. *I'll miss you,* she signed.

Erner was carrying a satchel, and he kneeled down and opened the flap. "There's room in here," he said.

"Keep out of sight," said Patch. "People have a thing about rats. Safest to stay hidden!"

Wren hopped inside, with one last sad look at Patch. She waved, and Patch waved in return. "Look after yourself, Wren," he said. Erner closed the door, and Patch listened as his friend's footsteps faded.

He was alone.

After a long restless night, Patch was awoken with a bowl of hot stew.

"Is it morning?" he asked the jailer – Furnel, the same burly man who'd been on duty the night before. Given that no natural light seemed to reach his cell, he had no way to tell if it was daytime.

"It is," said Furnel. "Your trial begins in an hour."

Patch ate the food, his last meal before perhaps ten years of confinement, or five if he was lucky. When he finished, Furnel manacled himself and Patch together.

"I know you're not thinking of escape now, lad," said Furnel. "But things change when the sentence gets passed and the reality of it hits home. Trust me."

He led Patch up the central steps of the Keep until they reached the ornate door to the Council chamber. Furnel knocked, and the doors swung wide to a cacophony of voices.

The chamber was full.

Around the walls, rising rows of seats made it feel like a theatre.

Rundel Stone sat in a chair at one side, and Patch was led to a stool in the middle of the chamber. He sat and looked around the room quickly, trying to find Erner – and there he was, three rows up on the left, satchel in hand. Patch thought he could see a tiny nose peeking out from the bag.

He would be judged by members of the Piper's Council, usually two of them. A door in the far wall opened, and his judges started to come into the chamber. He watched, anxious to see who was going to rule over his fate.

He stared as all five members of the Council came in and sat at the judges' bench.

Lord Drevis entered first, followed by Lord Pewter, Lady Winkless, Lord Cobb and Lady Rumsey.

All of them would preside over his case. They wore ceremonial robes, fold after fold of garments stitched with gold, silver and brilliant indigo.

Patch turned to Furnel. "Isn't it supposed to be just *two* judges?"

"For something this infamous?" said Furnel.

Patch gave him a wary look. "Infamous?"

"Aye, lad. You were big news for a time, when the rumours started about a rogue Piper. People were scared! They thought the Hamelyn Piper himself might have escaped! I'm not surprised the whole of the Council is here. And look at the size of the crowd!"

The clap of a gavel sounded from the judges' bench, and the chatter of the audience began to settle. The gavel was in the hand of Lord Drevis, the head of the Piper's Council. Drevis, like Stone, was one of the legendary Eight. Indeed, he had *led* them in their successful capture of the Hamelyn Piper, and as a result was probably the most famous Piper in the world. Another two claps of the gavel, and silence was finally achieved.

"The Court of the Council is gathered," said Drevis. "Accuser, state your case."

Rundel Stone stood from his seat. "This prisoner before you is Patch Brightwater."

"Prisoner shall stand!" called Drevis, and Patch stood, chain rattling.

"Thirteen years of age, Brightwater trained in this Castle," said Stone. "Last midsummer, his own failings led him to abscond after bringing shame on himself. He left the Castle, abandoning his training." The audience murmured darkly. "As the Council is aware, rumours began of a rogue Piper, playing the Dance throughout the land. A Piper able to change *form*!" The murmurs grew. "It transpires that Brightwater was at the root of the affair. However, the rumours of shape-changing were misplaced. He merely played the Dance in secret at various inns and taverns, to extract *moneys* and *favours*!" Stone addressed his next words to the audience, and spoke them with some relish. "His actions brought *disrepute* to the pure and glorious Art of Piping!"

The audience booed.

"The evidence?" said Lord Pewter.

Stone held up the two halves of Patch's broken Pipe. "The history of his crimes lies within the Pipe he used, one he had clearly crafted himself."

Lord Pewter gestured for Stone to bring the pieces to the bench. He took the broken Pipe and examined it carefully, then passed it to his colleagues. "A very traditional Pipe, but easy to get wrong," said Pewter. "I'm pleased to see how well you learned your carving, Patch Brightwater."

"Uh, thanks, Lord Pewter," said Patch. "It was cured over a hawthorn fire. Makes all the difference."

Stone glared at him. "The prisoner is to remain silent!"

"Come, come, Rundel," said Pewter. "I addressed him directly, his comment was allowed." He turned to Patch. "Think carefully, now, Patch Brightwater. Do you confess to your crime? Did you Pipe the Dance as the Virtus claims?"

There seemed little point denying anything. "I did," said Patch. A gasp came from the audience. "But it was not through greed, Lord. It wasn't riches I sought, only food and a bed to sleep in."

The Council turned to one another and entered muffled discussions. Finally, Drevis clapped the gavel and spoke. "Patch Brightwater, you have confessed your guilt. We must now consider the case for leniency. You have misused Piping, but I know your tutors thought well of you, and that previously you had shown yourself to be honest and of good nature – although not always of good judgement. Now, as you have done before, you have gone astray and chosen poorly." He looked to his colleagues. "We are all agreed?" They nodded. "This crime demands ten years in the dungeons of Tiviscan. The mercy of the Court allows us to reduce this to five years."

The audience murmured, nodding their heads. Erner gave him an encouraging glance. Patch looked to Erner's bag and could just about make out a thumbs up from a certain small paw.

Then a voice spoke: "Wait."

It was Rundel Stone.

"Yes, Virtus?" said Lord Drevis.

Stone got up from his chair and strode to the centre of the chamber. "I agree with your assessment of the prisoner. To my mind, he is indeed a *fool* more than a villain." Sniggers came from the audience. "However, there is one matter that I strongly disagree with."

"Go on," said Drevis, his eyes narrowing.

"This is a serious offence," said Stone. "When the Hamelyn Piper was imprisoned, the Dance was forbidden at once. In all these years, nobody has broken that law. Until now. Yet you wish to give the perpetrator a slap on the wrist?"

"Look at him, Rundel," said Lady Winkless. "There's no evil in the lad. Five years in the dungeons is already a severe punishment."

Stone shook his head, and when he spoke again there was a hint of anger in his voice. "You look at Brightwater, and see a boy who came here to study, a boy who then strayed from the path. I see *danger*. Here was a boy willing to play the Dance and ignore the law. Time has passed since Hamelyn, and people are starting to forget the horror of it. That cannot be allowed!" He looked around the chamber, the audience utterly silent. Yet, Patch noticed, Stone didn't look at *him*. "There has been *fear* since these rumours of a Dark Piper emerged, but before that, something curious had happened to the story of the Hamelyn Piper. On my search for Brightwater, for example, I saw an inn called The Piper and the Rats. The inn's sign showed a *jolly* scene, but it was the Hamelyn Piper that was depicted! Smiling! *Benevolent!*" His hand formed a fist as he spoke. "I spoke with some who even thought he might have been a hero. Who said the children had been taken to a wondrous place, to live happy lives. Who said that the people of Hamelyn must have done something to provoke him, or had treated their own children so *terribly* that the Hamelyn Piper needed to rescue them!" He paused, his anger seeming to overwhelm him for a moment. "How can that be? How can we have forgotten?" He looked around the chamber. Most would not meet his gaze. "The notion that the Hamelyn Piper was not evil cannot be allowed to stand," he said. "And so we cannot be lenient now. We cannot show pity. We must reassert the seriousness of what occurred in Hamelyn ten years ago. Brightwater's crimes must be treated with grim brutality. As such, I invoke the rule of multiple infractions!"

The Council all looked at Stone with stunned expressions, as the audience broke into uproar.

Patch bent down slightly to Furnel. "What does that mean?" he whispered.

"I think you'd best sit down, lad," said Furnel. "This ain't going to be pleasant."

Patch stayed standing.

"It's your right to insist, Virtus," said Lord Drevis, sounding almost dazed. He turned to the other Council members to discuss the matter, as the din from the audience continued.

At last, Lord Drevis clapped the gavel and the commotion in the chamber settled. "It is with sorrow that we must accept your request, Rundel," he said. "Patch Brightwater, your sentence will still be treated with leniency and reduced by half. However, the basic sentence is now ten years for each time you broke the law and performed the Dance." He looked to Rundel Stone. "In studying the broken Pipe, how many times did you assess?"

"One hundred and two," said Stone.

There was total silence in the chamber now. The faces of the Council paled, as the implications became clear to all.

"We will take it on ourselves to verify the figure, Rundel," said Drevis.

"Naturally," replied the Virtus.

"Patch Brightwater," said Drevis. "The sentence is ten years for each of the one hundred and two occurrences of your crime. You are hereby sentenced to one thousand and twenty years in the dungeons of Tiviscan, reduced to five hundred and ten by the clemency of the Council. Jailer, take him down." He clapped his gavel, looking somewhat ill.

The audience began its din once again. "God have mercy on you," shouted someone, "because Rundel Stone certainly won't!"

Patch fell back onto his stool, unable to take in what had just happened. He looked up to where Erner sat and could see him struggle with his bag as Wren tried to escape. "No!" Patch shouted at Wren. "Please! Don't!"

Someone from the audience laughed: "Beggin' won't help you!"

Patch kept his gaze on the bag. He saw Wren's paws, briefly. She signed something to him, then hid back inside.

Furnel dragged him out of the chamber and led him back down the steps, and through the dungeon gate once more, but instead of heading back to where he'd spent the night, Patch was taken to another spiralling staircase.

Down they went into the gloom below, passing level after level, and Patch thought, *How deep will I be put?*

Furnel took him down a long dank passage, one that

reeked of decay and was lined with cell doors. As they passed each door, shouts started up from behind: "Who d'ya have? Eh? Who've ya brought us?"

Furnel stopped at the last door in the corridor. There was a folded blanket on the floor, and Furnel picked it up and gave it to Patch. The burly jailer was subdued, and could hardly make eye contact. "It's not often I feel sorrow when I bring a prisoner down," he said, shaking his head. "This cell is the best I can do for ye, lad, given your sentence. Deep, sure enough, and at the very edge of the Dark. But it's by the outside wall of the Castle – so you have a window, such as it is." He unlocked the door and swung it open.

Patch stared. The door was several feet thick, as were the walls of his cell. He looked inside and saw that the cell was larger than he'd expected, perhaps five strides across. The "window" was an open hole barely the size of his hand, allowing a narrow band of light in from outside. The depth of the window showed that the outer wall was at least six feet thick, even thicker than the cell door. A bundle of rags was in one dark corner.

The stench in the cell was appalling.

"Your toilet is there," said Furnel, pointing to a hole in the floor. "You get food and water most days. There's your bowl and water jug." He pointed to a clay bowl and jug over by the rags. "Food and water tubes come in those holes by the door, see? Be sure you're ready to catch 'em." Patch noted small holes in the wall, and a mound of decayed food on the floor underneath. No wonder the smell was so bad.

Furnel unlocked the manacles on his and Patch's wrists. Patch rubbed at his chafed skin. "What happened to the last prisoner who was in here?" he asked.

"Oh, that reminds me," said Furnel. He walked across to the corner where the bundle of rags was, and lifted it up in his arms.

It wasn't a bundle of rags. It was a *corpse*.

Furnel carried it to the corridor and set it on the ground. Patch saw the dead man clearly now – ancient, and thin to the point of being just a collection of bones. "Innocent Jack, they called him," said Furnel.

"Why did they call him that?"

"On account of him being *innocent*," said Furnel. "Found guilty of murderin' a man through Piping, then the man showed up alive only last year." He shook his head. "Shame Jack died. His review was only a couple of months away. They'd probably have let him out!"

"How long had he been here?" said Patch, looking at the old face, its skin like parchment. *Must have been a long, long time,* he thought. *Perhaps it's possible to live long enough for the Council to come to their senses and let me go...*

"Jack was convicted when he was twenty," said Furnel. "So, let's see now –" his eyes went to the ceiling as he worked it out – "he'd been here almost fifteen years."

Patch stared at Furnel in shock.

"Time in here takes its toll," said Furnel. "Well, good luck, lad." He swung the huge cell door closed, and Patch heard the man's heavy steps vanish back along the corridor. Then he could *feel* the walls, unbearably heavy, crushing him…

He ran to the tiny window, stretching up on tiptoes to put his mouth to the slight draught that came in. Breathing deeply, he waited for the panic to subside.

He thought back to the message Wren had signed to him in the Council chamber: *Don't give up.*

But how could he not? Right now, there seemed to be only one thing that Patch Brightwater was certain of.

Like Innocent Jack, he would be in this place until he died.

8

The Hamelyn Piper

Patch's panic was just starting to lessen when he heard something that didn't help at all.

"Hey!" said a man's voice.

Patch pulled back from the window. "Who's there?" he said, looking around.

"Down here!" came the voice again, but it seemed to be coming from *everywhere*.

Aren't things bad enough, thought Patch, *without having to share my cell with the ghost of Innocent Jack?* "Who are you?" he said. "Please, just leave me alone!"

"Look, mate," said the voice. "We're going to be spending a *lot* of time together, so let's try and get along, eh? My name's Vague Henry."

"Are you…are you *dead*?"

Vague Henry sighed. "I'm your *neighbour*. Just look at the bottom of the wall. See the hole?"

Patch looked at the wall to his right. There was a dark area, smaller even than the five-inch window. It was level with the floor, and as he moved towards it he realized it actually *was* a hole. "I see it," he said.

"Stick your eye up to it and say hello!"

Patch put his eye to the hole. It was a long, dim channel cut through the thick stone wall, but at the other end – perhaps five feet away – was another eye, looking back at him. "Hello," he said.

"You've only got me as a neighbour, since you're at the end of the row," said Henry. "The holes are part of the plumbing, but it's a handy way to chat without having to shout and annoy everyone. So you're Patch Brightwater, eh?"

"How do you know who I am?"

"Word travels fast down here! Pleasure to meet you, Patch. We've not come up with a nickname for you yet, though. Not like Jack, your cell's previous resident."

"Innocent Jack," said Patch.

"Indeed! Used to be *Murderous* Jack, of course, before the whole innocence thing happened. Your nickname usually has something to do with why you're in the dungeons, see."

"So why do they call you Vague Henry?"

Henry paused. It was a long pause, and a strangely awkward one. "Dunno," he said.

Patch waited, but nothing more was forthcoming. "Uh… okay," said Patch at last, wondering if his question had been answered.

"What'll we call you?" said Henry. "Doomed Boy Patch? Bleak Young Patch? We'll get it. We've got plenty of time."

"Right," said Patch, the words "plenty of time" filling him with horror. He pulled away from the hole and lay on his back, staring up at the rough stone ceiling.

"Some advice for you," said Henry. "First up, when feeding time comes, the guard calls out 'tubes'."

"Furnel mentioned those," said Patch. "Why do they use tubes?"

"So they don't have to open the doors, lad," said Henry. "Be ready to catch it when it comes – especially the water! When it rains, you'll see the rainwater come in through holes like this one and run through grooves in the floor. See 'em? See where they lead?"

Patch looked to the floor and saw them. Grooves a couple of inches across ran towards the hole in the floor that Furnel had pointed out previously – the toilet. "I see them."

"Exactly. We get some of the, er, *waste water* from above us, and we're five levels down. So don't drink the rainwater, however thirsty you get, however clean it looks! And for your sake and ours, make sure your hole doesn't block up!"

"Will do," said Patch. "Henry, is it true that you can hear the Hamelyn Piper scream at night?"

"Oh, you'll hear him all right," said Henry.

"Doesn't it frighten you? Being so close to him?"

"The Hamelyn Piper? He's a wreck. His brain is nothing but mush by now. But no, I'm not frightened, not by him or any other Piper here. It doesn't matter how well a prisoner can lip-play to whistle up a Song. Hell, even if someone managed to get hold of a Pipe, it'd do 'em no good. They have precautions."

"Precautions?"

"Haven't you seen the depth of the doors and windows? If you look close, you'll see that every way out of your cell is lined with little furrows."

Patch looked into the hole that led to Henry's cell. Dark as it was, he could make out a slight twist here and there on the stone, a pattern carved into the rock. "Sound baffles?" said Patch. He'd heard of them in training – they confused any Songs you played, and took the edge off the magic enough to render them useless. They only worked for conduits that were long and thin, so they were no good as a general defence; they were more a curiosity of Piping theory. In here, though: perfect.

"Precisely," said Henry. "The workers down here are almost immune to Piping, lip-Piping at any rate, but the baffles make sure. It's why the walls and the doors are so thick, and why they feed us with the tubes. Inside your cell, you can't affect anyone else. So don't let the Hamelyn Piper frighten you. He's harmless now. Especially with what they did to him!"

"The Iron Mask," said Patch, nodding to himself.

When Patch was younger, his grandmother had often told him the story of the Hamelyn Piper, but only when he pestered her. She preferred to tell him about the adventures of the Eight as they hunted him down and caught him, rather than the horrors that had led to their quest in the first place.

She would say, "I don't want to frighten you, Patch."

And he would insist, "It doesn't scare me, Nan."

Eventually she would give in, and Patch would thrill at the tale. But he had lied to her about it not scaring him. He knew that once she was done – the instant his candle was blown out and the door shut – his courage would fail and he would lie in his bed and tremble, wondering when the long bony fingers of the Hamelyn Piper would wrap around the door handle.

She always began with the same words, words which, even when he thought of them now, brought back a strange combination of adventure and terror: *Have you heard of the town of Hamelyn, Patch? It was once overrun with rats…*

Have you heard of the town of Hamelyn, Patch? It was once overrun with rats.

Of course, *every* town has its rats, but one summer there were so many that the Mayor of Hamelyn brought in rat-catchers from all around, and they did their work. In the past, this had always done the trick.

But not this year.

At first the rat-catchers were happy. The more rats they caught, it seemed, the more rats they *saw*, and as they were paid for each rat they killed, there was real money to be made!

Then they began to grow nervous.

"It's not natural," they said to one another. "We catch a thousand a day, yet their numbers just keep rising!" They began to think the town was cursed, and one by one the rat-catchers left.

The townsfolk were angry with the Mayor for letting them leave, but what else could the Mayor do?

A Piper!

Much more expensive than rat-catchers, yes, but a Piper was the answer.

One thousand gold coins were raised and locked in the Town Treasury. By early evening the Mayor was sitting in the Town Hall surrounded by the most powerful people in Hamelyn, writing a letter to summon a Piper: *one thousand gold coins*, it said, *to the Piper who rids us of our rats.*

As he was placing his seal on the envelope, the door to

the hall opened wide. There stood a Piper so tall and so thin that he seemed to be built entirely of edges.

"I heard you had a problem," said the Piper.

"You did?" said the Mayor, wary. He looked at the letter in his hand. "And *how* did you hear?"

"From the twenty rat-catchers I met along the road," said the Piper. "But now I've arrived, and the rats will soon be gone! For five hundred gold coins."

The Mayor nodded, and tried to stop himself from grinning. *Five hundred!* he thought. *Only five hundred!*

He carefully placed the letter in his pocket before standing, and walked over to the Piper. "A hefty price," he said, looking up at the considerably taller man.

"Well, if you'd rather find another Piper—" began the stranger.

"We accept!" said the Mayor. He offered out his hand and the Piper shook it.

The Piper smiled. Those in the hall smiled back, even though they all thought that the Piper's teeth seemed a little sharp, and the smile a little cruel.

The Piper cleared his throat. From his coat he produced a long thin Pipe, and began to play. As he played, he took slow strides out of the hall, then along the street outside.

The first rats appeared from the shadows, watching him, but soon they followed in the same slow rhythm: step – step – step!

More and more rats poured out from every house, every street, and by the time the Piper reached the edge of the town there was a vast shifting carpet of rats coming after him. The Mayor and all the people watched this huge procession leave, cheering that the town would soon be free of its rat plague.

The River Weser lay ahead, beyond the walls of the town. At the river's edge, the Piper stopped walking. He raised his arms out to his sides, and the rats reached him.

The townsfolk shuddered, seeing from a distance how the wide column of rats engulfed the Piper, crawling up his coat then down the other side into the water to drown. It was almost an hour before they had all completed their final journey and the Piper was revealed again.

He lowered his arms and returned to the town. The townsfolk cheered and applauded. The Piper took an extravagant bow and smiled. The Mayor stood outside the Town Hall, waving to the crowd to make sure he would always be remembered for such a great success.

As the Piper reached him, the crowd fell silent.

"My job is done," said the Piper. "I will take my payment."

The Mayor summoned the Town Treasurer, who brought a bag that was so heavy it needed its own cart. "You have counted the coins?" asked the Mayor, and the Treasurer said he had. "Here is your payment," said the Mayor to the Piper. "Five hundred gold coins!"

The Piper opened the fastening at the neck of the bag and thrust in his hand. When he pulled it out, it was only *sand* that ran through his fingers.

A shocked gasp spread through the crowd. The Mayor stared at the Treasurer. The Treasurer stared at the bag; he darted forward and tipped the contents of the bag out. Nothing but sand!

"You try to trick me?" said the Piper.

"No!" said the Mayor, terrified by the malice he saw in the Piper's gaze. The Mayor looked to the Captain of the Town Guard, and pointed to the Treasurer. "Arrest this man!" he cried. "And bring five hundred gold coins from the treasury vault!"

The Treasurer protested as he was taken away. Soon, the Captain returned and shook his head. "There is only sand in the vault, sir," he said.

The Mayor was speechless. He looked at the Piper, who scowled.

"I see you have a thief in your midst," said the Piper. "I will return tomorrow to collect my payment."

The Piper turned and walked out of the town.

The Mayor looked to the Captain. "Find the money!" he said. Then he turned to his most trusted advisor. "You are now the Treasurer! Raise more, in case we can't find the missing coins!"

The next morning, the River Weser burst its banks downstream as the rat corpses blocked the flow of water. Fields of wheat and barley were destroyed. The townsfolk set about clearing the corpses and built pyres to burn them on. By afternoon the air was thick with the smoke of the pyres, and the stench of burning rat flesh.

The stolen money was not found; the previous Treasurer had refused to admit taking it, whatever unpleasantness was done to him. In the end, the Captain of the Town Guard stopped torturing him and concluded that he was innocent.

The new Treasurer, wary of the fate of his predecessor, managed to raise enough for the Piper's pay, but it was difficult. When the money was gathered, it was all witnessed by trusted men of the Town Guard, who then stood watch over the vault.

As dusk approached the Piper was seen coming along the road to town. This time the crowd was silent as he came. There was a fearfulness that was shared by all.

The Piper was brought to the treasury, where the vault stood closed. It had not been left unattended, not even for a moment.

"Greetings, Piper," said the Mayor.

"Greetings, Mayor," said the Piper. His smile seemed dangerous. "My payment?"

The Mayor nodded to the new Treasurer, who opened

the door of the vault and handed the Piper the first of the bags that were inside. The Piper untied it and tipped it out.

Sand.

"No!" cried the Mayor.

"No!" cried the Treasurer.

The Piper shook his head, tut-tutting. "Such a *terrible* crime problem you have here," he said. "What *are* we to do?"

The Piper's eyes were aimed directly at the Mayor, that sinister gaze drilling deep. The Mayor could see a darkness there, unlimited and uncaring. He cleared his throat. "We have no more money," he said. Suspicion and fear almost overwhelmed him. He thought of how the rat-catchers had been so wary of the rats, some of them believing the infestation was unnatural; he thought of the money disappearing repeatedly, with no apparent culprit.

He could see suspicion in the eyes of others around him, too, all looking at the Piper. But what could they do? People looked from the Piper to the Mayor, waiting for someone to speak.

"Don't worry," the Piper said at last, but in a voice that was far from soothing. "Tonight I will take my pay. I will take things that are often unwelcome. Things that *everyone,* at some point, wishes were gone. Could I be fairer than that?"

The Piper turned and left. Silence filled the entire town until he was far in the distance.

The Mayor looked to the Captain. "Ready your men," he said. "Guard the gates. Let *nobody* in tonight."

Night came.

In the distance, the pyres still burned.

The guards were ready. The townsfolk locked their doors.

It was midnight when the sound of Piping began. The music grew louder. The people of Hamelyn could hear their own children stir from their beds, laughing. The children came out, unlocked the doors and danced into the streets. The adults all found that they could not move, could not even *speak*.

They could only watch.

And the Piper, his eyes burning like the distant pyres, danced by each house and smiled a wide, sharp smile, and the children of the town followed him towards the town gates, dancing with unbounded joy. The gates were flung open by an invisible force, and the Piper led the children out of Hamelyn.

It was not until morning that the townsfolk could move again. They fell to the ground, wailing in horror at what had happened. Then they ran, seeking their children, following the road, seeing where the grass at the edges had been trampled by the dancing.

On and on they went, until the trampled grass veered onto a smaller pathway that went up Koppen Hill. Near the top of the hill, the trail ended by a sheer face of rock.

The children were not there.

The townsfolk heard the sound of sobbing, and found one small boy, who had been lame since birth.

"I couldn't keep up," he cried, again and again, despairing.

"Where are the others?" asked the adults. "Where are all the other children?"

"He promised us a Land of Play, with all the toys and sweets we could want," said the boy. "When the Piper reached this point, a doorway opened in the rock and they all danced inside. But I couldn't keep up! I was too late!" He burst into angry, desolate tears. "The door shut before I got to it!"

They found no sign of a doorway. In all, one hundred and thirty children had been taken by the Hamelyn Piper.

It took over a year to catch him.

The Pipers' Council assembled a group to track down this evil creature who had brought shame on their kind – a group who became known as the Eight, their exploits now legendary.

When the Piper was finally caught, he refused to reveal what had become of the children. Many wanted to see him die for what he had done, convinced he would never reveal the children's fate, but the Council kept him alive, and gave him the cruellest punishment they could devise. The Iron Mask: fastened around the head of the Hamelyn Piper, it prevented him ever using his abilities again, as no magic could escape it, Song or otherwise.

But it had one more function. Once put in place, whatever the Hamelyn Piper said next would be the only thing he could ever say again, unless he was to tell where the children had gone. When the Mask was fitted to the Piper's head, the Council addressed him.

"Piper of Hamelyn!" they said. "Do you still refuse to tell what you did with the children?"

"Aye!" the Hamelyn Piper cried, his eyes at first defiant; but then his eyes became defeated, and lost, as he finally knew that his reign of evil was ended, and the world would be forever safe from him.

They locked him in the deepest darkest place within the dungeons of Tiviscan, and "Aye!" is still the only word he speaks.

For he has never revealed where the children went.

"Sleep well," said a voice, bringing Patch crashing back to the present. He realized the voice belonged to Vague Henry, but those were the words his grandmother had always said to him as she left him in his bed.

He was a long way from there now, in this cold cell in the dungeons of Tiviscan. The dungeons that would be his home for the rest of his days.

"Goodnight, Henry," said Patch. He stood and looked around to see where best to sleep. The corner where the corpse of Innocent Jack had lain was, for the moment, ruled out, so Patch chose the opposite corner.

He lay down and closed his eyes, trying his best to cover himself in the meagre blanket he'd been given. Rather than consider what the future held, he thought back to the past again.

There was so much more to the Hamelyn Piper's story, of course; the quest of the Eight to catch him was, in itself, an epic tale of courage. But of all the things he'd learned during his training, the most shocking was the Hamelyn Piper's *next* crime, and how close it had come to triggering another war between dragons and humans.

It was shocking, because Patch's grandmother had never told him about it.

One week to the day after the children of Hamelyn were taken, there had been another atrocity: in the Dragon Territories, young dragons had vanished from an isolated school. One hundred dragon children, gone. The ten adult dragons who were their teachers and guardians were poisoned, and only one of them survived, managing to reach another settlement and reveal what had happened.

"A human came," the dragon had said. "A *Piper,* riding a griffin! He played his Pipe and the children followed him, flying over the horizon, laughing as they went."

The Hamelyn Piper had struck again.

When the evil Piper was finally captured, the dragons wanted him executed for his crimes. The refusal of the Pipers' Council was absolute, however, and tensions between Pipers and dragons, high at the best of times, increased. The dragons threatened war against the Pipers. One by one the many nations of the world made their choice: they would stand with the Pipers, whatever happened.

The last war between humans and dragons had been hundreds of years ago, and the loss of life had been horrifying; but suddenly, a new war seemed inevitable.

Yet war was averted. Just.

Among humans, meanwhile, the notion that the Hamelyn Piper had taken the dragon children was treated with suspicion, as if it was only a rumour invented by the dragons to stir up resentment. It was rarely spoken of, and this was probably why Patch's grandmother hadn't included it in her tales.

Humans had always feared dragons, and *fear* could easily turn to *hate*.

For many people, the hatred they had for dragons was so great that they could never have sympathy with them, whatever the situation. Even if their children had vanished.

For some, having fewer dragons would always be a good thing.

It took a while before he stopped feeling so cold, but Patch finally started to doze on the floor of his cell. Then, as sleep was beckoning, he heard it: from elsewhere in the dungeons came a terrible sound.

"There he goes," sighed Henry. "He'll keep at it until he's hoarse."

"Aye!" screamed the Hamelyn Piper, again and again, deep in the Dark. "*Aye!*"

Patch trembled, hands over his ears, but nothing he did blocked out the noise. It was two hours before the screaming stopped.

9

No Place Like Home

"*Tubes!*"

Patch's eyes snapped open. All he could remember was the nightmare he'd been having, the Hamelyn Piper's long fingers creeping along the floor towards him.

"*Tubes*, Patch!" yelled Henry. "Come on, get up! Tubes!"

Everything came back to him. He hurried to fetch his bowl and jug, turning to the door just as the metal tubes came in through the holes two-thirds of the way up the wall. Sludge oozed from the wider of the tubes, and water came from the other. He reached them in time to collect half of his meal, the rest having joined the rancid pile on the floor.

He looked cautiously at the contents of his bowl, pushing the food around with his fingers. It was a thick gloopy mush, with gristly bits dotted through it. Wary, he raised his fingers to his mouth and tasted it, ready for the most horrible flavours he'd ever encountered, but it was mercifully bland. Even after eating all of it, he was still hungry. He looked at the food that had fallen before he'd reached it, glistening on top of the rank heap that had been there yesterday – the remains of all the food Innocent Jack had presumably failed to collect before they'd noticed he was dead.

Surely he could salvage the rest of today's meal? Just scrape it off carefully, not taking any of the mouldy food below, or the *maggots* that were squirming in amongst it?

"No," he said to himself. But how long might it be before he took that next step, and ate the maggots and mouldy remnants without a thought?

What would he become in a year? In ten years?

He set down his empty bowl and walked to the tiny window, his only view of the outside world. The sun was bright, and on his tiptoes he could see the forest on the distant hills. He would never walk in a forest again, he realized; never feel the sun on his face.

He fell to his knees, sobbing hard, and there he stayed, lost to his misery. When he heard footsteps approaching up the corridor he was unaware of how much time had passed.

The footsteps halted and the lock in Patch's door clunked. He got up and went to the middle of his cell as the door swung open, and the first thing he saw was the purple and black of a Custodian Piper's robes.

It was Erner, carrying his satchel and a parcel. Behind him stood a guard even larger than Furnel.

Erner stepped into the cell and the door slammed closed, the noise reverberating for a few moments. He looked around and spotted the hole in the wall that led to Henry's cell. He walked over and fetched Patch's blanket, then went to the hole and blocked it up.

"Do you mind!" Vague Henry shouted, his voice muffled. "I'm trying to hear what's going on in there!"

Erner walked back to Patch. "Better if we can talk in private," he said. "I didn't come alone."

Wren's head peeked out of Erner's satchel. Patch held out his arm and she hopped onto it, then along to his neck, which she hugged.

Patch grinned, tears falling. "It's so good to see you," he said. "*Both* of you."

Erner nodded, smiling. "I've been enjoying Wren's company very much," he said. "Her Merisax is very good, considering how short a time she's been learning."

"She's a bright girl," said Patch. He glanced at Wren, who gave a proud nod.

"She is," said Erner. "Virtus Stone and I have been assigned duties elsewhere, and I fear Wren would be in too much danger if she came with me. I suggested leaving her with a trusted colleague, but she insists that I tell nobody else about her yet. Besides, she's desperate to keep you company. She should be safe enough with you, now that you're in your cell. I'll be back in two or three weeks."

"What about curing her of her curse?" said Patch.

"By the time I'm back, I hope to have a reply to *this*!" he said, and with a flourish he produced an envelope, complete with an official Custodian Elite wax seal.

Patch read the address. "Brother Tobias, Marwheel Abbey," he said.

"Indeed," said Erner. "I asked Virtus Stone if he knew of anyone capable of curing a Sorcerer's curse, given how... well, you know how it is with Pipers and Sorcerers."

Patch knew very well how it was. While the obvious course of action might be to ask a *Sorcerer* for help, the notion of a Piper doing so was almost unthinkable.

Sorcerers were few and far between, secretive and wealthy. They used a different, older form of magic that they thought was far superior to Songs, and so they looked down their noses at Pipers. In return, Pipers didn't have much liking for Sorcerers; they also didn't *trust* them. Sorcerers often had questionable morals and little regard for laws, although if it ever came to a clash between them and the Custodian Elite, the Custodians had the advantage of greater numbers – Sorcerers always worked alone.

"Didn't Virtus Stone want to know why you were

asking about curses?" said Patch.

"An apprentice is expected to extend their knowledge as much as possible," said Erner. "I ask him so many strange questions, he didn't bat an eyelid at that one. He just told me to contact Brother Tobias at Marwheel Abbey. I've kept my letter vague, and explained that a victim of a shape-changing curse needs help."

"Well, let's hope that Brother Tobias has the answers," said Patch, looking at Wren.

He'd better, she signed. *I want to be human again soon!*

Patch smiled at her, overwhelmed with gratitude that she would choose to stay with him. "In the meantime we can work on improving your Merisax," he said.

There was a heavy knock on the cell door. "Time!" came a shout.

Erner sighed. "Visiting prisoners is frowned on," he said. "And even when it can be arranged, they keep it brief. So, here –" he handed Patch the string-tied parcel he was carrying – "the wrapping is a new blanket – a warmer one – and there are a few other items inside. They're strict about what can be given to prisoners, so if I were you…" He leaned closer and whispered. "Unwrap it in secret!"

The door started to open again. Wren gave a tiny squeak of panic and ran down Patch's back, her claws digging through his thin clothing and into his skin. She clung there, out of sight, and Patch grimaced.

"Come on," said the guard to Erner.

Erner looked at Patch. "I'm sorry," he said. "I still can't believe what happened at the trial. I'll do what I can for you, but…" He shook his head.

"Thank you, Erner," said Patch.

Erner nodded, silent, then stepped out of the cell. The door closed with another thunderous slam.

Patch sighed with relief as Wren's claws stopped digging into his skin and she climbed back up to his shoulder. "Right then," he said quietly, raising the parcel. "Let's see what we've got here!"

Quietly in the corner of the cell, with Wren on the floor beside him, Patch untied the string. Inside was one of the tiny oilskin tents they'd used on the journey to the Castle, which folded up smaller than a fist. Patch found himself staring at it. No more cold nights, he realised, as long he was careful not to let the guards see it. There was also an apple, a curious little wooden box, and a small bag of wheat grains that had Wren's name written on it, in a scratchy style that Patch guessed was Wren's own writing. "Yours?" he said. She nodded, with narrowed eyes.

Touch it and you're dead! she signed, then pointed at the apple. *That's for you.*

Patch smiled and set the bag down beside her. He looked at the strange wooden box. "What's this?" he asked.

Fox and Owls, signed Wren. *Ever play it?*

"My grandfather tried to teach me once," he said. "I couldn't get the hang of it." He fiddled with the box until the top popped open. The inside of the box lid was a game board, and a dozen little pegs were the playing pieces.

Well, now I can teach you, signed Wren.

"We have plenty of time," said Patch, and the phrase didn't fill him with horror the way it had when Henry had said it. As he ate his apple and tried to remember how to set the board up for a game, Wren wandered off into the cell. After a while, Patch heard a crunching sound. Wren was on the top of the rancid food pile, merrily picking up the maggots and eating them.

Wide-eyed, he watched her as she polished off another of the wriggling grubs.

Wren noticed him watching. *You don't mind if I...* she started.

"No," said Patch. "You go ahead. Is it just the maggots, or are you going to eat the rest of the pile?"

Wren screwed up her little face in revulsion. *What, this mouldy old stuff?* she signed. *Don't be disgusting!*

They settled down for some Merisax practice, and after taking Wren through the signing of numbers Patch could tell she was distracted by something. "Are you okay?" he asked. "Do you want a break?"

Wren shook her head. *I've just been dying to ask a question*, she signed. *But it might be upsetting for you.*

"Go on," said Patch. "Ask away."

Why did you leave Tiviscan and abandon your training? she signed. *At the trial, they mentioned bringing shame on yourself.*

Patch took a deep sigh. "Ah," he said. "That."

You don't have to tell me if you don't want to, signed Wren.

"You may as well know," he said. "It happened at the Trials Ceremony, just before summer."

The trials?

"Each year, all the trainee Pipers engage in trials to show how well their studies have gone, and demonstrate their abilities. When a trainee reaches thirteen, though, it's a special time. That's when they can be chosen to begin training for the Elite."

Like with Erner? she asked.

"Yes. He was chosen, and did two years of training before passing his final trials to become an Apprentice. But it's not just the Custodian Elite. There are other specialities, you see. Those who excel in Arable Piping, for example, might be accepted into the Arable Elite. If a nation faces famine, say, or disease wipes out entire crops, the Arable Elite will help prevent disaster. I was like Erner. I wanted to join the Custodian Elite. They enforce the laws of Piping, but that's only part of what they do. They also act like the

Pipers of ancient days. They help those most in need, and bring justice to places that justice has forgotten. For that, a trainee has to be among the very best."

And you are, aren't you?

He shrugged. "I hoped so. Even when I first found I had a talent for Piping, I knew what I wanted to do. Pipers are mainly used by the wealthy. The bigger towns and cities can maybe afford them regularly, and the richest farmers, but for most people they're too expensive. The Custodians were always different. They're not paid by anyone. I mean, every Piper is expected to do their duty, do what's right, but Custodians apply basic laws of justice, even in countries that don't *have* those laws. In every civilized nation, the Custodian Elite have the power to make a difference, and defend the defenceless! If only there were more Custodians, the world would be a much better place to live."

And that was your dream? signed Wren. *To become one? Make the world a better place?*

Patch nodded. "When I first came to Tiviscan, the Tutors were very excited. I showed great skill in the Piping of *people.* Unprecedented, I was told! It's why I'm so good at the Dance. I could even affect *myself* with what I played, which I'd thought was normal, but for most Pipers it's nearly impossible. It's like trying to tickle yourself – it just doesn't work. They told me I could be anything I wanted to be, so I studied as hard as I could, and I tried my very best, because I knew that the *only* thing I wanted was to join the Custodian Elite. And then last summer, the Trials Ceremony came. With all the trials over, the ceremony began, and I knew I'd done really well. Every trainee, every Tutor, and the Pipers' Council themselves, were all gathered together, and at the very end of the ceremony the list of trainees selected for Elite training was read out."

Oh no! signed Wren, looking anxious. *They didn't call out your name!*

Patch shook his head in sorrow. "They called my name, all right. Just not as a Custodian. I couldn't believe what I'd heard, and I stood up, and I shouted. 'The Custodian Elite!' I cried. 'It has to be the *Custodian* Elite. No other will do!' But my trial results weren't quite good enough, and that was that. It felt like my world had ended." He paused, then looked at Wren. "Have you ever wanted something so badly that anything less just wouldn't do?"

Absolutely, she signed. *What happened next?*

"Being chosen for *any* Elite training is such an honour, you don't turn it down. Nobody had *ever* turned it down."

You turned it down? signed Wren, and Patch nodded. *That's all you did? It doesn't seem so bad.*

Patch winced. "I turned it down very, *very* rudely. To the faces of the Pipers' Council; in front of everyone. My disappointment had turned to anger, you see, anger that just bubbled out of me before I even knew what was happening.

I called Lord Pewter a stupid old drunkard who stank of rotting cheese; I yelled at Lady Winkless that she couldn't Pipe her way out of a sack. And I didn't stop there."

Oh dear, signed Wren. *That doesn't sound good.*

"The Council watched me in disbelief, with their mouths hanging open, as I insulted them one by one. When I finished there wasn't a sound. Everyone – the Council, the Tutors, the students, *everyone* – was staring at me. I couldn't believe what had happened! I did the only thing I could think of. I turned and ran. Away from Tiviscan. Away from Piping."

Wren put a paw on his hand. *You must have wanted to be a Custodian very much.*

"It was everything to me. A few days later I thought of returning, but I couldn't face it."

Wren nodded. *What branch of the Elite had they offered you?* she signed. *Arable?*

Patch shook his head. "It doesn't matter now." He felt a little distant for a moment, before snapping out of it. "My turn to have a question answered," he said. "How did you manage to get a Sorcerer angry enough to curse you like this?"

I was kidnapped, she signed. *The Sorcerer wanted a maidservant. This was last summer, too. As your life was changing, so was mine. When I almost managed to escape, he caught me, and that was that.*

"He turned you into a rat."

Exactly. I fled into the forest, terrified of the dangers around me from hawks and the like. I was even fearful of other rats at first, but they proved to be generous creatures. Stupid, but generous. I found a little rat community near some local wheat fields and stayed with them for a few weeks. Ten rats, terrified of the farmer's dog, half starved. They knew there was something unusual about me, and started to follow my lead. The dog was easy to outsmart, and soon everyone was well fed, but it came time for all of us to move on. As we travelled, we'd come across other rats, and they'd tag along. We snuck onto a barge transporting barley, and spent a week on it. I'd hoped we would make it to a warmer place before winter, but we were discovered and had to flee the barge. Turned out we were in the middle of the Breydram Valley, and winter came faster than I'd expected.

"Patterfall was your only refuge," said Patch.

Yes. We tried to push further downstream, but gave up in the end and stayed put. At first I thought we had plenty of food to last us through winter, but a population explosion put paid to that idea. Rats will be rats, and they just wouldn't be told.

"The villagers were terrified that you'd eat them. So was I, come to that."

They're much more mild-mannered than people believe. The villagers needn't have feared, but the rats didn't get the chance to prove it… She looked at Patch. *Would they have suffered?*

He shook his head. "I know the Dispersal is horrifying, but as far as I know the effect is instant. They wouldn't have suffered at all."

She nodded, tears in her eyes. *I didn't make a very good leader in the end,* she signed.

He picked her up and put her on his shoulder. She snuggled down, and they sat together in silence for a time, until they both felt ready to get back to the Merisax number system.

In the afternoon, shortly after the food and water arrived, Vague Henry shouted loud enough and long enough that he couldn't be ignored, and Patch removed the old blanket from the hole between their cells.

"Thank the stars!" said Henry. "Set something in front of it if you want to stop me peeking in, but please don't block it up like that. God help me if it rained!"

"Sorry," said Patch. "I forgot it was there." He gathered up the blanket and left it a little way in front of the hole, perched over the narrow channel in the floor so Henry couldn't see into Patch's cell. "That okay?" he said.

"That's fine," said Henry. "No harm done." He didn't waste time moving on to a subject he was clearly more interested in: "So, um, your visitor? A Custodian Piper, then? I saw that much."

"A friend," said Patch. "He came to commiserate with me on how things turned out."

"Oh," said Henry. "I just wondered if you were holding up okay? I mean, I thought he'd given you more bad news or something, since—"

"Since?"

"Since you've started to talk to yourself. And don't say you haven't!"

It occurred to Patch that if Henry thought he was crazy, he could chat with Wren as much as he liked without worrying about how loud he was talking. "Let me deal with things my own way, Henry," he said, smiling. "I'll be fine."

After a little more Merisax practice, Wren was eager to get started on Fox and Owls. She took the game board and rearranged Patch's failed attempt at placing the pieces.

Which do you want to be? she signed. *Fox or Owls?*

Patch shrugged. "Remind me of the difference."

Okay, signed Wren. *I'll start with the basics. There's only one fox piece, and two owls. Say you be the fox, then you move, and I move one of the rabbits, then I move both owls, then you move a rabbit and it starts again. Easy!*

Patch smiled, bewildered by the game but curiously happy. The cell around him had suddenly stopped being so oppressive.

He looked at the pile of rotting food and vowed to get it cleaned up soon. He faintly wished for a chair, or a mirror.

It feels more like a home than a prison, he thought. *Just because I'm here with a friend.*

10

Unwelcome Arrivals

Overnight it started to rain heavily. When they woke, the importance of Henry's warning about not blocking the hole in the wall became clear – the channel in the floor had turned into a murky stream, flowing towards the toilet hole.

Patch saw the opportunity to clean things up. He gritted his teeth and scooped up handfuls of the rotting pile of food, carrying it to the toilet hole and letting the filthy rainwater wash it away. Once finished, Patch used a little of the water from mealtime to clean his hands.

Outside, the weather kept getting worse, and with it the murky stream threatened to overflow its channel, but as the hours passed the flowing water became a little less filthy, and the stench in his cell began to fade.

Henry, meanwhile, kept trying to get Patch to converse. He seemed sure that Patch was falling apart, talking to himself and – God help him! – actually *laughing* occasionally.

"I'll be okay," Patch told him.

"I'm just worried," said Henry. "I asked some of the others if they could help, and all I managed to do was land you with your nickname."

"Which is?"

"The Mad Piper, I'm afraid."

Patch laughed out loud, which presumably didn't settle Henry's nerves one bit.

The heavy rain continued unbroken for the next two days.

Patch, meanwhile, was improving at Fox and Owls. At the start, Wren had always won within a dozen moves, but now it was taking perhaps twice as long for her to be victorious. In one game, his owls had taken *four* rabbits, and he'd clapped with excitement.

Then, after a particularly vicious thunderstorm that continued until dawn, the rain faded at last. The dungeon seemed oddly quiet with the rain gone. The drainage channel in the cell had little more than a trickle running through it.

When chatter started to grow from the prisoners along the corridor, it was hard to miss in the relative silence. With

Wren on his shoulder, Patch went over to the hole in the wall. "Henry?" he said. "What's the fuss about?"

"All this rain has caused serious flooding lower in the dungeons," said Henry. "They're having to move some prisoners from the deepest levels until it's sorted out."

There were footsteps in the corridor. For a moment Patch wondered if it was Erner again, but this time the sounds stopped short of Patch's door.

It was Henry's turn for a visitor. "Henry Trew!" called a voice.

"Yes?" said Henry.

"Ready your things, you're to be moved up a level." Other prisoners called out to ask if they would be moved too. "Shut up!" yelled the guard. "None of you lot are going anywhere."

The whole corridor complained.

"We'll be bringing a prisoner up shortly from a flooded cell," said the guard. "Keep the noise down or you'll not get a meal today! Now, hurry up, Trew!"

"I'll just fetch my things," said Henry. He came back over to the hole. "Patch! Did you hear? I'm getting an upgrade! Moving up a floor, until it's sorted out. Maybe they'll let me stay up there!"

"I'll miss you, Henry," said Patch. "Good luck upstairs!"

"God bless you, Patch. And I'm sure whoever they put here in my place will, um—" Henry paused, and Patch knew why – *any* prisoner from the deeper levels would likely be unpleasant company.

"It'll be fine, Henry," Patch said. He looked at Wren, who seemed fretful. "Don't worry," he told her. "I mean, how bad could it be?"

It wasn't long before they found out.

An hour later Patch heard the sound of rattling chains in the corridor, soon followed by the shouts of the other inmates: "Who's your prisoner, eh? We don't want no scum here!"

The clanking stopped at Vague Henry's cell. Patch and Wren heard the door open, and they both went to the hole and looked through. A narrow shaft of light from the window fell on the prisoner, who was shuffling into the centre of the cell.

You want me to go in there and take a look? signed Wren.

"No!" whispered Patch. "Stay here, where it's safe."

The prisoner stood in the light, but all Patch had sight of was the legs, chained together, thick manacles at the feet. The prisoner was facing the window, and Patch presumed the light was so unfamiliar that they were mesmerized. They might not have seen any sunlight in years.

The cell door slammed shut, catching Patch by surprise. He'd expected the guard to remove the chains before leaving, but apparently not. The prisoner's arms came into view, wrists also manacled with a long chain between them. That was when the sobbing began, deep and agonizing, as the prisoner fell to their knees and out of the shaft of light.

After a while, the prisoner's hands came back into the light, twisting around, almost playing with it. *Yes*, thought Patch, *this is someone who hasn't seen daylight in a while.*

Wren sneezed. Suddenly the shape in the gloom snapped up into a sitting position, chains clanking.

Patch and Wren pulled back from the hole.

Sorry! signed Wren.

Let's wait a bit before we have another look, Patch signed back.

The chains in the other cell rattled as the prisoner moved around within. Eventually the rattling stopped, and after a few minutes of silence Wren and Patch glanced at each other and nodded.

They looked through the hole.

An eye was looking back at them, full of desperation.

And there was something around the eye, Patch saw. Some kind of metal.

Iron.

Patch pulled back, and so did Wren.

"Oh," said Patch. "Oh no."

"Aye?" came a quiet voice through the hole. It sounded like pleading. "Aye?" More sobs followed, and then the prisoner spoke again, louder and louder, becoming more and more angry, the same word every time. "Aye! *Aye!*"

The other inmates knew immediately what this meant.

"Guard!" came the shouts. "Take him away! You can't do this! Anyone but him! *Anyone but him!*"

"*Aye!*"

"Guard! You can't leave him here!"

"*AYE!*"

"*Show us some mercy!*"

Patch grabbed the old blanket and stuffed it into the hole, pulling his hand out quickly – fighting the childish terror that the fingers of the Hamelyn Piper would close around his wrist. He lifted Wren from the floor and ran to the little tent at the far side of the cell. They stayed there all night, awake and shivering with fear as the Hamelyn Piper screamed.

Soon after dawn, Patch took the sleeping Wren from his lap and set her on the soft blanket Erner had brought. He went to the hole and pulled out the old blanket, then looked inside the other cell.

The Hamelyn Piper was asleep near the hole, and Patch could see the Iron Mask clearly. It seemed to be made from many smaller sections, forming a mesh that wrapped around the back of his head and obscured most of his face, save for his eyes and mouth. It looked grubby and tarnished, unsurprising after almost a decade of imprisonment. The Hamelyn Piper's beard – if that was a word that could be used for such a jumble of hair – had grown through the mask, and seemed to have been haphazardly cut quite recently. The guards had probably taken advantage of the move to do this most basic of maintenance.

As the other prisoners awoke, the complaints about the new arrival started up again, growing in volume all morning. The response from the guards came later – when the tubes arrived, it was only water that came, and no food. That night the Hamelyn Piper screamed again, and the prisoners complained again, and the only difference was the hunger that gnawed at Patch. Wren nibbled at her grain, offering Patch some, but he refused to take it from her.

"They'll feed us tomorrow," he said. "They'll have to."

But the next day, the food was still withheld. Complaints about hunger were now almost as loud as the complaints about the Hamelyn Piper.

The day after, the prisoners had learned their lesson. Any grumblings were quickly silenced by a scolding from the others, and the food came at last.

Once Patch's bowl and jug were full, Wren asked to sit in the tiny window as she sometimes did. Patch was quietly jealous, as Wren could scurry to the far end of the six-foot-long hole and see much more than Patch, who was limited to a tiny piece of sky and distant hill.

As he finished his food he heard Wren squeak urgently. He came to the window.

You need to see this, she signed, looking worried. She hopped onto his shoulder and he went up on his toes, straining to look out of the window. It took a moment for his eyes to adjust to the bright sky, but eventually he saw dark spots against the blue: birds flying.

"Starlings?" he said. Wren shook her head, agitated. He looked out again at the dark spots in the sky. It had to be starlings, he thought, with so many of them – a vast flock, coming over the distant hill.

Wait. The *distant* hill?

The trees on that hill were so far away they seemed tiny, yet he could see the individual birds, see them *flap*... How was that possible? He froze, staring at the dark cloud. He looked at Wren, and she nodded.

You understand now? she signed.

"Yes," said Patch, watching the dark cloud come ever closer. It wasn't a flock of birds.

It was *dragons*.

Thousands of them.

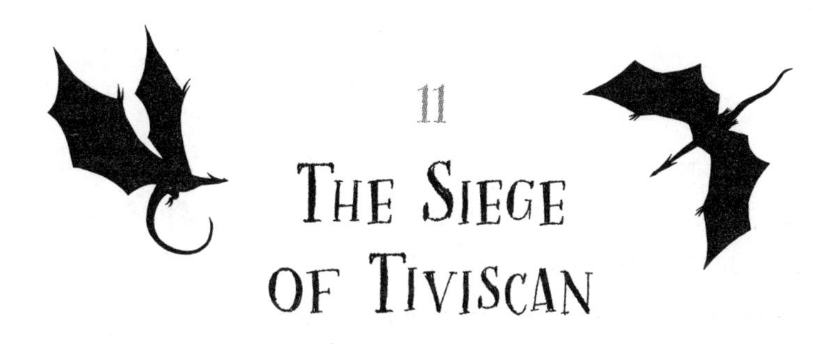

11
The Siege of Tiviscan

Warning bells rang out on the Castle battlements, something Patch had heard in the occasional drills during his training.

"It's been centuries since anyone dared attack Tiviscan," he told Wren. "They'll be readying the Castle defences now, with the garrisoned Pipers preparing the Battle Horns." Those huge horns were mounted permanently on the roof of the Keep, able to create barriers of turbulent air strong enough to protect against flaming catapult attacks, say – or to knock dragons out of the sky. He shook his head, stunned. "*Why*, though? Nobody wants war. What could they hope to achieve? Sending such a huge army?"

The dragons were obscuring more and more of the sky as they came ever nearer, the flock filling their little window now.

No, thought Patch. It wasn't a *flock*. That wasn't the right word.

The right word depended on the creatures in question: a *flock* of birds, a *swarm* of bees, or a *pack* of dogs. There was a word especially for dragons, too, and until now Patch hadn't understood why that word had been chosen, instead of something more appropriate for fire-breathers. Surely, he'd always thought, a *burning* of dragons would make more sense? Or a *firestorm*?

But seeing the dark cloud approach, blocking out more and more light, he understood at last why the right word was *darkness*.

A darkness of dragons was coming. And it wouldn't be long before they reached the Castle.

Wren scurried up to the far end of the window for a better view. After a moment, she came back. *Some of the dragons are carrying something,* she signed.

Patch looked past her, trying to make it out. Yes, there it was – small groups at the front were linked in some way, a shape hanging down below them.

"Are those…?" said Patch, squinting. "Are those *rocks*?"

Wren nodded. She hopped onto Patch's shoulder. Closer and closer the dragons came.

"What would they need huge rocks for?" He looked at Wren. "Not to—"

Wren nodded again.

Patch stepped back from the window and kept going until he reached the cell door.

The other prisoners were yelling to be released – "So we can help defend the Castle!" cried one, although Patch very much doubted their sincerity – and the general air of panic and doom was overwhelming. He sat at the base of the door, Wren on his shoulder, and waited.

The sounds of shouted commands, fearful cries, and angry prisoners were soon joined by another sound.

The beating of giant wings.

"Here they come," said Patch. He cupped his hands around Wren as a roar of fire came. Flame lit the window and the cell, then a black shadow flew past, heading up. After a moment there were screams and explosions. The dragons they'd been watching couldn't have reached them so quickly. He realized that some must have come in low, unseen, then shot up at the last instant to surprise the garrison. Certainly, he couldn't hear any sign of a barrier Song being played on the Battle Horns.

"I wonder if—" he started, but then the wall exploded and everything went black.

Patch felt something hitting his nose repeatedly, but all he could hear was a high-pitched continuous tone. He opened his eyes. The air was thick with dust. Wren was on his chest, slapping his nose with her paw.

Sit up, she signed.

"What happened?" Patch said – or *tried* to say, as his voice didn't seem to work. He clapped his hands but couldn't hear it. He was temporarily deafened; time to switch to hand-speech. *What happened?*

The dragons used their rocks, Wren signed, pointing at the wall.

Patch coughed as he looked. At least now he couldn't complain about having a small window. A large chunk of the wall had gone, taking the window with it.

His hearing was starting to recover. Wind howled past the damage in the wall, and there were groans and shouts from the prisoners and beyond, but it seemed that there was a definite lull in the attack. He set Wren on the floor and went to the hole, climbing up into it. The view was dizzying. The forest and hills were now home to the many dragons, bursts of flame coming here and there as shows of bravado. He looked up at the outside wall above him. "My God," he said.

The damage was considerable. Huge slabs of stone had fallen away, but the attack had been tightly targeted. He climbed back down to the cell floor and realized he was shaking. "This is madness," he said. "What could they possibly want—?"

He stopped talking and slowly turned his eyes to the wall of the cell next to them.

"They've come for *him*," said Patch. "They've come for the Hamelyn Piper. All these years they've waited, and finally they've come. Somehow they heard he'd been moved, and they must have known exactly where he was moved to!"

What will they do next? signed Wren.

Patch laid out his blanket and started to put his belongings on top, preparing to turn it into a parcel again. "I'm not waiting to find out," he said. "We're lucky that attack didn't kill us. If they do it again we're dead!"

Wren jumped onto the Fox and Owls board as he reached for it, his hand trembling. *What are you doing?* she signed.

"We're leaving."

How?

Patch pointed at the newly created hole in the wall. "That way." He nudged her off the game board and packed it up.

Wren looked at the hole. She stared at Patch. *We're climbing down?* she signed. *You're not serious!*

Patch nodded, trying to sound confident rather than terrified. "They'll assume I died in the attack, Wren! This is my chance of freedom."

You're crazy, she signed, and he thought she was probably right.

"I can lip-play a bit of courage into both of us," he said.

"And there's a climbing Song I know that'll help." He wrapped the blanket-parcel to leave plenty of string spare, and tied it around his waist.

But at that moment, the warning bells rang out again.

Outside, a lone figure was flying towards the Castle from the assembled dragons. Patch wondered how much damage the previous flaming assault had done to the huge Battle Horns. Not enough to put them out of use, it seemed – as the solitary dragon approached, the low pulsing hum of the Horns began, building a defensive Song. They'd been caught by surprise once before, and this time they were taking no chances.

The dragon representative carried a white flag in one front claw, and something else in the other.

A scroll! signed Wren.

"Their demands, I assume," said Patch. He climbed up into the hole again to keep sight of the dragon. This time, Wren scampered up with him. She seemed confident enough, he saw, climbing on the shattered wall, even in the blustering wind. A rat, he knew, could fall from such an enormous height and walk away after landing. For him, the result would be very different. *Messier*, for a start.

Patch watched the dragon as it came closer to the Castle. It wore a battle harness – a hardened leather chest plate on the front, and packs and straps on the sides which held equipment and supplies. The animal certainly looked fearsome enough. Patch could see what he thought were battle scars, discoloured areas on the creature's underbelly and flank. There had clearly been some trauma affecting its muzzle. And wings.

And tail, come to that.

It was male, Patch could tell, lacking as it did the giveaway spines on its back. It – or rather, *he* – came within a hundred feet of the battlements and stayed there, wings beating steadily as he tucked the white flag into the top of the battle harness.

The dragon unrolled the scroll he carried and began to read in an impressively booming voice. "By the authority of the Triumvirate of the Great Circle of the Red Sand, I demand that you hand over the prisoner known as the Hamelyn Piper. Failure to do so will be met with the displeasure of the dragons here gathered. You have thirty minutes to respond." He rolled up the scroll and turned to fly back to the other dragons.

"We have to go right now," said Patch. "If we're here when they attack again, we'll be killed."

Wren jumped onto his shoulder and gave him a thumbs up; Patch found the water jug on the floor, on its side but still with some water in it. He rinsed the dust from his mouth and licked his lips, ready to whistle up some courage.

But before he could begin, a deep rhythmic melody filled the cell. It was coming from the Battle Horns.

"That's an attacking Song they're building," said Patch, looking out to where the dragon with the scroll was still flying away from the Castle, barely a fifth of the distance back to the rest of the dragons. "Don't tell me they're going to—" The melody suddenly picked up pace, the underlying low hum from the Battle Horns pulsing now, rapid and deep. "They *are*!" he said, shocked. "They're sending their answer already! They're going to bring that dragon down!"

The dragon messenger looked over his shoulder and started to flap his wings harder. Too late, though – the sound from the Battle Horns grew so loud and so strong that it made the air shimmer and twist, and the space in front of the Castle took on a multicoloured sheen. The colours shot out towards the lone dragon like a rainbow turned into a torrent of flame, making a sound that was half-thunder, half-scream. The dragon was engulfed by the blast, and he tumbled hundreds of feet down through the air, vanishing into the dense pines in the forest far below. The crunch of impact made Patch wince.

Cheering began from the Castle walls, but in the dungeons a shocked silence fell. One prisoner shouted out: "We're dead! The fools have killed us all!"

The Battle Horns maintained their deep pulsing rhythm. Out of range in the distant trees, dragons were taking off and circling, gathering their numbers. "There are just too many of them," said Patch. "The Battle Horns won't be able to stop them all. They'll get through and the Horns will be abandoned. We'll be defenceless."

And then he heard a voice that had been silent all this time.

"Aye?" said the Hamelyn Piper, his voice almost mournful.

Patch looked out of the gaping hole and saw the rock-wielding dragons closing in. Behind them he saw *other* groups of rock-wielders, who were rising sharply at high speed, releasing their rocks well out of range of the Battle Horns. The air shimmered as the Horns did their work, but the rocks were flying up, arcing, coming down again, this time within the Castle walls.

There were crashes and screams, and the Song of the Battle Horns was silenced.

The dragons had already taken out the most important defence.

Cannons thundered from the battlements high above, but it was the rock-wielders heading right for the dungeon walls that Patch was watching now, almost hypnotized by the sight.

Wren's piercing squeal snapped him out of it. She scampered to the outer wall in the corner farthest from the Hamelyn Piper's cell, and he dived towards her as the rocks hit their target.

Impact after impact came. The cell shook violently. Stones shattered and flew. He tried to shield Wren with his body as he covered his ears with his hands. He yelled in terror, certain that he was moments away from a painful death.

The attack stopped.

Patch stood, shaking. On the floor under him Wren was holding her paws around her head. She peeked out and looked around.

There was no dust this time. It had cleared quickly in the strong breeze, because there was almost no wall now. The only remaining part was the small piece beside them that had miraculously remained intact. Patch looked up at the ceiling and saw a worryingly deep crack in it. He looked across to the Hamelyn Piper's cell. Much of the wall between the two cells had collapsed, and the external wall in that other cell was entirely gone. The Hamelyn Piper was on the floor, half-covered in rubble. A single word came from him, frail and almost lost to the wind. "Aye…"

Patch found himself staring at the most dreaded of Pipers, yet somehow he felt no fear of the masked man and started to walk towards him. He was aware of movement out in the distance. He turned and saw dragons holding their position in the air higher up, making sure of no further defensive assaults from the Castle, while a line of dragons formed some kind of honour guard, maintaining their height. Past the end of that line a group was coming closer, at the centre of which were three who wore incredibly ornate battle harnesses, flanked by black-armoured dragons.

The Triumvirate and their guards, Patch guessed. The rulers of the Dragon Territories, here in person to claim their quarry. They would reach their target soon, but Patch still walked towards the edge of the Hamelyn Piper's cell, drawn there by an irresistible need to *see*.

The attack had wounded the man badly. A large slab of stone had crushed his legs. The Iron Mask was visibly damaged at the front. Patch watched with horror and fascination as the Hamelyn Piper's hands came up and tore at the Mask, until the front opened outwards and it clattered to the cell floor.

Patch stared at the thin face, the Hamelyn Piper's eyes now locked with his own.

"Aye..." said the man, with a cough of pain that brought up blood. But the Mask's protective charms, the charms that had forced him to repeat the same word over and over, had no more hold over him now. "Aye...am..." he said.

Patch marvelled at how he felt no terror, even though he was in the company of the most evil Piper ever to have lived. And he realized what the man had actually said.

What he had *always* been trying to say.

It wasn't "Aye". It wasn't the single word of defiance

that the story claimed. Instead, it was only the first word in a sentence that he had never been able to finish.

Until now.

"I...am..." said the man, relief in his voice. He swallowed and took a breath, still looking directly at Patch. "I am not the Piper of Hamelyn."

The sound of wings announced the arrival of the black-armoured dragons. Patch stepped away quickly, knowing he was at their mercy, but they ignored him. Instead, they lifted the slab the man was trapped under and yanked their quarry from the rubble.

There was no fear written on the man's face, Patch thought, only a sense of *release*.

A short way from the Castle the Triumvirate waited. They gave their guards a nod. The dragon carrying the prisoner let out a deafening screech and flew high into the air, higher than the Castle battlements. The other dragon guards, together with the Triumvirate themselves, formed a circle. When ready, the prisoner was released, falling towards the circle in silence.

The circle of dragons aimed upwards and breathed their fire, creating a blast of flame that caught the man right in the centre and tracked the path of his fall.

All that emerged from underneath the circle were the blackened chains that had held him. Of the man, there was nothing left but ash, drifting in the wind.

Patch looked back to where the Iron Mask had fallen. He climbed over what was left of the dividing wall, then took the Mask and returned to his own cell.

Wren was angry with him, squeaking loudly to get him to come back. Fragments of stone fell on his head as he ran to Wren, and the moment he reached her a loud cracking came from the stone around them. Wren climbed up to his shoulder, scowling.

You scared me! she signed. *Promise me you won't do anything that stupid again!*

But before he could make any promise at all, the floor shuddered under them and shifted outwards in a sudden jerk. Patch found himself dropping down, a scream leaving his lips as he fell.

12
Not Quite Dead

Patch came to an abrupt halt, sprawled on his knees on the small section of cell floor that had broken away. It had landed on a wide rocky ledge jutting out from the sheer cliff the dungeons had been built into; beside them, in the jagged rock of the cliff face, was a crevice about ten feet high and two across.

He shared a look of bewilderment with Wren. She suddenly squealed with terror and pointed up: above them another huge chunk of wall was falling. Patch grabbed Wren and scrambled off the ruined floor, into the crevice. He winced as the falling chunk crashed into the space he'd just stepped out of, then stood with his eyes shut, not daring to look as debris rained down behind him.

There were other screams. He opened his eyes and

turned, staring as masonry and prisoners alike tumbled down past them. The piece of floor they had been on had already vanished, and the ledge that had stopped their fall had been sliced away from the cliff face.

They'd fallen fifty feet or so. Above them at least eight cells were open to the elements now – eight cells whose walls had gone, several having lost most of their floor. Shouts for help echoed around the devastation.

He put Wren on his shoulder and was suddenly aware of something in his other hand – he was still clutching the Iron Mask. He tied it to the parcel at his waist.

Very slowly, Patch bent his knees, keeping his back pressed hard against the rock. He worked his way as far into the crevice as he could, and found he could actually sit. Wren was staring ahead blankly, just as stunned as he was.

"I'll, um, wait until I stop shaking before I climb anywhere," he said.

It took a while.

As they waited, the shouts and calls echoing around the Castle above them grew less and less urgent. Apart from the occasional piece of stonework tumbling past them, the structure of the dungeons held together.

Soon they could hear gruff voices hollering to each

other, describing the damage and assessing what could be done to shore up the Castle until repairs could be attempted.

Patch wasn't shaking any more, but with all the activity that was going on he decided to wait until nightfall before risking the climb. As things stood, the Pipers would assume he'd died – certainly, he didn't imagine they'd be hurrying to hunt through the rubble for bodies. If people saw him climbing, that would all change.

In the distance, the dragon army was preparing to leave, apparently unhurried. There certainly didn't appear to be any sign of reprisal from the Castle – the dragons had come here to kill the Hamelyn Piper, and now that it was done the fight seemed to be over.

Far below, the forest at the base of the cliff showed the scars where the largest chunks of masonry had crashed to the ground. There was another scar that Patch could see – a smaller area further out, where the broken tops of trees were visible. He pointed it out to Wren. "Is that where the dragons' messenger fell, do you think?"

Wren looked for a moment then signed her reply: *Could he have survived?*

Patch thought back to the dragon dropping out of the sky, and the crunch of the impact. "I doubt it." The dragons had presumably collected their colleague's body during the attack. Patch felt a wave of empathy for the messenger, accompanied by a strong feeling of shame at how the Pipers had attacked him from the rear while he carried a white flag.

The dragon army rose and began the long journey back to their homelands. The darkness of dragons receded, until at last it looked like a flock of birds in the distance, just as it had when Wren had first seen it approach.

Once the dragons had gone, the sound of hammer on stone and the bawdy conversation of workmen drifted down to them.

Patch set Wren down beside him in the crevice, and a moment later she lurched to one side and grabbed a juicy beetle that had blundered too close. She tucked in, ripping the insect's head off with her first bite. As she crunched into the abdomen she noticed Patch's grim expression. She polished off the rest in two mouthfuls. *They're actually pretty good,* she signed. *A bit like caramel.*

"I'll take your word for it," said Patch.

As night fell the work on the Castle ceased. Patch and Wren risked a quick glance up and saw the roped-timber reinforcements that had been put in place, all rather impressive considering how speedily it had been assembled.

In the sky the moon shone through wispy cloud.

"I think it's safe to go," he said. He checked the parcel at his waist and took a moment to better secure the Hamelyn Piper's Mask. He lifted Wren back onto his shoulder. "If I fall, jump away from me. You'll survive the landing as long as I don't come down on top of you." Wren just gave him a hard stare. "Okay, okay. I won't fall. Right. Time to whistle up some courage. Quite a bit of it, I think."

Patch built the Song of Courage as best he could without a Pipe. As a very young boy, he'd stumbled onto some rhythms and melodies that made him feel a little braver; anyone who had ever felt emboldened by joining in a normal song of hope or patriotism could understand the kind of feelings he'd been able to create when he was young. The power of music was clear even to those who knew little of the Piping Arts. But as he'd learned the ways of the Pipe at Tiviscan, his eyes and ears had been opened to the *real* power that music could conjure.

He felt strength flowing through his blood.

Confidence. Certainty. Courage.

I can do this, he thought.

He stepped to the edge of the crevice they had taken refuge in, and looked down.

I can't do this, he thought.

He stepped back from the edge. It was a *long* way down. Long, and craggy, and *sharp*.

Are you okay? signed Wren.

Patch took a breath and nodded. "I've a little courage now," he said. "Next, I need help with the *climbing* part." He began the Song of the Climb, slowly building it up, the rhythm steady. In his mind, he could already feel the satisfaction of his hands moving over rock, finding purchase, knowing how much weight a handhold could support.

As he whistled, he put out of his mind the knowledge of where many Songs came from, where many had originated and been refined.

War.

Pipers had accompanied armies for centuries, and had also ventured on smaller missions: infiltration, sabotage. The Song of the Climb, for example, would have helped a group of fighters tackle terrain that an enemy thought impossible.

And while not all Songs had such origins, most of those that affected *people* came from the battlefields of history.

He whistled, eyes closed, until he felt a kinship with the rock itself. It would show him where to place his feet. It would guide his fingertips to where they would cling. He was ready to start the descent. He kneeled and lowered his legs over the base of the crevice.

The moonlight was unnecessary; instinct alone was leading him down the face of the cliff. Only the rock seemed real. Everything else faded away, coming back into focus from time to time and prompting him to change what he whistled. Whenever terror crept into his bones, he whistled for courage; when his sure reach for handholds faltered, he went back to the Song of the Climb.

When at last they were safely down, he stopped whistling and stared back up, unable even to *see* the crevice where the climb had begun. How long had it taken? Somewhere between hours and centuries, it seemed.

He looked at Wren, her expression one of awe. She hugged his neck.

Patch took her from his shoulder and gently set her down.

"We made it," he said, falling to his knees. Then he spent ten minutes retching, his last prison meal forced out of him in a thin stream of bile.

Where to now? signed Wren, when he'd stopped being sick.

Patch wiped the spittle from the side of his mouth. "Erner's letter, remember?" he said. "We go to Marwheel Abbey, to find a way to cure you! Unless you've decided to remain a rodent?"

No chance of that, she signed.

Now that the climb was over, Patch noticed how cold he was feeling. Tiviscan always enjoyed a mild winter, but his meagre prison clothing wouldn't do much to keep him warm. "I wish I had my coat," he said, rubbing his hands together. "Are you cold too?"

I'm all right, signed Wren. *Being furry comes in handy*.

"Well as long as we keep moving, I should be okay on the journey to the Abbey." He pointed to the trees ahead.

"We go that way through the forest. We have to get far from Tiviscan without being discovered. I'm an escaped prisoner now, Wren. I have to be cunning and resourceful! A day's walk will take us to the Penance River, which we can follow north."

And after I'm cured, what about you? She pointed to his waist, where the Mask was tied. *You're the last person to see the Hamelyn Piper alive. Perhaps you'll be famous!*

Patch shook his head, untying the Mask to take a proper look at it. "Obscurity is all that I want, Wren. If Rundel Stone found out I was alive, he'd make sure I went back to the dungeons." He held the Mask closer, peering at it. The parts that seemed damaged simply popped back into shape after some prodding, although the lock itself was beyond repair.

Every inch of the Mask's inner surface was covered in symbols that reminded him of the ancient magical textbooks in the Tiviscan library. He wiped it to see the runes more clearly, and was astonished at how much cleaner the metal was where he'd wiped. What he'd taken for tarnish seemed to be merely dirt. "The Mask came off the Hamelyn Piper's head just before the dragons took him," he said. "I don't even know why I picked it up. I should just drop this here and be done with it." Studying the metal, he could see that it wasn't welded together. It was made from overlapping pieces connected with *joints*, similar to the ones that allowed it to hinge shut over the wearer's face. He tried to move some of the pieces against one another, at first without success, but then parts of the Mask seemed to fold up. He tried again with another section, and this time the entire Mask flattened down into a rectangle the size of his hand.

He looked at Wren. "Interesting," he said. "Should I keep it, do you think?"

She nodded. *A souvenir*, she signed. *Of when you saw the most evil man in history finally get his reward!*

"I'm not sure that watching a man die is something I want a souvenir of, Wren," Patch said, but then it occurred to him – Wren hadn't heard what the man had said. *I'm the only one to know the Hamelyn Piper's last words,* he thought. *If I should even think of him by that name any more!* Suddenly the knowledge was a terrible burden: the prisoner had suffered a great injustice, if those last words had really been true, and worse – it would mean that the *real* Hamelyn Piper must still be free.

And if that was the case, surely it was Patch's duty to tell the Council? *They'd lock me up again*, he thought. *Whether they believed me or not, I'd spend the rest of my days rotting in a cell.*

He tied the folded Mask to his waist. He would need money soon enough, he reckoned, and strange magical objects always had value.

He put Wren on his shoulder and made his way through the light vegetation at the forest's edge, then through thicker bushes until they were in amongst the vast pines. By the time the first hint of predawn twilight was visible in the sky, they were far enough from the base of the cliff – and from Tiviscan – for Patch to breathe easier.

A little further on, the undergrowth became more challenging. The sky was brightening rapidly, letting Patch look further ahead to spot the clearest path. He could see a much brighter area beyond a thicket. "Is that a clearing?" he said. Wren shrugged, but as they got closer they could see splintered treetops high up, and a dark shape on the ground ahead.

The messenger? signed Wren.

Patch paused. Surely the dragons wouldn't just have left their fallen comrade? Yet as they got closer, they saw that it *was* the messenger, broken and still. The dragons had abandoned their sole casualty of the battle. "I don't understand," said Patch. "Why didn't they retrieve the body?"

That's really sad, signed Wren.

"This poor soul was attacked from the rear," said Patch. "Seeing that happen made me ashamed to be a Piper. But now this lack of respect from his own kind!" He scowled, surprised by how angry he felt. "It's not like dragons at *all*. During training I learned quite a bit about their culture.

When a dragon dies, the body is taken by members of the Order of the Skull – the most ancient and secretive part of their religion. The body is buried deep, in total secrecy, the location never revealed."

Wren frowned. *So a dragon's family don't even have a grave to visit?*

Patch nodded. "It's been that way for thousands of years. Mind you, humans have always thought various parts of a dragon have magical properties. There are plenty of idiots who'd buy any old potion if you pretended it had powdered dragon tooth in it. Can you imagine the trouble that'd be caused if there were dragon graves to rob?"

When Patch had first seen the messenger he'd noticed an odd discoloration on the scales, which suggested terrible old wounds; now, he could see the same thing around its closed eyes and mouth. The snout seemed misshapen, and was presumably broken. The wings were limply spread out, and one had a long bleeding tear near its base.

"A proud creature, reduced to this," he said. "Meeting its fate after showing true bravery, yet ending up mourned only by us, Wren. An escaped prisoner and a cursed rat."

He stepped closer. It wasn't very large for a dragon, he realized, its head perhaps four feet long and two across. Something nagged at him about the markings, especially those on the wings.

Couldn't we do something? signed Wren.

"Well, we couldn't exactly *bury* him," said Patch. "Unless we had a week or two to spare."

You could say a few words, she replied.

Patch nodded. He thought back to what he'd learned of their culture, then cleared his throat. "Today, we ask the Gods of Fire and Scale to look to the ground, and see this fallen warrior, that they may bring him to the Mighty Flame and—"

At that moment, Wren tapped his cheek. He glanced at her, irritated that she would interrupt such a solemn occasion, but she was pointing furiously towards the dragon. He turned his gaze to see what was bothering her.

The dragon's eyes were open, and looking right at him.

"Could you *stop* all the mumbo jumbo, please?" the dragon said in a deep voice. "I've already had a terrible day, and the last thing I need is *religion*."

13
The Messenger

It took a few seconds for Patch to get his mouth to work. The sudden reality of standing next to a living dragon, especially an injured and obviously *irritable* one, had quickly pushed him close to panic. He racked his brains to remember the most respectful form of address, and came up with *seken* – roughly the equivalent of *sir*. "I'm glad to see you're alive, Seken!" he said.

The dragon eyed him carefully and grunted. "Don't call me that."

Patch's eyes widened. "I'm sorry, I thought it was the correct term—"

"Oh, yes, it's the correct *term*," said the dragon, sitting up. "For a dragon. But I'm *not* a dragon, and after today I suspect I'll have nothing more to do with the pig-headed *idiots*."

"*Not* a—" began Patch, then his voice trailed off. He looked again at the creature, and those nagging feelings he'd had before resurfaced. Aside from the obvious tear, the wings were discoloured in places; the snout was misshapen, but he'd thought it had been badly injured in the fall and not looked at it too closely. Now that he *did* look closely, he saw a snout that ended in a hooked shape more reminiscent of a *beak*; he saw wings that were covered in the stubs of cut feathers, as well as areas of the thick leathery skin that dragons had. There were stubs of feathers around the snout too, but those were charred.

Now that the creature was sitting up, Patch could see that the legs each had densely packed brown feathers running down them. And while the front claws were very like those of a dragon, the rear were more like the feet of some enormous falcon, or…

Well, thought Patch. *Of course!* A smile crept onto his face as the truth dawned on him. The creature in front of him seemed to grow even more irritated because of the smile, but Patch couldn't help it.

Some features of a dragon, and some of a *griffin*. "You're a dracogriff!" he said. He glanced at Wren and saw the confusion on her face. "Half-dragon, half-griffin!" he told her. "I'm sorry, it's just I've never met a dracogriff before. Actually I've never met a *dragon* before, not really, or a griffin come to that, but when it comes down to it they're two a penny! A *dracogriff*, though! Now that *is* an honour."

Why is it an honour? signed Wren.

The dracogriff sat up suddenly, looking at Wren with astonishment. "Your rat can talk!" he said, wide-eyed. "I know Merisax hand speech when I see it! I've spent the last seven years as a bodyguard-for-hire in the Islands of the Eastern Seas. Merisax came with the territory. Is *talking* the nature of its curse?"

"Curse?" said Patch.

"Yes. As you approached, you referred to yourself as an escaped prisoner and a cursed rat."

Patch blinked. He looked at Wren.

Oh great, she signed. *We've only been fugitives for a few hours, and we've already given ourselves away.*

"Please," said the dracogriff. "You have no need to fear that I'd hand you over. I'm certainly no friend to Pipers. Even if you *are* one." Patch stared at him, open-mouthed. "I *also* heard you say that what they did to me made you ashamed to be a Piper."

"I did?" said Patch. "I did. Damn. I need to be more careful what I say in future. Being an escaped convict is harder than I thought."

"As I said, you've nothing to worry about from me," said the dracogriff. He held out his front claw. His *hand*, Patch corrected himself – that was what dragons and griffins called them, and it seemed impolite not to think of them as such. Patch offered his relatively tiny hand out in return, and they shook. "I'm Barver. Barver Knopferkerkle."

"Barver Nop-fur-ker-kill," said Patch, trying to get his mouth around it.

"That's it," said Barver. "Dragon surname, griffin forename. Your turn!"

"Patch Brightwater," said Patch. "Imprisoned a week ago, now free and hopefully presumed dead. This is my friend Wren Cobble, a girl cursed by a Sorcerer into the form of a rat. I taught her some hand speech when we met so that we could talk. She's a quick learner."

Barver looked closely at Wren. "Your markings *are* pretty," he said. "I especially like the red rings on your tail."

Thanks very much, signed Wren with a smile.

"A Sorcerer's curse, eh?" said Barver. "It always saddens me that Sorcerers are such *awful* people. Think of all the good they could do if they were nicer!"

Tell me about it, she signed.

Barver turned his attention to Patch. "Aren't you a little *young* to have been imprisoned?"

Patch felt himself bristle. "I'm thirteen," he said, as imposingly as he could manage. Wren suppressed a laugh, and he glared at her.

"I meant no offence," said Barver. "It just seems harsh, to experience such adversity so young." He looked up through the trees. Patch and Wren followed his gaze, and could clearly see the damage to the Castle through the branches. "I saw the flames burn brightly as the Hamelyn Piper was executed," said Barver. "I heard the screams as other prisoners fell to their deaths. Yet you lived. It seems fate has plans for you!"

"I hope not," said Patch. "I'd rather just find somewhere I can earn a living and get some peace and quiet. I reckon I've earned it."

"How did you survive the fall?" said Barver. "Humans must be hardier than I thought."

"I climbed down the cliff," said Patch. "How did *you* survive the fall? I heard the crunch when you hit the ground!"

"It was a bad one, I admit," said Barver. He slowly folded his wings up along his back and stretched his legs, wincing.

"Are you sure you should be moving anywhere for a while?" said Patch.

"I'll certainly not be flying for a few weeks," said Barver. "But apart from that it's just bruises."

"Incredible," said Patch. He and Wren shared an amazed look, and both raised their heads to the sky, through the broken treetops, thinking about how far Barver had plummeted.

"How much do you know about dracogriffs?" said Barver.

"That they're rare," said Patch. "Beyond that, not much."

Barver nodded. "There are two broad kinds. One is called a *higher*. The other is called a *lower*. Highers have a blend of the prettier aspects of dragons and griffins, but they're a bit delicate. Lowers have a blend of the more *durable* qualities. We're ugly, but very hard to kill. Naturally, dragons and griffins prefer the pretty ones, but I know which I'd rather be!" He grinned, and as he did his strange blend of features suddenly seemed to make *sense*. Wren and Patch both found themselves grinning too.

I like him, signed Wren.

"Me too," said Patch.

"So, my new friends!" said Barver. "Where are you headed?"

"The Penance River flows through the forest," said Patch. "Following it will take us to the Collosson Highway, and then to Marwheel Abbey. We've heard that someone there can help lift Wren's curse."

Barver grinned. "Then we should set off at once!"

"We?" said Patch.

"You don't mind if I tag along? I seem to have been abandoned, and I'll not be able to fly for quite a while. The company would be appreciated."

Patch looked to Wren.

Why not? she signed.

"Why not indeed," said Patch. "Although I have to say, Barver, you don't seem all that cross about the dragon army leaving you behind. I think if I was you, I'd be *seething*!"

Barver waved his hand like he was swatting a fly.

"I won't waste my anger on that lot," he said. "They weren't very keen on me accompanying the army when we left the Dragon Territories, but it seems they were even *less* keen on me going back with them." He shrugged. "As I said, dragons prefer the pretty kind of dracogriff. They tend to look at me as some kind of unfortunate *mistake*."

Wren was outraged and signed some things that made quite clear what she thought of the dragons.

"You should mind your language," said Patch, wincing. He noticed that the scroll of demands Barver had read out was still tucked into his harness. "When I saw you approach the Castle, I'd assumed sending you to deliver the demands must have been some kind of honour."

"I volunteered when nobody else came forward," said Barver. He frowned. "Makes me wonder if they all knew something I didn't." He shook his wings a little and stretched again. "Anyway, enough of all that! Which way is the river?"

Patch pointed towards an overgrown area of bushes that looked worryingly thorny. "That's the most direct way, so if we head over *there* –" he pointed towards a more accessible route – "it should be easier going."

Barver nodded and trotted off towards the wall of thorny bushes, flattening a path as if it was nothing more than tall grass.

Patch smiled at Wren, shrugged, and followed.

✶ ✶ ★

They could hear the soft murmur of flowing water as they approached the river. Barver paused and turned. "Can either of you smell something?" he said. "Bears, maybe? Or wolves?"

"Bears?" said Patch. He looked at Wren and she gave him a frightened glance, but following in Barver's trail made Patch feel about as safe as he'd ever felt in his life. "Oh, I don't think we've much to worry about on that score, Wren," he said.

"Actually, not a bear," said Barver. "Something *dead.*" He lifted his snout high and sniffed deep and long, turning his head this way and that. "Over there," he said. "*Human,*" he added, then led the way to a small rise covered in ivy-choked trees. He stopped and pulled at the ivy.

The corpse underneath was revealed. The skull grinned out at them, ragged remains of flesh clinging to it. It wore a long coat, which was torn in several places – gashes from sharp claws. Within the coat, little but bone remained.

Patch stared at the skull, and couldn't help imagining his own skull there instead. "Have I mentioned how glad I am that you're here, Barver?" Wren, who was also staring, nodded in agreement.

"It's at least a few months old," said Barver. "Probably a bear attack. A gruesome enough death, but quick." He pulled at more of the ivy, and discovered a hardy shoulder-slung leather bag, similar to Erner's satchel. "What do we have here?"

Patch picked up the bag and untied the fastening strap. Inside was a simple cotton tunic, a sheathed knife, a firesteel, a small waterskin, and the mouldy remains of an old hunk of bread – which he took out and discarded. "He just carried the basics of survival," said Patch. "Perhaps the poor soul travelled along the river, in search of a new life." He shook out the tunic. It was a little musty, but basically clean, so he set Wren on the ground before taking off his coarse prison shirt and putting the tunic on. It was a vast improvement. He gave the torn coat a sorrowful look. "Shame about that," he said. "It seems well made."

Barver shrugged. "It's not beyond saving. And a good wash in the river will shift much of the smell." He gave Patch a look. "Speaking of which…"

"What?" said Patch.

"Go to the river, Patch Brightwater, and scrape the dungeon stench from your skin. It makes my eyes sting even more than the odour of this corpse." He turned to the gnawed jumble of bones on the ground and looked at it, thoughtful. "In the meantime I'll see what can be done with that coat."

14
A Clean Start

Cold, was it? signed Wren.

Patch tried to nod in response, but it was hard because he was shivering so much. He'd stripped off and jumped into the river, but the water had turned out to be rather more chilly than he'd expected. Half-screaming, half-whimpering, he'd cleaned himself as quickly as he could before leaping out and returning to Wren.

He'd already untied his blanket parcel, leaving its contents on the fallen tree trunk next to Wren, so that he would have his blanket ready to wrap round himself. He dried off as best he could, then he dressed and put his meagre belongings back into the damp blanket. Wren hopped onto his still-trembling shoulder, and they returned to where they'd left Barver.

To Patch's amazement, Barver was holding the dead man's torn coat, stitching up the rips. Patch had never imagined that the clawed hands of dragons and griffins were capable of much dexterity, but Barver wielded a needle and thread with the skill of an expert.

Barver reached into his harness and produced another reel of thread. He smiled when he saw them nearing. "A few large slashes and a couple of minor tears, that's about it," he said. "I'll be finished shortly." He looked closely at Patch, his expression suddenly concerned. "Should your lips be *quite* that shade of blue?"

"The w-water was a b-bit c-c-cold," Patch said. "I'm not k-k-k-keen on being c-c-cold."

"My apologies, I should have thought!" said Barver. He set down his sewing and took a few steps forward, then with a broad swipe of his tail cleared an area of the ground down to the soil. He made a small mound of earth at the centre. "Stand back," he said, lowering his head to the mound. He opened his mouth wide and a gurgling noise came from his throat. He coughed and thumped his chest a few times. "Hang on, I'll get there," he said, and opened his mouth again.

This time, an intense flame poured from his throat, flowing over the mound of earth. It sounded, Patch thought, like a blacksmith's forge with the bellows being pumped. The heat reaching him was already significant, and very welcome.

Barver kept the fire coming until the earth started to glow, stones within it audibly cracking. "There you go," he said. "Get yourself warmed up!"

Around Barver's half-griffin muzzle there were blackened stubs, one of which was currently on fire. Patch licked his finger and thumb and reached out, pinching the stub to extinguish the flame.

"Thank you," said Barver. "My dragon and griffin features don't always work together. Griffin feathers on a fire-breathing face, for example. They don't last long, trust me."

Patch sat and let the heat fill him. On his shoulder, Wren stretched her paws out to the warmth. Barver held the coat up, examining his work. "I'll wash it when I'm done," he said. "Shouldn't take long to dry on a heated boulder." He returned to his stitching.

Patch and Wren watched him with an obvious bemusement. It wasn't long before the dracogriff caught their expressions. "Anything wrong?" he said.

"Sorry," said Patch. "But it's just...well, the sewing?"

"My mother taught me," said Barver. "For my wings." He unfurled his left wing a little. Patch and Wren looked, and saw that the tear they'd seen when they'd first found Barver was now neatly stitched. Barver traced his fingers along the line of the injury. "I treat my wings *terribly*," he said with a gentle melancholy. "Always have. They're about as hardy as those of a typical dragon, but I'm used to the *rest* of me being so much more resilient." To underline his point, he picked up a thick fallen branch from the ground and smashed it over his own head. "See? I was a clumsy youth and my wings often got torn. They heal better when stitched, and my mother got tired of having to keep doing it, so she made sure I learned. And I've had plenty of practice, believe me."

For a few quiet minutes, Barver stitched the coat while Patch and Wren warmed up near the glowing mound of earth. Patch opened out the blanket he'd used to dry himself, setting his belongings to one side and holding the damp blanket up to the heat.

Oh, show him the Hamelyn Piper's Mask! signed Wren, pointing at it.

"I don't want any fuss," mumbled Patch.

Barver had seen what Wren had signed, though. "The Hamelyn Piper's Mask?" he said.

Patch shrugged. "I was in the cell next to him. Like you, I saw him die, although I was *much* closer. His Mask fell off him before he was pulled from his cell. I picked it up."

"The actual Iron Mask of the Hamelyn Piper?" said Barver, fascinated.

Patch picked up the Mask and demonstrated how it unfolded. He tossed it to Barver.

"Astonishing," said Barver, turning the Mask over in

his hands. He reversed what Patch had done and the Mask folded up again. "We've seen history made today. A dark and evil thing, finally brought to an end." He shook his head slowly and gave the Mask back to Patch. "Well, the sooner I get this coat washed and dried, the sooner we can set off again." He picked up the coat and made his way to the river.

Patch put his belongings into the traveller's leather bag, and looked at the small pile of bones that was all that now remained of him. "This traveller was heading for a new life," he said. "Hopes and dreams, all brought to a terrible end." He shook his head. "Looking at those bones makes me think," he said, wistful. "However bad things have been, we're alive; we're luckier than that poor soul."

It makes me think, too, signed Wren.

"What?" said Patch.

Wren grinned. *Stay away from bears*, she signed.

They made good pace alongside the river, and Patch was glad of his new coat. Barver had managed to clean it well, and although a slightly odd smell still clung to it, the warmth it provided was more than enough to compensate. Spring wasn't far away now, but the air still had a deep chill to it.

As evening approached, Barver found a secluded clearing for their camp. Exhausted, Patch put up his little tent and lay down for what he thought would be a short rest before eating.

When Wren woke him with a loud squeak in his ear, night had fallen.

Patch came out of the tent. Barver was sitting by a small fire, holding a spit over the flames – rabbit, Patch saw. His mouth watered.

"Awake at last!" said Barver. "Wren was telling me all about your exploits, yours and hers both. She told me the story of Patterfall and of her own curse, and I gave her some tales of my adventures in the Eastern Seas." He took the spit away from the fire and sniffed the rabbit, then handed the spit to Patch, who tore off a piece of meat and ate it. It tasted sublime.

"That's *amazing*," Patch said around his mouthful.

"A few common herbs to bring out the flavour," said Barver. "Now, Wren… Shall we finish our game?"

Wren nodded and scampered over to where – Patch now saw – the Fox and Owls board was laid out. *I taught him*, signed Wren to Patch. *He picked it up pretty quickly.*

Patch ate his rabbit and watched the game, which was hard-fought by Barver. Wren's victory came in the end, but it was much closer than Patch had ever managed against her.

In the warmth from the fire, with his belly full, he realized with a degree of shock that he had a *future* to look forward to. Barver's mention of the Eastern Seas had made him think. The Islands of the Eastern Seas were mostly outside the influence of Tiviscan and, as such, uncertified Pipers could still work there if they were careful.

He could work there.

Of course, the Islands were also overrun with pirates and criminals, but it was something for him to consider: a future as a Piper, even if it wasn't the one he'd always dreamed of. But there was one thing he would need to do before even *that* future was possible.

He would need to make himself a new *Pipe*.

He'd already noticed plenty of mature boxwood bushes in the forest, so it wouldn't be hard to find some suitable branches that he could use.

A new Pipe, for a new life.

That night, he slept well.

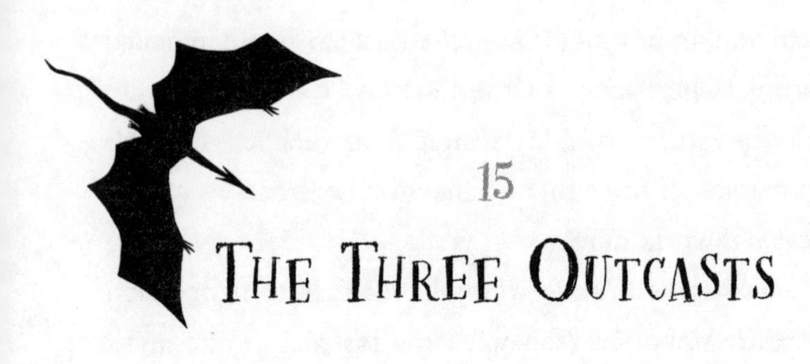

15
The Three Outcasts

The next evening, as dusk approached, they reached the Collosson Highway – a rather grand name for what amounted to a slightly-wider-than-normal muddy road. They were confronted with another smell in the air, but one that was rather more pleasant than a dead traveller: the smell of food cooking.

"Beef stew," said Barver, his eyes half-closed. His stomach gave a rumble so loud it echoed.

"Fresh bread," said Patch, his mouth starting to drool.

There must be an inn nearby, signed Wren.

"It's a shame the dead traveller wasn't carrying any money," said Patch, mournful. There was a curious tinkling sound to his left, and he turned to see a glorious sight. Barver was grinning, and in his hand was a small purse.

"Let this be my treat," said Barver. "Since I returned from the Eastern Seas I've not known many I'd care to spend time with, and now I meet a condemned criminal and a cursed rat and find them to be honest, decent and agreeable company. What do you say? We'll have a feast, and I insist on getting you a proper bed for the night. Then we'll reach Marwheel Abbey fed and rested."

A bed, thought Patch.

A proper *bed*. He almost wept.

The inn lay round the next bend in the road, and it looked as perfect as it smelled.

The innkeeper was petrified the moment he saw Barver, but soon enough Barver's friendly manner – and his money – smoothed things over. "A feast, if you please," said Barver, offering up a shiny golden coin. "And beds for the night."

"Will the smaller of our stables do you for sleeping, my large friend?" asked the innkeeper. "It's clean and warm, and you'll have it to yourself."

"Sounds perfect," said Barver.

The innkeeper spotted the rat on Patch's shoulder and frowned. Wren gave him a wave and bowed.

"Trained rat, eh?" said the innkeeper. "Clever."

"You don't know the half of it," said Patch.

The innkeeper showed them to a table at the back of

the inn. Patch had a tankard of small ale brought to him; Barver had a bucket of the same, and insisted on a thimble for Wren, the innkeeper delighted by the level of training this "pet" rat displayed.

Patch looked at Barver's bucket. "I would've thought you'd drink something stronger," he said. Small ale was a very weak brew of barley and oats, tasty and thirst quenching with hardly any alcohol.

Barver shook his head. "Anything strong irritates my fire ducts," he said. "This is just about right for me."

Patch nodded. "A toast," he said, raising his tankard. "To you, Barver, and to you, Wren! Only days ago, I was alone and in despair. Today, I'm happy and with friends!"

"Thank you," said Barver. "But I'd rather we raise a toast to my mother. She was the reason I recently returned from the Islands of the Eastern Seas, and it is her gift to me that is paying for our meal. To my mother!" He raised his bucket. "May she rest in peace."

Wren's face fell, and so did Patch's.

Oh, Barver! signed Wren, distressed.

"It's good for me to talk about it," said Barver. "In the dragon tradition, she left me what's called a Vanishing Gift – the money now in my purse. In her honour, I must spend it all within one month." He shook his head, his eyes moistening. "But I'd not spoken to her in years. We'd fallen out, which was why I left for the Eastern Seas in the first place. If my father had still been alive things might have been different, but me and my mother never spoke again. By the time word reached me that she was dying, it was too late. Her funeral ceremony had happened, and the Order of the Skull had taken her body to its final secret home."

They fell into silence for a moment.

"Then we *must* raise a toast to your mother," said Patch. They raised their ales and took a drink. "I'm so sorry, Barver."

Barver nodded, grateful. "She left a letter for me. I'd hoped there might be some kind of apology for the way she'd acted, but instead it was instructions for a last wish. I feel overwhelmed by it all. Things have been so rushed, you see. The day after I got back to the Dragon Territories, they began raising the army to claim the Hamelyn Piper. My mother had always been fascinated with him – an *obsession*, really. It seemed fitting that I should volunteer, and see with my own eyes what happened. I think she would have been appalled at how it turned out. Revenge is such an unpleasant thing."

Why was she obsessed with the Hamelyn Piper? asked Wren.

"She was an advisor to the Dragon Triumvirate. *Highly* respected. Even her relationship with my father hadn't tarnished her reputation, and dragons are very touchy about one of their kind falling in love with a griffin, believe me.

She'd first taken an interest in the Hamelyn Piper when the *human* children vanished, but when the dragon children were stolen her obsession was complete. And while the other dragons wanted war with the whole of humanity – as if it was their fault! – *she* was a voice of reason. Without her guidance, I think another war might have been unavoidable."

"Then we have much to thank her for," said Patch.

"True," said Barver. "But it was that same obsession which drove such a wedge between us. She became ever more distant, and was often cold to me. One question burned within her, the most important question of them all! *Why* had the Hamelyn Piper taken the children?"

Because he was insane, signed Wren. *Me and Patch saw him, remember? We saw his eyes! Crazy!*

Patch felt his cheeks redden, and wished above all else that he could just *forget* what the prisoner had said. He wanted to tell his friends the truth, but he also knew that doing so would lead to trouble. It was easier to pretend that the Hamelyn Piper *had* been mad, and so anything he'd said at the end was meaningless. "Did your mother ever suggest an answer to that question?" he said.

"Some claim the children were taken to a mysterious and beautiful place," said Barver. "To show that humans and dragons could live in harmony, and prevent wars from ever happening again. Fairy-tale nonsense! It's a miracle it didn't *start* a war at once, instead of preventing them in future. No, my mother didn't think any of the popular theories made much sense. If she had her own ideas about it, she never shared them with me." He took a drink of ale and sighed. "Then again, she stopped sharing *anything* with me. That was why we grew apart."

The food was soon brought out, and it was impressive. A pair of roasted boars at its centre, the table soon strained under the weight of cheese and bread and cake, nuts and fruit and bowls of spiced porridge, soups and stews and biscuits and salted fish.

Barver's table manners were almost a shock to Patch. He'd expected the dracogriff to consume the feast one vast mouthful after another, but instead he took his time and ate with delicate care. He didn't hold back on praise for the wide variety of dishes that had been cooked for them.

"Living out in the Islands of the Eastern Sea, you get used to decent food," said Barver to the delighted innkeeper. "This is all superb!"

They continued with the meal, Patch and Wren eating until they were almost in pain. Patch looked at his own plate, tempted by the various bits and pieces that were left on it. The idea of not eating everything he'd taken was unthinkable to him, but it would be a few minutes yet (and probably a belch or two) before he could fit anything else in.

He delved inside his bag and pulled out several pieces of boxwood that he'd cut from bushes as they'd walked. He studied the wood and chose the best pieces, straight and free of awkward knots. Before long, he'd planned out the new Pipe in his mind. The knife the dead traveller had carried in his bag was a good one, and Patch set about stripping the bark.

What are you working on? signed Wren.

Patch smiled. "A Pipe," he said. "I don't quite feel whole without one."

You've done this often? signed Wren.

"Twice before," he said. "Not everyone makes their own, but making it yourself lets you get to know it right from the start." He blew away some shavings. "I'll need some fine woodcarving knives, though, before I can really get to work."

I can't wait to hear you play it! she signed. She sat back and patted her stomach. *You know, after this meal I'll probably sleep for a month.*

Barver nodded. "It's a very welcome feast." He let rip with a thunderous burp that seemed to last for ever. Done, he gave a satisfied smile, while Patch and Wren laughed.

Barver started loading his platter up with food again, two-thirds of the feast now gone.

Patch mopped up soup with some bread. "What will you do, Barver?" he asked. "When we go our separate ways?"

"I'll fulfil the last wish of my mother," said Barver. "Her letter gave me instructions – there is a place I must go, and a second letter to open when I'm there. After it's done, I'll return to the Eastern Seas. There's nothing for me in the Dragon Territories. I've always been a bit of an outcast, but I think I prefer it that way." He smiled, and nodded to Wren. "And you, an outcast from your human form, but not for much longer! What will you do when the spell is reversed?"

I'll go home, she signed. *I miss my parents terribly, but I refuse to go back to them until I'm cured.*

"And you, Patch?" said Barver.

"Once Wren's free of the curse, I'll see her safely back to her home. Then—" He set down the stripped boxwood he was holding. "I'm making this Pipe because I feel incomplete without one, but I'll never be a true certified Piper. I'm an outcast, too. I can make a living, but it must be far from Tiviscan. Far from its *dungeons*."

"Well," said Barver, "if you happen to find yourselves in the Eastern Seas, just ask for me at any inn on the Islands. They'll be able to point you in the right direction." He raised his bucket of ale. "To the three of us! Outcasts all!" They each took a drink. Barver wiped the froth from his mouth. "There's an old griffin tale called The Three Outcasts," he said. "Have you heard it?"

"No," said Patch; Wren shook her head.

Barver looked wistful for a moment, then drew in a breath and frowned. "Probably better you haven't," he said. "It doesn't end well."

16

Marwheel Abbey

The next morning, they saw the Abbey long before they reached it. The road took them up over a high ridge, and on the descent they could see a wide expanse of farmed land with cottages dotted throughout. At the centre was a vast, ornate grey-stone building. A large central rectangular section was impressively high, and topped with densely packed spires. Around it, smaller annexes had their own profusions of smaller towers and pinnacles. The overall impression was that the architect must have had a considerable fondness for hedgehogs.

"Marwheel Abbey," said Patch. "Down there, Wren, lies the answer to your predicament."

Wren peeked out from Patch's pocket, where she was sheltering from the morning chill. She looked and nodded, returning to the pocket without a word. Patch could understand – she was nervous. There was a lot riding on this visit.

They reached the Abbey entrance – huge wooden doors, the frame intricately carved with flowers and animals. The doors were closed, and a bell-chain hung down next to the frame. When Patch pulled it a delicate tinkling came from the other side, followed by the echoing approach of footsteps.

A small inset hatch opened in the door directly in front of Patch, revealing the face of a young monk. "Yes?" said the monk.

"Would it be possible to see Brother Tobias?" said Patch.

"If you give me a moment I'll find out," said the monk. He caught sight of Barver and let out a curious noise, as if someone had trodden on a vole. He looked petrified. "Oh. I…um. Back in a minute." The hatch shut. Hurried footsteps charted his rapid retreat.

After a while, the hatch opened again revealing a different monk. He was much older, with blue, penetrating eyes on a lean and weathered face, the left side of which had a deep scar running from jawbone to forehead. With the man's gaze on him, Patch felt like a rabbit being sized up by a wolf. "I'm Brother Tobias," said the man. "Who exactly are *you,* lad?"

Patch opened his mouth, and suddenly realized that

giving his real name might not be the best idea. "Um... Henry," he said. "Henry...Smith." He felt a little wriggle in his pocket from Wren, and could almost *see* her exasperation; the way it had come out, calling himself "Archibald Fakename" would have sounded just as convincing. "And this is my friend Barver Knopferkerkle, a dracogriff."

Tobias nodded briefly to Barver, apparently unconcerned, then turned back to Patch. "I understand you wish to see me about something?"

"I'm a friend of Erner Whitlock, an Apprentice Custodian. He wrote to you about a problem regarding the victim of a curse?"

The man's eyes widened and he looked at Barver again. "Lord, really? That's one *heck* of a curse."

Patch glanced at Barver, who seemed bemused rather than offended. "No," said Patch quickly, "Barver actually *is* a dracogriff." He held open his coat; Wren poked her head out of the pocket and waved. "This is Wren. She's the one who needs your help."

"A rat, then!" said Tobias. "That's more what I was expecting. You'd better come inside."

Tobias opened the large main doors, and led them along a tall, arched corridor, which was spacious enough to give Barver no trouble moving around. Patch noticed a few fearful glances from the monks as they passed, but only a few ran off in terror.

"We've had some griffins here in our time," said Tobias. "But never a *dracogriff*. You're very welcome. Although, given recent events, you might find things a bit awkward for a while, being part dragon."

"Recent events?" said Patch.

"Yes," said Tobias. "Did you come to us from the south?" He nodded to Barver. "Did you fly?"

"A fall has left me too wounded to fly," said Barver. "For a week or two, at least."

"We came from the north," said Patch. "By road."

"Shame," said Tobias. "I'd hoped you could add to the news we've been getting from travellers on the West Road about an attack on Tiviscan Castle!"

Patch forced out a vaguely convincing gasp. "Goodness no," he said. "Was anybody hurt?"

"A dragon army assaulted the Castle, it seems," said Tobias. "The only fatalities were a few of the prisoners in the dungeons, one of whom was particularly noteworthy. The Hamelyn Piper!"

Patch gasped again. "Gosh," he said.

"The dragons finally got their wish," said Tobias. "And the Hamelyn Piper's secrets have now died with him. There's understandable anger that the Castle was attacked, but frankly the Hamelyn Piper's death is being widely celebrated. I suppose if he was ever going to reveal the truth about the children, he'd have done so by now..." They reached another set of double doors. "Ah! We're here. Come through."

The doors led outside to a walled garden. A solitary monk tended some of the plants, and looked anxiously at Barver.

"It's okay, Brother Jessop," said Tobias. "There's no reason to be scared."

"Morning," said Barver. The monk nodded without a word and turned back to the plants, trembling visibly.

"The infirmary garden," said Tobias, gesturing to their surroundings. "I'm a Healer, or at least I try to be. I've been running the Abbey infirmary for some years now, and we grow as many of the key herbs here as we can. Sit, sit."

There were stone benches in the middle of the garden. Patch and Tobias sat on them, while Barver hunkered down on the ground. Wren emerged from Patch's pocket and came out onto the bench. She stretched. *Come on then*, she signed. *Get down to business.*

Patch nodded. "So, Apprentice Whitlock wrote to you and explained?"

"That he had met someone who had been shape-shifted by a Sorcerer's curse," said Tobias. "That's the essence of it, yes?"

"It is," said Patch. "Rundel Stone himself suggested your name as Wren's best chance of finding a cure."

"Yes," said Brother Tobias, sounding annoyed. "Whitlock mentioned he was Rundel's Apprentice. I'm afraid, Wren, that you have come here with false expectations. I sent a reply to Apprentice Whitlock telling him as much, but not soon enough to save you a journey."

Wren sagged, and Patch didn't know what to say.

"What?" said Barver. "You can't just snatch away the girl's hope like that!"

Brother Tobias shook his head in sorrow. "I'm sorry. Rundel had someone else in mind, I suspect. Someone we both used to know."

"It sounds like you and Rundel Stone are old friends," said Barver.

"Old friends?" said Tobias. "Rundel doesn't really *do* friends. We were colleagues. But it was this *other* person I spoke of that is the true expert in matters of sorcery. I think Rundel sent you to me in the belief that I could take you to them, but I cannot. I made a solemn vow, a long time ago." Wren was staring ahead of herself, tears falling. Brother Tobias looked at her, a pained expression on his face. "I really am sorry, Wren."

"Please," said Patch. "Tell us where this expert is, we'll go and ask directly."

Brother Tobias looked at Wren and seemed torn for a moment, but he shook his head. "That's not going to work," he said. "Even if I broke my vow and told you, it would do you no good. The danger is too great. It's complicated, but there you have it. For your own safety, I'm not going to say any more. There are others who I think can help, however. Let me gather what information I can, and give you a list of names."

Patch put his hands out to Wren; she hopped onto them and went to his coat pocket to curl up.

Barver let out a deep sigh. "Well then, we must seek a cure elsewhere. Brother Tobias, we would appreciate those names as soon as possible."

"I think they are all a considerable distance away, I'm afraid," said Tobias.

"Not a problem," said Barver. "If I'm flight-ready soon, I'll take her wherever she needs to go."

Wren peeked out of the pocket and wiped away a tear. She shook her head. *You have your mother's last wish to deal with*, she signed. *I'm not going to make you delay that.*

"Nonsense," said Barver. He looked at Tobias. "Any hot springs around here? That tends to sort me out quick-smart."

"No hot springs," said Tobias. "But I'm sure we can do better than that." He called to the monk who was still tending the plants. "Brother Jessop? Could you find Brother Duffle and ask him to come out here?" Brother Jessop seemed only too happy to go. "Brother Duffle has experience with non-human healing. I insist you stay and let him help you, Barver. The Abbey can extend all of you hospitality for a few days."

Barver nodded. "I'd be very grateful," he said. He reached for his money purse and pulled out a coin. "I'll make a donation, naturally. Also, if there's any stitching or darning to be done I'll be only too happy to help."

Tobias gave him an odd look. "Uh…okay. The money is very much appreciated. The infirmary has been dealing with an outbreak of firefoot recently, various supplies are depleted. This will help considerably."

At that, a plump monk bearing an overwhelmingly excited expression entered the garden, heading straight for Barver.

"It's true!" cried the monk. He took Barver's hand and shook it repeatedly. "A dracogriff! Welcome! Welcome!"

"Brother Duffle," said Tobias. "This is Barver, our visiting dracogriff, and his friends, Henry and Wren – she is human, the victim of a Sorcerer's curse. A recent fall has left Barver unable to fly, and I thought you might take a look?"

"Absolutely!" said the monk. "Tell me, Barver, can you spread your wings a moment?" Barver did as asked, and Brother Duffle spent a few minutes looking over his new patient. As he did, he mumbled to himself. "I see, I see," he said at last.

"And your prognosis?" said Barver.

Duffle shook his head and tutted. "You've not been taking very good care of yourself! Your shoulder is in terrible shape, your wing skin is peppered with wounds that have never healed fully, and I suspect you've torn every muscle in your body at least once in your life."

Barver nodded, impressed. "You seem to know your stuff, Brother," he said. "But can you get me flying again soon?"

"Indeed!" said Duffle. "A poultice of my own creation will make short work of the old wounds, and a combination of hot rocks and massage will do *wonders* for your shoulder." He cleared his throat. "Um, could you just lie down for a moment, first?" Barver did, bemused. Brother Duffle stood beside Barver's head and took hold of his wing above the shoulder. "Just hold still," said Duffle. "This might… tickle." With unexpected force, he wrenched the wing back then pushed it forward.

There was a deeply unpleasant crunching sound, and Barver howled. He stood at once and backed away, glaring angrily at the monk. Brother Duffle toppled over, but the smile on his face was as broad as ever, and it soon widened even further – Barver started to move his shoulder, and suddenly grinned. "Good gods," said Barver. "What on earth did you just do?"

Duffle looked immensely chuffed. "Your *secundum humeri* had a dislocated *alae vallo*," he said. "Could have been like that for ages. I'm surprised you hadn't noticed."

"I have no idea what you just said," said Barver, stretching out his wings. "But you, Brother Duffle, are a genius!"

At the request of Brother Tobias, Brother Duffle led them out of the gardens and round to the side of the Abbey, which was dotted with a ramshackle collection of smaller stone buildings. He walked up to one and opened the door, revealing a large interior with a crudely built fireplace in one wall. Half the room was taken up by assorted piles of wooden boxes.

"The pigsties!" said Brother Duffle, smiling. "Oh, don't worry, we've not kept pigs at the Abbey for at least forty years. A fireplace was added so it could be habitable when necessary, although now it's mainly used for storage. Hence the boxes."

Barver peered into the nearest box and pulled out a piece of cloth, on which was embroidered "Grettings frum Marwel Abey". He looked in another box and pulled out a small misshapen lump of wood that, eventually, he identified as a model of the Abbey itself. A very *bad* model. "What is all this?" he asked.

"Souvenirs," said Duffle. "Handkerchiefs, little Abbey models, and other stuff. Some of our Brothers spend their days making them, and we sell them to visitors as a way to increase the Abbey's funds. Anything that's not quite up to scratch, we put in here. We might try and fix them, or, well...find another use." He gestured to the fireplace. "The Abbot often says that a wasteful heart is the first step to evil! Although please don't burn anything saleable."

"Understood," said Patch.

"I'll arrange a sleeping mat and bedding for later, and some candles," said Duffle. "For now, settle in and rest your weary feet. Barver, I'll return with my poultice shortly, and we can begin the rest of your treatment. The muscles in your shoulder will need a few days to settle before you can risk flight, but you'll soon be on the road to recovery." He bade farewell and left.

Barver chuckled to himself, moving his shoulder in circles and muttering, "Amazing!" every now and again.

Patch tapped gently on his coat, just where his chest pocket was. "Come on out of there," he said, gently. "Have an explore. I'm sure there'll be a nice beetle or two you can find."

Wren stuck out her head. Her eyes were still wet with tears, and her little nose was running. Patch went to the boxes and found one of the souvenir handkerchiefs. He tore a small square from one corner and gave it to her. "Here," he said. "More your size."

Wren took it and blew her nose. *I think I just want to sleep*, she signed.

"Don't be like that," said Patch. "It's not so bad. Once

Barver can fly and Tobias gives us his list, it won't take long to get you cured."

She shook her head, despairing. *But what if none of those people can help me either?*

"Nonsense," said Patch. He was trying to sound as positive as possible, even though he was thinking the same thing. What if she *was* beyond help?

A distraction was needed, so he took off his bag and rummaged for the Fox and Owls board. "You and Barver should play." Beside the board were the boxwood pieces he'd stripped ready for his new Pipe. A thought struck him, and he looked over to the models of the Abbey. Bad as they were, surely it meant the Abbey had some woodcarving knives? "Actually, I think I might pop out for a bit and see if I can borrow some tools. I can spend the time getting my Pipe made."

Will your Pipe take long? signed Wren. *I imagine it needs weeks of work.*

"Goodness no!" said Patch. "Carving it only takes a few hours. Then I can cure it and decide on a glaze." The thought of his new Pipe was giving him some much-needed optimism.

Wren blew her nose again, and set the mini-handkerchief down beside her. Suddenly, her stomach gave a little rumble. She looked up at Patch with a fragile smile on her face.

You're probably right about those beetles, she signed, and scampered off to hunt.

17

The New Pipe

Patch returned to the pigsties a few hours later. He'd managed to borrow tools from the small group of woodcarvers in the Abbey, on condition that he stayed in the workshop as he used them. His Pipe was a joy to carve, the boxwood having a particularly good texture that made it almost soap-like to work with. The central airways didn't take long to finish with the tools at hand, and the headpiece likewise was completed very quickly. This gave him plenty of time to cut the fingerholes – first the primary set, then the more intricate ones. Without feeling rushed, he took great care in their placement, although he was careful to keep his work out of sight to avoid awkward questions. As soon as he saw any of the other woodcarvers coming near, he swapped his Pipe for another piece of boxwood which he whittled into a crude bird.

Before returning to Barver and Wren he gathered a few more things he needed, including some hawthorn sticks and flat stones from the Abbey grounds. When he entered the old pigsties, an overwhelming smell assaulted his nose – a mixture of flowers, garlic, vinegar and sulphur. Barver was sprawled on the floor with his eyes closed, as Brother Duffle worked the muscles of his weakened shoulder. Some of the boxes of junk had been moved to give Barver space to spread out his wings, which were smeared in places with a greenish gloop that, presumably, was the source of the stench.

Wren, meanwhile, was dozing in front of a fire built up mainly from rejected souvenir Abbeys. They burned rather well.

Duffle nodded a greeting and stopped his massage. "That'll do for today," he said. "I'm going to make a start on an ointment for tomorrow, Barver. I have a few ideas I want to try." Barver opened his eyes, rose onto all fours and folded up his wings. He stretched, and an alarming crack came from his spine. "No, no!" said Duffle. "You should stay flat for a while longer. Your back is much more delicate than you think!" He lifted his near-empty poultice jar and went to the door. "See you tomorrow," he said, and left.

"See you, Brother Duffle," Barver called as the door closed. "Successful day, Patch? Or should I say, *Henry Smith*?" He winked.

"It went extremely well," said Patch. He set down his bag and produced his newly-carved Pipe, then played a simple scale and nodded, very happy with the sound. "I'm going to start the curing process now. How's your treatment coming along?"

Barver brought one wing up to his face and licked at the green gloop. "It's certainly *delicious*," he said, then grinned. "Brother Duffle gets *so* cross when I eat his poultice. It's doing my wings the world of good, I must say. Duffle told me it's laundry day tomorrow, so I'm going to sit in the laundry house and soak up some steam. It's the nearest thing to hot springs he can manage. A few more days, and he says I can try a small flight." He stretched his wings out as wide as the room allowed. "My shoulders and wings feel better than they have in years." He took another lick of the green poultice. "I know I shouldn't, but I just can't resist. It's too tasty."

Wren sat up and gave a big yawn. *I'll take your word for it*, she signed with a grimace.

"This from the one who loves maggots and beetles," said Patch, moving to the fireplace, where the model Abbeys burned brightly. He took the poker and tongs from beside the hearth and spread the Abbeys out. Once the fire was less fierce, he added his hawthorn and made a little chamber using the flat stones.

Is this for curing your Pipe? signed Wren.

"It is," said Patch. He produced a pot of sandy earth and poured half into the chamber, then laid his Pipe inside and covered it with the other half. He added a few more Abbeys around the sides, and sat back, pleased with his work. "An hour in there, and the Pipe will almost be done." From outside came the tolling of the Abbey's bells. "That's dinner time!" he said. "I'm off to the refectory. You want me to bring a bucket of anything back, Barver?"

"Yesterday's feast will last me a week," said Barver, licking more poultice. "I really shouldn't snack."

Bring some for me, signed Wren. *I've already eaten all the beetles I could find.*

When Patch returned from the meal an hour later, Barver was sleeping in front of the fire, with Wren curled up beside him. She greeted Patch with a wave, and ran over to see what he'd brought her – a little wooden bowl of stew, with a small hunk of bread. She tucked in as Patch checked on his curing Pipe. He prodded the stones and the sandy earth spilled out. With his hand wrapped in the bottom edge of his tunic he removed the Pipe and let it cool for a few minutes before examining it carefully.

"A good result," he said, testing various combinations of fingering. The notes from the Pipe were steady. "I've borrowed a pot of varnish, so I can get the glaze done once

I've sorted out the other ingredients." He reached for his bag and took out the varnish. As he did, the folded Mask of the Hamelyn Piper clattered to the floor.

Barver opened his eyes and sat up. "Can I take another look at that?" he asked. Patch handed it to him. Barver twisted the rectangle, opening it out into the Mask and studying it. "To think, this was created by Casimir himself! My mother read me the stories of the Eight, and I think he was my favourite!"

"I didn't think dragons were interested in the Eight," said Patch.

"Not usually," said Barver. "But my mother certainly was." He had a dreamy look in his eye as he spoke. "At first, news of the Eight was only rumour – a special team assembled to find the Hamelyn Piper and bring him to justice! It was an exciting idea for a young dracogriff, all that adventure and intrigue... But it was only once they'd succeeded that the tales of their adventures started to come out. Every week, it seemed, a new part of their exploits would be told! With her position as an advisor to the Triumvirate, my mother got copies of the pamphlets as they appeared, and I still remember them all. First was *The Call*, when the Pipers' Council brought in a dozen of the greatest heroes they could find, and tested them. Lord Drevis – a Virtus in the Custodian Elite at the time, not a member of the Council – was chosen to lead them, and one by one the heroes proved their worth or were shown lacking, leaving the Eight we all know. Next was *The Terror of Imminus Rock*, where the Eight hoped to find a great Sorcerer to help them, but discovered instead an island full of monsters! And then came *The Caves of Casimir*, where—"

"Okay, okay," said Patch, laughing. "I was only three when it was happening and too young to understand, but by the time I was seven I knew every chapter back to front. My nan must have been tired of reading them to me."

I loved those stories, signed Wren. *Our village had a copy of the collected pamphlets.*

"*Palafox, Corrigan, Kellenfas, Stone*," said Barver, reciting the names of the Eight. "*Casimir, Hinkelman, Drevis and Throne.* Casimir was so mysterious! A Piper who spent decades trying to understand sorcery, and called himself the Sorcerer Engineer."

Wren nodded with enthusiasm, but Patch decided not to comment. While Casimir had created the Mask and various other useful magical devices, Patch reckoned that the sheer courage and Piping skills of Stone, Palafox and Corrigan had been more important.

Barver went to the boxes at the back of the room and took a handkerchief, using it to rub at the Mask. "There are fine symbols engraved on the inner side," he said. "I don't recognize them. Do you?" He passed it back to Patch, who looked closely at the parts Barver had cleaned up.

"They're an old runic language," said Patch. "No idea what it says, but... Oh, that's interesting." In the places Barver had cleaned, the darkness in the engraved lines was glinting. "I'd thought it was just dirt in the engraving," he said. "It's not." He passed the Mask back to Barver.

"What, then?" said Barver, examining it.

"I think the letters are inlaid with obsidiac," said Patch.

At once Barver let go of the Mask, dropping it as if it was red hot. "*Black diamond*," he said, sounding angry.

Wren looked confused. *Black diamond?* she signed.

"It's the dragon name for obsidiac," said Barver. "The first humans to chance upon it in the Dragon Territories thought it was ordinary obsidian, just simple volcanic glass. But soon they realized it had magical properties, and because it was only ever found in the lands of dragons they called it 'drac-obsidian', a name which eventually became 'obsidiac'." He shook his head slowly. "Dragons, though, have long known that it is a dark, evil substance. Corrupting. Black diamond is a much more suitable name. Just as diamond is a rare form of beauty, black diamond is a rare form of darkness."

Patch picked the Mask up again, and fetched the knife from his bag. He used the tip of the blade to scratch at the dark glints in the runes. "Not leaving a mark," he said. "Pretty sure it's obsidiac."

Barver scowled.

Why do you hate it so much? signed Wren.

Barver sat down in front of the fire again, and added some more model Abbeys. For a moment he watched the flames in silence, then he looked at Patch and Wren with sorrow-filled eyes. "For dragons, black diamond is so dangerous it's something only the *gods* can use. Digging it up is a kind of blasphemy."

"I thought you weren't religious," said Patch.

"I'm not," said Barver. "But most dragons *are*. There is an uneasy peace between humans and dragons, but there are those who dream of more, of cooperation and coexistence, working together. Truly sharing this world. Black diamond makes this impossible."

What do you mean? signed Wren.

"Humans come to the Dragon Territories to steal black diamond, and dragons hate them for the blasphemous theft. Dragons *burn* the humans caught stealing it, and humans hate them for the killing. Black diamond creates a circle of hatred. The world would be a better place without it."

He fell silent again, watching the fire.

Wren turned to Patch. *When I was the Sorcerer's captive,* she signed, *I read some of the books in his castle. One mentioned an old legend that obsidiac could give unnaturally long life. Is it truly that powerful?*

Patch shook his head. "Don't believe everything you

read. Sorcerers are *famous* for wasting their lives looking for immortality. It is very powerful, though. An obsidiac-glazed Pipe is supposed to be as good as they come. The obsidiac is powdered and flaked, then bound in a resin varnish and used as a Pipe glaze." Absently, Patch started looking closely at the Mask again.

"Don't even think about it," growled Barver.

"Oh, I doubt I could remove it from the grooves," said Patch, still looking at the Mask. "It's known for being extremely tough, so unless I—" He trailed off, the tone of Barver's warning finally sinking in. "No," he said. "Of course not."

There was a cold silence.

After a few moments, Wren broke the tension. *What else can you use as a glaze?* she asked.

"Some flowers are good," said Patch, flustered. "But they have to be fresh. This time of year, the ash of feathers might be the best bet."

Feathers? asked Wren.

"Yes," said Patch. "Eagles are particularly effective." He frowned, wondering where he would get any.

"Eagle, hmm?" said Barver, his voice softer now. "How about *griffin* feather?"

"That's good too," said Patch. "Falcons as well, and buzzards. Has to be carnivores, you see, and—" He stopped, the penny dropping. "Ah," he said.

Barver was holding up three of his own feathers. "How many do you need?" he asked.

The following morning, Barver was awake the moment the dawn bells sounded.

"What's got into you?" said Patch, yawning. "Don't fancy a lie-in?"

"I'm off to the laundry," said Barver. "They get the fires lit early, so the water's hot by now. The laundry room fills with steam, Brother Duffle told me. I'll get half an hour before they need me out to get the laundry started. It'll do me the world of good."

"Well, I'll see you later," said Patch. With Barver gone, Patch went to where he'd hung his Pipe after glazing it the night before. The glaze, with its dracogriff-feather ash, had given the Pipe a rich dark colour, a deep reddish brown that Patch hadn't seen on a Pipe before. He touched it to test the varnish. "Dry!" he said, excited. He gave it a look over, then put it to his lips and played a few scales. "Good tone," he said. "Let's see if dracogriff feathers are up to the job!" He thought for a moment about which Song he should try. "A Lift, perhaps?" he said. "Yes. A Lift!"

And what's that? asked Wren, emerging from the folds of the blanket she'd spent the night in.

"Battle Pipers do it a lot," said Patch. "Lifts the mood.

Raises morale." He paused, thinking back. "When I told you about the ceremony at Tiviscan, and the moment I learned I wasn't to join the Custodian Elite, you asked me what branch of the Elite they'd offered me. I didn't give you an answer."

I noticed, signed Wren. *I figured you'd tell me when you were ready.*

Patch nodded, feeling sombre. "It was the Battle Elite. That was the branch that wanted me."

Not something you would consider? asked Wren.

"With Battle Piping, there are Songs with the power of cannon fire; Songs to set distant tents ablaze. But it's the Songs that increase hatred and bloodlust that are most valued. And I was so good at playing Songs that affect people, you see. That's why they wanted me. I'd dreamed of making a difference in the world, Wren. Making people better at *killing* each other wasn't what I'd had in mind."

Wren thought for a moment, then smiled. *I'm proud of you*, she signed.

"Thank you," said Patch. "Although I wish I'd just told them as much, rather than insulting them all and running away." He shook his head, then looked pointedly at Wren. "So...do I have a volunteer for the Lift?"

What, me? signed Wren. *No chance. That's an untested Pipe!*

"Oh come on, you're perfectly safe. The chances of a new Pipe actually going *wrong* are tiny."

Find another idiot to try it on, she replied. She scurried over to the door, pointing through a knothole. *One of them*, she signed. *They always look like they could do with a bit of cheering up.*

Patch joined her and crouched low to peer out. There was the usual solemn flow of monks, mostly individuals, sometimes pairs, quietly making their steady way around the Abbey in the time left to them before morning service. "I don't know," said Patch, although it appealed to a mischievous part of his mind. "A new Pipe is usually pretty weak. It might be hard to tell if it worked." He felt something tickle his hand, and looked down to see an ant crawling over it. "Aha!" he said. "Perfect."

Wren was sceptical. *How do you tell if an ant's morale improves?* she signed.

"Trust me," said Patch. "Ants are always good for practice. Plus I can keep my playing nice and quiet."

Fine, signed Wren. *Just make sure I'm not part of your experiment.*

"Don't worry," said Patch. "Stay beside me, we won't be affected. With things like the Lift it's a simple matter of moderating the direction, range and nature of your subject, to guarantee that the Song doesn't spill out beyond the desired target. Easy peasy."

Easy? signed Wren. *Isn't that what happened to make the villagers dance in Patterfall?*

Patch winced at the thought. "That was a lapse of concentration," he said. "Could happen to anyone." After carefully placing the ant in the middle of the room, he put his Pipe to his lips, furrowed his brow, then started to play.

The Lift was a very simple Song at its core, and Patch had always been good at it. No wonder, really – it shared many of its patterns with the Dance, although it didn't *direct* the subject in any way and was much less potent. All it did was perk them up, and the resulting effect varied considerably from subject to subject.

Patch built up the heart of the Song. It took him back to the days when he'd sat in the woods by his grandparents' home, whistling and seeing the effect it had on the wildlife as they drew near, intrigued and playful.

The little ant, which had started to march back towards the doorway, stopped. Its tiny head tilted up slowly, then moved down again; then up, then down. It started walking once more, but there was a definite *swing* to the motion, left and right, and it sped up and slowed down to the Song's rhythm. It began to take an extra little step to each side as it went, and from time to time it turned in a circle on the spot. It continued in the same way until it reached the door.

Wren looked at it, delighted. *That's one happy ant*, she signed. The ant tapped out the music for a moment, then made its way under the door and outside. Wren watched its progress through the knothole. Suddenly she turned back to Patch. *Hold on,* she signed. *I think your Song has spilled out a little!*

Patch stopped playing, and the Song faded gently. "Oooh, listen to that," he said, distracted by the Pipe. "The sustain is impressive! It usually takes a few more—"

Wren interrupted him with a cough, and pointed at the knothole. Patch crouched down to look out again.

The monks were still making their way around the Abbey, but now their pace had picked up, oh-so-slightly; from time to time, some had a bit of a skip in their step. The clearest change, though, was that most were smiling. There were even, shockingly, a few laughs to be heard.

Did you have another lapse in concentration? signed Wren.

"Not this time," said Patch. The Pipe was silent at last, and he looked at it with genuine satisfaction. "This packs a punch, let me tell you. Dracogriff feathers are now *officially* my favourite."

How long will the Lift affect them? asked Wren.

"That depends on the monk," said Patch. "Some, I imagine, will decide that they're *far* too serious for all that smiling. Others, well…it might stay with them for a few hours." In the distance, through the meandering monks, he caught sight of someone who definitely did *not* have a smile on his face. "Look who it is," said Patch. "Brother Duffle."

Duffle had a stern expression, but there was a hint of puzzlement there, too. He paused, looking at the smiling faces of the strolling monks. He shook his head and continued, making a beeline for the pigsties.

Wren frowned. *What's troubling him?* she signed. *I hope Barver's okay!*

"What is it, Brother?" asked Patch when Duffle reached them.

"There's a dire situation," said Duffle. "Brother Tobias needs you in the infirmary, right away!"

18

Desperate Times

With Wren in his pocket, Patch followed Brother Duffle to a small room within the infirmary. On one wall were shelves of old books, bottles and containers. Brother Tobias was standing by a table on which sat various sizes of pestle and mortar, and bunches of herbs and plants in the process of preparation.

"You can leave us, Brother Duffle," said Tobias. "Thank you."

"I'll return to Barver," said Duffle. "Some light massage as he takes in the steam, I think."

Once Duffle had gone, Tobias gave Patch a cold look. "*Henry Smith*," he said. "An interesting choice of name. As an escaped convict, you could have spelled trouble for the Abbey, Patch Brightwater!"

Patch felt his ears redden, but before he could ask how Brother Tobias had learned the truth, the monk turned and left the room through a second doorway. As he went, Patch could see he was holding something in his hand. He almost gasped to see it – a Pipe. What was a monk doing with a Pipe?

A moment later he *did* gasp, because through the doorway Tobias had left by, someone else entered.

Erner Whitlock.

"Patch!" cried Erner, hurrying over to him. Wren emerged from Patch's pocket and climbed up to his shoulder. "It's really you! And Wren! I thought you were both *dead*!" Erner flung his arms around Patch and gave him a hug, a look of immense relief on the Apprentice Custodian's face.

When Erner let go and stood back, Patch stared at him. "Oh no," said Patch. "Oh no, oh no, oh no…"

Erner looked at him, confused. "Why do you look at me with such horror? I can't tell you how thankful I am to see you alive! Virtus Stone and I were travelling to Yarmingly when news came through of the attack on Tiviscan. We heard that the Hamelyn Piper was dead, and that some prisoners had died too. Including the young lad who'd only just been locked away, they said! The Piper of Patterfall!" He shook his head, clearly distressed. "An awful thing to hear, Patch. *Awful*. When we arrived at the Abbey just an hour ago, Brother Tobias told me that Wren was here, accompanied by a dracogriff and a young lad calling himself Henry Smith—" Erner shook his head, smiling now. "I didn't dare hope, but here you are. Both of you!" When Patch and Wren still said nothing, Erner's confusion returned. "But still you look at me so strangely—"

Patch's mouth felt horribly dry. He kept glancing at the door, expecting Rundel Stone to enter at any moment. "Don't you understand? You've found me alive, and it's your duty to see me delivered back to the dungeons! Where is your master, anyway? I would have thought Rundel Stone would be *incredibly* pleased to be able to slap some manacles on me!"

Erner's smile dropped away. "My duty…yes. Perhaps it is. In all the relief of seeing you, it hadn't occurred to me. But Patch, please…I'll not tell a soul, not even the Virtus. Stay as Henry Smith, and you'll be safe. Nobody will know!"

Wren tutted. *Brother Tobias already knows*, she signed.

"Oh, ah, yes," said Erner, wincing. "Brother Tobias. I'm sorry. I blurted it all out when he told me you were here, Wren. I'll tell nobody else!"

"I know you mean well," said Patch, still glancing nervously at the doorway. "But Virtus Stone would never allow such a thing. Where is he, anyway?"

And what was the dire situation we were told about? signed Wren. *Was that just a trick, to get Patch to come here?*

Erner shook his head, looking grim. "No trick," he said. "You see, things have become rather complicated." He walked to the doorway. "Follow me, and I'll explain."

Erner led them through to the main part of the infirmary. Twenty simple beds were in a long hall, and each bed was full – there were men and women, old and young, being tended by three monks.

At the far end of the hall was a curtained area, and from there Patch could hear the sound of a Pipe. Once they reached the curtain, Erner pulled it aside. By the wall was a bed, and sitting on its edge was Brother Tobias, playing the Pipe he'd carried out with him.

Patch listened, impressed by the complexity of the Song Tobias played – a healing Song, and far more intricate than any he'd ever managed to learn. "Wow," he said.

Erner nodded. "Impressive, isn't it?" he said, his voice barely above a whisper. "Brother Tobias was a Piper before he took holy orders. He could make a fine living, yet he's chosen a life in the Abbey and to give his skills for free."

For the first time, Patch turned his eyes to the patient lying in the bed, and he almost jumped. There lay Rundel Stone, his eyes closed and his skin horribly pale. "What happened to him?" said Patch.

"We were called to the village of Yarmingly," said Erner.

"There had been a death, and the dead man was a close friend of the Virtus. The cause of death was obvious, and gruesome – several blows to the back of the head. We'd been there only a few minutes when Virtus Stone cried out and collapsed to the ground. Half-conscious, he ordered me to bring him here. I had to stop often and play a healing Song, just to keep him alive. Brother Tobias and his monks have treated him since, but he has not woken, and the cause of his condition is a mystery."

Brother Tobias stopped playing and beckoned them. "Quickly, Erner! He's coming round!"

Erner rushed to the bedside; Patch moved to follow, but Wren squeaked at him from his shoulder.

You should keep your distance, she signed. *Better Stone doesn't see you!*

Stone gave a spluttering cough, and opened his eyes.

"Virtus!" said Erner. "It's me, Apprentice Whitlock! Can you tell me what caused your collapse?"

Stone gripped Erner's arm. "An *enigma enicatus*!" he said, struggling for breath. "A death puzzle. A *box*, Erner. A small metal box. I found it under a book on the floor, near to where Ural lay dead. I felt its sting as I grasped it and realized my mistake too late!"

Ural…thought Patch. The name of Stone's dead friend was somehow familiar, but he couldn't quite place it.

Brother Tobias checked Stone's hand. "There! A small

mark, some kind of needle." He looked at Erner. "Did you see the box he speaks of?"

"Well, I did find this on the floor near the Virtus," said Erner. He reached into his pocket and pulled out a small metal cube, about an inch across.

"Don't touch it!" cried Stone. He knocked the box from Erner's hand. The effort was too much for him – he slumped back, and his eyes closed.

Erner looked at Tobias, shaking his head. "I already *did* touch it, Tobias, yet it did nothing to me."

"Death puzzles have specific targets," said Tobias. "You touched it without incident, but Rundel was stung. That means *he* was a target." He rushed to his room and returned with wooden tongs and a jar. He picked the metal cube from the floor and dropped it inside the jar, then held it up for a clear view.

Stone opened his eyes again, straining to speak. "Identify its targets, and you find the killer!"

"Forget finding the killer," said Brother Tobias. "Your *life* is the priority now, Rundel. Healing Songs can keep you alive for a time, but I fear I can't treat this, not fully. There's sorcery at work here." He paused. "You suspected as much, Rundel. You didn't come here to get help from me – you came to get help from *her*. Didn't you!"

Wren frowned at Patch. *Her?* she signed. *Who does he mean?*

"Yes," said Stone. "I sensed it was no simple poison. A Sorcerer's poison, needing a Sorcerer for the cure. You know where you must take me!"

Tobias looked away. "You're asking too much!"

"Please, Tobias!" cried Stone. "*Please!*" He tensed and cried out in agony, then went limp.

Tobias examined him. "Unconscious," he said. "And refusing to die. Stubborn as ever." He shook his head and hit the nearby wall in frustration. "That settles it, we have no choice." He looked directly at Patch. "I only pray that the expert we both seek has the answers we require."

"The expert we *both* seek?" said Patch. "Both?"

Tobias nodded. "You'll be coming as well. Wren's best hope is also Rundel's. I told you there was too much danger, and I meant it, but now Rundel's life is on the brink. Where we're headed, your dracogriff friend will keep us safe, to a point. We must leave at once. It's a full day's journey by horse, Erner, and while we're gone you must stay here and play that healing Song, to the best of your ability, for one hour out of every four. It'll be gruelling work, but it's the only thing that will keep Rundel alive. Can you manage it?"

"I can," said Erner.

"And, um, where exactly are *we* going?" said Patch.

"You've heard of the Gemspar Range?" said Tobias.

Patch frowned. His training had involved studying notoriously treacherous locations throughout the world, and the Gemspar Range was high on that list. "Home of vicious criminals, and unbounded danger," he said. "It has quite a reputation. There's also the mythical Witch who, legend says, makes the central peak of the range her home – Gemspar Mountain itself! A foreboding craggy deathtrap, by all accounts."

"Afraid of old myths, are you?" said Tobias.

"Oh please," said Patch. "I know there's no actual *Witch*, but the Gemspar Range is a hostile place, home to the worst smugglers and wrongdoers in the land. The Witch was just a story to frighten people away from the area. But those are all pretty *scary* old myths, Brother Tobias. Even *you* have to admit it."

"I'll grant they're unpleasant tales," said Tobias.

"Unpleasant?" scoffed Patch. "Horrible murders, horrible monsters, a horrible warty old hag of a Witch! Kept me up at night, some of those tales. She was said to have extra joints in her arms that she could make grow a hundred feet long. Her enemies would be strangled in their beds with their doors locked, the only clue being a sprinkling of soot from the fireplace. Her eyes were supposed to shine bright in the dark, so you could see her blink in the depths of the forest." He shivered. "Besides brigands, I'm surprised *anyone* wants to make their home somewhere so creepy! Your *expert* must really like privacy."

"That is certainly true," said Tobias. "She *absolutely* does."

"So, um, who exactly are we going to see?" said Patch, an awful feeling stirring in his guts.

Brother Tobias widened his eyes. "We're off to see the Witch of Gemspar Mountain!" he said.

Patch whimpered.

19
GEMSPAR

The Abbey possessed only five horses, and the group took three of them. Patch was given the smallest, a friendly black and white mare. He tied his bag to his saddle, and Wren opted to sit on his shoulder rather than be cooped up for the journey in his pocket. As well as Tobias, they were joined by a burly monk called Brother Madder, who was armed with a decidedly un-monkly broadsword.

Barver was reluctantly dragged from the warmth of his steam treatment, and looked rather grumpy when Brother Duffle led him to the front of the Abbey to join the others.

"Be careful!" Duffle told him. "Absolutely no flying, and if you *must* kill any brigands, don't strain your shoulder in the process."

"Okay, okay, I promise," said Barver, and Duffle waved

him farewell. Barver looked at Patch and Wren. "Bit of a rude awakening to have to leave that lovely heat and come out here," he said. "Duffle was vague about where we're going. Can you fill me in on the details?"

Wren told him everything. When she got to the part about the Witch, Barver went strangely quiet.

The presence of Barver unsettled the horses a little, so he kept himself to the back of their column, with Patch next, then Tobias, and Madder leading. They kept up a rapid pace, riding mostly in silence.

They stopped to rest only once, letting the horses drink from a stream and graze its banks. Patch took his Pipe from his pocket to take a look at some of the lowest finger holes – while playing the Lift earlier, he'd felt some rough edges on the mouthpiece that he needed to fix, but he'd not had a chance to deal with it until now. He used the tip of his knife to gently smooth the wood.

Brother Tobias approached him. "Ah!" he said. "Erner Whitlock told me you were a trainee Piper before you were put in the dungeons. I suggest you put your Pipe away, though. I have my Pipe with me, too, but I'll only use it if the worst comes to the worst. Be in no doubt: *Barver* is our protection in Gemspar. The brigands there have evaded capture from the Custodian Elite for a very long time. Anyone they see with a Pipe is likely to have a dozen arrows in them before a single note can be played. A dracogriff will give them reason to stay well clear of us."

Patch nodded. Before they set off, he made sure to put his Pipe in his bag.

By afternoon they could see the peaks of the Gemspar Range, and by evening they had reached the forest on the slopes of the first of the mountains. The path was rough, growing narrower with each passing mile, as the forest grew thicker.

Brother Madder held up his hand for the party to stop. "From here on," he told them, "there must be absolute silence. If anyone sees anything suspicious, they should draw my attention by clapping their hands together twice."

"And, um, what are we looking for?" asked Patch.

"Brigands. Bandits. Thieves," said Madder. "Given Barver's presence, anyone who attacks us will have to be especially crazed. That would make them especially *dangerous*."

Barver raised a hand. "I want to clarify the rules of engagement," he said. "Is fire breathing okay?"

"Feel free," said Madder.

"And am I allowed to *eat* anyone who attacks us?"

"Absolutely," said Madder, with a sly grin.

Patch and Wren stared at Barver. The dracogriff shrugged. "I'm kidding!" he said, although they weren't sure if he was.

From then on, Patch scanned the gloomy forest constantly. He saw nothing with his eyes, but his mind spotted dozens of non-existent, cut-throat villains hiding behind every trunk, every bush, every pine cone, every leaf. He broke out in a sweat as his anxiety grew.

The peaks of the Gemspar Range towered above, but it was another hour before the razor-jag tip of Gemspar Mountain itself became visible: bare black rock that seemed to cut and slice at the sky.

Behind him Patch could hear Barver's stomach gurgle continuously, the only sound coming from his otherwise stealthy friend. Patch slowed, dropping back a little from the others, and turned to Barver. Heeding Brother Madder's earlier warning of silence, he used hand speech.

Are you okay? he asked.

I think it's Brother Duffle's poultice, answered Barver. He rubbed his belly, looking queasy. *I don't think it agreed with me.*

Do you need to rest?

Barver shook his head. *It'll pass*, he signed, and sure enough it did seem to settle down.

The forest path began to weave as they ventured through a valley deep in the Range. Steep climbs became precarious drops, and the path led them through twisting high-walled gullies that Barver was only just able to fit through.

The narrow path, with high trees all round and little sky to see, gave Patch an increasing sense of claustrophobia. Then, as they rounded a series of tight bends, a clearing lay ahead. Patch smiled with relief and turned round to look at Barver.

Barver wasn't there.

Terrified, Patch clapped his hands twice. At the head of the group, Brother Madder turned and stared, seeing at once that their main protection had vanished. He guided his horse to Patch.

"Where is he?" whispered Madder.

"I don't know," said Patch. "He was behind me a minute ago."

Madder eyed the trees warily and went back around the bends they'd just passed. After a few moments he returned. "No sign of him," said Madder, his intense gaze darting around the trees. "We may be in trouble."

"You think somebody—" said Patch, disbelieving.

Wren was horrified. *Somebody nobbled Barver?* she signed. *How?*

"To the clearing, quickly!" said Madder, taking his horse to the front and picking up speed.

It was too late.

The vegetation around them erupted into life. Fifty well-armed bandits burst from behind every tree and bush, with a huge cry of "*Yaaaaarrgh!*"

They were caked in grime, and a smell like month-old pigswill filled the air. The bandits shook their various weapons at the travellers, growling menacingly as the leader stepped forward and addressed their victims. He was especially grubby, his hair long and matted, his blackening teeth on display as he grinned. Patch very slowly started to reach back to his bag; despite the warning Tobias had given, if they'd hurt Barver he was going to try and take out some of them before he was disarmed.

"Welcome to our forest, wanderers!" said the leader. His fellow robbers jeered and waggled their blades some more. "A dangerous forest, too! It's lucky that we chanced on you this day!" Another jeer came, with some coughing from the less-healthy members of the group. "Me and my friends wish to offer you protection against the evils here. A basilisk walks the woods!" A mock-scared "Wooooo!" came from the bandits. "An evil Witch haunts the mountain!" An "Ahhhhhh!" from the thieves. "Worst of all, the most feared band of murderous villains also prowls these parts!"

He paused for dramatic effect.

"And that's *us*!" he said, flourishing his sword as the brigands cheered long and loud. "Who better to offer you protection from our blood-keen knives, friends, than we ourselves? So if you would, a simple fee!" He paused again, and the grinning outlaws looked at him with anticipation, waiting for the punchline. "*All you have!*" cried the gloating leader, as every blade – long sword, short sword, knife and dagger – moved in to point steadily at the travellers, each blade-tip no more than a foot from flesh.

Patch's hand froze halfway to his bag. He looked at the brigand whose sword-tip was nearest his throat, and slowly brought his hand back to his horse's reins. Playing a Pipe would be *much* harder without fingers.

Madder, his broadsword half-drawn, gave an angry growl and shook his head. "Without Barver we have no chance," he muttered. He put the sword back in its scabbard and reached into his cassock, producing a small pouch. He threw it to the bandit leader. "Take it, and let us be on our way!"

The leader caught the pouch and looked at the contents. He raised an eyebrow. "This is all you have?" he said. "I think not!" He stroked his chin for a moment then suddenly looked at Madder's horse, pretending to be surprised. "Goodness!" he said. "A horse! And another! And a third! These should cover your fee, I think." The malice in his voice was matched by that in his eyes.

Madder gritted his teeth. "So if we give you our horses too, we can go on our way?"

"*If* you give us your horses? When we *take* your horses, then we'll see! Right, lads?" A sinister cheer came from his fellows.

"Might I ask what you did with our companion?" said Madder. "Is he alive?"

"Companion?" said the leader. "What companion?" He dismissed Madder's question with a shake of his head, and at that moment spotted Wren on Patch's shoulder. She was standing defiantly with her arms folded, glaring. The leader was fascinated. "What on *earth* is that?" he asked, then smiled. "What curious markings!"

From behind him another bandit – face wide with fear – cried out: "Dragon!"

The leader turned to him with a look of complete scorn. "Don't be stupid, man!" he said. "It's obviously a rat!"

But by then all of his men were staring past him with widening eyes, their bravado gone. Patch and Wren turned to see, and grinned: Barver was striding around the bend in the path. His expression was one of outrage – although, Patch saw, there was also a hint of glee at the reaction he was getting.

The dracogriff stopped, eyeing up the terrified brigands who, for now, seemed rooted to the spot. "If you've hurt any of my friends," cried Barver, "I will have to eat you. *Alive.*" There was a moment of silence, broken only by one or two sobs of dread. Barver let rip with a huge burst of flame and a thunderous roar, then charged forward. The thieves scattered at once, squealing like piglets as they fled.

Barver had set his sights on the leader. He seized the man by his feet and dangled him upside down. "I wonder how *you'll* taste," he said, leering.

"They're all fine!" cried the leader. "Your pals! All fine! Just our little…joke! Yes! A joke!"

But they weren't *quite* all fine. The horses had been seriously scared by Barver's fiery entrance, and were in a panic – particularly Patch's, which was hurtling around the perimeter of the clearing, whinnying in terror.

Patch was barely able to hang on to the reins; Wren was off his shoulder and clinging on for dear life to the saddle. The horse wasn't slowing – indeed, each time it caught a glance of Barver, the animal managed to go even faster. Patch reached back to his bag, trying to grip the horse with his legs so he wouldn't fall. At last, his fingers wrapped round his Pipe.

"Yes!" he cried, almost losing his balance. "Don't worry, Wren! I've got this!"

There was a Battle Song he knew, one that could be used against cavalry. It slowed a horse down, whatever the plans of the rider or the horse. Patch quickly looped the reins round his left arm and gripped even harder with his legs, leaving his hands free to Pipe. "Hold on tight!" he said to Wren. Her little face grimaced with effort as she clung to the saddle.

This was no time to be subtle, he knew; he went for it, and built the Song up as fast as possible. Finally, he played the key melody that would slow the horse down.

It stopped dead.

Patch kept going.

Over the horse's head he went, and the ground came up

fast to greet him with a hard, stony welcome. When his head stopped spinning, he sat up and looked behind him. There was his horse, slightly confused; and on the saddle sat Wren, giving him a thumbs up.

Patch stood, trying to ignore the pain in his shoulder and the smarting of his scraped knees. He went to the horse and took the reins, leading it back to Barver and the others.

All the brigands had abandoned their leader, who was now lying on the ground with his wrists and ankles tied, a gag in his mouth, and Madder's sword against his throat.

"So what happened to you?" Patch called to Barver.

"I had to go," said Barver, sheepish.

"What?"

"I had to *go.* Brother Duffle's poultice—" He rubbed his belly. "Sorry about that."

Wren jumped from the horse to Patch's shoulder and scowled at Barver. *We thought something had happened to you!* she signed.

"We're all okay," said Patch. "That's what matters." He looked at the brigand leader. "What do we do with him?"

Madder grinned, leering close to their captive's face. "What indeed!" he said. "All your friends have gone. And they won't be back."

The leader tried to speak through his gag. "Mmmpph!" he said. "Mmmph mmmpph!"

"A few years back I would've cut your throat on principle," said Brother Madder. "But I'm a man of God these days."

Tobias kneeled down beside him. "Maybe he can be useful," he said, pulling the gag down. "We're here to seek help from the Witch."

The leader laughed. "The Witch doesn't help people," he said. "Unless they want help to *die horribly*."

"You've met her?" said Tobias.

"None meet her and live!" said the leader. "We stay clear; she leaves us alone. You'd be wise to do the same. I've heard things screaming in the trees when I've got too close to her territory. You're idiots if you seek her out!"

Brother Madder pressed the blade of his sword a little harder against the man's throat. "Less of the backchat, scum. Is she easy to reach from here?"

"Follow the path until it splits, and you'll know which way to take. Trust me, you'll know..."

Madder took his sword away from the leader's neck and forced him to his feet. "You'd best run along now," said Madder. "Before I decide to kill you anyway. I'm sure God would grant me forgiveness if I asked nicely."

"Untie me, eh?" said the leader, his bound ankles making him wobble as he stood. "Please? Dangerous place this forest. Lots of undesirables, you know?"

Barver strode up to him and brought his head down until he was face to face with the trembling prisoner. For long seconds he studied the man. "You know what they say about the *eyes*," said Barver with a grin.

"They're the windows to the soul?" said the leader.

Barver shook his head and put the gag back over the man's mouth. "Tastiest part of the face," he said. The leader let out a muffled squeal and started hopping towards the trees, falling over every few hops. Barver watched him go, with a look of pure satisfaction.

Brother Madder swapped horses with Patch. "She knows me," said Madder, letting the animal nuzzle him. "And if I take her up to the front of the line, she'll not panic again."

Patch took Madder's horse, and went to put his Pipe in his pocket.

Tobias nodded to him. "Let me see it then, lad," he said. Patch handed the Pipe over, and Tobias examined it. "Your Song was a little stronger than needed, but given the situation it was impressive. Whitlock told me you were talented, and he was right."

"I have my moments," said Patch.

Barver tutted. "Listen to him! He's being modest. They offered him a role in the Battle Elite, but he turned it down, not wanting death and destruction to be his life."

Patch raised an eyebrow and gave Wren a pointed glance. "Do you share everything I tell you with Barver?" he said.

Friends don't have secrets, signed Wren.

"I too was in the Battle Elite," said Tobias, and Patch noticed the man's expression change suddenly, looking almost haunted. "You made the right decision, lad. The scars cut deep, and they stay with you for the rest of your days. And I don't just mean *this*." He gestured to the terrible scar that ran down the side of his face.

After another hour of travel they came to the split in the path that the leader of the brigands had told them about. On the path to the right, the forest continued without change, and songbirds perched among the leaves and tweeted happily. To the left, the trees were stunted, diseased things, the bushes spiky, and blackened by fungus. The only wildlife Patch could see were crows, sulking in large groups on leafless branches.

"Well," said Madder, with a wary smile. "He said we'd know the way to the Witch when we saw it."

They took the leftward path.

The peak of Gemspar Mountain loomed high above them. Patch felt uneasy when he looked at it, as if the sharpness of the rocks was pricking at his eyes.

As dusk approached, Brother Tobias held up his hand and called for a halt. "We're almost there I think," he said, sounding anxious.

"How should we approach her domain?" asked Brother Madder.

"The two of us will leave our horses and proceed on foot," said Tobias. He turned to the others. "The rest of you wait here. We're taking a great risk, and I can't say for certain how the Witch will react. We'll be back by dark."

With the horses tethered, Patch and his friends were happy enough to watch Tobias and Madder walk off to meet the Witch, but their nerves grew frayed as the light started to fail with no sign of the monks returning. Moonlight was all they had, lending yet another sinister edge to the forest.

What if they've been killed already? signed Wren, on Patch's shoulder. *Or eaten? Or turned inside out and rubbed with salt and then eaten? While still alive!*

"They'll be back soon," said Patch. "There's no need to worry. Barver will protect us."

From behind that tree? signed Wren.

Patch turned to look. Sure enough Barver was hiding behind a large oak, peering around it fearfully. "Oh, come out here, you big wuss," said Patch.

"I don't like it," said Barver, edging out from hiding. "All this creepy stuff. I just don't."

A low moan came from the forest ahead of them. Nobody said anything, but Patch stood up slowly and started to walk in the direction of the sound.

Wren squeaked at him. *You're going* towards *the sound?*

she signed. *Count me out.* She scurried down his leg and ran to Barver.

"It might be Tobias and Madder," whispered Patch. "Maybe they need our help." He felt for his Pipe, whatever use it might be, then remembered it was in his bag. "Barver?" he said. "Come on!"

Barver shook his head. "Uh uh," he said. "Absolutely no way."

There was another low moan, longer this time, followed by what could only be described as a *cackle.*

"Okay," said Patch. "So it's not Tobias and Madder."

Two bright circles appeared in the gloom, fifty feet from where they stood. Patch's legs wobbled. The light from the circles (Patch didn't want to think of them as *eyes*, not yet) made it easier to see the shape *around* the circles, and the two long dark lines on either side of it.

The shape was that of a bent figure. The two *very* long lines were about the width of arms, held out as if to embrace. Or to *grab.*

Patch backed away. The circles of light went off and came on again.

"It blinked!" said Barver.

The next moan was louder, longer, and far more ghastly. The cackle that followed was unmistakable. The dark figure shifted slightly, moving towards them one slow step at a time.

Patch kept backing off until he bumped into Barver, who was rigid with fear and staring at the wailing *thing* that was approaching.

Wren climbed over to Patch's shoulder again. They huddled together, the three of them, trembling and whimpering.

And the Witch of Gemspar Mountain drew ever closer.

20

The Witch

The Witch was wearing a black cowl. Its arms, ten feet long, ended in deathly white claws that twitched with each step it took. The disc-like eyes glowed in the midst of a face as craggy as the mountain itself, and under the eyes an oversized mouth gaped open, revealing discoloured teeth like ancient tombstones.

Patch could feel his sanity draining away, such was the terror he felt, and from the sound of her whimpers Wren was the same. The scariest noise of all, thought Patch, had to be Barver's hitched breaths: the dracogriff was paralysed with dread.

Then the Witch let out a hideous screech and Patch decided that no, actually, *that* was the scariest noise of all. As one, the group answered with their own long, drawn-out scream, which only faded when another voice cut through the air.

"Alia, stop it! They're with me!"

The Witch instantly halted. Without moving her mouth she answered in a voice that didn't sound anything like the cackling wails she'd been making so far: "Who said that?"

From the trees to the far left of the cowering group, Brother Tobias emerged, Brother Madder beside him.

"It's me! It's Tobias!" he said. "We need—" He paused and shook his head. "*I* need your help, Alia. Please. For old times' sake."

The Witch's long arms slowly lowered until the claws were on the ground. The light in the eyes faded. From behind the Witch, a second figure emerged in a grey hooded robe. It walked in front of the Witch's still form, then over to Tobias and Madder. Its hands – on the end of ordinary-sized arms – reached up and pulled back its hood.

Patch gaped. The figure was a woman, and a beautiful one at that. She was looking at Tobias with a defiantly raised eyebrow.

"Brother Tobias," she said. "I always knew some day you'd come walking back through my door." She frowned and glanced around at the trees. "Metaphorically speaking."

As Tobias and the woman spoke, Patch looked again towards the Witch, squinting to try and see better in the moonlight. He had a moment of realization, and all his fear vanished suddenly. With one eye on the newcomer in the grey robe, he walked towards the Witch.

Wren was on his shoulder, and she wasn't happy. *What are you doing?* she signed. *Stop!*

"It's okay," said Patch. "Take another look, Wren."

As they got closer, it became obvious. The frightening face was just paper, glue and paint; the terrible claws were jointed wood.

It's a puppet! signed Wren. *A big, horrible puppet!* She hopped off Patch's shoulder onto the "Witch" and vanished under the black cloth that covered it.

Barver arrived by Patch's side. "Never tell anyone about this," he said. "Not in the Islands of the Eastern Seas, anyway. I wouldn't live it down."

Wren reappeared on top of the Witch's head. *The eyes are lamps,* she signed, clearly impressed. *There are all sorts of levers back here!*

Barver reached out to one of the long arms and waggled it up and down. It broke off in his hand.

"Hey, leave that alone!" called the woman. She walked over, Tobias and Madder behind her.

"Um, sorry," said Barver. He half-heartedly tried to poke the arm back into position, and when he let it go it fell to the ground. "I didn't mean to break it."

The woman lifted the end of the arm and slotted it back

into place. "It's far more delicate that it looks," she said, tetchy. She stared at Barver. "And *what* are you?"

"The name's Barver," he said. "I'm a dracogriff."

She turned to Patch. "And you?"

"Patch Brightwater," he said. "Uh, human."

The woman shook her head, unimpressed, but then she saw Wren sitting on top of the Witch-puppet. "Ah! Now you…you're a different prospect entirely. Cursed, eh?"

Wren nodded. *I'm here so you can cure me*, she signed, but the woman waved a dismissive hand at her.

"No, no, stop all that," she said. "I don't understand a word."

Tobias stepped in. "Alia, this is Wren. She's part of the reason we're here. Everyone, this is Alia, the Witch of Gemspar Mountain."

"Obviously not the *original* Witch," said Alia. "So, the rat curse is *part* of why you came. What's the rest of it?"

"I need help with a patient who is close to death," said Tobias. "A poison runs through his veins, one that is dripping with sorcery."

Alia shrugged. "And why should I care?"

"The patient is Rundel Stone," said Tobias.

She scowled at him. "I say again, why should I care?" Tobias said nothing and just looked at her. After a few moments Alia sighed and shook her head, clearly irritated. "Oh all *right*. Give me a minute to pack up." She reached under the black cloth that covered the main bulk of the Witch-puppet, and pulled. The arms grew shorter and folded themselves under the cloth. She nodded at Wren. "Do you mind?" she said politely, and Wren hopped from the puppet to Patch's shoulder. Alia pushed down on the head, which retracted, and then shoved hard against what remained of the puppet. It pivoted down, and Alia gathered up the cloth and shut a lid. The entire puppet was now contained in a wheeled box, like a small handcart.

Wren couldn't resist giving a little round of applause.

"Everyone get your things and follow me," said Alia. She nodded to Barver and pointed to the cart. "Make yourself useful and push that. Just try not to damage it!"

She led them through the trees to a forbidding path between high volcanic cliffs. They emerged into a large open area, most of which was desolate. The peak of Gemspar Mountain loomed over them like a constant threat, yet among this desolation, next to the entrance to a cave in the side of the mountain, was an expanse of grass, perhaps eighty feet across, with various fruiting bushes and a vegetable patch, all surrounded by a fence. It looked like the whole thing had been cut out of a different landscape and dropped here.

Alia saw the bemused looks and smiled.

"Welcome to my home," she said. "The cave is ancient,

but the garden is my own construction."

Tobias was obviously impressed. "Does it not drain you, to sustain this kind of green magic?"

She shook her head. "The only magic needed for the garden was for the transportation of soil, Tobias. It gets plenty of sun and water, all free."

With the horses tied up, she led them into the cave. It seemed extensive, going back into the rock of the mountain for at least a few hundred feet, before bending away out of sight, the true extent impossible to tell. Lamps were burning everywhere, keeping it bright. Simple shelves were filled with glass jars of various contents, some of which were rather grim. Patch made an effort not to look at them too closely.

Barver still pushed the Witch-puppet, and Alia pointed to a spot by one shelf. "Over there, if you don't mind," she said, and Barver did as instructed. "The birds and insects around here are my eyes and ears. It's easy to tell when there are intruders in my part of the forest. Not very common, these days. My reputation seems to be enough discouragement."

"Why do you have the puppet?" asked Barver. "Surely you can just..." He made a spell-casting motion with one hand.

Alia gave him a warm smile. "Magic is an effort. I save my powers for the work that interests me. Lately I've not had need for elaborate magical defences. *Witchy* there is rather effective at chasing off strays. Also, she's considerable *fun*." She walked across to a large trunk and opened it up. It contained a vast number of little glass vials and bottles. "This is research," she said. "Out here, I refine my skills in peace." She gave Tobias a long, pointed glare. "In *peace*, Tobias. I wanted to be left alone, and never see any of you again. Why have you broken your word?"

Patch looked from Alia to Tobias and back again, feeling a very definite chill in the air.

"I kept my word," said Tobias. "Until I had no choice."

"And now you're here," she said. "Seeking help from the all-terrible Witch, even though I swore I would *kill* you if you came. *Any* of you."

Patch frowned, wondering who exactly Alia meant by "any of you". He shared a worried look with Wren and Barver.

Alia caught the look on Patch's face. She narrowed her eyes at him, making Patch's knees suddenly feel very wobbly. "Do I disappoint?" she said to him. "Did you want to see the old Witch, the *mad* Witch? I can pretend to be like that, if you want. I can be what the Council thought I was. A seeker of unnatural power, dabbling in things no Piper should touch! Things that even Casimir feared!" She clenched her fists and turned towards the cave entrance. As she went, the lamps within the cave dimmed as one.

Patch felt Wren's claws grip tightly to his coat, and he found himself putting his own hand on Barver for support.

Outside the cave, the moonlit sky was clear. Alia raised her arms, and clouds seemed to congeal out of the heavens.

"Power without limit!" cried Alia, and the clouds began to move in a slow spiral. Lightning flashed within them. "Unconstrained! Terrifying!" she cried, before shouting out a long series of incomprehensible words, each spoken with unmistakable rage. Lightning flared like none of them had ever seen before – tinged purple and red, it spread out in shapes like claws, bathing the whole forest in irate light.

She lowered her arms. Gradually, the lightning faded, and the clouds vanished. The lamps within the cave grew bright once more. She turned to Tobias and heaved a deep sigh. "Is that *fear* I see in your eyes?" she said to him. "I don't know what hurts me more. That you broke your word, or that you kept it for so long. That you really believed I could hurt *you*, of all people. You really did fear me."

Tobias suddenly looked rather fragile. "I kept my vow," he said. "I left you alone. But not because I feared you. I did it because you *asked* me to." She said nothing in reply, only looked at him with sadness. Tobias put his hand on her shoulder. "It's…it's good to see you again."

Alia seemed dazed for a moment. Then she stepped away, letting his hand fall from her. "I half-expected a visit from someone," she said. "Given what happened at Tiviscan."

"You heard about the attack?" said Tobias.

She nodded. "A little bird told me. I'm not surprised Drevis didn't come. I *might* have killed him."

"It was the Council who expelled you, Alia, and that was before Drevis was one of them. He was always on your side. And while Casimir was your greatest champion, don't forget that Rundel was also outspoken in your defence."

"Ah," she said. "Rundel." She let out a long sigh. "I *suppose* I can't let the old goat die, if I can help it. Back to the business in hand, then. Tell me what happened."

Tobias nodded. "His Apprentice brought him to me, close to death. My strongest healing Songs have kept him alive, but are unable to deal with the poison." He went to the cave entrance, where his horse was tied, and fetched the jar containing the metal box. "Here," he said, handing her the jar. "*This* is how it was inflicted."

Alia held the jar up. "*Enigma enicatus*," she said.

Tobias nodded. "A death puzzle. Rundel said if we identify its targets, we might identify the attacker."

"An *enigma enicatus* is a booby-trapped magical device," said Alia. "Difficult to make." She opened the jar and passed her hand over the top, back and forth. "Mmm. The *style* of the spells within it is unusual. You should take this to Ural. It's a very *engineered* form of sorcery. It'd be right up his alley. He might recognize the style, and point you to its creator. He knows much more about the Sorcerers of the world than I do." Tobias looked immediately wary. "Good Lord, Tobias, what is it?"

"Ural is dead," said Tobias. "Bludgeoned, without witnesses to what happened. Rundel was called to investigate, and was poisoned by the box when he picked it up."

Alia was stunned. "Ural Casimir, dead?" She closed her eyes, visibly distressed by the news. After a moment she opened her eyes again, and Patch could see they were wet. "Come," she said, venturing to a table beside her trunk of potions. "We must investigate the box."

The others followed, but Patch found himself frozen for a moment, distracted by a sudden realization. He'd thought the name Ural was familiar, and now he knew why. It was Ural *Casimir*, the Sorcerer Engineer. One of the Eight!

And there was something else he'd thought of, something that was surely impossible, but which made him look at Tobias and Alia with fresh eyes.

Wren jabbed his cheek. *Snap out of it*, she signed. *They're waiting for us.*

He nodded without a word, and went to join them.

Alia handed out pieces of rag to Tobias, Madder and Patch, and took one herself. "Each of you must spit in your rag," she said, and as they did she went to a corner where a hunk of cured meat sat. She cut some pieces from the meat and returned. "You first," she said to Patch. She took his rag, and wiped his spit over the surface of one piece of meat. Then, using a pair of tongs, she thrust the meat into the jar and pressed it against the box. Nothing happened. "Now you," she said to Madder. She repeated the process, and again there was no reaction.

"Can you be sure this works, Alia?" said Tobias.

"Hush!" she said. She took the rag from Tobias and wiped it over the third piece of meat. This time, when she pressed it to the box there was an audible *click*. She pulled the tongs away just in time to see a small needle disappear back into the metal surface. Black liquid dripped from the meat. She gave Tobias a dark look, and then tried her own spit with the last piece. Again, the click, and the meat was injected with poison. "As I feared," she said. "The targets include Rundel and the two of us. I give you one guess who else might be a target."

"Let's not get ahead of ourselves," said Tobias, giving Patch and the others a wary look. Alia saw the expression on his face and nodded. To Patch, the meaning was obvious: let's not talk in front of *them*. His suspicions grew almost to the point of bursting out of him, but he held his tongue.

"Now to identify what the substance is," said Alia. "Give me a moment." She took samples of the black poison from the pieces of meat, then added various liquids from vials she took down from the nearest shelf. A few minutes later, she nodded with satisfaction. “Moon-rot,” she said. “A nasty fungus, but the effect has been enhanced with sorcery as you suspected. No wonder your Song couldn’t quite deal with it.” She hunted through the vials in her trunk and selected one containing a bright purple liquid. “Aha!” she announced, standing up. “This should do it.” She took a long metal rod and touched it to the black poison, then swirled the rod in the purple liquid. The colour immediately changed to green. “This must remain absolutely still for at least eight hours,” she said, placing the vial in a tiny stand on the table. “By then it will have transmuted fully, and Rundel’s cure will be complete. I’ll come with you to Marwheel long enough to administer it, Tobias, not a moment longer. He’ll remain unconscious for a week, perhaps two, but he should live.”

“Thank you, Alia,” said Tobias. Brother Madder offered out the pouch of money he’d reclaimed from the brigand leader.

“No, no,” said Alia. “Keep it. You have need of it, I know, running your infirmary. You’ve been treating a firefoot outbreak recently, haven’t you? And doing a fine job, too.”

“You know about that?” said Tobias.

Alia grinned. “Oh yes, I’ve kept my eye on you, Palafox.”

That was it – Patch couldn’t hold it in any more. “Palafox!” he barked. “I knew it! I *knew* it!”

“Oh,” said Alia, wide-eyed. “Damn.”

Barver and Wren were staring at Patch. *You knew what?* signed Wren.

"*Palafox, Corrigan, Kellenfas, Stone...*" recited Patch. "*Casimir, Hinkelman, Drevis and Throne.*" Barver and Wren gave him bemused looks, but Tobias and Alia were watching him warily. "The names of the Eight," said Patch. "Kellenfas, Hinkelman and Throne died in the quest. Of the survivors, we have Drevis, now a Lord of the Pipers' Council. We have Stone, now a Virtus in the Custodian Elite. The other three sought new lives, away from the fame that their quest had brought. First, Casimir, the Sorcerer Engineer. Who does that leave?"

"Palafox and Corrigan," said Barver. "What are you saying?" He looked to Wren, and Wren shook her head and shrugged.

Patch heaved a sigh. "You two should have paid more attention to the tales of the Eight! Don't you know their first names?"

"Mmm," said Barver. "The stories only mention them once, but I *think* I do. Let's see...Palafox's name was T—" His mouth dropped open and he stared at Tobias. Then he stared at Alia. Then he fainted, crushing a chair.

Wren was staring too. *No way*, she signed.

Patch gestured to Tobias. "Tobias Palafox, Hero of the Battle Elite." He gestured to Alia. "Alia Corrigan, the Great Piper of Shielding Songs!"

And Rundel Stone's dead friend— signed Wren.

Patch nodded. "—was Ural Casimir, the Sorcerer Engineer."

Barver was back on his feet, looking groggy.

Patch looked at Tobias and Alia. *"That's* why you're all old friends," he said. "You were all members of the Eight. And someone's trying to kill you!"

Barver fainted again, narrowly missing a table.

"We don't know that for certain," said Tobias.

"I think it's clear!" scoffed Alia. "Someone finally decided to get rid of us, the last of the Eight. We ruffled too many feathers in our quest, and stepped on too many toes!"

"We did make enemies," said Tobias, sounding oddly proud.

Alia nodded. "We did," she said. She looked at Patch and frowned. "And now you know our secret. You must choose: swear to tell no one, or die in *terrible pain.*"

"The first one," said Patch quickly; Wren gave an emphatic nod.

"A good choice," said Alia. She nudged Barver with her foot, but he didn't stir. "That goes for you too," she said. "Unconsciousness is no excuse." Finally she turned to Brother Madder. "And what about you?"

Madder smiled. "I'm an old friend of Tobias, ma'am," he said. "I knew him before the Eight set off on their quest.

I've never betrayed his secret. And if I can be open, while Tobias has never told me the Witch's true identity, I'd come to that conclusion some years ago."

"Really?" said Alia, her eyes narrowing.

"Indeed," said Madder. "Whenever Tobias had a little too much brandy, and someone mentioned the Witch of Gemspar Mountain, or the name of Alia Corrigan, it was never long until Tobias spoke of a mysterious lost love, his voice filled with longing and sorrow. But you can trust me to keep it to myself, ma'am."

Tobias's cheeks were reddening.

Alia blinked for a moment, then coughed. "Well then," she said, and took a deep breath. Once she'd composed herself, she rubbed her hands together with purpose. "Glad that's all settled. We'll start out for Marwheel when Rundel's potion is ready, but in the meantime we have a certain curse to deal with! I must prepare!" She looked at Wren. "It's your turn, little one. Don't think I forgot you!"

Wren started to tremble. Patch rubbed the top of her head to reassure her.

"Have faith!" said Alia. "Ural Casimir saw that I had even more potential as a Sorcerer than as a Piper. Oh, *Ural*...how can you be gone?" She looked up to the moon, tears in her eyes. She wiped them away. "He believed in me. It was my destiny. Even though the Council declared me a witch and cast me out, I don't regret it one bit."

"Can we do anything to help you get ready?" said Patch.

Alia nodded. "We need a large fire, as big as you can make it. Take lamps into the forest, all of you, and fetch as much wood as you can. I'll start my preparations." She went further back inside the cave, where the shelves were laden with books, and began to consult her texts.

Patch and Wren looked at Barver, who was still out cold.

Leave me on the table next to him, signed Wren, and Patch did, taking a lamp and following Tobias and Madder outside.

After a minute or so, Barver's eyes opened. He sat up suddenly in near-panic. "Someone's killing the Eight!" he said. "One by one!" He blinked and looked around. "Where did everyone go?"

Wren gave him an affectionate smile. *Welcome back, big fella*, she signed. *Now go and get me some firewood!*

21
Awkward Truths

There was plenty of dry wood among the creepy gnarled trees in Alia's part of the forest. Barver's contribution to the wood gathering dwarfed that of anyone else, which was no surprise given that he could carry half a dozen actual *tree trunks* on each trip. It wasn't long before they'd assembled the bonfire a safe distance from the cave entrance and Alia's garden. The wood took flame readily, and soon the bonfire was well ablaze.

Alia came out of the cave carrying a small leather pouch, paper and some thin pieces of charcoal. She got everyone to sit facing the fire, then stepped closer to it and spoke a few garbled words. Taking a handful of some kind of powder from her pouch, she cried out in a high-pitched warbling voice and threw the powder at the flames.

There was a vast plume of yellow smoke, alive with sparks.

Alia walked to where Patch sat, with Wren on his shoulder as usual. The others were a few feet behind them, watching with interest. "Right!" said Alia, looking at Patch. She set down the paper and gripped a piece of charcoal. "I need background on Wren, please. You're her friend. You can speak this—" She waved her hands around madly.

"Merisax hand speech," said Patch.

"Oh yes!" said Alia. "That's it! I never quite got around to learning it. Go ahead, then. Ask her how this curse came about. I'll take notes." She was poised with her charcoal on the page.

"Oh, she's told me the story a few times now," said Patch. "She's the daughter of a wealthy nobleman, and last summer she was kidnapped by a Sorcerer and forced to work as a maid in his castle. She tried to escape, and *blam*!"

"Rat curse!" said Alia.

Patch and Wren both nodded.

"Where was this castle?" said Alia. "What was the Sorcerer's name?"

Patch looked to Wren, who'd never told him those details. She signed, and he translated. "The village of Axlebury," he said. "The Sorcerer's name is Underath."

"Okay," said Alia, writing it down. "What we must do is look for a chink in the construction of the curse. If we find something to pick at, we can try and build a *counter*-curse. We may be able to shatter the curse outright, but I make no guarantees. Building a spell, a hex, a curse – these are similar to layering the parts of a Piper's Song. Building a counter-spell requires those layers to be understood, to allow them to be cancelled out. First I need something of yours, little rat. Hair and nail." She produced a pair of sharp scissors, and Wren flinched. "Don't worry, I won't take much." Patch held Wren gently as Alia snipped a tiny bit of fur from her back. "Now, your paw." Wren held her paw out, trembling, and Alia cut the very tip from one claw. She put the clippings into a small square of paper, then folded it into a little parcel. "That'll do," said Alia. She handed the parcel to Wren. "You must throw it into the flames!"

Patch stood and carried Wren as close to the fire as the fierce heat would allow. She threw the parcel, but it fell short.

"I've got it," said Patch. He set Wren down and stepped forward; braving the severe heat he grabbed the little parcel and went to throw it into the fire himself.

"Wait, she's the one who has to—" started Alia, but Patch had already let go and the paper was in flames. Alia shook her head as Patch came back with Wren and sat down. "Oh, fine. Ignore me, I'm just the expert." The fire erupted into more smoke, white this time, the sparks filling the cloud with an astonishing range of colours. Alia smiled.

"Oooh, hang on! We've got lucky!" She gripped her piece of charcoal, ready to take notes, then turned to the others behind them, who were whispering. "Shush!" she said. "It's starting!"

Everyone looked on in awe as the coloured sparks in the fire began to gather into something recognizable.

A tiny run-down cottage in the midst of rolling fields.

"Wren!" came a voice, and Patch almost *jumped*. But the voice was from the fire, booming loud; suddenly a woman's face appeared, kind and concerned. "Where are you going, young lady?"

And there she was, a girl of thirteen – Wren, as she used to be. Earnest and smiling, she wore a long skirt, which was a little threadbare, striped with rings of red and white. Patch looked at the red-ringed tail of his rat friend and knew it was no coincidence.

"Mum," said Wren. "The time's come for me to get work. I know how hard things are for you and Dad, and I'm an extra mouth to feed. I have a plan, and I won't be talked out of it!"

Wren's mother hugged her. "How I wish it wasn't so," she said. "Don't be gone too long."

"Six months at most," said Wren. "I'll save as much of my pay as I can!"

The smoke from the fire darkened.

Patch gave Wren – the *rat* Wren, on his shoulder – a pointed look. "Daughter of a wealthy nobleman?" he whispered. She was staring at the fire, looking mortified.

"Shhhh!" hissed Alia. "We'll miss something!"

The smoke lit up again, to show human-Wren walking through the countryside, a determined expression on her face. In the distance was a castle – far smaller than Tiviscan Castle, but impressive all the same. The viewpoint changed, and now Wren was at the castle door, knocking.

A weary-looking middle-aged man, dressed in an elaborate robe, opened the door and peeked out. "Yes?" he said.

"You are Underath, the Sorcerer?" said Wren.

"I am."

"Sir, I was hoping to offer my services as a maid."

Underath looked astonished. "I've been seeking staff here for twenty years. Nobody's ever come before."

"I'm here," said Wren. "Do you wish to hire me? Yes or no?"

"Yes," said Underath. "But be prepared! Of the hundred rooms in the castle I use only four. Those four are filthy with use, and the rest are filthy with neglect! Pick any bedroom you choose; keep yourself to yourself. The kitchen is always well stocked. Can you cook?"

"I can."

Underath seemed elated at the idea. "Good, for I cannot! I've been living on salted meats and cheese and bread and wine. Cook whatever you will, and I'll be grateful to end the monotony. Come!"

The view changed again. They now stood on a high wall that ran round a courtyard, in the middle of which was a large dark-grey griffin. It looked up at the two humans with a wary eye.

"That is Alkeran," said Underath. "The courtyard is his, and his alone. Do not speak to him. He is quick to anger." They re-entered the castle, coming to a room where shelves of books filled the walls, potions and their ingredients cluttered tables, and sheets of paper littered the floor. "Here is my study. Keep the dust to a minimum, and tidy my papers. Beyond that, touch nothing."

Wren bent down and picked up some pages, looking at them with fascination. "Should I keep your writings ordered somehow, sire?" she said. "These notes are on necromancy, while these are on the history of prophecy."

"You can read?" said Underath.

"My parents taught me."

"How quaint to teach a girl something so useless to her! Just tidy the papers into one neat pile."

Wren betrayed no emotion, save for a brief narrowing of her eyes. She nodded, and looked with interest at the bookshelves, reaching out to them.

"Do not touch the books!" warned Underath.

"As you wish, sire," said Wren.

(The smoke of the fire weakened, to disappointed sounds from those watching. Alia reached for her pouch and threw another handful of powder into the flames. The smoke billowed up again, and the images began to re-form.)

The days passed. Wren, wearing the simple clothes of a maid, entered rooms filled with dust and spiderwebs, and she cleaned them; she cooked, she ate, she slept.

One day she went to Underath's study to retrieve his dinner plates. She heard snoring. Underath was asleep in his bedroom.

Cautiously she went to his desk. A great leather-bound volume of magic was lying open. She began to read it, concentrating hard. Then a light of understanding filled her eyes.

Again and again, as she collected the dishes from Underath's evening meal, she listened for the snoring and read what she could. At one point, deep in thought, she reached out to a spoon without touching it. She read aloud from the book and the spoon wobbled. A smile of utter delight crossed her face.

Day after day, she read; day after day, she could do more. She lit a candle without using a flame; she repaired a broken plate with words alone.

"Sire?" she said, as she brought Underath lunch one

day. "I have heard it said that Sorcerers often take on an apprentice, yet I know that you never have. Will you ever do so?"

"Perhaps," said Underath. "Young men of talent are rare, though. Ah, lunch! Good." He started to eat. "Actually, I have something to tell you. I'll be gone for a week. I shall ride Alkeran to a distant land, so you shall be alone. You have nothing to fear in this place, and I shall see you soon."

When she returned to her room, Wren cheered. A week to study freely!

Once Underath had left on his journey, she began to scrutinize his most precious books late into the night. In her room, she stood before an old ragged mirror: "Sire? And what if *I* was to ask…to be your apprentice?" She closed her eyes. "You can do this, Wren, you can ask him when he's back."

Finally, a shadow in the sky announced the return of the griffin, and of Underath. She went to greet him. The door to the courtyard opened, and standing beside Underath was a woman of cold beauty. When the woman laid eyes on Wren her smile contained nothing but malice.

"I have news, maid!" said Underath. "I am newly married! This is my wife. I have sought a companion even longer than I had sought a servant – a wife wise enough to keep within touching distance of my *superior* intelligence. I shall have no more need of a maid after today, but I will pay you well for the work you have done these last few weeks." He tossed a pouch of coins to her.

Crestfallen, Wren still had the courage to speak. "I was…I was going to ask to be your apprentice."

Underath laughed. His wife raised a sinister eyebrow. "You?" said Underath. "A girl?" He patted his wife's head, as if she was a pet. "It's not even right for a *woman* to be a Sorcerer, let alone a simple *girl*! Now run along and prepare a celebration meal for us!"

She did as she was asked. When she brought the first tray of food to the study, Underath guided her through to another room, one that used to be empty but which had been transformed into a dining room. An impressive table was laid out with plates and cutlery.

"See how I've been making changes to the castle already?" said Underath. "Nothing is too good for my beautiful wife!" He saw the food Wren carried – a wonderful-looking pie, bread, and soup. He smiled. "Thank you, maid. I know you're disappointed, but I wish you well, in all you do."

"I'll bring your best wines for the meal," said Wren. "And I've made some desserts, too."

She brought the rest of the food and drink to the dining room. Underath's wife was there, smiling her malicious smile.

"There's no need for you to tidy after, maid," said

Underath. "I grant you the night off, to let you gather your things ready to leave at dawn."

But that was not Wren's plan.

She returned later and, as she'd hoped, there was snoring from Underath's bedroom. This was, of course, why she'd made her meal with such care. They had eaten well, and now they would sleep well, too.

Silently she went into the study and chose four of Underath's books on sorcery, smaller ones that she could carry more easily. She crept out of the castle into the gloom of dusk, dressed in the red-ringed skirt she'd worn when she first arrived.

She froze when a voice spoke up behind her.

"If I'd not seen it with my own eyes, I wouldn't have believed it," said Underath. "You were right, wife!"

Wren spun round. Underath was standing there, his wife by his side.

"I told you she couldn't be trusted!" said the woman. "Look! Look what she takes from you!"

Wren hung her head, angry and ashamed. She dropped the books and the pouch of coins at her feet. "Keep your books. Keep your money. I can become a Sorcerer! I've always known it! I only ever came here because I wanted to learn!"

Underath shook his head. "I thought you were loyal," he said, obviously hurt. "Go. *Go.*"

"This is betrayal, my love!" said his wife. "She's the lowest kind of vermin! A *rat*! Why not make sure she never forgets it, dearest?" Grinning with malice, she placed her hand on her husband's arm.

Underath's expression was one of sorrow and regret, but it changed: oh so slowly, it changed. His eyes hardened, and he took on a look of spite and rage.

He muttered some words and began to wave his hands. A purple glow appeared round the tips of his fingers. He cried out, his arms pointing straight at Wren. The purple glow became impossibly bright and hurtled towards the girl, exploding around her.

The light faded, and when it was gone there was only a rat with a red-ringed tail. It squeaked in terror as it ran off into the trees, chased by the cruel laughter of the Sorcerer and his bride.

The sparks subsided. The smoke from the bonfire was now just ordinary smoke.

Wren hung her head. The silence was uncomfortable.

Eventually Alia cleared her throat. "Ahem," she said. "Yes. Um. There are details that don't *quite* match the account you gave, Patch."

"Don't I know it," said Patch, glum. He turned to Wren. "Kidnapped, were you? Wealthy parents, eh?"

Wren looked tearful. *I was desperate for your help in Patterfall*, she signed. *It seemed like such a little lie.*

Patch shook his head. "And you tried to steal his magical texts?" said Patch. "I can't believe this."

Wren gave him a defiant stare. *What?* she signed. *Are you upset that I can't reward you for your help? Is that why you became my friend? For the money?*

Patch was dumbstruck by the accusation. "Well!" he said. "Well, then…then I…" He felt very angry indeed, but he had a sudden fear that, perhaps somewhere deep down, he was guilty as charged. He hoped not.

"Enough!" said Barver. "You would risk your lives to save each other! Here we are, on the cusp of a cure for Wren, and you squabble over things that *don't really matter*!"

Long seconds passed before Wren and Patch found they could bear to look at each other.

"Sorry," muttered Patch. "I just thought you'd be more honest with me than that. *Friends don't have secrets*, isn't that what you said?"

There was a sudden *crump* from the fire. Everyone backed away as flames grew again, and colourful sparks exploded outwards with a loud bang.

"Something more for us to see!" said Alia. "Shush! *Shush!*"

The images in the fire resolved themselves, along with

the sound of rock grinding against rock, and the cracking of masonry.

Patch's face filled the image in the smoke, coughing as the dust of the attack on Tiviscan Castle filled his cell.

"Uh oh," said the real Patch, looking at the features of his past-self looming above him.

Alia seemed confused for a moment, but then she looked at Patch and mimed throwing the parcel into the flame. "A little of *you* has crept into the spell, it seems," she said. "Looks like you were a prisoner somewhere. Wait a moment...is that Tiviscan dungeon? It is! You're a *criminal*?"

"It's fine, Alia," said Tobias. "He—"

"You knew?" she said.

"I did. There's nothing to worry about, we just—"

Suddenly Tobias stopped talking. He stared at the fire, as did Alia.

As did all of them.

"Aye!" came a voice.

There in the smoke's magical images, the prisoner in the Iron Mask lay, his injuries obvious. His hands came up and tore at the mask, which swung open and fell to the floor.

"Aye..." said the thin-faced man, coughing up blood as past-Patch drew closer. "Aye...am...I...am..." The man swallowed and took a breath. "I am not the Piper of Hamelyn."

Then the dragons came. The man was taken, the expression on his face one of simple relief. He was thrown into the circle of fire the dragons made for him, and he perished.

With perfect timing, the images died and the smoke retreated. The bonfire's centre collapsed in on itself.

Everyone was staring at Patch, even Wren. *Especially* Wren.

Patch coughed. "Um," he said. "Ah. Yes. Didn't I mention that bit?"

22

The Children

You accused me *of dishonesty, eh?* signed Wren. *Take a look at yourself, you big dolt!* She hopped off his shoulder and went over to Barver, who was glaring at Patch.

Tobias seemed stunned. "You told nobody about this?" he said. "Even when you found out that Alia and I were part of the Eight, you still said nothing?"

Patch looked around at all the accusing eyes. "What *should* I have done? I'm supposed to be in the dungeons until I die. You want me to start blabbing about the Hamelyn Piper's last words, and get thrown back into a cell? I'm happier not doing that, thank you!" He folded his arms and scowled.

Alia, who'd been pacing furiously up and down, stopped and looked at Tobias. "The Mask was *off* him," she said. "He could say anything he wanted, and lie without restriction."

"You saw the same thing I saw," said Tobias. "You saw his eyes. Did it look like a lie?"

"Insane, then," snapped Alia. "He forgot what he was, perhaps. I don't *know*."

Tobias looked at her, a terrible doubt in his eyes. "Could we have imprisoned the wrong man?"

"Impossible!" said Alia. "We caught him with his Pipe, we knew the Songs he'd played! And the witnesses! The townsfolk of Hamelyn identified him, as did the child who was left behind—"

"The boy with the limp?" said Barver.

Alia gave a deep sigh. "That poor young soul." She clenched her fists. "You'd only need to see the look on that child's face to know we'd caught the right man."

"But his last words!" said Tobias, agitated. "He'd been trying to say that sentence, to deny he was the Piper of Hamelyn, for almost a decade!"

Alia put a hand on his shoulder. "You torture yourself for no reason, Tobias. Think back to the end of our quest. Think back!"

Tobias took a long slow breath, trying to settle himself. "We'd tracked the Hamelyn Piper down, in the Ice Fields near Port Hagen," he said. "He defended himself with a display of Dark Piping that was beyond anything I'd seen before."

Alia looked at him with an affection she'd not shown until now. "That was the day you got your scars. I thought I'd lost you—" She drifted to silence for a moment. "The Hamelyn Piper was caught in the same blast, yet he escaped uninjured."

"But we *had* hurt him," said Tobias. "When we found him again, he was dazed, bewildered. Barely able to speak. But the evidence was clear: he was the Hamelyn Piper." He nodded, the uncertainty gone from his face. "Whatever he said just before his death, it means nothing. We must listen only to the evidence, and the evidence speaks with one voice. It was him!"

Patch was trying hard to believe that the prisoner's last words had meant nothing, but he was finding it difficult. There was something else worrying him, though – something Alia had mentioned. "Wait," he said. "You said you got his Pipe when you caught him, and you knew what Songs he'd played. In all the stories I heard of the Eight, the Pipe had been destroyed, so the history of its Songs was lost. Which is the truth?"

Alia and Tobias shared a long look.

"She was, um, *mistaken*," said Tobias.

Alia frowned at him. "The Hamelyn Piper is dead," she said. "Perhaps the time for secrecy has passed."

"Alia," said Tobias, in a cautioning tone. "We *both* took a vow."

Alia looked to the ground, thinking. At last she shook her head. "We found the Pipe," she said to Patch. "And it told us what had happened to the children."

Barver, Patch and Wren looked at Alia, open-mouthed with shock.

Patch eventually managed to speak. "You know what happened to them—?"

"The Hamelyn Piper had *tried* to destroy his Pipe before he was caught," said Alia. "There were only fragments left. Rundel Stone attempted to extract the history of the Pipe's Songs from those fragments, even though we all thought it was impossible. But he found two Songs of immense power. One had been played on the night the human children disappeared. The other was played after the dragon children were taken. I saw Rundel's face crumple as he found out the truth. I watched as his heart grew cold and bitter. Hope had left him."

Barver was staring at her. "What happened to the children?" he said. "What happened?"

"Don't, Alia," said Tobias. "Please."

Alia ignored him. "Both were Songs of execution, old Songs that were once used to carry out death sentences. For the dragon children, it was the Song of Endless Sleep. This slows the breathing of the target until they fall unconscious and die. For the human children, it was the Song of Dispersal. The children of Hamelyn were obliterated, their flesh and bones scattered like dust across the skies."

Barver gasped. "And the Pipers' Council have known this all along?"

Alia nodded. "Yes. And the dragon authorities, too."

Patch shook his head. "But the Mask was going to force the Hamelyn Piper to answer that question! If they already knew the answer, what was the point?"

"The Mask's question wasn't about the fate of the children," said Alia. "We already knew their fate. It was about why he had done it, these senseless acts, these atrocities... *Why?* To get that answer, the Hamelyn Piper had to live – yet if the world knew the children were dead, his execution would have been impossible to stop! Then, the question of *why* could never be answered. So the Council ordered the fate of the children to be kept secret. The Dragon Triumvirate were reluctant to agree, and brought us to the brink of war, but they did agree in the end."

"And now it is over, at last," said Tobias. "The Triumvirate must have decided that no answer would ever come, and when the opportunity arose they made their move and killed the Hamelyn Piper. Whatever the Council does in retaliation for the attack on Tiviscan, they'll be secretly relieved that their most hated prisoner is dead."

"Even so," said Patch. "With his final words the Hamelyn Piper denied his guilt. Surely you must tell the Pipers' Council about this?"

"I will tell Rundel, and let him decide what to do," said Tobias.

"But you can't tell him about me!" said Patch. "Right now I'm listed among the dead. If he found out I'm alive, it would condemn me to a life of being hunted!"

"I'll not mention you," said Tobias. "It seems fair that we keep your secret, if you keep ours. I'll just say Alia conjured a way to see the Hamelyn Piper's final moments, and she told me what she'd heard."

"You think you could fool Rundel so easily?" said Alia. "Such magic needs a willing witness, and he'll want to know who that witness was."

"I'll tell him you have invented a new magic that needs no witness," said Tobias.

"He'll not believe you," said Alia.

Tobias thought for a moment. "He'll believe it if *you* tell him," he said.

Alia looked at him with a raised eyebrow. "You want me to wait around until Rundel wakens and speak to him? Just to keep this lad from the dungeons? Not likely! I have better things to do!" But the faces around her – Barver, Wren and Patch himself – were looking at her with the pleading expressions normally found on cold kittens or hungry puppies. She glared back at them, defiant at first, but her defiance gradually ebbed away. "*Oh very well!*" she snapped.

Tobias nodded. "It's decided, then. We'll let Rundel choose what to do, when he awakens."

The word "awakens" made Patch think of sleep; he couldn't hold back a yawn, and the yawn spread to Wren, and then Barver.

"The night is deep," said Alia, looking up to the moon. "Sleep, everyone. Especially you, Wren." She bent down and gathered the pieces of paper she'd brought with her, which were covered now in circles and arrows and hastily scribbled words. "I have my notes to study, to seek a flaw in Underath's curse. I will see you at dawn!"

23
The Cure

They slept near the embers of the bonfire. When dawn came, Alia woke them with a shout before walking off, a large earthenware jar in her arms.

Wren stretched and rubbed her eyes, but Patch knew she hadn't slept much. Neither had he.

Beside them, Barver was still snoring. Patch nudged him until he sat up with a start, one eye still shut. "How *dare* it be morning," muttered Barver.

Tell me about it, signed Wren. She looked over to where Alia stood, some distance from them, pouring salt from the large jar to create various shapes on the ground.

"She must have found a way to help you, Wren," said Patch.

I'm scared to ask, signed Wren.

They all watched Alia prepare, and at last she came over to them. "I'm ready," she said. "Wren, I'd hoped to be able to shatter the curse once and for all, but I fear it was too well constructed. Instead, I offer you this." She held up her hand, and in her fingers was a bracelet with intensely blue beads. "I did find a slight flaw in the curse, one that will let you be shielded from its power temporarily. This bracelet will give a few days at a time of human form. It's the best I can do." She put the bracelet around Wren's midriff. "Sadly it's not just a case of putting the bracelet on. It must be bonded to what is called your 'morphic countenance'. The process is painful." She looked at Barver and Patch with narrowed eyes. "And the two of *you* must not interfere, under any circumstances! It would put your friend in great danger. Do I make myself clear?"

They both nodded; Alia's stern gaze was enough to make anyone terrified of disobeying her.

"Make sure they do as they're told, Tobias," said Alia.

Patch felt almost sick with fear for Wren, yet he could do nothing but watch as Alia took his friend over to the salt symbols and set her down in the centre. She poured more salt from the jar, forming an outer circle thirty feet across. The circle complete, Alia stepped inside and began to speak. Patch couldn't place the language, a harsh and guttural tongue, all phlegm and spit. Her words turned into a chant.

"*Ree tee ko pak!*" she cried. "*Thagh pak skarra tak!*"

She raised her arms straight up as the chant grew in volume. A continuous low rumble began, and Patch could see the air within the circle shimmer.

Wren squeaked, and scratched at the bead bracelet with her hind legs, clearly in discomfort.

"*Ree tee ko pak!*" cried Alia. "*Thagh pak skarra tak!*" Her arms swept down suddenly, open palms held out to Wren. The air above the salt circle seemed to have texture now, moving like oil spilled in water. Patch looked to Barver, both of them deeply uneasy. The low rumble grew ever louder.

Wren shrieked, twisting in agony on the ground. Smoke started to rise where the beads touched her fur.

Patch stepped forward.

"We can't interfere!" said Barver, but Patch ignored him and went even closer. He moved around the outside of the circle. There was heat coming from it now, and the light within seemed to redden suddenly. Alia's chant continued louder and louder, and Patch saw her face…

He ran and fetched his Pipe from his bag. As he rushed back, Tobias stood in his way.

"You heard her," said Tobias. "Interfering could harm Wren!"

Patch pointed into the circle. "*Something's wrong!* Look at Alia, Tobias! Look at her *eyes*!"

Tobias looked. "Dear God," he said, backing off.

Alia's face was a grinning mask and her eyes were glowing red. Her chant took on an edge of madness – laughter burst from her mouth after every few words, a terrible insane *cackle*.

Wren was screaming now, writhing in pain, smoke pouring from her fur. Everyone was frozen, staring as the light within the circle darkened, until only the red glow from Alia's eyes remained.

"She'll be killed!" said Patch. He got as close as he could to the circle and stretched his foot out to the textured air. As he'd expected, the air formed a barrier. He looked at the swirling patterns directly above the salt and remembered how Alia had described the intricate layers of a Sorcerer's work, and how it was not so different from the layers of a Song.

He started to play the same counter-Song he'd played to save Wren back in Patterfall. To his amazement, he could see patterns forming on the barrier, patterns that changed as he played. He tried to create something that matched the shapes already there, hoping it would somehow negate them. Again and again, he tweaked what he was playing and observed how the patterns altered, and suddenly he struck lucky – a tiny gap seemed to open up, and widen. He intensified his playing, then reached out his hand. It *was* a gap, a break in the barrier wide enough for him to fit through, if he dived! He steeled himself and made the attempt, passing through the gap and landing hard inside the circle. He looked back at the barrier and saw the gap closing over. The noise was overwhelming, as if he was in the centre of a howling storm, Alia's yelling and Wren's screams only just audible. Wind whipped the black earth into his face, and he could barely see.

He tried to move towards Wren, but it felt like moving through deep mud. Then Alia's face leered at him, inches away. From this close, her eyes were even more terrifying – Patch could see a fire within, churning and flaring up.

"The deed is done, Brightwater!" she cried, cackling. "Look! The bracelet is bonded to her! She changes!"

"Wren!" he yelled. His friend's body was surrounded in smoke. "*Wren!*" He made to go to her, but Alia's hand gripped his shoulder.

"Leave her be, boy. Let me take a look at *you*!" Patch trembled with fear as Alia examined him from head to toe, those fiery eyes emitting a fierce heat. Loud as the winds around them were, Patch could hear her perfectly, as if she was speaking directly into his mind.

"I see you!" she said. "Your past! Your future! I see Tiviscan Castle!"

"That's in my past," cried Patch. "*Absolutely* my past."

"Perhaps!" she said. "Know this: should you ever return to Tiviscan, there will be a heavy price to pay! And what else do I see –" she studied him again, her grip on his shoulder painful now – "I see betrayal!"

"Betrayal...?"

"Yes, betrayal! The words come to me now, the *betraying* words. Listen and remember! The words I say next, Brightwater, burn them into your memory. There will come a time when you hear these words! A mouth that speaks them is a traitorous mouth, and will betray you to that which you fear most! When you hear them spoken, get away as quickly as you can! *Run!*"

Her frightening grin faded and she closed her glowing eyes. The wind dropped as she spoke in a gentle sing-song voice: "They thought they had us. But we're almost clear. Just the ridge to go. What's wrong with you? What's wrong?" Her eyes opened again and she stared at him. "An odd set of words, don't you think?" she said. Her voice shifted in tone, as if she was having a conversation with herself. "I agree, very odd! What say you, Patch? The lad's gone so very pale. The day's been quite a strain, I imagine."

She let him go and began to cackle once more as the howling wind returned. Patch fell to his knees, bewildered by what she'd said. Suddenly a hot blast of air hit him hard, flinging him backwards out of the circle.

There was silence.

He sat upright as a shadow fell across him. It was Alia, offering him a hand up. Her smile was utterly normal now, as were her eyes.

"That's got a bit of a kick, hasn't it?" said Alia as she

helped Patch to his feet. She dusted herself off, seeming rather high-spirited.

Patch looked to the salt circle. All signs of the barrier had vanished, and a dense mist was starting to dissipate. In the middle lay Wren: human, wearing the clothes they'd seen her wear as she'd tried to flee from Underath.

"It worked…" Patch said.

"It did," said Alia. "She'll be fine in a minute or two. I said you could trust me."

"Ye-ess," said Patch, not *quite* over how things had gone. "It was the glowing eyes and the insane laughter that were worrying me."

"Glowing eyes again, eh?" said Alia. She gave him an apologetic smile. "I lose track of things when it gets intense, so I can't remember what happens. Sorry if I scared you. I'll admit it gives me the heebie-jeebies, but that's just how it works." She frowned, as if remembering something. Then she whispered: "You tried to break into the circle, didn't you—?" She leaned closer, squinting a bit as she looked at him. Her eyes widened suddenly. "You *did* break in! Fascinating! And very *very* stupid of you."

"I was worried something had gone wrong," he said. "Sorry."

"Incredible that you managed it at all! But the *problems* it could have caused… For you, mainly. I didn't hurt you, did I? Or predict the day of your death, anything like that?"

"Um, what do you mean?" said Patch.

"You know. A prophecy. A warning. That kind of thing. I was really on form in there, I can tell you."

Patch thought of her prediction of betrayal, unsure what to tell her. "You really don't know what you did?"

"Not a clue. It often gets a bit intense, but that was a doozy."

"So...would giving me a prophecy be bad?"

"They're dangerous things, prophecies," she said. "Never straightforward. Tend to cause endless trouble." He was about to tell her the truth, when she added: "And I'd be absolutely *riddled* with guilt if I had, that's all."

"Ah," said Patch. It struck him that she didn't really need to know. Given that she'd been helping Wren, surely he could save her from her own guilt? "In that case, no. You didn't."

Alia smiled with relief. "Thank goodness for that."

In the centre of the circle, Wren was starting to sit up. Everyone turned to her.

"Hold on," said Alia. "Let her get her bearings."

Barver came to stand beside Patch, and they watched as Wren looked around her, nervous and confused. She scratched her nose, and then she stared at her hand for a good minute or so, bewildered.

Gradually, her wary expression was broken by a smile that grew and grew until, grinning broadly, she leaped to her feet. "Ha!" she cried. She jumped on the spot, then jumped again, laughing. She started to run, and hop, and leap, speeding around the salt circle and the ashes of the previous night's bonfire.

Suddenly her smile fell away. She looked down at herself, and the smile returned. "Phew!" she said. "Fully clothed!" She punched the air. "I was worried about that." She saw Patch and Barver, and her mouth opened in a look of utter delight. She ran to Patch and gave him a hug, then switched to hugging Barver. Then she hugged Alia, and Tobias, before hurtling over to Madder and giving him a hug too, whooping and laughing as she went.

At last, thoroughly exhausted, she returned to where Alia was watching her with amusement.

"Happy?" said Alia.

Wren nodded rapidly. "What a result!" For the first time, she noticed that the beaded bracelet was now on her left wrist. "How does it work, then?"

"When the beads are all blue, concentrate, wish it, and you'll become human for a while. Once invoked, you will remain human until the power in the bracelet runs its course. When that happens, make sure you're somewhere safe, as you'll become a rat again! Then you must wait until the power of the beads has returned before you can be human once more. The time will vary – days, at least. You'll know when it's ready."

Wren nodded, and took a closer look at the bracelet.

"A warning," said Alia. "Do not remove it, or allow it to be removed. The spell would break, and the only flaw in the curse would be closed. You'd be a rat, immediately, and no amount of magic would shield you in future."

"Understood," said Wren.

"See the colour fading on one bead?" said Alia. "Each bead changes to white in turn. When all have changed, you become a rat again. As I said, make sure you're somewhere safe when that happens."

"And will it always hurt so much?" asked Wren.

"Yes," said Alia. "Becoming human and becoming rat, both will hurt."

"Every time?"

"Every time."

Wren let out a deep sigh, and nodded. "Alia, is there any chance I might find a proper cure?"

"This is the best I can do." Alia looked to the ground for a moment, visibly upset that she had failed to do more. "At this point, only one other option remains."

Wren's eyes lit up. "Really? What?"

"Seek Underath," said Alia. "As the one who cursed you, he'll know exactly how the curse was constructed. He might agree to undo it himself."

Wren looked incredulous. "Isn't it just a *teensy* bit unlikely he'd help?"

Alia nodded. "He did seem the unforgiving type, I agree. But I'd suggest flattery. Tell him how *amazingly well-made* the curse was, and how only a *wonderfully clever* Sorcerer could unpick it. You never know, he might say yes. Assuming he doesn't just kill you."

Wren despaired for a moment, but suddenly she smiled again. "Oh, I think he'll be only too willing to help! He'll know he has no choice when he sees what powerful allies I've brought with me! The greatest Piper in the world, and the most fearsome beast you'll ever meet!"

She threw her arms out dramatically and gestured towards Patch and Barver, who instinctively looked behind them to see what Wren was talking about. It took a few seconds before they realized she'd meant *them*.

"Ah," said Patch.

"Um," said Barver.

Wren clapped, grinning. "Glad you're aboard!" she said. "Underath won't know what's hit him!"

24

AXLEBURY

Alia spent the next hour checking Wren for possible problems with the spell that had been cast, using an elaborate range of tests that included burning hairs plucked from Wren's head, and making her balance pine cones on her elbow.

In the meantime, Patch found a blank sheet of paper and a piece of charcoal on one of the tables in Alia's cave, and wrote down the words she had spoken in the circle of salt.

The prophecy.

They thought they had us. But we're almost clear. Just the ridge to go. What's wrong with you? What's wrong?

He stared at the words he'd written. Someone would speak those words, someone who would betray Patch to whatever he feared most, and Patch would have to flee at once. Alia had mentioned how prophecies could cause trouble, and he had to agree – he was already worrying about it.

He began to fold the paper up nervously, as if it was dangerous.

"What do you have there?" came a voice.

Startled, Patch turned to see Barver. "Nothing," he said, putting the paper into his pocket.

Barver nodded to the cave entrance, where Alia was now getting Wren to hop for as long as possible. "Wren's serious, you know," he said, keeping his voice low. "About confronting Underath."

"I don't think that would end well," said Patch. "From what we saw in the fire, didn't you get the feeling his *wife* was the scary one?"

"Perhaps, but if I can speak with Alkeran, his griffin, I may be able to learn our best course of action. There might be something we could offer, in exchange for help. You know, something valuable. And magical…"

Patch stared at him. "You mean the *Mask*?"

"I notice you still haven't mentioned it to Tobias or Alia."

"Of course not!" said Patch. "It's valuable! And essential to my future, since Wren's parents aren't *quite* as rich as she'd suggested, and are actually very, very *poor*. The Mask is the only thing of value I possess."

"So you won't part with it, even to help Wren?"

Patch grumbled to himself for a moment, his teeth firmly clamped together. "Okay, okay. If the Mask will buy Underath's help, then...fine."

Barver patted him on the back. "You have very high principles," he said. "You should be proud."

"Proud and poor," muttered Patch.

As they left Gemspar, Wren rode with Patch, and Alia with Tobias. Patch found himself half-wishing for bandits to attack again, just to see how the Witch of Gemspar Mountain dealt with them. *Spectacularly*, he reckoned, but in the end the journey was uneventful.

When they reached the Abbey, Patch dismounted and led the horse to the gate, with Wren still in the saddle.

Erner Whitlock hurried out to greet them, in his black-and-purple Custodian robes.

Patch was pleased to see his friend, and they gave each other a hearty hug. "Shouldn't you be arresting me?" Patch said quietly. "Before I run away again?"

"Why would I arrest you, Henry Smith?" said Erner with a wink. "How did it go?" Patch smiled and nodded to the rider on the horse, and Erner grinned. "Wren? Is that you?"

Wren jumped down from the horse, and hugged Erner. "It's me! The less ratty version."

"You're cured then?" said Erner.

"Sort of," she said. "It's temporary, but I hope to remedy that soon enough."

Tobias and Alia joined them. "We have the medicine to heal Rundel," said Tobias. "How is he faring?"

"No deterioration," said Erner. "Your healing Song has been doing its job."

"Good, good," said Tobias.

"What are your plans?" Erner said to Patch. "Will you stay a while at the Abbey?"

"When Rundel Stone wakes, I want to be as far away as possible," said Patch. "The sooner we leave, the better."

"Do you know what you're going to do?" said Erner.

"I'm not decided yet," said Patch. "But a new life in the Eastern Seas is an option."

Erner looked anxious. "A dangerous place, my friend."

"He'll be fine," said Barver. "I'll look after him."

"I'm sure you can do that very well," said Erner.

"We have some errands to run first," said Barver. "The letter," he added, looking at Patch – his mother's last wishes.

"And I need to see Underath," said Wren. "The Sorcerer who cursed me. It seems he's now the only one who can fully undo his work, so I have no choice but to face him! I've vowed not to return home until I'm cured, and I intend to keep that vow."

Erner was horrified. "That sounds far too risky, Wren!" he said. "Please reconsider! If only I could go with you, but it's not Custodian business. Even the most *stupid* Sorcerer would think twice before incurring the wrath of the Custodians by attacking someone under their protection."

"If I might suggest something?" said Alia. She gave Erner a quick handshake. "Pleased to meet you. I'm Alia. Magic expert, friend of Tobias, long story." She held up the little jar with the death puzzle inside. "The box which poisoned Rundel has an unusual magical style. I studied Underath's curse and noticed similarities. Not quite the same, so I doubt Underath created the box, but he might have suggestions as to who *did*. It's a starting point if you wish to find the culprit. So if you, as a Custodian Piper—"

"*Apprentice* Custodian," corrected Erner.

"Indeed, but it means that going with them to Underath *would* be on official Custodian business. Just an idea." She smiled, looking rather pleased with herself.

Erner grinned. "And a very *sensible* idea," he said. "It would mean a great deal to me, to be able to help my friends. I'll gather my things and return shortly."

As Erner headed back through the gate, Tobias stepped forward and shook the hands of Patch, Barver and Wren in turn. "Now we must get inside and minister to Rundel," he said. "Good luck with the journeys ahead, all of you!"

Madder bade farewell too, then he and Tobias led the horses into the Abbey grounds.

"I'll follow in a moment," said Alia. She turned to Wren. "You went to Underath to become a Sorcerer. How long have you known that was what you wanted?"

"I think I've always known it," said Wren.

Alia nodded. "Watching you in Underath's castle as you learned the basics of sorcery from his books, I saw your potential clear as day. I could understand if your brush with magic has put you off, but in a year or so it's quite possible that I would consider taking on an apprentice…"

"Really?" said Wren, excited.

"Someone like me," said Alia, wistful. "Eager to study hard. Dedicated and obedient."

Wren's excitement seemed to drain away entirely. "Oh," she said. "I thought you meant me."

Patch put an encouraging hand on her shoulder. "She *does* actually mean you, Wren."

Alia smiled. "Perhaps I should reconsider?"

"No!" said Wren. "I can be all those things. Absolutely!"

Alia nodded. "Well, if you do decide that sorcery is still your future… come and find me."

Once Alia had left, they sat on the grass by the road as they waited for Erner to return. Wren's attention was suddenly diverted as a large beetle struggled through the grass near her feet. "Ooh!" she said, picking it up and biting into the juicy abdomen. "Blaaargh!" she cried, spitting it out. "That's disgusting!"

Patch shrugged. "It's always been disgusting, Wren."

"As a rat those things are delicious," she said. "But as a human..." She spat again, and scrunched up her face. "Yuck! That's going to linger." She gathered herself for yet another spit.

Erner reappeared at the gate. He was leading three horses, and Brother Duffle walked beside him.

"I've commandeered Rundel Stone's horse for the trip," said Erner. "And I borrowed a third from the Abbey. It will speed up our journey." He handed one set of reins to Wren.

"Brother Duffle!" said Barver. "I'm glad you came to bid farewell!"

"You left this item in the pigsties," said Duffle, handing something to Patch.

Barver and Wren saw it and grinned. "Fox and Owls!" they both declared. Patch put it into his bag.

Brother Duffle gave Barver a serious look. "Now," he said, holding up a small glass jar. "An ointment for your shoulders and wing joints. Apply generously as required." He handed the jar to Barver, who placed it in one of his harness packs. "How about trying a few flaps to see how you look?"

"Okay," said Barver. "I'll try." He stepped away to give himself space, and then started to flap his wings – very gently at first, but giving a couple of really strong beats at the end. "Feels good."

"Everything looks fine," said Duffle. "You're almost there. Be careful though! Promise me not to overdo things! And can I say, it's been an absolute honour healing you."

"The honour was mine," said Barver, shaking Brother Duffle's hand. "And I promise to take things slowly."

They arrived in Axlebury three days after setting off from the Abbey. Wren was keen to reach Underath before changing back into a rat, so she could let the Sorcerer know exactly what she thought of him. As such, she'd been eager to push on at every opportunity. It had meant taking only a few hours of sleep each night, and Patch was exhausted by the time they rode into the village.

Axlebury was busy, an early market drawing traders and shoppers in the central square. Barver attracted plenty of interest on their arrival, but his cheery greetings were enough to settle the nerves of the wary villagers.

"That's Fendscouth Tor," said Wren, pointing to a large craggy hill some distance away. "Underath's castle is on the far side." All but one of the beads on her bracelet was entirely white now, and even that last bead had only the barest amount of colour left. "Oh hell's *bells*," she said. "I'm almost out of time."

Barver took a gentle hold of her hand, and looked closely at the bracelet. "You could change at any moment," he said. "I'm afraid we must wait here until it's happened. Underath will have to make do with *our* sharp tongues, instead."

Wren muttered to herself, but Patch caught Barver's eye – they both knew it was better this way, as Wren would accept Barver and Erner taking the lead when they reached Underath's castle.

Barver reached for his money-purse. "That inn over there," he said, squinting to read its sign. "The Old Raven. I'll get rooms for each of you, and a stable stall for me. We should rest for the night, and see the Sorcerer tomorrow. And, right now, it'll be somewhere private for Wren to, um, change." As he spoke, he did some shoulder exercises that Brother Duffle had suggested. His flight muscles were almost back to normal, and once or twice on the journey he'd attempted flying for a few seconds at a time.

Wren nodded. "That'd be welcome, but I think two rooms are enough. I'll have changed back soon, and I won't need a bed. I'd also rather not be alone once it gets dark. I'll probably have nightmares about owls."

With the rooms arranged, Erner took the horses to the stables to tend to them. Wren went up to one of the rooms for privacy, and refused Patch's offer to stay with her, so Patch and Barver ordered some small ale and sat in anxious silence at the front of the inn, sipping their drinks as they worried about her and waited for Erner to come back.

After a while, Barver took something from his harness and looked at it warily.

"Is that your mum's letter?" asked Patch.

Barver gave a big sigh. "Yes. The one I'm to open when I reach my destination."

"You haven't been tempted to open it in advance, then?"

"Of *course* I've been tempted," said Barver. "But I won't. Her instructions were specific. I must go to the place she's described, any time after the Scale Moon, and only read the letter when I get there."

"The Scale Moon?"

"The next full moon marks a special day in the Dragon Calendar, a few days from now. My wings are ready, I think. As long as I can remember the higher air currents at this time of year, I can ride the winds. If I set off soon I'll arrive just as the Scale Moon rises."

"And would you have the strength for a passenger?"

Barver frowned. "I appreciate the offer," he said. "The thought of going alone is—" Patch thought he could see his friend's eyes tearing up a little. "But my mother's instructions are to open the letter in a dangerous place called the Sun Canyon, in the middle of a desolate, harsh desert known as the Dragon Wastes. Nobody lives there. Nobody even *goes* there."

"I still want to come," said Patch. "If you can carry me for the flight?"

Barver shifted his wings a little. "That won't be a problem," he said. "But it's not *you* I'm worried about."

Patch nodded. "Wren," he said. "The last thing she needs is danger. If Underath cures her then she'll be happy for us to take her to her parents, but if not..."

"Then she'll insist on going with us," said Barver. "In which case, I think you must stay here with her. There's enough of my mother's Vanishing Gift left for you to stay at the inn until I return."

"You'd have to sneak off without telling her," said Patch. "And I don't relish the look she'll give me when she realizes what's happened."

Barver laughed. "Wren is courageous, loyal and very stubborn. I can only *begin* to imagine her anger at us for being so protective."

"It's good that she means so much to you," said Patch.

"She does," said Barver. "She reminds me of someone, you see." He shook his head slowly, looking sorrowful. "I was a lonely soul as a child. As the only dracogriff, the other children both feared and mocked me. I had one great friend. My young cousin, Genasha. I'd known her from the day she hatched. Independent, short tempered and rude!" He grinned.

"That *does* sound like Wren," said Patch.

"And honest, and loyal, and funny. Yes, Wren reminds me very much of Genasha." He fell silent for a moment. "The year before I left for adventure in the Islands of the Eastern Seas, Genasha died. Her blood thinned. It's a common enough disease in dragon children, but most recover. She did not." He closed his eyes. "My mother behaved very oddly after Genasha's death. She never once mentioned her name, and if I spoke of my cousin she would become cold. It seemed as if her heart had turned to *ice*. It was the breaking point for our relationship. Genasha's death hit me very hard, but my mother didn't seem to care at all. That's why I left home, and why I didn't speak to my mother again."

They finished their ales in silence, and the innkeeper came to fetch their empty tankards. "Another drink, lads?" she asked.

From above them came an awful scream, which was suddenly cut short and replaced by a few seconds of squeaking. Then there was silence.

The innkeeper looked up to the window of one of the rooms they'd rented. "That's your friend?" she said, eyes wide with panic. "We must help!"

Patch's throat was dry, hearing such a horrible noise

coming from Wren. "I can assure you everything is fine," he said. "Our friend has…a severe terror of spiders." It was the best he could come up with on the spot. "She must have seen one."

"Oh!" said the innkeeper. "Fair enough. They do get very big in this old place."

"I hope Wren's okay," said Barver, once the innkeeper had left.

Patch nodded. "I'm thinking two things," he said. "The first is that we shouldn't wait until tomorrow. We need to get to Underath right away and free Wren from this curse, whatever it takes."

"Agreed!" said Barver. "What's the second thing?"

Patch shivered. "That I'll have to get rid of every spider in my room to have any chance of sleep tonight."

Patch left Barver and went up to check on Wren. He knocked gently and entered. Wren was on the bed, curled up. Patch sat next to her and she climbed onto his shoulder, still trembling. He could see markings in the fur running around her midriff, and pointed them out to her: a series of grey circles, one of which was slightly blue. The bracelet was *part* of her in rat form, he realized – when the circles all turned blue, she would be ready to change again. "Is there anything I can do to make you feel better?" he said.

Absolutely, signed Wren. *Let's go and see Underath, right now.*

Patch nodded. "I was thinking exactly the same thing," he said. "First though, I have a little job I need to do here." He took his Pipe out from his pocket. "Let's see how my new Pipe handles these critters!"

Critters? signed Wren.

"You'll see," said Patch. He stood and opened the door, and also the door to the second room they'd rented, across the corridor. He started to play. He built a gentle Dream, but it sounded very different to the one he'd made for the rats in Patterfall. The note lengths, for instance, were far shorter. His target, after all, was much smaller than a rat.

It was the money spiders who appeared first, dozens of the tiny dots coming out of the beams above them and drifting to the floor, where they formed a line. Then the larger ones peeked out, intrigued, perhaps ten or fifteen of them emerging from between floorboards. At last, the real *biggies* came out of hiding from under the bed and behind the few bits of rough furniture in the room. Patch's eyes went wide; Wren stared at them. There were only four, but four was more than enough when they were that size.

Patch changed the Song slightly, and the eager spiders traipsed across the corridor to the other room, where the Song made them think the juiciest of all the world's flies awaited them. Journey completed, Patch closed the other room's door and returned. "When we get back, we'll all spend the night in here, I think," he said.

I'm not good with spiders, signed Wren.

"Me neither," said Patch. "I pity whoever rents that room next."

25
Underath the Sorcerer

With Wren on Patch's shoulder, they set off to Fendscouth Tor. They'd left the third horse – the one borrowed from the Abbey – back at the inn stables, getting a well-earned rest that Patch was quietly envious of.

The way was steep, through windswept scrubland. As they rounded the Tor, Underath's castle came into view, sitting on the edge of a forest that swept down towards a large lake.

"You two stay here," Erner told Wren and Patch. "This should be safe enough for you, while Barver and I speak to Underath, and see how things are."

Wren grumbled, but conceded that it was for the best.

Barver flexed his wings. "I think I'll try a bit of air time!" he said.

"Be careful, big fella," said Patch. "Are you sure you're ready?"

With a great leap and a huge grin, Barver took off. Patch watched with mixed feelings. It was a delight to see him enjoy himself so much, but being out of practice didn't lend itself to graceful flying. Soon, with a heavy landing, he was back on the ground.

"Feels good!" he said. He reached up and rubbed his shoulder.

Patch got off his horse and sat on a nearby granite outcrop. He was wearing his bag across one shoulder, eager to keep the Hamelyn's Mask close by rather than leave the bag tied to his saddle. Its value was too great – either Barver would manage to strike a bargain with Underath, with Wren's cure in exchange for the Mask, or the Mask would fetch a good price later and give Patch his chance at a new life.

Erner galloped towards the castle. Barver ran beside him, occasionally going airborne for a few seconds. At one point he veered off route and plunged down unnervingly before recovering.

Hmm, signed Wren. *I think I'll let Barver get the hang of flying again before I ask for a ride.*

With a while to wait, Patch reached into his pocket and unfolded the paper he'd written Alia's prophecy on. Wren stared at it.

I remember hearing those words! she signed. *I thought I dreamed it!*

"Alia spoke them in the circle of salt. She couldn't remember much and was worried she'd given me some kind of prophecy. She seemed so anxious about it, I didn't have the heart to tell her that she'd done exactly that. A prophecy that someone would betray us, but that we could recognize them by the words they would speak." He read the words aloud: "*They thought they had us. But we're almost clear. Just the ridge to go. What's wrong with you? What's wrong?*" He shook his head. "'Get away when you hear the words,' Alia said, 'as quickly as you can. *Run!*'"

Wren nodded. *I heard her*, she signed. *Then she spoke in a curious way, right?*

"Indeed," said Patch, thinking back. "Although pretty much *everything* was curious at the time. Her glowing eyes, for a start." *An odd set of words, don't you think?* Alia had said, almost conversing with herself. *I agree, very odd! What say you, Patch? The lad's gone so very pale. The day's been quite a strain, I imagine.*

He shivered at the thought of the fiery red eyes.

The words on the paper seemed to taunt him. He groaned. "I wish she'd not said anything. I'll be listening out for it every day and it could be years before it happens. Decades, even."

So ignore it! signed Wren. *From what little I know,*

prophecy is usually more trouble than it's worth.

"Ignore it?" said Patch. "Easier said than done." He folded the paper up and returned it to his pocket.

After a while, they saw Barver flying back towards them. Below, Erner was galloping on his horse.

Wren frowned. *Are they running away from something?* she signed.

Patch made sure Wren was secure on his shoulder before he mounted his horse, ready to speed off if necessary.

"Wait there!" cried Erner. He pulled up in front of them as Barver landed heavily, out of breath. Erner's concerned expression wasn't encouraging. "You need to see this," he said.

They left the horses grazing outside the main gate of Underath's castle and approached the entrance.

"The doors lay slightly open when we arrived," said Erner. "I called out and got no response, so entered carefully." He pushed the doors wide to reveal an entry hall. It was chaos inside. Every piece of furniture was upended. Glass littered the ground, and the smell of stale wine and ale filled the air. "This is what I found. Everywhere I looked is the same."

Wren stared at the mess in horror. *We have to find Underath*, she signed.

"His griffin is not in the courtyard," said Barver.

"Whatever happened here, it was weeks ago," said Erner. "There's rotting food on a table upstairs. I found his study. All his books were gone. I suspect the Sorcerer has fled."

Barver squeezed through the entrance and looked around. "We should search the whole castle. If Underath has gone, there must be clues as to his whereabouts." He sniffed the air, and moved towards another set of doors, flinging them open. The courtyard lay beyond. He pointed to a stone building within it. "The griffin's stable," he said. "There may be things we can learn about Underath there."

Erner nodded. "Patch, stay with Barver. You two take this half of the courtyard, check the various doors and cellars. I'll take Wren and search the other half."

"Agreed," said Patch. Barver hurried across the courtyard towards the stable. Patch let Wren climb onto Erner's shoulder, then went after Barver, finding him inside the stable hunting through shelves of the griffin's belongings. "You see anything interesting here?"

"Plenty of books," said Barver. "Alkeran was an avid reader. Mostly tales of adventure, but some philosophy too. Wait, look!" He moved to one wall and lifted some kind of large *ring* from the floor.

Patch realized what it was: a locking collar, to which was attached a formidable iron chain. "Did Underath use that for his griffin?"

Barver shook his head. He raised the chain to show that it was short, and not fixed to anything. "Presumably all that remains of a much longer chain," he said. "No, Alkeran was not a prisoner here. Griffins and Sorcerers are a good fit for each other, Patch. Both prefer isolation, and they can provide one another with a degree of safety. Alkeran and Underath are colleagues – perhaps even friends. The rust on this collar suggests it has not been in use for many years, yet Alkeran keeps it in his home. Interesting."

Patch nodded. "I'll start searching in the courtyard. I'll call if I find something." He left the stable and went to a nearby hatchway in the side of the castle. He opened it up, and there was coal inside. He looked to the stable again and saw a chimney, so the coal was presumably for the griffin's fireplace. Across the way, he could see Erner and Wren getting on with their search.

The courtyard had been out of bounds for Wren while she'd been living in the castle, so there was little advice she could offer Erner. They came to a row of doors, and Erner tried the first. It was locked; Erner took out his Pipe and played a rapid high-pitched Song. The lock thudded open.

Wren applauded, impressed. *I've not seen Patch do that kind of thing,* she signed.

"Thanks," said Erner, bowing his head. He opened the

door and a terrible stench of rot came from within. Inside were barrels, from which liquid was seeping. He closed the door in a hurry.

These must be the food stores, said Wren. *Underath magically restocked the kitchen from them, and the stores were charmed to be cold. Not any more.*

Erner frowned and went to the next door. Again, it was locked; again, Erner played to unlock it. He opened the door and entered.

A yelp came from one corner, and Erner stepped to the side instinctively as something shot from the shadows and thudded into the door frame, a puff of some kind of powder coming from it when it hit. Wren looked to where the object had fallen – it was a small leather pouch. She looked over to the corner, and there, wearing his favoured elaborate robe, stood Underath, terrified. He carried a bag filled with bread. Wren clenched her paws into little angry fists at the sight of him. She noticed how scruffy he seemed, his face and robes grubby, the hair on his head uncombed. He had always prided himself on his clean-shaven face, but now a ragged beard had grown.

Underath was distraught. "A Custodian Piper! Forgive me, I thought you were a brigand come to murder me! You caught me by surprise!" At that moment, he noticed Wren on Erner's shoulder. His face fell. "Oh dear," he said. "It's you, um, maid-person."

Wren scowled the deepest scowl she'd ever managed.

"Her name is *Wren*," said Erner. "I assume you are Underath?"

The Sorcerer nodded.

Erner glanced down to the pouch that Underath had thrown. He gave the Sorcerer an angry glare. "A Kaposher Pouch, eh?" said Erner. "If you're going to use that, you can't afford to miss!"

Wren had read about Kaposher Dust in one of the many books she'd pored over in Underath's study. It was a sleeping powder, difficult to make and highly prized by thieves – throw a Kaposher Pouch at an unwary victim, and they would be rendered unconscious in moments by the dust that puffed out.

"I am Erner Whitlock," said Erner. "I represent the Pipers' Council in an important matter." He rummaged in his shoulder bag, then held up the jar containing the little box that had poisoned Rundel Stone. "We shall discuss Wren's situation in a moment. First, tell me everything you can about this."

Underath took it, wary. As he examined it through the glass, Erner reached into his bag and produced a cloth; keeping one eye on Underath, he gathered up the Kaposher Pouch in the cloth and placed it carefully in his bag. "In case you get any *ideas*," he said.

Underath waved dismissively. "I have others." He

removed the lid of the jar and sniffed. After a moment, his eyes widened. "Oh no, this is a very nasty little thing. A death puzzle. Quite a complicated one."

"And did *you* make it?" said Erner.

"Absolutely not!" said Underath, sounding offended. He replaced the jar's lid and passed it back. "I don't make such weaponry. It's clumsy and brutal."

"I'm assured your style of magic is very similar," said Erner. "And remember, Sorcerer. I am here on Council business. I could make life difficult for you if you don't help."

"Make life difficult for me?" said Underath, with a sneer. "As if it's not hard enough already!" He glared at Erner, but soon bowed his head. "Very well. Look to the far north. Near Ygginbrucket, where a Master once lived. I was his pupil, and this *death puzzle* has his hallmarks. Hence the similarity to my magical style."

"The Master's name?"

"Sagharros. Died fifteen years ago. This box is of recent construction, so it definitely wasn't him. It may have been made by another of his students."

"And you're sure the box has nothing to do with you?"

"I swear it!"

"Mmm..." said Erner, stroking his chin. "Perhaps I will trust you more, once you undo the cruel curse you set on my friend here."

Underath looked back at them, pale. "I can't, I'm afraid," he said. "I'm somewhat indisposed. I have no magic to spare."

"We saw the state of your castle," said Erner. "What happened here?"

Underath scowled. "My *wife* happened," he said, venom in his voice. "She's long gone now. She took my griffin and left!" He looked at Wren. "Did you notice anything odd about her? For example, did I mention her name at any point?"

Wren thought for a moment. She shook her head.

"There's a reason for that," said Underath. "I don't *know* her name. Isn't that strange? I know *nothing* about her. I don't think I ever did. There I was, off on a trip somewhere, and the next thing I know I'm married, and *happy*, and not thinking straight, with no memory of how it happened."

Erner raised an eyebrow. "Did you drink much wine on this trip of yours, by any chance?"

Underath looked at him with scorn. "If only it was so simple! That woman hexed me! I still don't know how she did it, but she got the better of Underath. *She stole my heart.*" He sagged, shaking his head in misery.

"Pull yourself together!" said Erner. "So you lost out in love! You must still make amends to Wren!"

"That's *not* what I mean," said Underath. He reached

to his robe and unbuttoned it at the front. "She *stole* my *heart*," he said. He pulled his robe apart and exposed his chest. "Literally."

Erner and Wren gasped. In the middle of Underath's chest was a big hole, charred around the edges. "Nasty!" said Erner. The hole wasn't empty, though. "Is that…is that a *shoe*?"

"Yes," said Underath, seething. "She took my heart and thought me dead, but I had a little life left in me, and magic enough to keep death at bay. The shoe was a hasty replacement. All I had handy, really." He looked down bitterly at the hole in his chest, with its oddly pulsating shoe. "It takes every scrap of magic I have merely to keep going day by day. Slowly, the wound will close and the shoe will transform into a new heart, but it will take a year, perhaps longer."

"So you're refusing to undo Wren's curse?" said Erner.

"Look at me," said Underath. "I'm a wretch. I haven't the power to craft the undoing of a curse. Especially such a *fine* curse." He moved towards them, and reached out to Wren. She squeaked, and gnashed her teeth at him. "The circle around your waist… I see someone's had a go at fixing you already. Some kind of morphic deflector, I'm guessing. Interesting work, but not really a long-term solution." He looked up, a sly smile on his face. "There is one way I could help, however. For a price."

"What price did you have in mind?" said Erner, wary.

"My griffin," said Underath. "Get me my griffin back."

"If your griffin was happy to leave with your wife, then it's not for me to interfere."

"Happy?" said Underath. "*Happy?* Alkeran was her target all along. She told me as I lay there with my life's blood draining away. 'It was your griffin I wanted, Underath, not you!' For what purpose she wanted him I do not know, but that's why she took my heart – there is an old, dark spell to give control over a griffin. A spell that requires the heart of a friend, kept in a box and tied around Alkeran's neck..." There was a look of genuine loss in Underath's expression, a look that Wren had never seen or expected to see on the Sorcerer's face. In all her time in this castle, she'd never known that Alkeran was anything more to the man than just a handy means of transport. "He's a troubled soul," said Underath. "Nightmares plague him, of a time long ago when he was held captive. He's never told me more than that, but it's easy to see his pain, and his fear. I promised to keep him safe and I've failed him. So remove my heart from around his neck and free him. Bring my heart to me, and I can quickly regain my powers, but you must bring my *griffin* back too if you want me to create a cure."

Erner looked to Wren. "Can we trust him?" he said.

Does it matter? she signed, disheartened. *He obviously hasn't the strength to cure me, and we're not going to be able to bring back his griffin. I'm doomed!*

"Nonsense," Erner told her. He turned to Underath. "Do you have any idea where your wife may have gone?"

Underath frowned. "None, I'm afraid," he said. "Now if you don't mind, I'd like to gather some food and get back into hiding."

"Hiding?" said Erner. "Hiding from what?"

"From the mercenaries, of course!"

Erner's face fell. "What mercenaries?"

"Nastiest bunch of hired soldiers I've ever laid eyes on," said Underath. "My wife had some kind of deal with them. Gave them the castle when she left. They've made a terrible mess of the place. Didn't you notice them?"

Erner and Wren stared at him.

Patch searched a room storing equipment for horses – saddles, martingales, bridles. It looked as though no one had been in there for decades. He came out and walked over to the largest of the doors on this side of the courtyard, and as he reached out to open it something ripped through the air. It pierced the sleeve of his shirt and the strap of his shouldered bag, pinning him to the door.

A crossbow bolt. He stared at it, gobsmacked.

"Aw, look at that," came a voice from behind him. "See, your aim's way off!"

Patch turned his head as he desperately pulled his arm, and saw a mean-looking pair of men clad in well-worn leather armour. One of them smiled, showing off a mouthful of broken teeth. "We'll be with you in a jiffy, mate," he said to Patch, leering. He turned to his colleague. "Come on, get that reloaded."

"I'm harmless!" said Patch. "Just looking for Underath, that's all!"

"The old Sorcerer? He's dead, mate. Like you'll be in a second. This is our castle now. You're trespassing!"

Patch yelped and pulled as hard as he could, but he couldn't free himself.

"I can't get the bolt in," complained the man with the crossbow. "Why do they make these things so hard to reload?"

His colleague scowled. "You need to pull that lever back more." There was an audible clunk as the mechanism fell into place. "There you go!"

"Ta!" said the mercenary. He turned to Patch, who was still frantically trying to get free. "Right then, just you hold still while I murder you."

Patch whimpered and closed his eyes. A moment later the unmistakable sound of roaring flame filled the air, accompanied by hearty screams. When Patch looked again he saw two smouldering corpses on the ground. Behind them, Barver was grinning.

"That was a bit brutal, wasn't it?" said Patch.

Barver shrugged. "They caught me in a bad mood," he said.

"Don't worry, Wren," said Erner. "Patch will be safe. He's with Barver." He turned back to Underath. "We didn't come across anyone in the castle. How many mercenaries are there?"

"A hundred, maybe. They have dogs with them."

"Dogs?"

"You know," said Underath. "The big ones mercenaries love so much. War dogs."

"War dogs," said Erner, looking anxious.

Is that a problem? signed Wren.

Erner looked to the door. "We have to warn them."

At that moment, they heard a roar of fire, and screams. Erner ran out into the courtyard, Wren clinging tightly to his shoulder. Behind him, Underath hurried to the door and locked it, his muffled voice coming through the thick wood. "Good luck with that!" he said.

Barver came over to Patch and pulled the crossbow bolt out, freeing him.

"Thanks," said Patch. "That was a close one!"

The door the bolt had lodged in now started to swing open very slowly. The smile on Patch's face crumpled as he saw what lay in the large room beyond.

A long table, filled with bottles of ale and rounds of cheese, surrounded by benches on which dozens and dozens of unconscious mercenaries were slumped.

One of them snorted and opened his eyes. "Wha—?" he said. He looked at Patch. He looked at Barver. Then he looked at the smouldering corpses of his colleagues. "Awaken, lads!" he yelled. "There's trouble!"

Patch backed away as the mercenaries began to stir. He reached for his Pipe. He could try some battle Songs and take out a few of them, he knew.

"Oh don't worry," said Barver. "I can handle this lot!"

Then the growling started.

From the shadows within the room, two vast dogs emerged, almost as tall as the men around them. Their grey skin looked as tough as leather and much of it was without fur, giving them the appearance of being riddled with mange. Saliva was starting to drip from the mouths of both dogs. Their teeth were horribly long.

Barver was staring fearfully at them. As Patch watched

the massive dogs approach he knew the odds were firmly in the mercenaries' favour.

War dogs hadn't actually been bred for war, originally. It had been for *hunting*, and the prey they'd been bred to hunt gave them their other name.

"*Dragonhounds*," said Patch. He heard a shout and turned to see Erner running across the courtyard.

"Time to fly," said Barver. "Quit fiddling with that Pipe and get on my back! I'll grab Erner and Wren on the wing."

"Are you sure you can carry us all?"

Barver frowned. "We're just about to find out," he said.

Patch jumped on and held tight to the straps of Barver's battle harness. Barver launched himself into the air, straining hard to get speed. Ahead of them, Erner braced himself, arms raised. Barver grabbed him around the midriff and gained height immediately, setting Erner on his back.

"Where's Wren?" cried Patch, and then he saw her head poking out from Erner's robe. He took her and set her by Barver's neck, where a notch in the harness would give her some protection. She put her arms round a strap and held tight.

The dragonhounds prowled in the courtyard, and the mercenaries readied their bows. A bolt shot past them, and Barver attempted to get higher. Up they went, until they could get over the castle wall to the forest beyond, but below them the mercenaries opened another gate and allowed the hounds out.

"Tenacious, aren't they?" said Erner.

"We, um, killed two of their colleagues," said Patch. "I guess it annoyed them."

"Ah," said Erner. "I suppose it would."

"Where should I head for?" panted Barver.

Wren started to sign frantically, and Patch relayed the message. "See the lake in the forest?" he said, pointing. "If we fly over it, a large gorge lies on the other side of a ridge. They won't be able to cross it."

Soon they were flying just over the treetops, but the hounds were closing fast. If the dogs got ahead, it would only take them two leaps up a tree and Barver would be within reach.

"Go higher, Barver!" yelled Patch.

"I'm trying!" yelled Barver.

Erner took out his Pipe and tied his bag to Barver's harness. "Patch, we should ready some defences! If the hounds jump for us, a Push Song should be enough to deflect them! Hook your feet under the harness like this."

Patch nodded and watched Erner slide each foot under parts of Barver's harness straps. He tied his own bag to Barver and did the same as Erner with his feet. It was uncomfortable, but it gave him both hands free to Pipe. He set about building a Push Song, a simple defensive force that was the first battle Song any Piper learned.

Barver roared and picked up the pace, his great wings straining. On his back, everyone was watching as the hounds narrowed the gap, those frothing jaws even more horrible from such a short distance, the snarls terrifyingly near.

Then they were over water. Barver roared again, this time in triumph. Wren cheered and Patch laughed with relief. The hounds barked with rage for a moment before pounding along the side of the lake, but by now they were so far back Barver could just keep his current speed.

At the far end of the lake the forest rose sharply. "That must be the ridge," cried Erner. "Safety lies on the other side!"

"You hear that, Barver?" said Patch. "Head over that ridge, and you've saved us all!" He looked back and grinned at Erner. They both put their Pipes back in their pockets and unhooked their feet, holding on with their hands again.

"They thought they had us," said Erner. "But we're almost clear! Just the ridge to go!"

Patch froze, his blood turning to ice as Erner's words sank in. The words of the prophecy.

They thought they had us. But we're almost clear. Just the ridge to go. What's wrong with you? What's wrong?

He looked to Wren. She had one paw over her mouth, horrified. She shook her head slowly, back and forth.

Patch could hear Alia's warning: *There will come a time when you hear these words! A mouth that speaks them is a traitorous mouth, and will betray you to that which you fear most! When you hear them spoken, get away as quickly as you can! Run!*

It can't be, thought Patch. *It can't be.*

A moment of hope came to him: Erner hadn't said *all* of it, not yet.

"What's wrong with you?" said Erner, baffled.

Patch shook his head, not wanting his friend to say anything else; not wanting him to complete the prediction.

"What's *wrong*?" said Erner.

It was done. The traitor Alia had warned them of was Erner, however much Patch wanted to deny it. A terrible emptiness filled his heart as he realized what he had to do. Erner was watching him with utter confusion.

"I can't do it," said Patch, his vision blurred with sudden tears. "I *can't*." But he had no choice. "I'm sorry," he said, desolate. He gave Erner a sudden shove, sending his friend flying off Barver's back and into the lake below.

26

Still Not Quite Dead

Barver started to circle back. "What happened?" he yelled.

"Keep going!" shouted Patch.

"We can't go without him!" said Barver.

"*Leave him!*"

Barver turned his head to look directly at Patch, and he saw that Patch meant it, even if he didn't understand. He faced front and, jaws clenched, turned towards the far shore of the lake and the ridge beyond it, flying harder than he'd ever done before.

Patch looked at Wren, clinging to Barver's harness. She was glaring at him, eyes wet, shaking her head and trembling, but there was nothing he could say to her. He glanced back and saw Erner swimming towards the lake shore.

There was movement just inside the trees. The dragonhounds had made up most of the ground they'd lost.

"They're closing on us," said Patch.

"I know!" cried Barver.

"You need to go higher!"

"I *know!*"

It would be tight. If they were going to beat the hounds to the ridge, it wasn't going to be by much.

"I can't get the height," wailed Barver.

"You can do it!" said Patch.

Wren squeaked at him. *Your Pipe!* she signed. *Get ready to hit those dogs with something!*

Patch took out his Pipe and hooked his feet under Barver's straps again. He started to build another Push.

They reached the shore. The hounds were heading for the peak of the ridge. Barver was almost screaming now, putting all his might into squeezing out that last drop of height and speed. Wren and Patch watched the hounds.

The ridge: closer, closer.

The hounds: gaining, gaining.

The Push was ready. Patch held it, seeing the hounds get slightly ahead, watching them bound up the elm trees in front of them, and then…

Barver saw them leap, and swung right. One dragonhound had managed to jump higher than the other, and it was almost on top of Patch when he loosed the Push.

The Song hit the beast hard enough to stall its trajectory, and it fell just under Barver, howling as it flailed with its claws and plummeted out of harm's way.

Breathless, Patch turned to see what had happened to the second hound. His heart sank – it had found purchase. Its jaws were clamped around Barver's neck, and it was shaking its head violently to work its teeth under the scales. Its back legs were fending off Barver's arms, stopping him wrenching the hound away. Blood was already flowing. Barver roared with pain, but he was managing to stay in the air.

The trees vanished under them. Suddenly they were past the ridge and over a deep gorge. Patch raised his Pipe again, but he wasn't sure what he could use without risking Barver too. He decided to try something more direct: beside him, tied safely to Barver's harness, was his bag. He undid the fastening strap and took out his knife, putting his Pipe inside before fastening it again.

"Hold on tight," he told Wren. He unhooked his feet from Barver's straps and lunged past her, gripping Barver's harness as he swung the knife at full stretch, thrusting it deep into the dragonhound's paw. The blade went through until it scraped Barver's scales.

The dragonhound yelped. Livid, it pulled its jaws from Barver's throat and snapped towards Patch, snarling with rage, gobbets of bloody froth flying from its slavering mouth.

It was the respite Barver needed. He pulled higher just in time and they reached the other side of the gorge, skimming the treetops. As Barver gained a little more height, the hound clamped its jaws around his throat again and they veered suddenly to one side.

Patch's grip wasn't quite enough. He slipped forward and the hound swiped at him with its injured paw. The claws caught on Patch's shoulder and yanked hard.

Patch fell. Above, he saw that the dragonhound still had its grip on Barver's throat. Wren, barely managing to cling on, stared forlornly after him, just as they had watched Erner plunge barely a minute before.

He braced himself, but the first branch he hit took all the wind from him and knocked the knife from his hand. He knew there would be plenty of other painful branches before he reached the ground.

Patch stood as quickly as his shaky legs and rattled head would allow. He was in agony from head to toe, but nothing seemed broken; without the branches to slow his fall, he would certainly have fared much worse.

Although he'd been preoccupied with plummeting, he was certain he'd heard a crash nearby. He reckoned the battle in the air had lasted only a few more seconds after he'd left it.

Ahead, the tops of the trees had been broken here and there. He feared terribly for Wren and Barver. There was no noise, not even birdsong. Aware of every breath, every step, every crunch of leaf and snap of stick underfoot, he started to walk.

The treetops showed more and more signs of damage as he went. Then, there it was: a massive oak, once tall and proud, had been ripped apart by a great impact. The top third of the trunk had fallen to the ground, and the next third had been shattered. At the base, covered in broken branches and blood, was the still figure of Barver.

Patch remembered the first time he and Wren had met their friend, and how they'd assumed the dracogriff was dead, but this was different. The wounds on his neck glistened with fresh blood, and his head was twisted at an angle that filled Patch with dismay.

Yet the greatest fear of all struck him when he noticed one other detail.

The dragonhound was nowhere to be seen.

Suddenly Patch realized that his own breathing sounded horribly *loud.* He held his breath and listened; the only thing he could make out was his heartbeat. Something small hit him on the head. He looked up and saw nothing, but another object came out of nowhere and got him square on the nose. This time he saw it hit the ground: an acorn.

"Wren?" he whispered, squinting to see if there was any

sign of movement above him. He raised his voice a little. "*Wren?*"

He heard a distinct squeaking from above and peered harder, shading his eyes from the sun that was coming through the leaves. Nothing there...nothing *there*...

There! He could just about see Wren on a high branch, waving frantically.

"It's all right, I see you!" he said. His reassurance did nothing to calm her down. "I'm okay! A little bruised and battered, but—" He stopped, sensing something. Wren's squeaking grew even more urgent, and he realized that what he'd taken as *waving* was actually *pointing*.

A little whimper came from his throat when he heard the sound of the dragonhound's harsh panting behind him. He turned his head to see.

It was ten feet away, its muzzle soaked in Barver's blood. There was red on its flanks from open cuts. He turned fully to face the massive beast, its head higher than Patch's own. A vicious growl started up in the creature's throat as it edged closer to him.

He felt oddly *calm* as he watched slobber drip from the jowls of the massive dog. Its eyes narrowed, and the growl became even more sinister. The animal was preparing to devour him. The calmness he felt was the expectation of death.

He hardly noticed the high-pitched squeal from above,

even as the squeal grew louder and louder, nearer and nearer…

As one, Patch and the hound looked up to see a small shadow falling from the sky. Wren flopped onto the confused dragonhound's head and clamped her teeth deep into the fleshiest part of its ear.

The hound let loose a terrible yowl and shook its head this way and that with greater and greater violence, trying to dislodge the insolent rat. Wren's grip was firm, however, all four little claws clinging to the beast's sparse fur, her mouth dripping with the hound's blood just as the hound's had dripped with Barver's.

Back and forth the hound swung its head, yelping and angry, gnashing at the air. Patch backed away and watched in awe. The hound moved closer to the nearest tree and swung its head hard at the trunk, trying to catch Wren in the middle, but Wren was too quick, jumping to the other side of the head just in time. Without her tooth-hold on the ear, though, she was struggling to keep hold of the animal's fur.

The hound sensed she was in trouble and quickly spun for another attempt at crushing her against the tree. With a howl it smashed its head at the trunk once more.

Patch closed his eyes, unable to look, but when he opened them again he couldn't understand what he was seeing. The hound was motionless, its head pressed against the tree trunk, while Wren was on the back of its neck jumping up and down with her arms in the air.

Celebrating.

Then he saw: jutting from the beast's neck was the sharp end of a broken branch, still attached to the trunk. Blood started to gush from the wound. The hound gasped, and its legs buckled, but it remained skewered to the tree. A final sigh came from the dragonhound as it died. Wren took a well-deserved bow, and Patch applauded the monster-killer rat. *Nobody messes with Wren!* she signed, before her triumphant expression turned to concern. *Patch, you're bleeding!*

"I'm fine," he said, but the encounter with the hound had made him forget the all-over pain he'd been feeling after the fall. His shoulder was the worst. Wren was right, he saw – there was blood seeping through his shirt. He put his hand to his shoulder blade and felt where the dragonhound's claw had caught him. He pulled his hand back and saw the bright scarlet that covered it.

He wasn't good with blood at the best of times, but when it was his *own*, he was absolutely useless. "Oh," he said, and fell away in a dead faint.

Patch came round with Wren on his chest, squeaking at him.

Get up, she signed. *We need to check on the big guy.*

As he sat upright, she climbed up to his uninjured shoulder. He stood and started walking towards Barver's motionless form, and each step felt like the ringing of a death knell. He could see the fear on Wren's face, too.

Please let him be okay, she signed. Patch didn't even attempt to reassure her. Things were bleak, and he didn't think there was any chance at all that…

Barver sat up with a start and raised his arms defensively. "Yaar!" he yelled, his eyes still half-closed. "Where are you, foul creature?"

Wren squeaked with relief.

"Hello there!" shouted Patch. "We thought you were a certain goner this time!"

Barver blinked. "Where is it?" he said. His eyes settled on the dragonhound's corpse. He flinched, then realized that the beast was dead. "Wow. How did that happen?"

"Wren killed it," said Patch.

A slow grin spread across Barver's face. He looked at Wren, and she told him the story of the dragonhound's death. *All hounds shall tremble when they hear me squeak!* she signed.

Barver let out a delighted laugh. "I'll make a legend out of you, Wren!" he said. He stretched, turning his head from side to side; a great crack came from his neck joints, making both Patch and Wren wince. The blood on Barver's neck looked appalling.

"Hold on, Barver," cried Patch. "You should lie still for a while yet. You're badly injured!"

"What, this?" said Barver, gesturing to the wounds. "This is nothing. Looks much worse than it is, believe me." He turned to the massive tree he'd collided with, and whistled. "Now *that's* impressive! Luckily my head took the full force of the impact."

There was no answer to that.

27

The Dragon Wastes

It seemed somehow wrong to Patch. There he sat, while Barver – covered in a ridiculous amount of his own blood – treated the gouge on Patch's shoulder, using the ointment Brother Duffle had given him.

"I can't believe that jar survived," said Patch, as Barver packed the ointment away again.

Barver smiled. "I'm very careful." Patch couldn't help but look at the smashed oak beside them. Barver ran his hands over his own blood-soaked neck and winced.

"How is it?" said Patch.

"It smarts a little," said Barver. "But I heal quickly. My wings and shoulders have always been the exception. If the hound had gone for those instead of my throat, it would have been a very different result." He stretched out his wings and gave them an experimental flap. "They seem fine," he said. His expression grew serious. Patch could see something in his eyes – a question that he'd known was coming. "I think it's time you told me," said Barver, grim. "What happened with Erner?"

With a heavy heart, Patch explained about Alia's prophecy. Wren sat next to him, gloomy and silent.

"A tragic thing," said Barver when Patch finished. "I always thought I had a good sense of people. On our journey from the Abbey I had no such inklings about Erner. Still, you two knew him far better than I did. Could the prophecy have been wrong?"

It was very specific, signed Wren. *Every word he spoke was as Alia predicted.*

"And his betrayal, Patch?" said Barver. "What could that have been? Would he have sent you back to the dungeons, did you think?"

"I didn't have *time* to think," said Patch. "In my mind I could just hear Alia's instruction to get away as fast as possible. Now that it's done, I don't know if it was the right thing." He hung his head. "It certainly doesn't *feel* like it." In his mind, he could see Erner swimming to the shore, and wondered if his Pipe had been lost as he fell. If so, he'd surely been captured by the mercenaries; what fate lay ahead for him?

"We must move on," said Barver. "We can fret about

such things later, but first we must decide on our plans. What are we going to do now?"

Wren explained everything that had happened when she and Erner had seen Underath.

"Then our course is clear," said Barver. "I pledge myself to bring Underath's griffin home. And you, Patch? Will you join me?"

"Of course," said Patch.

I'm grateful, signed Wren. *But not until you've completed your mother's last request, Barver. I know how heavily that weighs on you. And then we must rest, for several days at least, before we set off to find the griffin.*

"It might be longer than a few days," said Patch. "We'll need time to prepare. And more money." He reached into his bag – still tied to Barver's harness – and took out the Mask. "Should we head to the Islands, Barver? We'll arrange to sell this as soon as possible."

"And so a plan emerges," said Barver. "To the Dragon Wastes for my mother's last wish, and then on to the Islands of the Eastern Seas. Sell the Mask, cure Wren, and have adventures along the way!"

"Some *safer* adventures would be appreciated," said Patch.

Barver grinned. "Understood! I'm sure we can manage that."

Wren suddenly scampered up to Barver's neck and gave him a hug.

Thank you! she signed. *I thought you two were going to take me to my parents and make me stay behind!*

"Leave you behind?" said Barver. "Unthinkable!"

Patch nodded, putting the Mask back in his bag, and as he did he noted Erner's bag was still tied beside it. He could hardly even *look* at it. They had left Erner behind, and the thought made him feel sick. Never again.

"We stay together," he said, "whatever happens."

The flight to the Dragon Wastes was a revelation. Without the need to race ahead of certain death, Barver could take his time, making use of rising heat and wind coming off hills to maintain his height. The speeds they reached seemed impossible to Patch, travelling in a single day what might have taken months on foot. By nightfall they had landed at the coast, overlooking the sea from a high cliff.

The sea crossing would be the most dangerous part of the journey, a hundred miles without a place to land. With the sun setting behind them, the darkening waters ahead looked ominous.

They camped, and foraged some berries before the last of the light had gone.

Patch and Wren were anxious as they set off over the sea the next morning, but the weather stayed calm and the air was warm. For hours they soared, and at last the land came into sight. Vast cliffs rose out of the water, the rock a mixture of oranges and reds.

"The Dragon Wastes!" announced Barver. "Rock and desert, a bleak wilderness. We fly on until we see the Hands of the Gods. There, we'll stop and locate the Sun Canyon." He was in his element, relishing the updraughts as he glided effortlessly above the dramatic and barren terrain. Soon, shapes rose on the horizon: features that dwarfed everything else in the landscape.

The Hands of the Gods.

Patch was awestruck. It was a formation of rock stacks, but even at this distance it was clear that they were immense. There were six wide stacks; on each, a further five stacks climbed high and ended in what seemed to be impossible curls and points.

Six hands, each with five fingers that ended in a *claw*.

"Impressive, aren't they?" cried Barver over the noise of the wind. "Tradition holds that the gods were once defeated by the great Lords of the Night Kingdoms, who turned them to stone. They reached to the sky as they died. They came back from the dead, of course, and had their vengeance. My mother taught me that the stones are a natural formation, worn down by ancient seas, but looking at them in person I can understand believing the old tale. We land on the highest claw!"

"Uh...on *top* of it?" said Patch, terrified; it seemed such a delicately balanced thing, but as they flew nearer he could see that there was no need for fear. The tip of the claw was at least a hundred feet across, and had stood solid for untold centuries.

Barver roared in glee as he touched down on the rock. "Feel free to dismount," he said, but he said it playfully.

No chance, signed Wren.

Patch was in complete agreement. Solid as the rock was, the sheer height was terrifying and the wind gusted hard. In the circumstances, the edge of the claw could never really be far enough away for his liking. "I think we'll stay on your back," he said. "If you don't mind."

Barver smiled. "Not at all." He broke out some of his rations and offered them around, little flecks of dried meat that had a strong fishy odour. Patch and Wren were reluctant at first, but it tasted rather like mackerel. They drank from their waterskins, and it was several minutes before Barver spoke again. "The Sun Canyon should be visible from here. It's almost as impressive in size as the Hands, but it's still very far away."

Wren was already squinting into the distance. *What does it look like?* she signed.

"It's a huge circle," said Barver. "With additional smaller canyons feeding into it like the rays of the sun." He strained to see, and at last pointed. "I have it! Are you both secure?"

Wren and Patch made sure of their grips. "We're good," said Patch. Barver ran to the edge of the great claw and leaped.

They landed where the instructions from Barver's mother indicated: at the northernmost point within the Sun Canyon.

Patch climbed down onto the brutal heat of the sandy ground, and Wren got onto his shoulder. "So what next?"

"My mother's instructions say that there is a triangular rock. We dig under the rock until we find something, and then I am to read the sealed letter." They glanced around, and Barver's eyes settled on a chunk of stone five feet high, a rough triangle. "You two had better get back," he said, as he leaned down and took the strain. With a roar of effort he flipped the stone over. He reached to his side pack and untied a short-handled shovel, offering it to Patch.

"Me?" said Patch.

"I...I don't know what's there," said Barver. "I could damage it."

Patch and Wren shared a look, but they said nothing. They were both thinking the same thing, though – Barver was wary of what he might find. Patch took the shovel and made a start, Wren standing nearby in the shade of a rock.

It wasn't easy work, as the sides of the hole kept collapsing. Once he was down three feet or so, the hole kept its shape. Patch stepped down into it and got on with the digging, as the pile of excavated sandy earth grew behind him.

Four feet down. Five.

Then he saw something.

He lifted out a tiny black pebble and held it up to the light, his eyes wide. "Volcanic glass," he said, looking at it in awe. "It could even be *obsidiac*. Black diamond." He set it on the side of the hole and continued to dig. "We could sell that, too."

"We'll do no such thing," said Barver. "Be very careful with it! We must return it to the soil when we've finished."

Wren scoffed. *You shouldn't be so superstitious,* she signed.

"I can't help it, Wren," he replied. "From an early age, they drill into dragon children that taking black diamond is a terrible crime."

Patch dug a little more. "Oh, hang on, I've got something else." It took him a few moments to free his new find from the dirt, then he lifted it up. It was a large shiny black chunk as big as his hand, very like the pebble he'd found before. "There's our answer," he said. "It can't be obsidiac. As far as I know, the biggest piece ever found was about the size of a chicken egg. This *must* be plain old volcanic glass, nothing more."

Barver stared anxiously at the black lump. "Is there a way to be certain?"

"Perhaps," said Patch. "They say it can make a Pipe sing by itself, but that could just be a myth. Give me my Pipe from my bag, would you?" Barver reached into Patch's bag and pulled out the Pipe, tossing it over. Patch brought the lump closer and closer to his Pipe until they were less than an inch apart. He shook his head. "See?" he said. "Nothing." But then he caught a slight whisper. He let them *touch*.

A sudden explosion of noise came from the instrument, deafening him – he dropped his Pipe and tossed the lump to the side, but the Pipe played on, intricate layers that he recognized from the Songs he'd already played on it.

The sounds faded. He looked up at Barver and Wren. "I, um, think that was a definite reaction," he said.

Barver was horrified. "My mother has led us to a stash of black diamond?" he said. "What was she thinking?"

"Well," said Patch, continuing to dig. "There's one way to find out. Read the—"

Suddenly he yelped and scrambled out of the hole. Wren held her hands to her mouth in shock.

"What is it?" said Barver.

"Nothing," said Patch. "A...an insect startled me. Read the letter."

"An insect?" said Barver. He started to walk towards the pit.

"No!" yelled Patch, moving towards him to intercept. "*Read the letter.*"

Barver frowned. He was reluctant but stayed where he was. He opened the letter from his mother and read aloud.

My Dearest Barver,

This is the hardest letter I have ever had to write. I love you, my son, and yet I drove you away. I drove you away to save you.

I owe you an explanation. Where else to begin, but with the Hamelyn Piper? That evil man rots in the dungeons of Tiviscan Castle, yet for me that wasn't enough. My need to understand his crimes became an obsession.

The question gnawed at my soul: why would anyone kidnap children, human and dragon, never to be seen again? There was never an answer that made sense to me.

And then, the year before you left, I discovered something. I may yet be proved wrong, but if I am right then there is one simple fact that outweighs all else:

I finally have the answer I sought. I know why the Hamelyn Piper did what he did.

Barver stopped and looked up from the letter, his eyes wet. "What have you seen?" he asked. "What's in the pit?"

Patch said nothing.

Go on, signed Wren. *Read it all.*

Barver looked back to the letter and continued:

One year after the Hamelyn Piper was captured, a novice scholar arrived at our home and asked that I follow him. I left you sleeping, my son, and did as the novice asked, for there was something in his eyes that told me that it was important, and that questions would have to wait.

He brought me to a cave outside the city, and within the cave was an old dragon, eyes clouded by sheer age. The old dragon sent his novice outside to wait.

"You are Lykeffa Knopferkerkle," the old dragon said to me. "An advisor to the Dragon Triumvirate."

"I am."

"You saved us from launching a war against the humans, after the Hamelyn Piper. You worked with Lord Drevis of the Eight, and secured peace."

"I did. Who are you?"

"My name doesn't matter. I am a scholar, and I had to meet you in secret to tell you something. It is a burden I would pass to you, for I can do nothing more about it. You are familiar with the Order of the Skull?"

"A little," I answered.

Barver stopped again. "The Order of the Skull," he said.

"The religious sect of dragons who deal with the burial of the dead."

"Yes," said Patch. "There are no graves in dragon culture, are there? The bodies are taken away and buried in secret."

Barver nodded and continued to read.

"The Order is based around a holy work, called the Book of Lost Names," said the old scholar. He produced a copy from beside him. "The rules for where burials may take place are specified in a single passage here: Chapter 4, verse 18." He opened the book and recited the passage. "The dry lands are not to be used for the rituals of burial. Only where plants may grow, and the earth is rich. In the dry lands, where heat is master, it is not just the dust of the ages that is left. There is also the shadow of memory; and for a child, this will be all there is." The scholar closed the book. "You see, burials must happen in fertile places, never in desert. Do you understand why?"

I shook my head. "I don't understand that part. What does 'shadow of memory' mean?"

The old scholar smiled sadly. "It means grief. The Order of the Skull believes that if they follow the rules in this ancient book, then the grief suffered by the relatives of the dead dragon will be lessened. If they break those rules, then the grief will be even worse, especially if it is a child who has died." He held up the holy book.

"But this is a translation," he said. "The ancient language the book was first written in is my area of expertise. Years ago, I realized that the translation 'shadow of memory' could be wrong. I kept my silence, however. I always thought it best that nobody knew."

I stared at the scholar. "Explain yourself," I urged. "What does nobody know?"

"The ancient word here translated as 'shadow' was more commonly used to mean 'dark', or 'black'. The ancient word here translated as 'memory' was more commonly used for 'unbreakable', or 'diamond'. Black diamond, Lykeffa."

"I do not understand," I told him.

"In the dry lands, where heat is master, it is not just the dust of the ages that is left. There is also black diamond; and for a child, this will be all there is." The scholar shook his head. "Don't you see? This text was never about grief. It was a warning. And it explains why the Hamelyn Piper took the dragon children!"

"Scholar," I told him. "I'm sorry, I don't understand what you're saying!"

The scholar had spoken with a quiet voice up to then. Suddenly, he shouted: "Black diamond is the bones of the dead!"

It seemed to Patch that the air had been sucked from

around them; breathing seemed more difficult, as the weight of the words settled. All this, and Barver had yet to see what Patch had uncovered at the bottom of the pit he'd dug.

I fell silent, shocked.

"This passage tells us what happens if a dragon is buried in desert," said the scholar. "Some small part of its bones will darken, and form black diamond. I believe this is why the Order of the Skull was created thousands of years ago, even before we first encountered humans – to ensure dragons are buried in ways that will not create black diamond, and so not create such terrible power to be misused. Yet the truth has been forgotten! 'And for a child, this will be all there is!' You see? The bones of a child, buried in desert! Pure black diamond! The dragon children were what he was after all along!"

"This is impossible," I told him. "What proof do you have?"

"Proof?" he said. "None! And now I am too old to do anything except pass the burden to you. Before the End of the Skies comes!"

The End of the Skies, my son. The old legend in which the earth gives up a vast store of black diamond, and all life is destroyed in the chaos that follows.

I left the old scholar in that cave and hurried home.

I was eager to forget what I'd learned, but again and again I would ask myself: why would anyone kidnap a hundred dragon children, never to be seen again?

And now the answer came: the bones of those children, buried in desert, will turn into the most dangerous magical substance that exists, in a quantity nobody ever imagined possible.

Yet why did the Hamelyn Piper take the human children? That I don't know, but I can guess. A war with the humans would have been unavoidable if only dragon children had gone.

I thought about what I should do. Without proof, this was just the ravings of a mad old scholar. Yet to prove it would need me to take a terrible risk. If I was discovered, it would mean shame, imprisonment, even death – and perhaps not just my own. You too would be at risk, simply for being my son.

I drove you away to save you from that. To save you from having to see your mother brought down; to save you from suffering the same fate.

And so, I sought the proof.

Seven years ago, when your cousin Genasha died and the Order of the Skull took her, I followed them, and watched as they buried her. When they left I committed an unforgiveable crime.

I stole the body from its resting place.

But I had to know.

Each year I have visited the site where you now stand, and so far no changes have occurred, but now illness has taken me. Soon it will be time to check again, and thereafter to return each year; this is what I ask of you.

I hope for all our sakes that the old scholar's fears were misplaced. I hope no change ever happens to those bones.

But if the worst comes to pass, you must find the bones of the stolen children and destroy them! You will need help, but the truth of black diamond must remain secret except to those who can be trusted completely.

I do not know how my dragon colleagues would react, so you must seek out Lord Drevis, the human I trust above any other. By capturing the Hamelyn Piper, the Eight saved us from far more than they ever knew. Imagine such evil power in the hands of so evil a man!

I love you. I wished to spare you this, but in the end it is a burden I must pass on. I know you have the strength to see it through.

You are all that stands against the End of the Skies.

Forgive me,

Your mother,

Lykeffa Knopferkerkle

Barver let the letter fall to the ground. He looked up at Patch and Wren, tears flowing down his pain-stricken face.

"What's in the pit?" he said. Patch could only shake his head, lost for what to say. "*What's in the pit?*" cried Barver.

At last the dracogriff moved slowly around Patch, and stood over the hole in the sand.

He kneeled and looked inside. There was the pebble of black diamond Patch had first found, and the larger chunk that had brought the reaction in the Pipe.

And beside them, beginning to blacken, was the skull of a dragon child.

28
Return to Tiviscan

Barver let out a terrible roar of despair.

"*Genasha!*" he yelled. "How could my mother do this to you? *How could she do this?*" He plunged his hands into the pile of sandy earth beside the pit and started to push it all back into the hole, covering the horrors within.

Patch grabbed Wren and quickly moved away to give Barver room to vent his anger.

The letter from Barver's mother was on the ground nearby; Barver glared at it, then let loose with a burst of flame, incinerating it. He flung his head back, the flames still coming.

Patch and Wren looked on, almost *fearful*, unsure if Barver was even aware of their presence.

When the flames stopped, Barver sobbed. He replaced

the triangular rock over Genasha's grave, then looked at his friends, heartbroken. "Genasha died holding my hand," he said. "When the Order of the Skull came to take her, it almost destroyed me. My mother made her excuses and left, telling Genasha's parents there was work to attend to..." He paused, then screwed up his face in disgust. "I tried to hate her, you know, for being so cold about Genasha's death. Eventually I left and didn't contact her again. I tried to hate her. And now..." He closed his eyes. "You should have told me, mother. You should have let me help you."

"She was protecting you," said Patch. "She hoped she was wrong about all this."

"But she wasn't wrong," said Barver. "My mother did what she knew was right, even though it caused such pain. She sacrificed everything in her quest for the truth – a truth that we are the first to really *know*. Somewhere in the world, in a dry and remote place, one hundred dragon children lie buried. And for what? For obsidiac. For black diamond. For power." He clenched his fists, visibly fighting his anger. At last he sagged, looking to his friends as he wiped away his tears.

We must do as your mother said, signed Wren. *Tell Lord Drevis.*

"Yes," said Barver. "My mother vouched for him, and that's good enough for me. But nobody else. The secret of black diamond cannot get beyond those we can trust."

Patch nodded. "Maybe Tobias and Alia would also be—"

"Nobody else!" said Barver. "Think, Patch! Can't you already *hear* the words, even from those we respect, those who mean well? 'We should take the black diamond and use it for good,' they would say. Tobias, perhaps, or Alia. Or Rundel Stone. That's a road to infighting, and the certain abuse of the black diamond's power. Not to mention war with the dragons—"

Patch thought about it, unsure – *couldn't* the obsidiac be harnessed for good? The dragons wouldn't have to know about it, and…

He shook his head, horrified by how easily his thoughts had taken that path. "You're right, Barver," he said. "The temptation would be there. It would always be a problem."

Barver nodded. "Some of Genasha's bones have already completed the change, and the rest is turning dark. It could be years before the bones of the stolen children have all transformed, or it might already have happened. Finding it will be a challenge! Still, the better it was hidden, the safer it remains, as it's unlikely to be *stumbled* upon. With the Hamelyn Piper dead, nobody knows where it is."

"If he truly *is* dead," said Patch.

"Enough of that!" said Barver. He sounded tired. "Tobias and Alia were certain of it. You're just tormenting yourself! The bones of the dragon children must be found and destroyed. We go to Lord Drevis at once. Agreed?" He looked to Wren.

Agreed, she signed. *Tiviscan it is, but I'll have to be the one who goes to meet Drevis.*

Patch heaved a sigh, and nodded. "True," he said. "I'd probably be recognized and arrested before I could even *see* Drevis, and Barver would cause utter panic. How long do you think it'll be before you can change into human form?"

Wren looked down at the circles in her fur, over half of them blue now. *A couple more days, maybe.*

"There is one more thing," said Patch. "Alia warned me there would be a heavy price to pay for returning to Tiviscan. That might not just mean *me*. We could all be in danger. Are you both absolutely sure you want to do this?"

Wren stood proudly on her back legs and solemnly quoted Barver's mother. *You are all that stands against the End of the Skies!* she signed. *I think that has to be more important than our safety.*

They landed well before dawn in forested hills over a mile away from Tiviscan, after two days of almost non-stop flight. Barver's shoulders had started to cause him discomfort, but with the help of Duffle's ointment he'd kept going.

During their journey, almost all of the bead-like markings on Wren's fur had become blue again. It wouldn't be long before she could change into human form; then she would set off to Tiviscan Castle and contact Lord Drevis.

In the meantime, they rested. Barver was exhausted, and fell asleep within minutes of landing. He was restless as he slept, muttering Genasha's name often, and calling for his mother. Patch took his little tent from his bag and set it up for himself and Wren, and soon they were asleep too.

When Wren awoke, she roused Patch and showed him that her band of markings was completely blue. Patch sat up and stretched. He looked outside the tent, and reckoned it was mid-morning. They'd had three or four hours of sleep at the most, and could have done with far more, but they had a job to do.

Soon they were all up and ready. They looked at each other, wary of how important their task was.

"We should get on with it," said Barver.

Wren nodded. *Time to change!* she signed. *Back in a minute.* She scampered off into the privacy of the trees. There was a blood-curdling shriek, and a few moments later Wren reappeared in human form, brushing down her clothes and looking somewhat flustered.

"Right," she said. "So *that* still hurts."

"How bad was it?" asked Patch.

"Like being turned inside out while somebody hits you with a mountain," she said. "Here I go, then. Wait here for my return, hopefully with Lord Drevis by my side. Wish me luck!"

They muttered a reluctant farewell, and as she went they found it very hard not to follow.

Wren walked through the forest and joined the road to Tiviscan. She could see the Castle ahead; wooden scaffolds encased the lower walls and the cliff face, as the work to repair the damage from the dragon attack continued.

For mid-morning, the town seemed empty and subdued. When she reached the main Castle gate, there was almost nobody around, and it set her nerves on edge. The gate itself was shut, so she knocked at the guard door.

The wooden flap in the door opened, and a Piper in Custodian uniform looked out at her.

"Yes?" he said, sounding fed up. He looked Wren up and down. "What is it, young peasant?"

Wren glanced down at herself, and had to admit she was a bit grubby. "I'll give you that one," she muttered under her breath. "But don't push your luck."

"I didn't quite catch that," said the Custodian.

"I have an important message to deliver to Lord Drevis," said Wren.

The Custodian frowned. He turned his head behind him. "Hey!" he called. "Dana! Get over here and listen to this!" He turned back to Wren, and she really didn't appreciate the dismissive look on his face. Another Custodian joined him – a woman, looking just as dismissive as he did.

"What's up, Klaus?" asked Dana.

Klaus smirked. "This... *person* wants to give Lord Drevis an important message." The two Pipers looked at each other for a moment, then turned to Wren and burst into laughter.

Wren felt a nugget of anger building inside her. She glared at them. "I mean it," she said. "It's important."

When the laughter faded, the woman sighed. "Lord Drevis is attending the Convocation, girl. He should be back here this evening. Who shall I say is asking after him?"

"My name is Wren Cobble," she said. "What did you say he's attending? A Convoc-what?"

The Pipers smirked, and Wren's nugget of anger grew. "A Convocation, girl," said Dana. "A gathering of the greatest Pipers in the lands!"

"Okay," said Wren. "Can you just point out where the Convocation is happening, so I can go and find Lord Drevis?"

Klaus shook his head. "Honestly, child. Just get yourself off home. We don't have time for games."

"I warn you!" said Wren. "This is of the *utmost* importance!"

The smiles vanished. The Pipers both narrowed their

eyes. "*Listen*, you insolent little pig," said Dana. "Run along, if you know what's good for you. Understand?" She shut the flap.

Wren seethed for a moment, then stepped forward and knocked repeatedly. This time, it wasn't just the flap that opened – it was the whole guard door. Wren took a few wary steps back, as both Pipers came out. They didn't seem at all friendly.

"That's *it*," said Dana. "You're coming with us. A night in the cells will teach you to show respect to your betters."

Wren let out a huge sigh. "You really did ask for this," she said. In her right hand were half a dozen daisy chains. She calmly threw one at each Piper, as they watched her with bemused scorn.

She'd made several stops as she'd come through the forest, so that she could gather and prepare a selection of useful flowers and plants. Underath's books had many complicated spells, far beyond her understanding, but she'd memorized a few humble little enchantments.

With the daisy chains, she'd tried a simple cooperation spell. She wasn't entirely sure it would work, but she kept her fingers crossed. As long as the targets didn't regard her as much of a threat, and so had their guard down, she reckoned she had a good chance.

Klaus bent down and picked up a daisy chain; so did Dana.

"What's this?" said Klaus, wide-eyed. His voice was oddly sing-song, like a dreamy child.

Dana grinned at her daisies. "Pretty!" she said.

Wren smiled. Her spell had certainly done *something*. "So, where is the Convocation taking place?"

The two Pipers nodded, their grins not slipping for a moment.

"In the Monash Hollow," said Dana. "The Council members are all there, as are most of the Elite Pipers from the Castle and many more who have travelled far." She waggled her finger at Wren. "Not us though. *We're* not there. We're *here*."

"It's not fair!" said Klaus. "A big party to celebrate the Death of the Hamelyn Piper, and we're missing it all! I mean, we've been helping out with preparations all week, but do we get to enjoy it?"

Dana shook her head. "Nuh uh!"

"Feasts and dancing!" said Klaus. "Games and challenges! And we have to stay here and watch the Castle." He frowned in a way that a grumpy five-year-old would have been proud of. "We're missing all the fun!"

Dana stuck out her lower lip and nodded. "Yuh huh!"

"Fair enough," said Wren. She was done here. She turned round and started to walk off.

"Hold up!" said Dana. She looked at Klaus. "Weren't we going to chuck her in a cell?"

The two Pipers blinked and shook their heads as if they had water in their ears. The spell was slipping, and *rapidly*. Wren delved into a pocket where she'd put some little bunches of clover stalks that she'd bewitched for an emergency. Quick as a flash, she snapped a bunch in two. "I can go about my business!" she said. "You should go and have some tea now!"

Dana nodded. "You can go about your business. We should go and have some tea now."

Wren felt a surge of pride at how well that one had gone, but Klaus was scowling at her.

"Hang about!" he said. "Is she...is she using *witchcraft*?"

Dana scoffed. "What, a good-for-nothing ruffian like that? Get a grip, Klaus!" They both shared a laugh, and then looked around with surprise. Wren, it seemed, had vanished.

"Where'd she go?" said Klaus.

"Fast runner," shrugged Dana. "Good riddance to her." She walked back through the guard door.

"I don't remember there being a tree out here..." said Klaus. He moved towards the tree for a closer look.

Wren felt like a bit of a fool, standing there with her arms stretched out to her sides as the Custodian Piper peered at her. The tree-glamour was the only magical disguise she'd managed to learn in all her time poring over Underath's books, and while the birds had always been fooled by it, she felt a huge relief that it had worked on the Piper too.

She felt something land on her arm.

"Ooh!" said Klaus. "A woodpecker!"

Wren gulped.

"Come on, Klaus," called Dana. "Your turn to make the tea."

"Yeah, okay," said Klaus, and off he went into the Castle, closing the guard door behind him.

Very carefully, Wren turned her head and stared at the bird. "Really?" she said.

The woodpecker blinked. For a moment it looked confused, and then, decidedly embarrassed, it flew away in shame.

29
Dark Instruments

Wren returned quickly to Barver and Patch, and told them about the Convocation. She was still rather cross about the way she'd been treated by the two Custodians, but she didn't mention it; nor did she say anything about the spells she'd cast. Tempting as it was to boast, she wanted to keep that kind of thing quiet for now.

Barver wasn't exactly impressed by the news. "Pah!" he said. "A celebration of the Hamelyn Piper's death is hardly a strong message of anger to send to the dragons, is it? They badly damage the Castle, and what's the response? 'You did a terrible thing, dragons, but also we're really happy about it thanks.'"

Patch nodded. "They clearly *are* happy about it," he said. "A Convocation is rare. There's an annual Spring

Festival held in Monash Hollow, but turning it into a Convocation makes it a much larger affair – with the greatest Pipers from near and far, not just ordinary Pipers and trainees."

"Well, that's where Lord Drevis is," said Wren. She looked at Patch. "Lead the way!"

Monash Hollow was a wide circular area of grassland to the east of Tiviscan, surrounded by woods. Barver, Patch and Wren took position on a neighbouring hill, giving them a good view of the Hollow that let them appreciate how big it was – at least half a mile across.

Even so, every part of it was covered in tents and people. There were plenty of non-Pipers at the Convocation, including people running food and clothing stalls. It was no wonder Tiviscan had seemed so quiet; most of the population were here, either making a little money out of the huge event or simply enjoying the spectacle.

The sounds that reached them contained celebration and excitement and – naturally enough – music. Patch could hear the playing of the Garland Reel, a traditional spring melody that accompanied the Garland Dance. He spotted those who were dancing, and smiled as he watched. The Garland Dance was essentially a *game* – pairs faced each other holding hands, dancing quickly sideways in a long line, and at different cues in the music the pairs had to change what steps they were doing. Those who got it wrong had to leave the dance, and as the music sped up the changes grew more frequent until only two dancers remained.

In the middle of the Hollow was a series of temporary structures, including a vast and impressive stage, which had been decorated as a towering mock-up of Tiviscan Castle made of painted cloth and scaffolding. It must have been at least a hundred feet high.

"Wow," said Wren. "Whoever did that has put in a *lot* of effort."

Patch looked at the throng, astonished by the sheer number of people. With a slight tremble he imagined how bad the toilet pits would be by the end of the day. "I loved the Spring Festival each year," he said. "But they were nothing compared to this! Look at how many Elite Pipers are attending! Such an opportunity for them to pass on their knowledge and experience. See that side?" He pointed to a fenced-off area where sheep grazed. "The Drover and Arable Elite are demonstrating their farming skills there. And if you look to the left –" there was a wide expanse of ground that had been churned up into crater-pocked mud – "the Battle Elite are showing off what they can do." He thought back to his own battle training. He'd learned that what generals most valued was anything that boosted morale or – when a fight was at risk of being lost – gave the fighters a frenzied bloodlust. Patch had hated those lessons. The role of the Battle Elite in war typically meant treating soldiers as nothing more than weapons: using Songs to stop them caring about their own lives. Yet he'd been fascinated by Songs like the Push, and its close relatives – blasts of destructive force could be launched with incredible precision by the best of the Battle Elite. Patch had never quite mastered the *precision* side of it, but the destruction part was fun, when lives weren't being threatened. "Whatever Song you can think of, somewhere out there will be a place for interested Pipers to learn more."

"What's the massive pretend Castle for?" asked Barver.

"Spring Festival always has a central stage for a tournament," said Patch. "I imagine the Convocation Tournament will be even *more* thrilling, given how many Elite are present. I mean, they've really pulled out all the stops with that stage, haven't they? Look at the size of it!"

"A thrilling tournament?" said Wren. "What kind of things do they do?"

"Lots of contests to pit the best against the best," said Patch. "For Custodians it might be chasing someone over obstacles, say. It can get very exciting."

There were Pipers on the stage as they spoke, but little movement. "They're not *doing* very much," said Barver, frowning.

Patch squinted until he recognized the uniform. "They're

Arable Elite," he said. "It could be a race to see who gets some seeds to germinate and sprout first, or who can get water to flow uphill the fastest."

The three of them watched intently. After a few minutes without any activity to speak of, a whistle blew and one Piper celebrated by leaping up and down.

"Germination race, probably," said Patch.

Wren shook her head in disbelief. "Gripping entertainment," she said. "*Gripping.*" Then she set off to find Lord Drevis.

When she emerged from the trees at the edge of the Hollow, Wren was half-expecting to be stopped and questioned by some more surly Custodians. Instead, the people were friendly and smiling, enjoying their day.

She headed for the mock castle stage first, thinking that perhaps the Council would be near the centre of the action. The stage itself was empty at that moment, so she went round towards the rear to see if she could spot anyone important-looking. She was sure she could hear activity going on further within the structure, and took a closer look at one of the large sheets hanging down around the exterior – canvas, it seemed, painted to resemble castle stonework. She was about to have a peek behind it when a hand grabbed her shoulder and firmly turned her round.

A large man was giving her a very disapproving glare.

"No access," said the man, his voice oddly emotionless. "Go."

"Oh, I was just—" started Wren, but the man clearly wasn't going to take any nonsense.

"Go," he said again, in that same impassive way. Wren noticed that his eyes didn't seem to carry any emotion either – not anger, or annoyance. Not even boredom.

"Go," said the man once more, giving her a shove.

"Okay, okay," said Wren. "No need for that. I'm going."

She thought about trying another part of the stage area, but there were other men around, dressed almost identically to the one who'd shoved her. Instead, she headed out into the crowd, passing a woman selling iced buns.

"Pay him no mind, my sweet," said the woman, smiling.

"You saw?" said Wren.

The woman nodded. "They've been helping set all this up, but they're not the friendliest souls. I suppose they just don't want anyone messing about near their centrepiece! Think of the work it took!" The woman looked up at the mock castle looming high over them.

Wren's gaze followed. "I suppose you're right," she said.

"Here," said the woman, handing her one of her iced buns. "No charge! You deserve some kindness after that."

Wren grinned and thanked her. She ate her bun, glancing around the Hollow, looking for any sign of the Council.

At last she saw a group of Custodian Pipers emerge from a particularly impressive tent. They were followed by five overly serious-looking men and women in robes that must have weighed a ton. As they neared the stage, she could see their faces clearly, and recognized them from Patch's trial. The Piper's Council! Her opportunity to speak to Lord Drevis would come soon enough.

Once they reached the stage, the Custodian Pipers and the Council members walked up some steps at the side. Wren watched from a little way back as the Custodians held up their hands, signalling for quiet. When the general hubbub had settled down, a Custodian spoke up with a loud, clear voice. "Ladies and Gentlemen, and Pipers in Attendance!" he called. "The Lords and Ladies of the Council will hereby make an announcement regarding the events to be held this evening! I give you Lord Drevis!"

There was a round of respectful applause. Lord Drevis stepped forward and addressed the crowd. "Welcome to you all! Today is the day that we shall celebrate an end to the saga of the Hamelyn Piper. It is with delight that I announce that tonight's feast shall be followed by a spectacle of fireworks and wonders arranged by the Battle Pipers of Kintner!" There was a great cheer from the crowd. Drevis settled them down with several waves of his hand. "Those yet to lodge their horses in the stables at Tiviscan please be sure to do so in advance of the display. Also –"

Drevis pulled out a sheet of paper and looked through it – "I've been asked to…to—"

He drifted off into silence. Wren frowned, puzzled.

There was a very low droning sound in the air, which varied rapidly as if an insect was attempting to fly into her ear. Wren looked around, expecting to see a swarm of bees or something similar nearby, but there was nothing.

Instead, she noticed curious behaviour in those standing near her. Slowly, everyone bowed their heads in silence, including Drevis and the others on the stage. The low droning grew louder and more rhythmic, and a melody began to take shape. Wren could see that it wasn't just those nearby who were affected. Within the vast Hollow, every single person was now standing utterly still, head bowed.

She looked to the person next to her, a Piper with a blue and grey uniform; she took the woman by the shoulder and shook her vigorously. "Wake up!" hissed Wren. The Piper didn't open her eyes. Worse, she felt stiff as a corpse, muscles locked in place.

This wasn't good.

Suddenly, the people gathered round the stage began to stride backwards in unison. Wren did the same, not wanting to be left standing alone. When they all stopped, the ground around the base of the stage was empty.

A group of men, dressed just like the one who had

shoved her earlier, spread out along the back of the stage, then reached up into the cloth drapes beside them and seemed to *pull* on something. The meticulously crafted mock castle began to come apart. Painted canvas fell away from the wooden scaffolds, and then those scaffolds fell away too, landing on the newly vacated ground.

What Wren saw being revealed underneath – something that had been hidden there all this time – made her tremble with a fear that was almost overwhelming.

Where the mock castle had stood was a curious collection of huge cylindrical shapes. The tallest and widest of them, in the middle of the structure, was a hundred feet high and four feet wide; the cylinders became ever smaller out to each side.

It was a *Pipe Organ*, and each of the Pipes was deep black in colour.

Wren stared at it, open-mouthed. The sound was coming from those Pipes.

On the stage, one final canvas sheet was pulled away to reveal a figure wearing a long hooded robe, sitting at a multi-tiered panel of keyboards and pedals that would have been more at home in one of the great cathedrals. Hands and feet started to fly up and down the keys and levers, and the low droning sound grew more and more complex, with higher notes added now, to create intricate melodies.

The hooded figure stood and walked to the centre of the

stage to take a bow, and even though the keys of the organ weren't being played, the music kept going – just as it did whenever Patch paused while playing his Pipe.

Wren looked around at the silent people and felt a deep chill as she realized what was going on. She tried hard not to react – drawing attention to herself could be disastrous.

"Time to go," she muttered. She backed away one slow step at a time. When she felt that she was at a safe enough distance from the stage, she made for the trees as fast as she could.

Once in the woods she ran, plunging blindly through bushes. When something loomed up just ahead of her, she screamed.

It was Barver. "Are you okay?" he said, looking just as panicked as she felt.

Barver was alone. "Where's Patch?" she asked.

"He fell into some kind of trance," he said. "I could hear those odd sounds, so I moved him down the other side of the hill until they faded. He went limp and collapsed. Then I came to find you." There was dread all over Barver's face. "What's happening, Wren?"

"Didn't you see it?" she said. "It was hidden underneath the fake castle."

"I left our vantage point to get Patch to safety," he said. "*What* was hidden?"

She told him.

* * *

They found Patch where Barver had left him, sitting behind an outcrop of rock. He was rubbing his head and moaning. Wren kneeled beside him. "Patch!" she said. "Snap out of it! We need you!"

Patch looked at her, finding it hard to focus. "Did I fall?" he said. "I don't—" He flung a hand to his mouth in shock: while they were far enough away for the organ music to have lost its power over him, it was still audible and he was able to pick out some of the familiar rhythms and melodies that lay within the intricate sounds. "Oh. Oh no."

"It's a Pipe Organ!" cried Wren. "The Pipes are vast, and they're dark black, Patch! The black diamond, the bones of the dragon children! It's already been harvested, and turned into a huge Pipe Organ! Everyone in the Hollow is under its spell!"

Patch stared at her, despairing. "An obsidiac Pipe Organ?" he said.

"Exactly!" said Wren. "There was someone at the keys, and surely there's only one person it could be!"

Patch shook his head, dreading what she would say.

"It's the *true* Hamelyn Piper!" cried Wren. "It must be!"

Patch wanted to run away, to just leave and not return, but he forced himself to take a deep breath. He slapped the side of his head quite hard. "Think!" he said to himself.

"Think!" He looked at Barver. "You're immune to the Song being played?"

"I seem to be," said Barver.

"It may be human-targeted, then," said Patch. "But why is Wren unaffected?"

She shrugged and held up her wrist, waggling her bracelet. "I guess I'm technically still a rat," she said. "With modifications."

Patch thought for a moment. "In that case, this is going to be up to you two," he said. "I can't get closer to the music or I'll be just as useless as everyone else in the Hollow."

"So what do we do?" said Wren.

"I'll fly down and incinerate him," said Barver.

Wren smiled. "I like that idea."

"No," said Patch. "He'll be ready to defend himself. The moment he saw you, he'd knock you out of the sky. Probably kill you in the process."

Barver tutted. "This is *me* we're talking about."

"Please, Barver," said Patch. "That Pipe Organ could have incredible power. It'd be like the Battle Pipes at Tiviscan, but ten thousand times stronger."

Another sound joined that of the organ music. *Voices.* "Go and take a look, Wren," said Patch. "Tell us what's happening."

She hurried up the hill and returned a minute later. "Some of the crowd are standing in rows and columns, like soldiers," she said. "They're moving suddenly every few seconds – both arms up, then to the sides, then down. They keep shouting every time they move, something I couldn't make out. The rest of the people are at the edges of the Hollow, standing motionless with their heads bowed."

Patch listened carefully to the music. He could feel it *pull* on his mind, but he knew he was just beyond its range. "Like soldiers—" he said, an idea forming. "Does the Pipe Organ look like it could be moved around easily?"

"Not a chance," said Wren. "It's just as big as the castle mock-up."

Patch frowned. "Then he needs an army. Unthinking, and controlled utterly by him. But the control would have to continue even after the Piping stopped, or they could never *go* anywhere."

"Is that possible?" said Barver.

"The permanent domination of the mind of another person," mused Patch. "A Song of absolute control, of *puppetry*. Making someone a mindless slave! That kind of thing isn't *supposed* to be possible."

"Wait!" said Wren. "A man stopped me going too close to the back of the stage, and I swear he was in some kind of trance. There was something *wrong* about him. Apparently he and others like him helped build the stage in the first place."

"Puppets!" said Barver. "It would make sense for the

Hamelyn Piper to recruit some before he came here, to help him prepare."

"Then such a Song must be possible after all," said Patch. "And he's attempting to enslave everyone in the Hollow, all at once!"

"Not everyone," said Wren. "Half of the people had taken themselves to the Hollow's edge."

"Did you notice a difference between them?" said Barver. "Those at the edges, and those being controlled?"

Wren thought for a moment. "Pipers!" she said. "It was the ordinary people at the edges, Pipers in the centre!"

"An army of Pipers," said Patch, dread filling him. "And among them the best of the Elite..."

Wren's eyes widened. "And surely he would arm them all with obsidiac Pipes!" she said.

"They'd be invincible," said Barver.

Patch listened to the Song again. Parts of it seemed familiar enough – he thought he could unpick those aspects if he had a chance. "He's gradually taking them over," he said. "How long it requires I don't know, but if he succeeds then silencing the organ won't be enough. They'll already be his soldiers."

"So we strike now, before it's too late!" said Barver. "Let me toast his noggin!"

Patch shook his head. "No incinerating unless absolutely necessary," he said, to Barver's disappointment. "The very *minds* of his victims could be at terrible risk if the Song simply collapses! We need a way to disable the Hamelyn Piper safely. Knock him unconscious, maybe, so I can get down there and try to reverse the Song."

The three of them thought in silence.

"I've got it!" cried Wren. She went to Barver's side and delved into Erner's bag, pulling out a cloth and carefully unwrapping something.

A leather pouch.

"This might be just what we need," she said. "Kaposher Dust. Underath had it."

"Ah!" said Barver, nodding. He took the pouch from Wren, feeling its weight. "I can throw the pouch at the Hamelyn Piper if I get close enough, but it's a risk. As long as it still has potency there's plenty here, but Kaposher goes stale easily."

"We should test it," said Patch, taking it from Barver. He reached to the ground beside him and picked up an acorn. With extreme care he untied the mouth of the pouch, then dipped the acorn inside and tied the pouch shut again. He tossed the acorn high into the branches of a nearby tree.

They waited.

They heard a squeak and a squirrel dropped out of the leaves, falling like a stone. It was out cold.

Satisfied, Patch gave the pouch to Wren. "You'll both have to do this," he said. "Barver, you must focus on flying.

Wren, you open the pouch up fully and throw it. Don't breathe the dust, whatever you do."

"And how do we get close, if he'll swat me like a fly?" asked Barver.

"I'll try to draw his attention," said Patch. "But I can't promise much, from so far way." He reached into his bag for his Pipe, but his fingers touched something else. He pulled out the Hamelyn Piper's Mask and unfolded it.

"If only we could slap *that* thing on him!" said Barver.

"Would it work?" said Patch. "Casimir built the Mask to block Songs passing through it, purely to stop the Hamelyn Piper lip-playing his way to freedom. It wouldn't prevent him playing that organ."

There was a thought buzzing in his head, however. He thought back to the stories of the Eight, as his own words echoed around his mind: *this was designed to block Songs passing through it.*

But that wasn't quite true – it wouldn't let Songs *leave.* The Songs of another could still affect the prisoner while he wore the Mask, so that the Pipers guarding him could use whatever was needed to restrain him.

It was a one-way barrier to the magic of music.

Patch folded the Mask, then unfolded it again. The action was smooth and took very little pressure. Fold; unfold.

He did it once more, but this time he twisted it in a

slightly different way, and the Mask was inverted when it opened. The curious markings in the metal – those runes that Casimir himself had engraved and inlaid with obsidiac – were on the *outside* of the Mask now, not the inside.

Barver and Wren were staring at him.

"You don't think—?" said Wren.

"It's worth a try," said Patch. He raised the Mask to his own head and put it on. He had an immediate sense of claustrophobia. With the Mask's latch broken he had to keep it closed with one hand. He strode towards the hilltop, Barver and Wren following. As he walked the music grew louder, but he could already feel the difference.

The Obsidiac Organ was having no effect; the Mask was protecting him.

"Do you have twine, Barver?" said Patch.

Barver nodded and produced some from his side pack. "Hold still," he said, and gently secured the front of the Mask.

Patch was the Piper in the Iron Mask, now.

He took his Pipe from his bag. "But can I Pipe while wearing it?" he said. "I'm going to play you some courage. Tell me if it works."

He began to create the Song of Courage; as he played, Barver and Wren straightened up and thrust out their chins, looking to the sky, determined and fearless. Yet for once, Patch himself didn't get any benefit from his Song.

"It's *definitely* working," said Wren.

"Good," said Patch. "I'll be your distraction. I'll hit him with everything I've got. It should give you a window of opportunity. But whatever happens once the Kaposher is thrown, get out of there as fast as you can and leave this place! Don't wait to check he's unconscious, just go! Get back to Marwheel Abbey: to Tobias and Alia, and Rundel Stone. Make sure the world knows what's happening here!" Barver and Wren both shifted uneasily, saying nothing; Patch hoped their courage wasn't about to override common sense. "Do you understand? Whatever happens, get away from here as fast as you can!"

Wren frowned. "But what if you—?"

"Swear it!" cried Patch. "Even if I get into trouble, there's to be no *rescuing* of any kind!" He fixed his gaze on them both. Eventually they nodded.

"I swear," mumbled Barver.

"Me too," said Wren, reluctantly.

"When the Hamelyn Piper is unconscious I'll tie him up and put the Mask on him," said Patch, taking the rest of Barver's twine. "Then I'll see if I can use the Organ and reverse the Song's effects. Now go! Hide at the rear of the Hollow, then wait for my signal. The Pipe Organ itself should give you some cover as you fly at him."

"What's your signal going to be?" asked Wren.

Patch grinned through the Iron Mask. "Chaos!"

30

THE SONG OF THE HAMELYN PIPER

Patch watched from the edge of the Hollow.

The civilians were standing around the perimeter with their heads bowed, all but forgotten by the Hamelyn Piper, whose focus was entirely on his new army. Now that he was so close, Patch could make out what it was these "soldiers" were shouting each time they changed position: "We obey you, Lord!"

The Hamelyn Piper was sitting at the organ, his arms moving in a frenzy over the keys. Standing along the back of the stage were a dozen large men, identically dressed; Patch assumed they were the ones Wren had mentioned, the Puppets. The organ's Song kept growing in complexity, the movements of the sleeping army becoming more refined as the Song grew ever richer. The Hamelyn Piper's control of his victims was increasing.

Patch gripped his Pipe. The Iron Mask felt more uncomfortable every second, making it hard for him to concentrate. He thought of that poor innocent prisoner, who had worn it for almost a decade, and scolded himself. He needed to ignore the Mask and focus!

His plan was simple enough. He'd promised chaos, and if there was one Song that had caused chaos in his own life, surely it had to be the Dance. And while the Hamelyn Piper had an army, Patch realized he could have one too – the unconscious civilians were no longer the target of the organ Piping. If Patch could reach them with the Dance, then delivering the chaos he'd promised would be within his grasp!

The Dance was a flexible Song; that was how Patch had been able to match it to the reels and jigs he'd taught the various bands he'd played with, after fleeing Tiviscan. Whatever the tune, he knew how to play the Dance underneath it. If it was a familiar tune for a well-known dance, those caught in the spell would perform the moves that the tune required.

He watched carefully as the Pipers in the Hollow repeated their movements again and again. A plan had taken shape in his mind.

He put his Pipe to his lips and started to play, hoping he was too far from the stage for the Hamelyn Piper to notice anything amiss. The feet of the civilians nearest to him began to tap out the rhythm he played. As expected, none of the Pipers were responding – they were lost to the Song of the Pipe Organ.

He risked playing a little louder to draw in more civilians, and then he moved along the perimeter of the Hollow. The civilians followed behind him in a line, like sleepwalkers, taking rhythmic steps with their heads still bowed. Each had a dreamy smile on their lips as, deep in their slumber, they enjoyed their dancing.

With perhaps two hundred recruits gathered, Patch turned and walked into the Hollow. He led his followers along the space between two columns of Pipers, who continued to follow their commands, oblivious to Patch and the civilians. When he was halfway to the Pipe Organ he changed his Song to include the melody of something everyone would know.

The Garland Reel.

At once, the civilians did as the reel required. They paired up and faced one another, two lines of dancers just fitting into the gap between the columns of Pipers.

Patch paid close attention to the sequence of movements the Pipers were following. It included a section where they raised one leg, balanced on it for a few seconds, then lowered it, before doing the same with the other leg.

Timing would be everything. He waited for that first

leg-raise to happen again, and when it did he played the musical cue for the dancers to separate and take three quick steps backwards. The civilians did just that, but now they bumped hard into Pipers who were all standing precariously on one leg.

Here it was: Patch's attempt at chaos. He could hardly bear to watch in case his idea simply fizzled out, but the line of Pipers teetered back and toppled – right into the next line, who also fell.

And the next.

And the *next.*

Patch couldn't contain his glee as the wave of toppling Pipers spread out and kept on going. The Pipers let out grunts and yelps as they fell, still trying to perform the movements that the Organ was commanding them to do. Unable to stand up again, they twitched their limbs and shouted, "We obey you, Lord!"

By the time the toppling petered out, a third of those in the Hollow lay on the ground flapping like landed fish. At the centre of the confusion, Patch let out a triumphant shout, laughing as hard as he could. He saw the Hamelyn Piper suddenly freeze, hands stopping above the Organ keys.

He had finally noticed.

The Hamelyn Piper jumped up from his seat and strode to the edge of the stage, his mouth gaping open. The toppling had failed before reaching those closest to him, and as the music continued to play within the Pipe Organ they kept on with their bizarre drill. "Who dares to defy me?" he shouted. "*Who dares to defy me?*"

"I do!" yelled Patch. He raised his Pipe and started to build another Song – a Push, just to rile the man even more. He launched it and for once his aim was good enough to knock the Hamelyn Piper off his feet, even from such a distance.

The man was stunned for a moment, but snapped out of it and pulled a dark Pipe from his belt, quickly weaving notes together, taking Patch by surprise with the speed and strength of the result. A pocket of air shot from the Pipe straight at Patch, sending him flying before he could move out of the way. Winded, he quickly picked himself up off the ground.

The Hamelyn Piper roared in anger and started to build another attack; Patch was building one too. They launched simultaneously and the two Songs hurtled towards each other. At the midpoint the Songs collided, and a deafening thunderclap echoed around the Hollow. The two Pipers set about forming yet another attack.

Suddenly Patch saw Barver closing in fast from behind the Organ. If the Hamelyn Piper hadn't been focusing on Patch, Barver would have been the target of those powerful Songs, but instead he and Wren had a clear run. It was only as Barver flew over the tops of the organ Pipes that the

Hamelyn Piper saw him, and by then it was too late.

The open pouch of Kaposher hurtled down towards him and exploded. A cloud of dust obscured the man, and some of the Pipers closest to the stage collapsed as the Kaposher reached them.

Barver and Wren saw Patch and started to head towards him.

"Go!" shouted Patch, waving at them to leave the Hollow. "*Go, now!*" He looked at the huge cloud of Kaposher obscuring the stage. The way that the pouch had *exploded* left Patch feeling very uneasy indeed. "*Get out of here!*"

They seemed to get the message, and began to turn.

Then Patch felt the cold edge of a knife at his throat, and a strong grip on his arm; his Pipe was wrenched from his hand. He didn't dare move, but he could see the sleeve of the arm holding him, with the colours of a Custodian's uniform.

The Hamelyn Piper's voice boomed through the air. "You fly *anywhere,* dragon, and he dies!"

A swirl of air began to spin on the stage, taking the dust cloud higher and higher until it dispersed. The Hamelyn Piper was standing there, the hood of his robe still hiding most of his face, but not his malicious grin. He was surrounded by a shimmer of air, the telltale sign of the protective shield he'd managed to create. The shimmer faded as the short-lived barrier vanished.

All around the Hollow, fallen Pipers were recovering and rising to their feet.

"Let him go or I will *burn* you," shouted Barver, maintaining his height.

"My *soldier* will slit his throat if you make any such attempt," cried the Hamelyn Piper. He waved a hand in a carefree gesture. "By all means try!"

Barver scowled but did nothing. On his back, Wren glared at the man.

The Hamelyn Piper gestured to his "soldier". Patch was pushed towards the stage and forced up onto it. He saw the members of the Council standing on the grass nearby, their faces blank.

"Now isn't *this* interesting," said the Hamelyn Piper. He pulled back his hood, and ran his fingers over the Mask covering Patch's face.

With the man's hood down, for the first time Patch got a good look at him, and all he could do was stare. Terrible scars covered his face, long healed-over but deep. The man's right ear was ragged, half-gone. But that wasn't why Patch stared.

He'd seen that face before, without the scars, but filthy and bearded. "My God," he said. "You...you look exactly like him."

"What are you babbling about?" said the man, raising an eyebrow.

"The prisoner in the Iron Mask."

The man's eyes narrowed for a moment, and then he smiled. "Oh, very good! *Very* good. You do seem to know a lot, don't you? And you have his Mask. However did you come by it? I thought it hadn't been found. I must try not to kill you, so you can tell me all about it later!" He looked more closely at the Mask, and his smile became a sneer. "Ah, I see what you did! Inside out, I'm impressed! Very clever. I wonder if Casimir originally made it that way, as a device for his own protection?" He looked around at his soldiers, only half of whom had managed to stand again. The rest were lying still. "You're little more than a *boy*, and look at all the trouble you've caused me. That will take time to fix." He shot Patch a look of sheer malice. "His Pipe if you please!" he ordered, and the Custodian – the *soldier* – holding Patch handed it over. "Beautifully made," he said, studying it. "The glaze is unusual." He raised it to his nose and sniffed. "Not sure what it's made of, but look at mine!" He held his own Pipe up for Patch to see. "Obsidiac glaze, of exceptional thickness and quality. Better than yours, lad." He put his own Pipe away, and gripped Patch's with both hands. "Shame," he said, snapping it in two and tossing the pieces to one side.

Patch felt as if he'd been punched in the stomach. He'd been getting to *like* that Pipe.

"I suppose you must be a trainee, studying at Tiviscan,"

said the Hamelyn Piper. "Imagine! Tiviscan's last hope, a child!" He leaned close to Patch, leering at him. "I know a way to deal with children, lad." Patch squirmed in the grip of the soldier holding him, and the Hamelyn Piper backed away. "But yes, of *course* the prisoner looked like me," he said, smiling. "Our mother would have been *so* disappointed by what I did to him."

"Your own brother?" said Patch.

"My twin, no less! It was always my plan to have him punished in my place. I played a Song of Forgetting and Piped away his memories, then kept him safe in a secret location. All I had to do was lead the authorities to him when the time was right! But the Eight made everything *so* much more difficult. They kept closing in on me, hundreds of miles away from where I was keeping my brother. It was tiresome! They almost got me, too. Left me with *this*." He ran his fingers over the scars on his face. "A present from the Eight. I've wanted to repay the favour all these years, but I had to be patient and not draw their attention. And what patience I have shown! Then some idiot started messing around, playing illegal Songs and making everyone worry about Dark Pipers. I'd intended to put my plans into action *next* year, but I decided to bring everything forward. Rundel Stone had started to ask awkward questions! I couldn't take the risk that he'd stumble onto something, or get the other remaining members of the Eight involved."

Patch gulped. The idiot messing around and playing illegal Songs had been *him.*

"Why are you doing this?" said Patch.

"To rule! This world needs a ruler who's truly worthy of the responsibility."

"And that's you?"

"Of course! There are so very *few* people deserving of power. The rest –" he looked out across the Hollow, at all the people under his control – "cattle. *Sheep.*" He leaned close again, and smiled. "Now, I *could* tear that mask from you and make you just another of my soldiers, but I wouldn't want you to miss the rest of the performance. I think you'll appreciate it. Right now, they obey my will for as long as the Song plays, but when I am done they will be mine *for ever.*"

Patch saw the fearful look on Barver's face, and on Wren's. They had to escape, he knew, escape and warn the world – and Patch had an idea, a way he could help them do it.

"I have one question," said Patch. He made sure he sounded absolutely defeated. "Did you ever think of your brother, condemned in the dungeon?" His voice grew quieter with every word, and the Hamelyn Piper drew closer to hear better. "Did you ever think about what he suffered?" whispered Patch. "Have you no *compassion*?"

The Hamelyn Piper put his lips right up to Patch's ear. "No!" he snarled with glee.

His glee was short-lived. Patch turned quickly and flung his head forward with as much strength as he could muster, catching the Hamelyn Piper on the nose with the full force of the blow. There was a satisfying crunch as the metal Mask hit home. The Hamelyn Piper fell to his knees with a howl, his hands covering his face, blood pouring out between his fingers.

At once, Patch flung his head backwards, connecting hard with the soldier holding him; the soldier's grip weakened and Patch tore free. He ran towards the rear of the stage where the Organ Pipes loomed high above him.

"Get him!" screamed the Hamelyn Piper, and more of his soldiers – the Puppets – strode with terrible purpose towards Patch. The Hamelyn Piper brought his obsidiac Pipe to his lips and began to play a Song that Patch recognized at once. A battle Song, and a powerful one – it wouldn't take long to complete, but Patch realized it wasn't going to be aimed at *him*: the Hamelyn Piper had turned to face Barver and Wren.

"Barver!" Patch yelled. "Do as you swore! Get out of here!"

He could see the hestitation on Barver's face, but there was no other choice. The dracogriff flew hard; seconds later the Song was launched, catching Barver a glancing blow. He tumbled; Wren only just managed to stay on, but Barver kept them airborne.

The soldiers were closing in on Patch, and only one route was left: onto the very Pipes of the Organ itself. He leaped high and got his fingers on the edge of the smallest Pipe, pulling himself out of reach just in time. His pursuers hoisted one of their number up after him. He backed away, climbing the taller Pipes as he went; ahead, he could see more soldiers climbing the smallest Pipes on the other side of the Organ.

On the stage below, the Hamelyn Piper was working on another battle Song to throw at Barver, but after a few seconds he stopped. "No, no," he said. "That's boring. I've got a much better idea, and I do love a challenge!" He put his Pipe away and hurried to his keyboards. He sat and rubbed his hands to warm them. "Let me see…" he said, and he feverishly worked the keys and pedals, adding more layers to the Song.

Barver and Wren were halfway to the edge of the Hollow.

The Hamelyn Piper turned to look at them and frowned. "Nothing?" he said, disappointed. "Mmm. That really should have worked on a dragon. Hang on! Were those feathers I saw? Was that some kind of beak? A griffin?"

He played a slight variation on what he'd added before, then stopped and frowned again. Barver was at the edge of the Hollow now. They were almost free!

The Hamelyn Piper grinned. "Of course!" he said. "How stupid of me!" He looked up to where Patch was scrambling to ever-higher Pipes, always just out of reach of his pursuers. "Taking control of a mind is so much easier one-to-one," he called. "Even if the target is a dracogriff!" He began to play again, laughing as he did.

Dismayed, Patch watched as Barver turned and started to fly back, helpless against the power of the obsidiac Pipe Organ. Patch felt a hand grab at his ankle, and he kicked it away, almost losing his balance. There was only one Pipe left to climb now – the largest of them all. He had little strength remaining in his arms, but he hauled himself up. This last organ Pipe was four feet across. He could feel the deep notes reverberate in his *bones*. Its edge was only a few inches thick and he struggled to stand, almost toppling into the gaping hole at its centre.

Barver reached the stage, level in height with Patch. The dracogriff's eyes were blank; on his back, Wren pleaded with him. "*Barver!*" she cried. "It's *me! Please!*"

She met Patch's eyes and shook her head in despair.

The Hamelyn Piper smiled at Patch, then looked to Barver. "Let's deal with your rider first!" he said. "Fly until you are above the rocks over there. Drop your rider onto them from a *great* height. Then come back here and eat your friend."

"NO!" shouted Wren. She tried to jump from Barver, but he grabbed her by the arm and held her dangling under him as he flew off.

The Hamelyn Piper looked to Patch's pursuers. "Leave him where he is," he instructed. "Let him watch his friend die."

Patch looked on in horror. Barver flew away from the Hollow until he was directly above a wide rocky outcrop. Up, up he went, a hundred feet higher, two hundred, three, all the while ignoring Wren's screams.

At last he stopped climbing. He held Wren up in front of him and looked at her.

Wren was distraught, tears flooding down her cheeks. She could see no emotion in his eyes, only cold obedience.

"Please," she said. "Barver—"

He dropped her to a certain death below, then turned back to kill Patch.

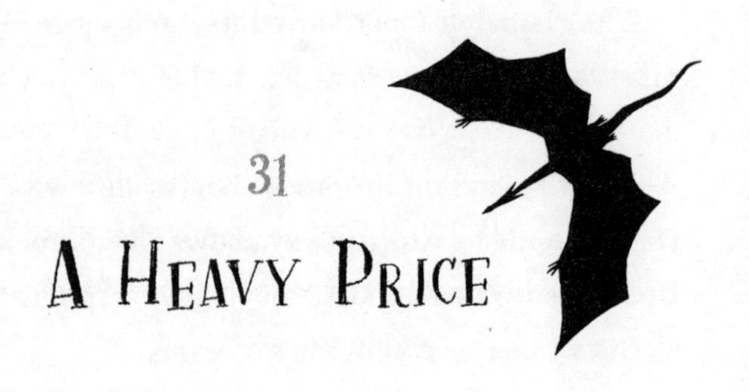

31 A Heavy Price

Wren screamed as she fell. Above her she saw Barver flying off, and she knew his target was Patch. She wondered if her dracogriff friend was still conscious of what was happening. If so, he would be suffering horribly.

She tumbled down through the air. She could see the rocks below her as she hurtled towards them, and she knew what she had to do.

Wren reached to her wrist and took hold of the bracelet that let her take human form. Alia's words of warning echoed in her head: *Do not remove it…You'd be a rat, immediately, and no amount of magic would shield you in future.*

She pulled hard, and the bracelet came apart. The beads scattered in the air, becoming ash. Pain coursed through her body as she changed – immediately, and for evermore – into a rat.

At this size, she was safe. She could fall from any height, and the air would slow her down, cushion her.

Wren Cobble, *rat*, flopped onto the rocks and looked across to the Hollow. Barver had almost reached Patch. She closed her eyes, unable to watch.

Patch saw her change, and understood at once what she'd done. Tears poured down his cheeks, knowing what it had cost her.

Get away from here, Wren, he thought. She was the only one who could warn the rest of the world now.

Barver would be on him in moments. Below, the Hamelyn Piper's laugh became ever more insane as Barver approached his target. There was nothing he could do, except stand and wait for the end to come, keeping his footing on the vast organ Pipe and its gaping core.

The *Pipe.*

Patch gasped as the thought came to him. He shook his head, angry with himself for not thinking of it sooner.

Taking a deep breath, he lifted up his right foot and gathered all the courage he had. He stepped forward into empty space and fell, plunging into the darkness of the Pipe's interior. It grew narrower lower down, jamming him inside; the sense of claustrophobia was unbearable.

He could hear the Hamelyn Piper's laugh falter, hear him scream at Barver to stop. But it was far too late.

Barver would seek his prey, whatever it took.

Patch closed his eyes. A moment later, everything exploded around him.

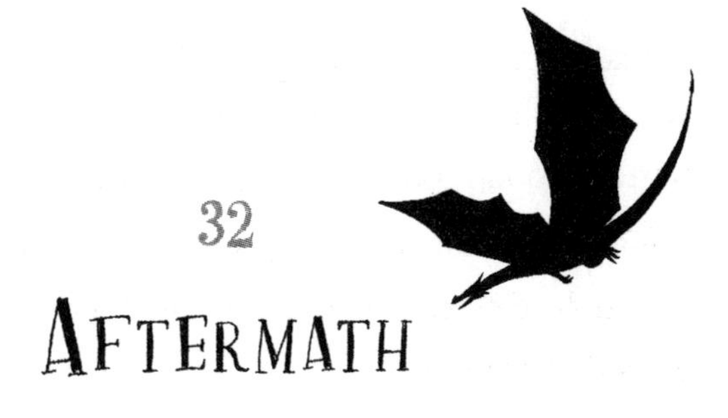

32 AFTERMATH

Patch opened his eyes and found himself looking straight at the face of a rat: Wren was sitting on the Mask peering into an eyehole.

Get up! she signed, and moved off him.

He sat up slowly. Pieces of debris fell from him – smashed organ Pipes and chunks of wood. He groaned, every part of him in pain. His lip felt swollen, and he had cuts and bruises aplenty. He started to work at the twine securing the Mask, eager to get out of it, but Barver had tied it too well.

Any bones broken? signed Wren. She was perched on a large section of smashed Pipe, a few feet away.

"I don't think so," said Patch. He looked right at her, and felt tearful. "I saw you fall," he said. "I know what you had to do. I'm so sorry..."

Yeah, signed Wren. She pointed to the markings around her midriff. The pattern of beads was still there, but they were all solid black now. *Being a live rat is better than being a dead girl.*

Patch reached out his hand to her, and she ran to his shoulder.

He stood, and they looked around. Everywhere in Monash Hollow, people were on the ground, out cold. In places, some were stirring, or sitting up and holding their heads. The Council members were on the grass near the stage, starting to rouse themselves.

"How long have I been unconscious?" said Patch.

I got back here a few minutes ago, signed Wren. *It was a long way to run on little feet. Half an hour maybe? I thought you were never going to wake up.*

Just in front of them a large pile of debris suddenly rose up, startling them both. A very familiar head emerged from underneath.

"What happened?" said Barver, blinking. "Why is everything blurry?"

"You ploughed head-first into the organ Pipes," said Patch. "Don't you remember anything?"

Barver frowned. He stood up, the debris falling away from him. "The last I remember I was escaping with Wren on my back!" he said. "And then I—" His mouth opened wide with horror. Huge tears welled up in his eyes.

"*Wren!*" he wailed. "*No! I killed her!*"

"It's okay!" said Patch. "She's here!"

"I can't see properly," said Barver, sniffling. "Talk to me, Wren! Let me hear your voice!"

Wren squeaked.

"She's a rat again," said Patch. "She had to break her bracelet and change back to survive the fall."

"But that means she'll never be able to change again!" said Barver, blinking away his tears. "We'll find a way, Wren. We'll find that griffin, and—" He was cut off by a shout from nearby.

"We have been attacked!" came the shout. "Get the rest of the Council back to the tent!"

Patch looked across and saw a group of Custodians; standing among them was Lord Drevis, who suddenly pointed right at Patch. "He wears the Mask of the Hamelyn Piper! Seize him!"

The Custodians ran directly at Patch. He held his arms in the air. "Hold on!" he said. "I'm not—" One of the Custodians tackled him; they hit the ground together, and the Mask popped open and came off. The Custodian pinned him down, but the relief of being out of the Mask was immense. Then Patch realized Lord Drevis was looming over him, staring.

"Good God," said Drevis. "Patch Brightwater. What have you done? Explain what happened here!"

"You were under a controlling Song, Lord," said Patch.

"Everyone was! Try hard, and you'll be able to remember!"

Lord Drevis glared at him, but then his glare faded. "There was another man—" he said. He looked around at the debris. "He played a vast Pipe Organ. He tried to seize everyone's minds! You fought him!"

"That's it!" said Patch. "It's coming back to you!"

"He was—" started Drevis, but then his eyes went wide. "No. *No.*" Drevis looked horrified. "Let him up," he ordered, and the Custodian released Patch and pulled him back to his feet. "I remember it now," said Drevis. "The Hamelyn Piper. How is that possible?"

"The prisoner in Tiviscan was his brother, Lord," said Patch. "He'd tricked you into imprisoning his twin, all those years ago."

"An innocent man," said Drevis, stunned. "I condemned an innocent man. Is the true villain dead?"

"He was at the keys when the organ was destroyed," said Patch. "He must have been crushed."

"Clear this area!" yelled Drevis. "Find the corpse! *Now!*"

They watched as the Custodian Pipers worked to clear the debris. Patch felt a dread building deep within him. As each piece of shattered Pipe and broken timber was thrown to the side, his dread grew.

When the stage was cleared, no sign of the Hamelyn Piper – and no sign of his Puppets – had been found.

They had vanished.

* * *

Lord Drevis ordered that the search be widened. He looked at the Mask he now held, then turned to Patch. “You were thought to have died when the dragons attacked,” he said. “Instead, the chaos gave you the chance to escape. But why take the Mask?”

Patch shrugged. “I honestly don’t know. But I’m glad I did.”

Drevis folded it, inverting it again. “It protected you,” he said. “Smart lad. And it’s lucky for us that you came back to Tiviscan. Now, there’s much you have to explain to the Council. Come with me.”

Patch looked across to Barver and Wren, who were clearly anxious. He signed to them: *Wait here.* Then he followed Drevis, who led him across the Hollow to a sumptuous tent where two Custodians stood guard outside.

Drevis held the tent flap open for Patch. Inside, the other four members of the Council sat on wooden stools around a central table. Each of them bore scratches that showed how near the stage they had been when Barver had destroyed the Pipe Organ. Some held small glasses filled with a brown liquid that Patch suspected was brandy; he could see more than one hand trembling a little.

Patch stayed by the tent entrance, but Drevis strode over to the others.

“Your memories have returned?” Drevis asked them.

"More or less," said Lord Cobb. "Imagine, all this time. An innocent man in the dungeons!"

Drevis said nothing, but Patch knew the comment must have pained him.

"Those Pipes were obsidiac glazed," said Lady Winkless.

"Impossible!" cried Lord Pewter.

"No, no, he's correct," said Lady Rumsey. She held a fragment up. "I've yet to do the sums, but the glaze is thick. There must have been a vast store! Goodness knows how he got all that obsidiac."

Patch kept silent – he would tell Lord Drevis what he knew about the source of the black diamond, nobody else.

"Wherever it came from, it's ours now," said Lord Cobb. "It's a source of unspeakable power, and it will be researched. I'll put our top people on to it!"

"The dragons may have something to say about that," said Lord Drevis.

"Let them," said Cobb. "One thing's for certain, that amount of obsidiac will be very handy in rebuilding the Castle defences."

Patch had listened to this madness long enough. "You must destroy every fragment!" he cried.

Lord Cobb frowned. "Who's this? We're discussing sensitive Council business! This is no place for a boy!"

Drevis gestured for Patch to come closer, and Patch saw Lord Pewter sit up sharply, eyes wide.

"This is Patch Brightwater," said Drevis. "*This* is who was wearing the Mask, and fought the Hamelyn Piper."

"Brightwater?" said Lady Rumsey, peering at Patch. "Didn't we lock him up?"

"We did," said Drevis. "He was in the cell next to the Hamelyn Piper – well, the Piper's *brother*, as we now know. Brightwater was presumed dead after the dragon attack."

"Well then, there's only one course of action!" said Lady Rumsey. "Guard!" One of the Custodians entered the tent. "Throw this criminal in a cell at once."

"What are you doing?" said Lord Pewter.

"The law demands it!" Lady Rumsey replied.

"Enough!" said Drevis. "He saved us all. I believe a suitable reward is appropriate for his courage." On the table in front of him was a small chest, which he opened. He took out paper and a quill, and wrote for a few moments. When he was done, he stood and showed what he'd written to each member of the Council. "Any objections?" he said. There were none, although Lady Rumsey looked slightly peeved. "Good."

Drevis passed the paper to Patch, and Patch read it.

It was a pardon. It absolved him of all guilt, and meant he was free. Tears rolled down his cheeks, and he didn't care. He folded the pardon up and placed it in his pocket, his fingers brushing against another piece of paper – Alia's prophecy, and an unwelcome reminder of Erner. Even so, the joy and relief he felt at being pardoned was so strong he thought his legs might buckle.

"Wait!" cried Lord Pewter, rummaging in the chest where Drevis had found the paper. He took out a small block of wood and what looked like an ink pad. "It still needs stamping with the Council Seal to make it official."

Drevis smiled and held his hand out. "My mistake. Can I have it back for a moment, Patch?"

Patch reluctantly took the pardon out of his pocket and returned it, feeling like it would burst into flames or simply vanish, but it was stamped and back in his grasp within seconds.

Drevis smiled at him. "When this immediate chaos abates, we must talk more. I'd like to know just how a disgraced trainee saved Tiviscan, and the world."

"The Hamelyn Piper is still out there, Lord," said Patch. "The world isn't saved yet."

"You saved it for today, at least," said Drevis. "That's all a hero can ever do."

At that, the tent flap opened and an out-of-breath Custodian entered. "Lord Drevis, your presence is needed."

"Good," said Drevis. He looked to the Council. "The hunt for the Hamelyn Piper is being organized in the Castle as we speak, and I must oversee it."

"But there are things I must tell you—" said Patch.

"It will keep until later," said Drevis, and he left.

"I suppose we too should make our way to the Castle," said Lord Cobb. He stood slowly from his stool and began heading out.

"Oh please wait," said Lady Winkless. "I need to sit a moment longer. I'm too old to be in such a hurry."

"Indeed," said Lord Pewter. "Allow us to finish our brandies, at least."

"Oh very well," said Lord Cobb. He turned back to the table, then stopped, gesturing to something on the ground near Patch's feet. He looked at Patch. "Did you drop your pardon, lad?"

But Patch still had the pardon in his hand. He looked down and saw what Cobb meant, and realized at once what it was. He checked his pocket to be sure, and yes – the pocket was empty. When he'd removed the pardon to be stamped, the paper with Alia's prophecy had come out too and fallen to the ground.

Lord Cobb picked it up and unfolded it. Patch had a curious sense of unease.

"'They thought they had us'," Cobb read aloud, in a monotone voice. "'But we're almost clear. Just the ridge to go. What's wrong with you? What's wrong?'" Lord Cobb looked up from the paper. "An *odd* set of words, don't you think?" he said.

Patch felt every drop of blood drain from his face. He could hear Alia's voice in his mind, saying exactly the same thing: *An odd set of words, don't you think?*

"I agree," said Lady Winkless. "Very odd."

"What say you, Patch?" said Lord Pewter.

Patch stayed silent, too stunned to answer.

"The lad's gone so very pale," said Lady Rumsey. "The day's been *quite* a strain, I imagine!"

An odd set of words, don't you think? I agree, very odd. What say you, Patch? The lad's gone so very pale. The day's been quite a strain, I imagine.

The precise words Alia had spoken. Patch had thought that those words were mere ramblings, but instead they had simply been a continuation of the prophecy.

There will come a time when you hear these words, Alia had told him. *A mouth that speaks them is a traitorous mouth.*

This was the first time the words had been spoken in their entirety. *This* was the moment the prophecy had warned him of.

This moment, and no other.

He felt sick with guilt. Erner had never been a traitor. The *Council* were the ones who had spoken the words. *They* were the ones who would betray him to whatever he feared the most.

When Erner had said it, Patch had most feared returning to the dungeons, being put back into the Dark by Rundel Stone.

But now…

His mouth went dry as he thought about what he feared most now. It was the leering face of the Hamelyn Piper that came to mind.

He looked at the Council, trying hard to keep his emotions from showing.

Get away as quickly as you can, Alia had said. *Run!*

The Council were still awaiting an explanation of what was written on the piece of paper. "Just the words of a song I heard," said Patch. "I wrote them down. Odd words indeed. Now, if the Council will permit, I think I need to go and get some rest."

"Indeed!" said Lord Cobb. "We'll speak again later, as Lord Drevis said."

Patch managed to smile. He prayed that it seemed genuine, because at that moment he wanted to scream and run from the tent.

"Absolutely," he said, and left.

Somehow he kept that smile going all the way out of the Council tent and across the Hollow.

He reached his friends. Barver was lying face down on the grass, his wings outstretched and badly cut. Wren was perched on his snout. "Ah, there you are!" said Barver. "How did it go?"

"Um," said Patch. "Yes. It went…fine. I was pardoned.

Which was good." He coughed. "How's your eyesight? Still blurry? Can you fly, do you think?"

"Oh, my eyesight's recovered," said Barver. "But flying? I doubt it." He sat up and used his hand to lift one wing, then let it drop. It was completely limp. "Something's broken in there." He picked the tip up and bent it right back, making Patch and Wren wince. "It shouldn't be able to do that, either," he said, with a shrug.

"Perhaps we should, um, journey to Marwheel and call in on Brother Duffle to treat you?" said Patch. "Right now?"

"Oh, I'd rather rest for a few days," said Barver. "We all should! You seem agitated, Patch. Do you need to empty your bladder or something?"

Wren frowned with concern. *You do seem agitated,* she signed. *What's wrong?*

And even though there was nobody close enough to eavesdrop, Patch leaned over and whispered to them both, explaining what had just happened.

Barver stared at him. Wren stared too.

"Alia warned me that prophecies were dangerous things," said Patch, frowning. "Never straightforward, she said. Tend to cause endless trouble."

"She was certainly right about *that*," said Barver.

"So," said Patch. "Marwheel Abbey, anyone?"

Wren hopped from Barver's snout to Patch's shoulder. *We should leave at once, but how can we get away unseen?*

Patch nodded to the edge of the Hollow farthest from Tiviscan. "We can reach the Penance River from that side," he said. "If we can sneak into the trees, it's forest all the way."

"Avoid the roads," said Barver. "Good."

We've done it before, signed Wren.

"Are we sure about this, Patch?" said Barver. "The prophecy already led us astray once. You say the Council will betray us to the Hamelyn Piper, but how? And what about Lord Drevis? My mother trusted him."

Patch shook his head, uncertain. "Drevis left the tent before it happened. Perhaps he's trustworthy, perhaps not. That must be for Tobias, Alia and Rundel Stone to decide, when we tell them what's happened here. Let *them* deal with the Hamelyn Piper. We have our own business to attend to."

"Yes!" said Barver. "Our own business – to find Underath's griffin!"

Wren looked dejected. *Alia said breaking my bracelet would leave me permanently changed. Nothing can be done for me now.*

"What kind of talk is that?" scoffed Barver. "We'll find that griffin, Wren, and all will come good."

"There's something we have to do first," said Patch. He pictured Erner's shocked face as he'd fallen from Barver and into the lake below, swimming for shore to an uncertain future at the hands of those mercenaries. "We have a friend to rescue," he said. "Agreed?"

Agreed, signed Wren.

"Agreed," said Barver.

The Hollow itself was emptying, people going back to the town and Castle. Patch led the way to the far edge of the Hollow, and they waited. When they thought it would be safe, they walked into the cover of the trees.

Their departure went entirely unnoticed.

So it was that the three friends – Piper, dracogriff and rat – began the journey that would take them, eventually, back to Marwheel Abbey. Even after they reached the Penance River, each step they took was leaden, as they fretted about Erner, and the Council, and the Hamelyn Piper.

"Look at us," said Barver. "Together we saved the world, but we're weighed down by worries!"

You should play a Lift and lighten our mood, Patch, signed Wren. *Like you did to the little ant and the monks in Marwheel.*

"My new Pipe was destroyed," said Patch, thinking of the terrible feeling of loss he'd suffered when it happened. "I hope you can spare a few more feathers, Barver, when I make a new one?"

Barver nodded. "As many as you require."

Can't you play the Lift without a Pipe? signed Wren.

"I can try," said Patch. But his lip, injured when the Pipe Organ was destroyed, was too swollen. When he tried to whistle, all that came out were flubs and raspberries. "Sorry," he said.

"Never mind," said Barver. "Do you know the shanty 'Farewell the Winter's Frowning'? It's popular in the Islands."

"It's popular everywhere," said Patch. He cleared his throat and started to sing, his voice unsteady. "*Farewell the winter's frowning*," he began. "*The sun's smile comes again.*"

As Patch sang the rest of the verse, Barver sang too. Wren joined in with tuneful squeaks.

They gave voice to the lyrics of hope and renewal, and as they did their singing grew ever more heartfelt. Soon enough, hope had truly bloomed within them; they smiled and laughed once more. And all from a simple shanty.

For there is a truth, one that is all too easy to forget:

There is magic in music.

Listen…

A
DARKNESS
OF
DRAGONS

Patch, Wren and Barver
will return for a second
spell-slinging, shape-shifting,
flame-throwing

SONGS OF MAGIC

adventure in 2019...

Check here for news:

@Usborne

@SethPatrickUK

@usborne_books

facebook.com/usbornepublishing

#ADarknessOfDragons

Acknowledgements

Patch, Wren and Barver have been waiting a very long time for me to tell their story. I thank them for their patience.

Thanks also to my agent, Luigi Bonomi, who encouraged me to follow my heart when I was dithering about what to work on next.

I'm indebted to Anne Finnis, Rebecca Hill and Sarah Stewart at Usborne for all their help and support in turning my early efforts into the finished work you have in your hands.

My final thanks, of course, go to my wife and children. Without you, there would be no music at all.

About the Author

S.A. Patrick was born in Belfast. When he was a child, he wanted to write video games, become an author, and have magical powers. The first two came true. If he does ever get magical powers, he hopes people like dragons and griffins because there'll suddenly be a *lot* of them around.

He has had four previous books published as Seth Patrick. *Songs of Magic: A Darkness of Dragons* is his first book for children.

Follow S.A. Patrick online

@SethPatrickUK

#ADarknessOfDragons

Grand Isle

Grand Isle

— A Novel —

Sarah Van Arsdale

State University of New York Press
Albany, New York

Cover art entitled "August, Prince Edward Island." Pastel on paper by Michael Goodwin.

Chapter 10, from Section 1, first appeared in *2 Bridges Review* under the title "The News." Fall, 2011, Volume 1, issue 1, p. 168.

"a piece of air with lightning in it," is from Judy Grahn's *Common Woman Poems.*

The quote from Vampire Weekend is from their song "Campus."

The poem "Pneumography" is by Sarah Van Arsdale.

Published by
State University of New York Press, Albany

Printed in the United States of America

For information, contact State University of New York Press, Albany, NY
www.sunypress.edu

Excelsior Editions is an imprint of State University of New York Press

Production by Diane Ganeles
Marketing by Kate McDonnell

Library of Congress Cataloging-in-Publication Data

Van Arsdale, Sarah.
Grand isle : a novel / Sarah Van Arsdale
p. cm.
Includes index.
ISBN 978-1-4384-4240-2 (pbk. : alk. paper)
I. Title.

PS3551.R725G73 2012
813'.54—dc23 2011030207

10 9 8 7 6 5 4 3 2 1

For Diana Cort Van Arsdale:
consummate grace under pressure

No worst, there is none. Pitched past pitch of grief,
More pangs will, schooled at forepangs, wilder wring.
Comforter, where, where is your comforting?

—Gerard Manley Hopkins

(i who have died am alive again today,
and this is the sun's birthday; this is the birth
day of life and of love and wings: and of the gay
great happening illimitably earth)

—e. e. cummings

Acknowledgments

One writes a novel alone, but a novel—or my novels, at any rate—could not be written without a community of writers. I'm very fortunate to have such a community, including those who have helped directly and indirectly with this book: Rachel Morton, Peter Bricklebank, David Groff, Richard Goodman, David Harris Ebenbach, Chris Bram, Draper Shreeve, Barbara Feldon, Elaine Sexton, Heather Sellers, and the inimitable "Ragdale Family." My thanks for sustaining me and allowing me to reach this occasion.

Thanks also to my agent, Molly Lyons; James Peltz and everyone at SUNY Press; Chuck DeLaney at the Sheffield School; the *Fiction Writers Review*, and Sally Henry and the Group.

I am also indebted to the Hambidge Artist Residency Program, the Ragdale Foundation, the Jentel Foundation, and the Djerassi Resident Artists Program, for giving me the time and space to work on other projects after this book was completed.

Thanks to Dr. Jessica Van Arsdale for serving as physician to the characters in an early draft; Peter Van Arsdale, luthier *par excellence*, for serving as stringed instruments consultant; Jeff Owens, artist, for on-the-spot and spot-on metal welding information; Steve Greco for soundtrack recommendations; and the Shelter Island (New York) Town Hall. Mad props to Hyacinth Parker and Zoe Morton for updating the youth language and culture. Any errors in this book are my own, not theirs.

Part One

One

Morning comes early to the summer camps on the eastern shore of the island, and on this Memorial Day, Tessa Bartlett tries to locate her feeling, now that she's back on the porch of Jake's summer cottage for another year; maybe she's a little nervous, or maybe she's a little smug. Happy? Sure. The house looks out to the bay and then to the shore that wraps around Grand Isle like a cupped hand, protective, full of water, waterbirds, and thick green leaves. Tessa watches the first sun ignite the flowerbeds along the brick path leading down the lawn to the dock.

From where Tessa sits, her bare feet propped against the porch rail, the late-blooming white tulips Jake agreed to last fall seem lit from within, as if they're exploding with their own internal light. This weekend, the spring flooding has subsided, and Jake has restored the dock to its summer spot on the speckled surface of the bay. There's a little wind, and Tessa can hear it rustling in the branches of the trees hanging over the porch roof. She feels fortunate, that's what it is, a little surprised, and hard on the heels of that, a flicker of her old feeling: undeserving.

She hasn't slept well, waking at two, at four, and finally at six, slipping out of bed so as not to disturb Jake, standing at the front window, watching the water. Now, her head hurts, and yet the day is so pitch-perfect, and the sun is so warm, that watching the tulips' heads bobbing on their green stems, Tessa wonders if this is happiness, sitting here with the flowerbeds and her good, strong coffee and her early morning moment alone. Soon, Jake will be getting up, and he'll come down the stairs in his running attire, his sneakered steps light on the stairs.

She ought to ask Jake about getting new cushions for the porch furniture today. The old ones were here when Jake bought the cottage from his uncle three years earlier, when Tessa was first getting involved with him. The place was a wreck, and since then, together they've made it more than habitable. The old cushions are faded nearly white from the sun, and all the life's been squashed out of them. She could make a trip into Wisconset this morning, and she probably should, because later today the guests will be arriving for their traditional welcome-summer barbecue, the first of the season.

She hears Jake first by his humming. The mood will be good: it's "La Habanera" from *Carmen*, and then screen door opens. "Good morning, my sweet," Jake says. He surveys the bright morning, the bay, the perfectly tuned day. "Another day in hell." She turns to look at him and smiles. She's glad to see him. She is. "Yes. It really is," she says, as always when he points out the beauty of the place with his happy sarcasm wishing she had a more clever riposte. "Just awful."

He looks good for fifty, with his compact body that he's kept trim, in his baggy t-shirt and running shorts, curly-haired, leaning into the porch rail to stretch his legs. He looks boyish, especially without the rimless, round glasses he wears when he's working on a violin or reading music. Sometimes she thinks he looks better than she does, despite her attempts to keep up with running and yoga classes, and despite the fact that she's six years younger.

He straightens, steps toward her, and she thinks for a moment he's bending to kiss her; instead, he takes a sip of her coffee. "Ah," he says, shivering in mock-shock at the strength of it. "One sip enough to stop your heart. I'll be back," he calls, trotting down the porch steps, then trotting backward, blowing her kiss, singing out the high lines of *Carmen*'s "La Habanera": "Mais, si je t'aime / Si je t'aime, prends garde à toi!"

Tessa stays on the porch for awhile, watching her luminescent tulips, drinking her coffee, appreciating the long sigh of open time ahead of her, when she doesn't have to rush to an early morning appointment with a graduate student, or, worse, with an anthropology faculty committee. The semester is finally, truly over, and for the next ten weeks she's free to work on her book on the early Arctic expeditions: how the Inuit ways of seeing the world changed with the arrival of those first, strange explorers. She knows it would be more marketable to write about what's happening there now, with the customs melting along with the ice, but she doesn't like thinking about that; it's too terrible, too real.

She stands, and stretches. She's got to get a decent night's sleep. Hands on her hips, she too descends the steps, walks out into the yard, scouting the area around the little gardening shed, looking for evidence of ferns and flowers beginning to push their heads up from the leaved earth. If the place had been built on a much bigger scale, it could be called a "compound": beyond the shed, nestled among the forsythia, sits the former canoe hut that Jake has renovated into a studio for his violin making, but this is his inviolable territory, and she's left it unplanted, each year letting the forsythia and the wild asparagus fern take over.

She turns back toward the water and her flowerbeds. The moment of the most intense light has passed, the sun diffusing across the lawn, the tulips now past that initial stage of saturation. The perennial beds look like hell, and she probably won't have time to pick up new cushions for the porch, because she'll be in the garden all morning, and everybody's coming at six.

She doesn't bother collecting her tools from the shed; instead, she just drops to the ground and starts pulling the weeds, inspecting the leaves of the plants, raking aside the dead leaves from winter with her hands. "If you want to put in a flower garden, be my guest," Jake told her that first summer, when she said she could imagine it lush with perennials. "Flowerbeds are overrated. All that work and nothing to eat," he'd said. "And don't think you're putting me on weeding duty. It'll be your responsibility."

Soon, she's worked her way up the beds that line the long, straight pathway from the dock to the porch, and she's making her way toward the shed, carrying a handful of detritus, stones and leaves and little sticks, and things are looking better, less neglected, and that's when she hears it, a small whimpering cry. She stops moving.

The closest house isn't quite close enough so that she'd hear a bit of crying from it, but she looks up there anyway, through the spit of woods to the next lawn. Sometimes the owner, Ivy Bless, is about in her yard, pretending to garden but mostly spying, Tessa thinks. But today, the house looks utterly empty.

Above her, the salty wind of the clear day breezing up from the southern, sea side of the island is picking up. She can hear it brushing through the needled branches of the tall pines that cluster around the yard. In the water, the dock creaks a little. There is no cry. She shakes her head, crouches to the bed that fronts the shed, which she'll fill mostly with annuals. Her hands are now covered with dirt, earth packed under her short nails. But then it comes again, she's sure of it. This time, the sound continues, and she turns toward the shed; she's certain it's coming from the shed.

As she stands, wincing a little as her knees straighten, the sound gets louder, and now she can hear that without a doubt it's a cry.

As she rounds the corner of the shed, the memory that still haunts her here comes back: the first time she and Jake came up to Grand Isle, when they'd been seeing each other just a few months, early spring, the flash of a cat bolting across the road, the thick thud of the tires as they hit. And then the rest of that trip, which she doesn't let herself think about. She has a flickering thought that what she's hearing now is the mewling sound of that cat, the ghost of that cat, and she even goes so far as to wonder why it would haunt her now. But then she's at the door of the shed, peering in.

It's dark inside, and smells musty, dirt and potting soil and manure, and something else too, a stronger, pungent smell. Everything is the way she left it last fall, her old pots lined up on a shelf, the rakes and shovels propped up in a corner, and the wheelbarrow tipped on its side, at Jake's suggestion, so that any errant rainwater or melting snow wouldn't collect there through winter.

She sees a motion down on the floor, and hears again the mewling, which she quickly sees isn't a cat at all, but is a raccoon, a tiny raccoon, too small to be on its own, and that's when she realizes that the smell is coming from the body of the mother raccoon, lying not far from Tessa's own feet. She gasps, presses her hand to her chest, frozen in that moment, having no idea what to do.

And then she hears Jake behind her, saying, "What's going on?" still panting a little from his run. He'll never learn to cool down slowly, preferring one last quick sprint down the driveway.

"Look," she says, and points into the shed, and he looks, and his breath catches, too, and he says, "What is it? A raccoon? Did you kill it?"

This is just the kind of thing he says sometimes that makes her wonder if she knows him at all. "No, of course I didn't kill it," she says. "I just heard the sound, and I came out here, and it was dead, and its baby is crying."

"God, Tess. Didn't I tell you to shut up the shed tightly last year? We have to do better than this." Jake exhales through his lips, making a sound a little like a horse. "Come on," he says, "we'd better go inside and call Dick."

"Dick? What's Dick going to do?"

"He's got a shotgun," Jake says, turning toward the house, and he's up the stairs already before she's left the shed. There is the baby raccoon, nuzzling its mother's fur, nudging the mother's body with its tiny nose.

She sprints across the lawn and up the steps to the house, letting the screen door slap shut behind her. Jake is already in the kitchen, dialing the old-fashioned rotary phone, but she reaches over and taps down the hook, severing the connection, even as she does feeling her own heart begin to pound. Usually, when his mood turns, she makes herself very quiet and very small.

"What on earth are you doing?" he asks.

"That's what I should be asking you," she says. "You're not really thinking of killing that baby raccoon."

He gives her one incredulous look, and for a moment she's scared of what he's going to say, or do, but he hands her the receiver, shrugging, then he takes a glass from the drainer beside the sink, turns on the tap, and lets the water run before filling the glass. He drinks the water down. He's still breathing hard.

"You can't keep wild animals around, Tessa," in the overly calm voice he uses when he's angry with her. "You don't understand how it is up here. That adult raccoon—"

"The mother," she corrects him.

"All right, the mother raccoon," he begins again, "is dead, and there's no sign of foul play. I mean, it isn't like it got hit by a car. There's rabies around here. Remember when they had to put those dogs down?"

"That was years ago," she says. "Anyway, they were Rottweilers."

"Okay, what bright ideas do you have? What else are we going to do? Even if it isn't rabid, we can't have a raccoon hanging around the house getting into the garbage. Plus, I don't want a wild animal that close to my studio. I've got thousands of dollars of tools and violins in there," he says, and turns on the tap again. He drinks another glass of water.

She stands against the counter with him, both of them looking out the window toward the shed. Soon, they see the nose of the baby raccoon appear in the doorway of the shed, then one small hand-like paw pushes open the door, and Tessa grasps Jake's arm. "This is terrible," she says, and he says, "Yeah."

She only says, *this is terrible*, but wants to say more, wants to tell him how she wants more than anything to go out there, cradle the raccoon in her arms, and sob. Instead, they stand at the window together, watching as the raccoon mewls a few times, looking up at the swaying pine branches, then wobbles away from the shed, away from the house, into the woods that run up to East Shore Road.

On Grand Isle, everyone knows each other, through avenues that are still a little unclear to Tessa. Torsten and Peg, who Jake has known for years in New York's in-grown world of artists and musicians and professors, own a low-slung, 1950s split-level on the eastern marsh just down the shoreline from Jake's place. Franci Weiseman, who along with her husband made up a foursome with Jake and his girlfriend of the moment, inherited a camp from her mother on the island's western shore, the marshy side where the other mainland shore cups around the island. And then there's Dick Grasso, the only one of their group with a flashy house on the southern, open-ocean coast, who will come to the party with his new wife. They all know each other and have known each other, their stories and memories predating Tessa by far, sometimes making her feel, still, as foreign as a visitor from the Arctic to the equator.

To offset that feeling of being the newest member of the group, she's invited, at the last minute, the new pharmacist on the island, Kenji Tanaka, handsome, middle-aged, who just moved up last October. Tessa and Peg have discussed how if he's straight—a determination not yet certain—he's a good match for Franci, but no one's mentioned that to either of them.

By the time the party begins, as always with the arrival of Torsten and Peg just a little too early, Jake has buried the mother raccoon, and sprayed the floor of the shed with disinfectant, and because she got such an early start on the flower beds, Tessa found that she did have time to get new cushions for the porch furniture after all, and everything feels righted, or nearly righted, Tessa thinks, turning the vegetables in the marinade, the oily vinaigrette making them slippery as eels. She's changed into her gray and black striped linen shift and her sandals, even though she's beginning to wonder, this summer, if she can still get away with exposing her legs.

The first summer she and Jake were here, Tessa hated it that Torsten and Peg came and went so easily, intruding, as she saw it, on the romantic bubble she and Jake lived in, and maybe even in a way spying on her, assessing her worthiness. Once she saw that she and Peg would be friends, it all changed, but tonight, she feels the flick of old annoyance when she hears Torsten's big Swedish voice boom out as they come up on the porch.

Tessa looks to the shed, but there's no sign the of the raccoon, *no evidence*, she thinks, and she lifts the heavy blue plate piled with cheeses and grapes and carries it out to the porch, smiling.

"Here, let me help you," Peg says, holding open the door. She looks older this summer. She's wearing her standard summer party outfit, a white t-shirt and her longish, gathered Mexican skirt, a string of heavy clay beads, glazed bright indigo. Like her husband, she has a head of hair that's entirely white. She's big-boned, and a little horsy, and Tessa always thinks she'd be good in an emergency, competent and take-charge.

Tessa turns her cheek up for Torsten's kiss. "Did you make it up here okay?" she says.

"Sure," Torsten says. "We drove up Thursday. It wasn't bad at all."

Tessa deposits the plate on the glass-topped coffee table. Everything looks right, down to the tulips she cut from the garden, their long green stems a little wavy through the glass of the vase, and she feels again the frisson of satisfaction she felt in the morning, which seems like a long time ago now.

"Tessa, didn't I ask you to put some music on?" Jake says, coming out of the house, Nina Simone's deep voice following him. He's wearing his own traditional summer-party outfit, khaki pants and a white button-down shirt, both softened by many washings. "I still can't do anything with her," he laughs, leaning in to kiss Peg's cheek, then clasping Torsten in a quick, manly embrace.

"Did you get new cushions?" Peg says, sitting down and patting the seat beside her. "They're nice."

"Thanks. I just picked them up today," Tessa says. The cushions, in actuality, are disappointing; apparently no one makes real cotton cushions for outdoor furniture anymore, or at least not for sale in a town the size of Wisconset, and she had to be satisfied with cushions covered in some kind of water-resistant plastic that makes an unpleasant crinkling noise when one sits down. As soon as she put them on the chairs and bench, she started missing the soft old ones, which are now stacked in the shed waiting for the next trip to the town dump.

She knows she should ask Peg about her summer work, making the illustrations for a book on North American birds, or joke about Peg's penchant for rearranging the furniture every year, but she has a sudden restless feeling, almost as if for a moment she can't breathe properly, and instead she holds up one finger to say, "Wait a minute," and turns toward the house, calling over her shoulder, "What can I get you to drink?"

"Just a lemonade to start with," Peg says. "Do you want some help?" But Tessa waves her offer away and escapes into the dim interior of the house.

Inside, she takes the pitcher of pink lemonade from the refrigerator, and removes the skin of plastic wrap from the top. She arranges the glasses and the lemonade on a tray, and then, as if she had just been busying herself with the lemonade as an excuse, she stands for a long moment at the kitchen window, looking out toward the shed. It wasn't Jake who told her to shut up the shed tightly when they left in the fall, she remembers. *She'd* told *him* that. She remembers precisely, because, as usual, she'd been afraid to say anything about his house, but she had, even warning him that animals might get in.

Outside, everything's still, the eastern shore now completely in shade, the trade-off of getting all that good, early morning light. The white clapboards of the shed stand out in the afternoon shadow, and when Tessa sees there is no sign of the raccoon, her thoughts drift: maybe she could plant something more permanent out there this summer, maybe hollyhocks, deep purple, magenta, glowing against the shed. She can hear the humming voices of Jake and his friends. She wants to stay inside like this and keep watch for the raccoon, but she can't, and she lifts up the tray and carries it outside.

Once she's back on the porch, Tessa's trapped feeling begins to lift. What was wrong with her? Now that they're here at the island, the tensions that were brewing between her and Jake in the city seem to have evaporated, and now, she's just happy to be here. She is.

She crosses her legs, takes a long drink from her lemonade, eats a few grapes. Torsten and Peg are clever and thoughtful and bright, and soon the conversation is sailing off just the way it should, touching on the relief they all feel to be out here again, the traffic problems on the LIE, and Tessa is happy sitting there among her friends, on Jake's nice porch with the new cushions on the wicker furniture, her flowerbeds ready for the summer. She can see the water turning that glassy, enameled blue that it gets just before dusk. Against the shadowy dark grass, the new white tulips seem to glow.

Soon, the others arrive, Kenji pulling down the drive in a Jeep that's seen better days, swinging gracefully out of the driver's seat, his hair, pulled back in a long, silky ponytail swishing across his back; he's like a new, black horse, Tessa thinks, with his black ponytail, wearing a black Mexican *guayabera* with silvery embroidery. He must be gay. He's brought a bottle of wine, and kisses Tessa's cheek, shakes hands with Jake. "Thanks for inviting me," he says, and not for the first time, Tessa wonders what kind of life he can have here, year-round, on this island. As he settles on the porch rail beside the wicker sofa, Dick bounds up the porch steps, holding the hand of his pretty new wife Jennifer, her summer slides scuffing against the wooden steps. She's wearing a short lavender shift, and Tessa imagines her considering what to wear to this party, weighing the pros and cons. Tessa can see a small Band-aid on the edge of one delicate toe.

The men smile at her, kiss her cheek. "What a pretty dress," Peg says, smoothing her own skirt with one hand.

Soon, everyone has something to drink, and they're having at the cheese and grapes and the big bowl of peanuts in their shells. To the side of the porch, Jake opens the bag of charcoal and rattles the black chunks into the belly of the grill. "I don't know why you refuse to get with the modern age and get a gas grill," Dick calls down from the porch. Even though Dick's speaking to Jake, Torsten waves his hand at this, as if Dick has proposed something so foolish it doesn't even bear a verbal response.

"Tessa won't let me," Jake calls back up, smiling. Tessa shrugs. They all know this about her, that in many ways she stubbornly refuses, as Jake puts it, "to pry herself from the twentieth century," lobbying Jake to keep the outdated fuse box, the rotary phone, the old phonograph. "You can bet which side of the cell tower controversy she's on," he says.

"Really, Tess?" Dick says, taking up a handful of peanuts and expertly shelling them with thumb and forefinger. "I thought only the townies were opposed. Don't you miss being in touch with civilization?"

"Oh, please, Dick, she's studying the Arctic in the nineteenth century, for God's sake," Torsten puts in. "And I bet she's happy to be out of touch with the university for the summer, as much as one ever is."

Jake douses the charcoal with lighter fluid, tosses a match in. The charcoal ignites in one great blow, and he jumps back a little. Peg and Torsten applaud, and Kenji shouts, "Bravo!"

"And for my next act—has anyone seen my trapeze?" Jake says. He picks up the lighter fluid and the charcoal and comes back up to the porch.

They all turn then at the sound of a car crunching down the driveway. It's Franci, in her old Saab, which, as Stiles—Franci's husband for twelve years—was always proud to point out, has been accumulating only about a thousand miles each year because it's only used at the island. "The engine is like a newborn baby," Stiles would say.

"Here's the newborn baby," Dick says, and indeed, when Franci emerges from the car, carrying a bottle of wine, he could be talking about her: she looks younger, renewed, closer to forty than to fifty. After Stiles left her, she had an affair with a woman named Leslie that lasted several years. It tested everyone's good liberal graces, Franci's refusal to label herself but happily living with Leslie—and with Franci's teenaged son—in her little cottage on the western marsh. Seeing her now, once again Tessa thinks the whole thing has been good for her, Stiles' leaving, the affair with Leslie, even though it ended. They can all see the evidence, the ten pounds Franci shed and the slightly darker shade of her hair. Everyone sees this except for Jennifer, who just sees another one of Dick's middle-aged friends approach.

"Hi everybody," Franci says, coming onto the porch. It's just now getting close to dusk, the day's light still reflecting back off the surface of the water. Jake kisses her cheek, saying, "You look terrific," and a murmur of concurrence ripples around the group. "Great earrings," Jennifer says, and Franci touches the big silver corkscrews self-consciously. "Thanks," she says, handing the wine to Jake. He reads the label out loud, with a passable French pronunciation, then lets out a low whistle. "Nice," he says. "Want to start with a glass?"

"Why not?" Franci says, brushing her hair from her face, her silver bracelets jangling on her wrist. "This is a party, isn't it?" She sits beside Tessa on the wicker sofa.

"Franci, you remember Kenji," Tessa says, but as soon as she does, she thinks this is too pointed—Franci met Kenji, as they all did, last August when he first came up to look at Grayson's. Anyway, he's probably gay. And maybe Franci is now, too, and Tessa has a giddy moment of thinking this would make them a good couple, as they shake hands, Kenji leaning across Tessa from his spot on the porch rail.

"Are these new cushions?" Franci asks, and Tessa and Peg laugh together.

"Nothing goes under the radar around here. Take a note of that, Kenji—welcome to the fishbowl," Peg says.

"There are spies everywhere," Tessa says.

"Duly noted," Kenji says, then leans close to Tessa and stage-whispers: "They'll never pry the code from me," and everyone laughs and relaxes a little.

Jake hands Franci a glass of wine; over his own glass, he looks at Tessa and smiles his crooked smile. "L'Chaim," Franci says, and "Cin-cin," Torsten and Peg say, and Kenji says, "Kampai." Everyone drinks.

"Where are you from, again?" Dick says to Kenji.

"New York."

"But I mean—" Dick begins. Tessa sees Jennifer leveling a look at him, and that makes her like Jennifer more.

"Brooklyn," Kenji says, smiling at Dick. Tessa sees he's practiced at this.

"Sorry," Peg cuts in. "What he means is, what brought you up to Grand Isle, especially to live here year-round? Isn't it just deadly in the winter?"

Kenji looks out at the water, then back. The way the water seems both still and moving: that's the feeling he wants to create in his new piece, to capture that in steel.

"New York just got to be too—*everything*. I wanted to get back to my metal sculpture, which I need a lot of room for," Kenji says. "And I spent my early summers with my grandmother, in a place kind of like this, Shimoda, on the ocean, in Japan." This last he says with a look toward Dick, who nods in satisfaction.

"Did I pass the interrogation?" he stage-whispers to Tessa, leaning down to her again, his ponytail sliding over one shoulder.

"For the moment," she stage-whispers back.

"Well, if you want to get away from it all, there's no better place than Grand Isle," Franci says. She isn't flirting with him at all, Tessa thinks.

Before Tessa can ask Kenji about his sculpture, "I almost had to call on your expertise with your shotgun today," Jake says to Dick. They're leaning against the porch rail, silhouetted against the background of the yard and the bay water. Tessa feels her chest tighten again; she hadn't forgotten about the raccoon, but she now realizes that she wasn't going to mention it; in fact, she realizes she was hoping Jake wouldn't mention it, as if what happened is a small precious thing she wants to keep for herself, a thought she can pet when she wants to, privately. "Oh? Were the terrorists trying to take Grand Isle?" Dick says. Everyone laughs, a little uneasily. "It wasn't the dogs, was it?"

"What dogs?" Tessa and Jake say simultaneously.

"Well, according to our ferry master, a pack of wild dogs was causing some trouble this spring," Dick says. "You know, taking down a couple of cows at the West Shore Farm, terrorizing the locals. Did you hear about that, Ken?"

"Sure," Kenji says. "It was on the front page of the paper, right next to the story about the cell phone tower. Or would have been, if Grand Isle *had* a paper."

"They think they came across the ice, and then got stuck here," Peg puts in. "It sounds like some of it got ugly, but they haven't been able to round them all up."

"Well, this wasn't anything quite that dramatic," Jake says. "Actually, it was a raccoon. Tessa found a dead raccoon in the shed this morning."

"You didn't touch it, did you?" Jennifer asks, leaning forward for a handful of peanuts. She's been carefully putting the shells on her paper napkin, and has built herself quite a nice peanut-shell mountain. Her hands are freshly manicured, each nail curving in a perfect sickle.

"No, of course not," Tessa says. "Jake buried it in the woods."

"I hope you were careful with that," Dick says. "You know there was that case of rabies a couple of years ago."

"That was nothing," Torsten says, waving his hand again. "Wasn't that in dogs, anyway? Rottweilers? Rabies have been coming and going around this island forever. That doesn't mean every dead raccoon is lethal."

"Rotties?" Jennifer asks. "I love Rotties!"

"Thank you, Torsten," Tessa says. "That's just what I told Jake. He wanted to shoot the baby." She feels a panicky rush as she says this. She certainly hadn't been meaning to mention the baby.

"Baby?" Franci says. "There was a baby raccoon too?"

Tessa looks over at Jake, almost pleadingly. There's that feeling again, that feeling that she can't breathe, almost like a premonition. "Shouldn't you put the meat on?" she says to Jake, and he pushes off from the railing, saying, "If you think it's time, my sweet, then it must be," and he disappears into the house.

"What did you do with the kit?" Kenji asks.

"With what?" A fog has clouded up her head, but then it clears a little. "Oh, it's called a kit? That's great."

"Not to mention the caboodle, which—yeah, which I have no idea *what* that is. But you want something even better?" Kenji asks. "A group is called a gaze."

"A gaze of raccoons!" Tessa says. "Perfect. They do. They gaze right at you." Now they're all murmuring their own favorite words for groups and young of animals: a mischief of rats, a surfeit of skunks.

"Anyway, it wandered off into the woods," she says, and remembers then its mewling noise as it nudged against its mother's body with its soft nose.

Everyone's distracted then by Jake's return from the kitchen, the platter of chicken and hamburgers in his hand. "*La viande est arrivé!*"

Franci leans forward to pour herself another glass of wine. "This Medoc is to die for. Really. Doesn't anyone want another glass?"

Soon the smoke of the barbecue, tangy and sweet, is coiling up into the swooping branches of the pine tree, and Jake and Torsten and Dick walk down to the water and step out onto the dock, followed by Kenji. Dick jumps up and down on it a few times, testing or proving its sturdiness. On the porch, Franci says Damian is home from his first year at Reed with his nose pierced and word of a girlfriend named Phoenix.

"A real girlfriend?" Tessa asks. In the past, they all know, Damian's been more than reticent about declaring his affections.

"I think so. I know there's something he wants to tell me, but hasn't yet. I think things with this girl might be, well, serious," Franci says, wincing a little, then smiling. "We'll see if it lasts the summer."

"Don't worry, Franci, Damian won't leave you for another woman until he's at least thirty," Peg says, and they all laugh.

"When he told me about her, he did say his heart will always belong to mommy," Franci says, and they laugh again. "What every Jewish mother wants to hear. Anyway, he has to stay with me at least until we finish painting the house, and we haven't even started the scraping."

They all drink a little, letting the wine lift them into deeper relaxation. "Franci," Peg says, "I've got to say it: you look terrific. What's going on?"

Franci pushes a lock of hair behind one ear. "Oh, it's just makeup. I made the mistake of going into Macy's before we drove up, just to get some moisturizer. I walked out a hundred and fifty dollars later with a big bag of useless stuff."

"You mean a little, teeny-tiny bag," Peg says.

"Yeah. Teeny. Once the girl put everything on me, I thought I really did look better. I asked her what it all was and she said first she used a primer, so I had to get some of that—"

"What was this, a makeover or your house painting project?" Tessa asks.

"At this point, fixing the face feels like an enormous job compared with painting the house," Franci says. "So, she started with the primer—"

"After a little sandblasting—"

" 'Would you like some sandpaper with that eyeliner?' "

"How about some spackle for those really tenacious wrinkles?"

By this point, the three friends are all in stitches. Jennifer laughs, politely, then rises, descends the porch, slips off her sandals, traipses across the lawn, and walks out onto the dock, where Dick swings his arm around her shoulder, kisses her cheek. From the porch, the women can see her toss back her hair as she laughs at something Jake says. Dick's nice to her, Tessa thinks.

And then Tessa turns for a moment, her attention catching on a small motion by the driveway. There it is. She knows she is the only one to see it, in the dusk, wobbling down from the woods alongside the house, determined, pawing open the door to the shed and disappearing inside.

Tessa doesn't call out. She isn't going to mention this to anyone, certainly not to Jake. She turns back to the scene by the water. Now Jake is standing with Jennifer at the end of the dock, pointing to something far off, something that Tessa can't see. His khakis and white shirt and Jennifer's pale lavender shift seem luminescent against the dark water. It strikes her that Jennifer is young, lithe and tanned, her hair haloed a little against the water. They turn together, her husband and this girl, and he looks up toward the house, sees Tessa watching him, raises his glass as if toasting her, and starts walking back up the dock toward the porch. Soon he's back at the grill, turning the meat again, and then cupping his hands around his mouth to make a more effective bullhorn, calling out, "Dinner's ready," to the people lingering by the water.

Kenji and Torsten and Dick and Jennifer, her sandals swinging from one hand, make their way up the lawn toward the porch, and Peg and Franci stand, picking up plates from the table.

They eat on the porch. There are just enough seats for everyone, with Dick perched on the rail. Jennifer smiles up at him. She really likes him, Tessa thinks, and for this, she likes Jennifer a little more, even though liking her feels like a betrayal. Of what? Unpredictable Marilyn, who she barely knew for a short time, and never felt comfortable with?

Peg laughs at something Franci says about Damian, about living with a teenager, then turns to Dick. "What's Cort doing with his summer?" she asks.

"Well, he's already here, mostly wanting to show off after his first year at UMass. Marilyn's got some kind of a summer teaching gig in Geneva, so he's stuck with us," he says, and Tessa thinks she sees a faint twitch of annoyance in Jennifer's lip. Spending the first summer of her marriage with the teenaged son in tow is probably not what she had in mind.

"And how about you, Tessa? Heading back into the Arctic this summer?" Peg asks, but then Kenji says "Look!" and stands abruptly, and all the attention swivels to him. He points down to the porch steps, spilling a little of his wine on the new cushion.

The baby raccoon is hoisting itself up to the bottom step with its paws, nose pointed up, sniffing the air.

"Oh my God, he's so cute," Jennifer says. "He wants some food."

Everyone watches as the raccoon crosses the bottom step and then continues to ascend toward the porch.

"What did I tell you?" Jake says to Tessa, and then, "Christ, this is the last thing we need," and he picks up the barbecue fork. Hitting it against the porch rail as he goes, he stamps loudly down the steps, and the raccoon scuttles away, down the steps, around the porch, and into the woods.

"Score one for the humans," Dick says, and everyone laughs. Jake, unlaughing, comes back, and takes a long drink from his wineglass, and sits again. He looks at Tessa. "I told you we can't have that raccoon hanging around. It's only going to be trouble."

Tessa doesn't say anything. If she speaks, she'll cry, so she bites into her hamburger, wipes her mouth with her napkin, without looking up. "It'll be fine," Torsten says, his deep Swedish voice soothing in the electrified air. "Don't feed it, and it will move on."

"Yeah, to our place, where it will feast on grapes and Gruyère," says Peg, and everyone laughs again.

When they're finished eating, Jake lights the citronella candles, even though it's too early in the year to worry about mosquitoes, and puts on Mozart's clarinet concerto, and they all sit together comfortably, watching the water go blue-black, the reflection of the last light looking almost oily on the water's surface. A few early fireflies wink out over the lawn. Dick moves from his perch on the rail to squeeze in next to Jennifer, and she rests her head against his shoulder. Kenji's on the other side of the porch from Franci, who doesn't seem to notice him at all.

In the growing dark, Tessa can just make out the white of the shed, but she knows the raccoon is in there. If left alone, maybe it will make a nest for itself in the old porch cushions.

The first point of the sickle moon rises over the water, and a few stars come out, and everyone keeps talking, their voices subdued now in the soft night air. The women pull sweatshirts or sweaters around their shoulders. Jennifer unfolds a soft lavender shawl from her bag. Tessa thinks that Franci no longer looks drunk, just sad in a vague way, as if she's misplaced something.

Maybe the new cushions aren't so bad after all; at least the wine won't stain them. She looks around with pleasure at the house, the bay, the garden, Jake, their friends. Maybe Torsten is right, and everything will be all right.

Even though Jake would hate it if he knew she were even thinking this, maybe while he's sleeping she can take a bowl of food out to the raccoon. Just because it's nesting in the shed doesn't mean it will get into his studio. What do raccoons eat, anyway? Everything? She'll have to look it up. The raccoon could turn on her. She feels her heart beat a little faster thinking this, sitting there on the porch, the light fading down at last to the blackness of night.

Two

The deck of the Crab 'N Claw perches over the rumble of water that falls into Fowler's Gut, affording a wide view: the river, the wooden row houses scaffolded to the rocky banks, the meadows and the bay beyond. The sound of the great sheaf of water unleashed by the spring's floods obscures the few noises from the town center, and out here, the air is fresh; you can almost feel the spray from the rushing water as it falls into the Gut.

On this afternoon, the day after Memorial Day, Damian arrives at the Crab 'N Claw a few minutes before Cort, passing through the cool, dim interior of the bar proper, muttering a muted "Hey," to the guys at the bar, year-rounders a couple of years older, the guys who work at the Greasy Gorgon and hang around the beaches and bars of Grand Isle, smoking pot, hot-rodding up Main: Rick Skiffton and Danny LaPlatte. They look him over, briefly, not really registering his face, just lifting their beer bottles in an abbreviated salute.

With a sigh of relief, he's out on the back deck, back out in the bright day, and he settles into one of the chairs, rolls up the hems of his baggy shorts a little, rolls up the sleeves of his ancient t-shirt, a hand-me-down from Leslie ("Lick Bush in '04"), leans back, letting the late afternoon sun hit him full in the face. He folds his hands behind his head, lets his eyes close on the view of the water. He emits a small sigh of relief at being back on Grand Isle, home from his first year at Reed, the protective army line of A's stacked up behind him. Okay, A's and that one B that he copped in Intro to Psych, which really he should have aced, seeing as how his mom has always talked about stuff like that, the "internal landscape," as his professor called it. It was the statistical part that busted him.

Still, now it's June, and his only duties for the summer are to work some hours at the ferry or Lantman's and, mostly, to help his mom scrape and paint the house. If anyone were to ask him, Damian would say that he doesn't mind helping his mom, but really, it isn't just that he doesn't mind; in fact, he's proud that he can help her like this, do something really concrete, help to offset how much of a dick his dad has been to her. And help her while he still can, he remembers with a chill like remembering a bad dream, only this is real. Of course he'll be able to help her, even with—*the diagnosis*—as he thinks of it. Perhaps his biggest job of the summer will be telling her what the doctor at Reed said.

"What can I get you?" he hears at his side, and opens his eyes. There's Britt, one of the summer kids, a couple years older than him. Like him, she's worked every summer since she was sixteen, and now she's pulled this plum job at the Crab 'N Claw.

"Oh, hey, Britt. I think I'll have a draft," he says, hands still clasped behind his head, until he realizes this looks arrogant. *Pompous*, he thinks, and he drops them to the table.

She squints at him a little. She's pretty, prettier than she was last summer, he thinks. Maybe she dyed her hair. "Sure, Damian," she says. "Um, do you have your license or something?"

"Yeah," Damian says, pulling out his wallet, slipping out his fake ID. "See?"

"Nice pic," she says, handing it back, smiling at him. "Okay, one draft."

He watches her go back into the restaurant. Was she flirting with him? He's never sure, and more than once he's been caught by surprise, to find a girl thought she was making her interest clear as day. But his curiosity about Britt is short-lived. He'd rather look at the water and think about Phoenix and the letter from her—a real letter, on paper, mailed with a stamp—which was waiting for him when he arrived on the island the day before, which he does, and in which activity he's still indulging when Cort appears, shouting, "Hey, Dickhead!" slapping his palm into Damian's, then grabbing Damian in a bear hug when Damian stands, jolted out of his reverie.

"Hey, Dickhead," Damian says back, wincing a little at this old routine of theirs. It's gotten old since the first year of college has passed, was old even when they got together in the city at Christmas break, and Damian's just glad Britt is still inside. "How's it going?"

"Okay," Cort says, settling into the chair beside Damian. They both rest their feet on the bench across the table from their seats, and Cort tosses a cell phone onto the table, dangles a set of car keys from his fingertips, before letting them drop as well, saying, "Summer time, and the livin' is easy."

"What, did your dad lose his mind and let you take his SUV?"

"Not only that—that ride is mine for the whole summer." Cort sits back as Damian had been before, hands clasped behind his head. "Dude, this is *real*," he says.

As usual with Cort's statements, there isn't much Damian can say to this, so he says nothing, just continues looking at the water, even though now, with Cort here, he doesn't want to revel in reminiscences about Phoenix, almost feeling that Cort can read his mind; he doesn't want Phoenix exposed to Cort's fantasies.

The cell phone lets out an anemic bleat, then stops. Cort picks it up, looks at it as if he's never seen it before, then slaps it back onto the table. "It's just the girls. I could tell you precisely what time they'll be arriving if you could ever get a goddamn signal out here."

Britt returns with two mugs of draft beer ("I caught her inside," Cort says with a wink) and Cort raises his mug to Damian. "To the return of the Dickheads," he says, and "To grand Grand Isle," Damian says at the same time, and they both laugh, and drink.

The sunlight hitting off the water makes a perfect watery pattern on the floor of the deck.

"So, buddy, how was it? When we last left off, you were all freaked out you were going to flunk psych, you had a hot English teacher, but you weren't getting too lucky in the extracurricular department."

"Thanks for reminding me, man." Damian says, rolling his eyes. "No, everything most definitely improved after Christmas break. And it was only a B."

"What was?"

"That psych grade," Damian says. He doesn't go on to fill Cort in on his other grades, his phalanx of A's marching him through the battleground of education.

Cort raises his mug again. "Hey, man, that's dynamite. I only got one B." Damian knows, without asking, that Cort's other grades were south, not north, of B.

"And you? How'd everything turn out in your great hunt for hotties?" Damian asks, not wanting to know, but wanting to wrest control of this portion of the conversation; if he's directing it, maybe he'll manage not to open his big mouth about Phoenix, manage not to offer her up like a sacrificial conversation piece.

"Oh, yeah," Cort says. "You know, UMass is loaded with opportunities. I mean, the Smith girls are right over in Northampton, and they're—" but he's interrupted in this line of thought by a giggle at the door to the deck, and then here are Betheny and Kylie, Betheny in cropped yellow shorts and a tight, yellow plaid shirt, Kylie in a short plaid shift, both of them seeming taller in their high wedge sandals. They're carrying iced glasses of Coke, which they delicately slide onto the table as the boys rise.

"Hey, look who's here," Cort says, taking each girl by the shoulders, kissing her hard and quickly on the mouth, then passing each girl to Damian, who kisses them on the cheek, demurely. *Faggot*, he thinks.

The girls sit on the bench. From her pink straw bag, Betheny fishes a flask from which she pours a generous stream into the Cokes, and the boys sink back into their chairs, each taking a long draught of their beers.

"It is like *so awesome* to have you guys back," Kylie says, slapping her palms onto the edge of the table. Her nails, Damian sees, are painted a dark maroon. "What a crappy, boring winter you missed!"

"And what was the crappiest thing about it, other than that we weren't here?" Cort says, throwing a wink toward Damian.

Kylie sinks back in her chair, pushing out her lower lip a bit in a way that makes her look slightly like a carp. "The main thing's I had to repeat American History *and* Earth Science just to graduate from good old Wisconset Regional High, so I was stuck back in that pit three times a week. And then I got busted by my mom smoking pot, and now my mom's saying I should just bag thinking about college and settle in for a life sentence working at Lantman's, like her."

Betheny rolls her eyes. "They don't want to hear about the troubles of those of us stuck here all winter," she says, then reaches into her bag, pulls out a pack of Camel Lights and a lighter. "Really, how was your first year?" she asks, lighting the first cigarette of their afternoon summit.

"Cort was just telling me about it," Damian says. "Seems he got a lot of—"

"A lot of good studying done," Cort cuts in, cutting a look at Damian. "Really, it was fascinating. I had this one class, The Nature of Science, that was all about how science impacts upon our daily life, you know? Like how we breathe, and how we hear, and how televisions and cell phones work."

The girls look at him, both of them aware that they're putting on a look of interested boredom (*isn't that an oxymoron,* Betheny thinks), looking like woodland creatures glancing up from their grazing, blinking a few times. Damian remembers a line from a short story in his Intro to Fiction class, something about what's going on in a girl's head being comparable to a bee buzzing around in a glass jar. It was a controversial line, the teacher had said, and had been criticized by feminists, and he could see why. But sitting here with Betheny and Kylie again, he can also see how it's true, at least of some girls. And, he remembers now, it was also true, what he'd told Cort, that the teacher *had* been kind of a babe.

Most of the conversation is carried on by Cort and the girls, with Damian offering up an answer or two but mostly trying to stay out of the volleying, which, once the girls start in on their drinks, launches fast and furious, the teasing back and forth that would, last summer, have ended up with the day skidding into evening and all of them at Dead Man's Beach, Damian pairing off with Betheny and Cort with Kylie, but which now Damian just observes, thinking he'd rather be home, or, really, anywhere but here. He pulls out his wallet, puts a few bills on the table, and drains the last of his beer.

"Listen," he says, not even sure if he's breaking in at a good time, "I've got to get home. You know," he says, forestalling their complaints, "it's really still my first week back, and my mom's got some special dinner planned."

"Okay, man," Cort says, and Damian's surprised, and a little hurt, that he doesn't protest, even though he's also relieved. But, "Oh, Dame, come on," Betheny says, pursing her lips into a pout, "it won't be nearly as much fun once you go."

"I know," Damian sighs, attempting an exaggerated ego as he stands, "but my fans are waiting."

"Well, but, like, you'd better call me," Betheny says, reaching for his hand as he passes the table, and it sounds to Damian like a threat. "I'll call you," he says, "really," believing as he says it that he will, even though he knows it's about the last thing he wants to do. He squeezes her hand, and from his vantage point, he can see down her halter top to the smooth tops of her breasts, "like two scoops of the most delicious vanilla ice cream," or something like that the author said in that same story about the bees in the glass jar. He feels his groin stir at this sight, and wishes he could will it away, but he can't, so he leans down, kisses her quickly on the cheek, then gets the hell out of there.

Three

Sometimes I dream of you, or sometimes, now, just of someone who looks like you.

This is what Franci thinks, when she wakes from a dream to the night-still dark.

It's not a dream of Leslie, but of Stiles—her ex-husband, Damian's father, a man she once loved so much it hurt her to think of him, but all that's so long ago now she has to work to remember something about him that was real, and not just her faulty, current imagination.

Franci wakes, and it's still night. It's too warm for early June, and sticky as August, but there it is: more evidence we've wrecked the planet. As plain as the evidence she now sees daily of the bare fact of her own mortality. As she slept, she threw off the summer blanket, and now she lies in the tangle of the damp sheets. She hasn't yet gotten out the fans, and there's no breeze at all in the small upstairs bedroom of the camp.

Franci has been given to waking once a night since the twin losses last year: her mother's death and Leslie's sudden departure, but, ironically, she is still a good sleeper except for that one, regular moment of wakefulness. ("Good sleeper," is a term Leslie used, and even though it has by now become part of Franci's vocabulary, she still thinks of Leslie when she uses it. Leslie told her she'd win the "Miss Sleepheart" contest, in which the contestants would vie for first prize by sleeping, their mattresses wheeled upright across the stage like a set in a musical, each lovely girl sound asleep, she said.)

She's still a good sleeper. It's just that every night she wakes around two, goes to the bathroom, returns to bed, contemplates her own mortality, and goes back to sleep.

On this night, she's more awake than usual, and she leaves her second-floor bedroom, a dark little square with pine paneling in the back of the cottage, and walks down the stairs, careful to be quiet. At Damian's room, she inhales, holds her breath, and opens the door. There he is, lying on his stomach, asleep, his big soon-to-be manly shoulders relaxed, his breathing even and steady, the sheets tousled down around his waist. He's only been home a couple of days; his body is still lithe, boy-slim, but there's more of him, more solidity. He's the most beautiful thing she's ever seen.

What is it she's looking for when she checks on him like this? She doesn't know, other than it's just to make sure he's really here, he's still her son, he hasn't transformed into himself at eight, or eighty. He hasn't disappeared in the night, like those kidnapped children one reads about, snatched out of their warm beds in predawn hours, no matter how big and strong he grows. Or, sometimes she feels she checks to make sure she didn't imagine the whole thing, didn't make him up, and isn't finding herself now, at forty-eight, both childless and alone.

But it isn't really for reassurance that she stands in the doorway like this, the only light the ghoulish green cast down the hall from the clock on the new kitchen stove. It's more a question of questioning the world as she knows it, and finding that it's just the same as ever; it's almost disappointing to her that she knows the world, if not her son, that well. She pulls the door closed, and walks down the hall to the living room, where she switches on the lamp that sits on the piano.

Here, she looks around, as if looking for something, and she even feels a little quiver of excitement, as if she might find something she's been missing, but the living room is just her same old living room, with the ancient knotty-pine walls, the built-in bookshelves filled with the same books, the small black piano, the comfortable, practical sofa. Damian's denim jacket lies where he tossed it onto the sofa back, his sneakers tumbled onto the carpet.

When her mother was dying, she assured Franci that she'd come to her when she, Franci, was old and in the hospital. "Don't be afraid, *shayna*, because I'll be there. You know how I know? I saw your *bubbeh* here. Really. She came in the room. So I'll come to you, too," Franci's mother the atheist said, even though she'd scoffed at the mystical all her adult life, rolling her eyes at anything like spirits or visitations from the dead or even at what she called superstitions like saying a *b'racha*, or prayer.

Four

From where he lies stretched out on the wooden chaise, Cort looks out over the slope of lawn to the dunes and beyond, to the big blue Atlantic. The house isn't on the beach, not for a lack of money, but because no house on Grand Isle is; it's a regulation from a long time ago. But it's just a short walk across South Shore Road, down the weathered steps, and through the dunes to Dead Man's Beach, which stretches three and a half miles, from past the Grasso's house as far up as the Kayak Shack.

Cort lies back under the shade of the awning, his orange juice and coffee on the little table next to the chaise, which Jennifer bought in Wisconset, gladly taking on the task of furnishing the new house. Still morning and the day is already promising to be very hot, a great beach day, Cort thinks. That's where she finds him, nursing an orange juice spiked with a splash of vodka, at the end of the first full week of his vacation from UMass, the first week in her new role as a stepmother, something she's joked with her friends about, as Cort is so close to her own age. One of her best friends, Faye, is dating a guy who's finishing college. Granted, he's a couple of years older than his classmates, having served in Iraq and then gotten sent back. But still, it creeps Jennifer out to think that Faye's boyfriend could, quite conceivably, go out drinking with Cort. What would they say to each other? What would they say about her, and about Faye?

Cort's left the glass door open, and she pointedly slides it closed behind her, not mentioning the air-conditioning. Maybe he'll get the point.

"Hey," he says, not moving from his position.

"Hey yourself," she says, settling into the Adirondack chair. Already, the day is warming up, and far down below, at the end of the steep wooden steps, she can see the water sparkling in the morning heat.

Jennifer slips off her sandals, props her bare feet up on the rail of the deck, and drinks from her own orange juice glass. "So, what's your plan?" she asks, then immediately regrets asking. It will sound like pushing, which it is; it will also sound like she wants Cort to get out of the house so she can be alone with Dick, or even just alone, which she does.

"I thought I'd make a couple of eggs after I have my orange juice," Cort says. He isn't joking, but then he understands this isn't the kind of plan she meant. He laughs a little.

"I don't know," he amends. "Dad said I've worked hard all year and I should take a little va-cay, so I haven't really made any plans. I might see if they're hiring at the ferry, or maybe at the Crab 'N Claw," he says, knowing he would never sink that low.

Jennifer nods, assuming Cort can see this from behind his sunglasses. He shifts a little in order to reach his juice.

"How about you? Got any big summer plans?"

"Well, Grand Isle Gifts is interested in some of my jewelry from Mexico, and I'm going to try and get a couple of places in Wisconset to take some things, and see how that goes." She touches her bracelet with one finger, distractedly. It's a silver bracelet she brought back from Oaxaca, embossed with a Mitla pattern, zagged lines like lightning bolts crossing the silver.

Cort takes another drink, swallowing hard. The vodka's a little bitter, and brings him back for a moment to the previous night, the beach, his hand down Kylie's shorts until the lights of the stupid Grand Isle cop car swept across the parking lot and Kylie freaked out and insisted he take her home. He's taken up a closer relationship with vodka ever since Christmas break, when his father announced his engagement to Jennifer. The wedding followed in February.

Out here, on the deck, the sun is very bright, and even though it's so bright that it makes Cort's eyes hurt, it also makes his muscles feel a little less tense, a little bit better.

Jewelry business. Right. Big freakin' deal. "That's nice, you've got a little business of your own going," Cort says.

Jennifer knows he's insulting her, but she ignores this, saying, "Yeah, it's interesting," and standing to stretch. She leans against the rail of the porch, orange juice glass still in one hand. "You want another juice?" she asks, turning to look at Cort.

She's pretty much a babe, Cort has to admit. The old man did all right, Cort thinks, then remembers his mother, remembers that he hates Jennifer on principle.

Cort empties his glass in one draught. "Sure," he says. His shot of vodka will be enough for now, and besides, he wants to watch her retreat into the kitchen. Nice little butt on her, in her little white shorts.

From the glass-topped table beside his chaise, he lifts the portable phone, punches in Damian's new number. Cell phone service is so spotty on the island, and the possibility of the town approving the tower anytime soon so remote, that Damian's mother has gotten him his own landline this summer, a small luxury compared to Cort's own newly rebuilt house, the huge deck, the lack of a requirement that he do anything like get a job. Still, it's the one thing Cort thinks he'd like to have: a private line.

"Yeah," Damian says into the phone.

"Hey, man, you up yet or what?" Cort laughs a little. It's nearly noon.

"Now I am, right?" Damian says. "No, man, I just came inside. We've been scraping paint all morning."

"Listen, you want to go down to the beach later? I'll pick you up."

"It'd have to be much later. This paint is a bitch," Damian says.

"Oh, man, come on. Doesn't your mom know that a guy's first summer from college is supposed to be all about kicking back?"

"Yeah, right. Listen, I'll call you later. Maybe around six we could go," and the phone goes dead, and that's where Jennifer finds Cort when she returns with his juice, lying in the chaise, tapping the phone against his thigh. When she hands him his juice, she can smell the vodka, a wispy hint of the sharp tang of alcohol, unmistakable, smelling at once sickening and clean.

Five

Crossing the Grand Isle common toward his pharmacy, Kenji Tanaka is the first islander to see the snow goose arrive, drifting down to earth, a speck first white, then dark, then white again as it tilts and leans into the wind. Even though it's the warmest morning of the year thus far, Kenji shivers a little in his sweatshirt, a shiver more of anticipation than of cold. His grandmother would know what to make of this, a single sea duck arriving on such a bright morning.

The goose lands smoothly, on the new grass of the common, and immediately begins picking at the grass with its bill, as Kenji watches. All winter, when he wasn't at the pharmacy or working in his studio—an outbuilding behind the Greasy Gorgon Garage—he's been studying up on the birds of the east coast, and knows this is a snow goose. He looks up again, but the sky's empty: no other snow geese on the way. The goose lets out one deep, melodious honk, and settles under the common's small cluster of white pines, tucking its bill under one wing.

As he enters the shop which is now his he inhales deeply the cool perfumey air, switching on the overhead lights, looking around to make sure Marie left everything in order before closing up for the night: the rows of perfume bottles, the glass cases reflecting back the light, the pearly gray carpet immaculate.

Since he answered the tiny ad in *Pharmacology Today* everything moved fast, and before he knew it, Kenji was moving his things to a rented house on Water Street, an easy walk from both the pharmacy and the studio, making a final inventory of the pharmacy with Grayson, signing the papers and taking the key. Now, he's still a little surprised to wake each morning and realize that he's made it here: his own pharmacy, and more important to him, his own studio, with his welding table and his tools.

Kenji doesn't mind going to the pharmacy each morning, doling out medications to Grand Isle's residents; he likes the crisp tidiness, likes feeling that he's helping his customers, especially the ones who come to him for medical advice that's really more the provenance of doctors; they trust him, and many of them can't afford a doctor. But he only went into the profession because his mother convinced him he'd never support himself on his sculpture—her fear of the great gulf of poverty waiting to pull her under particularly acute given that she'd seen her own parents killed by the North Koreans as they made their way across the river border into China.

That's Kenji's secret, even though he doesn't often think of it: 1957, his mother, fourteen years old, submerged in the freezing waters, hearing the shots ring out. She later made her way to Japan, married Kenji's father, a doctor from Shimoda, then moved to New York. Now, he tells everyone simply that he's Japanese, a fiction created the day he was born, and one he himself sometimes believes, despite having grown up with his mother's fear and grief an unremitting, piercing keen.

The morning passes to the bright shank of the afternoon and the pharmacy stills after the lunch rush, and with a moment to himself, Kenji stands behind the counter, watching the snow goose through the wide window, both of them still as statues.

In the early afternoon, Jake emerges from his studio humming the *Barcarolle* and finds Tessa on the porch, where she's about to doze off, reading *Book of the Eskimos*, a detailed narrative of Peter Freuchen's life in the Arctic. She's let herself sink into that white world; the night before, again she didn't sleep. In the book, the attitudes are outdated, the whole thing stinking of sexism, racism, imperialism, and yet, the descriptions of the broad swath of blue ice, of the tang of fermented seabirds, of the eternity of the landscape are so precise she's nearly there. But when she hears Jake humming as he leans against the porch rail, she looks up, embarrassed, almost as if she's been caught doing something she shouldn't, caught in her private world.

"Hey, gorgeous," he says smiling in a way she's come to think of as indulgent. "You were really somewhere else."

"Oh," she says, taking off her reading glasses, rubbing her eyes. "I was. I was in the world of the Inuit. What time is it?"

It's late for lunch, but this is their summer routine. They bring out a salad, and cold cuts, and a couple of glasses of white wine. He flourishes the cloth placemats down on the table. "God, this is the life," he says. "A good morning's work, and you here, and *lunch*. This stuff is great. Maybe we should put in a vegetable garden. Would you like that?"

"Sure," Tessa says, knowing that at some manic-y moment early each summer he says this; one year, he got as far as renting a Roto-tiller, but then he lost a commission, and his mood darkened before he even broke the ground.

"It feels so great to work on a real instrument for a change," he says, then tells her how the violin, modeled on an Amati, feels precious in his hands, as he replaces the sound post, his hands following the hands of luthiers stretching back centuries. There's something animal about him, Tessa thinks, how he so thoroughly inhabits whatever moment he's in.

But then, after they've eaten and she's sitting with her legs stretched over his lap on the wicker sofa, the mood shifts. "I really am serious about the raccoon, Tessa," he says, taking her bare foot in one hand and pressing right in the spots she loves to have pressed. "It's very sweet of you to want to take care of it, but it's just not practical. I don't want it getting into my studio. And you don't want it rummaging in the trash or digging up your flowers, do you? And if anything happened to you—these animals can be vicious."

"Jake, it won't do anything. And as for the trash, we've got those locking lids, anyway." He raises his eyebrows, turns down his mouth, looking so crestfallen she caves. "Okay. I won't invite it in to dinner," she says, and he presses the spot in her foot harder. "That's my girl," he says. "You know, if you wanted to, you could get a dog."

Tessa laughs. "I can't have a dog. How would I travel anywhere?"

"I don't know. Wouldn't it be great to have a little dog when we're up here? And in the city, you'd look adorable with one of those little dogs in a bag. God, I can just see it! It's perfect for you, a little perky-eared thing. We'd have to have the bark removed."

He pats her foot, drops it to the sofa, and stands.

"I really don't want a dog," she says. "Or any pet. Anyway, listen, I'm going to head into town and run some errands, and no, raccoon treats are not on the list."

"They'd better not be," Jake says, going back down the stairs, waving his hand without looking back at her. She watches him go, and sees it isn't that he's waving; he's shaking his finger at her, like a schoolteacher.

After washing up the lunch things, Tessa takes the long-cut to the common, first passing along the eastern shore, looking out to the bay; there's just one sail on the water. Then she turns onto Cross Island Road, and slows as she passes through the dense, green woods, the window rolled down so she can listen for bird song.

The pharmacy's the first stop on her list; she wouldn't tell Jake, but she's got to refill her prescription, even though she knows it's become a habit, a bad one; she started taking the pills when she tore her shoulder in January (racquetball, bad serve) and then kept taking them, and now she's concerned, worried even, at how long the nights are when she doesn't have it: galloping insomnia.

As she enters the shop, a lanky guy is coming out, and as he holds the door Tessa startles to see it's not a guy, not a man: it's Damian. Over the winter, he's turned the corner, and now he's an adult, she thinks, but doesn't say, saying only, "Damian, hi," holding back from all the clichés about how he's grown.

"Hi Tessa," he says, leaning down to kiss her cheek in a way that makes Tessa think, once again, of what a good job Franci's done in raising him. He's still teen-awkward, but self-confident, smiling as if he's really happy to see her, even though she's only known him a couple of years. "It's great to see you," he says, then, "Sorry, I'm kind of in a rush," and lopes away, down the shady block.

Inside, the pharmacy's cool, and Tessa's glad she wore her fisherman's sweater over her t-shirt and shorts. She tries to look as if she's just wandering the shelves, not wanting even Kenji to know what she's here for, which is ridiculous, because he's got to fill the prescription.

He sees her right away, as soon as the bell over the door rings with Damian's departure and Tessa's arrival; it's as if the air changes when she comes into the store, becomes *a piece of air with lightning in it,* he remembers from a poem.

From her tote bag, she pulls out a slip of paper, hands it to him. "It's from my doctor in New York," she says. "I tore my shoulder recently"—*well, if you call January "recently"*—"and sometimes it still kills me at night," she lies.

He reads the script and makes his face impassive. She's never mentioned a bad shoulder. Is she bluffing? Does she, like so many people, just need to find a way to sleep? He asks her to wait while he goes behind the counter, counts out the pills, makes up the slip. When he comes back, she's standing at the window, arms crossed, looking small with her big sweater hugged around her.

"Thanks for the dinner party," he says, handing her the crisp white bag. "Any sign of your kit since then? Or has Jake managed to maintain the borders?"

Tessa laughs a little. He sees that one of her front teeth is a little out of line, catching a tiny bit on her lower lip, giving her a slightly crooked smile. "I haven't seen it. I'm afraid now it thinks we're enemy territory."

"If I intercept any communiqués from him I'll let you know," Kenji says. "Here, you have to sign for this."

Tessa takes the West Shore Road all the way down to Dead Man's Beach, pulls into the parking lot. There's a stiff, bright wind, full of salt, but she ducks her head and runs up the beach, the water on her right, the marshes on her left. She can hear the redwings starting their long, watery evening trills, the rushes rustling as they settle and move, and she thinks again of Jake, how things have changed with him this spring, how coming here, this year, she's more aware that it isn't her house, it's his, despite how much work she's put into it. *His* garden, *his* shed, his goddamned raccoon.

She runs along the shoreline, where the sand is packed hard. There's the salty tang in the air, the cool mist lifting off the waves. When she reaches the far edge of the marsh, she stops, and looks out across the reeds and water. There are just a couple of ducks, gadwalls, a few bufflehead. She runs all the way back to the car, scooping her sweater up where she dropped it on the sand without breaking her stride, suddenly eager to see Jake, suddenly wanting—she doesn't know what, everything.

Six

From the waters of Bay Beach on the eastern shore, about ten feet off the raft, "Hey, Damian, come on in," Betheny calls, flagging her arms over her head so that she bobs up from the water, a quick, bright explosion of yellow bathing suit top and tawny skin, then sinks back down again. The polished, still water of the bay is the hard, clear blue of midday. The sudden, too-early heat has flooded the small beach with young mothers afraid to bring their toddlers to the ocean shore.

Damian walks in to his waist, then makes a shallow dive, propelling himself under the cold water until he feels his lungs go hot with holding his breath; the cold water feels great after the morning on the ladder in the sun, chips of old paint scattering into his hair. When he breaks the surface he's much farther from her than he expected. Good, he thinks.

"Hey," Betheny yells, a note of hurt belling out in that one syllable. Then she swims toward him, carefully keeping her head out of the water, while he treads his feet in circles.

When she reaches him, he falls back in a float, making a noise, "Ahhh," like a child's water toy with the air releasing.

"Isn't it awesome to be back here?" Betheny says. "It's summer! Time to get crazy!" and she flails her arms out again.

"Yeah," Damian says, floating. He'd like to just float like that in the big silence of the bay, but he knows Betheny, and he knows he won't be left in peace. Even last summer, when he hooked up with her at Cort's July Fourth party, he knew it was a mistake, and now he's paying still.

"Give me a ride," Betheny says, and then she's got one arm around his shoulder, and before he can refuse, she's on his back. He swims with her crabbed onto him like that, all the way back to the raft, where he deposits her and then hoists himself onto the raft's surface. This year, the sisal has been replaced with a square of green material like plastic grass. After the cold water, the sun feels good, and Damian likes the feel of the fake grass under his feet. He bends, and squeezes the remaining water from his hair; his hair is just long and curly enough for him to do this. Then he pulls up his swimming shorts, which, like all his shorts, reach to his knees in great baggy balloons and ride low on his hips, so low that it appears he could just step out of them without noticing and return to his natural, naked state.

Betheny lies back, angling herself on the raft in a pose that can only be described as seductive, one arm crooked above her head, one leg bent and the other lying flat against the raft floor. She's pretty, and she's wearing a yellow two-piece bathing suit that shows the curve of her breasts, her flat, unadorned belly, her skin all smooth and, Damian thinks, polished-looking. She looks like a model, or a statue, and in just that one small moment of seeing her lie back on the raft, despite everything, he feels himself get hard.

He perches on the edge of the raft with his back to her, letting his feet dangle into the cold water. The sun is so bright on the rippled surface that he has to shut his eyes, so he leans back, resting his weight on his hands behind him. Is he just tired from the days of scraping the house, or could it be the epilepsy? He still isn't entirely clear on what all the symptoms are, and he's taken to watching his own body's every sensation as if he's looking for clues in a mystery.

At Reed, he learned about bioluminescence, and now, sitting on the raft, he thinks of the slides the professor showed the class, the shiny blues and sparkling yellows, all the fish glittering under the water's surface as if touched by fairy dust. How Phoenix had listened to him explain bioluminescence as they lay side by side in her narrow dorm bed, and then had described for him a snorkeling trip to Puerto Rico, where she'd seen the Bioluminescent Bay, "lit up like it was a reflection of the night sky," she said.

"Damian," he hears now in a sing-song voice behind him. "What are you thinking?"

He's sure Betheny's never heard of bioluminescence. He's sure that in the classes she's taking at the community college, she isn't one of the serious front-row students; she's one of those girls who sits in the back, doodling pictures of animals or texting Kylie.

"What did you take this year at WCC?" he asks, knowing he's only asking so he can prove to himself that she isn't taking something like Wildlife Bio or Intro to Shakespeare. He winces at this, at how condescending he feels. Why is he sometimes so judgmental and mean?

She sits up at his interest, shakes out her hair and carefully places her hands, palms down, beside her on the raft. She crosses her legs at the ankle. "Intro to Business Practices, Business Writing, Intro to Literature, and Study Skills," she ticks off. "It was pretty lame, but I got to have classes all in the mornings, so I had my afternoons free to work at Luxurious Lantman's."

He nods. "What did you read in Intro to Literature?"

"Oh, I don't know. It was mostly short stories, I guess. And two fictional novels." She pauses. "The teacher made us all go to an opera in Wisconset, *La Bohème*. That was pretty amazing. Everyone said our teacher was a lesbian, so that made it more interesting, to look at her and think maybe she had this life, this whack life outside of class."

"Was she?"

"I don't know. I don't think anyone really knew, and she didn't look like one. I mean, she had long curly hair and wore skirts and everything. Lesbians don't look like that, do they?"

Damian kicks at the water a little. He knows that Betheny knew about when Leslie was living with his mom and him; she even met Leslie a couple of times. But he doesn't mention this, and he doesn't answer her question. Instead, "Did you read any Salinger?" he asks.

"I don't think so," Betheny says, and seeing that he's going to stay on the subject of school, she sinks back into her sun-bathing position on the raft, adjusting her straps to avoid lines.

Damian looks out at the water. On the shore, he can see the bathers at the beach, the littlest kids wading into the shallow waters, a mother bent nearly double at the waist, holding the hand of a little kid, walking in baby steps with him. The older children are running into the water, chasing each other in a game of water tag.

What's Phoenix doing right now? Damian imagines her in her father's house in San Francisco. She described it to him in such detail that sometimes he's sure she showed him a photograph, even though he knows that isn't true. He closes his eyes against the bright sun, against the parti-colored children on the pale yellow sand of the beach, against the deep blue of the water. He imagines Phoenix in her black cutoff shorts, her gray t-shirt. He can see how she's fingering the stone wrapped in a silver coil she wears around her neck on a leather thong. He imagines her lying on a sofa in the old Victorian she described to him, a *flat* she called it, in *the Castro*. Everything she's told him sounds exotic and somehow more real than his sewn-up, tidy East Coast life. About the only interesting thing that's happened to him was when Leslie lived with them, but then she left.

He imagines Phoenix coming here, just showing up out of the blue, and tries to send her a message by mental telepathy. When they parted, they agreed they wanted to try something different, that they wouldn't be emailing and texting all the time; it would be phone calls and real letters on paper, as much as they could, anyway. "I want everything between us to be real," she'd said.

He thinks about telling her about all this, the bioluminescent fish that aren't here, the imaginary photograph of her house, the imaginary letter, and he thinks how she'd like that, it would make her laugh, lying with her head against his chest, and she'd press her palm to his belly.

"Do you want to go with us? It isn't a big deal, just a house party over in Wisconset," he hears Betheny say, and he realizes she's been talking while he was lost in his fantasy. He turns, blinking in the sudden sun as he opens his eyes. She's rolled onto her stomach, and even though the twin heaps of her ass are perfectly shaped and round, this only makes him think of Phoenix, of how she wound her legs around him in the long meadow grass behind the dorms.

"Sure," he says, figuring this is easier than admitting he wasn't listening. "When is it again?"

Without moving, Betheny says, "*Friday*, Damian. God, were you even listening? Like nine. Cort's driving."

Great. Just fabuloso. Still, he's got no excuse, the long summer without Phoenix stretching out before him. And it isn't really like a date with Betheny, if it's just a party.

"Great," he says, standing. "I'll race you to the shore." And before Betheny can squeal in protest, he's up, diving off the raft, plunging into the water in his final, most perfect dive, a streak of boy, airborne for one moment, then gone.

Seven

Before dawn, Grand Isle slumbers through the gray fog that rolls in at night, most people in their dreamy boats still listing out at sea. The pack of wild dogs nuzzle one another in the leafy bed they've made at the center of the island's forest, waking from the hunger nibbling in their bellies.

In the dark, ferry master Claude Reigner wakes, and out of habit reaches for Mara, remembers, and rises alone with a sigh to switch on the coffee pot. He turns on the radio. It's always set to the station that plays the old songs he likes, Sinatra and Sarah Vaughan, and some of the songs remind him of dancing with Mara and some songs remind him of her laugh. With many songs, he hums along. It's been fifteen years.

Over on the eastern shore, Tessa and Jake are up before dawn so that Jake can return to New York for the weekend violin restoration workshop he's co-leading in the city.

In the kitchen, Tessa snaps the chain on the light over the sink, breaks eggs into a pan, the smell of coffee permeating the house. It's still so dark out that she feels as if she's getting up in the middle of the night, but she doesn't mind because finally she feels rested, so rested she's put on her running shorts and a soft green t-shirt, thinking she'll stop at Dead Man's Beach on her way back from dropping Jake at the train in Wisconset. She doesn't say a thing about the scraps she's been saving for the raccoon, sliced turkey and a bit of bread, and he doesn't mention the leg trap he's set.

Peg and Torsten's house sits right on the marsh, a mid-century construction of gray weathered wood and glass, the big floor-to-ceiling windows letting in the early morning bay-lit light, affording a view that spreads from the deck across the reedy marsh, and on out across the open bay. Peg too wakes to an empty bed; even before she's fully awake, she knows Torsten's out already for a morning paddle, and she luxuriates for a long moment in the simplicity of lying alone under the covers, in the air that's a little chilly because she always leaves the windows open and the June air is still cold from the night. As she often does when she's alone and half-dreaming, she thinks of her private dead, of BJ, whom she loved—and whom Torsten never knew about—and of Beau, her first cat, the orange tabby she still thinks of as her only real cat. She gets up from the bed, and stands at the wide, multi-paned window that looks out over the marsh. The sun's just up. She can see Smokey, the new cat, sitting on the deck, having his after-breakfast wash; she can see, far out on the water of the bay, the small red dot of Torsten's kayak.

Across the island, Franci wakes in her bedroom as she usually does here at the island with a flush of gratitude that's visceral: she's here, in this room with its plain plank walls, tiny ribbons of light eking through the cracks. By turning her head to the right, she can see out the window to the backyard, to her garden, the peonies bursting in big white and pink blooms, the roses ripening, and further off, the fence of cattails, a slip of brackish water, all of it under the pretty morning sun. The perfection of it makes her take a deep breath. For all the imperfections in her life (money, love, her mother gone, Leslie gone) she's got this: this house, this island, most of all her son—smart, kind, and healthy—*right?*—sound asleep downstairs.

In town, the fluorescent lights in Grayson's flicker, then flick on, and one by one across the island the early risers rise and begin the day. It'll be hot again, the sunlight saturating the trees now fully leafed out, the beach sand squeaking under Tessa's running shoes. Dick Grasso will do a little work in his home office, then find Jennifer sunning on the deck, and he'll surprise her with a picnic lunch. Damian will wake to the alarm he's set for nine, and in the bright sun he and his mother will scrape the old paint from the back wall of the house. Cort will sleep in, waking in the empty house near noon. At Lantman's Supermarket Betheny and Kylie will luck out and get to take their lunch break together, eating sandwiches at the wooden picnic table set on the little patch of grass by the parking lot. Betheny will turn to the sun, lean her elbows on the table, stretching back like a cat.

"I cannot believe we're stuck in there on this totally gorgeous day."

"I know, right?" Kylie will say, lighting a cigarette and flicking the match, still lit, across the parking lot. "What I wouldn't give to be able to just go to the beach on a day like this. Must. Have. Beach."

"Well, at least we have tonight to look forward to. I'm so glad those guys are back this year."

"And tonight," Kylie will say in a teasing, sing-song voice, "tonight you're hooking up with Daaaaamian." Betheny flips her plastic fork across the table at Kylie. "Shut it down," she says, and then, "Do you really think so?"

The day will be start-of-summer perfect. With the weekend alone ahead of her, Tessa will feel her tense shoulders loosen, and will think only briefly of how tightly wound she is when she's with Jake. Franci and Damian will scrape one side of the house, an old boom box propped on the back steps skipping between Vampire Weekend and Joni Mitchell, Barenaked Ladies and the Beatles.

Later, days later, weeks later, some of them—Peg, Tessa, Franci—will remember that long morning, how it opened with such a bright, hardened promise into the shimmering afternoon.

Eight

Let me out of this car. Let me out of this car. Let me out of this car. The night has just begun, they're barely to the ferry that will take them off-island and into the evening, and Damian's already chanting his mantra. Do any of these idiots even know what a mantra is?

How could he have been so dumb, so easily duped? He thought it was supposed to be a group going out, to some party in Wisconset, which would have been bad enough, but it wasn't that at all; it's feeling now like nothing other than a dumb double date, Cort at the wheel of his dad's SUV with Kylie Pickett beside him, practically on his lap already, and him in the back seat with Betheny.

Damian sits as far over on the seat as he can, close to the door, looking out the window. The sky is so bright with a nearly full moon that he can see the tips of the pines as the car slides under them; the salty air comes in the open window, and briefly, the scent of the sweet honeysuckle that lines the launch to the ferry, and then there's the clack of the car barging onto the ferry, Claude Reigner at the window, taking Cort's money, telling him to "drive careful." *Fat chance.* I will probably meet my maker here in the back of Cort Grasso's dad's dumb SUV, and die with Betheny in my arms, Damian thinks, smiling a little at the irony of this.

"What's so funny?" Betheny says, reaching over and ribbling his sidewaist with her fingers. "You having a laugh attack?"

"No," Damian says, gently removing her hand and returning it to her own lap. "It's nothing."

"Hey, I don't want any funny business going on back there," Cort says from the front seat in a fakely stern dad voice, winking at Damian in the mirror.

It's three hours earlier in San Francisco, just six p.m., Damian calculates. He imagines Phoenix at the end of a beach day with her friends, who are probably a bunch of very interesting people. Her best friend there was going to the Chicago Art Institute, and on scholarship, too. He imagines the two girls on a beach—"the sand is black, really black, and sequiney, like a dress," she told him—with their drawing pads, sketching the Pacific Ocean. The Golden Gate Bridge, looking huge from that vantage point, stapling the shore of Marin to the shore of the city.

Maybe he could call her later, when he gets home from this lame night. Or maybe he can get a signal in Wisconset; he could sneak her a text, but at some point in the texting he'd have to explain to Phoenix where he was, and with whom, and even though he's sure she'd understand, he knows enough about the distortions distance makes to know this would be a bad idea: *I'm out with Cort and a couple of girls . . .* Plus, there's their agreement to try, anyway, only to write letters and call. But it's already been three days since they've talked.

"Okay, the party has arrived!" Cort says, pulling into the parking lot of the Wisconset Danceria. "I thought you said there was a house party," Damian says to Betheny, even though now he knows there never was. Betheny looks over to Kylie in the front, as Cort pulls the SUV into a spot and cuts the engine.

"Oh, I had it wrong," she says. "It was last weekend. But come on, we'll still have a good time."

"Yeah, Dude, we can make our own par-tay," Cort says, getting out of the front seat, opening the back door for Damian, bowing like a chauffeur. "Come on, man, lighten up," he whispers to Damian. "You've got it made tonight!"

Inside, the bar is already packed, music blaring from the small stage. The girls settle in at a table, and Cort and Damian walk to the bar. "Listen, Damian, I'm telling you this as your best friend. I know Betheny's not the brightest bulb in the lamp, but look at me with Kylie. You don't have to have a philosophical dialogue with her. We're not looking for intellectual stimulation here," he says, emphasizing "intellectual," and making a none-too-subtle shaking motion with one hand.

"Right," Damian says, rolling his eyes.

"What happened, did you fall in love at college or something?"

Damian feels his face go hot.

"I knew it. Man, don't let that get between you and getting laid tonight."

The bartender hands them the drinks, and Cort pays, saying, "Let me get this one," but Damian knows this will go on all night, Cort paying but getting the drinks at the bar to make it look to the girls as if he and Damian are splitting the bills, just as he's acted as both guardian and dictator since they were kids.

And it does go on like that, Damian drinking as little as he can get away with in the booming music and crush of kids; he's never liked the swoony feeling of being really drunk, and now, with the epilepsy, he knows he shouldn't really drink at all. He lets Betheny pull him onto the dance floor, stomps his feet around and waves his hands in a way that looks, if not graceful, at least not as mechanical as he feels. Eventually, he lets himself relax, and doesn't even mind when Cort stumbles into him, nearly knocking him down, his beer spilling and splashing everywhere.

When the bar closes, a steady drizzle has started up; the fresh air feels good after being inside, and Damian breathes in deeply, stretching his arms over his head, as he and Cort walk to the SUV and the girls, giggling, shrugging their shoulders up against the rain, run. On the way home, Damian returns to the mantra in his head, *Let me out of this car, let me out of this car*, thinking of Phoenix, thinking of scraping the house with his mom, thinking of plunging into the indigo ocean waves at Dead Man's Beach. But he can't get out; this is his only ride home, and maybe Cort isn't that drunk; it isn't like Damian was keeping track or anything, it's just that Cort is well ahead of him, as usual.

If only Betheny would keep off of him, but here she is, taking his limp hand in hers, then twirling a lock of his hair around one finger.

Just after making the turn for the road that will lead down to the ferry and home, Cort pulls off to the side, saying, "Damian, man, you better take the wheel to get us across. You just know Claude's going to be sniffing for booze."

Damian has a moment's hesitation, but he knows that even so he's got a better chance of getting them all home alive than Cort does. He'll do anything to get himself home, plus, what are the chances he'll seize right now? He gets out of the back, and into the driver's seat.

And good thing, too, because sure enough as they pull onto the ferry, here's Claude, in his yellow slicker and rain hat, leaning into the driver's window, asking Damian if he'd like to pick up some hours working the ferry this summer, and the little knot of worry inside Damian's chest tightens; Claude is obviously checking them out to see if they're okay to drive the rest of the way. "Sure," Damian says, meaning it. Unlike Cort, he has to work in summer, even with the job of painting the house, and plus, maybe the work will distract him, help him stop thinking about Phoenix so much.

Damian points the SUV toward West Shore Road, toward the little green cottage on the marshy bay, but as soon as they crest the first hill after the ferry, "Hey, man, pull over here, at Massey's," Cort calls from the back.

"No, man, I'm getting out first anyway. I want to get home. I've got a phone call to make," Damian says, but he slows, thinking he'd rather have the hassle now than later.

Damian pulls into Massey's ice cream stand, and he and Cort switch places again, getting soaked as they pass one another in the headlights of the idling car, and as soon as they're back on the pavement, Cort turns down East Shore Road, veering away from the quickest route to Damian's house, heading down East Shore, passing Bay Beach, heading toward the southern shore, Dead Man's Beach, or what Cort refers to as "Laid Man's Beach."

"Wait a minute, you got to drop me off first, Dickhead," Damian says to Cort, leaning forward so he's talking right in his ear, using their old nickname, a name which, he realizes now, ironically, has developed a connotation of affection.

"Okay, Buzzkill Betty. Chill out. We don't have to stop. I just thought we all might like an extra little ride," Cort says, and from the back seat, Damian can see that Cort's sliding his hand farther up Kylie's leg, under her skirt. He looks out the window; even through the rain, he can see the whitecaps on the ocean waves, and he sinks into his favorite preoccupation with a certain final night at Reed, the dark smell of patchouli oil, the tiny clicking of the beaded curtain around Phoenix's bed in the breeze from their motion, the light in her room shifting from gray, to cream, the early morning signaling that their final night—the final night of the school year, anyway—had passed.

It will be just eleven-thirty in San Francisco when he gets home; he can still call Phoenix, and, giving up, Damian relaxes a bit, settling into the comfort of the leather seat, Betheny sulking in a little pout, as the island night grows huge and dark around him.

Nine

There's a flash of an animal against the black road, Cort's foot to the brakes, the steering wheel pulling hard to the right, and then the whole wet world wheels up before his face, fans down again, slow, like in a movie, and Cort's thinking it's happening just the way he knew it would, just the way he's heard, *Oh fuck, it's really happening,* he thinks, airborne thunderous reverberating crash everything so slow and so fast the car's ceiling tumbling under him glass splintering, the airbag exhaling against his chest. It all stops and somehow he's out of the car, which lies on its side broken and steaming and looking alive, and Kylie's beside him, screaming her head off, crying, so he slaps her across the face, hard, and that shuts her up. He's never slapped anyone before, but as he's thinking this he's thinking *How can he be thinking this*? And Kylie's tugging on the door to the back seat, and together they pull Betheny out through the back seat door, and *where is Damian*? *Where is he?*

Damian's crumpled up in the back seat, slumped down, and Cort, suddenly sober, pushes his phone into Kylie's shaking hands, saying "call the ambulance, damn it," and she punches the numbers in. For once, there's a signal. Betheny's useless, sitting on a rock outcropping, her arms folded against her chest, whimpering, and Cort clambers into the back seat of the SUV, *his dad's car,* and there lies Damian in the bottom of the well the car has formed, *no, no, no, this isn't happening, this isn't real,* crumpled up against the door, his legs and arms unnaturally askew. Still, he doesn't let himself think, and he pulls on Damian's shoulders, wraps his friend's heavy arms around his own shoulders and neck, talking to him, pulling him up, as if he's found the boy at the bottom of the sea and he's rescuing him, bringing him up from the water into the rainy air of night.

It isn't easy, but with the adrenaline running fast in his veins, with the muscles he's built up with soccer and weight-lifting, Cort manages to heft Damian from the car, up and through the open door, and to lay him on the ground. By this time, Cort is crying, even though when Kylie says, "Is he dead?" Cort says, "No, of course he isn't dead." Cort takes Damian's wrist in his fingers and tries to find a pulse, but he isn't really sure what he's looking for, and Damian's head keeps flopping over to one side and Cort keeps rolling it back so it's straight, whispering to Damian, "Oh man, come on, man." Betheny kneels by Damian's head, rocking back and forth, touching his face with her right hand, then wiping her wet hair from her face, her left arm pressed tight against her chest, crying. *Is she crying because she's in pain?* Cort doesn't know and doesn't care, because all that matters is that Damian won't respond, isn't there. That's the scene the ambulance drivers find when they round Dead Man's Curve.

And then Cort's world spins again, as the EMTs sprint across the meadow to the car, push Cort aside, and go to work on Damian, the girls silent now, Cort standing, holding his head as if he's going to drop, and he's going to be sick, and he folds himself in two, bending head to knees, vomiting until he feels the pressure of a hand against his back, and there's Cop Callahan, who's been the Grand Isle main cop as long as Cort can remember, now patting Cort's back, then straightening him up and sitting him down on the wet ground, saying, "Sit down, son, calm down, now."

"You okay?" Cal asks, just to say something, just to get the boy to speak.

"Yeah," Cort coughs, spits, then waves a hand in front of his face. "It's not me," he starts, but he's about to cry, so he coughs again, presses palms to his aching face. "It's my friend," he says.

"Don't worry. The EMTs are looking after him," Cop Callahan says. And then, because the scenario is so obviously what it is, and because, sitting this close to Cort he can smell the sweet-sour stink of booze, he asks, "Were you driving, son?"

The world is spinning again, and Cort feels he's about to be sick again, feels the rush of time running backward, of the accident undoing itself—*Can't we go back?*—leans his head between his legs, and his instinct for lying kicks in. "No," he says. "My friend was. Damian."

Cort can hear a little whimper at this from Kylie, and he shoots her a look, and she whimpers a little more as the remaining EMT approaches her. Cort isn't worried; neither girl will rat him out, both of them too scared of anything bigger, smarter, better off than they are. The lie threads out of him as naturally as the truth would, even though he doesn't have a chance to think that if Damian's dead no one needs to know he wasn't driving, but nor does he need to think this out. Damian hardly drank much anyway, and even if he lives, he certainly won't be charged, and anyway, doesn't it make more sense this way, isn't this more just? It isn't right that the driver, a few too many beers in his system, a little too daring on Dead Man's Curve, should live and the guy in the back seat, the kid who didn't even want to go out in the first place, the guy who would have been happy staying home and calling his girlfriend out in California or something, should be the one being shoved into the ambulance that's now wailing off the grass, toward the ferry and Wisconset hospital. Cort shakes his head; he's getting all mixed up. But Damian's got to be alright. He's got to be okay.

"Okay," Callahan says. From the look of the boy being loaded into the ambulance, he's sure he'll have to investigate, later, question the girls, see if anyone else at the bar noticed who took the driver's seat when the group left Wisconset, ask Claude down at the ferry—he's sure to remember who was behind the wheel. But for now, this is enough. It's enough. He's still got a long night ahead of him, one that's sure to stretch through to the other side of dawn. Later, he'll have to investigate Cort's claim, look into the angle of the car's descent, the pitch of the wheels and the pattern of Cort's small injuries, what appears to be the fractured arm of one of the girls.

But evidence is often silent as the dead.

The girls are huddled together by the rock, the EMTs herding the three kids with minor injuries into the back of the second ambulance, and they ride together like that to Wisconset, Cort holding his head in his hands, Kylie still crying, Betheny just looking dazed, eyes open wide to the larger, different night.

Ten

They told me the way that you're always afraid they'll tell you, in the orchestrated little nightmare you keep tucked away for an insomniac's worrying, until one night, the nightmare springs up to life, like the pop-up books I read to Damian when he was small, laughing with him in mock surprise at the cardboard chipmunks springing up from between the covers' folds.

The policemen stood at the porch door, ringing the bell, and I came grumbling out from my bedroom upstairs, my summer bedroom where the sound of the water hushes me to sleep like a lullaby. I pulled on my big corduroy shirt as I walked, thinking at first Damian had just forgotten his key when he went out, thinking, damn him for waking me up when I'd finally gotten to sleep, thinking that his first year at college certainly hadn't improved his ability to keep track of things, most notably keys and money, thinking I never should have gotten into the new habit of locking up at night. I looked into the darkened living room, and the moon was so bright that I could just make out the clock perched high on the bookcase. It was nearly three a.m.

I switched on the porch light, and there they stood, two pop-up policemen in their tidy blue uniforms, holding their pointy hats, as if such neatness could keep all the messy stuff of life at bay. I was impressed with how crisp their uniforms were, as if up here at the island I'd expected something more casual, more relaxed than the sharply creased officialdom of Manhattan.

I unlocked the door, pulled my shirt tighter around me. Under it, I was just wearing the boxers and t-shirt I sleep in, a habit of dress I adopted from Leslie, in the first years she lived with us, and in that moment, as I opened the door with one hand, the other clutching at my shirt, I thought of Leslie, and I longed for her presence as I hadn't since she left. I think I even expected to hear her footfall following me down the stairs.

But of course that didn't happen. Instead, one of the policemen said, "Mrs. Weiseman?" and I didn't correct him, didn't say, "It's Ms.," didn't say, "It's Wise-man." I just nodded. I knew what was coming, and I could hear a high-pitched whistle in my head, but I couldn't speak.

"Could we come in for a minute?" he said, and I held the door open and my shirt closed around me and I nodded again, and they walked into the miniature entryway of our little summer camp, filling it with their meaty blue presence. They were so big, these two men.

"Maybe we should sit down in the living room?" the one who'd spoken before said, and I nodded again, and we paraded into the living room. I was so cold. I thought about turning the heat on, but then I thought, no, this isn't real, this is only a bad dream, you don't need to turn up the heat when it's just a dream. Nightmare.

I turned on the table lamp. Damian made it in high school. It's an oblong of maple, with a shade with leaves pressed into the thick white paper. The older cop said, "Please, sit down," as if we were in his living room, not mine, and gestured with his hand, and we all sat down, and now I could see that the one who hadn't spoken yet was very young, maybe twenty-four. A new recruit, is that what they call them? A little older than Damian, I guessed, and I thought Damian would know. I'll ask Damian later, I thought, and the whistle in my head pitched higher. Mostly I wanted them to just leave, get out of there before they could say what it was they'd come to say.

The spokesman said, "Are you alone, ma'am? Is your husband or somebody here?"

"No," I said, "Damian—my son—is still out. It's just us," I said, even though I knew then that I'd just spoken about him in the present tense for the last time. There was now a blank swale of space, a cold air blowing right through me, and I couldn't imagine how I'd keep sitting there, in the little wicker rocker with the blue and white cushions.

"Is there a friend you could call?" the younger cop said, and sure enough, his voice still sounded like a boy's voice. His voice hovered on the word, "friend," and I thought how different his friendships must be from mine, and my brain hovered there for what seemed a very long time, wondering at how we could use the same word with such different meanings. I imagined him with other young men like himself, drinking a beer, clapping someone on the back.

They looked so out of place sitting like that in my living room. The older one, I could see now, wasn't much older. He had taken the club chair, and he looked too masculine against the pink and yellow chintz, much more masculine than Damian and his friends, lanky summer boys in their baggy shorts, everything about them loose and unevenly distributed, their hair brushing their shoulders like the hair of girls. Maybe it was the gun.

The young skinny one was on the brown sofa. They were both perched on the edge of their seats. I wanted to tell the young cop to sit back, tell him I'd gotten this sofa in its soft sturdy canvas when Damian was about six, knowing I'd have to wait years before I could have the delicate, clean kind of furniture Jake and Tessa have.

I guess it only seemed a long time I was just sitting there, looking around my living room, at the Oriental carpet Mom gave me when she moved into the retirement home, at the tangle of my plants clustered at the window. I could see that a few leaves of the hibiscus had dried and gone brown, and it took everything I had not to get up right then and cross the room and start fussing with them.

Instead, I looked at the older one, then at the younger. I wanted to hurt them both, suddenly. "Damian's dead," I said.

"Ma'am," the younger one started, and then the older one cut in: "It was very quick. The car he was in went right off the road at Dead Man's Beach. He died right away."

I looked at the clock on the bookshelf, and at all the books in their neat rows underneath the clock. The clock was from my grandparents' house, a big old mantelpiece ticker they'd somehow taken with them from Austria. It was precisely three o'clock.

How is it that I felt I'd been talking to those pop-up cops for an hour, hours? Both at the time and now, it was as if they came in and I just stared and stared and barely spoke, and everything was so slow, as if I knew what was happening the moment I heard them at the door and I was trying to stall; it was as if I had to make an elaborate dance to get from point A to point L or M.

But it was only about three minutes, the whole business of opening the door, bringing the cops inside, sitting down, switching on the table lamp, and hearing that my son was dead.

Remarkable, that it only takes about three minutes to hear your son is dead.

"Is there someone you could call? We need you to come down and identify the body. You shouldn't be alone," the older cop said again, and I thought of Leslie, but we hadn't spoken in what, six months? And right

on the heels of thinking of her, her solid presence beside me, not even really thinking of her as much as imagining her, seeing her, I didn't even say anything, just got up, picked up the phone from the coffee table, and dialed Tessa and Jake's number, almost to keep myself from calling Leslie.

Tessa answered, her voice thick with sleep: "Yeah."

"Damian's dead," I said, for the second time. The whistle was starting up again in my head.

"What? Franci? Oh Franci, no." I imagined her suddenly awake, eyes popping wide like in an old tv show, the camera focusing on her bedside clock, its hands pointing to the three and the twelve, Dick Van Dyke playing Jake in the bed beside her. "What do you mean?" Indeed. What did I mean? "There was an accident, I guess," I said, and before I could even take in what I'd said, "I'm on my way over," I heard her say and then there was just the hollow dead phone sound in my ear, and I thought about how the ear is shaped like a little shell, and I saw my finger tracing Damian's perfectly formed seashell ear when he was a baby.

The cops must have been horrified, that I would keep saying "Damian's dead," no euphemism, no dodging, no introduction for poor Tessa. "She'll be here soon," I told them, and they nodded, and then we all sat there in the still living room, the rain nibbling down the windows in long icy streams. I thought that I should probably call Stiles, but I wasn't even sure where he was. They must have told me the story then, my son's death already sliding into a narrative that would trail after me, and that, in the end, would change so many times over in its particulars that I wouldn't ever know what had really happened. But as I remember it now, it's as if we were silent, as if now there was nothing to say, and still I was waiting for Damian's step on the porch outside, heavy with his new weight, the weight of his becoming a man, and light, too, still light with his boyish grace.

Eleven

By the time Tessa and Franci get back from identifying Damian's body at the Wisconset hospital, Friday has thoroughly ended, and Saturday has begun; it's well after four a.m., and Tessa, unsure what else to do, makes them a pot of coffee. They sit together in Franci's kitchen, watching the enormous wet night through the screen door.

There's no attempt at sleep, even though the delicious, short-lived embrace of the shock may have made sleep possible, at least for a couple of hours. Instead, they wait for the time to pass, Franci occasionally saying something like, "I just can't believe Damian would drive drunk," then slipping back into the soft comfort of the shock. The rain continues outside, tapping and hissing on the back porch roof, at last lessening to a blurry mist as the backyard emerges in the graying light.

"Shouldn't you call Jake?" Franci says, remembering her image of the bedside phone ringing with her call. Why did she call Tessa, and not Peg? Was it only a few hours ago?

"He left for the city this morning. I mean, Friday morning. I'm not sure if I should call him now, or wait," Tessa says, looking up at Franci's kitchen clock. It's five-thirty. The clock face has a painting on it of a woman in a canoe, waving. Tessa feels the anxiety which is, by now, familiar to her, and which indicates that she's gotten herself into another Jake-impossible situation: if she calls him in the city, and wakes him, he'll likely be angry at having been woken. Or if she disturbs him and he's already at the workshop, she'll catch hell. But if she waits, he may be angry that she didn't tell him right away. And so she decides a compromise is best, and waits until it's six-thirty, and the day is beginning, the shapes of the shrubs and bushes in the garden becoming more visible, the sound of birdsong rising in the trees. There's no answer at his apartment in Brooklyn.

"He must be out for an early run," she tells Franci when she hears voicemail pick up. She doesn't leave a message, struck, suddenly, by what she'd have to say. Franci nods.

"Do you want to call someone, like a rabbi or something?" Tessa asks. It's always seemed to her that Jews, no matter how secular, would turn to their religion in a time of need, more than she would try to dig up her own long-severed Protestant roots.

"Rabbi? I don't even know where I'd find one, or what I'd do with one if I did."

As the sky lightens, they move out onto the steps of the back porch. Usually in the spring and early summer, a seasoned birder like Franci can be drawn outside simply by the sound of a birdsong that isn't immediately recognizable, thinking: a warbler's passing through! And usually, she's right, looking around in the canopy near the house to see a yellow-throat, a black-and-white, a cerulean flittering in the new leaves. Now, as they sit on the steps, the sky brightens briefly with a cleared morning, and then clouds over again. Franci isn't crying: in between talking about the accident and making plans of what to do next, she's listening for the birds, and each time she hears one, she stops, says, "Listen," and Tessa looks up to see a bit of brown and yellow rustling in the leaves of the trees.

Finally, at seven, Tessa calls Peg, whispering the news into the phone, and Peg, as Tessa had, simply says, "I'm on my way."

When Peg arrives, she walks right in, straight to Franci, and takes her in her arms. Everyone's crying. And then, "What about Stiles?" Peg says to Franci.

"Oh, God, I don't know. I just can't face calling him. Will you call him for me?"

"Of course I will. Where's the number?" But the only number Franci has for Stiles is the number of his Manhattan offices, and it's Saturday. There's a complicated maze of numbers to call in emergencies, and then the complications of locating him—he's at a meeting, out of the country, someone on the other end of the line says. It will take some time to track him down. When Peg comes back to the porch and tells this to Franci, Franci just nods.

Sometime in the mid-morning, Franci thinks of the epilepsy. Of course. That's the only explanation that makes any sense, and yet, the only pinprick of relief from the claustrophobic feeling that

Damian is dead comes from thinking this isn't true, this can't be right, he wouldn't have driven the car over the edge. He couldn't have. He couldn't have died.

And all through that first long day, and all through the coming days, she doesn't tell anyone about the epilepsy, doesn't want anyone to know; it couldn't possibly have happened that way. Couldn't have happened that way because it couldn't have happened. Couldn't be true.

Tessa and Peg don't leave Franci, agreeing that one of them will sleep on the pull-out sofa in Franci's living room the first night, the other the next, against Franci's insistence that this isn't necessary. Not necessary until Franci wakes the second night, screaming—literally, screaming, as Peg later reports to Tessa.

"Oh, dear God," Tessa says. "How's she ever going to get through?"

The day after the accident, the rain starts up again mid-morning and doesn't stop. Cort wakes late with the steady rhythm sluicing on the roof, for a moment disoriented by the rain, the soreness in his legs and arms and back, the light that surely isn't night, but that's the dark daylight of a stormy day. He looks at the clock: nearly noon. *Damian's dead*, he remembers, and now that Cort's awake, the accident spins out around him, again, the tumbling earth rising up before the windshield of the car. *Again*.

He closes his eyes, not to sleep, but so he won't have to see the room spinning, too. This room has only been his room since he got here this summer, and like the rest of the house, it's completely different from before the renovations, when it was his room and the house was his parents' house; *before*, when life was normal. When life was good.

But now, now it's like a fucking nightmare. The thing is, there is nothing he can do. His best friend is dead. And he was driving.

"I wasn't driving," Cort whispers, to practice saying it, although, even as he does, he winces a little at the feeling this gives him, the feeling like he wants to cry.

Somewhere far off in the house, the telephone rings, just once, and Cort listens to see if his father calls him, but there's just more silence.

The work began on the house last fall, after they left, and when they returned this year, this spring, the house was done, practically a whole new house built where the old one had been. Cort still has to work to remember where things used to be; the kitchen door has been transformed into a wall, the wall between the kitchen and living room now gone. Since coming up two weeks ago, Cort's had dreams about the house, disquieting dreams in which he can't find things, his high-school yearbook, his childhood dog, his mother. The house has become a maze.

Now, he has his own bathroom, off his room, so he goes in, washes up, then in his bedroom raises the window shades, so he can see the water. It's been raining all morning, and by now the grasses in the lawn that slopes down from the house to the shore are heaped over with rain. From his bedroom window, Cort can see the rain sheeting down in long gray swathes above the sea.

From his room, he can't hear much of what's going on in the rest of the house. His room is on the opposite end of the hall from the room his father shares now with Jennifer. For obvious reasons, Cort knows. One night he got up and wandered the house, and he could hear them in there, going at it. The old man.

Cort hears the front door swing open and slam shut; he crosses the upstairs hallway and stands at the window that looks down on the driveway. He sees his father and Jennifer getting into his father's red Miata. He can't see their faces, but he thinks they don't look too happy. It's still raining pretty hard, and his father holds the umbrella over Jennifer's head as she gets in the passenger side. She's wearing a pair of jeans, and a purple rain poncho.

He quickly returns to his room, pulls on his jeans over his boxers, and glides down the new, polished wood stairs to the kitchen. There's still some coffee; he switches the coffeemaker on to heat it up. In the refrigerator he finds some cold cuts, and some bread, and quickly fashions himself a sandwich, pours milk into one of the tall glasses with a swirly pattern embedded in the glass, piles everything onto a tray, and carries his food upstairs, before they can return and find him there. No telling where they've gone, when they'll be back. His mother would have left a note.

After eating, he takes another one of the pills they gave him at the clinic and sleeps again, pushing *what happened* out of his head as best he can. Sleeping is easier than he would have thought it would be. Maybe the rain helps, a crepitating pattern on the skylight over his bed, and maybe the fact that he was up until four in the morning, half-drunk still, and then, after his dad left him to join Jennifer upstairs, drinking more, watching the level in his father's good whiskey bottle slowly descend.

Late in the afternoon, when the rain has stopped, Peg insists that Tessa go home, get some rest. "You've been up since three this morning," she whispers when Franci goes to the phone to talk, again, to the police, and it's only when Peg says this that Tessa realizes how exhausted she is, and she gets into her car, urges the temperamental old Honda into starting.

The car takes her, almost by its own volition, not onto Cross Island Road, but down the west shore, the road curving along the water, and then, just before Dead Man's Beach, the ocean on her right, the sparsely planted oversized houses on her left, the road rises sharply, and up ahead is the accident scene, the meadow on the right, rolling down toward the blue Atlantic. After the rain, the sky over the ocean seems bright, too bright. When she gets to the beach, she makes a last-minute decision and turns the wheel, pulls into a spot, and stops. There's only one other car in the vast parking lot.

Now, she's back to not feeling tired. On the beach, the sand is wet, but the sky is clearing, skeins of pink and yellow cloud trailing over the horizon. She heads up the beach.

When she sees the figure approaching her, she has a crazy thought it's Damian, and almost cries out. But even before she takes a few more steps, of course, she knows it isn't him; it's Kenji. Even before she can see the details of his face, she recognizes him. As she nears him, she sees the broad, flat face, seeming to hold the secrets of the world, so like the faces of the Inuit. She thinks this, even though she knows it's ridiculous, it's just the kind of fetishizing she warns her students against.

She gives a little wave, feeling she's about to cry, just at the sight of another human being, alive.

"Hi," he says.

"Yeah," she nods, and before she has to explain anything, he says, "I'm so sorry about the boy, Damian. You must have known him well, didn't you?"

Tessa nods, feeling her eyes fill, and she wipes the back of her hand across her face. "Yeah. I guess the news is already out. I'm sorry, I'm just—I've been with Franci since this morning."

Kenji says, "It's just shocking, that this happened. Is someone with Franci?"

"Yeah, Peg took over. I've been up since three. I think it's just all hitting me now."

"Let's get you in your car; you ought to go home," Kenji says, and she turns, and they walk together back down the beach.

After a few silent minutes, Kenji says, "He shouldn't have been driving."

"No, it isn't that," Tessa says. "Of the two, Damian was much less of a drinker than Cort was. I'd have put my money on Damian getting everyone home safe."

"Oh. I—" Kenji begins, then stops. He was thinking of the boy's Depakote script he filled, but there's also the eerie feeling he gets sometimes that something just isn't right, just doesn't square. He thinks of his grandmother, a *miko* who straddled the spirit world and the world of the earth. He doesn't, really, believe in any of that, but if he did, he'd believe he had inherited it. Or a diluted, Americanized version of it.

Still, even if he had the gift, it wouldn't do any good now.

Tessa doesn't want to go home, but then she thinks of the raccoon, and suddenly wants more than anything to check on it, see if she can spy it nosing in the garden, or licking its paw after eating.

"Maybe you'll see the kit," Kenji says, when they reach her car, and she smiles a little. "That's what I'm hoping," she says. For once, her Honda starts right up, and she pulls out of the parking lot, up the sloping hill that's now become the accident scene. Around her, the wet meadows in the falling dusk.

When Cort wakes again, it's nearly evening, summer evening, and the rain has quit, and Damian is dead.

Cort rummages through the duffel bag he brought from school, finds the bottle of Scotch, and takes a drink. He did enough damage to his dad's bottles last night; he's on his own now. His nerves are shot, but he knows he has to go downstairs eventually, and anyway, he's starving. When he brought the bottle, he'd imagined drinking it with Damian and the girls, or maybe just with Damian, at Laid Man's Beach or something. It was supposed to be celebratory; it was supposed to be happy, for Christ's sake.

For Christ's sake. Something his father would say.

Cort pulls on his jeans again, a clean t-shirt, and crosses the hall to check out the drive. There's his dad's Miata, back from wherever he went with Jennifer. It's five-thirty, and still raining, the drops of water beading up on the waxed car, water dripping from the trees around the driveway, water shedding off the roof of the little-used, new garage.

Cort goes downstairs again, this time careful to make a little noise rather than being careful to be quiet, wanting to warn his dad and Jennifer of his approach so he won't find them in a clinch or worse, with their heads bowed in earnest, concerned conversation which will stop when he comes in the room, conversation, he'll be certain, about him. About what he's done.

He jumps from the last step to the floor, with a resounding thud, the way he did when he was a little kid.

The stairs bottom out to the living room, a wide expanse of polished hardwood and white furniture, the white alleviated by a few splashy pillows in blues and greens. A woven green sisal rug on the floor in front of the sliding glass doors. The living room, as usual, is empty, and Cort heads into the kitchen, also facing the ocean, also complete with sliding glass doors. His mom, an architect, designed the renovation of the house, and then his parents split up.

The kitchen is bright with the after-rain light. And here's Jennifer, standing at the counter with a cookbook open, a bowl, a few eggs, some other foods. She looks up as he comes in.

"Hey, Cort," she says. At least she isn't all fakey, at least she doesn't call him a nickname or anything. She doesn't try to give him a hug, or look all worried. In fact, she doesn't say anything more, and Cort just says, "Hey," rubbing his head with one hand, reaching for the fridge. He is suddenly very thirsty, and he also knows it's wise to have something to cover the Scotch.

"Have you been sleeping?" she says, and he says, "Yeah," then realizes he probably shouldn't just drink the orange juice out of the carton; this is a habit that always bugged his mom, and especially when they had company. Even though Jennifer isn't exactly company. Is she?

As he finds a glass, and pours, Cort thinks maybe he'll just go over to Damian's, where everything is more laid back, and then he remembers again.

Standing at the sliders, looking at the water, he drinks his juice in one long draught.

"Are you hungry?" Jennifer says. Why is everything a question with this girl? But he is. He's starving, even though he knows he shouldn't be; shouldn't he be grief-stricken and unable to eat or something? Like in that movie that Kylie made him take her to, where the guy's wife dies and he nearly dies of starvation or something.

"Yeah," he says, "I guess."

"Good. You've got to eat," she says, as if he's shown any signs of not eating. "I'm making a frittata and hash browns and salad."

"Chill." Cort isn't sure what a frittata is, but it's food, and he knows from the past two weeks that Jennifer's a pretty good cook, even if she does cook random things, like breakfast things for dinner and fried tomatoes for breakfast. Still, she's a better cook than his mom, much as he hates to admit this. In his head, he makes this fact okay by explaining to himself that his mother had more important things on her mind, like being an architect, for example. It's like his father has gotten a maid and a cook and a call girl all at once.

They're married, now, though. This is his father's wife.

She's still in her jeans, and a little blue shirt that reveals her midriff when she reaches for something. She is sexy, he's got to admit that, in a wholesome kind of way. She's got a great body.

Cort sighs without meaning to; the last thing he wants is for her to ask him what he's feeling. She won't do that, he thinks, but just in case, he walks away, into the living room. "Dinner will be ready in about half an hour," she calls to his back as he goes.

His dad's never been much for ceremony, and they hardly ever use the formal dining room, so they eat in the kitchen, as usual. The frittata, it turns out, is like a big scrambled-egg pie. It's pretty good, Cort thinks. He has a beer with his meal, acceptable, and after the first silent, tense moments, his father says, "So, we went down to the garage, and they think they can fix up the SUV, but it's going to cost a bundle. We'll have to think about whether it's worth it." Cort nods. The last thing he wants is to get behind the wheel again.

"And the police called earlier. They'll come over Monday, have you fill out a report. Give a statement," his father closes by clearing his throat.

"Sure," Cort says, feeling a sharp plunge of panic, and then the sudden pressure of tears. What's *wrong* with him? More to the point, what's he going to say? "I guess they want to know who was driving and all," he says, thinking even as he does, *Don't mention who was driving. Idiot.*

"Well, yes, I would think so." His father takes a drink of his wine. He hardly ever drank wine with his mom. "It does seem a little odd that Damian was driving, Cort. It's my car, after all."

"Dad, I know. I'm sorry. You know how Damian can be, when he gets something in his head. He's very convincing," he says, then lowers his eyes to the napkin in his lap. "I had a couple too many drinks. He wanted us to get home safe," he says, and this thought, this statement, this *lie* makes him so sad that the tears do come to his eyes.

"But Cort, if you'd had a few too many, didn't you think that probably Damian had, too? Why didn't you call? You know I told you I'd come to get you if this ever happened, no questions asked. Wasn't that our agreement?" His dad's voice is rising just a bit, even though he's still trying to sound like this is just a normal conversation. Jennifer doesn't say anything, just eats, delicately slipping forkfuls of frittata into her pretty mouth.

"Dad, I'm sorry," Cort says again, feeling the tears now pressing in on him, and he thinks then of his mother, of being a little kid, and crying into his mother's legs, in this very kitchen. Well, not this kitchen, but the first one, the old one. This reaction, this thought of his mother, is, at the moment, inexplicable to him. "I'm so fucking sorry," he says, and pushes back from the table, stands, bolts from the room, the feelings welling up in him like an animal, a big uncontrollable black bear that's going to swipe a paw at Jennifer's nicely set table and ruin even more of everything.

"Let him go," he can hear Jennifer say to his dad. His mom would have followed him. She's already left two messages for him to call her in Geneva. But in his room, he pulls on his sweatshirt and sneakers, trundles back down the stairs, and out the door. In the garage, he finds his bike, and hops on.

The rain has evaporated into a thick mist, and as he rides along East Shore Road, Cort can see the sky is clear, a few bright patches of rosy-blue shimmering behind the clouds. The road is straight, and perfectly flat, the newly blacktopped road of the rich, unpocked by potholes. On his right, the sea, behind the sand dunes, moving in its low lull. Left-hand, off land, Cort hears a far-off moaning that seems to come from deep in the island's forest; if he'd heard about the pack of wild dogs, he'd think it was them, but he hasn't, and so he isn't afraid. The only thing he has to fear, anyway, has already happened, and now the rain has done its job of obscuring this long, sad day, and now is lifting into the clear summer evening, and as he rides, hard, fast, along the smooth road, Cort cries, repeating again and again Damian's name, trying like hell to hear some response.

Twelve

When the phone rings late on Sunday afternoon, Cort has a moment between the phone's ring and Jennifer calling out, "Cort, it's for you," when he thinks—no, he knows—it's going to be Damian, calling with some crazy story about how everyone thought he was dead. It's only a split second, but it's so real to Cort that he lets out a sigh that is a sigh of relief before it collapses into a sigh of grief, and then he heaves up from the sofa in the "study"—a room Jennifer has lined with bookshelves, most of which remain empty—where he's been watching the only thing he can find on tv, a Mets game he really doesn't give a crap about.

As he nears the phone, he thinks next that it could be his mom, and he isn't sure if he's hoping it will be her or hoping it won't. She'll be hysterical. And then he thinks, it's Cop Cal, calling to say he knows the truth. There's that swing of panic in his gut again, and he starts to sweat, and picks up the phone.

"Yeah," he says, by this time knowing it won't be Damian at all. Ever.

"Hi Cort," Kylie says. Her voice is all muffled, like she's been crying.

"Hey. What's up?" He's never been so happy to hear her voice on the phone—in comparison with Cop Cal's call, this is great—but as soon as he does, Cort just wants to get away, back to the sofa.

"Nothing. I just feel so bad, you know, about Damian and all," Kylie says.

"Yeah. Me, too." Cort looks out the picture window, down the grassy bank to the beach. From everywhere in the house now there's a view like this: you can't get away from it.

"So, um, do you want to hang out? I had to work all day at Lantman's."

"I don't know," Cort says. The day's over already? He wants to say the weather's bad for doing anything, because that's how he feels, and he almost does say this, but that would be crazy, because outside, he can see, the sky is a clear plate of blue, and the sun has been saturating the island all day, and now the day's turning into one of those pure, soft evenings, warm and a little sweet. He's spent the day in the study, watching the tv images flicker and shift, not really thinking of anything, just watching the darkly blue and black memory of what happened repeat. If only he'd let Damian drive right from the start. Or at least let Damian drive to his mom's place on the West Shore. Or drop the girls in town, then Damian. Why didn't Damian insist?

"Come on," Kylie says, her voice rising in just a hint of a whine. "Just meet me at Bay Beach."

"Okay," Cort hears himself say, realizing he can't risk pissing her off, because if she's pissed off at him, she just might tell. Plus, seeing her will make a few hours pass, maybe help him stop seeing the pictures of the accident click over and over again in his head.

"Hey, I'm going out for a bike ride," he calls to Jennifer, hoping she's tucked away in some corner of the house where she can't hear him. But here she is, coming out of the kitchen, wiping her hands on a dishtowel, in her bathing suit top and a little skirt of some kind, barefoot, and Cort tries not to look at her breasts or her legs.

"Don't you want any supper? Your dad's stopping to get some fish. I was just making this yummy lime marinade for it," she says.

"No, really, that's okay. If there's any left over, I'll just have some later," Cort says.

"Okay. Well, have a good time," and Jennifer turns her back, and Cort, in spite of himself, watches her go, thinking he'd rather be anywhere than here, thinking, at least meeting up with Kylie tonight will pacify her, make her think twice before telling anyone the truth. And he'll probably get a blow job out of it, which at this point, he really could use.

The reeds and cattails at the edges of Bay Beach are already high; one reason this spot is such a draw for the teenagers is that the tall marsh grasses provide plenty of cover, if you lie down in the damp sandy patches that rim the bay. Or, you can walk up the path and slip into the dunes that lead to the beach. Cort waits for Kylie in the little parking area, sitting on the single weathered picnic table, watching the early evening sky turn dusky, the swallows sailing over the marsh in their last dives of the day.

Waiting for Kylie, Cort doesn't think about Damian, and doesn't think about the accident, except for the occasional, sharply focused memory, his hands under Damian's limp shoulders, the surprisingly heavy weight of Damian as Cort hauled him from the car. Mostly, he sees Jennifer again in that little skirt, licking a bit of lime or something from her lower lip.

And here's Kylie, on her bike, coming into the parking lot, wearing a tight green t-shirt, her low-slung denim skirt, and he knows that she's dressed for him, as if she needs to dress provocatively in order to get him hard, which she doesn't, because he is.

"Hey," he says, not moving from his spot as she dismounts, sets her bike into the rack. "Hey," she says back, stepping onto the bench of the table, sitting beside him.

Together, they look out across the parking lot, to Bay Beach, empty now.

"How're you doing?" he asks, for the moment really caring, seeing, suddenly, for the first time, how much of a disadvantage she's at: her mother is head cashier at Lantman's, for Christ's sake, her father took off years ago, she's just had to repeat most of twelfth grade, and she probably won't even make it to the community college in Wisconset. And she isn't sure it matters. Cort also sees, in this moment—because of the shock of the accident, the evening air all stilled around him, Damian's ghost breathing at his shoulder?—that Kylie could be much prettier, if she had money to spend on clothes and good makeup.

"I just feel so sad," she says, pressing her hands under her legs on the table, closing her eyes, and Cort watches as the tears leak out. "I can't believe Damian's just gone like that. I mean, like, he'll never come back."

This simple fact of mortality, in which Cort too has never quite believed, plainly stated like this, makes Cort's stomach turn cold. "Yeah," he says, putting a reluctant arm around Kylie's shoulder, pulling her against him just a bit, and she falls fully into his half-embrace. The living, human warmth of her melts the ice in his stomach a little.

"Plus," she snuffles into his shirt, "What if someone finds out?"

"What do you mean?" Cort says, not letting Kylie pull away.

"I just mean, if someone found out that you were driving."

"Well, nobody's going to find that out, right? Because none of us are going to tell." Cort turns to her, puts his fingertips on her chin, tilts her face to his. "We're going to forget it ourselves. Right?"

Kylie, accustomed to intimidation, nods.

"Now, tell me, who was driving?"

She looks at him skeptically, tucks her hair behind one ear, sighs. "Cort, you were."

"No." He takes her chin more firmly, turns her to look at him again. "Damian was driving. Why don't you practice saying that?"

"Cort, this is silly—"

"No it isn't," he says, feeling the panic again rising in him like bile. "Say it."

"Damian was driving," she says, and he drops his hand, pats her bare leg. "Good girl. You just start remembering it like that."

The sex is only going to confuse matters, will only make it more difficult in the coming days and weeks to separate himself from her. What the hell has he been doing with her, anyway? Still, without the sex, there's a greater chance she'll tell. Hell, she's got him blackmailed, but if the most he has to pay is getting a blow job, has he really got that bad of a deal?

Cort pulls her against him a little, and Kylie's hand falls to his lap. She sniffles a bit. He lets his hand trail down to the swath of skin on her back where her shirt rides up, then slips his hand under the waistband of her skirt. "Yeah," he says, "No one's going to find out."

Thirteen

On Monday evening, Tessa allows extra time to get the Honda to start and warm up before driving to Wisconset to meet Jake's train; the car's so finicky, and nothing annoys him more than when she's late. When she sees him step down to the platform, she feels again what she felt when she first met him: he's exactly what she's always wanted. He drops his bag to the pavement and, without saying anything, enfolds her in his arms, and she doesn't cry, but just presses her face into his chest, as if she could press out all her sorrow. Then they drive home across the island in the early summer evening light; Tessa fills him in on the details of the accident, tells him about how she's been staying with Franci; Peg's over there now.

"I wish I could have come home sooner," Jake says, as they drive off the ferry toward home. "Woody just couldn't handle leading the whole workshop alone."

"I know," Tessa says, though she isn't sure of this: *does* she know? Couldn't he have cancelled? Told Woody that his dear friend's son just died?

They're both subdued, Jake duly shocked, and solicitous of Tessa, insisting on cooking them an omelet with basil and tomatoes from the farmers' market, which they eat on the porch in the tangerine evening light. She sits next to him on the wicker loveseat, feeling the heat from his body, warm, familiar, alive.

In the morning, it's just getting light, the first birdsong starting, when Tessa feels Jake shift in the bed, feels his fingers trailing the back of her neck. She dredges herself up from the depths of sleep as best she can, but the sleeping pills have made her logy, and she barely hears him whisper that he's going out to work in his studio. She's asleep again before he's rustled into his clothes, back to a dream of cobbled streets, a window through which a dog leaps, then flies off into the sky.

When she wakes again, the sun is full up, and she's more than hungry. Ravenous. Lying in their bed, she can see the water, scintillating where the breeze shuttles past, and she realizes she's barely eaten since the accident. Is Franci waking hungry, too, or does a mother's need for food shut down when her child dies? And then she thinks of Kenji, on the beach, how otherworldly that seemed, the sand still pocked with rain, the sea rough and rain-moiled, the accident reverberating in the damp air.

Jake will be coming in soon, wanting his breakfast.

Downstairs, there's no sign of Jake, and Tessa puts the water on, measures the coffee into the French press. Just as she's pouring the oatmeal into the pot—Jake's latest regimen requires oatmeal every morning—she hears the front screen door squeak open, slam shut. He isn't humming, and she feels herself tense.

"Well, look who's up," he says, coming into the kitchen. He looks at the clock. "Let's see," he says, in a deliberate way that makes her think of her father's sarcasm. Here it comes, she thinks. "Eight-thirty. Well, I've been working since six. And how have you been spending your time?"

Tessa hears that there's a bit of jokiness in his voice. But she's feeling so out of sorts, she just says, "I just got up." Thank God for those pills.

"At least the kettle's on," Jake says, looking into the oatmeal and giving it a stir. "Haven't I told you that you need to keep stirring to get it perfect?"

"Yeah, you've mentioned that. I haven't slept much lately, Jake."

"So you were at Franci's the whole night, the night of the accident?" Jake asks. He's only been home one night since then; it's only been a couple of days, and yet, it seems so long ago that it takes Tessa a long moment to think—there was the night of the crash, Friday night, or rather, early Saturday morning. That long day, and then going home to drop into the bed here. And then there was Saturday night, when she stayed on Franci's sofa, after doling out her Ambien to both of them. In the long moment of Tessa considering all this, Jake's fear rushes in: "What, you have to think about it? Either you were or weren't, Tess."

"Jake, come on. Of course I was at Franci's," Tessa says, leaning against his back as he faces away from her and leans against the counter, and then, when he doesn't respond, turns to press the coffee and put the breakfast things on the table. The moment passes, the morning soured but not an irredeemable catastrophe.

"I just wonder why you didn't call me that night. Or the next morning, from Franci's."

"I did call. I called you at six-thirty in the morning. I also called you on Friday night, but there was no answer either time. I told you that. Jake, you're making me crazy with this. This is such a difficult time. It's terrible."

"I'm sorry," Jake says, but he doesn't sound sorry, not really. "You know, I had that faculty meeting on Friday, and then Peter and I had an early game of racquetball in the morning. But that's not the point; the point is just that I don't want to lose you, and I worry when I have to go away so much." He covers her hand with his, squeezes it, and there again is that flare of electricity she feels with him, which erases everything else.

That is, until they're sitting down, Jake beginning to warm again, telling her about his morning's work, when the phone rings. It's Franci, asking if Tessa will pick up a prescription for her that her doctor in New York has called in, for sleeping pills of her own.

Her voice sounds gray, a flat gray stone. "Sure, of course," Tessa says. "I'll bring it by later this morning."

"What'll you bring by?" Jake asks, when she sits down again.

"Oh, just a prescription for Franci," Tessa says, looking down at her oatmeal, aware that there's something in Jake's tone, something in what's going on that has the ring of danger, that she's done or said something that has incited him. He says, "Oh, right. The new pharmacist. I'm sure you're not sorry to have an excuse to see him."

"What?"

"You heard me."

"Jake, don't be ridiculous," Tessa says, but even as she's saying this, she's wondering, could he be right, or even just a little bit right? *No.* She knows herself better than he does. "Jake, I'm crazy about you. I don't care about some pharmacist, or anyone else for that matter."

"Okay," he says, raising both hands, palms up as if saying, "Stop." "I just know how it is with you. You're restless. You always have been. And I'm just saying, if there is someone else who's caught your fancy, let me know about it now."

He's gotten like this before, and by now Tessa knows what to do with it. She stands, walks to his chair, squats beside him, and looks up into his face. "Jake. There is no one else. No one."

"Okay, baby," he says then, and brushes her hair back from her face with one hand. "I just—okay. You'd better go pick up that prescription for Franci, then, right?"

Behind the pharmacy counter, Kenji's got his sketch pad; he's trying to get the dimensions and the angle right, unsure if the metals will bend to his imagination. He hears the jingle of the bell over the door, but the sound becomes part of the sculpture: somehow, he wants to incorporate that sound.

"Kenji," Tessa says. "Hey."

He looks up, startled, stands. He sees that she's placed one hand, palm down, on the counter. It's her right hand; he can see the thin metacarpals, tensed beneath her pale skin. Her nails are short, unpainted.

"Hey, Tessa," he says, trying, as he had on the beach, not to show how his heart rate is increasing at this proximity. *Tachycardia.* He loosens his ponytail, rubberbands it back again.

He sees that her eyes fill, sees her swallow hard on the tears. "I'm sorry. It's just—" she begins, then starts again: "Franci's in pretty bad shape," she says. "I'm actually here to pick up her prescription."

"I'll have it right up for you. Do you want to wait?" Kenji says, all business. She nods and drifts over toward the perfumes, toying with the makeup supplies, the fancy brushes with the faux-tortoiseshell handles and stiff boar bristles.

In the back, Kenji leans against the counter. Tessa Bartlett. *She's taken, she's taken,* he repeats to himself. He's already blown it once before, in New York, falling for a woman who was taken. He knows enough of psychology to know it's some kind of repetition compulsion. His mother, no doubt, is involved. *Great.* He still feels what he feels. He completes the paperwork necessary for the distribution of the pills to a third party, screws the lid on tight, sighs, slips the pill bottle into the waxy white bag, and staples it shut.

"Here you go, then. Thirty-four dollars and fifty-two cents." He allows himself to look at Tessa, to watch her face as she looks down into her big canvas bag. "Should I put it on Franci's account?"

"Oh, no, I'll pay cash," Tessa says, sliding two twenties from her wallet, then taking the change from Kenji. She signs. And sighs.

And then, "How's our little furry friend?" Kenji says.

"Oh." She looks quickly around the store, then leans in closer to him. He can smell something sweet about her, her soap or her shampoo, and he suddenly thinks that she isn't wearing anything but her dress, which is short, and yellow, and her sandals. "It's okay, I guess. I put out a bowl of scraps for it," she says, conspiratorially.

He drops his voice to a whisper, too.

"Good strategy," he says, widening his eyes, and she smiles. "Lull it into complacency, and then get it to defect."

She smiles, a dimmed, sad smile. "Thanks," she says, and she could be thanking him as any customer would, but they both know she's thanking him for the moment of levity, the moment of life-goes-on. Kenji puts one forefinger to his brow, tips the finger out, in a little salute that seems almost like a secret signal they share. "See you," he says.

"Okay." Tessa says, smiling again. They smile at one another at this, Kenji wishing he could think of something clever to say, but able only to smile back at her, and then she's gone.

Later, he leaves too, with Marie in charge of the evening hours. He walks over to his studio behind the Greasy Gorgon, and soon, under the bright lights, there's just the sizzle of the electricity, the fresh smell of ozone as the welding wire melts into the steel. The soft, cold feel of the metal in his hands, the magic of manipulating the iron into just the shape he wants, his imagination taking form.

Franci needs her, Tessa tells herself, and she repeats this all day, as she goes about collecting everything that's fallen to the side since the accident, in both her own life and in Franci's.

She left a living room window open during the rainstorm the day after Damian died, and the rain soaked the little Oriental rug, so now she has to bring it to the cleaners so mold won't develop and wreck it. And the raccoon is digging a hole under the shed, and she has to find some way to accommodate the raccoon without letting Jake see that's just what she's doing. And then the phone rings, and it isn't Franci, or Peg, but it's the Anthro department secretary back in New York, who *doesn't know*, and Tessa finds herself explaining that her friend's son died, but this only makes her feel worse, like the event, like Damian, is quickly becoming nothing more than a narrative. "How terrible," the secretary says.

Fourteen

Cort's at the round teak table on the deck, finishing his breakfast of eggs and Canadian bacon—his appetite remarkably undiminished by his shock, and guilt, and grief—when he hears the front doorbell chime, a long "ding-dong" that smacks to him of suburbia, which is, after all, how his house looks now, like a suburban pimple high on the slope above the beach. He doesn't move toward the interior of the house, knowing Jennifer will get it, and even though he doesn't hear her footsteps—she usually walks around barefoot—he senses that she's answering the door, imagines her standing there at the threshold, as if she's playing lady of the house, but not quite right for the role, standing with one bare foot on top of the other, holding the door with one hand dangling just above her head.

And then, just as this image is beginning to morph into one of his persistent soft-core fantasies of her, he sees a dark shape appear at the slider, and here she is, leading Cop Cal out to the deck. Cort feels his bowels go cold, and stands.

"Hey, Cort," Cop Cal says, putting his cop hat back on, a shield against the sun. "Hey," Cort says back, unsure what to do now that he's standing. He brushes his palm over his head.

"Can I get you anything?" Jennifer says, as if she's speaking a line from a play, stiff. "Coffee?"

"Sure, that would be great," Cal says, smiling at her, and Cort's stomach sinks: coffee means he's planning to stay a while, to stay and ask questions.

Cal and Cort watch Jennifer go back through the slider; neither comments, but Cort thinks, if this guy were any other guy in the world, he'd say something about Jennifer. Something. Not Cop Cal, though.

"Mind if I sit down?" Cal says, not pulling out one of the iron chairs at the table, waiting, as if he's the one who's younger and possibly in trouble.

"Sure, sure," Cort says. "Of course," and he motions to the chair, and both sit, Cort pushing his plate to the side.

"Gorgeous view from up here," Cal says, looking out over the lawn, the meadow, and down to the water. "Your dad did a great job with this place."

"Well, my mom," Cort corrects him. "My mom designed it."

There's a pause, a little moment of nothing, and Cort feels for a moment as if his mom herself has dropped into the silence, remembers briefly that he's supposed to call her back, but how's he supposed to figure out all that international dialing stuff? Later.

"Well, whoever designed it, it looks great," Cal says, and then Jennifer's back, setting a tray with two cups of coffee and a little pitcher in front of Cal. Where'd that tray come from? Cort's used to the one with the mallards on it, an old relic of the camp-style life they used to have here. This one is striped in green and white and pink; it looks like a girl's bathing suit or something. The pitcher he recognizes, though; it's a little silver thing with his grandmother's initials on it.

How can he think all this at the same time he's mesmerized by the fact that the table top hits Jennifer's thighs just below her shorts, making a little wedge of smooth brown skin appear there? And this, at the same time his mind is tearing up ground trying to think of what to say to Cal?

Once she leaves again, and Cop Cal has attended to his coffee, Cal pulls out a notebook from his back pocket. "Listen, Cort, I know this is very difficult," he begins, but at the sight of the notebook, Cort's ears fill with a rushing sound, and he can hardly hear anything; it's like the tide has suddenly taken up residence in his head. Then it subsides, and he hears Cal saying, ". . . from the beginning, when you left the bar in Wisconset."

Cort tells him the story, the one he's been rehearsing in his head, how when they left the bar, he tossed the keys to Damian, because he, Cort, wanted a little "backseat time" with Kylie.

"I know it was selfish," he says, and at this his eyes even tear up a bit, because if anything, he's haunted now by his selfishness, even though it's now visiting him in a different, much more disastrous, guise than he'd ever imagined it would. "You know how it is," he says, and Cop Cal nods a bit, more to encourage the boy than out of a real understanding. "I mean, it wasn't like Damian wanted to get any time with Betheny. She was all over him, and he's all like—well, let's just say he didn't exactly show appreciation." Cort shakes his head at this preposterous situation: how could Damian not care about a sure thing like that?

"Anyway, so Damian drove us back, and we got the last ferry, and then—" and in his telling of the story, here Cort's mind sticks a bit; wasn't there something else that happened? Oh yeah, they stopped to switch drivers again. Right. But then he wobbles forward in his fabrication: "—then, the next thing I knew, we were flying over the railing and into that big field right above Dead Man's Beach, and I saw the ceiling of the car flipping over . . ." Cort stops, shakes his head as if to shake the world aright again.

"Then what?" Cal asks, even though it's clear Cort thinks he's done with his story.

"Well, then I must have got out, I don't know how, and Kylie and I pulled Beth out, and then we realized Damian was still in there, and I went back and pulled him out. I thought he must be okay, I mean, Damian's so, I don't know—he's like always bouncing back, you know?"

Cal waits a moment, then asks: "And the steering wheel, was that a problem?"

"What do you mean?" Cort's head is swimming now, the rushing noise in his ears louder and more persistent than before. It's weird; he can hear Cal, but can't quite get himself over the sound, like the old box fan in his window when he was a kid blowing on *high*, rattling the wind into the hot room.

"I mean, did you have trouble pulling Damian out around the steering wheel," Cal says, knowing even as he repeats this question that he's offering Cort another angle on his own story, that he's almost warning him to think of the pitfalls of his lie.

"Well, yeah. Sure. You know, he was kind of slumped in there, so I could get his shoulders out pretty good, but then—" and that's when the physicality of the memory collides with Cort's fabrication, and he really can feel the weight—the dead weight—of Damian in his arms, how he flopped Damian's rag-doll arms around his shoulders, whispering, "Come on, help me out here, man," and a wave of nausea rises up in him, nausea at the memory of that dead weight, and Cort puts his hand to his forehead, presses his temples, leans down toward his knees until the nausea passes, and even though the nausea is real, he has presence of mind enough to think that this will impress Cop Cal, that Cal can't help but notice that Cort's feeling the dread of losing Damian, that Cort's loss is real.

"Okay," Cal says, folding up his notebook.

"I'm sorry," Cort says, head still in his hands. He means it, too, and feels his eyes fill again, even as he's thinking, *could this be it? Could it be this easy?*

"Okay," Cal says again, rising. He steps over to Cort, pats his bent back a couple of times. "Okay." He squeezes Cort's shoulder, hard. "We'll let you know if we have any more questions, but I think that should do it."

Cort looks up as Cal heads toward the slider. He wants to ask Cal if he's off the hook, but he's seen enough *Law & Order* and *CSI* to know this will look more suspicious than anything. "I'm just so damned sorry," he says, and Cal says, "I know," then disappears into the dim, cool interior of the house.

Left on his own on the deck, Cort leans back in his chair, in a pose of nonchalance that he doesn't feel at all. Instead, he can feel his heart pounding in his chest, like he's just done fifty push-ups for that damn coach at UMass. Now what? He can't be off the hook that easily, but then again, if Cop Cal really suspected the truth, wouldn't there be more of an investigation, like he'd be called down to the state police headquarters or something?

The day is big, and dry, and bright, the sea breezes having long since blown away any lingering dampness from the storm. Cort feels a little sick, still. He doesn't reach for what's left of his coffee, doesn't pour himself another cup from the thermos on the tray. He just leans back in the chair, and here comes the feeling of Damian, more than a memory, or a vision—it's so huge inside him that he feels he can barely contain it. It's some kind of longing, and some kind of pain, all of it gathered up into one big tornado of feeling, spiked with his shuddering anxiety. Cort sits absolutely still. He's certain that if he were to move right now, he'd explode.

The breeze from the water rustles through the colorful wind sock Jennifer has hung at the corner of the deck, lifting it just a bit. Cort breathes in, and out again, and the big feeling of loss and love pass, and by the time Jennifer returns he's almost back to just his low-level terror. She puts Cop Cal's coffee things on the tray, then bends to retrieve a napkin that's blown to the deck floor, and Cort's attention shifts from his reverie about Damian back to Jennifer's legs. The fantasies are always waiting there, no matter how much thinking of his father's new wife like that disgusts him. Still, there it is. There she is, standing in arm's reach from his chair, pouring coffee from the thermos into his cup. He could put out his hand right now, slip one finger under the hem of her shorts.

Instead, "You need anything at Lantman's?" he says, and this comes out friendlier than he intended. He'd wanted to put an edge to it, say something snappy and mean. And then he remembers: how's he going to bring stuff home, now that he's wrecked the SUV? And even if his dad would let him drive the Miata, he wouldn't want to.

"Let me think a minute," she says. "Just orange juice; we're nearly out."

"Okay," he says. "Orange juice it is," but he stays seated, watching her retreat again into the house, slipping from the bright, hot sun inside, where it's cool and dark as a grave.

Fifteen

The island's single religious venue is the Shore Chapel, tucked among the straight white birch trees at the end of Shore Lane, on the island's quiet, bay side, the side where Damian lived, not the side that spills onto Dead Man's Beach, the side where he died. It's not only a chapel but a historic marker as well, built in the 1700s of island stone, and it sits like a stone jewel box at the end of the dirt lane, meaning that access is difficult in winter and nearly impossible in early spring, when Shore Lane, like most of the island's back roads, becomes nothing more than two muddied tracks that will nearly suck the tires off a car or small truck.

It's taken just seven days for all the arrangements to be made; just as Franci thought that it only takes three minutes to learn your son is dead, Tessa now thinks it takes only a week to bury a boy. The day of the funeral is sunny, but not hot, a perfect June day, Tessa thinks as she steps from the car and into the mottled shadows that play across the hard-packed driveway and the grassy chapel lawn. Jake walks beside her, one hand on her shoulder, and Tessa presses her hand against the back of her navy straw hat, keeping it close to her head until she's safely inside. Jake is wearing his loose black trousers and his only jacket, the white linen one he'd once joked to Tessa was his "girl magnet," the jacket he was wearing when she fell in love with him. Inside the chapel, it's a little cool; the stone walls of the chapel throw a damp, chill air into the small, dim room. Tessa shivers.

Peg and Torsten have already arrived, bringing Franci with them, now in consultation with the minister at the front of the room. They're still standing, even though the pews are beginning to fill with mourners, and Tessa and Jake stand with them, a little awkwardly, no one sure what to say, so they all look over toward Franci, and Tessa whispers to Peg, "She doesn't look too bad," and indeed, at the moment, she doesn't, in a dark brown linen dress, and, in a departure for Franci, heels. She looks up, and, without smiling, waves to Tessa and Jake. She's wearing her new lipstick; Tessa can see, under the makeup, how pale she is.

Soon the music starts up, a kid Damian knew at Riverdale playing Bach's *Chaconne* on cello, filling the small chapel with the echo of the strings. There's a subdued shuffling as everyone takes a seat, and as Tessa turns to settle herself beside Jake in the row behind Franci, she looks over to the chapel door, just in time to see Kenji Tanaka come in. She notices how tall he is, seeming taller in a navy linen suit jacket, thin black tie, his hair back in its usual ponytail. Much as she wants to wave to him, Tessa knows that if she does, she'll never hear the end of it from Jake, so she turns, and sits.

What's wrong with her? She's never once let her attention stray from Jake like this, and this is hardly the time to start. The service is beginning, and Damian is dead, and she listens to the minister, who says a few specific things about Damian, about his humor, his compassion, and then says a few more general things which pretty much amount to how we can never really know what the hell is going to happen. Then Peg rises from beside Franci and goes to the front of the room.

"I *adored* Damian," she begins, unequivocally, boldly, and Tessa feels tears come to her eyes; perhaps its Peg's willingness to feel her love for Damian so fully in the face of never seeing him again that makes her cry now; perhaps it's just that the shock of the whole thing is finally catching up to her. Tessa clasps her hands around the small straw bag in her lap, trying to concentrate on the colored geometric shapes of light thrown onto her lap by the sun coming through the chapel's stained glass windows. Her bag is like a little box, off-white: *bone*, the color was called in the catalogue, the name of the color sounding clean, and ancient, and at the time, she pictured ivory tusks and the creamy piping of the navy linen suit she's wearing. She thought about how the clutch would match the suit. She certainly, at the time, didn't think she would be holding her clutch on her lap at Damian's funeral. Now, the color reminds her of the buttons on her mother's favorite sweater when Tessa was a girl, round bone buttons, tempting as candies. Even when she was an adolescent, Tessa wanted to put the buttons in her mouth. The sweater was red.

Peg takes her seat again, and another Riverdale kid is getting up, reading a poem Tessa recognizes as Hopkins, the words too unwieldy, she thinks, for a boy. "No worst, there is none. Pitched past pitch of grief . . ." Jake slides his hand over Tessa's hands, stilling them. She stops weeping, listens to the boy finish the poem, his voice cracking toward the end. From her straw bag, Tessa takes out her tissues, daubs her eyes, takes out her tin of mints, opens it, offers one to Jake, and takes one for herself. The peppermint snap brings her back where she belongs. Jake stands then, walks to the front of the chapel with his violin, and Tessa can see Franci's shoulders quiver as he starts to play, the meditation from *Thaïs*. Tessa watches Jake's face while he plays, giving himself over entirely to the music; this is why she loves him.

They all file out into the warmer air outside, and walk around the chapel to the cars. Tessa looks for Kenji, but doesn't see him. Was it really him? He's unmistakable, in this crowd. She thinks now that what it is about him, what she's drawn to, is that he reminds her of a gentle doctor who made house calls in an old movie. Of course, she thinks now, it's probably just the shock of Damian's death, and how he was the first person she saw when she finally left Franci's. That, and the way it feels as if Kenji is carrying a secret of hers. As if he sees something about her that few people do, something she wants seen.

Jake and Tessa hurry to their car so that they'll be the first ones to arrive back at their house, to make sure the preparations for the reception are underway. There's no graveside ritual, as Franci decided—wisely, everyone agreed—on cremation.

At the house, Tessa sees that the girls from the Crab 'N Claw have set up the drinks table on one end of the porch, and the food is laid out in the living room inside. One of the girls, Britt, knew Damian. The girls are wearing white polo shirts and black pants, the usual catering outfits the restaurant provides, but it's clear they understand this event is not the usual festive summer occasion. The accident has swung all of the island teens into the fierce truth of mortality, and they're still a little dizzy.

There isn't much for Jake and Tessa to do.

"It's so quiet. What kind of music should I put on?" she says, and moves toward the stereo hidden in the built-in bookshelves, but Jake stops her. "Tessa," he says, "don't," and so she busies herself with giving unnecessary instructions to the girls, about heating the hors d'oeuvres in the oven and where to put the trash.

The first wave of guests arrives all at once, a bright cortege of cars filing from the chapel along Cross Island Road to the bay. There's plenty of room for parking under the pines.

Dick and Jennifer, with Cort trailing behind them, are among the first to come up the steps and into the house, Dick holding the door for Jennifer, Cort stopping on the porch to talk with the girls. Jennifer's wearing a fitted linen dress, magenta, that makes her young complexion even prettier, Tessa thinks. She's got a darker shawl over her shoulders, her hair falling across it in a fringe. "I'm so sorry," she says, kissing Tessa's cheek, and Tessa's taken aback by this. It wasn't *her* son who died, and she only knew Damian a couple of years. But then she understands that Jennifer sees them all—Dick's old friends—as a group distinct from herself, and that she understands that they've all lost something, too. Something that she, Jennifer, never had and therefore didn't lose.

And then Franci comes in, with Peg and Torsten close behind. She looks a little unsteady, fragile, older. As much better as she looked at the party on Memorial Day, now she looks that much worse, looks as if she's aged back the ten years and then added five more.

"How are you doing?" Tessa asks her, and Franci just nods. The other people, those not in their little group, are starting to mill around, some unsure how to approach Franci, others hovering, eager to get their condolences over with so they can move away from the grief force field and get a drink. Jake appears, with a big glass of Scotch on ice, and hands it to Franci, who smiles a little. "Thanks." He puts an arm around her shoulders and kisses the top of her head, saying nothing, and Tessa thinks once again how lucky she is to have him, this man of hers. She feels so sorry for Franci in that moment, no husband, Leslie gone, her son so recently dead—*what is she going to do?*—that she feels the sorrow as a pressure in her chest, and she has to work to catch her breath.

"If you get tired of it all and want to sneak upstairs, go ahead. Or find me," she says to Franci, then steps back, to let Ivy Bless approach, who's come over from next door.

The teenagers stay out on the front porch by the drinks table, as if afraid to enter the house, and they *are* afraid: even under the best of circumstances, they're unsure what to say to any adult, and now, they have no idea what they'll say to Damian's mom. "Just say you're sorry, or that you loved him," some of their mothers told them that morning, but by now, after hearing all the things said at the funeral, they've forgotten that, and they stand and sit and lean around on the porch, waiting for it to be over.

"I just keep thinking Damian's on his way over, or Damian's going to call or something," Betheny says, squeezing her eyes tightly shut. Like the other girls, she's wearing a flowery dress, light, summery, something she'd have thought she'd be wearing to a party. Her left arm, wrapped in a cast she's painted pink, hangs from a white and yellow sling around her neck. "Yeah, I know," Kylie says. "He'd be all like, 'Hey, what's happening here?' and she laughs at this. When no one else does, she steps back toward the wicker loveseat, sits. *Stupid.*

"I still don't get it, how he went off the road like that," Paul, the cellist, who's come up from New York, says. "That was just so unlike him. He hardly even drank."

Cort sees again the wet road, hears again the wipers slapping the windshield, and sees something—what?—a dark thing about to bolt across the road. He feels the coldness in his belly give a wild surge, and he thinks for a moment he's going to be sick. Maybe even talking to Damian's mom would be better than this. "Yeah," he says. "It was weird," and he levels a look at Kylie and Betheny, now side by side on the wicker loveseat, Kylie picking at one of the strands of wicker until it comes loose, then tucking it under the cushion so no one will see. This tiny bit of vandalism makes her want to cry again. "I guess none of us really understand it," Cort says.

Betheny looks up at Paul, stares him right in the eye, having read somewhere that you can tell someone is lying if they look away. "Yeah," she says, nodding a bit. "It was just really random," and at this, Cort feels a small leak of relief: Betheny will not betray him. But Kylie's engrossed in picking at the wicker of the sofa, and Cort thinks that when she looks up, she's going to let loose with the truth. He should have called her to ask if she wanted a ride to the funeral. Or something. "Let's go inside," he says to the girls, and the girls rise as one silky animal, and the three cross the porch to re-enter the mourners' throng.

As the front porch draws more adults, the kids migrate inside, and soon there's a cluster of people at the drinks table, talking in hushed tones. Tessa takes a plastic cup of wine, then turns away, looks out toward the water, a hard bright blue in the noon sun. The driveway, shaded by the tall pines, is filled with cars; all of Grand Isle has come out to pay their respects, or to see who else has come. The flowerbeds look good, with the mid-summer flowers already blooming, thanks to the early heat.

Tessa turns, and sees a motion far up the driveway, up by the road. East Shore Road must already be lined with cars. She thinks for a wild, hopeful moment it's the raccoon, and then, she sees the motion is Kenji Tanaka. He's walking toward the house, his jacket open to reveal his thin, black tie. What if he mentions something about the raccoon? About how they've talked on the beach?

Tessa feels a little dizzy. She should, of course, stay out here and greet him. She should, and she shouldn't, and she doesn't.

She turns, quickly, and heads back into the darkness of the house, avoiding Kenji but also missing Stiles' arrival, as he's next, coming confidently down the driveway, shunting away his confusion and guilt grief by looking around appraisingly, taking in the improvements Jake and Tessa have made. How many years has it been since he was last up here? How long ago it seems that he was one of the group that at that time gathered on Peg and Torsten's deck, talking late into a summer's night, Damian and Cort racing each other to the water and back, while the grown-ups had their first drinks of the evening. He can almost hear the sound of it all, now, the voices. How did Damian get to be a college kid so quickly? How could he possibly have died?

Stiles sees the drinks table as he comes up the porch steps, stops, and asks the girl for a Scotch on the rocks. "Sad occasion," he says. "Yeah," she says, looking down, and he realizes she doesn't know he isn't just another island neighbor, but that he's the father of the dead.

Fortified with his drink, a bit unsettled by seeing he's nearly invisible here, at his own son's funeral, he makes his way inside, to the dimly lit, hushed living room, and there's Franci, in a baggy brown linen dress, looking, he thinks, terrible. Old. *Good God*—it hits him again—*their son is dead.* She's talking to a couple, the man's hand on the woman's back, a couple he doesn't recognize right away, and then he does: of course, it's Dick, but Dick with a young coltish girl, a very pretty girl. Well, good old Dick.

"Franci," he says, gliding into the conversation, and the three turn, the pretty colt smiling at him, the others looking, simply, stunned. Finally Dick puts out his hand. "Stiles," he says, awkwardly. "God, I'm so sorry. I didn't know you'd be here,"

"What are you doing here?" Franci says, the same thing, but more direct.

"Well, Lisa tracked me down in Amsterdam. They told me what happened. I asked her to call you—anyway, I'm sorry I couldn't get up 'til now. I'm so sorry, Franci."

Dick claps Stiles briefly on the shoulder with one hand, saying, "I'm sorry, old man. It's just unbelievable. Let's talk later," and leads his girl away by the hand. "It was nice meet—" she starts to say, then realizes they didn't meet, not really.

Franci is silent, and Stiles looks down into his drink. "He was my son too, you know," he says. "You could have called me."

"It's not my fault you were off somewhere," Franci begins, but she's exhausted, and the furrow of that argument has been ploughed so many times that it's exhausted, too. "Anyway, I left that to Peg, and your staff, and obviously they did reach you. Or someone did." Franci takes a drink from her Scotch. "Would you have even seen him this summer? It's just like you, to show up only after someone's dead," she says, not wanting to say this, not wanting to be this way, but unable to stop herself.

"Look, Franci," he swirls his drink a little, making the ice clink side-to-side in the glass. "Look, I'm sorry. I've done a lot of wrong things. But now, can't we just be kind to each other?" and he fixes her with his dark eyes.

"Right now, I don't know what I can do. And what I can't," she says, her eyes filling.

From across the room, Peg sails over, bringing a protective arm around Franci's shoulders. "Stiles," she says. "I'm really so sorry for your loss." And Stiles nods back at her. "Peg."

"Would you come into the kitchen with me for a moment?" Peg asks, and Franci nods, *yes.*

It's into the kitchen that Cort stumbles, still a little queasy, looking for some relief from the questions, the sympathetic nods and pats on the shoulder. He's reeling, and he looks it, pressing his palm against his cheek, as if he's in terrific pain.

There's no one in the kitchen, and he leans against the counter at the sink, turns on the tap, then cups his hands and splashes water onto his face. If only he could spit out the truth. Anyone seeing him would assume it's the grief that's making him woozy; grief, not guilt. He can't even tell the difference anymore, and just wants Damian to appear, so much so that he thinks he hears a sound at the back door.

He can imagine Damian standing there, opening the door a crack, motioning to Cort, rubbing forefinger against thumb to indicate he's got a joint for them to share.

But as real as this fantasy is, it isn't real enough, and instead, Cort turns, and sees Franci coming through the kitchen door, looking pretty woozy herself, but without the dramatics of pressing her hand to her head. She looks just like any other summer island mom, one of the summer people who, like his own parents, keep themselves in shape, who keep looking young in a way the year-rounders simply don't. But despite all this, even Cort can see, she looks like hell.

Hell. What can he say? But she bails him out, saying as she approaches, "Oh, Cort, I'm so sorry," as if it's *her* fault, not his. She comes to where he stands, and reaches her arms around his shoulders. She's weeping, and he's stuck, standing there uncertain what to do, reaching a hand around to pat her shoulder. "I'm sorry, too," he says, and feels himself choke up. He pulls away, feigns a cough. "I was just getting a glass of water," he says, "do you want one?"

Franci nods. She puts her Scotch down on the counter while Cort takes a couple of glasses from the dish rack.

"This is hell, isn't it?" she says, and he isn't sure if she means the funeral, the beginning of life without Damian, or meeting up in the kitchen, each of them now faced with the last person they want to see.

"Here," he says, handing her the water, as if it will really do anything. "I'm just so sorry," he says, looking down into his glass, feeling himself choke up again.

"Oh, Cort, it wasn't your fault. I don't want you to ever feel that." Franci puts her hand around his forearm. If it weren't for the epilepsy, she'd be convinced he was lying, convinced it *was* his fault. As it is, the idea that her son was driving still seems impossible to her, and she has to fight to tell herself that's the way it was. "It was an accident," she says. "You were just, well, there."

Cort nods. This is what he's always felt, and he remembers his mom explaining the divorce to him: *It isn't about you, you're just caught in the cross-fire.*

And then they're both saved by Betheny, hovering in the doorway. "Oh, sorry," she says, and Franci says, "Will everyone please stop apologizing?" intending this to sound funny, realizing too late she sounds panicked and shrill.

Cort puts his glass in the sink, and Betheny says to Cort, "I just, there's just some kids who want to talk to you," and he says, "Sorry," to Franci, leaving her there in the kitchen, where she leans back against the counter, overtaken by a feeling she can't articulate, a feeling that at first wells up inside her, a feeling that's beyond words.

But this is too much for her, her grief already threatening to take her under, it's all *too much*, and she turns to face the sink, swallowing hard, feeling as if she'll be sick. When Franci looks up at last, she sees a motion out there beyond the driveway: *Damian, Damian returned!* but she quickly sees instead it's the raccoon, nosing among the ferns and hosta, and this calms her, settles something inside her into a hot, bright coal.

Her back to the front door so she won't see Kenji come into the house, Tessa turns right, into the portion of the double living room that Jake made into a tiny library, with the soft yellow sofa and the floor-to-ceiling bookshelves.

Tessa sees the group of kids, the kids who were with Damian in the accident, in the corner of the library, and approaches, not really sure what she's going to say, just knowing she has to keep moving.

They're all silent, and would remain silent if she didn't say anything. "I'm glad you all could come. I'm sure it's a big comfort to Franci, to Damian's mom," she tells them, feeling as if she's making a speech. She's never known how to talk to kids. Cort rocks a little on the balls of his feet, hands deep in his trouser pockets, and the girls, Kylie and Betheny, look down at their feet in their pretty summer sandals. One of them is wearing a little too much makeup, and they both look awkward in their dresses, and Tessa has to work to recognize them as the island girls she's accustomed to seeing in their short-shorts and halter tops. One of them, she sees, has an arm in a cast, and she remembers that there were other injuries in the accident. Did Damian really go out with one of these girls?

"I'm just so sorry about what happened," Cort says, almost in a whisper, and Tessa sees him as he looked last year, when he was still more of a boy, and she puts an arm around his shoulders, in a gesture she hopes is motherly. "It wasn't your fault," she whispers against his shoulder—he's become that much taller than she is.

He's a modern boy, raised by a feminist mom, and isn't afraid of showing his emotions—especially if it means he'll solidify his cover, and he lets out a long sigh as Tessa pats his back in the way she would if he were a sweet-smelling baby lying against her shoulder.

The girls mumble something to her—she isn't sure what—and just as she's planning her escape from this group in which the pain is nearly palpable, there's a hand on her shoulder, and she turns, and there's Stiles, having just stepped into the room, bold, as if he never left, as if he belongs, as if he'd raised Damian himself. They've never met, but she knows it's him; he looks just like Damian, or like Damian would have in another thirty years, tall, lanky, loose-limbed.

"You must be Stiles," Tessa says, and introduces herself. He's good-looking in a way that's riveting. She's heard Peg and Franci talk about how Stiles' good looks were one of the problems: he could have any woman he wanted, and often did.

"Tessa," he says now, taking both her hands in his, looking deep into her eyes. "I hear you've been a very good friend to Franci."

"Well—I'm sorry, Stiles," she says, realizing with a bit of a shock that it's his son, too, not just Franci's, who has died, and much as she really doesn't like this man, her eyes fill. Beautiful Damian, son of this beautiful Stiles, but in a lucky twist of genes, inheriting Franci's goodness instead of Stiles' arrogance and calculation. "Me, too," Stiles says, still holding her hands, and she has only to think of a few of the stories she's heard in order to quickly find the shut-off valve for any attraction that he might have elicited: the time Franci arrived at a hotel in Barcelona to meet him, and found he'd taken up with the woman in the room next door, or the affair he carried on quite openly with a conference organizer all one summer, or the Christmas he left Franci and Damian in New York to go to St. Barts, alone.

But it's Cort who Stiles has come into the room to see, and Cort allows himself to be clasped by Stiles in a bear hug, and at this, Cort lets out a sob, a sob of all his grief, and guilt, and confusion, ashamed at the sound that emits from his monstrous mouth, and as quickly as it came, he swallows it again, claps Stiles on the back. "I'm sorry, man," he says, stepping back, wiping his eyes with his hands, and it's unclear if he means he's sorry for Damian's death, or sorry for crying out like that.

Out on the porch again, Tessa sees the water has changed from the bright blue of afternoon to the darker, oily waters of early evening. She imagines she can see the seam where the sea water flows in to meet the bay, the salty stuff of the ocean floor wafting over into the realm of the bay water, cleansing it, pure.

And then there's the voice she wanted to hear, was most afraid of hearing, Kenji saying, "How are you?" pressing his palm against her elbow. He looks at her, serious, concerned.

"I'm fine," Tessa lies. "I mean, terrible," and they smile a little at each other, as if they have a pact to tell the truth.

Together, they look out over the water, and Tessa's aware of Kenji's scent, a clean scent, slightly medicinal, and a little bit sweet. He drops her hand, but stays standing close.

"Well, it's a God-awful situation. How's Franci?"

"Oh, you know. Terrible. Everyone's terrible," Tessa says, laughing a little, but feeling her eyes fill. She swallows hard; she doesn't want to cry again.

Kenji nods. "Okay, how about the kit? Terrible too?" he asks, still looking out at the water.

"Oh, I haven't seen it lately. But it's been living in the shed," she says, nodding with her head, not wanting to point it out too clearly.

Kenji turns to lean against the porch rail, to face her, and Tessa turns toward him. "Tessa, I wish—" he starts, all his many wishes clouding up in a big buzzy cluster that makes it hard to think. *I wish I could comfort you, I wish mortality weren't true—*

He doesn't say this, just lets the word "wish" hang in the air between them. He can feel Tessa leaning toward him, and Tessa, for her part, wants to lean into him, as if he could hold her up against the wash of sadness she feels, a sadness that she knows isn't just for Damian.

Instead, "Tessa," Peg calls through the screen door, and Tessa turns away from Kenji. "Yes," she says. She knows that from the darkened house, Peg can see out much better than Tessa and Kenji can see in.

"The Emersons are asking for you," Peg says, gently, quietly, and Tessa's struck by how low her tone is, compared to the heightened tone on the porch. "I'll be right in," she says, and leaves, not turning to look at Kenji again.

What would it be like to live in a house like this? Kylie wonders, looking covertly around the library of Jake's house. Those are the biggest bookshelves she's ever seen. Could they really have read all those books? The colors of the books' spines are what draws her, first: they're so bright, lots of yellow books, and some red ones, too. They look great.

If Kylie could choose what to do, she wouldn't go to Wisconset Community College in the fall, and she sure wouldn't work at Lantman's for the rest of her life. She'd study interior design. She saw an ad in a magazine for a class she could take online, and went to the website. She thinks, now, looking at this living room, she'd like to be a designer when she grows up. *When she grows up!* How babyish that sounds. "I'd like to go into interior design," she's practiced saying in front of her bedroom mirror, in her room which she designed herself, the blue ruffled bedspread matching the blue ruffled curtains. With a valence. There are so many words to learn: *valence, molding, halogen.* Kylie pays attention when she reads *House Beautiful, House and Garden, Real Simple.* It's different than in school, having to learn about things that don't matter, things like history and French.

She'd like to get away from Cort and Betheny, even though she's afraid of what will happen if she leaves them alone. She'd like to go upstairs, see how they've got the bedrooms. They don't have any kids, so maybe there's an extra room upstairs that's a guest room, or something like that.

"I got to pee," she says, and even at this Betheny blinks back tears. "I'll be right back." Kylie slips out of the library, down the hall, and is just about to step onto the first step upstairs when she hears someone say, "There's a bathroom down here," and she looks up. It's an older lady, a big older lady, smiling at her. One of these summer people, like Damian's mom, no makeup, her hair completely white, like she hasn't even tried to dye it, in a baggy black dress, a big red necklace around her neck, big red earrings.

"Oh, sorry," Kylie says, hoping the woman won't bawl her out or something. "I was just looking for the bathroom," she says, even though of course, the woman knows this. Or does the woman think she, Kylie, was doing exactly what she was doing, trying to get a look at the rest of the house?

The bathroom—*powder room*, Kylie knows it's really called, because it's just a sink and toilet—is nicely done, too, like the rest of the house she's seen. It's all very simple, and looks very clean, and Kylie looks into the mirror, right into her own brown eyes. She's got her hair up, in a messy bun, and she inspects it, pulling out a few more strands of hair in the front. She reapplies her lipstick. *Burnt Umber.* What's up with Cort? Maybe she should have worn a shorter dress or something. He hasn't been paying any attention to her all day, all through the funeral, and even before. He's been all whack ever since the accident.

Well, maybe that's it between them. He was always stuck up, anyway.

Kylie opens the medicine cabinet. There isn't much in here, because it *is* just the powder room, and not the upstairs bath; that's where the good stuff is. Even in the cabinet, everything is tidy, like the "after" picture in a magazine article on organizing your bath. There's a bottle of aspirin, a small jar of lemon hand lotion, three tampons lying together in a little bunch, like logs. How weird to have tampons just out practically in plain sight like that, not even in their box. Isn't Mrs. Bartlett—or whatever her name is—afraid someone will see them?

On the top shelf, there's a stack of three little boxes with drawings of flowers, lavender flowers, on them. Kylie plucks one of these, examines it. She's forgotten all about the funeral, about Cort and Betheny in the library, about the big woman who directed her in here. *Bernwell's Lavender* it says on the box, and Kylie opens it. It smells sweet, and fresh, and clean, and Kylie closes the box, slips it into her purse, and shuts the cabinet door.

She takes another long look in the mirror, then leaves the powder room, heads back to the library, but Cort and Betheny are no longer there, and seeing this, she puts it together, or rather, the facts fall together in her head: Cort's been after Betheny all this time. Through the library window, she can see them on the porch, talking together, heads close. Talking about her? She feels something in her stomach go cold, and clenches her fist. And after that great blow job she gave Cort, a few nights after the accident.

And anyway, nobody here really cares about Damian, who is now just gone. And *where*? How can a person just be here, and then be gone? Nobody here is thinking about that, she's sure. Nobody's thinking about Damian. She flounces from the living room, slips down the hall, into the kitchen, and out the back door. No one notices, no one cares, and Kylie walks fast up the driveway in her heeled sandals, without thinking about how she'll get home, without really planning ahead.

Once she's gone down East Shore Road a bit, she stops, takes off her sandals, and steps into the sandy soil shouldering the road, then steps into the pines. She looks both ways, listens for the sound of a car, and hearing none, reaches up and pulls off her panty hose, sighing as she does, as her belly, held tightly in all this time, releases. She stuffs the nylons into her purse, running a finger along the smooth box with the soap in it as she does, then climbs back up to the road, sandals swinging from her fingers as she begins her long walk home.

If a car passes, she'll stick out her thumb. It's a perfectly pretty evening, not too hot, nice, and she knows she's a pretty girl in a pretty dress, and she knows she'll get a ride.

After the guests have gone and the girls from the Crab 'N Claw have cleaned the kitchen, the empty bottles nestled back in their cardboard box, the plastic cups tied into trash bags, Tessa and Jake take a couple of plates onto the front porch. "Pour me a glass of that wine, will you?" Tessa calls back toward the kitchen.

On the porch, she settles into the loveseat, so she can see the tool shed. She knows what's out there: the baby raccoon, waiting for her.

Jake comes out, balancing his plate and two wine glasses. He sighs as he settles into the chair, then looks down at the supper Tessa's put together from left over hors d'oeuvres, some good bread she got at the farmers' market, and a little potato salad.

Franci's gone to Peg and Torsten's for supper, and they'll see her home afterward, or maybe Peg will convince Franci to stay overnight, as she and Tessa discussed. Tessa can't help imagining how Franci's feeling, now that the well-wishing is over and she's on the verge of beginning her new life, the life without her son in it.

Jake sets to his meal, taking a drink from his wine. "The wine isn't that bad," he says. "It's terrible," she says, and they laugh, then fall silent. The porch seems very quiet after the rustling noises of the funeral meal.

"Okay," Jake sighs. "What is it? What's wrong?"

"Wrong? We just had Damian's funeral," Tessa says. "I just feel a little sick over it, that's all."

Jake nods, and keeps eating. Out on the water, a kayak paddles close to the shore; it's one from the conference center, a visitor to whom the shores of the bay are new.

"She'll never be the same, you know that, don't you?" Tessa says, and Jake nods, even though, no, he doesn't know this, and it hadn't really occurred to him.

The food settles Tessa's nerves a little, takes away the bit of a high she had from drinking early in the day without much in her stomach, and she casts her mind back over the funeral, the cold chapel, the drive home, the swell of the guests in Jake's house. She can't remember seeing Stiles leave. Or Kenji. She has to stop thinking about him, before Jake picks up on it. "Here," she says, "try some of this tapenade."

Later, as they get into bed, "Thank God that day is over," Jake says, and Tessa switches off the lamp on her side. The room is lit by the bay-light, the half-moon reflecting off the water. It's the brightest room in the house, with its wood floors painted white, the walls a pale yellow. She thinks again of that cat they hit on that first trip up here, how she'd assumed Jake would stop, and when he didn't, she hadn't insisted, even though that cat, twisting on the pavement as they sped on, haunted her. She should have known then that something was wrong, if she couldn't cry out, *"Stop!"* And, even worse, there is what happened on the rest of that trip, which somehow keeps her here as well. Has she stayed with Jake despite his moods in part because of this, somehow?—but that's crazy.

"Yeah," she says. He's lying flat on his back, and she presses herself against him.

"Are you okay?"

"I keep having a terrible thought," she says. "I hate to admit it. It's terrible."

"Go ahead," he says. "You know you can't control your thoughts. It does no good to try."

"I just keep thinking, at least she had him. At least she had the whole experience of having a baby and raising him. She had him, I mean."

"Yeah. But you can't think of it that way, Tess. Don't dwell on that." Jake shifts so that he's curled behind her, one hand resting lightly on her hip. "Don't I make you happy? Are you saying I'm not enough?"

"Of course not," she says, covering his hand with hers, bringing it to her lips. She brushes her lips across his fingers, and feels him press against her, and then push himself up so that he's leaning on one elbow, looking down at her.

Tessa turns to him. "Jake," she says, cupping his cheek in her hand. She can just make out his features in the light from the bay. "Of course you're enough. Don't be ridiculous," she says, and she thinks she can see him battling with indecision, and then he kisses her.

Tonight, Tessa wants to keep talking, but she kisses him back. Jake thinks she means she wishes she'd had a baby. That isn't what she means, not at all, but she isn't sure what she does mean. She means something else, something unspeakable: in spite of Jake, she still feels utterly alone.

While they make love, she can hear the wild dogs, far off, their howl rising in an eerie tendril into the dark island night. Couldn't she find some way to explain what she means about how Franci had Damian, how it seems, now, not to matter, really, if you have eighteen years or eighty. Or forty-four; no matter what, your life is just a wisp.

But Tessa doesn't say any of this, or try to. If she can't sleep later, she'll go downstairs and take a pill. For now, she concentrates on the feeling of Jake's weight upon her, comforting and unsettling in the half-dark of the bay-lit night.

Walking barefoot along the edge of East Shore Road, one of her fancy sandals swinging from each hand, the skirt of her new dress slipping around her bare legs, Kylie feels free, and even happy, as if this is just a new summer evening, and she's just out for a walk, as if she hasn't just left Damian's funeral, and left Betheny and Cort looking like they're about to slink off into the woods together or something. She's proud that she just left like that; it's like something Damian would have done. She feels she understands him so much better now, as if she always understood him but only now she can understand that she understood him.

Dusk falls, and not one car has gone by, and soon Kylie isn't enjoying the righteous bruise of betrayal, but she's starting to get nervous. She takes her cell phone from her purse, flips it open, but of course there's no signal, and she snaps it shut and drops it back in. Soon, the woods on either side of the road will be dark, and she's out here, alone. What was she thinking?

And then she hears it, far off, but close enough so that the sound runs a river of electric fear up her spine: the howl of a dog. How far could it be? She stops in her tracks, waits a minute, hears it again, this time trying to discern the direction it's coming from, but she can't, and so she can't tell if she'd be better off walking all the way back, back to the house, or if she should just keep going. What if the dogs are between her and town?

Just as she starts walking again, she hears another sound, this the one she wanted to hear, the low rumble of car with no muffler, and she turns to face the approaching light, standing with her legs slightly parted, her arm outstretched, thumb out, sandals clutched in the fingers of one hand.

Predictably, it's a car she recognizes, but not one from the funeral party; it's a low-slung black Camaro, with a spoiler bar on the back. Even before it slows to a stop, she can hear the bass booming from it, shaking the whole car, waking the whole woods. She bends to the passenger window, and from the dark interior Rick Skiffton's voice says in a low leer, "Hey. What's poppin' fresh, other than you?"

"Hey," Kylie laughs a little, flattered. "Can you give me a ride into town?"

"Sure, if you don't mind going the long way. Climb on in," Rick says, and Kylie opens the door, slips into the passenger seat, her sandals and little purse on her lap. "Thanks."

"Aren't you Kaz's sister?"

Kylie nods; Rick's still looking at her. "Yeah. You guys hung out a bunch 'til you graduated." As soon as Kylie says this, she remembers that Rick didn't graduate, but stayed back a year, then dropped out. Maybe it isn't too nice to remind him of this.

"Well, you sure have growed up," Rick says, letting his eye flick down to her bare feet on the floor of the car, then back up again to her face, giving Kylie the feeling both of being appreciated and being sized up. "I can't believe anyone would leave you dressed in such fancitude to find your way home alone," Rick says, still looking at her, not yet pulling back onto the road.

"Oh, this." In her panic, Kylie forgot she was so dressed up. "It was Damian's funeral. Did you know him? A summer kid?"

Rick nods his head, smiling a little, and Kylie wonders what's funny. "Sure," he says. "I mean, I saw him around. We got the call for the tow the next day—brand new SUV. That really bites the monkey." He fingers the leather gearshift cover. "Okay, downtown Grand Isle, relief is in sight," and he puts the car in gear, and they take off, Kylie pressing herself back into the seat with the velocity and letting out a little squeal of laughter.

"Aren't you afraid you'll get clocked?" Kylie shouts over the music, knowing that the island cops are famous for not doing much except laying in wait at dusk for teens and off-islanders driving too fast.

"Nah," Rick says. "I've never gotten caught. Grand Isle's finest is not exactly overabundant with mental acuity."

He turns the music down. "Hey, how'd it happen, anyway? The accident, the one that killed that kid. He was driving, right?"

Kylie thinks for a minute. Right. Damian was driving. "Right," she says.

"That sucks," Rick says, and a moment of a kind of reverential silence passes. "You don't need to get home with any, shall we say, prodigious dispatch, do you? Want to stop off at Laid—I mean, Dead Man's Beach?" Rick says. Kylie knows with certainty what this means: smoke a joint, probably make out, there in the parking lot, or out in the dunes. "Sure," she says, thinking the hell with Cort, and Betheny, everything.

The car shoots up the road, faster now, and Rick turns up the music, and the speed and the music together transport Kylie, make her fling her hand out the window to feel the rush of the air, shutting her eyes against the image of Cort and Betheny on the porch, against the image of Damian's casket in the front of the chapel. Then, just as she opens her eyes and tilts her head back again, Rick presses a button and the moon roof slides open, and the night sky, crowded with stars, fills up the little patch of space. She looks at him, and he smiles at her. "I thought you'd like that," he says.

Maybe this is all she's been needing, a change of scene, to stop hanging around with them and find some new people. And Rick is the perfect place to start, an older guy, with this great car and the way he uses words nobody else even knows: she's never heard Cort say "prodigious," whatever that means. He's part of a crowd that Kylie's stayed away from, most of them dropouts, working at the Greasy Gorgon or at the plant in Wisconset; there's something metallic about them. One time, one of those guys was arrested for molesting a kid.

They pull into the parking lot of Dead Man's Beach. There's just one car way down at the end, a new-looking convertible, probably with a couple in it, a couple of summer or weekend people. Rick pulls up so that the car's facing the water, cuts the engine, leaves the music on, but turns it down.

"Well, Kylie Pickett, look what I have here for you," Rick says, reaching into his jacket pocket and pulling out a Baggie of papers and pot. Kylie laughs. "How did you know that's just what I needed?"

"Oh, your pleasure is our business, here at Rick's Roadhouse." He opens his legs, sets the baggie between them, and starts rolling a joint. Kylie sees how skinny his legs are, like the rest of him, not like Cort, who is muscled from soccer and the more generalized "working out," he's always talking about. She feels a little shiver of excitement at the idea of Rick's skinny legs against her own.

Outside, the big clear night presses around the Camaro. Kylie can see the snack shack shuttered for the night, and she briefly wonders at how it looks so different, so quiet and sleeping now, as opposed to during the day, when it's crowded with kids and screaming mothers.

"*Voilà*," Rick says, smiling at her again. God, he's hot. And there's something cute about him, funny, even though he tries to make out like he's a tough guy. "And now, ve ezcape ze polize," he says in a phony French accent, holding up the joint and opening his door, and Kylie giggles again and gets out.

The night seems bigger, as they cross the parking lot. She's left her sandals in the car, and the sand and small pebbles prick the soles of her feet, but once they're on the path that leads to the water, the sand is smooth, and night-cool.

It's a little funny being out here with Rick Skiffton, and suddenly Kylie feels self-conscious, like she should say something. "How's everything down at the garage?" she says, then realizes she sounds like an idiot.

"Huh?" he looks at her, gives a small exhale of laughter. "Oh, just the usual malicosity. Each day a stunning replication of the day before," he says. "And that's how it will be tomorrow, too."

"Oh." Kylie knows she's said something wrong, but isn't sure what.

Out on the beach, it's a little cold, and Kylie, in her summer funeral party dress, shivers a bit, wishing she'd brought something warmer. Well, she didn't know she'd end up out here on the beach with Rick Skiffton.

"Come on," Rick says suddenly, putting out a hand to her, and she takes his hand, a little surprised at how quickly he's reaching for her. "Okay," she giggles, and he pulls her along from the beach into the dunes, where he motions to the soft sand, saying, "Welcome to my little house," trying for the fake French accent again, but this time not quite getting it, as the sentence is lacking any "th" sounds. He shrugs off his denim jacket, and puts it around Kylie's shoulders.

At this, she feels so completely taken care of that Kylie smiles up at him, and says, "Ze French accent iz so sex-y," even though she knows this will only hurry things along. But she wants to hurry things along, wants to get to the part where something definite has happened, like he's kissing her.

They nestle into the sand together, backs to the dune, facing the waves; Rick lights the joint, and they silently pass it back and forth. Kylie pulls the smoke deep into her lungs, and she feels the tension and sadness of the day begin to ebb away from her: the umpteenth breakfast fight with her mother about the accident, all those clueless people at the funeral, Damian's mom weaving around a little like she was drunk, Betheny suddenly treating her like she's an idiot. And how dumb Damian would have thought the whole thing was. And wasn't she afraid, too? Oh, yeah, on the road, waiting for Rick.

The one good thing to happen to her all day. Sitting close to him, she picks up his scent of oil and mechanic's grease, cigarettes: the thrilling, dangerous bad boy smell.

"That must have been pretty sad, that funeral," Rick says, and at this bit of understanding, Kylie feels her eyes fill. It would feel so good just to cry, but she doesn't want to wreck her mood, the happier mood she's been trying to achieve since Rick picked her up. She draws one finger delicately under each eye, so as not to smear her mascara. "Yeah," she says with a sniff.

And then Rick's arm is around her. "Poor baby," he says, pulling her close, and she lets her head drop to rest there. He's skinny, but strong.

"So you knew him, this summer prep?" Rick asks.

"Yeah, I *guess* so," Kylie says, and even though she hears the sarcasm in her voice, she can't stop it. "I mean, I *was* in the car at the time he was killed." Hearing herself sounding now like she's giving report to Cop Cal, she adds, "It sucked."

"Intense," Rick says, taking another hit from the joint. "How'd it happen, anyway? Were you all pretty baked?"

How'd it happen. The question Kylie's been rolling over and over in her head, even as the memory of rolling over and over in the car keeps knocking her down like a surprise wave out there in the surf.

"Yeah, we were. At least, Cort was—I mean," Kylie pauses, and then she thinks, why should she protect him? What's the point anymore? "Yeah. Cort was pretty buzzed, and so was Betheny. But Damian, he was like, not totally straight edge, but he just always seemed really kind of above all that. I'm not describing this too good. I mean, he wasn't stuck up or anything. It's more he was like thinking about something else."

"Huh. So how'd it happen then? I mean, if he wasn't even, um, imbibing?"

"Oh, you know, it was just one of those things. You know," Kylie says weakly.

"You can tell me, little girl. What is it? What's the big mystery?"

"I don't know. I shouldn't say anything more." Kylie shifts in the sand. Why is she protecting Cort, that dickhead? "Are you sure you won't tell anyone? Anyone at all? I swear. You have to really promise." Kylie looks up at Rick. His face is so close she can see the tiny stubble of dark beard along his chin. There's a little scar, shaped like a crescent moon, on his jaw.

"Even better than that, I'll tell you something hardly anybody knows," he says, leaning in a little closer to her, so close she can smell his scent, something musty, a little bit like a mushroom, or the soil in a potted plant.

He kisses her then, on the mouth, but quickly, no tongue. "Now, about your secret. Who would I tell?" he says, and she feels so safe with him there, wrapped in his denim jacket, his arm draped around her shoulder, the roach pinched out in his fingers without so much as a wince, that she knows she can tell him. She can finally tell someone the truth.

"Well, the thing is, Cort was really driving. We've just told everyone it was Damian, because like Cort pointed out, he'd be charged with like some kind of crime or something—"

"Vehicular homicide," Rick offers. He's familiar with the law.

"Right," Kylie laughs in recognition of the word. "I keep forgetting that word! So, since Damian is dead and all, he can't exactly be charged with anything, so it doesn't really make sense for everyone to think Cort was driving. I mean, what's the point?"

"Huh." Rick stares out to the water, which to Kylie now sounds louder than it did before, all roar. "Sounds like Cort's a tad mite reality challenged," he says, and she suddenly realizes how stoned she is, and feels for a moment like she's in a giant mouth out there on the beach, and she almost says this, but instead, Rick pulls her a little closer, and then he's kissing her, for real this time, and then his hands are moving up under her dress, and she lets the relief take her over, the relief of telling someone, the relief of finding someone to tell.

It's happening too fast, she thinks, and yet, it's Rick Skiffton, who she always liked, and she feels her underwear getting wet, and yet she wants to go back, to slow it all down, go back to that first kiss, stop now, but knows that she can't, it's too late now, now she's in it and it's got to run its course.

Above them, the stars crowd out the dark sky, and then the fog breathes in from the sea, and there's no sound anymore but the sound of Rick's breath on her neck, and now he isn't kissing her anymore at all, now it's just the waves turning and turning, the breath of the fog and the breath of the sea.

Part Two

Sixteen

A week after the funeral finds Franci sitting on the back porch steps, staring at the cattailed water, in the t-shirt and boxers she was wearing the night Damian died, the outfit she feels safest in. Peg and Tessa will be coming by later, arms loaded with greens and bread from the farmers' market, but for now, her ear is so precisely turned, listening for Damian, that she hears the mailman's step on the front porch, the squeak of the mailbox as it opens, then shuts, his footsteps retreating. She waits a little bit, not wanting to see him face to face, certain he doesn't want to see her (what do you say to the woman whose son just died?), and then she walks through the cottage, opens the front door.

Even though there's more news of torrential rains and flooding all along the southern Atlantic coast, here it's a simple, hot, blue day, the kind of day where it seems nothing bad could ever happen. She even has the feeling that Damian's inside, sleeping late, that soon he'll be up, pouring himself a big bowl of Froot Loops in the kitchen, slopping the milk onto the table.

How could she have let this happen?

He's been dead now for two weeks and eight hours.

Eight days after he was born, she had him circumcised, in what was probably her last Jewish ritual. Shouldn't there be some kind of a counterbalance for this? Should she have done something the eighth day after he died?

As much as Franci loathes the prospect of interacting with anyone except Peg and Tessa, the thought of receiving the mail gives her an excited chuff that settles in an emotional borderland between anxiety and grief, a feeling reminiscent of waiting for a new lover's phone call, or for the results of a medical test. As she thinks this, opening the front door, arrested by her thought and in no hurry at all, she remembers her mother's last weeks in the hospital, how once, half-lucid, she looked up at Franci and said, "The doctor said it was positive," smiling, her face glowing with happiness. It had been Peg to solve the puzzle: Franci's mother wasn't in the present day, when for her, "positive" meant "cancer," but was back in her youth, when "positive" meant "baby." Meant Franci herself, in fact, and Franci had wept to think that she'd seen an echo of her mother's expression upon hearing the news she was pregnant with Franci.

She steps into the relative cool of the front porch, immured by the deep green elephant vine, and opens the mailbox, even though she knows as she does that this will ruin having something to look forward to, until tomorrow. No, until Monday. Her anticipation isn't anything concrete—she doesn't think there will be a letter from some authority announcing that there was a terrible mistake and Damian survived—but she doesn't worry about this. She'll settle for anticipation, in any form.

She opens the mailbox, pulls out what's there, and sits on the glider, toeing herself back and a forth a little; there *is* comfort in rocking. The mail contains the usual circulars, which she ordinarily just throws out without even looking at them, but now, she reads through each one, page by page. Lantman's is having some special deals this week: hamburger is $2.29 a pound; chicken, free-range and antibiotic-free, is $7.99. Damian would like that. "Free the chickens," he'd say. "Let them range!" She turns the page. A picture of flats of pansies. She reads every item, looks at each picture, matching picture to price and back again, then carefully folds the circular and sets it beside her. Whole minutes have passed.

There was that terrible moment, was it only two weeks ago, when Damian told her about the epilepsy, and she thought he was going to tell her he had a fatal disease, lymphoma or HIV. When she thought he was going to tell her he was going to die.

She picks up the mail from her lap again, carefully reading each of the three circulars, each of the bills, puzzling over the abbreviations on the cryptic electric bill, taking a deep breath when she feels the trembling, now becoming familiar, in her chest. There's a manuscript for her to edit, something she agreed to in the time *before*, all of two weeks ago. She sets it aside without opening it.

There's something from the hospital in Wisconset that looks like a bill, and this fills Franci with a rage that burns so hot she has a fantasy of the envelope catching fire, but she opens it, reads it through. Everything is covered by her insurance, after the deductible. *Great.*

A thought comes to her, unbidden, triggered by the thought of the insurance, medicine, the accident: if there is any question about who was driving, if anyone—other than Franci—suspects Cort was really behind the wheel, shouldn't she tell Cop Cal about the epilepsy, which she's coming to think could have been the cause? Shouldn't she make sure that the whole story is known?

But at this thought, Franci's suffused with exhaustion. No. She cannot pick up the phone, cannot call, make an appointment, drag out Damian's condition as if trying to make sense of the insensible.

She goes back to the mail. She has two hours before Tessa and Peg will be here. The condolence notes. There are five. She reads the return addresses without opening the envelopes, then organizes them alphabetically, by last name. They're all from people she doesn't know well, people who didn't come up for the funeral, all except one: *L. Morgan*, in a distinctive ribboning script.

Okay, she thinks, and settles it in the middle of the pile.

The first two notes, predictably, make her cry, just with the preprinted, anonymous words: "In Sympathy," and "With Our Thoughts." She rubs her fingertip across the embossed daffodils on the front, crying, lets them drop to her lap. *I don't want to be doing this.* She looks out over the old front garden, which looks bountiful and terrific, everything leafing out, the generous peonies and the climbing roses.

There's a card from Dick and Jennifer, the usual platitudes in Dick's scrawl, nothing about how Cort was in the car, how it was Dick's new SUV that got wrecked, or how now, grief has stitched them permanently to one another. Nothing in the note asking Franci to please not pursue any fancies of further investigation, and yet, Franci knows that's part of what the note says. Franci closes her eyes, letting the sun hit her face, the light behind her eyes going red. Damian couldn't have been driving, could he? Damian, with his bouncing step and his funny fakey laugh at her terrible puns, Damian drawing cartoons on the back of restaurant napkins, always losing his homework, and later misplacing his wallet, his keys, Damian at six running down the ramp to the L train, arms splayed wide, calling out, "I can fly, I can fly," Damian with his worry about her, his secret dread, his relentless unrequited love for his father, his tousled sleepy head. Damian, her baby, her boy, her son. Damian's never coming back to be laughed with, chastised, or fed. Damian's gone. Damian's dead.

The card from Leslie is enveloped in heavy white paper, which Franci opens carefully, careful not to let it tear. Inside, a thick white card, with a little blue watercolor painted on the front. At first, Franci isn't sure what the painting is of. She inspects it, tracing it with a fingertip, as if the meaning of the design will penetrate her skin and tell her something. Then she sees it's a little sailboat, on a lake. Hand painted, by Leslie.

She opens, and is disappointed before she even begins to read: it's very brief.

Franci,

He was lovely, perfect in every way, and there's nothing anyone can do to make this anything other than a tragedy. I'm thinking of you, and of Damian, who is still with me in many ways.

L

Okay. What did she want, or expect, anyway? A declaration of Leslie's love, her regret at having ended their relationship? *But I loved you*, Franci wants to say. She adds the card to the pile, goes on to the next, this one from the publications department at Memorial Sloan, where she does a little editing. It has a soft-focus photo of a bouquet. Everyone is very sorry for her loss.

After she reads all the notes, Franci sits for a long time, suspended on the porch glider. From inside the house, the phone rings, the answering machine clicks on. Franci's turned the volume down, but she knows her own voice, recorded weeks ago, is brightly talking, as if her voice, severed from her grieving body, remains in the well-lit past of *before the accident*, saying to leave a message, giving the number of Damian's landline. She knew she should have gotten with it and switched to voicemail years ago; if she had, she wouldn't be haunted now by her own voice.

It's eleven in the morning, and now it's very hot, and Franci sits in the green viney shade on the porch glider another twenty minutes, thinking she's thirsty, thinking maybe she'll have a glass of ice water. But for now, she's crying, again, the mail in a tidy pile beside her, her toes touching the porch floor, hands dangling between her knees.

Seventeen

The most difficult days, Peg knows, are those after a funeral and before the world rights itself and forces the mourner to stand, to move a tentative foot in a wobbly forward motion. And so she's the force behind Torsten and Tessa and Jake that insists they don't leave Franci on her own much, insisting that she practically live at their houses, the two couples forming a phalanx against the tide of Franci's loss.

"We hang by a thread," Peg says, during the third week after the funeral. She and Franci are sitting at Peg's redwood picnic table on the deck under the sweeping, dark-limbed pines. Peg's brought out a plate of cookies and her watercolors and brushes, hoping she'll be able to add the wash to her blue jay drawings while they talk, and knowing it's easier to talk when at least one person's hands are occupied. It's still early in the summer evening, the sweet soft air still warm with the day. Out on the open bay water, past the reedy marsh, they can see a motor boat tugging a water-skier, spinning in wide circles.

"I know," Franci says. Since the accident she's known this more than ever before, and she finds an odd comfort in Peg pointing this out, as if Peg has joined her hyper-consciousness of mortality.

Franci reaches for the plate of cookies, but instead of taking one, she just spins the plate in a little circle, bit by bit. She looks so different now, Peg thinks, so different than she did the night of Tessa and Jake's first party of the summer, when they were all thinking how good Leslie had been for her, even though that had taken some adjusting on everyone's part, and even though it hadn't lasted. She looked young on that night as the summer began.

"He was a beautiful boy," Peg says, opening her paint box and dipping her brush, and this makes the tears come to Franci's eyes again. "Remember when he was about eight, what he said about coming over here?" Peg says. Franci shakes her head, no, even though does. She wants to hear it anyway. "It's always funner with you, Peg," Peg says, and they laugh, Peg's voice trembling.

From inside the house, they can hear the sound of Torsten cleaning up the dinner things, water running in the sink, the dishwasher spurting to a start.

"You're so lucky to have him," Franci says.

Peg smiles, looking over her shoulder toward the house. "Yeah, he's pretty great. I was lucky," she says, and then sees that Franci's weeping, silently, looking out at the water. She thinks of Tessa then, how Tessa's changed, too, since the accident, but instead of seeming paralyzed in grief, if anything she seems less cowed, more willing to do or say what she wants and the hell with Jake and his overreactions.

On the shore across the bay, a few lights wink on, even though there's still plenty of light. The last peepers of the season start up, and Peg reaches across the picnic table, covers Franci's hand with her own.

"I just don't know what's wrong with me. It's the weirdest feeling, like I'm out of my body or something," Franci says. Her hand is very cold.

"That's because the shock's worn off," Peg says, her own eyes filling. "Now you've just got the reality of it: one minute he was here, now he just isn't. You're grief-stricken, Franci."

The sound of the peepers begins to rise. Franci takes a deep shaky breath, lets it out. "My life is all different now," she says. She could elaborate, but in her mind, she sees the differences unfurling before her, and she's struck dumb.

"Yeah," Peg says. "In many ways, it is. In how many ways, you have no way of knowing right now. Don't try to figure it out all at once."

Franci nods, reaches again to spin the plate of cookies a little. She wants to say something to Peg about the epilepsy, how she knows it was probably a seizure that threw the car off the road, but she doesn't; she still hasn't mentioned it to anyone, as if by keeping the secret of Damian's epilepsy she can hang onto her own secret, the crazy idea that he wasn't driving, wasn't at fault, as if this somehow will ameliorate her grief. Instead, "How do you know so much about this, Peg? I mean, your parents died a few years ago—"

"Six years for my mother, ten for my father."

"Right. But you know something about sudden death, Peg, and don't try to bluff me. What is it? What happened?"

Peg hears again the voice of BJ's sister on the phone, saying, "Just like that." How can she tell Franci about this? Telling anyone would be even more of a betrayal of Torsten. All these years she's thought that keeping her affair to herself, especially after BJ died, was a way of making it less bad, with the justification that at least everyone wasn't whispering about Torsten behind his back.

"Yeah, I do," Peg says now, with a sigh. There's a shout from the water-skiers, indecipherable. "I just"—she looks again over her shoulder to the house. "I just can't go into it, I suppose," she says, looking back, but then she sees the look on Franci's face, that look that she's melting into her grief, as if she's drowning and waving wildly for something, anything to save her.

Peg leans forward, brush still in hand. "I had an affair," she whispers, and the utter change on Franci's face is worth all the risk of this, because Franci goes from grief to shock to an outright laugh, a huge surprised "Ha," springing forth from her, a sound Peg had thought she'd never hear from Franci again.

"I don't know that it's hysterically funny," Peg says, in mock affront. Half-mock.

At that moment, Torsten appears at the door, slides open the screen, steps onto the deck. "I thought I'd take an evening kayak," he says. "Would either of you like to join me?" Franci and Peg shake their heads, no, Franci feeling she's about to dissolve again into giggles, or tears. The two women watch in silence as Torsten ambles down the slope to the water, sets up in the boat, and paddles out into the open water. He turns, waves, and is gone out across the twilit bay.

"Peg, honestly. I can't believe you would keep that from me. Does Tessa know?"

"No, of course not. And she never will." Peg fixes Franci with a glare. "No one knows." She re-dedicates herself to the blue jay on her paper, which is becoming several shades of blue—indigo, cerulean—just like in life.

"Well?"

"Well what? Do you want some of this bug stuff? It doesn't smell too bad," Peg slides a tube across the table to Franci.

"Well, what *happened*, Peg? You can't just tell me you had—" Franci looks around comically, over her left shoulder into the piney woods, over her right toward the water—"had an affair and leave it at that."

"Oh, I don't know. It was just an affair. You know, man meets woman at a conference, there's a spark, and they foolishly follow through with it. Haven't you ever read any literature?" Peg hears the sharp edge in her voice, but she can't seem to control it, now that she's presented her affair with BJ as entertainment, offered it up just to get a laugh out of Franci, even if the circumstances are somewhat extenuating.

"Peg," Franci says. She picks up a cookie from the plate, more confirmation to Peg that she was right in telling.

"I'm sorry. I shouldn't have even told you. I've never told anyone, and it was a long time ago, twenty years or something. I've mostly forgotten about it," she lies.

"And Torsten never knew?"

"Mr. Magoo? Never."

Out on the water, the motorboat is spinning almost silently in lazy circles, the water-skier trailing behind, one arm held out like a sail. Torsten and his kayak are now just a mote of red on the water.

"I was about forty. Forty-one. I went to an illustrators' conference, and met BJ there. There was instant chemistry. He was younger, ten years younger. Oh, Franci, it was all so predictable, and it sounds so boring, now. Torsten was up against the deadline for his second book, and of course I was feeling neglected. That's why he didn't go to the conference with me in the first place."

"Maybe it's predictable for some people, but you? I never, ever, would have guessed."

"Why? Because I'm not a svelte and sexy young thing?"

"No," Franci says, scrutinizing Peg. *Yes.* "It's more about your character, I guess. I mean, I just never have seen you flirt or anything." Franci doesn't add, "unlike me."

"Unlike you," Peg says, and they laugh.

"I guess if I'm in this deep, I might as well finish," Peg says. "So, we saw each other for about a year, meeting when we could, sending letters—"

"Letters?"

"Yes, if you recall the Paleolithic custom of taking pen to paper—"

"But weren't you afraid Torsten would find them?"

Peg looks down at the flagstones between her bare feet. Over the years, she's been careful about keeping her feet in good condition.

"I got a post office box," she whispers.

"Peg!"

"Well. The whole thing got pretty serious, and we talked about getting married. He had just divorced before we met. Of course, I was crazed with conflict. I didn't *want* to leave Torsten. And then, the week that I was to tell Torsten, to tell him about the affair, to tell him I was leaving him, I got a call from BJ's sister." The peepers' noise is falling now, as more lights come on along the arm of shoreline across the bay.

"He died in a boating accident out in Oregon. It was sudden, something about an unexpected rock outcropping. I never really got the details. I just remember the sister saying it happened 'Just like that.' *Just like that.* She'd found my letters when she went through his things and figured out how to contact me."

There is a long pause as the two women look out at the marsh and the bay, the opposite shore still lit by the last light. They can see a single great blue heron stalking the water's edge, nearly lost among the tall cattails and reedy grasses.

"Peg. I'm sorry. God. It isn't easy, any of it."

"No."

Another silent pause. There's an animal rustle at the base of the pine trees, and Smokey meows, once, insistently, from inside the house.

"Thanks for telling me the story, Peg," Franci says at last. "But you know, the whole time I've just been thinking of Damian."

"I know that," Peg says, holding up the painted jay for Franci to see.

The broad bay stays lit late, and out on the water, Torsten keeps pulling on the kayak paddle, away from the house, not wanting to go back, not just yet. Out here, in his kayak, he feels graceful, or at least something approaching grace. Out here, he can make the kayak do what he wants, and it obeys, turning left, or right, quick and light.

Finally, he turns in an arc to head back home, and then, just for the fun of it, turns again, and again, his boat making tight circles in the water.

And then he heads back. It's later than he thought, and in the dusky half-light, he can see the darting bats swoop down over the water. He's avoiding Peg, but he'll come out of it. It's just that he knows that Damian's sudden death has reminded her of BJ, all those years ago, and it's hard for him to shake off the memory of finding that packet of letters, the obituary clipped from a Portland newspaper, which suddenly explained his wife's odd behavior.

The hardest thing wasn't knowing she'd taken a lover. The hardest thing was that he had no way of comforting her. He'd just taken on more of the household chores, and he'd held onto her tightly while she slept, his arms clasped around her shoulders, some nights weeping, silently, for them both.

Driving home, Franci's new mantra, beating now in her blood, *Damian's dead, Damian's dead* is subdued some by her thoughts of Peg and Peg's affair. Franci shakes her head a little, the warm summer air coming in the open window of the car. *Peg? An affair?*

When she comes into the cottage, she steels herself against her instinct to listen for Damian, to look for a note from him, or evidence of his quick departure, a glass with a little milk in the bottom left on the table, or a scattering of books on the sofa. She steels herself against this impulse to look for him, knowing to expect it, and thinks: this is the beginning of letting go. You know the impulse will be there, but you train yourself not to look, not to listen, not to expect.

But, as she has every night and morning since the accident, she walks into his downstairs bedroom. Just as she left it. Just as *he* left it, the covers pulled up in a halfhearted attempt to make the bed, the pillow with the white sheep leaping forever across a green background, his red and white jersey hanging over the closet door, his sneakers and assorted clothing tumbled askew on the throw rug.

His room is utterly quiet, just the way he left it when he went out to the party in Wisconset. How will she ever do anything in this room, like pick up the clothes lying on the floor, or take the sheets off the bed? What would be the point? His phone, the old-fashioned black push-button she got for his landline. What if someone left a message on it, she thinks, wondering why she hasn't thought of this before.

She picks up the receiver, guesses at his password (F-R-O-G), taps it in. One message—she feels a punch to her stomach as she hears the date: June 8, the night of the accident. She presses the "1": out comes a sweet, lilting girl's voice. "Hi, Damian. Hi, it's me, Phoenix. Hi. Well, I've been thinking about you, and I just wanted to call. I really miss you. I don't know if we can go the whole summer without seeing each other. In case you don't have my dad's number it's 413-255-8036. And you have my cell. I miss you, Beastie. I'll be around tonight and tomorrow night. Okay. Namaste."

Namaste? Beastie?

Franci wipes her hand across her teary eyes, and plays the message again. It's like a message from the Other Side, from the life that would have been continuing, the life that would have been. The life that should have been, the one in which Damian would be telling her about this girl, maybe showing her a photo, admitting to her his questions, his reservations, his obsession. They'd go to a specialist in the city, find out how to manage the epilepsy, which eventually wouldn't be frightening but would in Damian's hands become a mark of distinction. The life in which, every morning, they'd get outside with the scraping and painting equipment, sanding down the old blue paint on the exterior of the house, then, by July, painting over it in the new yellow. Maybe she'd catch him smoking pot, and they'd argue. They'd take their plates down to the water and have a supper picnic, and maybe this Phoenix would come to visit for a few days. And on, beyond this summer—but Franci stops herself from thinking of that.

Franci picks up one of Damian's notebooks lying near the phone and plays the message one more time, this time carefully writing the phone number on the cardboard back, with one of his pens. She knows as she does that now she's started to disturb his room, there's no going back.

She writes the number with something approximating hope, or maybe just imagination, as she doesn't for a moment believe she'll be able to make the call.

What would she say? Would she use the phrase that Peg heard, "Just like that?"

Even after the funeral, after he's interviewed Cort and examined the evidence and had Marty type up his report and send it in to the state office, something nags at Cop Cal, a buzzing in his ear like a mosquito in the room. It isn't that the kids' injuries weren't consistent with Damian driving, but the ME said the injuries were "not inconsistent." Could've happened another way, one of the girls or Cort behind the wheel. Even though he's handed in the paperwork, a few weeks after the accident Cal decides a trip to visit one of the girls is in order. Just to check. Just to make sure.

Kylie's house sits in an open field near the center of town; it's an old square farmhouse, but not a big farmhouse like the ones on the water, or even those closer to the ferry dock; inside, the rooms are cramped, and dark, and because the house is situated in an open field, with just a few old lilac bushes huddled up to its siding, in the summertime it bakes in the sun, the heat filling the small rooms with the mustiness of summertime. In winter, it's worse, with the cold sneaking in around the weather-stripping Kylie's mom puts up every year, and the radiators clanking on, loud but ineffective.

Upstairs, in her attic room, under a soft-focus poster of Taylor Lautner, Kylie sits cross-legged in her bed, staring out the back window. From here, she can see a sliver of the bay far off, just beneath the horizon line. She's looked out at this view all her life.

Despite the earplugs pulsing "Rolling in the Deep" into her ears, she hears a car pull into the drive, pushes onto her knees to look out the other window, and feels her stomach go cold: it's the Grand Isle cop car. *Oh. My. God.* Did Rick blab? She never should have trusted him. She stands, legs shaking, looks in the mirror over the dresser, gives her lips a swipe of gloss, brushes the loose hair from her eyes, takes a deep breath to steady herself. She waits until she's called downstairs, trying to remember what Cort told her to say, telling herself it doesn't matter if she lies.

"Kylie," her mother calls. "You'd better get your precious butt down here right now."

Cop Callahan looks bigger in the small living room than he did by the car the night of the accident, seeming even to dwarf the oversized plaid sofa and matching recliner.

"I just can't believe you'd do something so stupid," her mother says, without preliminaries, when Kylie comes into the living room, as if they haven't been over this ground several times already.

"How're you doing?" Cop Cal says.

"I wouldn't be too concerned about how *you're* doing, young lady," her mother says. "You've got much bigger things to worry about."

Kylie doesn't roll her eyes at her mother; she knows her mother's right. Instead, she shrugs. "Okay, I guess."

"Okay. Listen, now that some time has passed, I've got to ask you a few questions, about what happened."

"She'll answer whatever you want to ask," Kylie's mother says, and Cop Callahan smiles at her. "Mind if we sit down?"

"Of course. I'm sorry. Can I get you anything, a coffee or something?"

"Sure. Thanks." When her mother's out of the room, Cop Callahan turns to Kylie. "I know this is hard, but why don't you just start by telling me what happened when you left Wisconset. You were at the roadhouse, right?"

Kylie feels herself relax a little. Maybe Rick didn't tell. She knew he was more trustworthy than Cort. She tells her story the way she's been practicing, starting with the truth: going out to the parking lot, Damian insisting on driving, Cort resisting, then Damian whispering to him. She also knows, but doesn't say, that at the time this pissed her off, because she knew this meant Cort would be in the back seat with Betheny. She leaves out the crucial bit of the story, that in the end, Cort won the argument, drove them all as far as the ferry landing on the Wisconset side of the water.

Instead, "You know, Damian's very responsible," and then she remembers again: he's dead. "I mean, was."

"Yes," Cop Callahan says.

They left the bar, and drove to the ferry. Kylie says nothing about how after they drove off the ferry and rounded the first bend in Ferry Road, Cort started insisting that Damian now pull over to switch drivers back, and they did, Kylie now pressed up tight against Cort as he drove. But she's careful to leave this part out of the story, and instead, her voice starts trembling when she gets to part where the car lurched off the road. "It was so weird, it was like a movie or something, like we were just sailing out over the meadow. I could see the whole ocean like coming through the windshield right at me," Kylie says, and then she draws in a long, shaky breath. "It was so scary," she says, and Cop Callahan waits, waiting to hear her say something to indicate that Cort, and not Damian, was driving.

"And then it all stopped, and we all got out of the car, somehow, except Damian was still in there." She pauses, remembering the scene, Cort clambering up on top of the toppled car, reaching down into the back seat. And she remembers that she has to remember this differently, and she imagines Cort leaning into the *front* seat. Yes, that's right. She nods a little, once, twice. "Cort reached right into the front side door, you know, the passenger door, and he kind of yanked Damian up like that, but Damian was all floppy." By the time her mother comes back into the room, Kylie's crying.

"I'm sorry," Cop Callahan says, and then, to her mother, "Thanks."

"I don't know what you're thanking me for," Kylie's mom says. She's wearing her sleeveless top, her tight white summer pants. Her hair's been done, and her makeup's on; she's got a date tonight. But her mouth is drawn in a tight, flat line across the bottom of her face, and before Cop Callahan is out the door, her mom's questioning her again, "How could you have been so fucking dumb?"

Kylie responds to this by flopping down into the sofa, picking up the remote. She knows better than to switch the tv on, but holding the little plastic box in her hand is comforting: she knows that if she wanted to risk it, in a split second the room would be filled with the light and noise of the television world. Instead, she listens as her mother goes on, then stops, saying, "I don't have time for this," and her mother grabs her keys, her purse, and is out the door.

Alone, Kylie still doesn't turn the tv on. Instead, she stays on the sofa, running Cop Callahan's visit through her head again. Did she say anything wrong? Anything that might *incriminate* her? And then the wave of it washes over her again: *Damian's dead*. There's no undoing it. And one day, she'll die, too. She can hardly stand the queasy, restless feeling this gives her, right in the pit of her stomach, like she's going to be sick, like she's got to get away from it, and she gets up, goes into the kitchen, where she stands at the fridge until she sees something she thinks she might want.

Cal climbs into the patrol car, settles into the seat, sits for a long moment, watching the house, then pulls the belt across his middle and starts the car. When they were at Wisconset Regional, Kylie's mother was pretty, one of the prettiest girls in the school. He drives, because driving often clears his head and because Marty's at the station, watching over things. God knows his years here have earned him the right to drive the island roads when he needs to be alone and think.

He rolls the window down, letting the sea air into the car, as if the air will cleanse him of his uneasy feeling, but it doesn't, it only makes his face feel cold. He takes Cross Island Road, then finds himself on East Shore Road, then heading down island, coming up on Dead Man's Beach just like the kids that night.

As he approaches the curve, he slows, even more than usual, peering through the windshield at the big, bright day. There's something amiss, but he can't quite say what it is, and he sails past the spot, looks out at the sea, then heads back to the station, thinking he'll have lunch at the diner today, thinking today is Wednesday, and it's meatloaf.

Eighteen

How does a boy die in a car wreck? Shouldn't it take a lot to kill a big healthy boy, take more than a half-ton of metal sailing over an embankment and landing upside-down in a meadow, by the sea?

Standing beside her bike on the cliff overlooking Dead Man's Beach, Franci can make out the bright colors of the people on the beach. She could have been among them; she would have been, maybe with Damian, or with Tessa and Peg, a beach picnic on a hot afternoon.

But here she is, standing beside her bike on the cliff. From here, she can see the long blue waves curling into their white breakers. Out in the dunes, a cluster of color, teenagers, she knows, smoking pot. It's no different now than it was when her parents first started coming here when she was in high school. The day is hot for early summer, the first really hot day, a real beach day, and here she is, in her jeans and a sleeveless black t-shirt, soaking up the sun like a black hole. *Good.* She should suffer much more than that, for God's sake: she let her own son die.

Didn't the car have to pack onto the rocky cliff awfully hard, tumble over like the machine that it was? Wouldn't Damian have had to be flung against the car's roof with the force of a bullet, or a train? How did it feel, the impact that crushed his neck?

Franci rubs the back of her hand across her eyes; she's crying, again. Again, and again, and again; she'll never be done grieving, and she's only just begun.

She can hear the sound of the crash, again.

The cliff is pretty high above the beach; there's the guardrail, *the guardrail that failed*, she rhymes in her head, or did she say it out loud? When she was a little girl, she heard her mother say that rhyming was a sign of psychosis, and she was always afraid that her tendency to make up rhymes indicated some scary mental illness. *Well, Mother, what would you tell me now?*

The cliff spills down into a sloping meadow, grassy and green, a long meadow which leads to the long flight of wooden steps which in turn lead down to the beach, the way her thoughts now lead one to one to one in their jumble-jump. Franci lets her gaze wander across the grasses. They are many shades of green. Why don't people who live in very grassy parts of the world have the same impossibly large number of words for "green" as do the Eskimos for "snow"? Only, she knows from hearing Tessa talk about her research in the Arctic, they're not called Eskimos anymore, and she hears Damian in her head chiding her, "Pop culture shock Mom, they're Inuit."

The only way to survive middle age is by having a son who's smarter than you, she hears herself say in her head.

The bright sun flattens everything. Out in the water, Franci can see three dots of color: a man and woman have apparently gone into the waves, and there's another dot out there, swimming along the shoreline, staying close in, but swimming in a vigorous Australian crawl, as if intending to swim the circumference of the island. Leslie, Franci thinks, even though she knows this isn't possible. But it's the kind of bold thing Leslie would have done, would do, *did*, swimming the island's circumference, and Franci feels a pinch of regret at not having called Leslie herself, at having chickened out by asking Tessa and Peg to take that on. And then, Leslie's card, which Franci still hasn't answered, and probably won't.

At the thought of Leslie, at the thought of all the condolence notes she should be answering, Franci feels any energy she'd had drain from her, sagging her shoulders, slumping her muscles. She lays the bike onto the gravel of the shoulder, steps over the guardrail, and lies in the grass, on her back. It's the hot middle of the day; there's no shade, and she lets the sun soak right into her dark clothes. Maybe this way she'll feel something other than grief, even if it's only heat. Maybe the heat will sear her grief to her, she thinks, and lying there imagines her grief for a moment like a plastic skin over her skin, her clothes, mottled, clear, puffy like the skin of someone who's been badly burned and won't survive.

Lying in the meadow grasses, she returns to her question: why did Damian die, when she knows the human body withstands a great deal, without giving in? She sits up, arms around her knees. It took her mother a long time to die of cancer, and she was nearly eighty, trembling down to a hospital-gowned wisp in the white hospital bed, which looked bigger with every one of Franci's visits.

The sky is an immaculate blue, with just a few wispy clouds, high up. "Up in the sky, where the dead reside / that's where you are to me / up where the bright plane / cuts a white incision . . ." Franci remembers from a poem she wrote, years ago, after Stiles left her. She recites the words, and the recitation makes her voice crack. "Up in the sky, where the dead reside," she cries. The poem came out of an assignment in a creative writing class she took, to write about one of the elements, and she chose air. "Pneumography," she called it, and she sees then Damian's chest rising and falling with his breath as he slept in her arms, just after he was born.

This soothes her, this image of Damian breathing. Her own breathing becomes less ragged, and the sky opens its big blue heaven to her grief.

Franci wakes; she's fallen asleep there, in the grass, just like that, in spite of the heat. Her clothes are damp with her sweat. It doesn't matter. She stands, then, and crosses the grass toward the water, looking down. She keeps her gaze focused on the grasses, as if she'll find something here, and soon, she starts looking earnestly, dropping to her knees, parting the grasses with her hands, patting them down. There's a cluster of Indian paintbrush, the stems grown long already. More grass, thick and deep. She isn't thinking that she's looking for something, but she is, and then, there it is: glinting in the sunlight, a bit of twisted metal. She picks it up, then drops it immediately: it's so hot it burns her hand. It's a fragment of a fender, she thinks.

Kneeling in the grasses under the hot sky, Franci tries to imagine Damian behind the wheel, the car plunging toward the sea, rolling over on itself in the meadow, the meadow the last thing Damian saw, as it rose up to meet the car.

But no. She can't get it out of her head: Damian, in the back seat, not driving, the girl he didn't like, Betheny, pressing against him, and Damian, head back, eyes closed, just wanting to be home. But what does she know? How much does any mother know her nearly grown son?

She combs through the grasses with her hands, even though she's aware that if anyone saw her, she'd look mad. Maybe she is. Maybe there is no coming back to the land of the sane after this.

She feels the sharp pinprick of glass in her palms, shards from the car's headlamps or windows, and then she sees something else glittering in the sun: a CD that must have fallen from the car when it rolled, "Vampire Weekend," imprinted on it. She stands, and spins the CD around on her finger, imagining the music coming out of it in this way, imagining that this was the last music her son heard. She knows the music of teenaged boys, having at times listened to Damian's music, having played some of the CDs, just to see what he was listening to, back when he was in high school and wasn't talking to her much.

How am I supposed to pretend
I never want to see you again?
How am I supposed to pretend
I never want to see you again?

Standing under the hot white sky, the small sound of the waves below, Franci listens in her head to the music Damian listened to, watching the car plunge again and again through the guardrail and into the meadow, watching it until it's no longer an imagined scene, but is something real to her as memory, as if she's there with him, in the car as it flew up into the air and then landed back on earth.

And if she had been there, what could she have done? What would she have done, folded him into her arms protectively? Whispered some secret of life into his shell-shaped ear before he had to go? If she had to choose like that, what would be the one thing she'd want him to know?

Franci doesn't want to walk away from the meadow, but she must; the patches of sweat are blossoming on her back and chest, and she feels dizzy standing there. She drops to her knees, combs up a handful of the glass shards from the grass, then stands, and stuffs them into the pocket of her jeans. She picks up her bike from the gravel, slips the CD into the pouch on the handlebar, and walks the bike away, looking not back at the meadow, but out to the dark and sparkling sea.

Nineteen

The Fourth of July comes and goes on Grand Isle with little fanfare, something Franci's grateful for; no one she knows feels like a party, and yet if it were their custom to have one, it would be obvious they were skipping it this year, and skipping it, really, for her. Plus, it falls on a Wednesday, making everyone undecided about which weekend should be the holiday weekend, and so Peg has Franci over for dinner on the Fourth, a low-key meal, *just a meal*, Torsten insists, as the fireworks pop across the island, setting the dogs, wild and tame, to howl.

The weekend after the Fourth, Tessa takes Jake into Wisconset for the evening train; this time, he'll be gone a week, to the annual Early Music Festival in New York. As soon as she gets home, she gets out of the car, sets her canvas tote bag on the border where the driveway and the grassy lawn meet, and walks out to the shed in the evening dusk, without even going into the house first. It's close to dark, but the light is still reflected off the bay water, making everything in the garden shimmer; it's been a bright day, with a small rain shower as she returned from the ferry, and now the tall Asiatic lilies are bursting with the last light, and the grass has taken on that cellophaned look that makes Tessa think of estate gardens, stone fountains, girls from the 1920s in white togas acting out Greek tragedies.

The shed looks dark from here, tucked as it is among the pines that line the drive. For a moment, Tessa's afraid of approaching it, and she thinks of the pack of wild dogs. Would wild dogs really attack a person, out on the beach, say, walking alone in the morning light? Or out here, in one's own yard?

But the yard is silent, and Tessa shakes off her fear, approaches the shed with false confidence, careful lest the baby raccoon should be there and she should scare it off.

She opens the door to the shed, propping it open with the rake, wishing there were more light. In a moment her eyes adjust, but she doesn't hear the mewling of the raccoon. She doesn't hear anything, and she thinks, it's dead, isn't it? And then she remembers seeing Damian in the Wisconset hospital, laid out on a table as if he were alive, and Franci standing stock still beside her.

Tessa picks up the flashlight from the spot where it's kept, a little measure of thinking ahead of Jake's, a clever plan, as they've had to use it more than once, for things like putting a rake away or finding the lighter fluid for a rare after-dark barbecue.

She switches the flashlight on, and follows the triangle of light across the shed, until she comes to the bed of old porch cushions. There's no raccoon there, dead or alive, but there is a blooming patch of red, blood that's soaked the cushion through. For a crazy moment, Tessa thinks this somehow has something to do with Jake, that it's some kind of a premonition: *Jake is going to hurt me*. There's still no sound, and gingerly, Tessa steps into the shed, and pushes at the cushion with the toe of her sneaker. The blood still looks a little wet, a bit shiny, and is still bright red. But there's no raccoon here, Tessa now knows; she can feel it.

But what could have possibly happened? Tessa tastes a bit of bile rise in her throat, and she looks around, panicked, then steps backward out of the shed, keeping the flashlight with her as she makes her way toward the steps to the house.

It's nearly dark. As Tessa crosses the lawn to the house, she can see the white lilies standing out against the dark lawn and darker water, glowing in the dusk. She sees her bag sitting where she left it. It looks like a relic, like something from the civilized world left here on the grass by mistake, and she picks it up and carries it inside.

Inside, at first the house seems quieter than ever before, and Tessa stands in the center hall for a long moment, without turning on the lights, just watching the rooms as her eyes adjust. There's a certain night-time bay light that makes it bright enough to see—or maybe it's just that the room and its things are so familiar that she can see them even in the dark. From here, she's smack between the doors that open to each of the living rooms, the formal one to her left, the friendly room to her right, with the old stereo and all the books. Surely there's a book somewhere in there that could tell her what to do? But she doesn't know what she'd begin to look up: raccoon, blood, fear?

She sets the flashlight and her bag on the hall table, and as she does, she hears something, something scratchy and not quite right-sounding coming from the formal room, and before she can be too afraid to see what it is, she steps into the room, switches on the lamp, and sees it, the raccoon, huddled on the sisal rug by the pale yellow club chair, licking its paw so intently that for a long time, it doesn't look up at her. But then it does, with a look of such pain and fear that Tessa cries out, "Oh. Oh, no," clasping her hand over her mouth, even though as she does this, she thinks she's like a heroine in an old movie.

She takes a few steps back into the hall, panicking now, thinking that by now, Jake is on the train, and even if she could reach him, what would he say? That she should have known this would happen. That she should shoot it, probably. Here it is, in his house, bleeding on his furniture, and now Jake will have to find out, and what will he say? What will he do?

If it hadn't been for the accident, she could call Franci, and Franci, ever-capable, a little stern, would be right over, knowing just what to do, but now, she certainly can't call Franci, given that she's still under the care of both Tessa and Peg. And tonight Peg's taken her into Wisconset for a movie and a meal, coaxing her out into society, as if she, Franci, is herself a wild beast.

And so Tessa finds herself at the kitchen table, thumbing through the slim island directory, looking up "Tanaka," thinking even as she does that this is a bad idea, but unable to stop herself. *What else can she do?* she thinks as she finds the number, and punches it in, listening for the scratching sounds from the living room, watching the kitchen doorway for the raccoon.

Kenji is home when the phone rings, slicing cherries from their pits, his fingertips bloodied with the juice, while the green beans steam, and he lets the phone ring once, twice, three times, not in any hurry to answer it; and yet, what if it's her, even though he knows he shouldn't think this, knows it won't be her; why should it be?

But, remarkably, it is. "Hello," he says, after clearing his throat. What could she want? Certainly not what he hopes. And instead, it's something almost better: the raccoon at her house, remember? Well, it's come into the house, injured, and she doesn't know what to do.

"How badly do you think it's injured?" he asks.

"I think it's his paw. It's bleeding. But he looks kind of okay."

"Isn't Jake around? What does he think you should do?" Kenji says, hoping his interest in her husband sounds convincing.

"Oh, he's at a violin festival thing. He won't be back until next weekend. Besides, he doesn't—" Tessa stops herself just short of saying, "He doesn't know about the raccoon," and instead switches lanes. "Anyway, I just thought that you might be able to think of something . . ."

"Well," Kenji says, thinking he'd been planning to go to his studio after eating, "Do you want me to come over and take a look?"

Tessa's on the back porch, sitting on the top step, staring out over the lawn and the water, when she hears the gravel in the driveway disturbed by the tires of Kenji's Jeep. It's a soft sound, not much more noticeable than the sound the dusky breeze is making through the leaves of the maples and the pine boughs and she barely notices it, but she notices it quite strongly, and all this (noticing that she shouldn't, by rights, hear the sound at all, but noticing that she does) fills her with such a mix of dread and longing that for a long moment she's frozen there, unable to move, thinking, *my God, what am I doing*, yet unable to stop herself.

She hears then the sound of his voice, close and yet far at the same time, calling out somewhat timorously, "Tessa?" and then, here he is, and his presence, in his full, three-dimensional self, only confirms for her two things: one, she's been imagining him so much that the reality of him is somewhat shocking, and two, that now he's here, she's even more certain that what she hasn't wanted to be true is: she's terribly attracted to him. And then, three: she's in big trouble.

"Hey," she says, standing, running her hand through her hair. "God, I'm sorry for dragging you over here. I'm sure you have other things to do than to bail out misguided animal lovers—" Even as she's saying this, Tessa catches herself. Why on earth is she sounding so helpless, so apologetic?

"I'm glad you did," Kenji says. "I've been curious about this rogue raccoon all along. Where's the suspect?"

"It's in the living room. Or was. I've been out here since I called you."

Tessa just wants to stay out here on the porch with him. She wants more than anything for Kenji to sit beside her, close, and watch the big night with her. If she were to say this to herself, she wouldn't know what she means, but that's what she wants. But instead, she stands, and walks toward the house. He holds the door for her.

Inside, she turns toward the living room, and switches on a lamp. The raccoon's still there, where it was before, licking at its paw, looking up at them a bit furtively, with that same look of terror on its face. "I think I've found it," Kenji says, almost whispering, and bending down into a crouch. She sees then that he's got a leather bag slung over one shoulder, not quite a doctor's bag, but a bag that could be like a doctor's bag, a bag that could possibly hold some doctoring things, Tessa thinks.

The raccoon hisses as Kenji approaches. "Do you have an old towel?" he asks, and Tessa says, "Of course," and goes into the downstairs bath, rummages in the cabinet under the sink, and comes back with one, white with blue stripes.

"Here," she says, handing it to him, and sees he's dropped his bag onto the sisal rug, has taken out a couple of vials, and is inching toward the raccoon. He takes the towel from her. "Thanks. Do you mind holding him, once I sedate him?" He looks up at her, and she thinks, God help me.

"No," Tessa says, and she doesn't: if anything, being the one to hold the animal will make her feel less like the helpless maiden.

It's quick, and sure, how Kenji throws the towel over the raccoon, injects it with something, and there's a squealing little shriek, and then he passes the toweled animal into her lap, and it goes quiet, and for a moment Tessa thinks he's killed it. He wouldn't do that, would he?

No. Kenji brings out one small paw, and then opens one of the vials, dabs at the wound, opens another one, dabs again, holding the cotton ball pressed tight to the raccoon's wound.

And then the raccoon begins to squirm, and she rises awkwardly from the floor. Just as Kenji gets to the door and opens it, the raccoon turns in Tessa's hands, latching its teeth into the soft flesh of her hand as it explodes from Tessa's arms to land on the porch floor in a scrabble of nails and hissing spit. Tessa cries out, "Hey," and then, "Damn," and then the raccoon is gone into the night.

Tessa waits until they're back inside to show Kenji the bite, thinking, first, that he'll tell her she was stupid to have let it bit her. She even thinks of maybe not showing it to him; she's embarrassed by it, and yet, it hurts like hell. "It bit me," she says, simply, and holds out her hand to him.

"My God, it did," he says, taking her hand. The raccoon's sharp little teeth punctured the skin, and already a bloody bruise is rising there in the soft pad between her thumb and forefinger. Kenji says, "Damn. I'm so sorry. Sit down here," motioning to the club chair, switches on another lamp, and sets about repairing this wound just as he had the other, except this time, she gets up and fetches bandages, and he wraps a long strip of gauze around her hand, like a part of a mitten. "God, Tessa, I'm so sorry," he says again. "I never should have asked you to hold it."

"Yeah, what did you sacrifice me for? I never hurt anyone," she says, and they laugh a little, feeling their status as co-conspirators deepen.

"It's the revenge of the pharmacist. Or no, how about the Sino-Japanese war? Which side were you on, anyway?"

She shakes her head at him. "Kenji," she says, turning serious again. "It's not your fault. It's not a big deal."

"Well, no, but you should see a doctor."

"What, because of rabies?"

Kenji nods, still not looking at her. Stupid idiot, he thinks. Another thing he's fucked up.

"Don't you think the whole rabies thing is a little exaggerated?" Tessa touches the bandage around her hand. It's so clean, and white, and smells medicinal. "And don't you have to go in and get several shots?" She doesn't ask if it will heal by the time Jake comes back up from the city, or how she'll explain this if it doesn't.

"Yes," Kenji says. "You do have go in more than once. And it has to be reported to the state. And you shouldn't wait until you start foaming at the mouth."

She smiles back at him. "But I can't just go to the island clinic, right?" Tessa says, thinking, if she did, somehow it would all get back to Jake: the raccoon in the house, the bite, Kenji here with her.

Kenji walks toward the door, but once there, he stops. "I'll look into it in the morning. You don't have to get the shots immediately; it can wait until Monday. I'll take you, I mean, since Jake's still away. God, it's the least I can do after offering you up like lunch to a wild animal."

"Yeah, you're right," Tessa says, "I didn't know when I called you I was taking my life in my hands." She's laughing a little as she says this, and Kenji laughs, too; they look at each other a moment too long, and then they both turn away.

Standing at the open screen door, watching him walk to his Jeep, watching him fold himself into the front seat, he looks to her like a teenaged boy, a boy just on the verge of growing up, rather than a man with all manner of occult concerns and abilities. "Thanks, Kenji," she calls out after him.

Inside, Tessa throws out the wrapper from the bandage, wishing there were more to be done here, wishing there were more evidence of Kenji's presence. There's the clump of fur he cut away from the raccoon's wound, and the wide bandage on her own hand, which is now beginning to throb.

Twenty

Franci wakes to the silence of the midsummer island; the bullfrogs and the peepers have gone, everything stilled. It's just Franci in her bed, waking, again, in her old t-shirt, restless, waking to see the fat half-moon arcing across the sky. The first night that Leslie slept with her in this bed was on a weekend when Damian, then just twelve, was staying over at Cort's. In the midst of making love, Leslie stopped, saying, "Look, look at that moon," and they lay together, watching the moon in its drift, Leslie trailing her fingertips along Franci's waist.

There's no sleeping for Franci anymore, not real sleeping. She doesn't want to take the Ambien, preferring this, these long hours when she's alone to think about Damian, her son, her lost boy.

She rises, and goes down to the dark night kitchen, where the moonlight is spilling in from the back porch. She pours some of the pinot into a jelly glass, and takes it with her into her study, where she sits at her desk, feet folded under her in her big wooden chair.

There's the familiar clutter of her desk, the dictionaries and Gray's *Anatomy* and style manuals closed and shelved, and the laptop, which now sits at the rear of the desk, its blue light pulsing, as if it could comfort her, as if it's alive.

There's the Visible Man that Leslie gave her teetering on his stand in the back corner, the greenish clay paperweight Damian made for her in kindergarten, a rough-hewn clay iguana from Mexico. And papers, mountains of papers: bills paid and to-be-paid, her calendar under there someplace, notes to herself about Damian, about work, about plans for a day trip or a party with Tessa and Peg. All the stuff of her previous life.

And the little mountain of glass shards she plucked from the accident scene, which has now become the centerpiece of her desk, occupying the space where once she worked on manuscripts.

Again, Franci sees the SUV tumbling over the embankment, Damian pressing his hands to the ceiling of the car, watching the ceiling spill over him like the ceiling of the sheet-tents he'd make on a rainy afternoon here, in this very room.

She has to do something, or she'll go mad. She has to go forward; the summer has inched along, peepers giving way to silence, the moon waxing and waning. And Franci's remained lodged in the night of June 8th, lodged in the back seat of that car, pressing her son to her chest.

But she can't work; she's sent the manuscript she was editing back to Johns Hopkins, unfinished, unpaid. *Grave.* That's all her mind is good for, now, making up morbid rhymes. Still, she sits at the desk, as if waiting for something, looking around the little room. She still hasn't taken down the kite Leslie gave her, a yellow and blue paper kite shaped like a bird, which hangs from the beadboard ceiling above her head. The walls are beadboard, too; this room was at one time a little porch. There's a long, narrow window that looks out onto the backyard and the bay, and the breeze from the night water comes in, smelling damp and grassy.

Sitting in her old wood desk chair, Franci pokes at the pile of glass with one finger. She had thought everything on cars was made of Plexiglas now, but this is the real thing. Tiny shards of the glass thread into her finger, but she doesn't care. When she was a girl, she cut her hand on a windowpane that fractured when she pressed too hard trying to open it; she thought a bit of the glass would travel through her bloodstream to her heart. She doesn't remember how old she was, or why she was so desperate to open the window. Her mother would remember the details. Wouldn't she?

For a long moment, sitting there, Franci wishes now that a bit of the glass would kill her that easily. She's going mad, isn't she? But there isn't any place else for her mind to travel; her thoughts make their way from Damian to the night of the crash, then back to what she has now, what she's left with: this little pile of glass and a mind that's gone flat. Couldn't she die now?

But no. First, she has to write to Cort, tell him—something. She isn't sure what it will be.

Franci looks in the cabinet to the side of her desk, finds a small padded envelope, nondescript, manila, the kind of envelope she uses to send CDs of her editing to Sloan or Hopkins.

She opens the mouth of the envelope, presses the envelope to the edge of the desk, and with the edge of her palm, sweeps the pile of glass in. Most of it falls into the envelope, and what sticks to her hand, she sucks off. She's crying again. Franci then addresses the envelope, finds her stash of stamps, puts on enough postage to get it where it's going, and takes it to the front of the house, where she tucks it beside the hallway phone, into the spot where she lets the outgoing mail accumulate.

She takes her jelly glass of wine upstairs with her, gets into bed, feeling she's done something, almost as if she's moving ahead.

Twenty-One

Claude Reigner was one of the first to know about the accident. After he brought the kids over on the last crossing that night, he shut the engines down and walked to the cottage, rubbed Ben-Gay on his aching shoulder, both like and entirely unlike Mara used to do, then settled into bed, shutting down his own creaking engines, only to be rousted in minutes by the crackle of the emergency radio, Cop Cal's young officer saying there'd been an accident, they needed the ferry for the ambulance.

Right away, he thought *but Damian was driving*, as if this could explain the impossibility of an accident. While he waited on the bridge for the red pulsing light to appear through the rain at Sexton's Hill, as if mistrusting his own memory, he looked at the entry he'd made in the log: *Damian at the wheel.*

Since the accident, he hasn't spent much of the slow moments as he usually does, making notes in his meticulous log or penciling answers into his crossword puzzle book, finding a five-letter word for *worry* or an eight-letter word for *matched set.*

Rather, he's looked out at the bay water, puzzling instead over the things that don't make sense. He doesn't like to think this way, but now Mara's not around to nudge him back, he does: he thinks of all the changes on Grand Isle, the big houses going up, thinks of the kids he's seen turn bad out of boredom and those who turn bad due to a lack of love; he thinks of losing Mara. It's like probing an achy tooth with his tongue; since the accident, mostly he puzzles over how the good die young. He's stumped over how Damian could have gone off the road; he's known both kids since they were small, and he knows that while they were something of a pair the way kids thrown together for summers get to be, they certainly weren't bookends. Cort, horsing around with the dock lines, pretending to climb over the rail, then always saying "thanks" at the crossing's end, but giving what Claude knows is the fake smile reserved for the help. And Damian, head in the clouds, chattering with Claude about inventions to make the ferry better, such as having more "commodious accommodations," to make Claude comfortable on the bridge, as he advised when he was six. Damian, at nine, asking if he could read Claude's log book. "There's too much private information in there," Claude explained, telling Damian what he didn't tell anyone, that he noted not just times of crossings and the schedule of the tides, but also who crossed when, with whom. The log book holds a record, to the second, of each arrival and departure, fuel used, monies received and paid out, an almanac of wind, and heat, and rain.

And with a hand no less meticulous he tracks the comings and goings of the people of Grand Isle, sometimes elaborating on what he observes, other times allowing a few words to fill in. On a certain Wednesday a year previous: "Dick Grasso, without Marilyn," followed, over that summer, by a complete record of the dissolution of their marriage as told in ferry crossings.

If anyone had asked, Claude wouldn't have had a ready answer as to why he kept these records; he just liked observing the people of Grand Isle and their habits, he'd say, even though, if he looked a little deeper, he might know that he found comfort there, in watching over the troubled waters of those whose lives seemed so glass-smooth at first unknowing glance.

Now, he still meditates on that crossing in June, runs over again who said what, how he bent in close to see Kylie Pickett in the front seat, obviously drunk and giggly; how he leaned in to get a sniff of Damian's breath, even though he knew Damian wasn't one to take chances. Even though he knows there are things that happen that bear no explaining, like Mara. Even though he knows anything could have happened that night. Even though he knows the log book doesn't lie.

Five in the morning on Sunday and it's turned blustery, as if the early heat of the summer created more pressure than the island's atmosphere could hold, and, pent up, it's exploded in this windy tug of rain.

In the control room at the ferry dock, Claude keys the numbers in to rev the ferry's engines, pleased again by the ratchety sound of the machine doing its work. He opens up the waiting room, where in winter and on rainy days like this, foot passengers congregate, steam rising from their coffee and their coats. He plugs in the coffee pot, straightens the few plastic folding chairs, then starts when he hears a quick rap on the door. When he sees it's Cop Cal, he isn't surprised.

"Morning, Claude." With the silence that comes of familiarity, Claude says nothing, just takes down another coffee cup, and motions Cal to sit in one of the chairs.

"It's terrible, what happened," Claude begins, and Cal nods.

"The worst part of my job," Cal says, "is pulling a dead kid from a wreck."

"You pulled him out yourself?" Claude says, feeling the relief of his suspicion ebbing away.

"Well, not quite. Cort did that. But we got there pretty quick," Cal says, not adding that Damian's body was still warm to the touch, that he still looked as if he could come round, if it weren't for the terrible, unnatural bend in his neck.

Claude nods, suspicion back.

"How's Franci holding up? She hasn't gone off-island since."

"About like you'd think, I guess. Lucky she's got those friends, Peg and Tessa." Cal shifts in the seat, and Claude hands him a cup of coffee, light, the way he likes it.

They talk of other things, the crowds that ferried over for the funeral, the cell phone tower, the town budget that'll come up in the fall.

"Want another cup?" Claude asks, then checks his watch. "Joyce Rexman will be coming in soon for the five-thirty."

"Is she still working those crazy hours at the hospital?" Cal asks, shaking his head. "Pretty girl like her."

Claude keeps quiet; he doesn't gossip about what he learns from ferrying his passengers back and forth.

"So," Cop Cal says, pulling his notepad from his back pocket. "I wanted to check with you, see if you remember anything when they came over on the ferry."

"You mean, Damian and Cort and the girls? You mean, like who was driving."

"Yeah."

"Oh, Damian was driving, I remember that. I had a few words with him, just to check, you know."

"Sure."

"He seemed fine. You know, he was a good worker the past couple summers. I never figured him for a big drinker or anything like that. Never had to worry about him when he came onto the ferry late, even though he's only had his license a couple years. Now, that other one, Cort Grasso, him I'd worry about more."

"But he wasn't driving, right?"

"That's right. It was definitely Damian behind the wheel." Claude takes a drink from his coffee, and Cal makes a note, folds up his notepad, jams it into the hind pocket of his uniform pants.

"Okay, then," he starts, but then Claude says, "Definitely Damian was behind the wheel, at least when they came onto the ferry."

"What do you mean?"

"I mean, they had to switch drivers anyway, right? Didn't Cort have to drop Damian off at Franci's place out on West Shore Road?"

"Yeah, of course," Cal says. Another tear in the fabric of *case closed*, even though he doesn't have much reason to think that anything happened that night other than what the kids say happened. "But they must have been heading to Dead Man's Beach before calling it a night," Cal says. All he has is a hunch; there's no getting away from the evidence: the girls' word matched up with Cort's, and the injuries would be consistent with either being an unbelted back seat passenger or the driver, up front. If Cal pursues this crazy thought of his, that Damian wasn't driving, he'll look a fool, unless he has something more to go on than a bad feeling and a prejudice against the richest summer kid. He'd have to start all over, call the ME's office in Wisconset, and they'll start asking questions about why he didn't ask this sooner, why didn't he investigate the scene, if there was any suspicion at all? Why would he take the word of the kid who was driving his father's SUV?

Cal steps back out into the blustery gray morning; the waves are whipping up and over the dock, the ferry rocking with the tug and splash. He feels the real answer about why he hasn't looked further into the accident whisper to him, so softly he can't hear it over the noise of the coming storm; it's soft as the whisper the wind makes whistling up to East Shore Road, up to the new, big houses that have taken over the cliff that looks down to the sea, the whisper of the linen dresses of the summer people as they pass along the common, the whispering sigh of the women in line at Lantman's when they learn there are no porcini mushrooms or Pecorino cheese. It's the whisper he's heard all his life, the steam heat hissing on in his frigid bedroom, hissing along with his parents' kitchen argument, his mother bitching: *why isn't there ever enough?*

Cal slides into the driver's seat of the police car, adjusting his belt with all its equipment, then sits for a minute, as if waiting for something. He should investigate further, but if he does, and if Cort's found to have been driving after all, what will that do to the island, to both the summer and winter residents? What will it do to the girls, Kylie and Betheny? What will it do to Franci? He's so reluctant to admit it that it's barely a thought, but it's there: Cort's dad is one of the island's most powerful summer people.

Cal starts the car, wipers on high, and heads back to the station, carefully braking as he rounds the curve at Dead Man's Beach. The rain is really coming down now, as it must have been at the time of the accident, the pavement fully wet. It wasn't necessarily the booze bubbling up in the driver's blood, clouding his reaction time, jellying his legs and arms. Couldn't it just have been the rain?

Twenty-Two

"Morning, Ken—leaving Marie in charge today?" Claude begins, when he sees who's coming on the ferry on Monday morning, and then he sees Tessa in the passenger seat, and "Oh, hello Tessa," he says, his tone changing just a bit, from something jocular to the more formal, the shift of language as it's changed for the summer people.

"Yeah," Kenji says. "I've got to pick up some welding things in Wisconset—"

"And I couldn't kick my Honda into life this morning," Tessa adds, hearing how this sounds even to her like an unnecessary excuse.

"You're lucky to have such charming company." Claude leaves it at that, taking the bills from Kenji, "You'll want your receipt, I suppose," he adds, handing Kenji a ticket stub.

That's how easy it is to have an affair, even on a small island, as long you're good to the ferry master, Claude thinks, even though he never would have figured it, never would have thought Tessa, who always seemed to really be in love with Jake, would even look at anyone else. But then, there's no accounting for what goes on among the summer people.

The air is clear, and Claude can see all the way to the mainland as the ferry lurches into the waters.

Once they're on the ferry, and he dares look over at Tessa beside him in his Jeep, Kenji thinks she looks a little pale. He looked it up as soon as he got home from her house that night, and he was right that she could wait on the rabies shot. It seemed the best thing, to encourage her to wait a couple of days, encourage her to talk it over with Jake.

"The rabies seems to be holding off," Kenji says, peering at her. He reaches over, takes her chin in his hand, and for a moment she thinks he's going to kiss her, but he turns her head left, then right. "Yeah, no evidence of foaming. No whiskers or mask appearing yet. You've still got some time."

Tessa makes a growling noise low in her throat, ending in a short bark, and Kenji gives a mock-startled look, and then they're at the mainland, and go bumping off the ferry.

Instead of getting on the highway, Kenji takes the water-side road that slips along the shore to Wisconset, passing the marina, under the shrieks of the gulls; a few sails dot the blue water. They've got the windows down. Everything on the other side of the road is awash with summer green; it seems that since her last trip off-island, the green has deepened, painted with another, darker layer of color.

Tessa asks about Kenji's sculpture, and "It's kind of brutalist," he says, and she laughs. "But you seem like the most unbrutal person."

"Damn. All those years of cultivating my machismo, wasted. No, brutalist, looks kind of like a car crash, but charming: an artistic wreck. Really. But you'll have to see it. Instead, I want to know what all this is about the Arctic. Isn't it kind of hard to study something that's disappearing?"

"If I could manage to sit at the desk for more than ten minutes at a time, maybe I'd get something done," she says, but she immediately hears her own criticism of herself, and this repels her; *stop*, she tells herself, and switches course: she describes for him what she saw in the Arctic, how the icebergs were tinged with a blue so unusual it seemed unreal, how the icebergs were so huge—even just the part you could see—that it made her dizzy to be in a little boat beside them. How seeing the glaciers made the entire system of the earth real to her in a way it hadn't been before: "It was like I was seeing a truth about life, like seeing a baby being born, or watching someone die. *It's true, it's true!*" she slaps her palms to her knees, in what kind of emotion she wouldn't be able to say.

Kenji laughs. "I know just what you mean."

"Unfortunately, it's also true that soon it'll be gone. I hear that it's a different place there, now. When I was up there, it was August, and we got blocked in by a brigade of rogue icebergs; that doesn't happen anymore, at least not in summer."

"Just the end of the world, right? Nothing a total, abrupt halt to modern life won't fix," Kenji says.

The clinic is generically like any such clinic in any small city in North America, with a small waiting room populated by an assortment of the sick: a too-skinny teenaged girl, knee jiggling, engrossed in a tiny electronic device in her hands; a big-bellied man slumped over his suspendered shirt; a couple of college girls, summer people—their manes nicely brushed, freshly washed, whispering to one another while managing a flurry of texting in their hands. One other woman of roughly middle age, two young children seated on the chairs on either side of her, looking tired and harassed. Kenji feels a flicker of pride, walking in with Tessa, as the heads turn and they're appraised; this offsets the uneasiness he often feels in these white, northern towns, where he's usually the only Asian anyone's seen, except the staff at Szechuan Fire. He guides her into the room with the slightest pressure of his palm flat to the small of her back.

Once she tells the clerk her reason for being there, holding up her bandaged hand as if it's evidence, she and Kenji take their seats, and neither one reaches for a magazine. If she loved him back, Kenji thinks, wouldn't she be holding his hand now with her good hand—Jake or no Jake? He imagines how cool her smooth palm would be in his hand.

After she's called away, he walks over to the entrance, takes out his cell phone. After three rings, Marie picks up the pharmacy phone. He repeats his story of needing to pick up welding wire and Argon/CO_2, but Marie doesn't understand any of this, doesn't care.

"Sure, Kenji, don't worry about it," she says, brightly. The Grand Isle Clinic pharmacy will cover any emergency prescriptions, just as they do on Sundays. "Fine, fine," Kenji says, nodding, as if nodding will somehow add conviction to his words.

Back in the waiting room, Kenji finds himself sitting with an old copy of *National Geographic* on his lap, waiting, and there is such a deep pleasure in waiting for Tessa that he sees her before him even as he's thumbing through the pages of photos of coyotes on the open plains. *Canis latrans.*

She comes out, at last, smiling her crooked smile. She holds up her hand, almost triumphantly. She's so small, there in the big white hallway, in her little striped dress, looking almost like a child. She comes over to him, and he stands, and to his great surprise, relief, and terror, she presses up onto the tiptoes of her sneakers and kisses him on the cheek, a long kiss, pressing his head against her lips with her good hand.

"Well," he says. "Everything okay, then?" And she laughs. "Yes. They gave me the shot, the first one. I have to get two more. And the nurse bandaged me up."

He picks up her hand and turns it, side to side. "I'd say you're pretty well mummified," he says. He gently drops her hand back down. "We don't have to worry about foaming?" He's joking, of course, but Tessa feels a chill: she does feel as if she's becoming, if not rabid, certainly changed. Nothing, she knows, will ever be the same after this, no matter what happens. And this, seeing that something enormous is about to change, feels much more dangerous than the raccoon's bite.

She shakes her head, suddenly frightened, and shy, and they walk together out into the bright parking lot.

All the long ride home, Kenji is thinking of that touch, feeling still her fingertips on his cheek. Tessa isn't really thinking on the way back to the island, she's just a welter of feeling, in particular a growing dread of what Jake would say if he knew of this trip, along with a pleasantly claustrophobic feeling of being in the interior of Kenji's rattly Jeep, smelling a little of old cigars and newspaper.

When Kenji pulls into her driveway, she's a little startled to find herself home already. She wants more than anything to just stay in the car with him like this, but instead, she puts her hand—her right hand, the unbandaged one—on the door pull, starts to say, "Thank you—"

"Listen, Tessa," Kenji says, and this is enough to stop her. "Look, I want you to come by the studio sometime, if you think it's okay with Jake." And he looks at her then. She's always known, of course, that his eyes are dark, but now she sees how black they are, black as the eyes of an animal.

"Sure," she says, the confusion, which by now is becoming familiar, rising inside her. "Maybe we could both come by. I mean, maybe I could bring Jake." Kenji looks back down again, nodding, as if he'd been expecting precisely this. Through the open window, she can hear the tall pines rustling a little in the island winds. "Kenji," she says, "I love having your friendship. Really."

"Yeah," he says, looking back up at her again, and Tessa says, "Thank you. Thanks," and then she does open the door, leaning her weight against it as if it's the heaviest thing in the world. Standing in the driveway, she waves her bandaged hand a little at him, and he waves back before turning, then pulling up the drive and back onto the road that will lead him back to town.

Three years before, when Jake first told Tessa that his uncle was selling his camp on the island, she pictured a summer camp, the kind she'd gone to as a little girl, a main lodge with long wooden communal tables and little cabins scattered about. She remembered stumbling around in the rocky wood-smelling darkness in Maine, needing to pee and unable to find the outhouse. Peeing in the dark under the stars, and then worrying that somehow someone had seen.

She looked at him across the table, her soup spoon halfway to her lips. She'd made a cold tomato bisque, even though it wasn't yet summer, and even though she felt she was cheating the hours allocated to her research while she chopped and then pureed.

"A camp?" She knew she was putting on what she thought of as her quizzical wife expression, wrinkling up her eyebrows and smiling a little, an expression she learned long ago from old tv shows.

Jake laughed, said, "Not that kind of camp," as if he knew what she was thinking, as if he could see the summer camp in Maine, with the smell of something musty that never went away. "You wouldn't know this, but up there they're called camps. Really it's a little summer place, like a cottage."

"And you think you should buy it from him?"

"That's what I'm thinking. I've hardly been there since I was a kid; I can barely remember it. But Peg and Torsten have a place right down the shore, and Dick and Marilyn have a place there, too. Wouldn't it be great to have a place on Grand Isle, right on the water?"

And so they went up, for the weekend. On the drive up, he put in a CD of Mozart's clarinet concerto, and she watched as the long flat fields of the mainland bunched into hillocks, then mountains, then flattened again. How had she gotten herself into this situation, involved with her older sister's friend from music school, who was so knowledgeable and charming, and who, she was now just beginning to see, had a way of slicing her words with the blade of his wit, or his intelligence. Cruelty? It was hard to tell. Every time she thought he was making fun of her, or being controlling, he'd do something so endearing that she'd be reeled back in again. He was romantic in an old-fashioned way, bringing her flowers and leaving her quirky notes decorated with his little drawings, singing arias to her while they waited for the subway.

They ferried over the grayish waters of the bay, then pulled into a motel near the dock, a slightly broken-down place, but it was the only choice on the island in the off season. The one good place, the Marble Rock Inn, was closed until Memorial Day weekend.

It was very early spring, and everything was damp. Along the dirt roads to the camp, Tessa could see the trunks of the trees stained with rain. There was still a winter chill to the air, and if the sun hadn't been out, one could imagine snow. When they came down the long sloping driveway in the early morning, Tessa didn't even see the squat little house that was falling into disrepair, a green shingle missing here and there, a section of pipe lying across the small patch of grass. All she saw was the wide swath of the bay, open to the pale blue sky.

The slam of their car doors echoed across the water. Tessa's shoes slipped a little on the soft carpet of pine needles. She was wearing capris, and the damp grass tickled at her ankles. A few winter birds, chickadees and sparrows, chirped in the high pine trees. They were so close, she could see their faces.

While she looked up into the trees, Jake walked around the old camp. Like many of the camps, it was painted dark green, with white trim, and plywood boards painted white still covering the windows from the winter. The paint was peeling, heavily, having come off the window frames in long strips to lie on the pine-needled ground. He circled the camp, then came back to where Tessa was now looking out over the water, shielding her eyes with her hand.

"Tessa, this is great!" he said. "I cannot believe how much better it is than I remembered. Can you picture it, fixed up? Come on, picture it."

"I can picture it," she said, laughing. She turned to face him. He wasn't that much older, just six years, but he had an avuncular way about him that made her feel both protected and, though she couldn't admit it yet, patronized. He was almost forty-seven. They'd been seeing each other just four months. She looked into his face. He was going to buy the cottage, she thought then, in that way that inevitability makes something knowable. He was going to buy the cottage, and he still wouldn't know her the way she wanted him to.

"It's going to be a ton of work—it won't be any cakewalk buying it, either, but what a great opportunity." He took the flashlight from the glove box in the car, humming "Golliwog's Cakewalk."

He pushed away from the car, and gingerly walked up the porch steps, testing them. From under an empty terra cotta pot on the porch, he slipped out a house key, jiggled it into the door handle, and the door opened.

Inside, the house was dark, and musty, a bright smell that made Tessa sneeze. In a tool box near the back door, Jake found a hammer and a screwdriver and they took these tools back outside, and together they pried the white plywood from the windows, stacking it alongside the steps to the porch.

When they went back in, the place looked bigger. A central staircase disappeared into the darkness above. There were two small living rooms; in one, there was a sofa, and two easy chairs, all covered with white sheets. A bookcase with some paperbacks and a couple of board games moldering on the shelves. They walked down a dark hallway and into the kitchen at the back of the house.

Jake turned the faucet, but the water hadn't been turned on for the summer yet, and there was just a noise like wind being blown through a long empty pipe.

It was only when Tessa spoke that she realized they'd been silent except for Jake's humming since coming into the house.

"What do you think?" she said. She didn't know at that point that if their conversation could be transcribed, she'd see how often she asked Jake a question and how infrequently she made a statement of opinion; she didn't know yet that his moods could change like quicksilver.

"It's smaller than I remembered it," he said again. "But I think it's pretty damn fabulous." He leaned against the kitchen counter and crossed his arms.

Even with the shutters taken down, the kitchen wasn't bright. It was still morning, and the kitchen, in the back of the house, wouldn't ever get bright, not even in the afternoon when the sun finally made its arc across the water.

She crossed the kitchen and stood next to him, leaning her head against his shoulder. "I think it's a sweet house."

"That's because you're a sweet girl," he said. He kissed the top of her head, but he didn't break his arms apart to embrace her, and they stood for a long time like that. He was thinking about the work involved in owning a camp; his uncle had been coming up here for years, doing the maintenance himself, and still the place was falling apart. He'd seen how much work his friends had to put into their places; when would he have any time for his violins?

She was thinking about how she could feel his muscled shoulder where she leaned her head against him. She was thinking about his smell, a smell like hay lying out in the sun.

How much are the taxes, he thought.

I'm pregnant, she thought.

She wasn't sure why she hadn't told him yet. When she first missed her period, she hadn't thought much of it; she chalked it up to the tension of entering the final stretch of her evaluation for tenure. It seemed that suddenly everyone in the department wanted something from her. Plus, at forty, her periods could be starting to falter and skip, she thought.

But now, by this weekend, she was sure of it. She'd visited her doctor, not telling Jake.

Now, she thought she could feel something in there, growing. She knew it was too early for this, but she felt as if she was ballooning up from the inside out, and she was surprised that Jake couldn't see this, couldn't sense it when he saw her undress or when he was making love to her. But she didn't say anything. It was almost as if by not saying anything, she could make the baby disappear.

The plain fact was, she didn't want a baby. She wanted to go back to the Arctic, before it was gone, and to go back again, and again.

They stood in the kitchen like that for a long time.

"Let's go upstairs," Jake said, and he switched on the flashlight and she followed him up to the second story, which was dark and a little spooky. She was careful to hold on to the railing, and felt a little queasy going up. On the landing, he turned and took her hand.

"I think there are two bedrooms," he said, leading her into the one in the back. It was small, with slanted attic ceilings. Two single twin beds. He swept the circle of light across the wooden floor, up the wall covered in paper with tiny, delicate lavender flowers.

Her queasy feeling increased, and she suddenly felt she needed the bathroom, but she remembered there was no water, and thought, no, she'd better hold it. "I remember this room," he said. "This was my cousin's room, where we slept." And then he turned, and opened the door of the front bedroom.

"Hold this for me," he said, handing her the flashlight, and he opened the windows, then pushed open the shutters, and the light from the bay flooded into the room.

This was the best of the rooms, with a double bed with spool posters, covered in a white chenille spread, and the floor painted a bright, hard blue. They stood together at the windows. From up here, they could see the water stretching out before them, wide and open, crinkling with light in the morning sun. They could see, on the far shore of the bay, the conference center with its string of tiny cabins perched high above the water, and far to the right, heading out toward the Atlantic, a single sail.

"I'd forgotten about this view," Jake said, leaning one hand against the ledge just above the window, and that's when she felt it, a cramp low in her belly, like monthly cramps only worse, and she tried not to say anything, tried to hold it in, but then another one came and she reached out for his arm. "I—" was all she could say.

He sat her down on the bed. She could feel the blood, wet and warm between her legs, and she thought that the blood would soak through to the white spread covering the bed. She could smell the dark upstairs smell of dust and floorboards and something else, too. It smelled like something dead.

"What's wrong?" he asked, solicitous. He was watching her face closely in that way she loved.

"I'm pregnant," she said. She hadn't meant to say this; it just came out. Another cramp came then, like a huge fist gripping her insides, and she cried out again. Her pants would be ruined with the stain.

"I think I'm losing it," she said, and her eyes filled. He laid her down onto the bed. He was a violin maker, not a doctor or even a veterinarian or even a farmer's son. There was no phone, not for miles, and now he could see the blood seeping out into the lime green of her pants.

But he was the man, and he had to think of something. There wasn't even any water in this house. He sat on the edge of the bed, holding her hand. He wiped her forehead with a corner of the bedspread, and it came away wet. She was pale, and then she started to shake.

He moved, as if to rise, thinking he'd lift her in his arms and carry her to the car, but she clung onto his hand, and she looked so frightened and wild-eyed that he couldn't go.

He smoothed his hand over her forehead, waited with her silently, and she knew then that in spite of everything, his condescension, the way he could be sharp with her, that he loved her. He'd change; he'd have to change, because now she couldn't leave him with this, this cottage, the memory of this moment, the baby neither of them wanted bleeding into the old, soft bed.

They left the camp that afternoon, and stayed at the motel. From the motel, she called her doctor, who said as long as the bleeding had stopped she should take it easy and come in when they got back to the city. These things happen, more often than you'd think, he'd said, but after they got home and he examined her, he told her there was something wrong, that her body couldn't support a baby, couldn't "sustain" it, he said.

His office had been too cold, overly cooled by the air conditioner pumping away in the unexpected April heat wave.

She didn't want to tell Jake about this, even though she knew he'd be glad, relieved that she wouldn't suddenly change her mind and start pressuring him to have a baby with her. At night, she'd lie in bed and imagine her fragile female systems in there, as if they were made of tissue paper instead of real tissue, pale pink tissue paper crumpled up to form a weak uterine lining, a pair of ovaries like paper drums, paper-straw fallopian tubes.

Now, Tessa leans against the porch rail, listening to the sound of Kenji's Jeep fade. It's true, what she said: she does love having his friendship. She's happy here; she's making a life with Jake. They have a history; this is what matters, this is what's real.

Twenty-Three

The water is still, as it often is in the late afternoon, and Franci, from her spot on the back porch steps, picks up a flat pebble from the step below, and side-winds it out across the lawn. It skims the surface of the water once, then drops. In the same moment, she has a vision of Damian, at about five, standing beside her at the water's edge, as she showed him how to flick his wrist just so to make the stone defy the laws of gravity for a moment. "Look, the house is a stone's throw from the water, literally," Stiles said in the memory, Damian looking up and saying, "Yeah," laughing only because they were laughing, too young to know what was funny.

Tuesday afternoon, and she's already looked at the mail, already spent a few hours in her study staring at the manuscript she should be working on, not making one mark. The storm has left the air even heavier with humidity, as if it isn't really done raining, but just gave up with all the business of lashing wind. The marsh looks storm-tossed, littered with floating branches and twigs, and the garden's a rain-soaked mess.

She lights a cigarette, inhaling greedy lungfuls and then watching the smoke steam out from her nostrils. She gave up smoking when she was pregnant, and she had thought she'd never go back to it. Then again, she thought a lot of things, things that were no longer true, and wouldn't be.

Even though she's known among her friends as the consummate list-maker, Franci doesn't bother with making a list; she knows what she has to do this week: cancel the reservation on the room at the conference center she'd been planning to use for Damian's twentieth birthday party, cancel the reservations for their annual trip to Montreal; disconnect the new land line. And call the girl who left the message. Phoenix.

But for now, Franci sits on the porch steps, thinking about the things she has to do. Maybe she'll make one call today. She tamps her cigarette out into the planter, and in one move, before she can chicken out, she gets up and opens the screen door to the kitchen, but just as she's picking up the phone book to get the number for the conference center, she hears a knock at the front door, so she's a little confused, a little off-balance, when she goes to the front door to open it.

Through the screen—she rarely shuts the glass-paned door—she can see a girl, about eighteen, in overalls, cinnamon-skinned, her blondish hair cultivated into heavy dreadlocks. Now what, Franci thinks, and opens the door, prepared to give directions to the conference center or to tell the girl she doesn't want to donate to Greenpeace.

It's only when Franci opens the door to speak the girl, to get rid of her, that she sees the girl's suitcase, an old plaid thing that must date to the 1960s, and then she sees the telltale straps of a knapsack over the girl's delicate shoulders.

"Mrs. Weiseman?" the girl says. She smiles, and Franci sees she's got good, straight, very white teeth. Her eyes are a startling green.

"Yes?"

"Is Damian here? I'm a friend of his."

Oh. Oh. No. "Are you Phoenix?" Franci feels her face tightening from the effort of this conversation, even though it's just begun.

"Yes," Phoenix says, warily. She has a tiny, delicate silver hoop piercing one eyebrow. "Is he home?"

Franci doesn't answer. "Come in," she says, and Phoenix lifts her suitcase with apparent effort and lugs it into the entrance, blinking a few times at the sudden darkness. "You can put that down here," Franci says, pointing to the bare wood floor under the coat hooks. Damian's denim jacket is still hanging there, next to the now-rumpled brown linen jacket she wore to the funeral.

Phoenix deposits the suitcase and shrugs off the knapsack, then stretches her arms over her head and yawns. "Sorry," she says, "it was a long trip. And man, it's so hot."

"Let's sit down," Franci says, and Phoenix follows her into the living room. Franci sits in the same chair she sat in when the cops were here; it's the only chair she sits in now.

The living room is filled with light reflecting from the water at the side of the house, igniting the lemon lilies that Tessa brought over, standing straight up in their vase.

Phoenix sits on the sofa, spreading her arms out to either side, and leans her head back. "It's great to be off that bus!" she says. Franci catches with surprise the familiar, old smell of patchouli oil: do kids really still use patchouli oil?

Franci wants to lie to this girl, to tell her Damian's out, tell her that he's gone to see his father, or he's run away with Betheny. Anything but the truth. Instead, she leans forward, elbows on her knees, until Phoenix looks at her.

"What?" the girl says, sitting up a little straighter, squinting her eyes warily. "What's wrong? This *is* Damian's house, right?"

"Yes. I'm his mother," Franci says. She'll always be that, won't she? "Phoenix, Damian was in a car accident. He died." And for the first time in the many times she's said this in the past weeks, Franci doesn't cry. She can't break down in front of this girl, who is so young that Franci can see the downy hair along her arms, delicate as a spider's silk. In the pocket of silence that follows, Franci sees that Phoenix is very beautiful, in a way that years ago would be called "exotic," but now is nearly ordinary. And, despite the squirrel's nest hair, she's well-kempt, her skin clear and unblemished, eyes alight with intelligence, humor, kindness. She's been cared for. Right away, Franci sees why this girl appealed to Damian, and she's filled with a rush of love for him.

"He died? Damian died?" Phoenix slaps her hands into her lap. "But I just got here. That can't be right." She shakes her head a little, side to side, as if by shaking her head she'll make this untrue. Only then does Franci feel the tears sting her eyes.

"No, it isn't right," she says, taking a shaky breath. Why did this girl have to show up now? Couldn't Franci have at least had a couple of weeks to suffer alone, to lie on Damian's bed and sob for him, without having to worry about taking care of some freaked-out teenager who imagines herself in love?

"It isn't right, but it's true," Franci says, almost cruelly, with a low note of anger in her voice. She leans back into her chair and looks up at the mantelpiece clock on the bookshelf, more out of habit than out of wanting to know the time; there is no time in this timeless bubble of the world without Damian.

And then Phoenix begins to cry, her face melting as Franci watches, and the girl makes no effort to stem the flow, but cries with her mouth gaping open, her face reddening and bare, until soon she's sobbing uncontrollably, sitting straight up on the sofa, like a baby.

At first Franci sighs at this, but she is, after all, a mother—is she still a mother?—and she gets up and sits next to the girl and takes her into her arms, holding her, smoothing her hand along the girl's trembling, convulsing back, until the girl's crying subsides and she hiccups once, twice, then falls into a deep, dead sleep.

Franci gently moves herself out from under the girl's weight, pushes one of the small chintz pillows under her head, and pulls the thin Mexican blanket over her. The afternoon light has shifted, and the lilies look dull and ordinary and comforting in the tall glass vase, and Franci returns to her post on the back porch, where she can watch the night descend.

When, later, the phone rings and Franci answers, she tells herself it isn't really that she's hiding anything; it's just that she doesn't mention Phoenix to Peg.

"Are you sure you don't want to come over? We're just going to grill some chicken, and there's plenty here," Peg says. Franci can hear Torsten in the background call out, "Tell her we raided Lantman's entire poultry department. We left not a feather."

"I'm okay, really. I've had dinner with someone every night this week. You and Tess have been terrific," Franci says. "But I have to start adjusting on my own now."

"Have you spoken to Tessa?"

"She called earlier. She invited me over too, and I declined her invitation as well." Franci plays with her cigarette pack, tapping it against the doorjamb. She hasn't smoked in front of any of her friends; it's her little secret, her small personal way of hurting herself. What does it matter, now, if she dies of lung cancer like her mother did? "Really, Peg, I'm just looking forward to having some pasta and watching *Idol* and going to bed. I'll be fine."

"If you insist. But you'll call me if you can't sleep, won't you? We'd love to have you stay over if you ever want." Franci can hear Torsten in the background: "There's practically a whole guest wing she'd have to herself."

"I will. And I'll call you and Tessa in the morning."

As Franci's hanging up the kitchen phone, Phoenix appears in the doorway, looking sleepy and stunned.

"Hi," Franci says. "Do you think you'd want some dinner? "I don't know," Phoenix says, stuffing her hands in the big pockets of her overalls. "I feel hungry, but I feel sick, too. I can't believe it," she says, and her face puckers again with tears.

"Come on," Franci says, going to the doorway and putting an arm around Phoenix's shoulder. Several platitudes rush into her head at once: *It'll all be okay, It's not that bad, is it?* But as soon as each arises, she dismisses it, again and again with the realization that it isn't okay, that a terrible, irrevocable, impossible thing has happened, and it is done, and nothing will make Damian live again. So instead, she says, "Come on, let's have a smoke."

Phoenix gives her the most skeptical look Franci has ever seen, her eyebrows reaching high up toward her hairline, her eyes rolling down incredulously. "Oh God, I don't mean that," Franci says, laughing a little, and then she catches herself. Laughing a little. How can a person laugh when her son is dead?

"I mean these," she says, waving the pack of Camels. "Come on," she says again, and turns toward the back door.

Outside, on the steps, it's as if Franci and Phoenix are in their own little intimate universe, a little time-stopped blister of grief. They sit and smoke and look out over the garden and out to the water. They can hear the small waves of the brackish bay splash against the tall beach grasses. Without preamble, Franci says, "You would have loved him when he was little. He was curious about everything, and I couldn't believe how he soaked up the world, like he just opened his eyes in the morning and drank in everything he could until he fell asleep. He was thirsty for everything. I'd answer one question and he'd be on to the next, asking me things like why are June bugs called June bugs when we only see them in July and what is an atomic bomb and what does "ahbright" mean?

"Ahbright? What *does* it mean?"

Franci laughs a little, again, a short snort, and again, she catches herself, and feels her eyes fill. "I'd recited Hopkins' 'God's Grandeur' to him, I guess I glossed over the enunciation, and he thought it was one word in the line, 'with Ah! Bright wings.' "

Phoenix nods. "He recited that poem to me a couple of times," she says. She takes a long draw on the cigarette and coughs a little. *Damian memorized it? When?* But instead of asking this, Franci says,

"Have you ever smoked before? God, I don't want to give you this awful habit. I thought all teenagers smoked."

Phoenix waves her hand, the one with the cigarette, then pushes back a clump of her matted hair. "Don't worry. I've been smoking one thing or another since I was about nine."

"Oh, come on. That isn't true. You're just trying to sound cool," Franci says.

Phoenix looks at her and smiles, and again, Franci thinks how nice her smile is, with those good, straight teeth. "Yeah. You're right. I've smoked cigarettes before, though, and pot. Not often."

They're silent again, just the buzzing of the peepers and the lapping of the water, and the occasional mysterious sound of an animal rustling in the garden. The groundhog, Franci thinks, the groundhog that was so oddly out at night—was it only four weeks ago?—when she stood out here until Damian woke and brought her back inside.

Phoenix maneuvers her cigarette end so that it's resting on the tip of her index finger, ready to be flicked across the lawn. She looks questioningly at Franci, who says, "Go ahead. Why not?" and they watch the orange wick spin out over the dark grass, into the night, where it lands in the pebbles of the beach and glows for a few seconds longer before disappearing.

"So," Franci says. "How long were you going to stay?" She reaches to the pack of cigarettes and lights another from the lit end of the first.

Phoenix's lip trembles, and Franci can see silent tears leak down her cheeks. Okay. So it will be this way for awhile, and isn't that right?

"I don't know. My dad—well, Damian thought I had like this perfect life in San Francisco, with these really hip parents and everything, but it isn't like that. My dad's gay, and he's really preoccupied right now with his boyfriend, his shrink, his house. You know. And my mom's in LA. She's an actress," Phoenix says, making it clear with her intonation that she doesn't think much of her mother's profession. She wipes the back of her hand across her eyes.

"So, I just figured, I missed Damian so much, I'd come find him, and I'd just see what happened. If it wasn't cool here, fine, I'd go along to New York, where my friend Lisa has a summer sublet." Phoenix takes a long draw on her cigarette, then slowly exhales, watching the smoke dissipate into the night island air. Franci does the same.

"I mean, I don't know now. I guess I could still do that. I mean, I don't want to impose on you, not with everything you're going through."

Franci looks at Phoenix. It's her turn to look incredulous. "Phoenix, I would be happy if you'd stay with me a few days. Really." The two turn then to look at the water. Any protocol either has for social situations has been suspended. It seems to each that they're locked in a tiny world governed by its own rules for behavior, rules which they both seem, intuitively, to understand.

"Okay," Phoenix says.

"Okay," Franci says, then takes in a deep breath. There's that feeling in her chest and stomach she's had all week, a hollow feeling, just-about-to-cry. She lets her breath out, then steps on her cigarette. "Let's eat something," she says, and they go in to the warm, lit kitchen.

It's funny, but in a good way, to cook for someone again—to cook for a teenager. Franci hands Phoenix the jobs she used to give to Damian, chopping garlic and snapping the ends of the green beans. She's got a load of food that Peg brought from the farmers' market, and now, finally, she has a reason to cook it.

After dinner, Franci sets Phoenix up in Damian's old room, stripping the bed without mentioning that she hasn't changed anything in here since the accident. She puts on the plain yellow sheets usually used for guests, not the goofy green ones with rows of sheep that Damian insisted on continuing to use long after they lost their elastic edging. Franci opens the window and props the box fan in to keep it from falling shut, explaining the quirks of the cottage, apologizing for the hot water heater that will boom on during the night, warning Phoenix of the scritch of squirrels on the roof and the first-light birds that will wake her, babbling about the house and coming morning to keep the roil of her feelings at bay.

Hours later, long after Franci has gone upstairs to bed, Phoenix steps out onto the back porch, then into the night garden. The air is still, and clear except for a few misty ribbons trailing around the lilac and the bushy peonies. Phoenix stands for a moment at the water's edge, thinking of just plunging in, fully clothed, but she doesn't; instead, she turns the Adirondack chair so it faces the house, her back to the water, and she settles in, her feet tucked under her bottom, like a princess, or a hen. Even in the dark she can see where the blue house paint is scraped off in spots, up high, where Damian was working on the ladder before the accident. She's wearing her usual sleepwear, a t-shirt emblazoned with the words "My Parents Got Divorced And All I Got

Is This Lousy T-Shirt." Over this, she's wearing Damian's old cotton bathrobe, a dark green watch plaid, which she found in the closet.

This is the house where Damian spent all his summers, all the years before she knew him. On the second floor, she can see the inky window of his mom's bedroom, and beneath that, the windows of the kitchen, glowing with the milky light from the fixture over the sink. The narrow downstairs window that's in Damian's room, the room where she tried, and failed, to sleep. Phoenix imagines Damian coming out the back door, imagines seeing his figure appear on the screened porch, the chiaroscuro of screen almost obscuring his shadowy form. If she concentrates hard enough, can't she make this happen? How dead could he be, really, if she can imagine him this clearly?

She looks above her, up to where the air is clear, and the stars are hard, and bright. Is Damian up there?

Where *is* he?

A motion at the porch door draws her attention back to earth. Someone is there, and for a moment, Phoenix thinks that her imagining *has* brought Damian back. What will she say?

But it isn't Damian's broad shoulders, his lanky, slightly stooped form; instead, it's his mother. She opens the screen door and stands on the top step. Around them, the night hisses.

"But how did it happen?" Phoenix asks, without any preliminaries.

Franci knows it's pointless to pretend she doesn't understand the question, or to lie, or to do anything but just tell Phoenix the truth.

She sits heavily on the top porch step. She's wearing her boxers, her corduroy shirt over the t-shirt she sleeps in. She'd been dreaming, not of Damian, but of Leslie, and she'd rather not have to sit here and talk to this girl. She'd rather just come out here and think about Damian. But here she is, in a situation she agreed to—even asked for—and she's got to follow through with it.

She pulls out her cigarettes. The night is cool. There's a little breeze coming off the water.

"Well, he was driving," Franci begins, feeling her voice quaver at this—how could she have let it happen?—"and apparently he lost control coming around a curve—a curve that's known for being dangerous—and the car went into a meadow and flipped," Franci says, swallowing hard. "He was killed immediately, they said."

Phoenix nods, not looking at Franci.

"Who was he with? What happened to them?"

This is the part Franci doesn't want to tell her. "Just some friends, some island kids. You know. Kids he's known a long time."

"A girl?"

Franci nods, her mouth full of smoke. "Two girls, one other boy."

"He was on a date?"

"It wasn't a date. Really. It was just, you know, some old friends. It was a group. Phoenix, he told me all about you. He told me how smart you are, and how he had wanted to go with you to California, and I've never seen him so interested in someone."

Phoenix leans her head back, looking up at the stars. "He said he was in love with you," Franci lies, justifying it in part because now she's met her, she knows without a doubt it's true.

"He did?" Phoenix says, still looking up. She can't see it when Franci nods.

"So then what about those other kids? Did they die too?"

Again, there's a little pause, in which Franci for a moment thinks she could change the truth of the world just by saying it differently than the way it happened. But this passes. "No," she says. "Just Damian."

Phoenix looks at her, steadily, waiting for more.

"The other kids were fine."

Together, they listen to the hissing sound get louder. It's the crickets.

"That's it," Franci shrugs. "I'm sorry if maybe it isn't romantic enough for you, but it's just that, another teenager killed in a stupid accident. Not much more to say than that." She rolls the ashes of her cigarette against the porch step. Why does she want to be mean to Phoenix? She can't seem to stop herself.

Phoenix turns away, looking out over the lawn. A few fireflies blink against the night.

"Don't be getting all mad at me," Phoenix says. "I wasn't the one driving. I wasn't the one in charge of his summer. I wasn't the one making sure he had a safe ride home," she says, quietly, still looking away.

"Fine. Don't you think I torture myself enough with that? Don't you think maybe that's why I can't sleep at night?" Franci flicks her cigarette out across the lawn, the way Phoenix did earlier in the evening, in the happy honeymoon period that seems to have evaporated forever. Now, because Phoenix is facing the house in the Adirondack chair, Franci by necessity flicks the burning bit in her direction. "Sorry," she says, but it's unclear just what she's apologizing for.

Phoenix doesn't say anything; she just keeps her gaze steady out across the lawn, as if some answer will come loping across the grass to her.

They sit in silence for awhile. There are just the stars above, the peepers, the occasional splash of something mysterious in the water.

"I'm going in," Franci says. "Would you lock the door when you go to bed?" She can't see it, but behind her back, Phoenix makes a face, imitating Franci's words, as if Franci is her own mother, nagging her. When Franci's gone, Phoenix leans her head back against the top of the Adirondack chair, the starred mouth of the island night sky opening to her. The answers help nothing.

Across the bay, she can hear the howl of the wild dogs go up into the night air, the sound lifting her to her hands in the chair, and she stares up into the night sky, afraid to move, believing with all her heart the sound is the cry not of dogs, but of Damian.

Twenty-Four

At Sandy's Snack Shack at the edge of the Dead Man's Beach parking lot, the shade is provided by roofed picnic areas, each table and bench painted a glossy, bright white and sheltered by a pitched cedar shingle roof. It's here that Cort's called Betheny and Kylie to a summit so they can keep apprised of interviews with Cop Cal, and report any gossip heard, anything that might indicate what he fears most: *someone knows*.

"Well, nobody's visited me," Betheny says, her good hand wrapped around a waxy milkshake cup, which is sweating beads of water in the heat. "Cop Cal just called, asked me a couple of questions, and that was it. No one seems very interested."

"Yeah, I mean, it isn't like someone's going to call you out of the blue and say, 'hey, wasn't Cort driving?' " Kylie says.

"Hey, shut it, will you?" Cort says, looking over toward the table next to them, where a married couple is trying to get some hotdogs into their two little kids.

"Oh, get over it," Kylie starts, then waves her hand in front of her face. "A wasp!" she cries out, leaping up, still waving, and they can all see the little yellow creature hovering around the edges of her milkshake cup, where finally it lands, and begins to crawl toward the straw. "Oh God, I hate those things," she says, still standing, crossing her arms as if for protection, or maybe in defiance, over her midriff, which is exposed between her blue bathing suit top and the low-riding line of her yellow terrycloth shorts.

"Jesus." Cort says, picking up the cup, flicking the wasp off with a napkin, handing the cup back to Kylie. "Thanks, Cort," she says in a sing-song. "My hero," and they sit again.

"The two important things are that we all tell the same story, and that we keep the rest of it to ourselves." Cort swallows, hard, to keep his voice from breaking. There's a small worry buzzing in the background of his anxiety, like he's forgetting something about the story, but what? He shakes his head, goes on. "I mean, there are some people on this island who would just as soon blab something like this—" he starts, but then there's the loud rumble of a car's approach, and they turn to see Rick Skiffton pull into the parking lot in his jacked-up Camaro, Sugarcult blaring from the open windows.

"Speak of the devil," Betheny says, watching the car jerk to a halt next to the guardrail between the parking lot and the Snack Shack tables. "Hey kids," he calls out. The married couple turn, and glare. "What's going on?" Rick shouts over his music.

"Nothing," Cort says, thinking, *there's no need to yell. Idiot.*

"Party on the beach," Rick calls out, still loudly, and Cort realizes he's stoned out of his mind. Not that he needs an excuse to act like an idiot.

"Great," Betheny says, not sure if she should sound sarcastic or excited. She's laughing a little, cutting a look over to Cort to see if he's laughing, too, and when she sees he isn't, she drops her laugh down into a smile, rolls her eyes at him. "Paartay!" Kylie calls out, tilting her head back. The couple at the next table have gone back to the work of wiping the kids' faces clean of mustard and ketchup and crumbs, with the occasional glare at the teenagers.

"There's a bunch of people coming," Rick says. "I've scored some great greenery," and he motions with his hand as if he's smoking a joint.

Three weeks ago there would have been nothing Cort would have liked more. An afternoon with a little weed, some easy local girls, and him smarter and set for greater success than any one of those suckers.

But now, there's nothing Cort wants less than to trudge out onto Dead Man's Beach, past the lifeguard station, out to the dunes, to set up camp with Rick and Kylie and "a bunch of people," which probably means the two Jennifers, Allen Sherman, God knows who else. All people who *don't know*, Cort thinks.

But to not go would alert Rick, and everyone else, that something's up, so he's the first to say, "Sure, let's move," and before he can stand, Kylie's bolted to join Rick in the front seat of the car. "We'll meet you on the beach," she calls, and "Don't ditch out on us," Rick yells, looking right at Cort, lingering for a long moment.

The stare Rick levels at him sends a chill through Cort; he's always a little nervous around Rick, always thinking that Rick's envious of him and Damian and the other summer kids, the ones who leave each Labor Day for suburban houses or sprawling apartments, for a life of children's matinees and housekeepers, the rhythm of dinner at six and parents watching over homework, and later, a life of money to spend taking girls from Chapin or Brearly to museums, theater, dinners out.

As the car peels away, Betheny laughs, shaking her head. "Kylie. God, what a twit. I can't believe she was like my best friend."

"Yeah, that's what worries me. Are you sure she hasn't told anyone?" Cort says, then says, "How's your shake?" and Betheny nods as she drinks down the last of it, still not standing, not in any rush. She doesn't say, "Thanks."

Cort thinks, but doesn't say, that this is what worries him also about Betheny, that she's an idiot too, just slightly less of an idiot than Kylie is; at least she's made it into Wisconset Community. Or maybe it's just that she's a prettier idiot; she's just as capable of spilling the truth at just the wrong moment. *Girls*. This is what keeps him hanging out with her, buying her milkshakes: the worry that she'll break away from him, that she'll *tell*. And her word would be taken much more seriously than would the word of Kylie, who everybody knows exaggerates. But he also stays around Betheny because of something else, because the world is now split into two distinct camps, the much smaller camp of *people who know*, just him, Betheny, and Kylie, and the much larger camp of *people who don't*, otherwise known as everyone else in the entire world.

Plus, now that Kylie's stopped spending any time alone with him, there are no more blow jobs or quick screws in the dunes.

From here Cort can hear the waves coming in to the shore, but he can't see the ocean; all he can see, from here, is the parking lot, wavering in the hot sun.

"She went on a date with Rick on Saturday," Betheny says.

"A date?" Cort laughs. "What the hell does that mean?" He's surprised by his pang of something like jealousy. And fear.

"Well, I guess not a date really. You know how it is. She told her mother it was a date, and her mother was all like, 'Oh, how nice, oh, you're feeling better after the accident, oh, you're dating again.'"

"Yeah, her mother never was that thrilled about me," Cort shifts on the bench. He's wearing his long khaki shorts and a faded blue t-shirt. He looks the part of the teenager at rest, the college kid on summer break; he knows he looks as if he just walked out of a clothing catalogue, Ralph Lauren or Abercrombie and Fitch, and all he can think is how far his current reality is from that. How much trouble he's in.

Betheny pulls a pack of cigarettes and a neon pink lighter from her canvas bag. The bag is pink, too, and holds God knows what, Cort thinks. Girl beach things. Suntanning lotion, a bottle of water, cell, whatever it is girls think they can't live without for a few hours.

At the far edge of the parking lot, he can see Kylie and Rick get out of the car and disappear from the open parking lot into the dunes. God knows what she's saying to him.

"You done with that?" he asks Betheny, and she nods, smiling up at him. She's pretty. He drapes his striped beach towel over one shoulder, tosses their cups in the trash, then hops over the guardrail that separates the Snack Shack from the parking lot and begins the long walk to the dunes.

Cort and Betheny follow Rick and Kylie down the narrow path through the dunes to the beach, the flat sand alive with color, and noise, and the motion of people, mostly mothers chasing their toddlers to the water's edge, a few of the nerdy summer kids, the ones who don't smoke or anything, lying on their blankets with their summer books.

There's a bunch of slightly older guys playing volleyball, the kind of guys, Cort knows, his dad wanted him to be, assumed he would be, the guys who are just back on Grand Isle for a couple of weeks before starting a college internship or their first job or before getting a jump on grad school. They're the guys Cort and Damian have been following all their lives, always just a few years behind, trailing after them through middle school vacations, high school summers. Until now. "When we come back that final summer of college," Damian had said to him, "they won't even recognize us."

Cort wasn't sure what he meant at the time, and Damian himself probably didn't know, but this is what comes to Cort now, plodding along behind the others, looking up occasionally to appreciate Betheny's tight butt in her white shorts.

Out in the dunes, far from the crowd, far from the water, they find the small collection of teenagers with a couple of coolers, sprawled on towels and blankets in the sand, and they set up their own camp,

Betheny pulling a folded towel from her pink canvas bag, then stripping down to her suit, removing watch and rings to avoid tan lines, seeming oblivious to her cast, which must be hot and itchy in the sun. The girls lather up with the tanning oil, then spread it on the backs of the boys, and Cort applies a line of zinc to his nose, which always burns in the sun. Betheny and Cort sink into their towels with sighs, elbows propped on knees, facing the sea, as if exhausted.

From here, all they can hear is the ocean.

Rick lights up a joint as soon as they're settled, passes it to Cort, the four newcomers sitting in a row, staring out to the blue, moving ocean, silent together in their silent thoughts, Cort thinking about how Damian would have loved this day, brilliant, blue, sharp-lined, and the queasy feeling in his stomach recedes a bit with every toke. Everything will be okay, he tells himself. And again, in his head he tells Damian he's sorry, but even as he's thinking this, he isn't too sure if his regret is for the accident, or if it's for the lie.

Beside them, the others, Rick's sidekick Danny, the two Jennifers and Allen Sherman, a fat guy none of them really know too well, are already sacked out on their blankets and towels, and the four new arrivals smoke their joint as if working to catch up.

"Did you guys hear that Debbie Rocksmith got busted?" Rick says.

Cort looks at him, passes the joint to Kylie, sitting between them. "Who's that?"

"You know, man, she was like two years behind us. Blonde, kind of hot—" he cuts himself off. "Oh yeah, you didn't go to Wisconset. I always forget that about you, man."

Cort shrugs, thinking it's not a good sign that someone thinks he actually attended that Podunk excuse for a school, even though he can hear in Rick's tone that he's bestowing this as if it's a compliment.

"But hey, can you keep a secret?" Rick continues.

"I'm very good at keeping secrets," Kylie says, raising her eyebrows at Cort and Betheny. "Right, guys?"

She's going to tell, Cort thinks, and all he can think of to say is "Shut up, stupid," which he does, and Kylie rolls her eyes at him. If Rick were alert at all, this would awaken him to the fact that something's up, but Rick is distracted by reaching across the others to Betheny for the joint while simultaneously hanging onto his soda can, and these two activities thoroughly engross him until he's reclaimed the joint, taken a hit, and embarked on his tale of how he "kind of inherited" Debbie Rocksmith's stash when she was busted, although by the end of the story, Cort's sure it's really just that Rick stole it.

Looking out at the blue water, Betheny lets the smoke roll into her lungs. She'll have to go to her job at the supermarket later, but she won't think about that now; instead, she soaks up the blue morning, thinking she'll save this up for later, to think about when she's standing in the icy market under the florescent lights, ringing up the purchase of some rich summer cow with screaming brats in tow. Whenever she shuts her eyes at home, in bed, lights out, she sees the accident again, the dark interior of the car's backseat, Damian tumbling over her. But here, she closes her eyes, and the bright sun makes a red sheet of color, blanking out everything.

For her part, Kylie's thinking that Cort might be a little jealous, even though he hasn't shown it. If Cort and Betheny are going to be so weird about the accident, she'll show them. They think she's dumb, but she's a lot smarter than she acts sometimes, she thinks, and thinks she'll find a way to get them back. Get back at them. In between tokes, she looks down at herself, sucks her stomach in, making her navel ring jiggle a bit, and she quickly becomes fascinated with this, until she realizes they're all watching her watch herself.

"You're so queer," Betheny says, and they all laugh, and even Kylie, knowing she's being made fun of, dissolves into helpless giggling, and soon they're all as collapsed as the others, and they lie there together on the sand, like a pack of beached sea creatures, barely speaking, moving only as necessary to shift position to ensure even tanning or to make themselves more comfortable, interrupted only by the occasional *pling* indicating a communiqué on one of their devices.

Cort's head is aching as he lies on his back on the beach towel; the towel is striped, red and white. It's one of a set of three towels his mother bought three years before, the last really good summer they had here. One for each family member.

He's lying on his towel, one arm draped over his eyes, the other lying by his side, one of Betheny's cigarettes between his fingers. The sun is hot, but he likes it; it's as if the sun could saturate his skin, could burn through his grief. His guilt.

Cort hears the sounds of the girls getting up, running to the water, Betheny, and Kylie, and the Jennifers. Cort doesn't really care about any of them, except insofar as they do or do not know what happened in the car that night, and even as the other guys prop up on their elbows to watch, discussing the various physical attributes of the girls, Cort stays supine in the sun. He hears Terry and Allen Sherman get up, hears the *thwack* of the football as someone catches it. The beach slowly goes quiet, and soon is silent except the shuffle of the waves sucking against the shore, the shrieks of girls and gulls far enough to be not piercing, but lulling.

And then he feels a weight sinking into the sand, the sand shifting beside him, a shadow falling across his bare chest, chilling him. At first, *Damian*, he thinks, but then he hears Rick's raspy voice, smells his stale cigarette-and-grease-monkey smell that persists even out here, on the bright, clean beach.

"Hey man," Rick says, quietly.

"Hey," Cort says. "That was some legit weed. Thanks, man."

"Oh, that's nothing. I know where to get the best, and only the best for my friends."

Cort doesn't say anything, doesn't say, *hey man, you're blocking the rays*, as he would to anyone else. Instead, "Well, it was great," he says, knowing this is weak. Lame.

There's no response for so long that if it weren't for the shadow across his chest, Cort wouldn't be sure if Rick's still there. "A truly killer buzz," he adds, for good measure, thinking for a moment of the film clip he watched in Intro to Psych, about how the animal that's at a disadvantage tries to mimic the stronger animal to avoid becoming prey.

"Glad you liked it. Glad to be of service," Rick says. "You know, I like helping people. I know a lot of guys wouldn't just offer to get everyone high without asking for some, ah, recompense, if you know what I mean."

"Yeah," Cort says, "you've always been generous like that. You're a great guy, Rick," he says, marveling at how he can say this, sitting up now, lacing his hands around his knees, blinking in the sun.

"Of course, there are times when a guy wants something in return. Something more than a little pussy in the dunes," Rick says, nodding toward the girls, who are still playing in the waves.

Even though Cort's no longer lying in Rick's shadow, he still feels chilled. "Well, that's commerce for you, right? Buying and selling. Nobody gets nothing for free."

"I'm glad you understand me," Rick says. "A guy like you, for example—there's a lot you have to offer. And," he says, coolly drawing a cigarette pack from the waistband of his shorts, "a lot you have to lose."

Even though Cort doesn't want to know the answer, he knows he has to ask: "What are you getting at, man?"

"Let's say there's something I know you don't want known. Let's say I have it on good authority that you have engaged in some serious duplicitude."

Cort feels the chill flood through him.

"Come on, man," Rick says, laughing a little, bumping Cort's shoulder with his own. "I know you were driving," he says, in a friendly way.

"What are you talking about? You mean the accident? Damian was driving, man, not me."

"Okay, you want to play it that way. You keep up that story with everyone but me, okay?" Rick's no longer laughing. He takes a drag on his cigarette. "And if you keep me happy, I'll keep up that story, too."

What is this, an old Law & Order *episode?* Cort thinks, but it's real, this conversation is real, and he's got to see it through. "What do you want?" he asks. "How much?"

"Oh, come on, Cort, it's not like that. Not like I'm blackmailing you or something. I've got a little favor to ask. It'll hardly take any time at all."

Cort feels relief in a backwash that meets the dread. Sure, of course. What could it be, helping him out with some legal problem at the garage? Helping him negotiate a deal on a car? "Sure, Rick." He feels again like he often has around Rick, like a little kid, babied by his mom and dad's money, humiliated.

"Sure," Rick says. "It's nothing. Just a set of keys. A little, lightweight set of keys I think you probably have hanging in your dad's front hall, that nice new front hall that my dad did the tiling for."

Fuck you, Cort wants to say, but doesn't, as he realizes what this is, as he sees this *is* blackmail, after all. He knows the keys Rick means, even though he can't imagine how Rick knows they're there. And Cort's stuck; Rick's made that much clear.

"What do you say? We'll work out the details later, okay?"

Cort watches as the girls come running up from the water, slicked and sleek as seals.

Lying on her stomach, the beads of cold seawater having evaporated from her suit and skin, the cast on her arm seeming not to have suffered much from the water, Betheny pulls her watch from her bag, groans, and flops back down again. "It's three-thirty," she says. "So?" Kylie says, turning her face to the other side.

"I have to be at Lantman's at four."

"Oh, shit, I'm supposed to be there at three."

"Just like girls," Rick says to Cort, although in Cort's lingering high, the meaning of this is unclear. Just like girls to have jobs, or to be late for them?

"How are you going to get there?" Rick asks.

"I've got my mom's car," Betheny says to Kylie. "I'll take you."

Kylie is standing, pulling on her shorts. "Rick, can't you drive me?"

He shakes his head. "After that weed, I am definitely auto-impaired," he says.

"So? That's never stopped Cort from driving, especially—" Kylie begins, but is cut short by Cort standing suddenly, a bolt of adrenaline coursing through his veins.

"I'll take a lift with you, too, Beth," Cort says. "Man."

They gather up their things, leaving Rick lying on the sand with the others, settling in as if convalescing, and make their way back across the beach to the parking lot.

"Listen, Kylie, no more jokes," Cort says as they cross the hot sand.

"Oh, God, do you think Rick cares? Or any of those other people?"

"What do you mean? Did you tell Rick?" Cort pulls Kylie by the arm, twisting the skin of her arm in his hand.

"Cut it out. No, I didn't tell anyone," she lies. That's about the last thing she's going to tell Cort. "Anyway, I don't see what the big deal is. It isn't like they can do anything to you now."

"Sure they can," Betheny says. "For one thing, they could arrest Cort for drunk driving, and probably for like killing someone in a car accident."

"Vehicular homicide," Cort says as they reach the path to the parking lot. He's looked it up on the Internet, and pretty much, if anyone finds out he was driving, he's fucked. "Plus, you two could get into some kind of trouble for keeping it secret all this time," he says.

"Really? Ow," Kylie pauses to grasp onto Cort's arm, standing on one foot, inspecting the bottom of the other foot, where it seems a small bit of glass or a sharp shell fragment has embedded itself.

"Jesus." Cort says, shaking her off after a moment. "You don't seem too worried about this, but you'd better be."

"Cort, will you drive, just to the common? I've got to change on the way," Betheny says, and Cort feels the cold keys pressed into his hands. *No, I can't,* he wants to say. *I can't ever drive again.* Instead, he unlocks the door, passes the keys to Kylie, and clambers into the back.

"Let Kylie drive. Kylie loves to drive," he says, even though he knows she's the worst driver among them—or was. He settles into the backseat, feeling his chest expand, and then tighten. If anyone says anything more, he's going to start to cry.

Franci doesn't have to convince Phoenix to take her bike and go out for a ride on Monday; Phoenix is just as eager as Franci to get some time alone, and sailing along on the black-topped road that inclines up to the sky, she feels Damian with her, and imagines him riding behind her, spreading out his arms into the clear, salty air, an image which makes her eyes burn and fill, but she's heading fast downhill, the wind blowing back her tears and drying her face.

Dead Man's Beach is a whole different scene than that at the beaches Phoenix is used to in San Francisco where it's black sand soaking up the heat from the sun, a cluster of gay men down by the rock cliffs on their bright blankets and towels, a couple of hippies smoking a fat joint, an older woman with binoculars, and Phoenix and her friends, with their pastels and their pads of drawing paper, their thermoses of lemonade, a little pot in a baggie which they may or may not smoke. The City glittering across the bay, stitched to the headlands by the Golden Gate Bridge, swaddled in a bank of fog.

Here, for one thing, the sand is bright white, clean-looking, and the water is blue, bright, hard. All the colors are different from home, and Phoenix notices this, and is glad; how could she have anything normal around her, now, now that everything has changed? Now that Damian is dead, she makes herself think.

Walking her bike along the road above the dunes she can see a crowd of teenagers. Phoenix only sees them as a cluster of colored suits and splashing; that's all she needs to see in order to make her way away from them; she turns the bike straight into the dunes, bumps down to a patch of beach that's clear of chaos. Here, she drops the bike and her pack, spreads Franci's Mexican blanket on the grass-spiked sand, and lies down, feeling the tears again leak out of the corners of her eyes.

When will she stop crying? How long does it take? A month ago, she imagined this beach, this hard blue water, but she didn't imagine sitting here alone, she imagined sitting here with Damian, one of his long arms looped around her shoulders.

Phoenix, still in her cutoffs and oversized black t-shirt, watches the teenagers—her peer group, she thinks—down on the beach. From here, she can see them behaving just as they should, just the way she learned in Soc 101, the class where she met Damian, the two of them the only students who refused to reach into the envelope the teacher passed around in the experiment which proved that nearly the entire class would willingly allow one of their own to receive an "F" in the course, unearned and unwarranted, if it meant saving themselves from the same fate.

"Of course this is just an experiment," the teacher had said, "but it does show how a group will believe they have no recourse, no ability to stand up to authority."

After class, Damian and Phoenix slapped high fives in the hallway. "Resist authority, man," Phoenix said, with just a note of irony.

"I can't believe it," Damian said, gesturing widely with his arms. He had a thin leather thong tied around one wrist, and seeing it, she knew she'd fall in love with him. She knew this was it. "These idiots are as bad as the idiots back home," he said.

Now, it's immediately clear that these are precisely the same idiots Damian talked about, clustered in the usual teenage scene: the boys lying like water mammals on their towels, and the girls—her subgroup, she thinks, feeling her mouth pull down in a parody of a grimace—giggling and chattering like a flock of startled songbirds. The few who do venture into the water do so only holding hands with one another, squealing, and once they're in, they paddle helplessly, carefully holding their heads aloft like poodles, one of them with her arm in a permanent salute above the waves, encased in a pink cast.

If Damian were here, Phoenix would laugh.

She lies on her back, imagining the warmth of the sun cleansing her, imagining that it's a way for her to still communicate with Damian. He is *somewhere*, isn't he? Somewhere more specific than the vague "everywhere" as her father explained back when he told her about how AIDS had killed so many of his friends, when she was little.

And then she thinks: the girl who was with Damian when he died. She sits bolt upright, and looks over at the kids again: there she is, the skinny girl in a pink bikini, blonde ponytail bobbing like something out of Phoenix's father's beloved campy Annette Funicello movies, the pink cast on her left arm. The girl has what her grandmother would call "a nice figure," what any guy would call "stacked."

Of course. Of course Damian couldn't have been faithful to her, wouldn't have been. They had something at Reed, but then he came home to the island, and turned out to be just like any other boy, susceptible, horny, dumb. There's a squeal from the beach: "Riiiiick," one of the other girls calls out, as a skinny guy, older than the others, wearing cutoffs, not swim trunks like the rest, swoops her up in his arms, walks into the water carrying her, her arms around his neck. He pretends he's going to throw her in the water, but then carries her back out again, and she slaps his butt, then runs, and he tackles her in the sand.

Teenagers at play, Phoenix thinks. Will she ever play again?

Are these the girls who were in the car with Damian? What was really going on between them? And how can she find out? How can she get at the truth of what she was to Damian, to know whether any of it was real at all? What was happening when he died?

And then she remembers: the epilepsy. The seizure Damian had, that last week at school, when they were together in her room. She knows enough to be pretty sure that seizures mean you shouldn't drive, and with this realization—why didn't she think of this before?—Phoenix feels a kind of relief, an explanation for how Damian could have gone off the road.

Phoenix rises from her spot, sheds her cutoffs and t-shirt, stripping down to her one-piece, black suit. She knows the kids will see her and start whispering, but now, invigorated by the idea of forming an idea, she doesn't care. She pulls her dreads back into a heavy pony, walking down the hot sand, crosses to the water, and walks right in. Franci was right when she said the water would be warm; this is nothing like the icy waters of the Pacific. When she's waist-deep, Phoenix folds herself into a dive, and pushes through the waves, and that's the moment when it occurs to her, not the plan of how to find out from the girl if she was sleeping with Damian, but something else altogether, something much more frightening, more *real*: her period is not just late; she's skipped.

Twenty-Five

While Tessa waits among the other summer residents on the train platform the Friday after she's bit by the raccoon, she decides she won't try to hide her injured hand. By now, it only has a single, large Band-aid on it. It's her left hand, and she's tempted to hold it behind her back, to shield it from Jake's view, but she knows this will only raise his suspicions; any prevarication on her part always catches his attention.

Instead, she'll be bold about it, and by exposing it to him, maybe she'll throw him off. Maybe if he sees the bandaged hand, it will distract him from the truth of what happened: the raccoon in the house, Kenji there, the raccoon's teeth sinking into her fleshy palm, just like Jake warned her.

The train's appearance is always so sudden to Tessa, and it is sudden again, a whisper of sound and then here it is, the iron horse, blowing up to the little platform, discharging its passengers, then disappearing down the tracks. Everyone watches it approach, but no one watches it leave.

And here's Jake, in his jeans and his white linen jacket, looking around eagerly, looking around for her, his duffle over one shoulder, a violin case in each hand. He waves with his head, like a happy golden retriever, holding the cases to his side triumphantly, and she waves back, with her right hand, her good, undamaged hand.

He's humming Beethoven's Ninth, putting the violins in the backseat, then swinging into the driver's seat, kissing her quickly and hard, then gunning the engine, swinging out of the train station parking lot fast, making her gasp and laugh out loud. Maybe everything will be alright.

Once on the road, reaches for her hand. "What happened here?" he says.

"Oh," Tessa says, careful to look him in the eye because she knows that liars don't look people in the eye when they lie. "I had a little run-in with the grass shears."

The bully necessitates lying, she thinks. If Jake weren't so damn controlling, weren't so pathologically jealous, she wouldn't have to make up a story like this; she could tell him the truth, just leaving out the bit about Kenji Tanaka. Or not; there's nothing wrong with her friendship with him; in most relationships you can have a friend, without anyone going nuts over it.

But no, she won't dwell on this. He's in such a good mood. He pops a CD in, and out spills Tchaikovsky, and they ride in the clear, blue evening.

On the ferry, they stand at the railing, with the other passengers, she leans against him, his arm around her shoulders, while he tells her why his mood's so good: at the Early Music Festival, he landed a new commission for a Castagneri restoration: "A Castagneri, Tessa—from 1745. Think of that, the mystery of it, over two hundred years old, and now in my possession for a moment." And then he makes her laugh, launches into his parody of the subway announcements he suffered while in New York: " 'Service is interrupted on the *brouchbrouchbrouch* line. As an alternative *broucckbroucckbroucck*.' As an alternative do *what*? Kill yourself?" and on, until she's laughing, hard.

"Well, you're in a good mood, considering," he says, then picks up her hand from the railing. "Are you sure you don't want to see a doctor about this?"

"Oh, I did," she says, turning to look at him. She figured she'd have to explain. "I went to the clinic. I just figured it was better to get it looked at, and plus I thought I should get a tetanus shot."

"Poor baby," Jake says, nuzzling her hand a bit. His solicitation incites her guilt, but then she thinks of how it will be if he finds out the truth, and then she pushes the guilt away. "I'm just glad you're back," she says, and it's true. Any whisper of a feeling for Kenji has vanished. It's safe, now he's here. He's back, and she's safe at last, and by the time they're disembarking at Grand Isle, everything feels better, feels back to normal, even better than normal.

When Jake is like this it's hard for her to imagine him the other way, hard to imagine that the surly, condescending man is the same as this man, handsome and charming and quick. After they bump off the ferry, Jake pulls over at Massey's, without putting on the directional, just slides off the road and into the dirt parking lot, fast, making Tessa laugh in surprise.

"I know just what you need," he says, and he jumps from the car. She watches while he orders at the window. She loves him, loves the slope of his back, the line of his waist down his leg, loves his white button-down shirt and his beat-up jeans and his old-fashioned tennis shoes, which he wears with no socks.

And she loves it that he returns to the car with two ice-cream cones, one, for her, dipped in sprinkles. Mint chocolate chip. "I knew you'd be a sprinkles kind of a girl," he'd said to her that first summer. Now, "You make me so happy," she says, meaning it.

Twenty-Six

Phoenix wakes to the sound of scraping, metal on wood, an annoying, insistent noise that merges with her dream of an oyster knife scraping against a bone, the bone of a baby, her baby, Damian's baby. But when she wakes, she realizes quickly it wasn't that, it was a real sound, something from outside the house. Is it someone trying to break in? She looks at her phone. It's nearly noon. Is Franci back?

Lying on Damian's bed, Phoenix realizes she's still in the same position she fell asleep in, *shavasana*, corpse pose, still in her t-shirt and cutoffs. But she still isn't dead, she's alive. And could it really be possible that she's got something alive inside of her, too? But they were so careful, every, every time. Except that once, when they went hiking, and there was that meadow, and Damian was so sweet to her, so tender, kissing her practically the whole time. Reciting that Hopkins poem to her between kisses. Oh, God.

She gets up from corpse pose, gets up from the bed, and walks down the dim little hallway to the kitchen. The scraping sound is louder out here, and draws her through the screened back porch and into the backyard.

Outside, the light is a deep golden summer light, reflecting off the bay. The scraping continues, and Phoenix turns, looks up, and sees Franci on the middle rung of a metal ladder, scraping the blue paint off the shingle siding. She shields her eyes. Franci hasn't yet noticed that Phoenix has come outside, that she, Franci, is being watched. Her hair is pulled back in a dark blue bandanna, and Phoenix can see the concentration lining her face. Or is it grief?

"Hey," Phoenix calls up, and Franci nearly topples from the ladder. "Sorry," Phoenix says, going to the foot and holding it steady.

"That's okay. I thought you were sleeping," Franci says, gingerly toeing her way down the ladder to the ground, the scraper gripped in her hand.

"Yeah. I don't know what's wrong with me," Phoenix says, lifting her hands to her head, pulling her dreadlocks up and back, as if this will wake her up further, and even as she's saying this she's realizing that she does know, now. Of course: her nervous stomach, her afternoon sleepiness. It wasn't just the long bus ride, the shock.

"I guess it's just the long bus ride, the shock, you know, of—well, everything. You know," she says.

"Yeah," Franci says. "I know." From the porch steps, she takes her cigarette pack and matches, offers the pack to Phoenix, who takes a cigarette out. Franci takes one for herself and lights them both. "God, I am such a bad influence on you," she says, exhaling. "I can't believe I'm actually offering cigarettes to a teenager."

They sit together on the steps of the porch. Instead of working on the editing projects she's got for the summer, maybe she could just write an instruction booklet for the grief-stricken. Assume position, and start inhaling noxious chemicals, Franci thinks.

"Damian told me he was going to be painting the house this summer," Phoenix says. This is why Franci likes having her around; Phoenix keeps telling her things about Damian, things she didn't know, and no matter how small these things are, Franci wants to hear them. Everything.

"That's right," Franci says. "We started up there," she says, getting up, pointing to the uppermost spot where the ladder leans, about five feet higher than where Franci was, above the single, wide, second-story window, the window to Franci's bedroom. Phoenix stands, too. "He was on the top rung, up there. You can see where he started," she says. "I can't make myself go up that high." How could she have let him stand on the ladder, that high up, that precarious? How could she have put him in harm's way like that? What if he'd fallen?

"It looks like a lot of work," Phoenix says, looking up at the house, imagining Damian up there, shirtless in the afternoon sun, the sound of the metal working against the painted wood.

"Yeah," Franci says. "I know I'll never get it done myself. I'm too slow, and anyway, I'm so afraid of heights only the bottom half of the house would get done. Damian said a drunken bunny would work faster than me," she says, remembering how he made his rabbit face when he said this, making fun of her but at the same time making her laugh and swat him with a paint rag. He had run in mock fear back to the ladder, climbing it so quickly that Franci was sure he'd fall to the ground, thinking of the seizures, and she'd called out, "Damian, you're going to break your neck."

Franci and Phoenix stand staring at the house, as if waiting for it to tell them something, but all it tells them is what they already know and haven't fully absorbed: Damian's dead. Franci watches the ghost-memory of Damian, lithe, graceful, running up the ladder, t-shirt riding up from the back of his baggy shorts, and Phoenix watches her imagined ghost of Damian, the curve of his arm as he scrapes, tiny blue flakes raining down onto the ground beneath him, like bits of the very sky above come home to earth at last.

And then, as if this has taken all their remaining energy, in silence they return to sit again on the porch steps and smoke. "What are you going to do now?" Franci says.

"I thought I'd finish my cigarette," Phoenix says, without laughing, and Franci isn't sure right away whether she's joking or not, so she just smiles a little, cautiously.

"I'm kidding," Phoenix says. "I guess I'll head out tomorrow. I mean, you've been great to have me stay here and everything, but I know I'm in the way," she says, looking out at the water.

"Where will you go? To see that friend in New York?"

"Yeah. I could take a bus down there and see if she's around."

"You can't do that," Franci says, the panic in her voice startling them both. "I mean," she says, more calmly, "you can't just go to New York City without a place to stay or anything. God only knows what might happen."

"Yeah," Phoenix says, even though to her the idea seems exciting, going to New York City with no idea what might happen. At the moment, it seems the only way she'll be able to get over losing Damian like this, but she's smart enough to know that Franci's right, she can't just arrive in New York City, not even knowing if Lisa's still there. She has to figure out what to do. "I don't know. Maybe I should just, like, go home. Back to San Francisco."

"No," Franci says, and this time her voice isn't panicked; it's firm. "No," she says again. "Stay here."

"Here?" Phoenix looks at her with utter skepticism.

"Yeah," Franci says. "Stay here. Look, in exchange for room and board, you can help me paint the house. It's perfect. You can stay in Damian's room." Franci feels so much enthusiasm at this idea that she has to stop herself from adding, "We'll have fun!"

In the silence that follows, Franci's sure Phoenix will launch into a monologue about why this is a bad idea, why she has to go to New York or San Francisco, but she doesn't. "Okay," she says, with a little shrug. "Why not? I helped my friend Lisa paint her parents' place last summer." She takes the last drag from her cigarette. "Shouldn't we use an ashtray, at least?"

Franci reaches behind her, takes a potted geranium from its dish, and settles the dish between them. "There. But if you're going to stay here, we both have to quit smoking. This is terrible. I can't believe I'm such a bad influence."

Phoenix half-turns to look up at the house. "I can do the top," she says. "I'm not afraid of heights. I'm not afraid of anything."

In the late afternoon, "Look, I need to take a break," Phoenix says, climbing down the ladder, landing on her sneakered feet in the grass. "Can I ride your bike downtown?"

"Wouldn't you rather drive? Or do you want me to drive you? What do you need?" Franci asks, even though, as she's asking, she knows she shouldn't be, knows she's intruding. *None of your business*, Phoenix could easily say.

"No, I like riding. I thought I'd pick up some strawberries and stuff and make strawberry shortcake for tonight," Phoenix says, this excuse coming to her now.

"Oh. Okay." Franci reminds herself this girl is a teenager, and even if she isn't Franci's teenager, Franci's still in the precarious position of the adult, the representative of the adult world, and she has to tread carefully, watch out not to startle Phoenix away.

The town of Grand Isle isn't much, and isn't far from Franci's house, but Phoenix takes the long way 'round, riding Franci's old ten-speed, along the south shore, where she can hear the ocean's roar, then up into the meadows that overlook Dead Man's Beach. Taking this route takes her about an hour, following the black-topped roads that roll up, then down in gentle slopes. Everything is green, and then there's a sudden swatch of blue sky and bluer sea between the trees, and then she's riding alongside the water, until, finally, she comes to the center of Grand Isle: an old-fashioned town square, tidy as a town reproduced in miniature, a grassy square flanked by the shops that feed the island, painted white, pale blue, dark green: Lantman's Grocery, Szechuan Fire, Bayside Books, Grayson's Pharmacy. In front of the last, Phoenix props the bike against a free-standing flower box; Franci has told her no one here locks a bike, except tourists.

Inside, the pharmacy is cool, and scented with the perfume from the long glass counter along the side of the store, jammed with every perfume imaginable. After the ride, the bright, cool interior and the heady floral smells make Phoenix a little dizzy, and she looks around, not wanting to look as if she's looking, because she doesn't want anyone to ask her what she's looking for.

There it is, up by the register, by the pharmacist's part of the store. She adds a Peppermint Patty in part to throw off the attention of the man behind the counter, in part because there's something about the pharmacy's atmosphere that makes her long for mint. The pharmacist, the first other nonwhite person she's seen on this island, looks at her just long enough to make her shift her weight side to side.

"Hi," Kenji says, in his easy manner, but he feels ill at ease, feels that glaze of premonition: this girl isn't only new on the island, she's important, somehow, by which he means: related to Tessa.

"You must be up at the conference center," he says.

"I'm staying with Franci Weiseman," Phoenix says, thinking, that'll shut him up, and it does, because Kenji Tanaka, either with his quick mind or his sixth sense, figures it out. It must be Damian's girlfriend, who, he's heard, came out for the funeral from California. That the details of the story have eluded him he doesn't know, and to him, it doesn't matter whether the girl boarded a bus after hearing Damian had died or before.

But to Phoenix, of course, it makes all the difference, and still, standing in the pharmacy, the air shimmery with perfume, she thinks the pharmacist must be assuming this; she can see in his eyes the assumption, and she thinks then of the bus ride, of how luxurious it was, even though she didn't know it at the time, to ride along, looking out the window, thinking of Damian, in the present, living tense, like a film tripping on itself repeatedly, imagining the details of their reunion.

"Twelve twenty-eight," the pharmacist says, and Phoenix hands him her money, without fumbling in her pockets for the exact change.

In the downstairs bathroom, when Phoenix looks at the little stick and sees that it's pink, not blue, she checks the package directions again. Maybe she had it wrong. But there it was: pink = pregnant, and Phoenix wonders who thought this system up. Why not lavender, or neon lime green for that matter? But then she feels the shock of it: she's pregnant, and what on earth will she do?

Phoenix goes back to Damian's room, and lies down on his bed on her back, hands at rest along her sides. "And now, let's practice being dead," her yoga teacher had said, and Phoenix had shut her eyes and tried to think about nothing, just nothing. It gave her the creeps.

Now, she likes it. Franci, according to the note she left pinned to the front door, is out in the kayak. Before she closes her eyes, Phoenix lets herself look around Damian's room.

It's his room at their summer place, not his room at his regular home in Manhattan, so it looks spare in the way a summer camp room would. It's a small room on the ground floor, with three windows, one facing the front of the house, one nearly covered by the lilac to the side, and one facing the water. Lying on Damian's bed Phoenix can see, with her head propped up against the headboard, out to the water, a slice of blue water, above it a slice of paler blue sky.

The room itself is tidy enough that it's clear a boy had been living in it only about a week. Just enough time to allow a duffel bag, half unpacked, to get a little dusty lying on the floor at the foot of the single bed, a small hillock of dirty clothes beside the laundry basket, which still holds the remains of Damian's first load of laundry for the summer, laundered and folded by Franci, with the admonition, "You know I'm only doing it this once, because I love having you back, right?" Damian's jersey, white with red sleeves, hangs from the partly opened closet door. Phoenix has been saving this shirt all this time, resisting her desire to press her face into it in order to inhale his scent; she knows there's a limited amount of his scent in that shirt, and she doesn't want to use it all up at once.

So she lies still on her back, making do with the boy-smell that permeates the room, some mix of a man's sweat, the sour dirty laundry, maybe a trace of chlorine from the college pool. Phoenix lies in *shavasana*, thinking this must be a good way of communicating with Damian, now that he's dead. "Beastie," she says to him, "I'm pregnant," and she feels the tears come to her eyes. "I don't know what to do," she whispers. She knows she could ask advice from any number of people: her father (*ha!*), the college counselor she saw for a little while in December, when she got the news that her mother went into another detox place, maybe even Franci. But any of them will only tell her what *they* think is best, and Phoenix knows they'll all just say one thing, the practical thing, which is probably the right thing: abort.

This would be a good time to call Lisa, who Phoenix has known practically all her life. But for one thing, the signal out here is so spotty she'd have to bike around the island just to try to catch it. She could email her. But Lisa may not even be in New York still.

No. She'll have to figure this out alone, and pressing her hands against her belly, she thinks of how this wasn't what she wanted, none of this, not at all. She imagines a fetus in there, swimming around in its fluidy sac, the fetus made up of her genes, and Damian's. Not a baby, yet, just a collection of growing cells.

Phoenix lies in *shavasana*, but she isn't dead, and no amount of lying still will stop what's happening inside her, the steaming-forward of cell division, cells forming, cleaving, forming, eventually morphing into the shape of a human being, the shape of a baby.

If anyone had looked in, he might assume she was sleeping, and might further assume, from her cutoff shorts, her toe ring, the tattoo of an ancient Celtic symbol on her wrist, her matted dreadlocks, her skimpy, worn Indian shirt, and the small silver ring piercing her brow, that she was not only sleeping but had sunk into a drug-induced coma. Someone watching wouldn't know it wasn't that, but was shock, grief, and the energy necessary for cell division: it was life.

Franci drags the kayak up onto the grassy slope of lawn, turns it belly up, and wipes her face on the sleeve of her t-shirt. She knows she's a mess; she couldn't care less. In the house, she looks into Damian's room and sees Phoenix lying there on his bed, perfectly still, dead asleep. Good, she thinks, the girl needs to get some rest. In sleep, Phoenix's face is softened, the recent grief and its attendant anger, the adolescent leave-me-alone erased. Franci closes the door as quietly as she can, then goes into the downstairs bathroom to see if she needs to restock any supplies for Phoenix. She's thinking, *toilet paper? Toothpaste? Tampons?* And so she doesn't see the evidence Phoenix has left, the girl's subconscious knowing more than her conscious mind ever could, like a marionettist behind the curtain pulling up on the strings, making the girl drop the cardboard box and applicator right onto the uppermost layer of the trash.

But Franci's preoccupied, still wandering a bit, still somewhat dazed, as if Damian's death were a physical blow that's left her, five weeks later, staggering.

And so she doesn't notice anything in the bathroom except that there is just one extra roll of toilet paper, no extra soap, and she starts making a list in her head, but when she gets to *soap*, she feels exhausted, and goes to the living room, lies on the sofa, and, like Phoenix, falls asleep.

It's late afternoon on a bright July day, and by this hour the sun has crossed the island, so the house is in shadow, the rooms cooling rapidly; the rooms of the house where Damian spent his summers, where, had he lived, he might now be napping too, or where he might be in the kitchen with Phoenix, scooping up a couple of bowls of ice cream. Soon, it will be evening. Soon, Phoenix will wake, stretch, and then remember: *Damian. The test. The stick glowing pink.* She'll then be shot through with panic that she left the trappings of the test in the bathroom, where Franci might see them, and she'll come out of Damian's room, see Franci lying on the sofa, facing in, so dead asleep she's barely breathing.

But for now, for this moment, Phoenix sleeps, and Franci sleeps, and Damian's ghost sits on the front porch, chin in his hands, shaking his head. What can he do to help these two? He's always hated to see a girl cry, starting with his mother, when he was a kid, and his parents fought all the time, his father slamming out of the house. His mother would shut herself into their bedroom, the closed door just about the most frightening thing Damian could imagine.

"Mom?" he'd say at her bedroom door. "Mom? You okay? You want an ice cream sundae? I'm making one right now. Mom?" Until she came to the door, opening it just a bit, wiping her cheeks with the back of her hand, then reaching down to tousle his hair. "Smackers," she'd say, and pull him close, and much as he wanted to just fall into her clean-smelling warmth like that, like he did was he was a little kid, he'd pull away, preserving a bit of his dignity, saying, "Mom, okay, enough already. Do you want that sundae or what?"

He'd like to go in and wake her now, but Damian's ghost knows she needs her sleep, so he stays on the porch, shaking his head. He should have let her hug him more. And now, there's nothing he can do to help.

Twenty-Seven

By nine a.m. on Saturday the air is already so warm that a mist hangs over the water of the bay, heavy as silk, promising the kind of sultry day that the people of Grand Isle usually escape by escaping the city. There's no talk of relief in the forecast. In Tessa's garden, the plants look healthy, richly deep green, the hollyhocks beginning to shoot forth their bright, courageous flowers, the leaves of everything thick with humidity.

From her usual spot on Tessa's porch, in the wicker rocker, Peg says, "I haven't been able to raise Franci since Friday." Tessa, in her summery polka-dot skirt and sleeveless black t-shirt is half lying on the wicker sofa with her bare feet propped up on the coffee table. Despite the heat, they both have coffee in hand.

"She called this morning," Tessa says. "She seemed okay. She said she just needed some time to herself. She promised to call if she needs anything."

"I'm sure there comes a time when you just want everyone to go away and leave you to your grieving," Peg says, and thinks again of BJ's death, and the mourning she kept hidden from Torsten.

"Yeah," Tessa says. She wants to say something about Jake, how she's realized, this first weekend he's not in the city, how nervous she feels around him.

The slightest breath of a warm breeze ruffles the leaves above the house.

"I just don't know if it's so good for her to be alone. Don't you think she could get maudlin or something? I mean, what is she doing, lying on his bed? Going through his things? How is she going to do all that?" Peg says.

"I don't know." Tessa takes a drink of her coffee, which is good, and strong. She knows her preoccupation with her own problems is insurmountably self-absorbed but she can't seem to shake it.

"You make the world's best coffee," Peg says.

"There's always still coffee, I guess," Tessa says, and they laugh a little, sadly, and then they're silent a long time, while the breeze picks up a little and there's almost some relief from the muggy air.

"Okay, what is it?" Peg asks, and Tessa's afraid that if she looks up, she'll cry, so she looks into her coffee cup.

"Oh, it's Jake. As usual," she says, lowering her voice even though he's well out of range, out in his studio. They can hear him playing, violin notes so sweet that it doesn't seem possible they evidence anything but a dear, sweet man.

"Tessa, you know we all love Jake—"

"I know. I'm sorry. I don't mean to turn you against him or anything."

"That isn't what I'm saying. I mean, we all love him, but face it, he's a handful. We've known him for what, fifteen years? Twenty? We've seen what his moods can do."

"His temper, you mean," Tessa says, shifting on the sofa to sit up. Now there is no breeze at all, no relief from the heat.

"His temper," Peg says. "You know why he's never married?"

Tessa looks up. "He's told me about Lizzie, and Alice. They always had their eye elsewhere."

"Think about it, Tessa. He was the one who tore through all those other relationships. As far as I knew, Lizzie and Alice were both just regular, perfectly nice women. Neither one of them was a flirt, or anything close to it. The man just can't trust anyone."

"Really? Why haven't you told me any of this before?"

Peg doesn't have a ready answer. Why indeed? Why is she suddenly telling people things she's never dreamed of telling before? Why did she tell Franci about BJ, for example? "I guess because this summer you seem less happy together, you and Jake. He's hardly ever here. And, I guess, because of Damian, though I'm not sure exactly why."

"The way that death makes you consider what's important?"

"Something like that. The way death makes me open my big mouth, is more like it. Ah, death, the big mouth opener."

Tessa shifts against the cushions. "I hate these new cushions," she says, and Peg says, "I wonder if we should just go over there."

"We really shouldn't. Maybe she really just wants to be alone."

"Listen to us. We're acting like we don't even know her," Peg says, looking down at her watch. "Let's go over and take her to the farmers' market. That's a good excuse, isn't it?"

Tessa shakes her head a little, putting her coffee mug down on the table. "It's a bad idea," she says, standing. "You drive," Peg says, heaving herself up from the chair.

Franci's house has always looked to Tessa like a real camp, funkier than Jake's place, cluttered inside, and always before she's felt a little pigeon-puff of pride when she compares the two. For one thing, Jake's house has light, real light, the kind that saturates everything, making you feel as if you're on a little boat when you look out at the water, and Jake's obsession with fixing it up has meant summers spent in hard labor, resulting in a house that's tight and tidy. But today, Tessa sees how Franci's garden, even though this summer it's in a bit of neglect, is a crowded, wild profusion of color, where her own is too neat and predictable.

She turns off the car, looks over at Peg. Franci's car is in the driveway. "She must be home," Tessa says.

"Okay," Peg says, keeping her hands folded in her lap.

"What's the matter with us? She's our best friend. What would we want in her situation?" Tessa says.

"I don't know," Peg says. "I don't think anyone can ever tell what they'll want when something awful happens."

"Yeah." Tessa drums her fingers against the steering wheel, then reaches around for her bag, taking the keys from the ignition. "Let's go," she says.

They step onto the front porch, the elephant vine now thick enough to make it a cool little green world. The glass-paned front door is open. Tessa presses her face against the screen. "Franci? Hey, Franci!" she calls, and then, just as she's about to pull the door open and step inside, a girl appears before her, obscured through the screen.

"Hi," she says. "Franci isn't home. Can I help you?"

She doesn't open the door, and Tessa and Peg stand on the porch, nonplussed.

"We're her friends. I'm Tessa, this is Peg," Tessa says, then waits for the girl to explain herself.

"Hi," the girl says, offering nothing more. Tessa can see her eyes are puffy, and her face is red; she's clearly been crying.

"Are you a friend of hers?" Tessa says, finally.

"Yeah, I guess you could say that. You want to come in?"

"Well, I don't know—," Tessa starts, but Peg breaks in: "Where'd Franci go?"

"She said she was going to the library, and then the farmers' market. She said she'd be back about noon."

"That's okay," Tessa says. "We were on our way to the farmers' market anyway. We'll just meet her there."

Back in the car, the air conditioner on "high," Peg looks at Tessa, says, "What the hell," as if it's a statement, and Tessa just shakes her head, as if the appearance of this girl is part of the overall mystery of sudden death, as if Damian's death has caused the whole world to wobble off-kilter, and now there's no telling what will happen next.

Franci's reluctant to go to the farmers' market, but on this second Saturday in July she forces herself to; the longer she waits, the more difficult getting out will become; she'll turn into one of those unbearably self-absorbed women who live in their grief, never satisfied with anything. Since Phoenix arrived, she's barely even seen Tessa and Peg, preferring to stay in their little bubble of grief, as if living in their tiny universe could somehow keep Damian alive, or at least, keep his ghost around.

Grand Isle center looks just the same as it does on any other Saturday, the air heavy with the unseasonable heat, but Franci likes the heat, wants the weather to stay the way it was the day that Damian died, as if it will keep her there, caught in that time straddling his life and his death.

The town common is ringed with pickup trucks, from which the farmers offer huge bushel baskets of broccoli, and spinach, and cut flowers. By this point in the summer, the abundance is magnificent: giant white onions swinging from their bright green shoots, perfectly formed bunches of carrots, leafy crowds of basil, all of it looking huge and clean, all of it appearing to be, as it is, the very stuff of life.

The whole thing is a little too perfect, and much too colorful, and Franci feels her head begin to swim. The last time she was here was the week before Damian arrived, loading up on all his favorite early summer things. She could easily list his favorites, and she does, without thinking, each item trailing behind it a memory: Damian, at three, surprising everyone with his love of fresh steamed peas; Damian, at fourteen, sitting down to a plateful of new potatoes with butter. He started cooking when he was about eleven, experimenting with what could be done with tomatoes, and eggs, and flour, asking Franci to buy things like truffle oil and balsamic vinegar. Franci feels a smile ghost up her mouth, and then catches herself: *he's gone.*

So it is with a mixture of guilt and wistfulness and her now-ever-present grief that Franci arrives at the market, looking for all the world like her usual summer self, in her khaki shorts and her white t-shirt, her eyes hidden by her dark glasses. As she begins her tour of the produce, she thinks this isn't so bad, really. She recognizes some of the farmers' stands, and exchanges pleasantries with a few; not all the farmers are from the island, and some of them don't even know of her own status, the celebrity conferred upon her by tragedy.

And then she sees them, before they see her: the girls Damian was riding with the night of the accident: Betheny, and Kylie, a boy she doesn't quite recognize, and Cort. Except for Damian's funeral, it's the first time she's seen Cort this year, and she can see he's become more of his father, Dick—there are points in a child's life, she knows, when he takes on more of the look of one parent than the other. When Damian died, he looked just like her, she thinks.

They're a raggedy group, with Cort looking a shade tidier, a shade better cared-for than the others, well fed, teeth neatly arranged by expensive orthodontia. He's wearing a blue t-shirt, and Franci's caught for a moment by the brilliant shade of blue, something between navy and royal, and she remembers a word from her editing work: *watchet.* Cort's even wearing Topsiders, for God's sake, Franci thinks.

Next to him, the girls who were in the accident look a little cheap: Kylie, a swarthy girl whose skin looks a little grimy, with her slightly flabby midriff exposed under a flimsy paisley-patterned shirt, and Betheny in her brilliantly white short-shorts, showing off her smooth, tanned legs, her long hair recently highlighted with broad blonde streaks, even with the clunky cast on her arm a real Queenie type, Franci thinks, remembering the story by Updike. Franci hasn't seen these kids since the funeral, when they were just sad shadowy figures skulking quickly into the back of the church. She hasn't replied to the condolence note Dick sent, pushing that particular task further and further down her list of necessary jobs to be done.

If they'd seen her first, she's sure, they would have turned suddenly as a flock of starlings, but as it is, she's upon them before they distinguish her from the several other summer island women of a certain age browsing among the tomatoes and cabbages.

"Hi Cort," Franci begins, striving for a breezy tone, the shock of seeing him catching her breath. Thank God she never mailed that envelope with the shards of glass. What was she thinking?

"Oh, Mrs. Weiseman," Cort stammers. "Great to see you," he smiles at her as he has for the past fifteen years she's known him, ingratiating, in a smarmy way that's always reminded her of the character of Wally's friend on the old *Leave It to Beaver*. A kid neatly ensconced in a summer community every year, and taught in no uncertain terms that he's decidedly better than the year-round kids, but choosing every summer to hang out with them, using them, even using her own Damian—as a foil for a date with a girl, as his fall-guy, as his patsy. *Sap. Dummy.*

"It's great to see you, too," Franci says, sounding to herself almost imperious, even though—*how could she have let this happen?*—is the only thing she can think. *What kind of mother am I? Was I?* The other kids shuffle a little on the pavement, the lanky boy chewing on his thumb, Kylie trying to get Betheny's attention, pointing to something across the common, and at this, Franci is infuriated. "How's your summer going?" she asks.

"Oh, great—" Cort begins, then cuts himself short, realizing too late his mistake. "I mean, it's okay. You know, it's just not the same."

Is it his youth or his native lack of compassion that prohibits him from saying what it is they're not saying? Franci doesn't know, and doesn't care. "Yeah," she says. "It's like there's a big empty place where Damian used to be."

At this, the girls hang their heads, almost in a parody of shame, or grief, and Cort nods. "I know just what you mean, Mrs. Weiseman," he says.

"No, you don't," Franci says then, surprising herself. "You don't have any idea. You are such a self-absorbed, arrogant little idiot you couldn't possibly know what this is like. You're just going about your summer as usual, screwing around down at the beach, drinking too many beers on a Friday night, driving what's left of your father's car. You have no idea what you've done. None." She spits the words at him in a long stunning hiss, so quietly that no one around them can hear, but the crowd feels the heat of her anger and parts around the little group, some heads turning back to look.

Cort's so taken aback by this that he just shoves his hands into the pockets of his khaki shorts and stares back at her. The dread that's become constant expands in his chest as he inhales, and looking into her eyes, he sees something there beyond the woman's anger, beyond her rage: she *knows*. He's sure of it.

Franci, to her credit, stands her ground, doesn't turn on her heel to walk off in a huff. She's so angry now she could easily start swinging at Cort, but for one thing, he's bigger than she is, and for another thing, even in her rage she isn't willing to risk public humiliation. She must remain above it all. "I'm sorry," Cort begins in his usual ass-kissing tone, but then he changes his approach, or maybe it's that his true self is liberated by Franci's tirade. "I'm sorry, Mrs. Weiseman," he begins again in another tone. "Look, I'm really sorry about what happened to Damian. I loved that guy—you know that. But what's done is done. Nothing can bring him back, and I'm only eighteen years old. I've got to start living my life."

"It's barely been five weeks," Franci says, very slowly, pulling each word out of herself, feeling, to her great dismay, her voice begin to tremble. Looking at him, saying this, her suspicion that he was driving solidifies, becomes, now, knowledge. He was behind the wheel. She's certain of it.

"It's been over a month. Look, Mrs. Weiseman, I'm so sorry about Damian, you'll never know. I feel you. But it wasn't my fault—I wasn't even the one driving," he says, and then sees, by looking at Franci's face, that he's said the thing that's exactly the right thing, and exactly the wrong thing, too. "You need to go on living," he says, backing away from her, into the crowd, the girls following behind him, tugged in his wake through the bright summer crowd.

As they move away, toward the benches that rim the park where Danny LaPlatte and the Jennifers are hanging out, Rick drops back to keep pace with Cort, letting the girls go ahead. As Rick slows his pace, Cort slows, too, and Rick knows he's got him by the balls. It's about fucking time.

Now who's smug? Rick thinks. He says, "Hey man, why don't you go get us a crappacino at our grand new purveyor of caffeine?" He nods across the common to the coffee shop that's opened this summer.

"Sure, what do you want?" Cort says, even though as he says this, he's realizing he's only affirming the change in power between them; he should pull away, he should refuse; he should tell Rick to go fuck himself, but he can't. Rick knows too much, and knows how to use what he knows. Cort's stuck.

"Well, I'll have a mocha, skim, two shots of espresso, whipped cream," Rick says, watching the surprise on Cort's face as he says this. The little prick never imagined Rick was familiar with things of this world as sophisticated as the choices available in an espresso shop.

"Sure, man," Cort says, but before he can head off, Rick checks to see the girls have bolted ahead and are now giggling with the Jennifers, Danny lighting a cigarette. "Wait a minute," he says. "There's one other thing I'd like. I'd like you to meet me tonight by the Kayak Shack. That's not too far from your daddy's new place; you should be able to get there on your little bike. Let's say midnight, okay?"

Cort feels his stomach drop. Is this a set up? What's Rick got planned?

Rick watches Cort's face blanch white, and laughs. "Don't worry, Candy-ass. I'm not going to show up with Danny and gang-rape you. Bring that ring of house keys, is all. We're going to see how well you can fulfill your end of our little deal. And you can prove you're not really a jackass of all trades."

This isn't reassuring, really, but Cort nods. "Okay man, but that's got to be the end of it," he says, even though as he says this, he knows he doesn't have much to go on, much right to talk like this, with such bluff and bluster, and he moves across the common toward the coffee shop.

It would be perfect if this was the spot where Tessa and Peg appear, to prop Franci up after her confrontation with Cort, but the timing is just a bit off, and instead, Franci stands there, alone, the people of Grand Isle congregating and parting again, and she looks down at her shopping list, because she knows that to do what she wants, to drop her head into her hands, would only attract more attention. Let everyone think this was some small conflict, a rude teenaged boy and a cranky middle-aged woman fighting over sidewalk space. With the back of her hand, she wipes off her cheeks as best she can without removing her sunglasses, and stares down at her list, imagining the scene as if from an aerial view: the bright green of the common grass, the pickup trucks, the swarming Saturday shoppers, and herself, Franci Weiseman, alone, a still point in the midst of all that rush.

Tessa and Peg circle the common, looking for a place to park, making three passes before they luck out, and with each pass Peg reports to Tessa that there's no sign of Franci, and then: "Wait. There she is, at the Ormonts' stand." Tessa stops the car to let a group of teenagers cross the street, saying, "Isn't that Dick's son? Cort?"

"Yeah," Peg says, and they're both silent, thinking of Damian, thinking of Cort as Damian's killer. "How come he was never arrested?" Tessa asks.

"What do you mean? Why should he be arrested?"

"Oh, I don't know. I just can't get it out of my head that he should have been arrested for something," Tessa says.

"I know. It seems impossible to me that Damian was that dumb. There's a spot."

Tessa slides the car into the spot. They both see Franci at the same time, get out, and approach. "Franci," Peg calls, a little more loudly than she'd wanted to, and when Franci turns, Peg thinks it's a damn good thing they came to see her today. She looks like hell.

There is cheek-kissing, and Tessa takes one of Franci's bags. "What kind of friend are you, making us come gunning for you at the farmers' market?" she says. "Where have you been?"

Franci looks from one to the other. "Oh, God," she says. "You know who I just ran into? Cort. It was terrible."

Peg drapes her arm around Franci's shoulder, tugs her close, pats her back a few times.

"Come on," Tessa says. "Let's get an iced tea."

With their tall paper cups of tea, they sit on a bench on the common. From here, they can hear the hubbub of the market, and it's comforting to all of them, this continuing life around them, all the gorgeous vegetables and irrepressible life of the earth. And the tea is icy cold.

"Okay, Franci, you are not to venture out to something like this without us. You are not to be a lone wolf," Peg says, and they all laugh a little.

"I know. I just suddenly got scared that I'd become one of those women who never gets over something. I'd get to be like Ivy Bless, or something, living on other people's gossip, never leaving the house for fear I'd miss something."

"Okay, great, but who's the girl answering your door?"

"Oh. Oh, God." Franci looks down at her feet. "You went by my place."

"Well, we didn't just intuit your whereabouts," Peg says. "Who's the girl?"

"Damian's girlfriend?" Franci asks, more than says.

"The one you told us about at the beginning of the summer? What was her name? Phoenix?"

Franci nods. "She just showed up," she says, not admitting that she's been there for several days. "I didn't know what to do."

"Let me get this right," Peg says. "Damian's girlfriend shows up on your doorstep and you don't tell either one of us? For days?"

"Well, no. I mean, yes. Yeah. She didn't know—I mean, she was coming to see him, for God's sake." Franci leans her forehead into her palm. She takes a deep breath, lets out a long sigh.

"Oh, Franci," Tessa pats Franci's back. How do we stand it, keeping the hardest things to ourselves?

"Well, that sounds pretty much like a nightmare," Peg says. "I guess I shouldn't even ask how she took it?"

"Yeah," Franci says, swallowing hard. "Yeah, it was awful at first. But then, I don't know, it's like we were both in the same place, if you know what I mean. All we do is talk about Damian and sleep, pretty much." *And smoke cigarettes*, she doesn't say. She has to draw the line somewhere.

"Well, everything keeps changing, doesn't it?" Tessa hears herself say, really meaning *everything*. Her, too.

"Well?" Peg says, and Tessa and Franci look at her, saying simultaneously, "Well, what?"

"Well, let's go meet her, properly, I mean. We've already waited long enough to meet this girl we didn't even know existed until now."

Twenty-Eight

When Tessa gets back from Franci's, she's still a little bit baffled: imagine a girl just turning up on your doorstep like that. What on earth will Franci do with her? She's preoccupied with this, coming up the porch steps with her farmers' market bags, and doesn't notice Jake there, slouched in one of the wicker chairs, waiting for her. She's startled when she hears him say: "I just had a very interesting conversation with our neighbor," without any preliminaries.

Tessa's gotten used to Jake being away on the weekends; she'd almost forgotten he was here, almost forgotten this *is*, after all, his house, not hers. There's a sweet breeze lifting off the water of the bay, rustling the leaves around the porch.

Tessa knows it's trouble, just from the way he's sitting, with hands pressed under his thighs, not reading or working on a violin or anything. He's clearly been waiting for her.

"Yes?" Tessa says, not wanting to risk saying anything more.

"When I came out of the studio this morning, I heard Ivy Bless calling to me from her yard. She was quite agitated," Jake says. Tessa slides the bags onto the wicker table and leans against the porch rail.

"It seems Mrs. Bless saw a man coming and going from this house, my house, last week when I was in the city."

"A man?" for a moment, Tessa's scared: a burglar? "What do you mean, a man? Who was it?"

"She wasn't sure who it was. You know, she's an old lady, Tessa. Her eyesight likely isn't what it once was, right?"

Tessa sinks harder onto the porch rail. Where is this going? What's going on? And the feeling of what's going on, the reeling of being caught in a vortex takes her, for the briefest moment, back to the kitchen of her childhood, the slam of the door as her father stormed out for the night.

Jake is looking at her as if he's really seeking an answer. "Well? Isn't that right?"

"I'm sure that Mrs. Bless' eyesight isn't what it once was," Tessa says carefully.

"Right." Jake stares out across the lawn toward the water. "Right. And yet, she did see someone. A man. Coming to my house, staying a bit, then leaving, last week. In the evening. She was quite sure of the date. It was Friday, she said, and she knew this because Friday is the day when her sister comes and they go for their walk on the beach together."

Tessa's chilled, perched on the railing, the bay breeze on her back. She's in a t-shirt and her floaty skirt, not having anticipated how quickly the temperature on the island can drop on a summer's day.

"I still don't get it. Who was it? Was it a burglar?" She crosses her arms over her chest. Even though, she knows.

"Well, Tessa, I don't know. I would hate to think that you had a gentleman caller while I was in New York, but it certainly sounds that way."

At this, Tessa feels herself go cold, colder than the bay breeze warrants. In fact, the clouds have now passed from the sun, and the sun is warming her back. It was the day that she called Kenji about the raccoon, the day the raccoon had bit her hand, the day everything, for her, really started to change. The day that delineated her defiance.

"Well, I don't know anything about any gentleman caller," she says, and then stops herself. Why not tell the truth? What, at this point, does she have to lose? Jake. That saturating relief of the moments when he forgives her, when he returns to himself, opens his arms to her. But the only way for this relationship to continue is if she stands up to him.

"There was one afternoon," she begins, shifting on the rail, "when I called someone because the raccoon got in the house."

"The what?" Jake says, half standing, then sitting again. "The raccoon got into the house? When was this?"

"About a week ago."

"And you didn't think to tell me? Didn't I make it clear to you that I was concerned about precisely that?"

Tessa turns to look at the bay. She can feel that she's about to start crying, feels the trembling, quivering in her throat. She won't cry, though, she won't.

"For Christ's sake, Tess, don't tell me you were feeding it all this time. Just don't." Jake says, leaning forward now in the wicker chair. A couple of blue jays, high up in the pines, scrabble and cry, then go silent. Tessa sees one fly down to the lawn and pick a few times at the grass.

Tessa really doesn't have to say anything; Jake will just keep at her, and eventually he'll tell her everything that's happened. And he does.

"Oh, now I see it," he says. "Now it's clear. It was Tanaka, wasn't it? I knew you had a crush on him. Of course. Mrs. Bless said she thought he rode up in a Jeep."

Tessa looks down at the porch floor. It's scattered with twigs, and a few leaves blown there by the day's rains. Blown there by the night's winds, she thinks, even as she knows she should be concentrating on what Jake is saying, preparing for something. Preparing for the worst. Still, she can't help it; she lines up her feet, in their black flip-flops, side by side. "Heels touch, toes touch," she hears a yoga instructor say in her head.

"It certainly wasn't a 'gentleman caller,' " Tessa says at last, launching out into the silence. "First of all, I wasn't feeding the raccoon all this time," she lies. At least this can't be proven. Exactly what is the accusation that she's trying to answer? Maybe she'll get out of this, somehow. "But one afternoon, right after I took you to the train, I came home, and the raccoon was in the house." She looks up. Jake is still staring out across the lawn, not looking at her.

"Jake, I didn't know what to do. I was scared. It was right there, in the living room, and it was bleeding, and it snarled at me. I didn't know who to call, or what to do," Tessa feels the tears gathering again in her throat, but she won't give in to them. She won't.

Jake looks up at her, saying nothing.

"What?"

"Nothing. I'm just waiting to hear the rest of this story."

"Jake, I swear. I knew that Peg had taken Franci to Wisconset, and Torsten was in the city."

"And I don't suppose it occurred to you to call Dick?"

"Dick?"

"Yes, my dear. Dick, my friend of twenty years, Dick, my friend who, as you know, has a shotgun?"

"Jake, I hardly know Dick," Tessa says. *And I don't like him*, she wants to add, but doesn't. Standing up to Jake is one thing; telling him how she really feels about Dick is another.

"Well, assuming for a moment that your motive in calling the local pharmacist was indeed innocent—an assumption I don't for a moment buy—what happened when he got here? He wrote a prescription for the raccoon?" Jake smiles at this, and Tessa smiles, too, hoping this means there's a break in his anger, but then she sees it's not his genuine smile, not the smile she wants to see.

"He came in, and he was actually quite good with the raccoon, and kind of caught it, and wrapped it in an old towel, and took it outside. And then he left." Tessa shakes her head. This is too much, she thinks, and yet her overriding feeling is that she still just wants him to turn back toward her, to drop it and sling an arm around her shoulders, kiss her hair.

"Look, this is ridiculous," she says. "Jake, I love you. I am not interested in the pharmacist, or the butcher or the baker or the candlestick maker, or anyone else for that matter. You're being ridiculous."

"I'm being ridiculous?" Jake gets to his feet. "Right," he says, stretching his hands above his head. "Right." He walks to the porch rail where Tessa is sitting. *He's going to hit me*, she thinks, and in her imagination, she can see him lifting his hand, the palm of it coming toward her face. "Listen to me, Tessa," he says, lowering his voice, looking her dead in the eye. She thinks of this phrase, "dead in the eye," and thinks how that phrase is both chilling and trite, even as he's going on, his face inches from hers. "You'd better think very carefully about whether you really want this relationship, and about what you're after here."

He turns then, picks up the bags, and goes into the house, and Tessa's left sitting on the porch, in her black t-shirt and summer skirt, alone in the sun and in the warm breezes from the bay.

Part Three

Twenty-Nine

It's all a little cloak-and-daggerish, thinks Cort, waiting for Rick in the dark, the air thick with the smell of mud and stagnant, reed-choked water. He's propped his bike against the rack. From here, he can just barely see Peg and Torsten's house, dark as he expected, having heard from his dad they were going to Manhattan for the weekend. Around him, the bay water's quiet; he can see just a couple of lights on the other shore, at the conference center. Probably some girls at a late-night yoga class, he thinks, but as he's beginning to sail off into a fantasy involving complicated poses, he remembers why he's here, waiting for Rick Skiffton by the water in the dark.

He hears a low, far-off rumble: Rick's jacked-up car. Jacked-up, and probably jacked, too, he thinks, pressing his lips together, hard, to keep the queasy feeling down. He thinks of that short story he read in English class, about the guys going to a lake to get into trouble. "Very bad characters." His teacher made a big deal of that. In his pocket, he's got the keys, a copy he made of all the keys, all labeled and ready to go.

The rumble approaches, and Cort sees the flash of headlights through the trees, then darkness. The engine quits, and there's the slow roll of heavy tires on the deep, thick mud.

"Well, glad to see you know what's good for you," Rick says, getting out, letting the car door fall shut quietly.

"Hey," Cort says. It's all he can think of to say.

"Did you get the keys to our future?" Rick stands in front of Cort, and Cort sees now something he's never really noticed before; for all Cort's soccer-pumped, organic-fed girth, Rick's got some height on him, some muscle, and tonight, a hunting knife cupped in a sheath hanging from the belt that circles his slim hips.

"Here, man. There're all here." Cort hands him the keys, dangling from the plain ring.

Rick takes them, holds them up to see them better in the dim light from the moon. "Nice. Nicely labeled, too. Good work, boy."

Cort shuffles his weight foot to foot, hating himself for feeling proud to get this compliment from this scumbag.

"Let's go," Rick says, and Cort says, "What do you mean? I've done my part. I'm out of here," and zips closed his sweatshirt, turns toward his bike.

"I said, 'Let's go, pussy,' " Rick says, putting one hand on Cort's shoulder, pushing down, dropping his voice. "You're not going to puss out on me, are you?" Rick says. "Let's move," and by now, Cort knows what's coming, and he follows Rick along the shoreline toward Peg and Torsten's house, which, he can see through the mist, sits unguarded, unlit, dark as the shell of an animal, a shell Cort wishes he could now crawl into, where he'd feel nothing, nothing at all.

Inside, Cort watches as Rick moves through the dark house, not even a flashlight to guide him. The living room is paneled in old knotty pine boards, the furniture with prints of pine boughs, pine cones, and *he must have the eyes of an animal,* Cort thinks, and for a brief moment imagines Rick as one of the wild dogs, stealthy through the dark trees of the living room. The kind of thing Damian would think, Cort thinks, and misses Damian then with a searing pain like a light through his head.

He isn't sure what to do while Rick makes his rounds, so he stands in the middle of the room, a room he's visited at least a couple of times every summer since he was a kid. A couple of times, he and Damian had sleepovers here, Peg serving up French toast with ice cream for breakfast, Torsten taking them out in kayaks later in the day. Alone in the living room, Cort bends down, peers at the collection of photos on the low bookcase. There's one of Damian and Franci, when Damian was a kid, at a Fourth of July thing. *Damian. Damian.*

"Hey man, look at this," Rick calls in a rough whisper, and Cort follows him into the bedroom. Everything in this house is on one level, something that seemed exotic when Cort was a kid. Rick's standing in front of the dressing table, where Peg has a forest of what Cort knows, from Jennifer, are called "jewelry trees," each hung with necklaces and earrings.

"You can't take that, man," Cort says. "I mean, there's got to be some cash or something else. That's her stuff."

There's a long pause, and Cort thinks of the dog he had as a kid, training the dog, and how the dog would stand stock still when it was torn between what it wanted to do and what Cort wanted it to do. "Hey, chill. What's with the premature exasperation?" Rick says. "She's got it, and I want it." There's another long pause, and Cort's eyes flick around the room, desperate to find something to distract Rick, some other thing for him to take that won't be noticed.

"But you're right, man. She'd notice this stuff, and I want to keep this place as an ongoing source, if you know what I'm saying."

Cort lets out the breath he's been holding. "Let's look in the kitchen. They always kept grocery money in there," Cort says, remembering as he does that Peg called it the "fun fund," taking out a few bills to take Damian and Cort down to Sandy's Snack Shack those few times she had them for a weekend. Why did they stay there? Was it when his parents were fighting, and Franci was away?

In the kitchen, there's more light from the bay, and Cort quickly finds the money drawer. Thank God, there's a pile of twenties, and then a couple of hundreds clipped with a note, and Rick judiciously leaves two twenties there, as a decoy, he says to Cort. Rick opens the kitchen cabinets until he finds the booze, takes out a bottle of Maker's Mark, a bottle of Johnnie Walker, and then, to Cort's vast relief, heads to the sliders that lead onto the deck.

When they're on the deck, the automatic light switches on, and Cort hurriedly locks back up again, Rick already darting into the woods, down the narrow path, fast as a wild dog through the mist-soaked night trees. By the time Cort gets to the kayak stand, Rick's opening his car door; Cort feels his stomach reel. "Just remember, I know a couple of things about you, man," Rick says, then smiles and winks. "I'll see you around."

Cort stands by the kayaks, hands in his sweatshirt pockets, listening to the roar of the car as it hurtles along the island's dirt roads, the night swelling up around him.

Thirty

It's just starting to rain on Monday morning and Tessa's in the bedroom, having changed into her jeans and t-shirt, still barefoot, getting Jake's things ready for his next trip. He's only been home a couple of days, but summer is the busy time for music festivals; this time, he'll be gone another week, to teach the restoration intensive at the Strings Festival in D.C., and then they'll have the rest of summer without interruption, save for impromptu suppers with Franci and Peg and Torsten, languorous afternoons on the porch, or out on Dead Man's Beach, rocking in the surf.

Now, Tessa presses Jake's t-shirt into her face, inhales his scent, and she feels like crying with disappointment. It won't be like that, not this year. They've barely made a rapprochement since the fight on the porch. She can't repair this thing in him, whatever it is. She picks up his jacket, the off-white linen jacket she loves.

She'd never have thought she'd be packing her man's suitcase for him, never have thought she'd be smoothing the wrinkles from his jacket, then plucking through the pockets in preparation for a quick pass with the iron. How did she become such a *housewife*?

And that's when she finds it: *evidence*, she thinks, bringing two ticket stubs out of his jacket pocket. They're dated for the night that Damian died, an eight o'clock show at the Film Forum. More than once, Jake has launched a dissertation about how trite old movies are, how we think they're good only because we romanticize the past.

All About Eve. Tessa can't help it: she imagines Jake in one of his happy moods, holding open the theater door—for whom? For a young woman, a pretty young woman, maybe a violin student or someone from his gym. She lets out a sigh that's almost a groan, feeling now the exhaustion from the past week. She doesn't want more work. More *tsuris*, as Franci would say.

And yet. Tessa rubs her fingertip across the edge of the tickets. And yet. If Jake is having an affair—and there's still no certainty of this—couldn't this let her off the hook?

Stop it. What hook? She thinks of that poem, about the fish hook, the open eye. Surprisingly, Margaret Atwood. But just as Tessa's distracting herself with those lines, Jake advances up the stairs, and before she can stop herself, she says, "Did you go to a Bette Davis movie?"

She thinks he looks a little bit stunned, standing there at the doorway to the bedroom, but maybe she's imagining it. Is he scrambling for an excuse? In the next moment, like magic, he turns the conversation back around, saying, "What?" looking incredulously at her. "I thought I heard you ask if I went to a Bette Davis movie, but to me, it looks more like you're just looking through my things. I thought we cleared this up long ago."

Once, the first winter they were together, she read a card he'd had on his refrigerator, signed with a row of "x's" and the name "Annie." That was the first time he'd really gotten furious with her. "I just looked at it because it was on the fridge, and it was such an interesting-looking card," she'd lied at the time. They'd only been seeing each other a short time, and the truth was that she was worried the card was from a rival, one of the other women he'd been dating before her.

"You did not," he'd said. "You opened that card because you didn't trust me. And why not? Don't you know that people who don't trust are by and large themselves untrustworthy?" At the time, the argument had spun Tessa around so fast she was breathless, soon defending her innocence, and only after they'd made up and gone to bed did she lie there, wondering, still, who Annie was.

Now, the room is soaked in the rainy late afternoon light, the pale lemon walls reflecting the light back, and Jake has that same look on his face, but Tessa thinks, as she always has, that she can discern too a look of such fear that she can't just get angry back at him. "Jake," she says, about to explain herself, as if she needs an explanation, and then she thinks, oddly, of the raccoon, and of how frightened it had looked in the shed when she first found it, cornered. Now, now that Damian's dead, that bright first week of summer seems so long ago. She hears herself say, "Jake, come on. I was just cleaning out the pockets."

"Well, in the future, why don't you just leave that to me? You don't see me cleaning out your pockets, do you?"

There's that familiar long gulf inside her, the gulf into which she would ordinarily plunge in silence, or which she'd fill with placating noises. Instead, "No, I don't," Tessa says, her heart beating faster at this. "I don't see you cleaning out my pockets," and she sees, in that moment, that he's leading the conversation away, and like a trained dog, she's following.

"No," she says, firmly, almost as if she's talking just to herself, moving toward the windowed wall, the jacket still hanging from her hand, saying "No," now in answer to her own internal question.

"No. I'm not getting distracted from what I was saying. The tickets caught my eye because you've always said you detest old movies, and you've used Bette Davis as an example. So it seemed quite odd to me that you'd go to a Bette Davis movie, and not alone, and that you wouldn't mention it."

"I cannot believe this," Jake says, shaking his head. He's shaking it, *no*, but he's also quivering, as if he's quivering in rage. "What on earth gives you the right to question me like this? You don't have any idea what you're talking about, but you'd better reconsider your position pretty damn quick."

"I mean," Tessa goes on, even though she's by now afraid she's pushing him too far, "I mean, you were upset that I got help with the raccoon and didn't tell you. If that's so important, then why didn't you tell me about this?"

Jake's face has gone red, and his voice, rather than getting louder, is getting quieter, angrier, and Tessa's stunned that she's gotten herself into this position with him, and yet, she's stunned further when he advances toward her, his face inches from hers, and says, almost under his breath, "you idiot."

"I'm not an idiot," Tessa says, even though, as she says this, she's thinking what an idiot she is. She's begun to cry; hard as she tries not to, she can't seem to stop herself, her chin trembling. "I'm not, and you have to stop treating me like one," she says, hearing her voice come out all weak and quavery, and then there it is: the cold smack of his hand across her cheek, stunning her further, stunning them both.

She puts her hand to her face, thinking as she does that this is just what she's seen women do in the movies. The movies. She isn't in a movie. Jake has taken a few steps back, his hands now resting on the back of the chair, the old wing chair she had reupholstered last summer in a yellow fabric sprigged with white flowers. He's looking down, and he keeps looking down, as he turns, and leaves the room. She hears his footsteps, and she stands still, hand to her face, listening to him descend the stairs.

It's funny, almost, how, with one small exception, Jake and Tessa don't talk about what she quickly starts thinking of as "the incident." She drives him across the island, in silence. The afternoon is tired, the rain having let up, clouds bundling above from the sea. She drives onto the ferry, and then to the train in Wisconset. There, in the parking lot, Jake leans across the front seat to kiss her goodbye, and he touches her cheek lightly, brushes her cheek with his fingers, whispers, "God, Tessa, I'm so sorry. That was awful," and then kisses her other cheek, and the tears come to her eyes, but here's the train in its big grinding noise, and then he's out of the car, and gone.

Before she pulls back onto the street, Tessa checks her reflection in the rearview mirror. There is no sign of Jake's hand on her cheek, even though she feels the ghost of it there.

Tessa notes her remarkable skill at repression as she makes her way through Wisconset. She has no idea what to do, now, so she heads to the Wisconset Free Library to do some work. In the big reading room, sitting at one of the three long tables, she settles in to work on her manuscript, consulting the library's special collection of works from the journals of Louise Boyd, detailing the ten thousand miles she trekked across the Arctic Ocean, searching for Roald Amundsen, who in turn had been lost searching for Umberto Nobile.

While she works, the rain streaks down the tall library windows, and soon Tessa's nowhere near Grand Isle, or the northeastern coast of America; she's feeling the snow beneath her feet, watching the sun arc down close to the horizon without disappearing.

When she leaves the library, the rain has let up, leaving streaky clouds high above. As soon as she gets in the car, there's the memory: Jake's face pressed so close to hers, his hand coming, unbelievably, toward her. She turns the radio on to try to snag her thoughts away. There is no one she can tell this to, is there? She passes the trailers and dreadful little camps that lead back to the ferry road, then drives back onto the ferry, smiles at Claude when he takes her money.

Once they begin to move, Tessa gets out of the car, and walks to the rail of the ferry boat, where she can see Grand Isle in the distance, a green lozenge that looks happy and hopeful. The gulls that always follow the ferry's wake are following the ferry's wake. There is no one she can tell this to, she thinks again. Among her friends, men don't hit women. *There's no excuse for wife abuse,* she thinks, and the old phrase almost makes her laugh. Even though she knows better, has even argued that domestic violence cuts across all lines of class and race, still she thinks that real abuse happens in those trailers that line the road to the ferry. This isn't *abuse*, for God's sake.

And yet. She can't tell Franci, or Peg, or anyone back in New York about this. About what? They had an argument, that's all. Don't all couples argue? And wasn't it good she was standing up to Jake, at last, fortified by the jolt of Damian's death?

The air is damp. Her cheek still stings a little. She has two weeks to sort it out, two weeks before Jake's return. And then it occurs to Tessa that despite her best efforts, despite pushing Jake to the point that he'd hit her, she still was led off-course, and still didn't get an answer about the movie tickets.

The ferry continues plowing back toward Grand Isle. She can smell the salt from the ocean, as they cross over the familiar water.

When Peg and Torsten get back from Manhattan, they don't notice anything amiss; there's no broken lock on the door, no sign of anything awry, and they unpack their bags in the bedroom. Peg hangs the earrings she brought back on the jewelry tree, straightens the rest of her things, shakes off a frisson of something.

"What's wrong?" Torsten says as she comes into the kitchen where he's already making a sandwich from the good bread and the cold cuts they got at their favorite deli.

"Nothing," Peg says. "Just a funny chill." It is nothing, but still she thinks that now, each passing year brings her closer to the chance it could be something. One day, it will be something, and she shivers again, reaches for the bread.

"We've got to get some wine in," she says. "We should have stopped at Humphreys."

"Harrumphreys," Torsten says.

"Oh, you just don't like him because he flirts with me."

"That's right." Torsten finishes building his sandwich with a flourish, and hands it to Peg. "For you. Let's take the fun fund and go to the Wine Warehouse after lunch."

When Peg rifles through the kitchen drawer and comes up with only two twenties of the fifteen she knows were there, she has a moment of terror: she's losing her memory, just as her father did. But then Torsten says they probably frittered it away on groceries, and anyway, didn't they dip into it for the trip to Manhattan, and together they convince themselves that the money was spent, if not prudently, at least well.

Having money enough, they absorb this loss easily, with no repercussion beyond Torsten muttering something about Peg always moving things around, and Peg saying they've got to be more prudent with their spending.

They don't notice, but the twenties rest heavily in Cort's mind, and every night he wakes from dreams each of which has scenes of violence more graphic than the one before. A rickety house, a blood-splashed car. Damian, in danger, and Cort's own feet stuck to the sand. The phone wakes him from one such dream, and it's Rick, calling to say he wants Cort's help again; this time it's Joyce Rexman's place, while she's working the night shift at the hospital; Cort's got it "on good authority" that she's got a stash of prescription drugs, OxyContin and Ativan, anything you'd want.

It's easier this second time, and that's what nerves Cort out the most. Tiptoeing around her house, seeing her clothes tossed on the bedroom chair, her white tomcat pacing around their legs, it's freaky, it's creepy, and Cort feels again Damian's presence there, like Damian's watching him, and when he comes home near dawn that night, he doesn't sleep at all.

Thirty-One

A false positive, Phoenix thinks, in her spot on the ladder, scraping. That's what it must be. That's the only answer, the best answer. She learned about false positives and false negatives in her Health Issues class back in high school, thinking at the time it was a good metaphor; she could use it in a poem, or maybe in a story.

Any kind of test can result in a mistake, a false negative, a false positive, and in the section of the course on pregnancy, she learned about how the emotional state can trigger all kinds of things, making the whole system go haywire. Even worrying about your period can make you skip, the teacher said, making it funny, saying, "In what may seem an especially cruel joke to play on young ladies who are worried they might be pregnant, worry about pregnancy can actually become so stressful the body shuts down the reproductive system, and you don't get your period," she said, and the girls laughed, partly out of thinking this was funny, partly out of nervous recognition.

That could be it, couldn't it? Sure, her breasts are sore and she feels bloated, but maybe that's just from not having her period so long.

When this idea comes to her, Phoenix is up on the ladder at the second-story window, and Franci is down below. Near the ground, Franci's at work on the bottom edge of the house, scraping her way around from back to front, first sitting on a little gardening stool, then rising to stand. By now, the boards along the bottom of the back porch are scraped smooth, and Franci's making her way around the side of the house, toward the front, the side that faces the street.

Phoenix has Damian's radio up on the top of the ladder with her, tuned to WILD. The music is less than satisfactory, mostly the pop version of the kind of music Phoenix prefers, rap and hip-hop, bluegrass and old folk. Still, it's something to focus on as she works, something other than the thought that's become her constant companion, which is that she's pregnant and she's frozen, unable to tell anyone, unable to take any action, even though she knows this inaction is a kind of action. Thanks to the laws of physics, everything is always changing, and so there is no way to not change, to make a nondecision. She knows this, and yet she's hanging, like a cocooned caterpillar, waiting.

But maybe she isn't pregnant. The more she thinks this, the more convinced she is. She's got to get herself another pregnancy test, which means she has to get herself into Grand Isle, alone. She carefully backs down the ladder, paint can in one hand, radio in the other, and walks around to the side of the house where Franci is scraping.

Franci doesn't like any music while she works, doesn't want any distraction from her thoughts, which are not purely of Damian, but which are purely of her life; seemingly random scenes tick in front of her like a film clip, but cut with an abundance of shots of Damian's last days on a continuous loop: the night she couldn't sleep and he came out to the yard to get her, or how she stood in the spring twilight waiting for the bus to pull into the station in Wisconset. Damian coming down the bus steps, taller, heavier in the shoulders, more of a man. The argument they'd had shortly after his arrival, Franci saying she wanted to spend time with him, Damian saying he just needed to chill and hang out on the beach by himself.

Franci thinks of this side of the house as mysterious. There is no neighboring house on this side; beyond the lawn, the woods slope off into the marshy wetlands bleeding into the bay. The trees crowd up close to the house, and because there's little light here, no flowers bloom on this side. Franci's never had much patience for shade plants, feeling that the little reward of a small lavender blossom of a hosta isn't worth the trouble, investing her gardening time and dollars instead into the bay side and front of the house, into tiger lilies and lemon lilies and dahlias and bulbs, lots of bulbs.

Damian was always afraid of this side of the house. She doesn't know that this fear continued even on this final visit, his childhood fears of the gathering gloom around the south side of the house following him into adolescence, and on to college. She doesn't know how sometimes, at home in New York or away at college, he'd dream of the camp, and in every dream there would come a point where he'd be looking out the upstairs side window, a window that doesn't exist, onto the woods, and there'd be something menacing out there, burglars or animals, something stronger than he is, something from which he can't protect his mother.

Damian took this dream with him, and now, Franci doesn't know why, but she finds herself wondering about the dreams of the dead, how strange it seems that the whole secret world of dreams dies when someone dies, and she's startled when she hears Phoenix say, "Hey."

"Oh," Franci says, turning from the forest, where she's been staring without realizing it.

"Sorry, I didn't mean to scare you."

"That's okay. I was just dreaming."

In the dim, cool interior of Damian's room, Phoenix gathers up her wallet, her shades, a book she's borrowed from Franci—*The Lost Daughter* by Elena Ferrante—not because she thinks she'll get a chance to read but because she never leaves the house without a book, just in case. At the front hall table, she feels as if she's forgotten something, and stops, looking down at the telephone table. There's a stack of mail there, addressed, stamped, and she picks it up, rifling through it as she walks out to the front porch to get the bike: it's mostly bills, a couple of real-looking, old-fashioned letters, a CD envelope; she'll take it all to the post office for Franci—that'll be one less thing for Franci to think about.

On the bike, Phoenix feels free, alone, no knapsack, her things in the basket between the handlebars. Franci didn't make her wear a helmet, thank God. She's got her dreads banded together behind her head; maybe she should cut them, start over with the whole hair thing. She can feel the cool island breeze in her face, and she's glad she's wearing Damian's worn blue t-shirt and old khaki shorts, even though they're maybe getting tight. She erases the thought from her head as soon as it arrives.

Around her, the island's a green and blue bubble, and as Phoenix rides she thinks it's like a convex ball; she can almost see the island as if she's floating up above it, looking down: to the south, the big Atlantic Ocean pushing its white-capped waves toward the ocean beach, the still waters of the bay along the west and east. She imagines she can see the ferry plowing through those still waters to the island's northern cusp, trailing a dark roiled river behind it. She imagines the house, with Franci now walking into the backyard, standing to stare out at the water just as she'd been staring out into the tangled trees.

And Phoenix, herself, on the rickety old ten-speed, pedaling toward the little cluster of stores that make up the town of Grand Isle.

Phoenix rides her bike right past the drugstore; she knows she can't go back and buy another pregnancy test there, if she wants any privacy at all on this island. She spins into the gravel parking lot of the post office, and, still straddling the bike, creaks open the mailbox, slides in Franci's mail. Next, she wheels into the parking lot of the island's single grocery store, racks the bike, and goes inside. She finds the pregnancy test quickly, and then wanders the store: is there anything she could make that would get Franci to eat more? In the produce section, thinks of a salad of oranges and red onions, and what's the other thing? *Dill.* She finds them all, pleased with herself: it's a little exotic, a little different. Maybe Franci will like it.

There are just three registers, and Phoenix pushes her cart into the only one open, the only one with a bored-looking teenager leaning over the belt, tapping a text into her phone.

Phoenix plucks her things from the cart and sets them carefully on the belt, not trying to hide the pregnancy test, knowing that to try to hide it will only make it more visible. She watches as the girl drops her phone into her apron pocket, then rings up the fruit, watches as she drags the pregnancy test across the lighted pad, and sees then she's got a pink cast on her left arm: one of the girls in the car. Sure enough, the girl looks up to see who's buying this, her eyes sparkly with the excitement of gossip, or at least, of news.

"Oh," Betheny says, as if she's surprised, as if she's putting something together in her head. The girl she saw at Dead Man's Beach, who wasn't even wearing a two-piece suit. And what's with that hair? Is she black, or what? Her skin's darker than just from a tan. There's no doubt: she's the same girl from the beach, who was just lying by herself on a dumb Mexican blanket, reading a book. Who reads a book unless they have to?

This girl, that's who. But Betheny can't just come right out and say, "Who are you?" so she says instead, "Nice day, isn't it?" to which Phoenix replies, "Gorgeous."

"That's seventeen twenty-nine. It's the pregnancy test that makes it so much."

"Oh, that's okay." Phoenix hands her a twenty.

"Are you just here for the summer?" the girl says, and Phoenix nods, giving the girl the dumb look she's practiced for times she doesn't want to talk, holding forth her hand for her change.

"At least in summer it doesn't totally suck," Betheny says. "You should come down to Dead Man's Beach sometime, Friday or Saturday night."

"Sure," Phoenix says. "I don't know how long I'll be here, though. I'm really just here for a little while," she says.

"You're Damian's girlfriend, aren't you?" the girl says, putting the bills and coins into Phoenix's hand. "Two seventy-one is your change." Brother. The island really is that small, that this random girl in a grocery store knows right away who she is.

Except she isn't a random girl; she's one of the girls Damian was going out with that night; well, that settles it—there's no way he was interested in someone like that. Phoenix picks up the plastic sack. "Yes," she says, and then says it again. "Yes." Before Betheny can say more, Phoenix is out of the store, not knowing that the next customers coming into Betheny's lane will be Cort, with Kylie, and Rick and Danny LaPlatte, loading up on beer and chips and salsa in a jar, Cort pulling out his wallet to pay for it all, Rick carrying the case of Rolling Rock out to his car, into the bright dirt-paved parking lot.

Outside, the day is already going hot, the air heavy in a way Phoenix has never felt in San Francisco, even in the warmer shoulder seasons of autumn and spring. She tucks the plastic bag into the handlebar basket. She's suddenly so tired all she wants to do is to spirit herself somehow back to Franci's, back to Damian's room, to lie on his narrow bed, think about him, and sleep. But she's got the bike, the grocery bag, and she mounts up, pebbles plashing out from her tires as she leaves the parking lot for the smooth paved road.

Soon, she's gliding along the bay under the hot sun, nearing the house, and she's feeling better, as if all she needed was a little air, a little exercise. Maybe she really isn't pregnant after all, she thinks, relieved to think this, but then she feels a sob in the back of her throat: Damian's gone. In order to not think about this, she instead makes her plan for entering the house, how she'll pass by Damian's room and toss the pregnancy kit in, maybe slip it under her pillow, then proceed to the kitchen with the groceries.

As she's plotting this out, she's rounding the curve that leads to the straightaway where Franci's cottage perches by the water; she's wondering how long it takes for gossip to filter up from the ranks of supermarket teens to adults on an island this size, and she's watching the handlebar basket precariously full of oranges, onion, the dill's topknot poking out the top.

It's taken about two seconds for the gossip to go from Betheny to Kylie, Kylie giggling the news to Rick and Cort and Danny as she catches them up in the parking lot: it's Damian's girlfriend from Reed. This is what the carful of kids sees as they approach her from behind, a dark-skinned girl in khaki shorts, baggy t-shirt, roped dreadlocks lying against her back like a living creature, wobbling a little as she makes her way. They've got Usher pumped up loud. Inside the car, "That's her!" Kylie calls out, and Rick careens the car side to side, just to give her a little scare.

And that's when, distracted by the car, the pumping music, the secret she's hoping isn't true, Phoenix feels the front tire of the bike lift, and then the bike skids off the road, floats up over a ditch, and Phoenix feels, for one glancing moment, close to Damian again. The grassy ground rises up in a great green wall to meet her in a long, still moment, long enough for Phoenix to close her eyes and fly.

She lands with a thud onto the ground, and she lies there for a long time, just as she fell, afraid to move, afraid she might jar something loose. Is she okay? She pulls herself up to sit, and the world spins a little, then rights itself. *The fetus*. If it *is* in there, is it okay? She stands, puts her hand to her head, right where it hurts, and feels that it's wet. There's blood on her hand, and then she sees the sharp rock poking up from the grass where she must have landed. She isn't far from the house; she can see it from here. She's shaking all over. The car has continued on; she can't see it anymore. It wasn't like it hit her, but you'd think they might notice and come back.

When Phoenix gets to the house, Franci is on the front porch, leafing through the mail, in the shade of the elephant vine that makes a green wall around the porch. As soon as Franci sees Phoenix, she stands, then rushes down the porch steps, taking the bike, saying, "What happened? My God."

"Nothing, really," Phoenix says. "I'm okay." She pushes a loose dread back from her forehead. "I just miscalculated, and lost control of the bike." They both look down at the bike. The front tire's gone flat, and the frame is twisted.

"God, look at your bike. It looks like Dali painted it. I'm sorry—" Phoenix says, and then she starts to cry, and Franci puts an arm around her, draws her close for a moment.

"Don't worry about the bike. It's so old it's probably better to put it out of its misery," she says. "I'm just glad you're okay."

Franci takes the grocery bag from the bicycle basket and leads Phoenix into the cottage, sitting her on a kitchen chair. "Let me see that cut on your forehead," Franci says, putting the bag on the table. Phoenix allows herself to be examined, still crying a little. "Does anything else hurt? Do you think you're okay?"

"Yeah," Phoenix says at last. "I'm fine." But before she can stand, Franci is at the freezer, taking out an ice pack, then pressing it to Phoenix's forehead. "Hold this," she commands, and then, "Let's get this stuff in the fridge, and then we'll see if we should take you in to the clinic." She opens the bag on the counter. Phoenix remains sitting on the kitchen chair, elbows on knees, pressing the ice pack to her head, more like an injured old football player than a summertime teen.

"You know, you really don't have to buy anything for yourself while you're here," Franci says, taking out the cardboard box that holds the pregnancy kit without looking to see what it is. "That's our deal. Room and board."

"No, it's not that," Phoenix says. The almost gentle cramping starts low in her belly as she says, "It's a pregnancy test," she kind of moans. "I think maybe I'm pregnant."

"You what?" Franci says, so mildly it sounds as if she really didn't hear. Or thinks she didn't. Franci looks down at the box.

"I think I'm pregnant. Or, I don't know," Phoenix says, waving her hand in front of her face. "Maybe I'm not, anymore, I mean."

"Phoenix, are you okay?" Franci says again, but this time with more concern, turning from the counter. "You're going to the clinic," she adds, decisively, and Phoenix, wobbly, the cramping setting in for real now, doesn't resist. "Okay," she says, and stands up into the biggest headrush ever, her knees nearly giving out, but Franci props her up and gets her to the car.

How would Franci have thought of the fetus had she learned of its existence first, and then of its being in danger? Like so many other things, she'll never know. As it happens, she hears of its vulnerability in the same moment that she hears it may exist, and she's immediately protective, not thinking that maybe it's best to let it go.

But *Damian*, is Franci's first thought, when the penny drops in the kitchen, pregnancy test in her hand, Phoenix moaning out: "I think I'm pregnant." *Damian*, not even really a thought, more like a feeling of his presence there, at last, in the kitchen again. Damian standing by the counter while she cooked, a few years before, arguing with her about his father. Damian slurping up the sugary milk left from his Froot Loops, mid-afternoon. That's how the memories are, slipping into the bay of the present like fish, quick and silver-fresh.

Franci loads Phoenix into the car, driving very carefully.

Thirty-Two

In the clinic waiting room, Franci tries to look as if she's concentrating on a magazine, but keeps stealing glances at Phoenix, next to her. Phoenix feels her glances and says, "I don't know why we have to sit here. Nothing's wrong. Really."

"Phoenix," Franci says, turning to face her. "Look. You're pregnant, for one thing—"

"You don't know that. I only said maybe I was pregnant."

"You said you took a pregnancy test and it was positive. You said you haven't had your period for two months. You said you're sick in the mornings, and you've been sleeping more than a drugged cat," Franci says.

"Okay, but even if I am, that's no reason to go to the emergency room. Do you know, like, what it costs just to set foot in here?"

They look around at the small room. She's been in this one plenty of times to know that inefficiency trumps expertise every time: *Damian's twisted ankle and bad bee sting, the time he and Cort skidded out on their new skateboards, the time*—it's already been forty-five minutes since they filled out the papers.

"Phoenix, you are in my care, as long as you're living with me. If there's anything your father's insurance doesn't pay for, I will. I'm taking care of you, okay?"

Phoenix, who has wanted to hear someone say this all her life, says nothing, because if she says something, her voice will crack, and she'll cry, but she doesn't have to worry about this, because the door swings open and a nurse calls, "Phoenix Kearney," and Phoenix and Franci stand, then approach. "Are you her mother?" the nurse says, and Franci says, "Yes," to which Phoenix gives her a look, raising one eyebrow expertly, and Franci widens her eyes, as if to say, "keep your mouth shut." If the nurse had been watching this exchange, it would only serve to prove to her the veracity of Franci's lie.

In the examination room, the two wait, just like a real mother and daughter, Phoenix sitting on the examination bed, Franci standing, then sitting on the black doctor's stool. She tells Phoenix how she remembers going to doctors' offices with her own mother, as a child, how, while they waited, her mother would get on the scale, or make conjectures about the uses of shiny instruments on the metal tray; Phoenix laughs. "She sounds like fun."

"Fun? I was mortified."

Eventually, the doctor sails in, brisk, and Franci is banished to the hallway for the exam.

When the doctor calls her back into the room, Franci can see that Phoenix looks better, not so worried; she's no longer covering up her worry, it's genuinely gone.

"Phoenix asked me to go ahead and tell you what I told her," the doctor says. "She does appear to be pregnant, and I don't think the bike accident did any harm. We'll do an ultrasound to make sure, but everything seems fine."

Franci's relief nearly stuns her. *Hooray*, she wants to shout.

"If she wants to keep the pregnancy," the doctor says, "she should be able to. I'll put her on a few days of bed rest, and from then on she should just take it easy, and start seeing a doctor. If she doesn't want to keep it, abortion is still an option at this stage. I'll write down the name of the clinic in Wisconset where you could go." He's already writing on his pad.

Phoenix nods, vigorously. All the color's come back to her face.

"Well, I guess she'll have to make that decision," Franci says, not meaning it, meaning, really, that the only thing she wants is for Phoenix to have the baby. Already she's got a plan for this. Already she can see it as if it's happening before her eyes.

"I'll go see about the ultrasound," the doctor says, and leaves the room.

For Torsten and Peg, midsummer means settling into their work; it's the time when Peg can finally focus on her new illustrations on the deck, and Torsten can stay camped in the living room, secure in knowing Peg won't bug him to enjoy the beautiful days.

Instead, he saves his outdoor time for his crepuscular paddles, at dawn and dusk. On this morning, he gets out of the kayak, while it's still in the water, steps onto the moss-slipped rocks. The morning air is bright around him, a light, bright morning, with just a whisper of the fall's chill that still won't come for weeks. He's thinking of the work ahead of him today: his chapter on the sixteenth-century Norwegian poets, and then he stumbles into the water, quite safely in the shallows, so if anyone were watching, his falling would have looked more comical than tragic, a big man brought down—by what?—to land—*kersplash*!—right on his keester, feet and hands kicking and splashing. He grabs the edge of the kayak to right himself, but the boat, still unmoored, is little help, and he wobbles, falls, again. Even as he's falling like this, it's as if he sees his wobbling from afar, as if he's watching himself in a cartoon. *What is happening?* is the thought in his head, and he's got no answer, as the sky spins around him, a blue vortex streaky white with clouds.

Torsten rights himself, shakes off the shaky feeling in his hands, and drags the kayak up the shore and hoists it onto the rack. Hands on his hips, he appears to survey the water, but really, he's taking an internal inventory. This was just slipping on the rocks; it wasn't a stroke, that blizzard of warning of the coming collapse of age and then the final spill into darkness. He just slipped on the rocks, but at this point in his life it fills him with fear. *Dread.*

He makes his way up the slope to the house, where he knows he'll find Peg, sketching something, listening for his step even as she pretends not to wait for him.

On the terrace, Peg is sketching the marsh for the cover of the bird book, and she's in her favorite part of the process, when she's just playing around with ideas. She's sketching in the redwing blackbirds mostly from memory, as it's late enough in the morning that they've settled their singing and flitting from reed to reed, when the phone rings inside the house. She doesn't answer right away. Torsten will get it. But then she remembers Torsten isn't there, he's out in the kayak.

So Peg reluctantly abandons the drawing, the morning light, and goes back into the dim, cool house. It's Tessa on the phone, calling to tell Peg what Franci has just told Tessa: Phoenix is going to stay.

"Stay? What do you mean?" Peg asks, looking out the window over the kitchen sink to the water.

"I mean," Tessa says, "She's going to live with Franci for the rest of the summer. She said there was more, too, but she'd wait to tell us in person. She sounded so much better, Peg."

Peg hears something off in Tessa's voice; this is good news, but Tessa isn't telling her something: something's wrong. But she ignores it. She wants to get back to work. Outside the window, she sees a flick of a redwing and thinks of her drawing, of what she needs to do to get the line right.

"That sounds like a good idea," she says.

"Well, I don't know," Tessa says. "I wonder if it wouldn't be better for Franci to just have some time to herself. Anyway, I was wondering if you'd like to go into Wisconset for the afternoon, maybe tomorrow?"

Oh. Tessa wants a consultation, probably about Jake. He's probably being a bastard to her, like he's been with every woman Peg's seen him with. Today, she doesn't have the patience to try to untangle Jake's cruelty, Tessa's willingness to put up with it.

"Listen," Peg says, "I was just working outside. Can I call you back?"

Back on the terrace, the early morning light is brightening, and soon, Peg can see, it will be flattened out into the boring light of day. She settles back onto the wooden chair, takes up her pad of paper. Now, the idea of a wide view of the marsh seems silly, predictable. Peg sighs. Tessa knows better than to call her early in the morning. She tosses the pad of paper back onto the table, stands, stretches her arms over her head, leaning first to the right, then to the left, and then she hears it and knows right away it's a catbird, squawking from the branches of the pines high above the deck of their summer house, and when she looks up from her drawing pad there it is, natty in its gray suit and darker gray cap, polished and ready for a day out. She lifts the binoculars from the picnic table and looks through them, able to see, this close, the detail in the bird's perfectly smooth feathers.

The morning is warm enough that Peg has toed off her tennis shoes. The water ramps a little against the shore, and the high pine tops sway a little, making sharp shadows drift across her drawing paper. Out beyond the house, a solitary great blue heron rigs along the shore; the whole house has a little of the look of a heron, built low into the marsh, the deck leaning like a wing out toward the water, the wood of the structure having grayed to a herony color, the whole thing camouflaging into the cattails, the pines, the surrounding water's edge.

Peg watches the catbird jump from branch to branch, wondering again—for the thousandth time?—how it is that birds manage all they have to: song, flight, nest building, and then she hears a noise from the house, turns, and sees the silhouette of the cat, her new cat, her fourth cat, standing on his hind legs at the door, front paws dangling at his chest in what she thinks of as his kangaroo pose, alert. Then she hears the catbird meow once more, and she turns to see it fly off, launching from the low branch into the trees surrounding the house.

When she looks back to the house, Peg can see, through the scrim of the screen, Torsten, having come back from his kayak through the kitchen, now coming into the living room, bumping his thigh against the back of the sofa; there's a thud followed by a little grunt of protest. He stands at the screen door.

"I don't know why you move the furniture every summer," he says, but he says this mildly, as if continuing an old conversation. "Just when I get used to it, it's time to leave again."

"It makes me feel better," Peg says, shielding her eyes with one hand. She's told him this before. She can't quite see him, standing in the dim interior of the pine-paneled room. On the terrace, the sunlight is very bright, and she has a sudden thought—a premonition?—of sitting here after his death, looking into the house through the screen like this, and seeing the same big shadowy form. Won't she always be seeing some image of him there, after so many years?

"It's your way of reclaiming the house every spring," he says. She thinks he must be smiling a little, the way he does when he's pleased with his own insight.

"Why do you ask me every year?" she says. Then, "Why don't you come out here?" She pats the table as if to indicate more clearly what she means by "here."

He slides open the screen door, stepping onto the terrace in his bare feet, then stands a moment, blinking in the sun. Just as she says, "Torsten, the cat," the cat bolts from the house, a gray and white streak hurtling across the flagstones, brushing past the big terra-cotta planters, scuttling over the picnic table and leaping to the trunk of the pine, where it lands and clings about five feet above the ground, eyes wide, tail puffy as a raccoon's.

Peg and Torsten stare at the cat, all three of them frozen in surprise, and then Peg rises, slowly, whispers, "you idiot," and, as quietly as she can, she approaches the cat, who is still cemented by all four paws to the bark of the tree.

Silently, she calls upon the ghost of Beau, her first cat—and, as she still thinks of him, her only cat. She imagines Beau, the great marmalade weight of him, the feeling she had of understanding him, and she calls upon this feeling of communication as she approaches this new cat, this stranger.

But this cat isn't Beau, and just as she reaches touching distance, the cat looks down his shoulder at her, widens its green eyes, and leaps beyond the tree into the woods, in the same direction as the catbird.

"Beau," Peg says, out loud, as if cursing, not because she's thought this cat is Beau but because, for so long, for fifteen years, the name "Beau" came to mean, simply, "cat," so that even now, she still tends to call any cat "Beau," particularly in an emergency.

"Peg," Torsten says, the same way he said her name when Beau died, that awful summer years ago, when everything was going wrong. "Peg," he says again, and she turns to look at him, standing there, arms hanging helplessly at his sides.

"Why did you let him out? What on earth is the matter with you?"

Even now, she can hear—or more accurately, feel—her father's voice in her own voice, and she can hear what she would say next, if she really had inherited all his worst traits, starting with "You stupid idiot. Why can't you do anything right?" and maybe "I don't even know why I married you."

But she doesn't say these things. Instead, she feels tears come to her eyes, returns to the picnic table, and bends to put on her sneakers, slowly and firmly tying the laces.

"I'll come with you," Torsten says, reentering the house for his own sandals.

She wants to say, "Don't bother," or "Haven't you done enough damage," but she doesn't. Instead, she takes off in the direction of the cat, into the pine forest that surrounds the eastern edge of their house.

In the forest, there is no sun; it takes several moments for her eyes to adjust. In the dim interior between the trees, the forest is unfamiliar to her. It smells clean. Why doesn't she ever walk in here when they're up at the island? She never has a reason not to, except that it's always so pleasant on the terrace, and there's always something else demanding her attention, illustrations to work on, or things to fix up around the summer cottage. Now, there's the talk of the pack of wild dogs, which this year has been enough to keep her close to home.

She calls the cat. "Smokey," she calls. Her other cats all had dignified, literary names: Beau for Baudelaire, because he had a French reticence about him, handsome black tabby Baldwin, and then the black and white kitten they'd rescued when Beau was old. Flannery.

She'd let Torsten name this newest cat, in the hopes that he'd get a little more attached to it than he had to the others. It wasn't that he didn't like cats; he would talk to them, give them a pat. He even built an elaborate playhouse for this cat, Smokey, last summer. But he doesn't love the cats the way Peg does, and she still feels a little guilty about bonding so tightly with them, as if her closeness with the cats belies her distance from Torsten.

Now, she's saddled with the name, calling "Smokey," into the pine forest, and sounding to herself more like a ten-year-old girl than a sixty-five-year-old woman, hair gone white, in her baggy blue jeans and work shirt.

In the woods, she hears something, a mewl, but she knows without looking up it's the catbird, not the cat. There's philosophy in that: the important thing is knowing when it's the catbird, and when it's the cat. She takes a few steps farther into the pines, the piney carpet soft and silent beneath her feet.

Torsten is her catbird: renowned scholar of Swedish history, but still, after forty years in America, a little slow in English, a tall shambling bear-like man. She suits him physically, as she's tall for a woman, "big-boned" as her grandmother had politely put it, but she's quicker with the language, and quick to figure things out, and there are times when she marvels at his slow, deliberate manner, shaking her head at how he can be unsure about how to read a map or figure the tip in a restaurant.

She had her cat, when she fell in love with BJ, with his lithe, aging dancer's grace, his rapid-fire articulate speech.

Just like that.

Just days after the news about BJ, she found old Beau lying in his sick sphinx pose under her desk, and she took him in to the vet's, holding him in her lap while the vet injected the poison into his thick, warm pelt. And then he was gone.

The tops of the pines tremble in the wind, and Peg hears the far-off sound of the rowboat creaking against the dock. It's all about knowing when it's the catbird and when it's the cat. Torsten is her catbird, her nearly perfect, utterly lovable and devoted companion, but he'll never be her cat.

"Smokey," she calls again, and hears behind her Torsten's heavy footsteps, the scrape of the lid peeling up from a can of cat food. A solution she hadn't thought of: their old trick for getting Beau inside, who was so trustworthy he most often came and went at will from house to the wild world outside.

She stops walking. She hears the mewl of the catbird high in the branches, and then she looks up. It isn't the catbird; it's the cat.

Smokey, lying comfortably along the lowest branch of the pine, just above her head. She approaches him cautiously, but he's done running away, and he tilts his head toward her, the way Beau used to. She would tilt her head at Beau, and he'd tilt his back at her, in a communication that so perfectly transcended the boundaries of species it often brought tears to her eyes.

Now, she tilts her head back at Smokey, then takes him down into her arms. She holds his front paws in one hand so he can't spring away into the forest, and she follows Torsten into the house, where they'll all have something to eat and she'll resume her work for the day.

Thirty-Three

There's a gap of a week between Tessa's summer sublettors, and in this week she decides to go into the city for a couple of days, while Jake's at the Strings Festival, to see her little apartment on the Upper West Side, try to remember who she is without him. Try to figure out what to do.

Plus, she doesn't want to stay on Grand Isle and take the chance of running into Kenji Tanaka. She knows she should at least call him, tell him she was wrong, she can't have him as a friend, update him about the rest of the shots she got, but the thought of calling sets up such a storm of confusion in her that by the time she's thought it through, it seems easier to just leave town.

It's another rainy summer day when she drives herself to the station, leaves the car, rides the rattly train all the way to Penn Station without once opening *The Ice Museum.*

Instead, as she watches the wet landscape pass beyond the window, she thinks of the Arctic, imagines herself an Inuit woman, sewing a walrus-skin parka with a needle carved from bone and a thin strip of sinew.

The city, once she arrives, is a shock. It's hot, and holiday-quiet, and airless after the open light of Grand Isle. Her apartment, empty just a week, feels baked and abandoned. The faucet coughs out a chuff of air when she turns it on, before spilling forth a stream of brown water. It's several minutes before it runs clear.

Tessa switches on the air conditioner, puts on clean sheets, and sleeps in her own bed again. She feels half like a stranger, returning to her old life as if trying on an old coat for size. Will it fit again?

Mostly, she misses Jake here, misses their early days together, when she was falling for him fast and hard and he was elusive and charming and lean and bright. During the two days she's there, Tessa elbows her way into the crowds at Fairway, wanders into Central Park. She troops up and down sweltering Broadway and Columbus and Amsterdam to look in the store windows and watch the few people on the uncrowded August streets. In Verdi Square, there's a man playing a big button accordion, sad, European-sounding songs, and she sits for a long time, in the hot shade, listening.

Everywhere, it's stifling; it's hard to breathe in the humidity. Then finally the sky opens and the rain begins, and Tessa rides across town to visit her favorite room in the world, the Asian room at the Met, so wide and white, the statues so large it's like being in the Bering Strait. She sees the one friend who's in town, a talkative friend she knows won't ask much about Tessa's own life, and she hears the news and gossip. She sees her life is waiting for her, again. Her lonely life, but *her* life, nonetheless, and Tessa makes up her mind, even though she doesn't know she'll be able to hold to it when she sees Jake again, sees his crooked smile, feels his fingertips against her skin.

By early afternoon, the day Tessa heads to the city, the rain is beating down onto Grand Isle. Along the eastern shore, Jake and Tessa's empty house and garden stand as if abandoned, the plump hydrangeas shaking their heads with the steady beat of the rain, the tall hollyhocks bending down. In the shed, the raccoon nestles into the old cushions, protected, warm, the rabies just beginning to tickle the base of his brain.

Across the sandy road, Rick and Kylie wait in Rick's car, obscured by the screen of scrub pines, the windows cracked to let their cigarette smoke escape. He jangles the key ring in his fingers.

"Just like I told you," he says, when they see the car emerge from the drive and turn toward the ferry road. "Going back to the big bad city."

At the door, the key Cort gave him goes in, but won't turn. "Damn him," Rick whispers. "Damn your fucking boyfriend." Soon there's the sound of breaking glass at the back door, the shattering noise muffled by the rain. The doorknob turns by the hand shoved through the glass, the door opens, the wet sneakers puddle onto the kitchen floor.

Kylie tugs at Rick's denim shirt, pressing her hand over her mouth to stifle her giggles. "Ow," he says, pushing her away from him. "I cut myself."

"Oh, poor baby," Kylie says in mock concern.

Rick walks to the sink, turns the faucet, and holds his cut hand under the water. It isn't bleeding badly, but, for all his macho bravura, he's the kind of guy who takes bleeding, and all matters concerning his bodily functions, quite seriously.

"See if there's any paper towels around here," he says, and Kylie, shivering a little in her baby-t, her ponytail damp with rain, presses her lips together, scans the kitchen, drops her crocheted purse to the floor, then tears a few towels from the roll on the counter, which is held on a wooden dowel topped with a wooden apple, painted green. She shoves them unceremoniously at Rick.

Once he presses the towel to his wound sufficiently to stop the bleeding, Rick can attend to the house, but because of the rain it's darker than he expected it would be, and he knows better than to go around turning on the lights. The house is secluded, set back from the road, but still, you never know who might be watching. He didn't think to bring a flashlight, but there's enough light so that he can find his way, and he walks carefully toward the front of the house, not wanting to bump against something and get a bruise.

"Come on," he says to Kylie.

"Wait a minute. How come you're so sure they're not coming home?'

"Look, I have my sources that tell me the mister is away for like a week, and that the lady of the house has gone to the city for a couple of days. That gives us plenty of time to enjoy the fruits of their labors."

At this, Kylie casts a look around; she's always wanted to be able to freely explore someone's house, to see how other people live. Especially summer people.

The short hallway is dark, but in the living room, at the front of the house, there's more light, the silver light from the water and the rain. The house has a double living room; to the right, it's a formal room, with a white sofa and a glass coffee table, and a big wooden and glass cabinet on the wall facing the water. Rick presses the towel one more time to his hand, then opens the cabinet: a flat screen, a stereo; CDs neatly stacked on one shelf. He looks at the titles of the CDs, but there's nothing here he'd want; it's all classical and old, Bob Dylan and Joan Armatrading and other people he's never heard of, but he knows they're old. He knows they're not what he wants. He switches on the stereo, pushes the button for the CD to play, and immediately recognizes the music, like something the band would play on the

Fourth at the bandstand in Wisconset. He knows this! He picks up the jewelcase: *Carmen*, by Bizet. "Man, I can't believe they have this."

"Yeah, like you really you like this stuff," Kylie says, and he doesn't hear or ignores the sarcasm, and says, "Yeah. Listen." He turns it up, and the music follows them through the house: the preview notes of "Toreador."

He'll take the CD after it plays, but other than that, he doesn't really want anything from this house; he isn't breaking in to steal as much as he is just breaking in so he and Kylie can have a nice place to screw and so he can look around. Sometimes it's better just to look.

The next room, Kylie following in his wake, is like a tiny library, the walls bright with floor-to-ceiling books on the shelves, a pale yellow sofa and matching easy chair, a desk off to one side.

"Do you think they've read all these books?" Kylie says.

"*I* sure as hell don't know," Rick says.

A big mirror hangs from the wall that faces the water, and Rick stares at his face in the rainy light reflected back. It's still raining, but now it's getting brighter out.

The book titles all look pretty boring, a bunch of books about music, some books in French. He finds some books about the Arctic, and flips through the pictures. There's a lot of ice and snow. And then he comes to Wescott & Williamson's *Anatomy and Physiology*. He stuffs the paper towel into his back pocket, takes the book from the shelf, and, opening it, sits on the sofa. "Jeez," he says, and Kylie perches on the sofa back to look over his shoulder. "Gross," she says at the illustration of the intestine. "That stuff is sick," she says, but he keeps flipping through the pages, which reveal, one by one, a deeper and deeper layer of the body: *fascia, muscle, tendon, bone, marrow*. He finds the page for the heart, and studies it. His own heart, he's been told by the doctor, has a hole in it, a tiny hole.

Kylie looks around the room from her perch; she doesn't feel like getting up, even though she does kind of wonder what's in that desk. Couldn't that be where they keep a little cash on hand? But it gives her the creeps, being here, in the house where they all came after Damian's funeral. She plays with the curl of hair that waves around Rick's shirt collar, and soon he looks up at her. There's something about being here, in this house, that turns him on. "You want to screw?" he says.

She throws her hands in the air, lets them slap down to her legs. "You are about the most unromantic guy I've ever met," she says, sighing.

Rick turns, letting the book fall to the sofa. "What do you mean? Don't you want to bonk? Isn't that the whole point of coming here? Isn't that why I imperiled myself?" he says, holding up his injured hand. The bleeding has stopped, and now there's just a dark smudge along his palm.

"Sure," Kylie says, softening her voice a little. She sure doesn't want him getting mad at her, especially way out here, in the pouring rain, where she would be stranded if he decided to take off without her.

"Listen," he says, "it's the *Intermezzo*. God, I love this shit." He lets his eyes drift closed a little, reaches up to her shoulder, brushes her hair back. He cups her head with his hand, then pulls her toward him and kisses her hungrily. "How about this: let's see what the bedrooms look like," he says.

Upstairs, the rooms are small, tidy, and clean. No clutter, Kylie notes. They look like the rooms in the magazines she reads, with the painted wood floors and the lace curtains and the stenciled walls.

"Not bad," Rick says, standing at the window facing the water in the front bedroom. It's a new window, and takes up almost the whole wall, but because of the rain, he's sure no one can see in, even if anyone were looking. He unbuckles his pants and lets them drop, then pulls his denim shirt and the white t-shirt underneath over his head in one motion. Kylie watches from the edge of the bed, still fully clothed in her own hip-hugging girl jeans, and her baby-t.

He sits beside her, kisses her once, and soon he takes off her clothes, too, and then he's inside her, and she thinks, shit, she forgot again about the condoms.

Afterwards, he reaches for his shirt, finds his cigarettes and lighter in the pocket. "There's no ashtray," Kylie says. "What are you going to use for an ashtray?'

"Come on, Kylie. We've already broken a window. What difference do you think a few lousy ashes make?"

Rick sits up, leaning his back against the wooden headboard, carved with a frieze of apple blossoms. From here, he can see the rain pelting down onto the water of the bay. Outside, the air is bright with the rain.

"Here, if it makes you feel better, I'll use this," he says, picking up a little plate from the bedside table. He turns it upside down to empty the paperclips it's holding onto the table. On the bottom of the dish, "Italy, 2003" is written in black paint.

Later, they make their way downstairs, Kylie still wishing that once, just once, Rick would lie with her in his arms after fucking her, like she's read about in *Cosmo*. In the kitchen, Rick sits at the table, tilts the chair back onto its hind legs, runs his hands over his chest. "Can't you make me something to eat, woman?" he says in a mock-caveman way, and Kylie shakes her head at him, then opens the refrigerator, thinking this is what it would be like to be married, this is what it would be like to have someone need her.

She finds some eggs, and some onions, and some bread, and makes them both a meal that looks more like breakfast than anything else.

"Rick, this is so wrong. What if they come home?" she says, breaking the eggs into the hot butter in the pan.

"They're not coming home," he says, for a moment allowing himself a flick of fear that they are. They can hear the branches of the trees, heavily leafed for summer, swishing about in the rain.

"What are you doing tonight?" Rick asks her while they eat.

"Nothing," she says, reaching up and putting her hair back into its ponytail. She slides her hand all the way down it, to make sure it's smooth and straight. "What did you have in mind?"

"Oh, well, Danny and I are peregrinating ourselves to Wisconset for a little boys' night out. I just wanted to make sure you'd be okay."

The rain is letting up, but she can still hear it pattering on the tin roof of the house. Now it's really getting dark, and soon the house will be alone, left just the way they found it, except for the messed up sheets, the cigarette smudge, a bloodied paper towel stuffed into the cushions of the sofa, the broken window pane.

By the time they leave, the rain has stopped, and together they walk up the driveway to the road, where Rick stashed the car. Far off in the distance, there's a howl, like wolves, and they stop, Kylie touching Rick's arm, Rick standing stock still on the sandy road. "Oh. My. God." Kylie says, looking at Rick, while Rick looks off into the distance, as if he can see the sound. "What the hell is that?" she asks.

"It must be the dogs. Didn't you hear about that, the pack of wild dogs that came over from Wisconset like in March, before the bay opened up?"

Even on the night she stood out here after Damian's funeral, the dogs didn't sound like this, this close, this much like a person wailing into the night, or, it isn't even that. The sound comes up again. It's getting dark, the sandy road damp from the rain, the air around them misty.

"You can walk home from here, right?" Rick says, and Kylie feels a bolt of fear: the dogs, the cold fear in the pit of her stomach, like when she was little and listening for her father's car to pull in the driveway, late, long after everyone else was asleep, the lurch of the door opening, the angry voices rising up the stairs. She knows what she should say, knows she should say, "Sure," but she's so scared in this moment, scared of the dogs, scared of Rick, scared of Cort finding out that she's told someone who was really driving, scared of Damian's ghost that sometimes visits her in the night, that she can't speak.

Rick pushes her shoulder with his hand. "Kylie, yoo-hoo, kidding!" he says, waving a hand in front of her face. "Jeez. You really think I'd do that? Leave a girl out here for the dogs?"

Kylie manages a little laugh. Of course he was kidding. "I know. Of course I know you wouldn't do that," she says, but there was a moment when he would've done that, wasn't there? They get into the car, settle into the bucket seats, Rick turns up the volume on the stereo, and the music slides out of the windows as he makes a U-turn, then heads down Cross Island Road, toward the center of Grand Isle. They can't hear the dogs anymore, but Kylie will forever remember the long, high howl.

Tessa comes back from New York so she'll have a few days to straighten herself out before Jake returns on Sunday, and as she passes through downtown Grand Isle she knows she should stop and pick up some milk and things, but instead, not wanting to run into Franci, or, worse, Kenji, she keeps going. Even though she knows there's no visible mark on her cheek, she still feels the impression of it. Plus, she's sure she has a different look about her now, a look of someone who's been to the city and back, and she doubts her ability to pretend that nothing's wrong, or that the only thing wrong is the usual thing wrong.

Tessa makes her way through the back streets of Grand Isle, passing the neat Colonial houses behind their white picket fences, each front door painted a different, bright color—one of the charming and at the same time cloying affectations of Grand Isle proper, and for the first time, Tessa entertains the fantasy of living in one of these homes, being able to walk to the common or Lantman's; she imagines herself as a young woman, just out of graduate school, living in a studio apartment or a rented room.

She can see that Cross Island Road is already dark, but she turns left onto it anyway; it's quicker to cut through the island's wooded center than to take the peripheral roads that run along the shores.

Tessa doesn't switch the radio on; she prefers the silence, looming around her, like a huge, protective animal. She thinks of the days she's just spent, unsure which is greater, her guilt for keeping the raccoon's bite a secret, or her guilt for Jake's slap on her cheek, for having gotten herself into such a bad relationship in the first place, for having stayed there so long that now, even her finely tuned sense of direction can't get her out.

And here, then, is her own road, but even as she approaches, she hears a knocking in the engine of the car, and then she feels something slip to the side, something inside the engine, an odd feeling, like a bone slipping its socket, and the car rolls to the side of the road, and stops.

Tessa tries restarting the engine, but nothing happens when she turns the key, just a terrible screeching noise, like a door opening on a rusty hinge. *Stupid idiot*, she hears Jake say in her head. She takes her cell phone from her bag, flips it open, but as usual, there's no signal.

There's nothing for it but to walk the rest of the way. It isn't far; maybe a mile from here, which may take her twenty minutes. A half hour. Surely she can manage that.

She gets out of the car, and stands for a moment in the road. By now, it's dark. It's a dirt road here, well maintained but sandy, being so near the beach. The road itself is pale, and Tessa can see well enough to get herself home. The trees, after all, are short beach pines, few of them over ten feet high, and furthermore, she knows this road, knows that there are four roads leading off it between here and her own driveway. Down each of the roads lie a cluster of summer homes, most of them inhabited now, and if anything really bad happened on her way, she's certain she could run up to one of these houses and ask for help.

Don't be silly, she tells herself, and sets out, her canvas bag slung across her chest. She's wearing her summer clogs, which make the walking a little unsteady at first, until she gets the hang of it.

Tessa straightens her back as she walks, breathing in the night air around her. See? She's fine, she thinks, even though she's listening closely for the night sounds of the forest. The creak of a branch overhead. A rustle in the piney underbrush. The far-off sound of the surf, receding further as she walks. The night seems to grow darker as she goes, rather than getting brighter. Shouldn't it be seeming brighter, seeming easier to make out the shapes of things as her eyes adjust?

But it's as if there's a cloud across her vision, and Tessa can just make out the edge of the road, the shapes of the trees. Where is that first turn? Shouldn't she have passed it by now?

Tessa looks at her watch, but there's no moon, and it's too dark to see. She thinks of the house, tries to visualize it waiting for her. Did she think to leave the porch light on? She can't remember. She tries to visualize it with the porch light on, welcoming her home.

And then she hears the dogs.

It starts as a low howl, so low and far-off that at first Tessa thinks it must be the wind, a wind coming through the trees, but then she stops walking for a moment, takes off one clog, shakes out a few sandy pebbles, and then she can hear that it is the dogs, moaning like the packs of sled dogs waiting in the bare patches of yard in front of the shacks in Iquaalit. The dogs' howls go up like a cry, like the wail of the newly bereaved.

And getting closer.

Tessa looks around, a little wildly. Don't run, she thinks, and quickens her pace. Wait. Is this foolish? Is she closer to the car or to home? But she can hear from the howling that the dogs are distinctly behind her, maybe not yet on this road, but coming from the direction of the car. All she can do is pick up her pace, and she takes great wide strides, even as she feels weak from fear.

Tessa walks as fast as she can the last half mile, listening for more dog sounds, relieved when everything goes quiet, then feeling her heart race again when the barking resumes, each time sounding closer.

By the time she's at her driveway, Tessa's running, and she can hear the dogs approaching. Do packs of dogs hunt people down and kill them? She isn't even sure, but she doesn't want to find out this way, and she sprints down the drive, nearly tripping on the ruts in her clogs, cursing a little, then coming up the front steps. She did leave the light on, she sighs in relief, and opens the front door, and immediately knows *something's wrong*. Someone has been here. Someone has broken in.

The house, nestled in its tidy bed beneath the swaying pines, the front rooms lit by the porch light, is utterly still, with a stillness born of the previous, recent and unsanctioned activity there: Kylie and Rick Skiffton's footsteps through the library, their rustling in the sheets, the clatter of the forks and knives as they ate the meal Kylie prepared from Tessa's larder.

"Hello," Tessa calls out, feeling her voice run high and reedy so that it almost comes out as "Hell-ow."

But here she is, entering Jake's house at dusk, no car, and clearly someone has been here—is still here? she wonders as she makes her way down the hall to the central stair, still calling "Hello," thinking maybe Franci came by for something, for some reason, and she climbs the stairs, still a little shaky from the fear and adrenaline of running the last hundred yards from the road, thinking the dogs were at her heels.

Walking up the stairs, she can hear them out there, a howl, a few barks.

She switches on the bedroom light, and there's the evidence: the bed's all rumpled, the covers pulled lazily up over the sheets, made but made badly, and now Tessa feels the icy bolt of fear melt a bit. Kids.

Kids messing around in what they thought was an empty summer house, and Tessa's so tired now anyway that she sits on the bed, kicks off her clogs, then allows herself to lie back on the bedspread, not caring that it's sullied by some island delinquents. She imagines calling the police, but then she imagines the scenario, knowing what will happen, kindly Cop Cal and some young pup interviewing her, asking her where she was coming home from. The cops asking if she'd called her husband, or if she wanted to call a friend.

No. Tessa sits up, sees the cigarette stumped out in the little dish that Franci and Stiles brought Jake back from Tuscany, and feels her jaw tighten and her eyes fill. Hasn't she been through enough for one day? For one summer? But no, apparently she hasn't; the clean sheets on the bed were the last clean ones in the house, she knows, the guest bed stripped from the one night Franci stayed over, all the other sheets waiting in the basement by the washing machine, and Tessa sighs, rises, strips the bed, carries the sheets down the stairs, seeing the evaporation of her well-laid plan of coming home and figuring out what to do next.

At the top of the cellar stairs, Tessa switches on the light, feels a frisson of fear as she descends to the smell of water and dirt, smelling of everything once moving stopped, smelling, she can't help but think this, of the grave. She thinks then, horribly, of Damian in his grave, the wet grasses of the Shore Chapel cemetery tamped by the rain, the dogs pacing in the woods just beyond.

A house like this, a former summer camp, shouldn't by rights even have a basement, but someone long ago was thinking ahead. Still, this cellar is purely utilitarian, the walls made of layers of exposed rock, the dirt floor covered only with wood pallets. A washer and dryer in one corner next to a wooden table Tessa never uses for folding; she never wants to stay down here that long.

Now, she stuffs the sheets into the washer, adds detergent, and just as she switches the water on, she sees it, a swiftly creeping motion by the wall, by the door that leads from the cellar to the driveway, an animal running along the edge of the wall, skulunking under the door to the outside. A sound comes out from Tessa, part wail, part shudder, and she switches the washer on and makes quickly for the stairs, careful not to trip and fall, thinking even as she reaches the first steps of how it would be to trip, to lie injured on her back on the wood pallets as the animals of Grand Isle creep into the cellar, the raccoon and the wild dogs and whatever that creature was that she just saw. Snakes.

But she makes it safely to the kitchen. At the top of the stairs, she shuts the cellar door firmly behind her, breathes for a moment. For God's sake, she's acting like she's in some horror movie. You're a grown woman, for crying out loud, she tells herself, then surveys the kitchen, standing stock still, her back against the cellar door. A frying pan, her best one, lies in the sink, along with the metal spatula, a couple of plates. She was right, after all; it was just a couple of island kids using her house for their love nest. Right?

In the living room, Tessa sinks to the yellow sofa, suddenly enervated again. As nervous as she is, she can barely keep her eyes open right now, and she lies back on the sofa, lets her eyes drift closed, thinking she'll just rest for a little while, while the sheets wash downstairs. Thinking, for a moment, she can hear the dogs pacing the perimeter of the house.

While Tessa sleeps, a dead, dreamless sleep, the raccoon skulks back to the cellar door, bellies its way under. In here, it's found a better shelter from the rain and the dogs, a nesty spot in a forgotten cardboard box of old life jackets and towels, and it nestles in, curls up to sleep, the thrum of the washer becoming the swishing beat of its lost mother's heart, and there the raccoon, one floor below Tessa Bartlett, sleeps.

Thirty-Four

When Franci gets back to the house from running necessary Friday errands, Phoenix is napping in the hot afternoon; Franci can hear the whir of the fan going. She unpacks the vegetables, then goes down to the shore and takes out the kayak, slips it into the water, pushes off from shore.

Only once was she afraid for Damian in the canoe, when he was about seven, and they'd gone all the way around the cove, nearly to the mainland side. As they headed back, Franci saw the sky bruising with dunderheads gathering out toward the sea. The wind picked up, and soon Franci was paddling hard to get them in before the storm hit, Damian delicately putting his paddle in, pulling it out, utterly unaware of the danger. "It's so much easier in the canoe than in the kayak," he said when they reached the shore. "You don't have to paddle as hard." And Franci had laughed at his naiveté and at her relief that he didn't have a clue how close they'd come to being tumbled into the bay water, struck by lightning, or worse.

The fat drops of rain began as they hustled across the lawn and into the house, she remembers now, and digs her paddle in. Now, it's a clear summer afternoon, and as she paddles she's a little disappointed to realize there won't be rain to bring that other afternoon back to her some more.

I wasn't the one driving, Cort had said to Franci at their run-in at the farmers' market.

How many times since the accident has Franci played back in her head the invitation from Cort to Damian to accompany him? Now that Phoenix has arrived, Franci knows with even greater certainty that Damian didn't want to go; he could barely tolerate Cort and those two girls even before he had a girlfriend. She imagines him trying to beg off, but being unable to; she taught him his manners too well, she thinks, and paddles harder.

Because if it isn't Cort's fault, it must be her own. Franci imagines Damian having his one beer of the evening, Cort knocking back God knows what. She can hear Damian telling Cort to hand over the keys: "Come on, man, you know you shouldn't drive like this," but in the end, backing off, again, because she raised him to be a man unlike his father, unlike Cort, raised him to be diplomatic rather than aggressive, to use a convincing argument rather than force, and a convincing argument never works with a drunk. And backing off because of the epilepsy; he knew he was prohibited from driving.

Out on the water, Franci thinks again of Damian's last conflict: he should keep drunken Cort from driving, but he himself shouldn't risk seizing at the wheel. She remembers him, baffled, at ten, trying to come up with a perfectly balanced decision about splitting Thanksgiving between his newly divorced parents, or at four, torn between giving a present at a party and keeping it for himself.

With all her thinking, Franci's brought the kayak nearly to the Grand Isle Marina that forms a brace against the back of Lantman's. In the distance, she can see the ferryboat steaming through the waters. She knows that, according to Cop Cal, Claude Reigner said that Damian was driving when the car came onto the last ferry that night. Shouldn't that appease her? Her son drove himself to his own death. Isn't that enough?

She's saturated in her grief, mired in her misery, and she will never be anything else. At the thought of living the rest of her days with this feeling, Franci feels a flicker of anger: she's too young to live this way for the rest of her life. The next moment she is relieved to be feeling something other than the stunning, relentless grief, and then she feels guilty at feeling that way. How could she possibly want to let go of her grief for her son?

And there is the bay, the big hollow clear sky, the heron startled into flight, the beautiful summer day.

He should be into this, shouldn't he? Cort tells himself to concentrate, concentrate on the way Betheny's butt moves ahead of him as they trek up the beach, concentrate on how she has to work her legs to keep her balance in the sand. She looks great, as usual, in a polka-dot wraparound skirt that's real short, a little pink t-shirt over her bathing suit top, swinging her casted arm easily. Walking up the beach behind her, laden with the cooler and the towels, Cort starts wondering at the difference between her and Kylie, at how come it is that Kylie seems so much trampier, and yet he wouldn't exactly want to bring Betheny home to meet the folks, either? He can just imagine his dad asking her about what she's studying at WCC, and her shrugging her shoulders, adjusting her bra strap, telling him how bored she is with school.

Still, she was good enough for Damian last summer, wasn't she? At least he's sure Betheny hasn't told anyone the truth of what happened, and she won't, either, as long as he stays on her good side, which means, of course, as long as he doesn't dump her now.

He's never really thought about dumping a girl before. Either a girl is available and he gets to have a nice lay every now and then, or she isn't. Only once, his senior year in high school, did he find himself in the awkward situation where a girl he was screwing thought that they were really boyfriend and girlfriend, and he'd had to be a little cold to her, to get her to understand it wasn't like that.

If everything were normal, he wouldn't even be thinking about dumping Betheny. It isn't like there's a lot of other choices here on Grand Isle; any of the summer girls his age are either doing some kind of summer internship someplace, or they've already hooked up with some guy, some older college guy, or even some graduate student or something. There's Britt, but she's been dating Jonathan Beck since forever.

But of course, Cort reasons, if everything were normal, he wouldn't even be screwing Betheny, because she'd still be Damian's, even though he obviously didn't know enough to appreciate what a good thing he had there.

So it is that Cort finds himself in the penultimate week of July, following Betheny into the dunes, loaded down with beach towels and a cooler filled with a six-pack. How come he isn't more excited about this? She turns left off into the dunes, running ahead, turning back to look at him and laugh. "Catch me if you can," she calls back over her shoulder, and he takes a few false running strides ahead, as if in pursuit, but then she turns, leans down with her hands on her knees, catching her breath, and he can see her breasts in the cleft of her t-shirt, and he feels himself start getting hard, and then he imagines how it will be, and then, once he starts thinking like this, he thinks, thank God, he's not so far gone after all.

All he has to do is keep it going with her until the end of summer. Once he's back at school, the whole thing will have blown over. It's just that he can't break it off with her now, can't stop it with her, because if she gets pissed off at him, forget it. The jig is up, as his dad would say.

Betheny stands and slowly pulls her t-shirt over her head, teasing him, pulling it back down again, then tossing it to him like she's doing a striptease, which is sexy even with the cast on her arm, then unties her skirt and lets it drop, then squeals and runs down toward the water, looking back over her shoulder to make sure he's following. Cort feels Damian's ghost on the beach towel next to him, and he just wants to stay there, talking to his pal, telling him again how sorry he is, how sorry he is for everything. But he's got to do this, and beside, Betheny does look pretty good in that suit, and Cort's soon on his feet, walking down to the water's edge, plunging in to the waves after Betheny, trying to keep his mind on what's happening here, trying to keep his interest up.

Thirty-Five

In the morning, the light coming in the curtainless living room windows is so clear, pellucid, that Tessa wakes very early, to a feeling of optimism, a rising feeling she hasn't had in a long time. She lets her eyes drift closed again.

And then remembers: she's on the sofa because of the break-in, the dirtied sheets, the dogs, her car abandoned. Jake's hand coming toward her. Damian.

By the time she gets up, gets the coffee on, she's reconciled these two moods, and decides she may as well pursue the optimistic one. After breakfast she puts some Colombian music on the stereo and sets about a major cleaning of the house. It is still possible to make things work with Jake, isn't it?

The Memorial Day party seems a long time ago now, and as Tessa shoulders open the front door to hang out the hall runner, she surveys the front porch, and finds it hard to remember that cluster of people in the balmy evening twilight, Dick and pretty Jennifer, Peg and Torsten, Franci looking so young and happy. Tessa drapes the runner over the porch rail. And Jake. She can't seem to locate her feeling for him at that time. Wasn't she feeling happy to be starting another summer on Grand Isle, lucky to have this house, these friends, this man?

Crossing back inside, wrestling the vacuum from the downstairs closet, Tessa feels a stab of guilt. She hasn't called Franci in days. She doesn't want to pretend that everything with Jake is okay, but nor can she burden Franci with her own bad news. Right? When will Franci come back from her exile of grief?

As she cleans, Tessa sees the house has really gotten filthy. Everything's gotten away from her this summer. There's still a small bloodstain on the rug in the living room where the raccoon waited, hissing at Kenji and her, and she remembers then that whole afternoon, Kenji's arrival, his departure, every moment playing out before her. She doesn't want to erase the stain, doesn't want to lose all evidence of his presence here, and if she were certain Jake wouldn't notice, she'd leave it. But she knows that even though Jake now knows about Kenji coming to the house, it would be verging on insanity to allow for anything that will remind him, and she gets out the stain remover and the bleach.

It's midmorning when the nose of Tessa's vacuum finds the book, nestled under the desk in the front room, the desk that Jake uses for the business of his violin restoration, writing invoices, balancing books. She switches off the vacuum, bends to pick up the book, and her first thought is that it's something of Jake's, some *evidence*, she thinks, even though, as she's thinking this, she knows it's ridiculous. It's just her guilt, and guilt at what?

It's a new book, a small, slim volume called *Poems of New York*, with a nice cloth cover. Tessa's never seen it before. She opens it, turns quickly to the title page, and sees there, in curly script, the words, and when she sees them, it's as if she's been looking for them for all the past five years, as if she knew she'd see them one day, eventually. "Sweet Jake of New York," she reads, "Thanks for my summer of love." There's a scrawled signature at the bottom that Tessa can't quite make out, but it seems to start with a "B," and the date: it's dated three weeks ago.

Tessa's first thought is that the handwriting is the tidy girl-cursive she's always thought evidences a cheerful yet somewhat dumb mind and a chesty figure. She remembers finding a passel of letters in a high school boyfriend's locker, reading through them. They were in that same kind of handwriting, and Tessa thought at the time this was the handwriting of a big-breasted girl, a girl "well-endowed," not a flat-chested girl like herself.

Tessa, sitting in the desk chair, the vacuum at her feet like a patient dog, looks out the window that faces the driveway. It's still early, just past eight o'clock, but already the day is warming up; she can feel it, even through the shade of the pines.

And here, she holds in her hands an answer of sorts. It's not so much that Jake is clearly seeing someone else; it's more that as she imagines asking him about this, she sees the scene spool out before her and she knows how it will go: somehow, she'll be to blame. There will be another slap, or worse. And even if that doesn't happen this time, it's too humiliating to go on and bring him this in her trembling hands, especially after she's given up her friendship with Kenji just because of his jealousy. It's too humiliating. Isn't it?

She's got to leave him, and leaving him will mean leaving this house she's come to love, will mean fracturing the circle of friends here and in New York, will mean uprooting herself yet again to start a new life, again.

And first, before any of that, she's got to see about repairing the car. It's already late, and tomorrow is Sunday; there's no putting it off.

Tessa waits for the tow truck by the stranded car, leaning against the fender, looking up at the lacy leaves against the blue sky. Now, there's nothing threatening out here on Cross Island Road; now, the air is rain-rinsed, sweet. A jogger huffs "hello" as he passes. There's no sign of the wild dogs, just the summer gulls screaming in the sky.

The guy driving the tow truck looks a little familiar to Tessa, but she can't quite place him, except as one of the Grand Isle year-rounders, a good-looking young guy, skinny, a kid she's seen around over the years but never taken much notice of. She climbs into the cab with him, very aware suddenly of her knee-length skirt that swirls over her legs, her old sleeveless black t-shirt that's a little too tight.

She smoothes the skirt over her thighs, puts her bag on her lap. "I've seen you around Grand Isle, haven't I?" she asks, figuring conversation will be better than silence.

"Yeah," he says, putting the truck into gear. "You don't mind a little music, do you?"

"No, go ahead," she says, not wanting him to think she's some kind of stuck-up summer person, but dreading the blast of rock or hip-hop that's about to burst forth, shocked when it isn't; it's "La Habanera," and Tessa has to work hard to suppress her surprise. Rick smacks a cigarette from a pack, lips it out, and she's so nervous—not nervous about the break-in anymore, but unnerved knowing that now, she has decided to leave Jake—that she hears herself saying, "Could I have one of those?"

He looks at her uncertainly, as if she's just asked him to sell her some coke. "I'm not—" she begins, but isn't sure where that sentence would end, and anyway, he says, "Sure," and holds out the pack to her, and she takes a cigarette. One hand on the wheel, he lights hers, then his.

"Hey," he says, "I see we have something in common," and just as Tessa's thinking he means they both like to smoke—despite her small coughs at the harsh tickle in her throat—he holds up his hand, the left. It's bandaged, like hers, only sloppily, a loose looping bundle of gauze that's pulling off in spots.

She laughs, and holds up her hand. "What are the chances?" she says, and then, at the same time, they say, "How'd you do that?" and they both laugh a little.

"Just horsing around with my girlfriend, you know," he says. She nods, as if this makes some kind of sense, as if making out often results in injury. *Ha, ha.*

"I was bit," she says, but as soon as the words are out, she thinks, *stupid, stupid.*

"No shit. What bit you?"

"Oh, it's nothing. Really."

"No, I mean it. I'm interested in all those kinds of things," he says, but Tessa isn't sure what he means by "all those kinds of things"—bites, accidents, animals?

"Oh, it was just a raccoon," she says. Why has she been able to lie with such alacrity to Jake, but not to this stranger?

"Wow," he says. "This sure seems to be the summer for calamatatious collapse."

"Yeah. Have you been having a bad summer?"

"Well, no, not that bad. I mean, this was the first thing that's happened to me," he says, holding up the hand again. "But I mean, like it all started out bad with that kid who got killed in the car crash, right?"

They're well into the woods now, Tessa sees, the sun and shadow dappling the road. In here, far from the sunbaked beaches, it's cool as a cave. "Damian," she whispers, more to Damian than to the guy driving the tow truck.

"Yeah, that's right. I never really knew him."

"No? I did," Tessa says, still whispering, turning to look out her window. "I knew him."

"Yeah? Did you know the kid who was driving, too? Man, that must be one formidable load of remorsitude."

"What do you mean?" She feels the way she does when a student is trying to make a logical argument but is missing a few of the necessary intellectual building blocks.

"You know, the guilt," Rick says, exhaling long and loud. "I mean, he's got to live with that for the rest of his fucking life."

"Oh, no, it isn't like that," Tessa hears herself saying. "No, Damian was driving. Damian, the one who was killed. He was driving." But there's something in her insistence, the forcefulness of her insistence, that makes wonder if she's wrong. She feels a little shiver run through her, shakes it off.

"Yeah? I guess I got it wrong," Rick says.

He flicks his cigarette butt out the window, and only then does Tessa realize she hasn't smoked any of hers. She crushes it out into the open ashtray.

They pull into the Greasy Gorgon, and Tessa alights from the cab to the ground, thinking as she does this ground is like new ground, this place is like a new place, the world is made new. She's leaving Jake, and she's got to figure out what to do.

The repairs take the better part of the afternoon, but Tessa walks over to the farmers' market, picks up just a couple of peaches, a tomato, not buying much, because now she knows she'll be leaving soon; she doesn't want to be there when Jake gets back. While she waits for the car, she reads *The Frozen Deep*, sitting in the slick air of the garage's waiting room. When Rick appears in the door, telling her the car is ready, she looks up, a little disoriented; she's been so thoroughly immersed in the world of the glaciers and the icebergs that this, Grand Isle, doesn't seem quite real.

She pays Rick, pulls out onto West Shore Road, knowing what she needs to settle her decision and figure out what to do, and heads down to Dead Man's Beach.

On the island, most of the summer people don't have the mail delivered to the house; instead, they prefer the excuse to go down to the post office on Saturdays, lending more shape to their days while still affording them the illusion of being so carefree that they don't worry if they miss a day, or even a few days in a row.

So it is that Dick and Jennifer Grasso come home late on Saturday afternoon, having ridden their bikes into town, the duffel bags on the back of the bikes stuffed with vegetables from the farmers' market and imported olives from the health food store, and the mail, a great wad of mail.

Jennifer drops the mail onto the kitchen counter and sets to putting the food away, keeping a few things out which she'll make into supper for herself and Dick. God only knows where Cort is, she thinks, but she doesn't ask. If she doesn't ask, maybe Dick won't try to find him. She knows she shouldn't think this, but she can't help it:

this summer, her first summer married to Dick, is not going anything like she thought it would.

"I wonder where Cort's gone off to," Dick says, looking around for a note, and Jennifer sees that he looks a little lost, sees that he really wants more than anything for Cort to come back, to really come back. She sees that he wants this even more than he wants an afternoon alone with her.

"Why don't you check his room?" she says, not wanting to, but hearing her friend Faye's voice in her head, telling her to be magnanimous. "You have to be more generous than the kid," Faye had said. "You have to act as if you love him, or else you'll lose Dick."

Dick's gone upstairs without a word, and as he doesn't come back down for some time, Jennifer goes ahead with preparing the meal, which is fresh crab salad. She knows Cort would probably prefer a hamburger, but she's got to the draw the line somewhere, and she's not going to risk packing on the pounds to suit his tastes. By the time she hears the footsteps of father and son coming down the stairs, the tray is prepared and the table on the deck is set, and she's carrying the pitcher of lemonade out into the sun.

"Hey, let's take this out with us," Dick says, handing the stack of mail to Cort. It's huge, but Cort takes it in one hand, fingers the three glasses up in the other, and follows Jennifer outside. No matter that he has to blink several times in the bright sun, no matter his mounting dislike of her; still, he watches her lean down to place the pitcher on the table. She turns, and bends to the potted plants, and he can see that under her white shorts she's wearing a darker thong. This—his response to her—makes him hate her even more, and he sits heavily at the table, trying to look away, slapping the stack of mail down onto the wrought-iron side table.

Here, in the shade of the table's umbrella, it's cooler, and there's a little breeze coming off the bay.

They eat. There isn't much conversation; Jennifer and Dick tell Cort about their ride into town and back, uneventful except that they could hear the dogs howling in the distance.

"I just don't get it about those dogs," Jennifer says. "I mean, why can't someone just catch them or something? Don't they have some kind of tranquilizer gun?"

"They disperse whenever anyone gets near them," Dick explains, reaching for the salad.

"Well, but what about those tranquilizer guns, like they used when that guy climbed into the lion's cage in Japan?"

No one answers. Cort wolfs down his crab salad, taking a second roll, then a third. He's starving, even though he shouldn't be, considering. Considering what? That Damian's gone, or considering the fear that he'll be caught? Considering that now he's involved in an even bigger crime, accessory to breaking and entering? He still isn't sure which preoccupies him more, and his head roils with all the thoughts.

Cort finishes eating before his dad or Jennifer, and he turns then to the stack of mail, flipping the junk, one by one, to the floor of the deck. Condolence notes from his aunt in Kentucky, his uncle in California. He can tell they're condolence notes just by the look of them, and he tucks them under his plate to not read later. A few such note-looking things for his dad, one addressed to "Mr. Richard and Mrs. Jennifer Grasso," which makes Cort feel like tipping the whole damn table over the rail of the deck.

And then, something addressed just to him, a CD envelope. It's immediately apparent that this isn't computer-generated junk mail, or anything approaching that kind of precision, but rather is hand-lettered, no return address.

Cort slips this in with the condolence notes, looking up to see if his dad and Jennifer have noticed it, but they're busy eating their salads. Jennifer eats slower than anyone he knows. He sorts through the rest of the mail, the feeling of the letter lingering in him, as if he can taste it; he can't help thinking it's a note from Damian, a letter from the Other Side.

"Cort?" his father is saying, and he looks up from the mail.

"Cort? I said, is there anything interesting in the mail?"

"Not really," Cort lies. He has no idea what's in that letter, but he's sure it isn't boring.

Down the meadow, down to the water, the bright day is quieting toward dusk, and the redwings are beginning their evening song. He's got to get away from them, someplace he can open this damn thing, and the restless feeling he's had since the accident shimmies up his legs, and he says, "If you don't mind, I think I'll ride down to Dead Man's Beach. I just want to be alone for awhile." He takes his mail with him, leaving his plate, stuffs the letters into his back pocket, and walks from the deck around the house to the garage, then spins out of the driveway, and peddles to the beach. Whatever else, it's obvious his dad and Jennifer don't want him around; he can see that he's only in the way. He's no dummy; how can you have a romantic dinner for two with your teenaged son sulking around? It isn't even his own house anymore. And while it's nice to have a little something going on with Betheny, it's getting harder and harder for him to forget about Damian when he's with her. Every time he sees her, it's like Damian is there, too.

And most of all, he knows now that he won't be able to dodge the truth, to dodge the charges much longer. If anything, he's got to get out of town fast.

Out near the beach, the sky is still bright, the gulls wheeling over the parking lot as Cort pulls in. There's just one car in the lot. Good. He can get a little peace and quiet out here, ease his mind a bit, figure out how best to play this hand.

Once he's on the beach, Cort sees that the evening is August-warm, the light opening out for one big exhale before the sky shuts down for the night. He finds a spot slightly up the dune, and pulls the tab on the envelope. He reaches inside, until he feels a searing pain in his fingertips; it's such a surprise and so sudden and sharp that tears come to his eyes, but he pulls his hand back out, and looks at it, and sees splinters of glass covering his fingers.

Immediately, he knows what it is and who it's from. Cort pinches the envelope open and peers inside. When he sees the glass, he knows with even more certainty it's from Rick; the smashed glass is just the kind of thing he'd send. How crazy is he, anyway?

Cort pitches the envelope back behind him into the dunes, then wipes his hand on his shorts, which does nothing to remove the glass, just digs it deeper into his skin.

He just has to get this over with; he has to get the hell out of here. But for now, he sits in the dunes, thinking over and over: *what have I done? Jesus H. Christ, what have I done?*

The parking lot of Dead Man's Beach is empty when Tessa arrives, so she parks near the path through the dunes, then walks only as far as she needs in order to see the water. Perched up on a sloping dune, facing the waves, she feels as if she can see everything, as if she's one of the early Arctic explorers, having sledded with her dogs across the vast icescapes to find this, the monstrous open sea.

What she has discovered, instead, is something else altogether. She has to leave Jake, leave the island, remake her own, solitary life again in New York.

She turns into the dunes; the evening beach is nearly empty, and the cool air feels good on her skin.

She hears a gull cry, looks up, and there's someone sitting in the dunes: Cort, appearing in the cleft of the dunes like some Inuit hunter waiting for his prey.

Tessa nears. "Cort. Cort," she says, loudly, so he'll hear. She has no idea what she's going to say, just that she has to say something. He turns toward her. "Oh, hi," he says, in a way that strikes her now as a little shy, and she realizes that even though she feels like a newcomer to these people, that to him, she's someone he's known since he was a kid.

"Hey," she says. "What are you doing out here?" She isn't sure she has much to say, but she sits anyway, both of them facing the water, which by now is going lavender as the sun slips closer toward the horizon line.

"Nothing," Cort begins, but Tessa can see right away he's going to make some kind of conversation, and she feels acutely the anxiety and frustration and need to act that have increasingly become her companions this summer.

Tessa fingers her hair from her eyes. "Cort, my car broke down today, and I had to have it towed into the Greasy Gorgon," she says, watching his face for a response. "A guy named Rick drove me, and he said he thought you were driving the night, you know, the night of the accident. Isn't that weird?" The word "weird" sounds funny to her own ears, clunkily old-fashioned; she doesn't even know if young people still use this word.

Cort closes his eyes, or rather, he lets his eyelids slowly descend, and shakes his head again, but this time, he isn't smiling. He lets out a long sigh, and Tessa thinks she hears the trembling in that sigh that would indicate tears, if he were a girl. When he opens his eyes again, he turns to face her. "Yeah," he says. "Yeah, right, I was driving," he says, sarcastically.

Tessa feels her eyebrows lift in surprise, and then she hears the sarcasm.

"What do you mean?"

"What do you think I mean? Of course I wasn't driving. The cops did their investigation thing, why isn't that enough? Anyway, it doesn't matter. I'm getting out of here."

"Are you going back early? To UMass?"

There's a pause, Cort looking out at the waves, Tessa looking at Cort. "Yeah," he says, finally. "I'm going back a little early, just to get out of here." He looks down at his sneakers, toys with his shoelaces. "I don't know."

"I don't know what to do, either," Tessa says, resting her chin in her hands, elbows on knees. "I don't know what to do," she repeats, meaning, this time, about everything, even though she does know, and for the first time all summer, she feels a little bit lighter, a little bit of relief. The wind, heralding the evening, is picking up a bit, and suddenly the beach is autumn-cold. Cort doesn't offer any suggestions.

"Okay, Cort," she says, standing, brushing the sand from her pants. She looks at him then, his head hanging, staring at the sand. When she was a girl, she used to think that there was someone with answers, someone who knew what to do. Now, she knows that's a fantasy of children; there's no one steering this boat we're all in.

"Thanks," Cort says, still not looking up, and then he does, and she sees now that he *is* crying. This big lug of a guy, crying out here on the beach. "I'm sorry," she says, and reaches down to press her palm into his shoulder. It's the shoulder not of a boy, but of a man, a man who has to make decisions and face the results.

In the parking lot, there's less light, and Tessa hears the first howl of the dogs, feels a flicker of fear, but gets into her car, starts it up, and pulls onto East Shore Road, heading home, or rather heading to Jake's, to pack up her things and make her plans.

Thirty-Six

On Monday Franci takes Phoenix to a follow-up appointment at the hospital in Wisconset, where they learn the fetus seems fine, and Phoenix seems fine, and she's back to having a decision to make.

Afterward, they get into Franci's car, which has been baking in the parking lot. They open the doors to let some of the hot air escape, and then they get in, neither of them saying a word. All the long drive back to the island, through the trip on the ferry, and the drive around the curving island roads, they say nothing, until they reach the house, and then, before they leave the car, Phoenix says, "I want to keep it," and by then, Franci's lost track of whatever the conversation was back at the hospital; she's so sunk into her thoughts, afloat in memories of taking Damian to that hospital when he was nine, and six, and thirteen, that at first, she stares blankly at Phoenix for a moment before coming round.

"What?" she says, her hand on the door.

"I think I want to keep it," Phoenix says, looking down at her hands, which are folded in her lap.

Franci feels excitement—something she thought she'd never feel again—swell up inside her. "Oh, Phoenix, you don't have to decide that right now," she says, thinking, *keep it, keep it, keep it*. "Really, if you want to get an abortion, we can drive up to the women's clinic. It isn't a big deal," she says, meaning the drive, not the procedure.

"No, really," Phoenix says, toying with the braided macramé bracelet on her wrist.

"I had one of those when I was a teenager," Franci hears herself say.

"What?" Phoenix looks up, one eyebrow raised. "An abortion?"

"No, Silly. One of those macramé bracelets. My best friend, Rachel, gave it to me when we were sophomores in high school, right before she moved away. I wore it for about a year before it finally fell off."

With one finger, Phoenix spins her bracelet around her wrist. Hers is studded with yellow and blue beads; Franci can't remember, but thinks maybe hers didn't have beads.

"I really want to keep it," Phoenix says. "You've got to remember, I've known for a couple of weeks. I've had some time to think about it. I mean, it's Damian's baby. It's all that's left of him."

They sit together for a long moment, saying nothing, and then Phoenix says, "But what about the epilepsy?"

"What?" Franci says.

"I mean, what if it's genetic? Isn't it genetic? Shouldn't I at least consider that?"

"What epilepsy, Phoenix?" Franci has an odd sensation, as if the world is tilting sideways, and she thinks for a minute that if the car doors were open, they'd both go tumbling out.

"You know," Phoenix says, then looks at Franci and stops. "Oh my God. You don't know. He never told you, did he?"

"Yes, Phoenix, he did tell me. I didn't think anyone else knew."

"But didn't you think that's what caused the accident? I just assumed that was it."

Franci feels her carefully constructed belief about the accident start to fall. Damian the cause of his own death. She feels the tumbling feeling again.

"Oh, Phoenix," Franci says, pressing her palms into the steering wheel. She imagines Damian at school, so far away from home, so far away from her, hearing this from a doctor, a stranger. Did he know how this would affect his life? He must have. Franci feels such a deep longing for him, to hold him tight against her, to enfold her arms around him the way she did when he was little, when he'd leap into her arms and press his face against her neck and say, "Mommy, don't leave me," and his being alone with this news at Reed and his being alone in the world of the dead become one thing, and the moment of her feeling this lasts forever, and she doesn't even realize any of it is happening, doesn't realize the tears are running down her face, doesn't realize Phoenix is pressing her shoulder with her hand, until Phoenix says, "Come on, let's go inside. I really have to pee."

"Okay," Franci says. She takes a deep breath, and the terrible moment is gone. "I just want you to know that you can still think about it, if you want to. Come on," she says, and pushes herself out of the car, hoping Phoenix will follow, which she does.

Inside, the house, having been shut up all afternoon, is warm, and Phoenix follows Franci into the kitchen, both of them pulled by the somewhat cooler air off the bay that's blowing into the kitchen from the back porch. They sit on the back step, and Phoenix takes her pack of cigarettes out from her embroidered bag, taps it twice against her knees, and then hands it to Franci.

"Here," she says. "I guess I shouldn't smoke anymore, right?"

Franci raises her eyebrows. "Phoenix, that's about the dumbest question I've ever heard," she says, and then she laughs, snatching the pack of cigarettes away and in one motion, tossing it out across the lawn, where it sails in a wide arc over the tangled beds of lilies, to land on the shore, down by the water. Phoenix and Franci laugh. "I'll go pick it up in a minute," Franci says. "But first, didn't the doctor say bed rest? Let's at least get you set up on the chaise." She cranks the handle of the old chaise on the back porch, arranges a nest from the chintz pillows. Once Phoenix is settled, Franci sits on the edge of the chaise, and smoothes Phoenix's hair from her forehead. "What would you like to read? I have Salinger's *Nine Stories*, you might like that," Franci says. She can't seem to stop talking, or moving; she's so excited, she feels she must do something, even though her excitement also means that she keeps feeling her eyes fill with tears.

"Yeah," Phoenix says, "Salinger will be great."

Phoenix remembers Damian saying the *Franny and Zooey* character of Lane Coutell was like his friend from the island, Cort. Now, Cort is one of the last people to see Damian alive, one of the few people who knew what was really happening in that car. And yet, Phoenix is suddenly so tired that she doesn't want to know any more than she already does. Damian loved her, she knows that with all her heart, and that's all that matters. That, and having this baby, even if she does give it up to Franci's care, as she knows she must.

By the time Franci locates *Nine Stories* and returns to the porch, Phoenix is asleep. She sits on the step and starts reading, then remembers when Damian read it last summer, he said Lane Coutell was like Cort. And then she thinks: of course Damian was driving, and had a seizure. Of course.

As deep as her grief was just minutes ago, her relief at this sudden acceptance is equally deep. Damian was driving. Cort hasn't been lying. There was a reason—it wasn't just a dumb drunken frat boy. It was science, it was medicine, it was Damian's own body, the body she's loved more than any other, rebelling. It was unavoidable, it was—*necessary* is the word that comes to her, even though she wouldn't have been able to explain why. "Oh, Damian," she says out loud, to the air, to the water, to the sky.

She rises from the porch, tucks the book beside Phoenix, who has one hand curled near her mouth, and even though she knows the fetus is yet just a cluster of cells still puzzling into a recognizable form, Franci imagines the fetus inside her, her grandchild, with a tiny fist curled by its mouth, too, beginning the long, slow climb toward being born.

Thirty-Seven

The burr of his phone wakes Cort from a dream which seems to have nothing to do with anything, out in a kayak circling an island, Grand Isle but not Grand Isle, a dream he used to have when he was a kid. Big waves, tiny fish.

"Yeah?" he says, reaching up to the window to push the curtain back. Outside, it's bright, and hot-looking already.

"How's my favorite accomplice?" Rick's voice sounds greasy, even coming through the phone, and Cort pulls the phone away from his ear. Great. When you finally do get a signal out here, it's the last person you want to hear from.

"What do you want?" he says, unguarded by sleep.

"Oh, that's not a very nice way to treat the keeper of your classified information, is it now?"

"Listen, man, I've done what you wanted. You've got all the keys. Our deal is over. Shut it down."

"Well, I think not, my friend. Your key didn't work at the last place. I cut my hand when I had to break the window to get in. I need my hands for my work, you know. It's how I *earn* my money."

Cort feels the lurch of panic surge through him. Rick *did* send him that envelope of glass. He must have. What else is he capable of? The acid of anxiety rises in his stomach. "Sorry, man. I thought I had them all straight."

"Well, listen, I want to hit the next one tomorrow night, and I need some assistance with it. Namely, your assistance. Over on the West Shore. Your little buddy's place, that little cottage. We'll go when she's asleep."

"You mean Damian's house? You want to break into Damian's?"

Cort, still holding the curtain back with one hand, looks longingly out the window at the big, bright day, the slice of water down there, winking like an eye. How different this view was at the summer's beginning. How terribly different everything is now.

"I can't, man. I just can't do any more," Cort says, at first meaning just that he can't break into Damian's—now Franci's—house, not after everything she's had to deal with. But he means, too, he can't keep on being Rick's patsy; that, and he can't stay mired in his guilt and grief. He almost means he isn't up to the simple, devastating task of living.

He knows that it's the end. There's a long pause on the other end of the phone, and then the line goes dead.

Franci comes into the kitchen to find Phoenix thumbing through the little Grand Isle phone book. "What are you looking for?" she asks, and at once curses herself for asking. The surest way to get a teenager to clam up is to ask something, she knows.

But Phoenix looks up from the book, one finger pressed to the page to keep her place. "The Grand Isle Clinic," she says, looking Franci right in the eye, as if daring her to stop her.

"Yes?" Franci asks.

"Yes," Phoenix says. "Yes, I really meant it when I said I decided. I'm keeping the baby. That's my decision. I need to get a prenatal exam," she says, as if that's it—one prenatal exam and then wait for the baby to arrive. Franci almost laughs, both at Phoenix's lack of knowledge and at her own relief. She wants to swing out her arms and shout thanks to God, or to Something. There must be a *b'racha* for this; her mother must have said something when she found out Franci was pregnant with Damian. But she just says, "As long as it's your own decision. That's the important thing, Phoenix," knowing as she says this that what's really important is that she, Franci, will be having a grandchild.

Once the appointment is made, they go into Damian's room together, and stand in the doorway. Since Phoenix's arrival, the room has changed; the sheets on the bed have been washed, slept in, washed again, and Phoenix has had to push some of the clutter aside to make room for her knapsack, towering in one corner, a pair of jeans and a couple of her t-shirts discernable from Damian's only by their color and cut lying scattered on the chair, the dresser, the bed. It's no longer his room.

"It isn't his room anymore anyway," Franci says, feeling the choke in her throat. But it's true. Damian's gone from this room, gone from the house, gone, as far as she can now tell, from the whole island. The world. This world.

"I'm sorry," Phoenix says, leaning against the doorjamb.

"No, I don't mean that. I just mean it's time for you to move in. If you're going to stay the rest of the summer, and you're going to keep the baby, you need a proper room. And this is the only one. Besides, what else would I do? I'm not going to maintain it as a mausoleum; that's sick."

"I know. You don't want to end up like Mrs. Glass, right?"

"Right. And you know Damian wouldn't want to end up entombed like Seymour."

"Right." Phoenix nods, but still doesn't push away from the doorjamb, until Franci says, "Come on," and walks into the room, the first time she's come in here at all since picking up Phoenix's message back in June. Has it really been that long?

Together, they move Phoenix's things into the living room, then set to their work. It isn't as bad as Franci's imagined it; this is just Damian's summer home, and doesn't have the years of collected stuff his room at home will hold. She shelves that thought as they empty the drawers. There's no sorting to do here; it's just socks and boxer shorts, t-shirts, jeans, and even though each piece of clothing sears through Franci with a memory—buying it, laundering it, in some cases actually even seeing it worn on her son—she feels the sadness, but she doesn't succumb. She knows she's just going to box it all up and donate it to the Wisconset Shelter, so she brings her sharp professional eye to the job, the eye that edits medical texts for errors in punctuation and fact. Or that used to do.

It's the closet that's more of a problem. Here, Damian's summer jackets hang empty: his sweatshirt, his parka. She sees him in the parka, early summer, early fall, calling to her from the kayak, the air fresh and promising. Promising.

"Do you have any boxes?" Phoenix asks, and Franci turns, for one short, stunning moment having no idea who Phoenix is or what they're doing there. "In the basement," she says, and Phoenix is gone, and Franci presses her face into Damian's sweatshirt, still on its hanger. It's filled with his boy-scent, the scent of detergent and sweat and milk that's been spilled, the scent of her son. She inhales as deeply as her choking chest will allow, and then lets out a cry, not even thinking of Phoenix, not thinking of anything, just letting her grief exhale.

Take a deep breath, now, she hears her mother's voice in her head, some half-forgotten memory of scraping her knee, or learning to swim. She feels what she's sure is her mother's hand palmed to her back, and she takes a deep breath. *There.*

Franci takes the sweatshirt from the closet. She doesn't pull it on over her head; she knows she'll fit into it, but that it will also be a bit too big. She folds it and sets it aside, and then Phoenix is back with the box, and they put in Damian's sneakers, and all his other clothes.

Phoenix isn't intrigued by Damian's wardrobe; having no memories of Damian's summer wear, she doesn't care so much about that, but when they get to his knapsack, the one he used for school, she feels a prickle of fear. This will be hard, she thinks, and she doesn't realize it, but she lets out a sigh.

There's a notebook in the bottom, the notebook he used for sociology class, the class where they met. She thumbs through the pages. There are his meticulous notes, in his tidy handwriting. He was careful with everything. Well, almost. There are a few drawings in the margins, sailboats, pine trees, cliffs, and then, taking up half a page, a drawing that is unmistakably of her. "PHOENIX" is written in his blocky capital letters under it.

"Look," she says to Franci, and Franci looks. "Okay," she says, and now she's sighing too, putting the palm of her hand to Phoenix's back. "Okay. Let's keep that for the baby."

Soon, the room is stripped of Damian, and Franci and Phoenix pack the things into the car, then drive to Grand Isle's single housewares store where they buy new ticking-striped curtains, a matching bedspread, and a blue cotton rug. "This must be that nesting thing," Phoenix says as they wait at the cash register, and Franci reaches over and pats her back again. "I guess I'm nesting vicariously then," she says. Nesting, or grief; grief, or denial. At least she isn't crying.

When Peg calls Tessa, she knows right away that something's wrong on the other end of the line, and isn't surprised when Tessa says, "Peg. I've got to tell you something."

Tessa keeps her story shorter than she'd thought possible, whittling it for Peg's sake into only the necessities: she's going back to New York tomorrow, before Jake returns on Wednesday. When Peg asks,

"What happened?" Tessa feels again Jake's slap on her face, sees again the inscription in the book, hears again Jake's voice going high-pitched with condescension. The shame over the slap, and finding the book, threatens to swallow her up, so she just says, "It's just been enough things over the summer. I'll explain it to you later, but really, I can't stay here anymore," and at this, she feels her voice crack, then swallows hard. "Jake's driving his own car up from the city tomorrow, and I won't be here. I can't."

"Oh, Tessa, you can't go back to New York. You'd melt. And anyway, where will you stay? Isn't your place sublet for August?"

"Yeah," Tessa sighs. "But it's only a little more than a month. I can bunk in with Cassie. She has kind of a guest room in her apartment in Inwood."

"Don't be silly," Peg says, without pausing. "Of course you can't go back to New York in August. God, what a thought. Stay with us."

"What?"

"Stay at the house. Really. We're going to Izzy's wedding in Boston this weekend, and Torsten's got that conference coming up. And it would be a pleasure to have you when we *are* here."

So Tessa finds herself not packing up the car and barreling onto the ferry, but merely driving down East Shore Road, past Ivy Bless' house, past the Sheffield's camp, past the place where the land begins to give way to the marshes, pulling at last into Peg and Torsten's driveway in the dusk of this, her first night out, her first night on her own.

When Jake returns from New York, he'll find her note, and he'll find everything changed. Knowing him, he'll probably just lock himself up with a new violin project and never speak to her again. And that's okay with Tessa, or so she tells herself, sitting on the deck of Peg and Torsten's.

In the house, she settles herself in what Torsten calls the "guest wing," a bedroom and bath set up a short flight of steps at the back of the house. Once she's living in it, Tessa thinks the house is like a wooden puzzle, mis-pieced together.

Tessa doesn't mind losing the view of the bay, or the big window that lets in all that light. Here, now, she now enjoys the dark, sleeps late, rises, goes back to work on her book. She's now on the part where the explorers are making their way through the Northwest Passage. She's trying to unfreeze the frozen past, to melt the ice that packs up around the ship, securing it for the season. The question she keeps coming up against is *what went wrong*? Sure, it was cold, but did the men wear itchy wool pants? Did their feet get soaked, then freeze? How did they have enough to eat? How did they survive?

On her first evening alone, Tessa takes her supper out to the deck, looks out over the marsh. From here, she can see the shoreline of the bay as it curves around to where the freshwater meets the sea. Lifting Torsten's binoculars to her eyes, she watches the great blue heron unfolding, an origami bird cut from the water. Far out there, she can see the place where the waters meet in a foamy seam of whitecaps.

She puts the binoculars down, and eats her spinach salad. It has sliced anise, and pine nuts she found in Peg's kitchen. Jake won't come by, won't try to convince her to return, no matter how much she wishes for and dreads this.

As the sun goes down, the air grows cooler, and Tessa thinks that soon she'll go inside for her sweatshirt. But for now, she'll stay out here, watching the marshland recede into evening, listening for the rustle of the animals: meadow vole, deer, raccoon.

Even though Tessa's car isn't in the driveway, Jake enters the house calling "Hello! I've returned from the wars!" but there's no answer. *Good thing I drove*, he thinks, and to tamp down his disappointment that Tessa is apparently nowhere around, he thinks that the least she could have done was arrange her schedule so she'd be here to greet him. For God's sake, he's been gone most of July, and can finally settle in for what remains of the summer.

Humming "La Habanera," he leaves the violin cases in the front hall, takes his duffel bag upstairs, tosses it onto the bed, and leans against the window to look out at the bay. The windows were a great idea; he can remember how dim this room was when he first bought the place. The violin restoration business has really paid off; he showed all those people who told him it was a crazy idea—Dad chief among them. If he can just keep the commissions coming in, he can pretty much do what he wants.

Like at the Strings Festival. Doing what he wants. He shakes this off, this memory of the girl's slim legs, her bright laugh, the way she looked at him as he talked about the delicacy of edgework, about how by fine-tuning the bridge, he could pull out the instrument's sweetest sound.

Jake's come back with a new commission: a Mittenwald. Probably—okay, possibly—by the Klotz family. With his expert touch, the cracks will seem to disappear completely, and if he can find a good copy of the Klotz label, it will be much more valuable. Much.

Jake doesn't unpack his clothing; instead, he walks downstairs, picks up the violin cases, and makes his way out to his studio, noting that the lawn needs mowing; didn't he tell Tessa to take care of that? He passes the tool shed, almost stopping to look inside, see if there's any evidence of the raccoon, but he continues on to his workshop. He unlocks the door and turns the knob.

The smell is what hits him first, the cloying, nearly sweet smell of something dead. And then he sees it: a small raccoon, bloated, lying belly up under his workbench, dead, ballooned to such a girth it appears ready to explode.

Jake steps back outside. He can hardly breathe, and feels the nausea rising in his throat, and with it, the rage. Tessa. Tessa and that damned raccoon, as if she'll save the whole world of injured animals and needful things. Like the first dead raccoon of the summer—the one he thinks of as starting off all the bad things of this summer—this one probably also came upon the poisoned bait Jake set out for them. Why can't they go die in the woods?

And even though he wouldn't be able to say how he knows she's left him, or even *that* he knows it, he doesn't need to read or even see the note she's left on his workbench; he knows she's gone, and he knows why. He knows, for a quick, clear moment, as he stands and retches into the forsythia bush, one hand holding the workshop door closed as if the stench will escape to find him, that it's the way he keeps his heart locked up in a case of its own that's made her leave.

Jake knows this, and yet it will be a long time before he's more than just aware. He sets about cleaning up the mess, getting a plastic sheet from the tool shed, shoveling the raccoon's body onto it, dragging it outside to the woods, all the while with his face pressed deep into the crook of his arm. He'll have to set out more bait, especially at summer's end, when they'll all be looking for shelter, looking for a way inside.

Thirty-Eight

It's so early in the morning that it still feels like the middle of the night when Cort finally hears the bleating of the alarm clock and reaches out a hand to tap it down. It wasn't necessary to set it, anyway; he's pretty much been awake the whole time, first closing his eyes in a failed attempt to sleep, then watching the night-filled room, thinking about his plan, thinking about what to say, thinking, as always, of Damian and the night he died.

He sits at the little antique wooden desk in his room, a desk too small for him that Jennifer installed, and on a pad of lined legal paper, he writes to his dad, saying that he has to get off the island, he isn't sure where. And then, he tries to think ahead—September's more than a month off, but he can't imagine showing up at UMass again in the fall, clapping his dorm buddies on the back, ordering up a kegger. *Fat chance.* "Please tell UMass they shouldn't expect me in the fall," he writes, even though writing this fills him with dread. He has one long, hollow moment of wishing he could go to his mother, wherever she is now, but he sees that scenario spilling out too clearly: her dramatic embrace, followed by a lecture, followed by a rush to the door for a conference or a meeting she's late for.

What will he do? Where will he go?

He only knows he has to get out of here, and fast, just start moving and not look back.

He could just text Betheny once he's off-island, or email her, but a letter seems more serious, proper almost. If he's going to stop being such a dick, he'll start here, and won't leave her with a text. But writing the letter to Betheny is harder than he'd thought it would be, and he finds himself slipping into a reverie, imagining taking her with him, the two of them hitting the open road together, the two of them against the world. But he knows better: for one thing, she'll never leave Grand Isle; for another, he'd be putting her at risk, and for another thing, he wants to be alone. At first, he isn't going to tell her any reason for going, but then thinks that's worse, for her. He thinks maybe it'll be easier if he makes something up, maybe it will hurt less that way, and he writes something about joining the Army, even though he's sure he isn't that desperate.

And then he writes to Damian's mom, which at first is almost like writing to Damian, and he closes his eyes, and feels Damian so close Cort thinks he feels Damian's hand on his shoulder, imagines Damian leaning down to the desk, correcting his spelling, telling him it's ridiculous to expect Betheny to believe he'd join up.

He writes, in his best schoolboy hand, "Dear Mrs. Weiseman," hearing the echo of all the times he had said "Mrs. Weiseman," knowing he was the only friend of Damian's who called her that, but figuring it was a safe way of sucking up. So,

"Dear Mrs. Weiseman," he writes, and then he finds himself writing:

> I'm sorrier than you'll ever know about what happened to Damian, and the thing is, you've been right all along about a lot of things, and I don't know how to make good on any of it. I can't stand it, what happened, and I think about it all the time. And that's why you won't be seeing me around Grand Isle anymore, this summer, or probably ever. I don't know where I'm going, but I have to leave, and maybe by leaving it'll give you some peace. I hope so. Probably you will never be able to forgive me in your heart, but I hope one day you can.
>
> Sincerely Yours,
>
> Cort Grasso

When he writes "Sincerely" he stops for a moment and thinks of what that really means, and it's true, he feels *sincere*.

The final letter, in some ways, is the easiest: he addresses it to Cop Cal, using his official name and appellation: Calvin Callahan,

Chief of Police. In it, he says again he's sorry for the accident. And then he says he lied at the scene. He knows but doesn't say that by coming clean, the DA may go easier on him. If it comes to that. He's so mixed up he doesn't know what he should do; he's getting out of town, and yet, if anyone wants to find him, he'll make it easy for them. "I'll let my dad know where I am," he writes. He looks at the clock; he's got to get out before Rick does anything. He writes a line about Rick, the impending B&E at Franci's place.

He'll start by heading north; a couple of his buddies from UMass are working on someone's dad's house up in Canada, building it from the ground up. This thought reassures him; it's a fantasy that comes from his other, normal life, college kid working a summer job. His head is spinning now, and feels like it's about to split in two.

He reads the letters over once for spelling errors, and as usual finds none. Then he folds them, sliding each into an envelope he also pilfered from his dad's study, sticking the stamps on the ones to Betheny and Damian's mom.

He doesn't have much to pack. He knows he can't be weighted down on this trip, wherever it takes him. He's got to travel light. He takes his wallet, with his driver's license in case he wants to cross to Canada, even though he's sure he'll never drive again. He crams some clothes into his big knapsack. His phone, with his music. And then, just when the pack is nearly full, he scans the little white "distressed" bookshelf (Jennifer again), for Salinger, *Franny and Zooey*. Damian had always been after him to read that. He looks for it, and there it is, because his only books, really, are the ones from when he was a kid or the ones Damian has given him. He tucks it into the top of the knapsack, shoulders the whole thing onto his back, and makes his way with very little noise down the new, polished staircase to the door.

In the kitchen, he takes some provisions from the fridge, and secures them in the insulated bag he's used many times for trips far easier and more innocent than this. At the last minute—how could he be so dumb?—he remembers money. His own ATM card is nearly bled dry. He's in serious need of a cash infusion, but thinking of this phrase, a phrase he and Damian used to use, he feels like crying. He finds his dad's wallet on the hall table where he always leaves it, and he can't help but feel the little ripple of excitement when he sees that his dad must have just made a withdrawal: there's a pile of crisp twenties tucked inside. He takes these along with the credit card he knows his father uses least, and then, just as he's about to head to the door, he scrawls another note: "Dad, sorry about the money. I'll pay you back, I swear."

At the door, he has to disarm the new alarm. Is Jennifer paranoid, or what? Outside, it's brighter than he'd thought; the sky above the water is already white and pink with dawn. He gets his bike from the garage; everything he touches is wet with dew, but the sky is now so light he can see it promises to be one of those clear, perfect island days with a bright sun and a big blue sky hanging over everything.

But he won't be around to see it. He awkwardly clambers onto the bike, the knapsack and the insulated bag throwing him off balance, then peddles laboriously down the long drive and toward the common. It isn't far. Around him, the island's beginning to stir, with the squeaking of the birds, the sea breeze lifting up across the cliffs, and far off, the howl of dogs.

The police station's still darkened; it's not like there's enough crime to warrant staying open 24/7, Cort thinks, not knowing that Cop Cal and Marty are out already at a crime scene; Cort lifts the door on the mail slot, the ocean breeze cool and salty in his face, and takes a deep breath. Is this the right thing to do, or is it not? Dumb/smart, dumb/smart . . . it's hard to know for sure. Cort slips the letters in, hears the clap of the little door slap shut.

He hesitates again at the postbox, when he pulls the handle down, and is about to drop the letters in. But then he hears a car approaching from far up the main road, and he lets the letter drop, wheels his bike to the back of the post office and props it against the wall, gets out onto the road, and puts out his thumb so Joyce Rexman, on her way in to her early shift at the Wisconset hospital, will see him in time enough to stop.

Not long past dawn and Cop Cal's standing at the muddy bank of Fowler's Gut, feet cold in the sneakers he tied on fast when he got the call that woke him from his sleep. When he sees the body floating in the water, he folds one arm across his barrel chest, rubs his hand across his face, shakes his head, feels a sob rise into his ribs, not for this boy in particular, not so much for Rick Skiffton, but for all the lost boys of summer, for Damian, and Cort; for his own Nate who hasn't called in months, even for the lost boy of his own youth, dear dead Fritz—

But that was then, and now—now, he directs the EMTs to go ahead, retrieve the body, and they pull it with a sucking splash from the shallows to the shore. The sky's just starting to lighten, a strip of brilliant blue and white bordering the horizon where the river tumbles to the sea. It'll be another beautiful day. Behind him, the rickety row houses, built into the hillside tower on their stilts, laundry flapping from some of the porches that face the river and the hill, the occupants just starting to stir, readying themselves with coffee to begin another day in the fluorescent lights of a telemarketer's warehouse, or in the salty greased-up air of a fast-food place, or cleaning the houses of the rich.

What are the chances he'd be loading not one but two boys into ambulances this summer, both of them too young to die, both of them dead? Cop Cal turns away, shaking his head. Rick Skiffton was just as familiar to him as Damian was, for different reasons, none of them good. If he wanted to, Cal could run down a list of offenses, starting with petty theft when the kid was eight, nine, ten, progressing to school bus threats and vandalism, then skipping school, smoking pot at Dead Man's Beach, a stint at the juvey hall, a record extending behind and then in front of him, everyone on Grand Isle knowing where he'd been and certain, really, what was still to come.

The EMTs do their job, and the ME in Wisconset will take it from there, finding a stab wound to the chest, or an overdose of drugs. Or both. Cal shivers, once, bends to inspect the dune grasses growing in the muddy bank, sees nothing, no evidence; just a couple of old cigarette butts, a Styrofoam cup, a scattering of broken glass.

Watching the ambulance lumber up from the river and then turn toward the ferry, Cal's sure the burglaries around the island's shore will now come to a halt. But first, isn't there some consideration to be paid the dead, some recognition that this was once a kid, a baby with huge dark eyes, long girlish lashes, and dear, round head who made women coo when they stooped to his stroller on the street? Cop Cal saw it himself: even little Rick Skiffton was adorable, sweet, innocent before he learned the hard lessons often taught by poverty.

He turns back again. The musky water of the bay is lapping on the shore. Rick Skiffton, found in shallow waters, water filling his lungs, God only knows what took him down. An overdose? A drug deal gone awry? Cal almost doesn't care—no, it isn't that, he thinks with a heavy sigh. It's more just that he's tired. Two boys, one summer. Whoever it was said life is short wasn't in this line of work. This September, he'll be fifty-five.

At Lantman's, Cop Cal's never paid much attention to the clerks, the girls and occasional boy behind the register or stocking shelves with cans of evaporated milk, boxes of oversweet cereals, plastic beach toys in spring and pens and notebooks in the fall. But today, having gone back home to shower and shave, put on his uniform and prepare properly for the day, he scrutinizes the girl at the register ringing up his can of Maxwell House and jar of Cremora, her arm in a pink cast.

"You're Betheny, aren't you?" he asks, knowing the answer before she speaks. The one girl in the car he didn't interview, only spoke to on the phone. When she nods, she hands him his change, looking away from him, blinking too quickly, in a way that makes him think she's got something to hide.

As the doors slide open and he steps back out into the heat, there's something bothering the back of his brain, a little worry mouse he's felt before when something just doesn't quite add up. What is it? Something about the girls who were in the car.

As he slides into the driver seat of the patrol car, he remembers Cort saying he wanted a little "backseat time" with Kylie. With Kylie, right? And yet, who was in the front with Damian when they came across on the ferry?

He's got a pile of paperwork to fill out on the Skiffton kid, but he's asking himself these questions without realizing he's pointed the nose of the patrol car toward the ferry dock. He pulls in, shuts the engine, gets out just as the ferry's pulling in.

He waves to Claude, and Claude ambles down from the bridge. They sit together on the bench by the dock, and before Cal can say anything, Claude says, "You'll never guess who I took over to Wisconset this morning."

"Okay, Claude, there's nine hundred and fifty-one people on this island. Give me a hint."

"Let's see." Claude looks heavenward. "We won't be too sorry to see him go. And maybe his leaving will help put something to rest."

"Cort? Cort Grasso?"

"That's the one. On the first ferry of the day. He was riding with Joyce—she said she'd picked him up hitchhiking. He's gone."

Cop Cal's too stunned to come up with a rejoinder. Cort's gone. Does this prove that Cort was in the wrong? Even if this is so, it doesn't prove that Cort will be punished.

"Well, that *is* a piece of news," is all he can say. He knows that Claude knows why he's telling him this; they're the only two, Cop Cal thinks, who suspect the truth of what happened in early summer, the night the kids' car swung off the curve at Dead Man's Beach. And they both know the risks that would have been involved in a more full investigation.

"I'd have thought he'd just go back to college in the fall, a kid like that," Claude says, meaning, of course, a kid whose dad owns the biggest house on Grand Isle.

"Maybe something was eating him," Cop Cal says. "Or maybe he's off to sign up for the services; maybe he just wanted to serve his country."

"Listen, Claude, I've got another question about that night, about the accident. You said Damian was driving, right?"

"That's right."

"Which of the girls was in the front with him? Did you notice? Do you remember?"

"Sure, of course I do. It was the Pickett girl, Kylie Pickett. I know, 'cause I thought it was a little strange at the time, that she wasn't in back with Cort. You know, those two were, well, I guess they sure don't call it "going out" anymore, but you know what I mean."

There's his answer. If Cort wanted "a little backseat time" with Kylie, and that's why he insisted that Damian drive, why was Kylie in the front?

"Did he say anything this morning, when you saw him?" Cal asks, knowing already the answer.

"Are you kidding me? He barely said 'good morning,' as usual."

Cal stands then, calling "thanks," over his shoulder. He's got to make it back to the station, wrap up Skiffton's death.

On his way to the station, the radio crackles, Marty telling him that already Skiffton's cause of death's been found, and it isn't any big surprise, an overdose of crack.

Cal pulls into the drive of the station house, the gravel spraying around his angry tires. The town better approve the paving this year. He unlocks the door; it's still early, not quite eight. As he pushes the door open, a note falls from the letter drop, and he stoops to pick it up.

Another night marking another day when Tessa hasn't come by the pharmacy, but another day too that Kenji's resisted his urge to call her. Urge? *Need.* And still, he stays away. Night comes slowly to Grand Isle, and in the cooling evenings Kenji walks the shore, looking for beached scraps of metal, watching the sea ducks on the waves, then goes to the studio, wrestles with a sheet of steel, rummages in his collection of metal odds and ends. He doesn't call Tessa.

And then, one bright afternoon in early August, Rose Allemand comes in, her red hair tangled up in a collection of barrettes. "Did you hear?" she asks, breathless.

"Hear what, Rose?" Kenji busies himself with reorganizing the toothpaste display.

"Well, just that one of the couples of Grand Isle literati has split," she says, cocking one hip to hold her oversized patchwork bag.

"Really? And who would that be?" Kenji loosens his hair from his ponytail, then pulls it back again. He realizes that his interest is partly feigned, but partly real: could it be Tessa and Jake?

"Tessa and Jake. You know, the anthropologist and the violin maker. Apparently she's moved out and she's staying over on the east shore someplace."

Kenji rises, a tube of Crest in one hand. "Okay," he says. He will not express any interest, will not ask even one of the myriad questions that come swirling into his head, such as *when*.

But, "When?" he says, thinking to himself, *think, think, think.*

"I thought you'd want to know," Rose says, smirking a little. But she isn't one to torment her victims. "Just this week, I think."

"Okay. Listen, Rose, I've got a lot of restocking to do today, so if you—"

"Yeah, I need something for my insomnia. I think Bach Flower has something that's supposed to be good." They walk over to the display. It's still stocked as it was at summer's beginning, with the exception of those bottles Rose herself has bought.

She deliberates, then selects one, saying, "I see our snow goose has moved on."

"Yes," Kenji says. Indeed. "I hope that portends well."

"Why would it portend well?"

"You said when it first landed it meant bad luck, or something."

"Oh, right. Well, it did, didn't it? You'd have to say more bad than good has happened this summer. But that doesn't necessarily mean good luck now it's gone. It could just mean that fall is coming."

Alone again in the store, Kenji watches the sunlight saturate the windows, whiting out his view of the Grand Isle common. Tessa won't be coming in, even now that she's left Jake. He was part of her leaving him, but not in the way he'd wanted; he was just a trigger.

Tessa's gone, as gone as the snow goose, and maybe it's better that way. He turns away from the window, to go back into the pharmacy's cool interior rooms. He's never before understood his fellow pharmacists who find themselves dipping into the supplies to shore up the frailties of their own emotion, but now, he scans the bottles on the shelves.

It doesn't take long for Cort to get so far inland that he doesn't even think of the ocean, the smell of salt, from the rustle of the dune grasses, the slip of sand under his bare feet so that he no longer expects it at every turn. Every time someone stops to give him a lift (usually truckers, never women), he tells a different story: going to surprise his mom, or hooking up with a girl. He passes through the cities of the Eastern United States, thinking he could stop in any one and set up a life; they're all pretty much alike.

Before long he'll be up in Canada, tracking down his buddies, getting on the work crew; this won't be hard, because he's young, and strong, and good-looking. He's got the kind of honest face that people believe. The money he took from his dad's wallet will only get him so far, and soon, he's sure, his dad will cut off the credit card. He's got to get a job.

It's late at night, past eleven, and he's gotten pretty far, when he sees the taillights of a car stop a little ways ahead, then weave backward toward him, and he sees it's an SUV. It looks a lot like his dad's did, before he cracked it up. He has one crazy moment of thinking Damian will be driving, that Damian has come to pick him up, and it'll be just the two of them out on a road trip, laughing about the crazy thing that happened this summer, when everyone thought Damian was dead. But it's just a middle-aged guy in a polo shirt and khakis.

Before Cort gets in, when he's still opening the door, saying, "Thanks for stopping, man," the guy, rubbing his eyes with the palms of his hands, says, "Listen, kid, could you drive? I've been driving all day, and I'm beat."

There's a pause, seeming longer for Cort than it could really be. A long empty maw of a moment, a moment of seeing another car flare past in the night, a moment of praying for the man to take his hands from his face and show Cort that he really is Damian, Damian come back as an angel to save him. Not a random guy come to make him drive.

And then, "Sure, I can drive," Cort says, and they negotiate the change of seats, haul the knapsack into the back, and Cort takes the wheel, heading them into the mysteries of the night.

Rick Skiffton's funeral's a small affair. That it's held at the Shore Chapel is the only thing it has in common with the service held for Damian;

the chapel's services for the dead are free, if the family can't pay. But the little church isn't stuffed with mourners; there's just Rick's mom, his sister in the front row, the row that says: you're next. Farther back, Kylie, and her brother, Kaz, Danny LaPlatte, and beside Kylie, Betheny, holding Kylie's hand, thinking this is too much death in one summer, thinking she can't take much more of this. She thinks of that opera at school her English teacher made them go to; she thought she'd be bored out of her mind, but ended up crying when the girl died. Thinking of this now she feels like crying, again, feels a gasp of air in her chest so big that she could sob.

There's no violin keening for the mourners, no boy reciting Hopkins' poetry. For Rick Skiffton, there's just the minister saying a few cursory words about the brevity of life. But at the end, recorded music comes on, and Kylie recognizes it right away, the music Rick played at the house where they broke in. The Intermezzo from *Carmen*. At the reception in the chapel basement afterward, she asks, but no one can tell her who chose it; no one knows why it was played. Later, there's just family at the open grave.

After the funeral, Kylie, Betheny, Danny LaPlatte and the others gather at the Crab 'N Claw to toast Rick. They end up shooting pool, Danny and the guys drinking beer, Britt sneaking jello shots to the girls. Without telling anyone where she's going, Betheny steps out onto the deck, alone, stretches her left arm, newly released from the cast, rubs it a few times to get the circulation going, and then presses her palms against the rail. She wants to cry, but she's cried enough for one summer, hasn't she? Besides, she doesn't care about Rick so much; it's shocking, more than anything. It's more the other losses, the letter from Cort, and of course, bigger than anything, losing Damian. She looks down the gully to where the river tumbles toward the inlet. No one's going to bail her out of this life, of shooting pool on Friday nights, working at Lantman's, or, if she's lucky, as a secretary in the industrial park in Wisconset.

She hears someone come onto the deck. "God, I could really use a smoke," Kylie says, throwing herself into one of the deck chairs, lighting a cigarette, and flicking the match over the edge.

"Aren't you hungry?" she says to Betheny. "I ordered us some fries."

"Kylie, how can you just go on like that? Rick just died."

Kylie shrugs. "I know that, Beth. I just feel like if I stop for one moment, I'll really lose it."

Betheny pulls out the chair beside Kylie, and together they sit listlessly with their backs to the restaurant, facing Fowler's Gut, where the lights of the row houses shimmer in the evening mist. There's a slight chill in the air, just a whisper that this summer will end. Betheny pulls on her denim jacket, which is a little too thin to be much help; at least it covers her left forearm, pale as sand where the cast had been. Kylie shivers a little, cold, but not wanting to put on her sweatshirt and ruin her look, which today involves a black wraparound shirt that ties in the front, and low-slung dark jeans.

"Can you believe Rick would be so dumb to actually shoot up?" Betheny says, thinking, she herself believes it.

"Well, yeah," Kylie says. "I mean, he was so, like wanted to do everything, all the way. He was kind of a dick."

"And Cort turned out to be a dick too, just like all of them," Betheny says.

"Like I couldn't have predicted that," Kylie says, stubbing out her cigarette, reaching to play with her pack of Camel Lights. "Cort Grasso always was, always has been, and always will be a dickhead of the most superior kind," she says, laughing a little at her double entendre on the word "superior." She lights another cigarette, and then offers the pack to Betheny, who waves it away, then locks eyes with Kylie and motions the pack back toward herself.

"Okay, what did he do to you?" Kylie asks, thinking, *at last. What goes around, comes around, and you ain't been around 'til you been screwed around*, as her stepfather always said.

Betheny exhales a mouthful of smoke. "More like what he didn't do. All he did was leave me that letter. Not even at my house; he mailed it from the Grand Isle Post Office, which is like five hundred yards from my house."

Britt appears at that moment carrying a basket of fries and a salad, and hands the salad to Betheny and the fries to Kylie, who proceeds to douse the fries in ketchup.

"And he didn't mention any of this to you?"

"Not a word. In his letter to me, he said he'd just decided. And of course I'd given him a great blow job Saturday night. That's what really pisses me off. He knew then. He must have known then, but he wanted to get one more hummer in." Betheny looks with disdain at her salad, as if she has no intention whatsoever of getting close enough to eat it.

Kylie feels a twinge of jealousy at the thought of Betheny giving Cort a blow job; not so long ago, that was exclusively her territory, wasn't it? But in the end, she had the better deal, at least for awhile, bombing around the island with Rick in his Camaro. But at the thought of Rick, she gets that cold feeling again, the one that reminds her that one day she, too, will die.

"Well, you saw what he did to me," Kylie says, intending only to add more fuel to Betheny's fire of hating Cort, but Betheny cuts in, saying, "Look, Ky, I'm sorry about all that. It was the wrong thing to do, for me to hook up with Cort like that. I don't even know how to explain it; it's just that Damian, and the accident, and then you hooking up with Rick and all. I don't know."

"It's okay, really," Kylie says. And it is. They've known each other since first grade. Kylie pushes the basket of ketchup-soaked fries toward Betheny. "Just one," Betheny says, smiling. "Yeah, right," Kylie says, taking just one, too.

"It's got to be okay," Kylie says then.

"What do you mean?"

"Well, somehow we've got to get ourselves over to Wisconset all winter to start the new year at WCC."

"You mean, you're going? Your mom's letting you?"

"Well, two classes, she said. Whoop-de-doo." And Kylie twirls a fry in a circular motion, then pops it into her mouth.

"You're so queer," Betheny says. "Go inside and tell Britt we want another one of these, would you?"

"Oh, alright. I have to pee anyway."

Alone again on the deck, Betheny looks out to the inlet. The fog is coming in. Damian would probably have something poetic to say about that. But he isn't here, and now, neither is Cort, and it hits Betheny at last that they never were her ticket out, although either one of them, conceivably, could have been. She's got no ticket out, except starting WCC in another week. It's up to her; she's got to be the one to haul herself up, and out. And if she's strong enough, maybe she can bring up Kylie, too.

Cort just saw a chance to get laid, or a way to keep Betheny from telling the truth about the accident, and Kylie just saw a good time with Cort for a couple of summers. Rick just saw a girl he could get busy with. Betheny knows that she herself didn't see it coming with Damian's new college girlfriend, didn't see what would happen that night they drove back from Wisconset, didn't see all the sorrow that summer would bring.

But Damian, he saw everything.

The dogs pace along the northernmost edge of the island. The summer has been one of plenty for them, with a high population of rabbits, voles, and summer residents who leave their trash out carelessly, often with a good portion of barbecued meat in it. The dogs are, if anything, looking healthier than when they started out last spring, skittering across the ice.

No one's bothered them. The Fish and Game people have tried, but they only got one. Soon, in another few months, the water will be frozen over again, and they can make their way back to the mainland, maybe head up north, into the woods. And long before the passageway freezes, the summer people will be gone.

Thirty-Nine

Peg and Torsten's August First party feels a little unreal this year, an upside-down mirror image of the party that kicked off the summer, as if the people standing on Peg and Torsten's deck, moving among one another, talking, laughing, are really just reflections in the glassy surface of the bay.

Tessa brings a platter of marinated vegetables out to the deck, and opens the lid of the grill. Again, she has a moment, as she often does, of thinking she's doing it wrong, waiting for someone—Jake, for example—to bark at her. Even after all these days at Peg and Torsten's, she hasn't quite gotten used to the gas grill. What if it's too hot, and everything gets seared?

Stupid idiot. The fact that this is what she most often hears in Jake's voice in her head doesn't intimidate her; instead, it serves to spur her on. *I'm not,* she says back to it, silently skewering the vegetables and placing the kebobs on the grill.

Tessa stays close by the grill, still a little unsure what her role is here. At least here, at Peg and Torsten's, she sleeps better than she has in a long time, and without any of her pills.

It isn't exactly festive. Peg and Torsten have always had a party to kick off the last bit of summer on Grand Isle, but in past years, these have been the happiest of affairs, kayak races, silly games like charades, or music and readings on the deck while the sun drifts down to the horizon and the fireflies come out.

Not this year. Tessa looks around the deck. Their ranks have dwindled. Even though Damian wasn't at the first party of the summer, he was there in the way that the living are always with us even when they're not around—Franci was talking about how he'd come home with news of a girlfriend, and how they were going to paint her camp. He was there, still safe under the penumbra of the gods of the living.

Jake, of course, is missing, too, having not been invited. Peg assured Tessa this was what she, and Torsten, and Franci wanted. Tessa turns the vegetable kebobs carefully, and then hears Peg calling out, "Tessa, come on, try some of this tapenade. Sit down with us, for God's sake."

She does, settling into one of the Adirondack chairs that face out to the marshy bay, as they hear Franci's car come down the drive. Then the slam of the car doors, and here's Franci, coming up the steps to the deck, clutching a pair of wine bottles by their necks. "Just in time, I see," she says. Even in that one phrase it's obvious Franci is trying hard, whistling while pushing a Sisyphean rock uphill. Still, she looks better than the last time Tessa saw her, a little less worn, a little less drawn, a little less like she's been up all night crying. She's wearing a gray and black striped linen shirt, and black jewelry, and jeans, and Tessa again marvels at the ability of anyone to get herself dressed, to buy a bottle of wine, to drive a car, after someone—her *son*!—has died. There's a long, quiet pause, in which everyone is too aware of the loss they're all rowing against. *Pull, pull.*

Phoenix lingers behind Franci, hanging back a bit. She's more petite than Tessa remembers, but just as pretty, in her denim shorts and a thin, gauzy blouse cut in a v-neck in a kind of Indian print, a style of shirt Tessa remembers wearing when she was young.

"You all remember Phoenix," Franci says, one hand on the girl's shoulder.

Everyone says hello, and they all wave a little from their chairs, and Phoenix waves back. "Hi everybody," she says, and then there's the sound of another car coming down the drive, and everyone turns to see Kenji's Jeep appear. Tessa, on the far side of the deck, feels a twirling ball of feelings, all at once: dread, excitement, sadness, joy, and she covers this by saying, laughing a little nervously, as he comes up the steps, "You drive that thing like you're in the outback."

"You should see me throw a boomerang," Kenji says, and hands a bottle to Peg. He feels, finally, as if he's beginning to belong to this group, even though he hasn't seen Tessa alone since before she left Jake; he kisses Franci on the cheek in greeting, then pulls back, unsure if this is too much.

"Okay, wine all around then," Peg says, and Phoenix says, "Except me, please. Sorry. Do you have any seltzer or something?"

"Right-O," Peg says, shooting a look at Tessa. "Tess, Kenji, will you help me with this?"

And then, just as Tessa rises, they hear another car approach, and they all turn to see Dick and Jennifer pull up in his red Miata. The top is down, and Dick waves with one hand, and they can see Jennifer smile behind her sunglasses. Peg and Tessa and Kenji wave, then slip into the kitchen.

"Well, I guess that means she's decided," Peg says.

"Decided?" Tessa asks, and Kenji answers, "To have the baby." They both look at him in surprise, and he shrugs, raising his eyebrows as if it should be obvious to them how he knew this.

Peg says, "Why else would she be drinking seltzer, and plus, didn't you notice she looks a little plumper?"

Tessa is still distracted—by the echo of the first party of the summer, before everything changed. She still thinks often of Jake, and not just of the times he bullied her; she thinks too of the long evenings on the porch, or how elegantly he'd hail a cab, open the door, usher her in, kiss her in the backseat as they sped uptown. She's still not sure she's done the right thing, leaving him. And she's distracted by what Rick Skiffton said about the accident, how he thought Cort was driving—and right before his own body was found in Fowler's Gut, too. She holds the bottles while Peg pours Phoenix's seltzer and finds the corkscrew and mumbles under her breath about never being able to leave something in the same place, as Tessa feels herself pitching into the never-never-land of not knowing what to do.

"Give me one of those. You're hanging onto them like they're a life preserver," Peg says, and as Tessa hands her a bottle, Peg looks at her. "Uh, oh. What's going on?" Peg sets bottle and corkscrew onto the counter. The kitchen's big oblong window that looks out onto the marsh is filled with the light of early evening.

"Peg, nothing. Really. I just—it's just so disorienting seeing everyone again, here, you know, not at my place. I mean, Jake's place."

"I know, ducky," Peg puts a hand on Tessa's shoulder. "You did the right thing," she says, then turns back to the wine. Kenji says nothing to this; it isn't his place. For now, he's got to find a small corner in which to tuck his feelings for Tessa.

"Let's get this bottle opened, and then we'll all feel better," he says.

"We have to start with Franci's, 'cause it's a far sight better than whatever we have around here," Peg says.

Peg gets a few glasses down from a cabinet. The light in the room is shifting to a purplish tint. Smokey meows once, and leaps up onto the counter. "Switch on that light, will you, so I don't spill this all over the place," Peg says, and begins to pour.

"Has Dick heard from Cort?" Tessa asks.

"He finally got a call, after being out of his mind with worry for those first days. I guess Cort just hitchhiked up to Canada. He even thought about joining the U.S. Army, can you believe that?"

"Oh, God," Kenji says under his breath.

"I know," Peg continues. "Haven't we lost enough boys to these wars? But now he's got a job for the rest of the summer, something with kids and sports, of all things. I guess he's trying to make his peace with everything that happened. We have to remember he lost his best friend, right?"

Tessa nods, feeling a chill run through her. *So did I*, she thinks.

Peg says, "Smokey, get out of here," unceremoniously lifting the cat from the counter and dumping him onto the floor. To Tessa, she says, "Don't worry so much. For now, have a glass of this wine—" Peg pauses to look at the label, then whistles. "Nice." Peg opens the second bottle, hands a clutch of glasses each to Tessa and Kenji.

When they emerge, evening is settling over the marsh, everything going a hazy lavender. Dick and Jennifer have settled into deck chairs, Jennifer with the dark shawl she wore to Damian's funeral wrapped around her bare shoulders. From one of the butterfly chairs, Franci motions to Tessa to come to the chair beside her. "Sit down, would you?"

"Sure, but take this first." She hands her a glass of wine, then hands the lone seltzer glass to Phoenix. "Thanks," Phoenix says. She does look a little rounder.

"Well, this should be nice, Franci says. "It's a 2002 Rosso di Montalcino." She'd been saving it to share with Damian when he turned twenty-one, in another year. A year from now. A year that won't ever happen. Now. She doesn't mention this, just swallows hard.

"Compared to this, anything we have is the vintner's equivalent of Schlitz," Torsten says.

"I'd like to make a toast," Dick says, sitting forward in his Adirondack chair, which isn't easy as the slope of the seat keeps drawing him back. *Oh, brother*, Tessa thinks.

"Oh, brother," Peg says.

"No, really. This summer has been hell, and I know we'll never be the same. I mean, the loss of Damian is just—well, unspeakable. Still, I want to say that I love every one of you, and I'm just glad we've got each other."

Everyone raises a glass, and together they drink.

"Thank you, Dick," Franci says. Looking at him now, in the dwindling light, she can see Cort in him, see what Cort will become, and seeing the physical resemblance reminds her again of what she'll never see in Damian, growing into his body, becoming entirely him*self*, whoever that would be. Would have been. She has one moment now of blinding, mute rage, but then she raises her glass.

"And, well, I have something else to tell everyone," Dick goes on, clearing his throat. "I got a call from Cop Cal a couple of days ago. It seems they wanted to ask Cort some more questions about the accident, so I told him how to reach Cort." There's a hollow gasp all around; sitting next to her, Tessa puts her hand on Franci's arm. "Franci, I probably should have told you this privately," Dick goes on, "but I just found out myself, right before we came over here, that Cort's told the police that he was driving. Cort was behind the wheel."

The silence is filled only by the soft breeze rustling the cattails in the marsh, the hum of a motorboat.

Peg is the first to speak. "Good heavens, Dick, why are you bringing this up now?"

"Like I said, we just found out, right before coming over here. We're as shocked as you are."

"What does this mean for Cort?" Tessa asks, feeling as she does she's asking on behalf of Franci, who is stunned into silence.

"They're not sure. He's cooperating, and partly it'll depend on whether Franci wants to press charges." Franci still hasn't looked up from the spot she's staring at on the floor of the deck. "I'd understand if you wanted to, Franci. I mean, depending on what happened that night, Cort will have to pay somehow."

The rich golden light of evening is saturating the deck, and despite the shock they're all feeling, the light makes everyone look good, Tessa thinks, makes everyone look as if they're lit from within. Is this life? Or is it just the light of the setting sun? She feels tears come to her eyes, and blinks them back hard.

"Oh," Franci says, low, so low Tessa's the only one who hears this, and it sounds to Tessa like a low, shortened keening, like the last vestige of Franci's keening. "Oh," she says a little louder, less like a moan, more like a word. "Oh, Dick, I don't know." Franci sees for a moment Cort as a little boy, at about five, or four, chasing after Damian on the beach, crying to Franci as a wave came up faster and bigger than he'd expected, Franci lifting him from the water in the nick of time, clutching him up into the air as Damian, unafraid, played on in the water. She's aware that everyone's watching her, waiting for her to say something. "I don't know," she says at last. "Dick, I've known him since he was a baby. Let's think it all over, later."

There's a murmur as everyone begins to speak again; there's muttering, a sigh, Kenji asking how the accident happened, then, all of them together making up a new story of the accident, that rainy night that seems both very recent and long ago mutating into yet another version of itself as they speak. Drinking, the wet road, a flash of a wild dog crossing swiftly in front of the car.

Phoenix sits on the arm of Franci's chair, and Franci looks up at her gratefully.

"For now, I have a toast, too," Franci says, standing, and everyone leans forward. Peg, perched on the wide arm of Torsten's Adirondack chair, slips her hand around his shoulder.

"Or, I guess it really isn't a toast," Franci corrects herself. "It's more an announcement. Phoenix is going to have a baby. Damian's baby." Her voice breaks.

There's a chorus of "oh," and "well, well," and other exclamations, but before the questions can start, Franci, glass still raised, voice trembling, shouts out "L'Chaim," even as she begins to cry, and Phoenix puts an arm awkwardly around her waist, leans her head on Franci's shoulder, and the others echo back to her, as is their tradition, their own proclamations: "Cin-cin," "Kampai," "Cheers."

The air is chilly and fresh, smelling promising, almost smelling like fall. The crepuscular light softens until everything is still, then suddenly ignites the cattails and rushes with the day's last light; the heron shrugs open his papery wings, unfolding over the marsh, rising above the pale beaches, the cliffs, the waterways and bay, up into to air, the clear blue air where the dead reside.

Vermont, 1997
Oaxaca, 2011